# BLOOD
## OF
# THE HUNTED

Marc R. Micciola

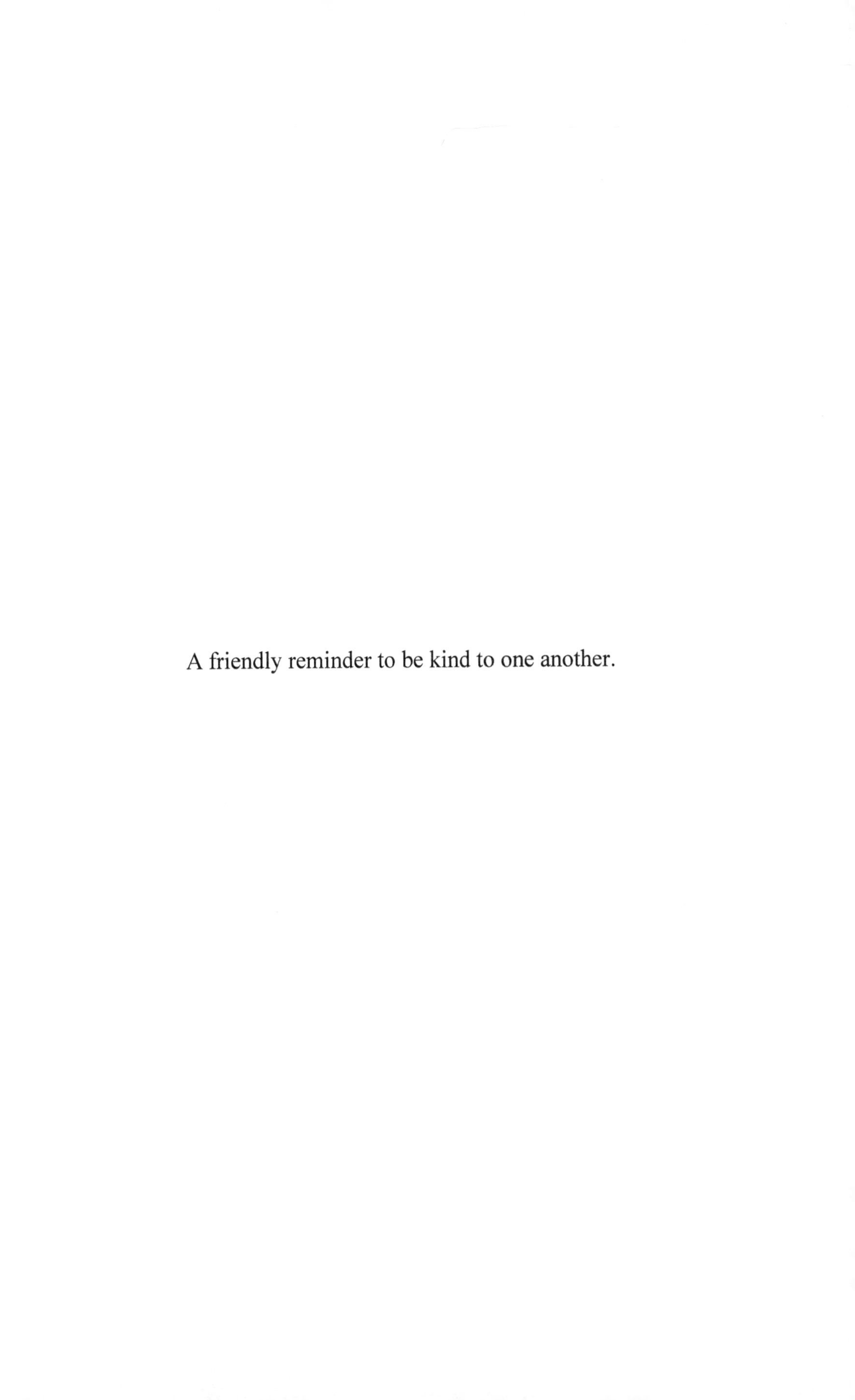

A friendly reminder to be kind to one another.

# Prologue

## Weylyn

Cloque, Fleuris  |  November 1789

I tried to ignore the hateful screams coming from the crowd. The insults were shouted in both the common language and Fleuran, with someone even yelling a curse in the old language priests used. Things had already been thrown onto the stage by people who hoped to strike the lycan that was tied up for all to see. I kept my hood high so that I could remain as hidden as possible. I tried to slouch to hide my height while being sure to avoid eye contact with those around me. I had always been proud to be a lycan, and the lack of horns or colored skin was doing wonders for me right now. My satyr friends — as well as the sprites I knew — would have a much harder time blending in with the crowd today than I would. That was if anyone had taken the risk to come. Uncle Benen had refused to allow Brina and me to leave the house, but I snuck out the window late last night and hid in an alley until afternoon came. I could have gone to Ossian's house, but the satyr would have just tried to keep me inside like Uncle Benen had. I couldn't stay away. I couldn't hide. I needed to be here for him. Even if the smartest and safest thing for the Tóráin in the city was to stay inside, I had to be where I was. Deep down, I knew all of the Tóráin felt the same way. We couldn't abandon him now, not when he needed us the most.

Tears started to fill my eyes as I watched the soldiers bark out instructions to the witches, the women casting spells to torment the brave lycan they had restrained. I was mad at myself for doing so, but I looked away. I looked up, blinking away the water from my eyes as I stared at the looming image of the Sainte Mère Cathedral. I inspected the spires and the stained-glass window high above us as I tried to gather myself. The gothic church's shadow stretched over nearly the entirety of Dame Square, swallowing the crowd in darkness despite the sun shining brightly in the afternoon sky. After taking a deep breath, I forced myself to look back down at the stage. The image I saw would give every single Tórán who had braved the crowds today a great pain in their heart. The lycan before me meant a lot to our community. He was always empowering those who were deemed devils simply because they were different. We all knew we were hated, but that lycan made us feel like we were worth something. He made me who I am today, and now I had to watch someone take him from me. Today, they were executing the most important person in my life: my father.

The pain I felt was not only the anticipation of loss, but also the knowledge that I could do nothing to stop it. All I could do was stand there, at the front of the crowd, and stare up at my father. He was tied up to two poles and spread uncomfortably. The witches had forced him into his feral shape, no doubt to make him appear to be the monster they would portray him to be. Humans continued to throw food at him, some even threw stones. No one stopped them. The officers and witches weren't focused on the wrong doings of humans today. Their eyes were fixed on our kind. '*Diables*', they called us. Beings from another world that many would see eradicated if it were up to them. Today was about sending a certain message to our kind, while sending a completely different one to their own. We were to be humbled and defeated, while humans would be propped up and celebrated. A story would be told on that stage, and none of my kind were supposed to enjoy it. I stared at my father's face, hoping he would look up and lock eyes with me. For a moment it seemed like it would happen, but I was shoved from behind and forced to turn around.

"I knew I smelled a stray *chien*. You *salauds* aren't allowed to mingle with us up here. Back of the crowd, *Diable*."

I looked back over my shoulder at my father to catch him looking right at me. I refused to show weakness. "I'm staying right where I am."

One of the young men who had confronted me raised a fire poker in the air, but he never got around to actually hitting me with it. A slender hand attached to a lean arm grasped his wrist and he grew red in the face.

"Rosey!" he whined. "What are you doing? He started it!"

Rosalie — my very best friend and one of the few people I knew I could trust outside of my father — was a human. Not even a witch. She was just a regular, wonderful, human. Her parents had helped mine for years since I was a pup. We grew up together, and despite my clear edge in strength, she was always rescuing me from ignorant assholes. The teen harassing me dropped his weapon and used his other hand to reach for Rosalie's shoulder.

"Don't call me Rosey, " she said as she grabbed his outstretched hand and twisted his fingers roughly. "And I highly doubt Weylyn started anything. Leave us alone or your father will find out just how much of a *petit con* you've been."

The boy's face scrunched up before he left through the crowd, massaging his injured hand. His friends followed him, prompting Rosalie to let out a deep sigh before fixing her dress. She grabbed a hold of my arm, laced her fingers through mine, and looked up at my father. The two of us stood there, trying to send him our strength for what felt like hours until trumpets sounded. Up the steps came King Louis, soaking in all the praise the majority of the crowd was giving him. He eventually waved at them to quiet down so he could speak, and I knew that what came next would make my blood boil.

"*Gens de Cloque!*" King Louis shouted with a pompous grin on his face. "I have been a just king, have I not? I have been a gracious, and bountiful king, have I not? Under my rule, all have prospered! Yet we still have...*ordures*...that want to see that lovely life tarnished. This *monstre* murdered ten officers. *Dix protecteurs*! For that heinous crime, the only plausible sentence is death! But first, we will make an example out of him!"

The crowd roared. The group of witches and officers stood ready now, surrounding the stage as torturers began whipping my father. He kept his fur covered head held high, defiant despite his pain. The people whipping him moved on to more forms of torture, dragging on the inevitable much to the enjoyment of the crowd. They cut at his ears, pulled his teeth, removed his fingertips, and even branded him with the royal sigil of Fleuris. Not once did my father cry out in pain. Not once did he give them the satisfaction they wanted. What they were doing to him had brought tears to my eyes yet again, but I also felt a sense of pride in seeing the strength my father was showing. The torturers looked at the king with lost expressions on their faces, prompting King Louis to rise from his chair and draw the saber at his waist. He began carving his prisoner. He sliced at his arms, and then his legs, then his back, and then his chest. All that and yet, still, there were no cries out for mercy or even a grunt from the pain. Now visibly angry, King Louis grabbed my father by the snout and shouted at him.

"Why must you defy me? You're dead, *Diable*, there's nothing to fight for anymore! Scream like I know you want to! Show everyone the *lâche* we know you to be!"

His face was bloodied and swollen, but at that moment I knew that he was looking at me. Our eyes finally locked, and I squeezed Rosalie's hand. I took a small step forward, but Rosalie held me back. I looked down to see her crying as she shook her head. Bringing my attention back to my father, I found my eyes to be drowning in tears so much that it was hard to see. It all felt so hopeless...until he howled. Right in the face of the bastard that had committed so many wrongs to him and his kind, my father howled to the sky. Howls broke out from the crowd, followed by screeches and whistles from the harpies and other creatures who had come. King Louis was beside himself from this display. He drew his pistol from its holder, placed the barrel between my father's eyes, and fired.

The world around me evaporated into nothing until all I could see was my father's body limp on the stage, held up only by the ropes around his wrists and ankles. My eyes were locked on the horrid sight until Rosalie began pulling me through the crowd as more whistles, and screeches, and howls flooded the city. I barely paid attention to the chaos that was erupting as Rosalie and I pushed our way through the crowd. We eventually escaped the large mass and slipped into an alley.

"We need to get clear of here. My house is close enough, and we'll be safe there." Rosalie tried to pull me, but I stood my ground.

"My father is...he's..." Rosalie came forward and put her hands on my face. The contact had me snapping to attention. "Uncle Benen. Ossian. Darby. They...I have to tell them what happened."

"Yes. But not right now. Right now, we need to get you off the streets." The general noise of a boisterous crowd turned into loud screams and gunshots. "Weylyn!"

I nodded furiously. "Yes. Right. Okay. Your house first then."

The two of us ran off into the city, but the sounds of the riot that had broken out in Dame Square followed us for some time. I barely saw what was in front of me, Rosalie holding my hand and guiding me most of the way. I couldn't shake the image of my father, torn apart, with a bullet wound leaking from his head. I still couldn't believe it. My father was dead.

# Part One

## The Gunpowder

# Chapter One

## Weylyn



I woke up so quickly the room spun. I was breathing heavily, and a cold sweat covered my body. I let out a disgruntled groan as I sat up in the bed. Resting my arms on my raised knees, I let my head hang loose. My damp hair fell around my face as I took a few deep breaths to try to settle myself. It wasn't until I heard a voice that always found a way to bring me peace that I finally began to calm down.

"You okay?" I looked up and found Rosalie sitting at the edge of the bed.

I didn't give her an answer. Well, not with words anyway. I closed my eyes before rubbing them, all while letting out the biggest sigh I could muster.

"Nightmares again?" Rosalie asked as I tossed the sheets off of me.

I swung my legs over and came to sit on the edge of the bed. Rosalie shuffled over until she was close enough to put her hand on mine. She didn't get upset that I chose to remain silent. She knew the answer to her question anyway. The woman knew me well enough to know when my sleep had been invaded by horrors. After some time spent in silence, I squeezed her small hand and gave it a gentle pat before standing up.

I made my way over to the bowl of water sitting on a fancy table and gave my face a good splash before finally responding. "Every year. Every November. It's like he refuses to let me forget."

Rosalie handed me a towel, having gotten up from her seated position to join me by the fancy table. "You shouldn't forget. He sparked something that day, something that had been dying for a spark for dozens of decades. He's why we're doing this."

"I know, I know." I began getting dressed, recognizing that Rosalie was already prepared for our meeting. "All I'm saying is that I could do without the nightmares."

The door to my room opened after a quick knock. In came Brina, tall and proud like always. She ran her fingers through her short, blonde hair as she shot a toothy grin our way. "Ready?"

Rosalie brought the long braid of her fiery red hair over her right shoulder before putting her hands on her hips and nodding. I put my arms through my coat and gave it a quick brushing with my hands to have it as clean as possible. We were seeing a queen after all. I had no love for monarchs; however, Queen Sophia was supposed to be different from all the rest. That is, at least when it came to people like Brina and me. Tudrose was a country unlike any other, and it was very important that we make a good first impression. I nodded at my two dear friends and extended my arm out, insisting they lead the way. Brina took the role of leader and Rosalie followed, with me not too far behind. We went down a few hallways and then descended a couple staircases until we finally reached two large iron doors, each with a massive rose engraved on them.

Two guards stood on either side of the entryway holding tall halberds. They brought the weapons together in an 'x' and blocked our path. "Seems to me that someone's lost."

Rosalie stepped forward and smiled. "Not at all! We were told to come to Queen Sophia's throne room this morning, so here we are."

The duo looked at each other, then they began scanning Brina and me. It was the same looks we were used to getting back in Fleuris. Their eyes fixated on everything about us that made us different. The easy one was our height; all lycans were tall. Next was our ears, short and pointed. If humans were close enough, they could spot our common gold-colored eyes. The overall posture of a lycan is slightly different from a regular human too, our backs hunched just a bit and our knees almost always bent just a little. Every inch of Brina and me was looked over twice before the two men shook their heads.

"Since when does royalty meet with wild dogs?"

Brina crossed her arms. "Wild dogs? Last time I was called a wild dog was when I spent the night with that painter. However, when she said it, I believe she meant it as a compliment. I doubt it's crazy to assume that you didn't. It's a shame really. I thought Tudrose was different from everyone else."

"We are." The voice from behind us had the two guards bring their halberds back to their sides and stand as erect as possible. "However, there are those who have yet to adjust, even after all these years."

Queen Sophia stood there with her arms crossed and an eyebrow raised, staring holes through the two guards at the doors. She kept her eyes fixed on the duo for a short while until dropping her arms down to rest her hands on her hips. The white gloves she had on were a bright contrast to the vibrant red dress she wore. It was tight at the chest and waist, flowing outward the closer it got to the floor. Her blonde hair fell down over her shoulders like a waterfall of silk and her hazel eyes were somehow both intimidating and inviting. She cleared her throat and the two guards rushed to open the doors for her.

The room was nothing like anything I had seen before. A long red carpet led all the way down the long room to a tall throne with three banners hanging behind it. Lengthy windows lined the place on either side, allowing a large amount of sunlight to illuminate every corner of the royal room. Large stone columns stood in front of the windows, holding up what appeared to be a second floor above us. At the very end of the hall, high above the banners and the throne, was a stained-glass window displaying the royal crest of Tudrose. Chandeliers hung from the intricate design of the vaulted ceiling and two more soldiers stood guard on either side of the throne. Queen Sophia had walked past us while I was taking in the sight of the royal chamber and was now about a quarter of the way down the hall before she stopped and turned around.

"Well? Are you coming or not?" She had a kind smile on her face, the ruby on her necklace sparkling in the morning sun.

I took the first step forward, Rosalie and Brina following close behind. The four of us walked all the way down to the throne. Queen Sophia seated herself before waving away the two guards. They remained there for a moment, no doubt wondering if their queen really wanted to be left alone with us. That was until Queen Sophia cleared her throat like she had at the doors, sending the reluctant duo scampering for the exit. She brought one leg over the other and gripped the armrests of her royal seat, before sending another bright smile our way. "My sincerest apologies for all that nonsense. I assure you, the majority of Tudrose is less ignorant than those you have been exposed to. Shall we get right to it then?"

I looked over at Brina, and then Rosalie. The two of them nodded, urging me to be the one to speak for us. I had thought that perhaps it would be best for Rosalie to speak — seeing as she was the human among us — but I took a deep breath and gathered myself before addressing a monarch for the first time in my life. "Your apology is very much appreciated. I'm sure Tudrose is a more accepting place than Fleuris. In fact, it is because of this that we chose to reach out to you. We are incredibly thankful for you choosing to meet with us, and we promise to not take up too much of your time."

Queen Sophia grinned and waved away my promise. "You do not need to worry about silly things like that. Say what you need to say, however long it takes for you to say it. I would not have agreed to meet you if I had wished to hear you speak for only ten seconds. If I remember correctly, you want my help, yes?"

I nodded. "Yes. You see, as you probably already know, Fleuris and its neighboring countries make life for every Tórán a difficult one. There are many injustices committed daily in these nations, and my people are suffering. We have been suffering for a very long time now, and our efforts to stay the bleeding in Fleuris has done little to put an end to it. For nearly ten years we have fought for lives that are endured instead of enjoyed. Even before that, atrocities of the greatest degree have been committed against beings like me, and we feel it needs to be brought to an end. We've tried revolts. They only result in more of us being tortured and murdered. We need a real plan. We need help. That's why we've come here. The Resistance is asking for Tudrose's assistance in bringing an end to the mistreatment and subjugation of the Tóráin and their supporters in not just Fleuris, but in her neighboring countries as well."

Queen Sophia plucked an apple from a plate nearby and took a large bite out of it. She stared at me while she chewed, then she swallowed, and then she took another bite. I was starting to wonder if I had said something wrong, and I was quickly beginning to regret ever coming here. The entire idea was a long shot, not to mention embarrassing. I hated having to ask anyone for help, and this still sort of felt like asking someone else to fight my battle for me. I was about to bow and leave, but after swallowing her third bite Queen Sophia motioned at me with a hand now holding a half-eaten apple.

"You are the leader of this revolution of yours, correct?"

"I am." I stood more erect, trying to look as leader-like as possible.

"What are you willing to do to achieve this world you dream of? This world where beings from two different worlds live in prosperous harmony."

I was nervous. I didn't know if I should give a specific example, or a general one. After realizing I had taken a painfully long time to answer, I went with the one that seemed best. "I'd do anything to see that dream come true."

She took another bite out of her apple and began shaking the leg which sat upon the other. The ruffles of her dress bounced in silence as the room filled with the deafening crunch of Queen Sophia chomping on the red piece of fruit. She took another bite as she turned her attention to the windows to her right. She stared out at the morning sun until all that was left of her snack was a chewed-up core. After bringing her attention back to me, she tossed the core back onto the plate beside her and leaned forward. With her elbow resting on her knee, her face now resting in her hand, she smiled.

"Weylyn, was it? Your dream is a twin of my own. I do not know what information reaches your ears south of The Great Canal, but I have brokered treaties with Fruberg, Linne, Czermak, and, most recently, Weidel. The treaties were purely political and have seen your kind given more rights and better livelihoods as a result. I have tried these peaceful conversations with the other countries that make up Kosavros, but they are so stuck in their ways of doing things. They are stubborn and defiant, willing to fight to keep things the way they are. There are many who benefit from the pain your kind endures, and they will not see their riches and lifestyle vanish." Queen Sophia uncrossed her legs and straightened out her dress with her hands before standing from her seat. "I had been considering military action, despite my hatred of violence. However, I know Tudrose would be alone against the other nations and together they would be quite the problem. I think there is a way for us to make the path to seeing our dream realized a bit easier, if you're up to the task."

I hesitated. I had said I would do anything to see this dream of ours come true, but I was starting to get a bit worried about what she might suggest. The thing is, this all came down to trust and I didn't know if I had any for Queen Sophia just yet. Sure, she said the right things, and she didn't come off as someone who wished ill on my kind. However, the Tóráin had been betrayed by humans before. It was hard to ignore that type of pain. Thankfully, I wasn't here alone. I felt Brina's strong hand on my shoulder and Rosalie's dainty fingers weave through my own. They had convinced me to come here, insisting that we would find a friend and ally in Queen Sophia. I was surprised as any when word came back that Queen Sophia had agreed to see us, fully expecting to be rejected and tossed aside as usual.

I looked at Rosalie, her olive eyes staring up at me. I took a deep breath before inclining my head as a sign of respect for Queen Sophia. "What do you need from me?"

The Queen of Tudrose brought her hands together with a smirk on her face before calling out for her guards. I immediately prepared myself for an attack, and I

felt foolish for doing so. Queen Sophia gave me a quizzical look before looking
past me and addressing the two soldiers who had entered the room. She called for a
table, a map, and some wine; all three things were less threatening than a leaf on a
tree. It didn't take long before everything she had asked for was brought before us.
A server poured some wine for Queen Sophia first, before pouring cups for
everyone else. Brina rejected hers of course, seeing as she had sworn off alcohol a
few years ago. She was swiftly brought some water and, once everyone had a drink
in their hand, Queen Sophia got to explaining her plan.

# Chapter Two

## Weylyn



I was a fool for thinking my second time on a ship would go better than my first. My stomach lurched from the rising and falling of the waves, making me sicker than I had been in years. This was Brina and Rosalie's second time on a ship too, so at least I wasn't alone in my turmoil. Well, I shouldn't say turmoil. The view was calming, and the spray of the salty ocean waters did keep my nose clean, so it wasn't all that bad. Knowing that our trip had not been in vain also did a good job combatting any sourness towards our watery adventure. Our meeting with Queen Sophia had gone much better than any of us could have expected. Brina wasn't too thrilled with the plan we had decided on, but she was quick to admit that no plan of her own was better. Rosalie hadn't really said much about it, other than she believed it to be our best plan. Regardless of the tough road ahead, it provided us all with a new level of hope, something that had been fading for some time now.

I looked out at the open sea and thought of what lay ahead, both excited and nervous to discover how everything would end up. After all, our side of the plan was only the beginning, and much more would be required of both The Resistance and Tudrose by the end of it all. A lot of this plan relied on the beings that inhabit the countries of Kosavros, both Tóráin and humans. It was up to me to bring them all together. I had promised my father on the day of his death that I would never stop fighting for a world where anyone — no matter who they were — could live prosperous and happy lives. Every decision I have made since the day my father was killed had led me here, and I was hoping that the path I was on was the right one.

It helped to know that I wasn't alone in my fight. Rosalie was by my side without hesitation the moment I decided to join The Resistance. Brina was quick to join me too. My cousin was just as angry as I was at what they did to my father. She would have joined me simply because of that, although what really pushed her my way was that her father, Uncle Benen, was killed during the aftermath of The Great Riot. Many died along with him, but they were all inspired by my father's defiance on that stage. My father had shown all of the Tóráin a strength I think many of us didn't know we possessed. His kindness and the amount of care he had for those who called themselves Tóráin had him admired by many. My father was incredibly strong and very protective; he was the most fearless lycan I ever knew. He was a father to the Tóráin community in Cloque, even befriending some of the witches and officers of the city with that damned charm of his. The day my father was killed, it seemed as though the shadow cast on the city square by the Sainte Mère Cathedral spread outward and enshrouded the entire city. From there it spread to every corner of Fleuris, even reaching further outward to neighboring nations. Conri the Defiant became a name every Tórán admired and respected. Being the son of such a being came with a large amount of responsibility.

As we sailed through the choppy waters, I reflected on those responsibilities and wondered if I honored enough of them to make my father proud. I thought of all the good I had done as the leader of The Resistance, but it wasn't long until all the mistakes I had made came flooding in faster than I could manage. Every good deed done came with a failed attempt beside it, making it hard to see any type of progress in our fight. Sure, we did a lot of good, especially during The Great Dread after the Diables Loyalty Act; yet there was a bunch of pain during that time as well. We saved hundreds from firing squads, but we also failed to save thousands. When the conscriptions started during the wars, we would do some good only to have it followed by more negative outcomes. I remembered amidst the depressive spiral I was in that Rosalie had always pulled me out of them. It didn't do much when I said the things to myself, but when Rosalie reminded me of all the good we've done I would feel able to breathe again. I almost left my spot on the main deck of the ship to go find her, but I figured it best to let her rest.

I stared out at the evening sky instead, the sun having faded in the west and the stars shining brightest in the east. I chose to try to imagine Rosalie's voice filling my head, and I was happy to find her words become like a spell as the waves crashing against the hull of the ship soothed me. It took a while, but I managed to get myself out of that depressive mud. Rosalie's voice, whether it came from her own mouth or my memory, always found a way to calm me down. It worked even better when I conjured her image before my closed eyes. I silently debated on whether it was her gentle eyes or warm smile that had broken the spell of hopelessness I was under, but I eventually abandoned the struggle. I was just happy to not have a shadow of negativity enveloping me anymore. After all, this trip had provided a great measure of hope. It also provided a great measure of work, but I was prepared for the task at hand, and I knew the others were ready too. We all saw a possible light at the end of the tunnel, and we were going to fight our hardest to see this dream of ours realized. No matter what we had to do to get there.

"Rosalie will be mad if she finds you awake." Brina came and leaned on the railing beside me.

"I'm not tired." I was compelled to yawn directly after stating this, my body betraying me.

"You barely slept on the way to Draca. Bullshit you aren't tired. You know, we aren't going to have too many chances for a good rest for who knows how long."

I sighed, wiping the spray of the sea off my face. "I know, Brina. I just...I don't know."

"Don't know about what? I thought you were a fan of this alliance with Tudrose. Aren't you happy?" Brina was facing me now instead of the water with her arms crossed over her chest.

"I am. Truly, I am. We just don't know what's going to happen and if this plan fails, I really don't have any other ideas. It's scary to think that our greatest hope in nearly ten years could be our greatest failure. My mind doesn't let me think of anything else."

Silence. Nothing but the sound of the waves crashing against our ship could be heard. I was starting to think Brina had just left me here by myself until I took my eyes off the churning waters and looked over to where I expected her to be. I had looked over just in time to catch her wrapping her big arms around me in a tight hug. She didn't say anything for a while, and it wasn't until I wrapped my arms around her that she spoke.

"Everyone fears failure. It can be a crippling force that ends all forward motion. But failure isn't the end of something, it's the beginning of a new lesson." Brina broke our embrace, keeping her hands on my shoulders as she tried to lock eyes with me. "We've failed before. It's never stopped us from fighting. We've adapted and found new ways to keep people safe. As hesitant as I am about all of this, I do believe we can make this plan work. But if it doesn't, and we fail? We'll come up with something else. Don't let fear eat away at you. We need you. I need you."

She was right. I would never admit that, seeing as she would hold it over my head for who knows how long, but it was true. Anyone in my position would be afraid, but we did always find another way. This plan of ours was just another fight that needed fighting, and The Resistance was full of courage. If anyone was going to pull this off, it was going to be us. Tudrose too of course, but their involvement relied heavily on us completing our part of the bargain. In order for us to do that, we would need all the strength we had. I patted one of Brina's hands and nodded.

"Thanks." I sighed and gave a quick glance at the starry sky above us. "You know, I think I'll give sleep a try."

I forced a smile, getting one in return as Brina set my shoulders free. I gave her shoulder a quick pat before making my way to the beds below deck. I stopped a few feet away from the open hatch when I noticed I was alone. I turned around and saw that Brina hadn't moved.

"You coming? I doubt you've gotten much more sleep than I have."

Brina reared her head and sniffed the air as a spray sprouted from the sea. "I think I'll watch the waves for a little bit, if my stomach allows me to. Don't you worry about me. I'll probably end up sleeping more than you anyway. Get some rest, Weylyn."

"Alright. Well, goodnight then. Don't fall overboard. I'd have to fish you out and we both know how much I suck at fishing."

Brina laughed. "I'll be extra careful, I promise. Goodnight."

I waved goodbye before lowering myself onto the ladder that led below deck. I walked past the rows of cannons on either side until I reached the steps down to the lowest level. I was greeted by the snoring of sailors, all asleep in their makeshift beds of wood and hay, one stacked upon the other. Making my way through the aisle, I reached Rosalie. She was sleeping on the bottom bed, the one above her vacant. I didn't trust the rickety structure to hold me, so began making the floor as comfortable as it could be. There was a free bottom bed to the left, but I didn't want to force Brina to sleep on the floor. I approached Rosalie's bedside slowly so as to not wake her, when I heard someone whisper loudly at me.

"Hey! Be careful there. That one's a puncher she is."

A grizzly man with a short beard and bald head was sitting up in his bed a couple cots over. The lamp hanging nearby shined on his face just enough for me to catch the beginning of a welt on his right eye.

"That's what you get when you don't understand when a woman says she is perfectly fine sleeping in her own bed by herself." Rosalie was propped up on her elbow, blinking as her eyes adjusted to the soft light of the lamp. She had a wicked scowl on her face too.

The man raised his hands in the air in surrender and turned over, going back to sleep nursing his bruised eye. I took my place on the floor between the empty bed and the one Rosalie was occupying, prompting the woman to sleepily call out in a huff. "Um, what are you doing? There's a bed right there."

I sighed, suddenly tired and wishing to just lay down, wherever that was didn't matter to me anymore. "Let Brina sleep there. I'm fine on the floor."

Before I knew it was being dragged off the floor towards her bed. "Nope. Unacceptable. Share my bed then. I'm cold anyways."

I climbed onto the low cot and cuddled close to her, most of me still hanging off the bed as I wrapped my arm around her waist. "What happened to wanting to sleep alone?"

Rosalie slapped my thigh and brought her finger to her lips to shush me. "Be quiet, my little fireplace. It's time for sleep now."

I shook my head and gave her a squeeze, prompting her to push herself into me even more. It took some time, but our situation actually became comfortable. I allowed myself to bury my nose into her hair and rested my hand on Rosalie's belly. Her scent, her soft snore, and the rise and fall of her stomach lulled me into a peace long enough to feel ready for sleep.

# Chapter Three

## Olwen

Cloque, Fleuris  |  December 1, 1798

We assumed that the trip to Draca and back would take roughly fifteen days. Today was the sixteenth day since Weylyn and the others left, causing my anxiety to run rampant. It was entirely possible that they simply stayed in Draca a day longer, or a storm delayed their ship over in the port city of Comaine. However, my mind quickly and continuously brought forth possibilities that involved everyone either imprisoned or dead. The whole thing was a massive risk that I wasn't entirely comfortable taking, but Weylyn was convinced by others that it was our best option. We do the best we can with what we have — which isn't much — but Weylyn always wished to do more. He hasn't been the only one to realize that despite all our efforts, things haven't really changed much in the last ten years.

We would free those we could, sending most out of the city to start a new life; we even sent some to other countries entirely. We stole from the richest humans and gave to the poorest members of society, with our kind making up a large part of the less fortunate. Humans had their own derogatory names for us all throughout the continent, but Tóráin was an old name we used to identify the group of different races that came to this world so long ago. It's a word in our language — Séúbua — that means 'Hunted Ones'. Every Tórán — "Hunted One" — wasn't overly fond of the term, however it was better than what everyone else called us. Still, it was a shame that after all these years, we've had no reason to come up with anything else. It wasn't done in such a feral, barbaric manner anymore, but we were still hunted like animals. Humans just went about it in different ways now. Imprisoning us under lame or even false charges was their favorite form of hunting us, among other things. Knowing this was debilitating and often cast a dark shadow over my head. Every day of the last eight years of my life I've given my blood, sweat, and tears for The Resistance; it was frustrating beyond comprehension to know that we were barely any better off than when I first joined.

It was because of this admission that I agreed that we needed to do something that would truly change things. The idea of forming some type of alliance with the most Tóráin-friendly country was the best thought anyone could come up with. Still, the longer they all took to get back here, the more I would believe that my greatest worries had come true. That would be the last thing I needed tossed on my plate. Staging another rescue — or worse a funeral — was just something I was growing tired of doing. The only thing that had gotten me through all those difficult, depressing experiences were my friends. I truly didn't know what I would do if they didn't show up. I was hoping they would arrive before tonight's events, but time was slowly passing by, and I would not be able to wait here much longer.

We had decided that we would meet at The Dame, right in the middle of the famed Mascarons Bridge. I had brought tiny stones with me this time to throw into the river to pass the hours. Just as the sun was setting in the west, causing a soft orange glow to fill the spire-touched skyline, I heard a whistle. It wasn't an ordinary whistle; it was the song of a sparrow. I spun around to find three people coming down the bridge, all with large hoods covering their faces. It was them. I knew it was. All my composure left me as I quickly embraced Weylyn the moment he moved his hood so I could better see his face. I set him free just as quickly, feeling my cheeks flush as my embarrassment consumed me. I quickly went and hugged both Brina and Rosalie as well, so as to not raise any questions.

You see, I had loved Weylyn for years. Every day during that time I have tried to set aside these emotions, but they always keep coming back. I could never confess these feelings to him, knowing full well his heart belongs to another. My feelings for him would only complicate things anyway, and so I kept them to myself as much as I possibly could. This moment had been a bit of a slip up, but I didn't beat myself up over it. We had been apart for the longest time since I had returned from the war roughly two years ago. I was simply glad that he had returned from a trip I didn't believe was very safe. Nothing more to it. Thankfully, nobody chose to point out the awkwardness of me lunging into the lycan's strong arms, so that was good.

"Olly, we have good news!" Weylyn whispered loudly.

I tried not to swoon. He was the only one who called me Olly, and every time he did it made me feel lighter than a feather. I looked over at the sky to avoid his eyes and realized that I didn't really have time to hear what he had to tell me.

"Olwen, what's wrong?" Rosalie must have noticed I was tense.

"Oh, just running late for another rescue. Quite an important one really. I was actually hoping you would get here in time to help maybe. After all, it is Keagan we're freeing."

Brina rolled her eyes and put a hand to her forehead while Weylyn swore under his breath.

Rosalie crossed her arms and allowed her eyes to roll too. "Another brawl, I would imagine."

"If it was just another brawl, he would be out in a couple days with some cuts and bruises from the jail keepers having a good time beating up a chained lycan. If you're going through the trouble of rescuing him, this is worse than that. I'm right, aren't I, Olly."

I had missed hearing his voice say that name. There was nothing more that I wanted than to just go to The Flying Pig and listen to Weylyn talk for hours on end. I blinked quickly a few times to snap myself out of the fantasy I was envisioning and allowed myself to breathe before responding.

"Yup. Keagan did indeed get into another brawl, only this time he went too far. Those who witnessed it say it was an accident, which I believe by the way. Keagan is an angry brute, especially when he's drunk, but I can't believe he did this on purpose. Making a long story a short one, Keagan killed a human. We all know they wouldn't give a damn if it was another lycan, or a satyr, or any other race of the Tóráin. Kill one of those? Ah you'll get let go eventually. Kill a human? Well, they torture you in private for a while before torturing you at sundown. All that before the eventual execution of course."

Weylyn's face became like stone and all signs of joy and happiness that were visible moments ago were now gone. He took a quick look at the setting sun himself before locking his eyes on me.

"We don't have much time. Lead the way, Olly."

I put my own hood up before turning around and walking at a brisk pace towards where they planned to execute Keagan. It was a fair distance from our current location, but we couldn't run and draw attention to ourselves. My dear friend would just have to endure whatever heinous acts were being done to him. Keagan was strong. Not just physically, but mentally too. Sure, he was a bit of a firecracker, but he was also very stubborn and headstrong. He was one of the higher-ranking members of The Resistance, despite his amazing ability to be the least discrete individual we had. Keagan was brazen and rough, often offending others, especially when he was drinking. Weylyn usually kept a good eye on him to limit his problematic encounters, but the lycan rarely ever listened to me despite our close friendship. I had even told him to leave the pub with me that night, but he refused. I foolishly left him there, angry and annoyed at him for things he had said earlier in the night.

Now, it was my responsibility to make sure the damn fool didn't lose his head. No one knows what the humans and the witches under their command had done to him already, but the body can mend cuts and bruises. Even broken bones could eventually heal with time; however, a severed head was something nobody could recover from. So long as we got to Bastion in time before the executioner did his job, we would have time to set our friend free. It wasn't going to be easy, seeing as there would be many guards. The place was crawling with them. Thankfully, I had help from the rest of The Resistance carrying out a plan I had devised earlier. With Weylyn and the others helping now, I think we have a much greater chance at getting Keagan out of there without anyone else being in danger of losing their lives. I ran through as many possibilities I could think of as we quickly made our way down the street, hoping to be prepared for anything. With a rescue as dangerous as this one, it did you good to be well prepared.

# Chapter Four

# Weylyn



I knew being gone for so long was a mistake. As we swiftly made our way past the houses sat on the edge of The Dame, I berated myself for ever leaving. Keagan was like my brother. I took him in when everyone else said he was too much of a risk. I cared for him like one would care for a family member, and now he could possibly die in the same manner my father had all those years ago. It was something I wished not to think about, but my guilt forced me to recognize the situation for what it was. There was no guarantee we would be successful in freeing him, but knowing that Olly was the one who had come up with the plan to save him gave me some hope. She hadn't even told me it yet, but I trusted her. The level of trust I had for her was what eventually convinced me to leave for Tudrose. I was foolish to believe she could keep a hold on Keagan though, seeing as the ill-tempered lycan barely even listened to me.

    We made our way across the slight bend in the street and were welcomed by the daunting sight of Bastion in the distance. The large castle was compact, its walls high and thick. Olly and I had broken into it before to save our good friend Nolan, but we barely made it out alive. Thankfully, General Rosspier and his minions loved to make executions a show for the public, so breaking into the prison wasn't necessary this time around. Bastion had a stage where they would publicly torture and execute criminals they deemed worthy of such charges. If people were saying this was an accident, then I believed them. Keagan's exterior is rough and unpleasant, but underneath that is someone with a loving heart and a mind for peace. His temper gets the better of him often and it usually gets him into scuffles, but never did I think Keagan would kill some random person in a pub. Whatever had happened, I knew Keagan wasn't the monster he was undoubtedly being treated as. We needed to save him.

Our group of four approached the drawbridge, the only way in or out of Bastion. Many others were trickling in with us, but the majority of the crowd had already formed in the fair-sized courtyard of the prison. We were at the very back, about one hundred and fifty feet from the front of the stage, but all of us could see who was displayed on the raised platform. They had Keagan tied up to a pole, his hands bound above his head. I spotted at least two witches off to the side, both of them, no doubt, keeping Keagan in this awkward in-between stage. It was a new form of torture they had developed for us lycans, forcing us to be stuck in the middle of our shifting process. Keagan's jaw was barely halfway into a snout, and only a few of his fingers were long and clawed. His right shoulder was larger and hairier than his left, and his spine curved and straightened out multiple times in the brief minute I had watched him. As we pushed through to get closer, it was easier to notice that this was not the only form of punishment our friend had endured. His right eye was swollen and the skin on his body was so bruised he was more purple than white. Blood trickled all over him from an endless number of cuts on his body. Even closer now than we had been before — roughly fifty feet away from the stage — I noticed burns on his skin as well.

I tried to keep my composure as I slightly leaned down to Olly, keeping my eyes straight ahead so as to not raise suspicion from the fifteen or so guards surrounding the stage. "What exactly is the plan here?"

Olly leaned in towards me so I could hear her whispers. "This crowd isn't just ordinary folk from the city. Many of them are our own. When they untie Keagan and take him over to the guillotine, many in this crowd will charge the stage. Our human allies will gather on the drawbridge to prevent them from raising it. We all know they wouldn't risk hurting their own. I've got Moya and Dwyer ready to fire at the witches to scare them off. Rosalie, you can make for the drawbridge with the others. Weylyn, Brina, and I will rush the stage and free Keagan."

"And our escape?" Brina whispered right behind us.

"Dive back into the crowd and flood out the exit with them. Hopefully we get lost in the chaos of it all. I know it's not the best, but it's what we've got."

"It's good enough for me, Olly." I reached back for Rosalie's hand and I was happy to feel her grasp it. I couldn't turn around, but I knew I had her attention. "Rosalie, start easing your way to the back. If we don't find you afterwards, meet us at The Flying Pig."

"Be careful." She gave my hand a tight squeeze before breaking free.

Thankfully, we didn't have to wait too much longer for two guards to come over and untie Keagan. They had humiliated and damaged him enough in their eyes, and now it was time to move onto the main event. The witches stopped their torturing and forced their prisoner into the form that resembled the likeness of a wolf. They dragged Keagan over to the guillotine, the fighting spirit in the lycan driving him to struggle in their grasp. He managed to break free of one of the soldiers, sending the man on his back. The witches were quick to restrain him; Keagan went rigid after the duo shouted out spells. I was growing impatient, waiting for the crowd to charge just like Olly had said they would. It wasn't until they were lowering him into the stocks of the guillotine when I heard shouts from the crowd and a few howls nearby, followed by gunshots. The two witches went running, one of them having been caught in the shoulder. In a swift moment the entire crowd around me lurched forward, with even those who did not wish to participate being taken by the wave of people. I quickly allowed myself to change, knowing my feral form would be much more useful in such tight quarters than a sword or pistol. Brina must have had the same idea, her wolf-like form coming into my vision from my left side.

The two of us, along with Olly, pushed through to the front line of the crowd. The guards were struggling to keep everyone at bay, unable to get their rifles pointed in the crowd's direction. The three of us pounced on the closest ones, removing them from the equation. Brina and I used our brawn and our claws, while Olly used her knives. Being lycans, it was easy for us to overpower our enemies, but as a sprite Olwen had to use her speed and finesse to be effective. She was a very capable fighter and had proven herself over the years as a member of The Resistance, as well as a member of the army during the wars. We made our way onto the stage swiftly and got to Keagan just as he headbutted the only remaining soldier trying to restrain him. Without the witches forcing it onto him, he had reverted to his tame form.

The large lycan struggled to keep himself upright when he spotted us, his bruised face twisted into a sour expression. "About bloody time you showed up."

Before we could say anything, Keagan's eyes rolled into the back of his head and he fell forward. Brina and I both caught him before he hit the stage floor, each of us putting an arm over our shoulders. Olly assessed the scene quickly before pointing over to the steps that led off the stage and into the chaotic crowd. To keep ourselves more hidden, Brina and I shifted back into our form that resembled a human. Together, we carried Keagan's limp body in the direction Olly had gone. The moment we got into the thick of the crowd, Olly whistled a quick tune loud enough for everyone nearby to hear. In a lurching motion, the crowd began making its way toward the drawbridge. Shouts and army whistles could be heard all around Bastion as soldiers struggled to get a handle on the situation we had caused. They tried to move our human allies away from where the portcullis could drop in an effort to keep everyone inside the prison. Thankfully, The Resistance stayed strong, and we slipped by the soldiers as the crowd rushed onto the drawbridge. There was no time to look for Rosalie, she would find us later. Olly weaved through the thick mass before us while Brina and I shoved our way through. Finally free of the thick section of the crowd, it was easier to spot us. Even though we were in our tame forms, we still stuck out thanks to our shirts being torn from changing. We looked around for only a few seconds before Olly led us into an alley.

"In here. Quickly before someone sees us." Olly lifted the heavy sewer cover and waved us over.

I sent Brina down first, then lowered Keagan down as gently as I could. I made sure Olly went next, allowing me to be the final person climbing down the ladder. With everyone inside, I slid the iron cover over our heads. It was pitch black for a moment, until my eyes adjusted. It was still hard to see, but it wasn't impossible to navigate. However, we weren't in the dark for long. I heard Olly muttering to herself until she let out a loud happy squeal as light filled the sewer tunnel. She was holding a thick stick about the size of her forearm, with a magical flame flickering on the end of it.

"What in the world is that?" Brina asked as she shaded her eyes from the glow, her eyes having to adjust once more.

Olly smiled while pointing to the shaft of the torch. "A special thing I had Genevieve make for me. A torch that doesn't need a spark to light! Just rub away the rune and boom, you got some light for a little while."

"You know where you're going?" Brina grumbled as we began following Olly down the sewer.

"Of course, I do. I essentially grew up in these sewers. Pays to have an exit strategy as a thief. We'll be at The Flying Pig before you know it."

I looked over at Keagan's battered face and a large wave of pity and guilt filled me. We had saved him, but he needed a healer quickly. "Will Odran be at the pub? Keagan needs to be tended to."

Olly turned around and began walking backwards. "Yes, Odran will be there. Let's just hope he hasn't started drinking yet."

Olly turned back around and I tried to be positive. Keagan was strong. He would be okay. He had to be okay. I needed Keagan for what was coming.

# Chapter Five

# Weylyn

Cloque, Fleuris  |  December 2, 1798

"How is he?" Rosalie asked as she put a comforting hand on my shoulder.

"Odran said he should be fine in a week or so. He just needs rest," I answered.

Rosalie came around to sit in my lap. "It turns my stomach to see him like this. We had our arguments, but I'd never wish this type of abuse on anyone."

"Keagan's a tough bugger," Olly interjected as she chewed on a piece of apple. "He'll be fine."

"Olwen is right. All we have to do now is wait," Brina said before taking a large bite out of a loaf of bread.

"Yes well, while we wait," Olly grabbed a chair and spun it around before sitting down and resting her elbows on the back of it. "Why not tell me about this good news you have?"

Any bit of excitement I had before arriving was overshadowed by my concern for Keagan. Actually, the whole situation surrounding tonight had me thinking about the risk I had agreed to take on the behalf of others. I almost, for just a brief second, wished that I had never agreed to even go to Tudrose. I looked to Rosalie, then to Brina. Both of them gave me an encouraging smile and nod. Bringing my attention back to Olly, I took a deep breath and cleared my throat before telling her the outcome of our time in Draca. "Queen Sophia has agreed to help us in our efforts to make life better for all of the Tóráin. Not just in Fleuris, but in other countries as well."

Olly's olive-skinned face lit up, her lavender eyes glinting with excitement. "That's wonderful news! Well done. All of you. You should all be very proud."

I scratched behind my ear and avoided Olly's gaze, my dear friend noticing that everything wasn't so wonderful quite quickly. Before I could say anything, the sprite was sitting more upright in her chair, looking to get reactions from Rosalie and Brina too. "What's wrong?"

"We had to make a deal with her," Brina announced, saving me from saying it.

"What sort of deal? Come on you three, you're beginning to make me think this good news of yours isn't really all that good."

I eased Rosalie off my lap and stood from my seat, silently insisting for her to take it for herself. She sat down and I walked a few steps over to Keagan's bed. We had removed his tattered clothes and Odran had cleaned his wounds. Surprisingly, only a few fingers and his nose were broken; everything else was just going to be severely sore for a while. I bent over and removed the cloth on Keagan's forehead, dunked it in the bucket of cold water nearby, and then squeezed as much of the liquid out of the cloth as I could. Gently, I rested the newly cooled cloth back on his forehead. Having bided my time long enough, I turned around to face everyone and put my hands on my hips.

"In this deal we've made, Queen Sophia gives us an army. We have been assured this will not be a conquest for Tudrose, merely a cleansing of the oppressors of our kind in the selected nations. However, she will not attack until the countries are weakened from within somehow. Tudrose is strong, but their ruler is uninterested in losing so many of her citizens to a war she does not need to wage. It's our job to go to Tulp, Korblum, Stelpina, and Malvene in order to raise resistances there like we have done here in Fleuris. We need to assure people, humans and non-humans, that Tudrose can free them from the horrible lives they lead; that it's in their best interest to help weaken the nation they reside in. It will be a difficult task, one that could take quite a bit of time to complete. Regardless, this is what we have agreed upon. What do you think, Olly?"

The sprite put her palm on her forehead and tapped her small, brown antlers with her fingers. She continued tapping as she absorbed everything I had just told her. I valued her opinion on this the most, knowing that she would be honest whether it hurt me or not. It was why we were such good friends. I gave her all the time she needed to come up with a response, respecting the fact that I was asking a great deal of The Resistance. Olly finally stopped tapping her antlers and took one final bite from her apple, tossing the core onto a nearby table.

"It's quite the deal, Weylyn. We're risking a whole lot while Queen Sophia keeps her hands clean. Having nothing but her word to assure us that after all our work is done, she'll finally help us, isn't ideal. However, if you trust that she will be true to her word, then I'll trust the same thing. Do you have a plan on how to start these revolutions?"

I wouldn't say I fully trusted Queen Sophia, but I had no other choice than to do just that. We couldn't continue doing the same things. We weren't going anywhere. This was our road forward. Thankfully, I had thought about how we could start during our trip back. "I figured we could split up, each taking two countries. I would start in Malvene. It's been a while since I've heard from him, but I believe Ossian still lives in Leonessa. The satyr was a very good friend to my father. He did leave Fleuris when the riots started, but he's been supportive of The Resistance in his letters. My hope is that he could help me figure out what to do in Malvene. From there I'd move north to Stelpina. You could start in Tulp or Korblum. That's all I really have right now."

I could tell as I was telling my plan that both Brina and Rosalie were surprised by it. It had crossed my mind to maybe tell them on our journey back home, but I hadn't been entirely sure if this was what I wanted to do. Honestly, I still wasn't sure, but I knew Olly and I could come up with something that would work. However, the sprite took her time to respond, giving Brina and Rosalie time to voice their transgressions.

"You don't really think I'll let you go on your own do you?" Brina exclaimed.

I rolled my eyes. "How many times do I have to reassure you that I am fully capable of taking care of myself?"

"Why does it have to be you and Olwen?" Rosalie chimed in, taking my hand in hers. "Who's going to look after things here? You know full well that Brina would follow you anyway. You, Brina, and Olwen, all gone? You can't be thinking of leaving Keagan in charge."

I brought myself to a knee so my eyes were more level with Rosalie's. "You're right. Both about Brina and the three of us leaving. No, I wouldn't leave Keagan in charge. You would be a much better candidate."

"Hold on now. First off, if this does happen, one of Brina and I are going with you. You shouldn't go anywhere on your own, you're way too important to —" Olly cut herself off, eventually shaking her head in an apparent attempt to clear it. "The Resistance needs you alive, Weylyn. Next order of business is this thing you call a plan. It's more akin to a whimsical idea than a plan, but I will admit it has some promise. I might be able to connect with an old army friend by the name of Rooney. I saved his life in Korblum. I heard he had settled in Tulp's capital, Leuw, so I guess I could start there. That still leaves each of us with a country where we have zero connections, which isn't great. And finally, my last bit of input here, I'm not entirely sure Rosalie should be given that responsibility. No offense."

Rosalie put up her free hand, the other still holding mine. "None taken. I agree. The Resistance needs to be led by a Tórán. You're better off with someone like Dwyer than me, as much as it pains me to say it."

I took a moment to absorb everything that had been said. I wanted to please everyone and let them know that their opinions mattered. It was how my father used to handle things and it had become how I handled things too. The Resistance was more than just one person, and so more than one person had a say in what we did and how we did it. After rising to my feet, I removed my hand from Rosalie's and rested it on her shoulder instead. I took a deep breath before addressing everyone's concerns. Brina, as much as I would like for you to remain here and watch over Rosalie instead, you're welcome to come with me to Leonessa. Olly, it seems like you have a good idea of where to start so I'll agree that Tulp should be your first stop. As you said, it isn't great that we are lacking in contacts within Korblum and Stelpina, but perhaps we'll discover something during our times in Tulp and Malvene that can help in that regard. We'll figure it out when we get to it. For now, we have a place to start, and that's better than nothing. As for the concern of Rosalie handling things here in Cloque, there isn't anyone else I trust to do so. Dwyer may be effective but he's no leader. He wouldn't be able to handle the stresses that come along with keeping things together. Rosalie, it'll be tough, but you'll have allies like Dwyer, Odran, and Moya to rely on. Even Keagan has his uses. It has to be you that leads them though. It can't be anyone else."

Silence filled the room for a short while. I could see on everyone's faces that what I had said wasn't fully acceptable in their minds. Each of them struggled with something, but it wasn't any of them that broke the quiet that had swallowed us whole.

"Right well if Brina is goin' with Weylyn then I better go with O' and make sure she doesn't die."

We were all surprised to see Keagan sitting up in his bed, rotating his left shoulder and grimacing. Another friend of ours that we had saved a few months ago had endured similar punishment, and they had slept for nearly four days as they recovered. Keagan's strength was always talked about, mostly by Keagan, but what had been said appeared to be true. Don't get me wrong, it looked like Hell had chewed him up and spat him back out, but there was life in his eyes. It was a sparkle that usually died when people endure the type of torture he had gone through. Rosalie jumped out of her chair and spun around to face the red-haired lycan, her hands placed firmly on her hips.

"You'll be going absolutely nowhere until you've given yourself time to heal."

Keagan scoffed, leading to a brief coughing fit that ended with bloody spittle erupting from his mouth. "I'll be doin' exactly what I want to be doin', Rosey-dearest. I'll heal on the road."

I quickly stepped in between the two of them, cutting Rosalie off. Had I not done so, she almost certainly would have given Keagan some new bruises. I shook my head at Rosalie and she rolled her eyes before turning back around and returning to her seat. She crossed her arms aggressively. "Fine. Go on the road and die for all I care, you ignorant brute."

Olly extended her hand at Keagan. "Ladies and gentlemen, the ever so charming Keagan, Prick of Fleuris."

"Charmin', yes. Prick of Fleuris? Doubt that's right. Everybody loves me. Just ask around. More like 'Prize' of Fleuris." Keagan chuckled as he tossed the blanket off himself and swung his legs over the edge of the bed.

We all watched as he tried to stand. Well, all of us save for Rosalie who seemed to truly care less if the lycan died right then and there. Everyone knew not to call Rosalie, 'Rosey'. The name brought back horrifying memories of her uncle and she usually punched, kicked, or — in one case — headbutted the person who called her it. While Rosalie stewed in her chair, Keagan miraculously stood up on his own. He was weak, struggling to keep his balance, but I had every belief that he was actually better than he looked.

"You're sure you can travel?" I asked Keagan as he reached over at the table and snagged a cup of the local brew, downing the mug in a few gulps.

"Oh you cannot seriously be considering sending him with me!" Olly was visibly upset, her eyes wide and her arms firmly crossed over her chest.

Keagan laughed. "Oh I can do more than travel. Give me a few days and I'll cause all the riots you and O' want."

It was my turn to cross my arms now, glaring at Keagan as he sat back down on the bed. "No riots, Keagan. I mean it. We aren't going to cause problems, we're going to fix them. Our job is to find what's stopping the Tóráin and their human allies from forming a true resistance against those who oppose them. Then, we remove whatever is stopping them. We help them as much as we can, inspiring them like we were inspired. I don't want you going if you're just going to give Olly a headache and a mess to clean up everywhere the two of you go."

Olly threw her hands in the air, no doubt realizing that I was indeed considering allowing Keagan to go with her. The sprite was even more capable than me to take care of herself; however, it would do us both some good to have one of our own to rely on during our journeys. Plus, I didn't think leaving Keagan in Fleuris with Rosalie was a good option.

"I can't make any promises on the headaches, but if what you need from me is to give the citizens of a couple countries a good ol' kick in the ass, then I'll do just that." Keagan leaned back to lay on the bed with his legs hanging off the edge.

"We aren't going to be kicking anyone in the ass, you boor. We're going to help people. We both know that you're barely capable of helping yourself. Take your physical condition out of it and I still don't think you're the right person for this." Olly grabbed a small handful of hazelnuts and peeled the skin off one of them before popping the snack into her mouth.

"I think he is." Olly gave me a look I was expecting for saying such a thing. Brina mirrored the sprite's expression and I think Rosalie was ready to punch me.

"You can't be serious. You know how much trouble he is, Weylyn," Brina said as she plucked a new piece of bread from the table.

I gave my attention to only Keagan. He had straightened up in response to what I had said, and his bruised face was focused on mine. I caught his eyes and saw the same thing I had seen the moment I met him. He was rough. He was rude and unruly. But, at his core, he wanted a better life for himself and every other Tórán in the known world. He wanted to help. Maybe this would be good for him.

"I appreciate all of your concerns, and I want you to know that I understand all of them. However, I still believe that the best plan for us is as follows. Brina will come with me to Leonessa to meet with Ossian. Olly and Keagan will go to Leuw and search for Olly's friend Rooney. Rosalie, you'll stay behind and keep things going here in Cloque. It isn't perfect, but it's my final decision. I hope you can find it in yourself to support it."

Keagan nodded, thanking me for my decision, before lowering himself onto his back again. Olly let out a grunt and a few grumbles in annoyance, but she did not argue with me any further. Brina just came forward and put a hand on my shoulder for a moment, patting it before using her hand to break off a piece of the bread she was holding. Rosalie rose from her seat so that the two of us stood close to each other. She placed both of her hands on my chest and looked up at me longingly.

Her green eyes grew misty and I thought she might cry. Before she could, she blinked quickly and gathered herself.

"When do you plan to leave?" Rosalie asked.

I kissed her forehead to comfort her, knowing this would be extremely difficult for both her and The Resistance. "Tomorrow, I'd imagine. The sooner we begin the sooner we'll finish."

"I'll gather coin and provisions for the four of us." Brina tossed the bread she had been eating back on the table where she found it.

"I'll make sure that Dwyer, Moya, and Odran know what's going on. No details of course, just enough for them to function well enough. They won't take to a human leading The Resistance very well. Even if it is Rosalie."

I waved my hand at Olly. "They'll get over it. I'm going to get Rosalie home safe and then get some sleep. Make sure you all get some too. Don't know how many relaxing nights we'll have ahead of us. Best take advantage of this one."

"See you in the mornin', boss!" Keagan waved from his sprawled out position on the bed.

"See you in the morning, Weylyn. Sleep well, Rosalie." Brina gave Rosalie a quick hug and smacked my arm before leaving through the door.

Olly stood where she was, fumbling with her fingers before speaking. "I may have my doubts about some parts of this plan, but I'm not against what you've chosen, Weylyn. I'm with you. Always. I hope you know that."

I put a hand on each of her shoulders to make sure she looked at me. "Olly, you never have to reassure me of that. We all have our opinions. It doesn't mean we're against each other when those opinions don't align perfectly. I'm with you too. Always. Get some sleep alright?" I looked over at Keagan and shook my head before bringing my attention back to my dear friend. "I have a feeling you're going to need it."

"And whose fault is that?" Olly chuckled and gave me a firm hug. "Just kidding with you. Once everything is ready for tomorrow, I'll get some rest. Promise."

She released me from her embrace, and I shot a smile her way. She returned the gesture before turning around and yelling at Keagan to get into his bed properly and let her see to his wounds. "I won't have you falling apart on our trip, so stop being such a stubborn ass and let me help you."

It was the last thing I heard as Rosalie and I left the room and closed the door behind us. We made our way down the old stairs that led up to the few rooms The Flying Pig offered its patrons, and then wound our way through the tables set up on the main floor. There were a few people still here, most of them passed out in their seats either at the bar or at their table. I waved over at Terrence behind the bar before opening the door for Rosalie and me to brave the streets of Cloque together.

33

# Chapter Six

# Rosalie



I tried my best not to think of how this could be our last night together in a very long time. Knowing that Weylyn was leaving only had me hugging his arm tighter. The streets had grown dark, with only the moon and random lanterns on people's windowsills left to light our way. Of course, Weylyn could see in the dark much better than I could, so it probably didn't bother him as much. You would think that not being able to see everything around you would be unsettling, but I felt safe with Weylyn. I always have. Ever since we met all those years ago, I felt an overwhelming sense of comfort around him. I trusted him with my life, so letting him guide me through the dark paths of Cloque was easy.

He led us through the shadow-filled streets until we finally arrived at my house. It was small, but it was home. I had left my parent's house only two years ago, needing a place of my own. Of course, with my mother already being ill, my father got sick as well. Now I was bouncing between the two places, enjoying my independence at one while taking care of my parents at another. I would need to relieve my friend Claire tomorrow and thank her for watching over my parents while I was away, but tonight I needed to be here. I needed to be with Weylyn. Not only did I need him to give me the strength and confidence to run things while he and the others were away, but I also needed to hold him and kiss him just in case I never got the chance to do so again. Fleuris was a terrible place for Tóráin, but the neighboring nations were no better. Some of them were even worse. Any of them would easily kill a lycan trying to incite unrest in their country.

Weylyn pulled me in for a hug and kissed the top of my head, almost as if he knew what I was thinking about. He knew I worried for him. It was why I went with him to Draca. I couldn't bring myself to sit here while he went to a new country asking for them to wage war on Fleuris and others. Not to mention it was my idea, so if anything were to happen to him, I would have been even more devastated. I forced my way into that quest, and I was beginning to wonder if I should force myself into this one too. Again, as if he could read my mind, Weylyn moved me out of his embrace so he could kiss me.

"Before you try to guilt me into taking you with me again, can we at least go inside? It's quite cold for me, which means it's much too cold for you."

He wasn't wrong. After all, it was approaching the winter months. It had snowed slightly back in Draca, but it would not begin to snow here in Cloque for at least a couple more weeks. The cold only made me wish to go to Malvene even more, their winters known to be more manageable than ours. Despite my eagerness to plead my case, I honored Weylyn's request and held off my debate until we were inside. I reached at my neck and pulled the string necklace over my head, grabbing hold of the key that was attached to it. The lock stuck, so I had to wiggle it a bit, but eventually it gave way, and I opened the door. I asked Weylyn to find the lantern for me so we could have some light in the place, and a few moments later a soft orange glow filled the small apartment. Weylyn sent me a big smile before making his way over to the hearth to get a fire going so that we could warm up.

"I'm going to change into clothes that don't smell so bad," I announced.

"Why don't I get the tub full of some warm water and we wash the stink off our skin too?" Weylyn lit a match and tossed it into the kindling he had set up in the hearth.

"Won't that take a while?" I was tired. I just wanted to lay down and be with Weylyn for however many hours we had left.

"Won't a warm bath feel wonderful?" Weylyn asked as the crackling of the warm fire filled the small apartment.

A warm bath did sound lovely. "Oh fine. But I'm still getting these clothes off of me. You'll just have to keep me warm until the bath is ready."

"It would be my honor to keep the fair lady warm." He grabbed the kettle and made for the door, going to grab water from the rain barrel that was outside.

I made my way to the back of the apartment where I kept my clothes. I only had four dresses and one was too fancy for everyday living. Thankful that I didn't have to put any new clothes on just yet, I quickly removed my cloak and tossed it on the floor. I untied my boned corset — something I hated wearing — and it followed my cloak to the floor. I pushed the fabric off my shoulders and allowed my simple dress to fall to the dusty floor with the rest of my clothes. I then removed my undergarments and stockings after kicking off my boots. Within the time it had taken me to undress, Weylyn had returned to the fire and set the kettle on it to warm the water up. He approached me with a large blanket and wrapped me in it. Bending down, he put one big arm under my legs with the other around my shoulders before lifting me into his arms. I cuddled into his warm chest and allowed him to carry me to the bed laid out by the fire. It was just a simple mattress on the floor, but it was comfortable and warm.

We laid in silence while we waited for each pot of hot water to reach the right temperature before pouring it into the tub that sat about five feet away from the bed and the hearth. We cuddled and kissed. I grew upset that he was clothed and I wasn't, so I removed his shirt. He complained he would be cold leaving to get more water from outside, but I told him it was only fair. I wanted to be close to him, not his clothes. I wanted to feel the hair on his chest on my cheek as I listened to his heartbeat, the rhythm different from a human's. I wanted to be able to feel the muscles on his back and stomach too. His shirt just got in the way of that. Luckily, it didn't take as long as I thought it would to fill the bath and I quickly made my way into it the moment Weylyn had declared it ready. I leaned on the edge of the wooden tub as I watched him undress. He climbed in the bath behind me, and I leaned into him, enjoying the warmth which the water and he himself provided.

"So about me coming with you."

I could hear Weylyn's eyes roll behind me. "I know I brought you with me last time, but this is different work, Rosalie. I don't want to be away from you for a single day, but this has to be the way things are. If we have any luck, our time away will only be weeks, maybe a month or two at most."

"I know, I know." I nuzzled my head under his chin. "I just worry. About you, me, and everything that surrounds us. I can't help but feel I'd be more useful out there with you than trying to keep things running here. You really think it's the right decision to have me lead The Resistance while you and the others are gone?"

Weylyn brought his head down next to mine so he could kiss my shoulder before squeezing me tighter than before. "I do. You've been doing this as long as I have. You care for my kind. You know how to keep things quiet while keeping them efficient at the same time. Plus, you won't be alone. The others will help you when you need it. Olly will make sure everyone is on board before we leave."

"Is Olwen even on board? I mean I don't blame her for thinking the way she does, but it's clear she isn't really for me watching over things."

He kissed my neck now, then my cheek, before speaking softly in my ear. "Olly views The Resistance as an army. It's just how she is. She doesn't see a lieutenant ready to bark orders and lead people into battle. What she doesn't understand is that The Resistance needs something different right now. We need someone who will keep everyone calm while the rest of the world gets a little crazy. After what happened with Keagan, we need to keep a low profile for the next month or so. You're the only person staying behind that I trust to make that happen."

Mention of Keagan soured my mood. "Ugh, why did we go through all that trouble for the bastard anyway? Sorry, I didn't mean it like that. I know why we saved him. I don't want anyone to die, I'm not that cruel, I just don't see what you see in him. To be honest, I'm thankful he's going to be Olwen's problem and not mine."

Weylyn laughed. "Keagan is a...special lycan. Not everyone understands him. To be honest, I too am thankful he won't be here to give you trouble. It's partially why I allowed him to go with Olly."

"You don't think I can control him?" I ran my hand along Weylyn's leg, stopping at his knee.

"I'm sure you'd do a wonderful job at that, but the lycan's talents are better served with Olly than here. We need the utmost quiet here in Cloque, and that fool is anything but. Let's just be thankful he won't be a problem for either of us for a good while."

"Now that's something I can get behind," I said. We laughed before cuddling into each other more, sinking a bit deeper into the water.

It was silent for a moment, until Weylyn brought his hand to my chin and guided my lips to his. "So, you'll stay then?"

I sighed in between kisses. "Fine. I'll stay. But you can't leave just yet." I spun around in the water and wrapped my arms around Weylyn's neck. "You owe me plenty of loving before you get my permission to leave."

Weylyn put his hands on my hips before running them up my sides. They brushed the sides of my chest before one hand made for my back and the other went to my hip again. Kissing me during his exploration of my body, he bit my lip softly, pulling back until it escaped his teeth. "I will give the beautiful lady whatever she wants."

I smiled at him before I took his bottom lip into my teeth and bit down gently, pulling back until it fell out of my mouth. Our noses grazed each other before I kissed him. "Good boy."

# Chapter Seven

# Olwen

Etoile, Fleuris  |  December 8, 1798

If the torturers in Bastion had removed Keagan's voice our trip would have been a more peaceful one, but alas I was left with a traveling companion that never shut their mouth. Keagan loved talking, especially when the subject of conversation was himself. He acted as if he hated when I tended to his wounds every night, but I knew he loved the attention. Every day I considered robbing him of that attention and leaving him to handle his injuries on his own, yet each time we stopped for the night I was quick to check in on him. The truth was that I couldn't have my only support on this trip be an anchor. If Keagan was going to accompany me, he was going to pull his weight, and he couldn't do that if he was bleeding and limping everywhere we went. While his ability to be of use was definitely my top reason for tending to him, it wasn't the only one. Even though he can try my patience more than anyone, Keagan was a very dear friend of mine and I liked it when he wasn't hurt. I had the thought that the more I tended to him, perhaps he would heal faster, and I wouldn't have to see someone I cared about be all battered and bruised all the time.

We could have taken the train even a little of the way, but we all agreed back in Cloque that it was too risky. Word would have been spread quickly to watch for any suspicious activity from our kind within Cloque, but also outside of the city in about a twenty-five mile radius. Even horses would draw too much attention to us, and that was the last thing we wanted. We were all safer to just travel by foot and avoid as many towns and cities as possible by taking old roads through the wilds. Eventually we would have to return to the civilized world and today was such a day. It was actually easier to cross the border into Tulp from the nearby city than out in the wilds. Soldiers watched the wilds much more closely, expecting everyone who would avoid the cities to be hiding something. So, knowing that, Keagan and I had made our way into the border city of Etoile.

The city was named after the star shaped citadel at the center of the place. It was an old castle, one of the oldest ones in Fleuris. A few high-ranking nobles, as well as the local magistrate lived there while the Duke of Etoile resided outside the city in a nearby villa. A good chunk of the city's garrison also called the citadel home, with their commanding officer watching over them. Magistrate Tristan Frollo was a vile man who was known for doing horrible things to my people, and it was he who ran the city. It was well known that he was a member of a group of humans that still believed all the Tóráin should be removed from this world. He treated every race that wasn't human like meat, caring little for their livelihoods. It was why the city of Etoile was home to mostly humans. The Tóráin still travelled here, either to pass through or sell things at the markets, but barely any stayed here for very long. Doing so ran the risk of being picked up by Frollo on some made up charge, and that was the last thing you wanted. You were lucky if he killed you the next day. He was known to torture our kind for fun, sometimes even selling us to rich nobles who had fetishes that involved non-human partners. And when you were caught, there was little to no chance of you escaping. Etoile housed one of the strongest witches in the entire world: Ravenna. Frollo had taken her in and raised her from a young age, and so she was as loyal to him as a child would be to their blood father. It was rumored that Frollo had actually murdered Ravenna's mother and stolen the poor girl, but you ran the risk of being killed asking questions about that.

With Ravenna by his side, Magistrate Frollo did whatever he wanted to do to any Tórán that entered Etoile. Knowing this made our journey into the city a stressful one. We would have to venture through the entire breadth of the city to get to the border, and then we would have to get past the soldiers that watched over it. Keagan wished for us to just take our chances in the wilds, but I knew this way was better. It didn't seem that way to Keagan, and he vehemently argued his distaste for my plan, but he eventually conceded. With or without him, I was going to brave the dangers of the city. Keagan cared too much to let me go on my own, and so he was obliged to follow me. That was one of the few good things about Keagan. He was rough on the outside, for reasons I somewhat understood, but he had one of the biggest hearts. The lycan was prickly and it took a long time for him to trust people — even his own kind — but when he did you were his family. He took the role of protector when it came to those he cared for, always doing his best to make sure they were never harmed. He took great pride in keeping others safe.

Wishing to make sure I was safe, Keagan walked beside me through the crowded streets of Etoile. We kept our hoods up and our cloaks wrapped around us. It was cold, so at least we didn't stand out being so covered up. Many others among us were wrapped in various types of clothing, some of richer taste than others, so we actually blended in quite well. Sure, I had my green skin and my horns, and Keagan had his height and odd posture, but everyone was so busy with their own lives that we managed to pass through unseen. That was until we got close to the citadel. We could have avoided it, but it would have taken us longer to get to the border and neither of us wished to stay in the city more than we needed to. Soldiers patrolled the streets in groups of four, holding their rifles upright just like they taught us in army camp. They all had their eyes moving back and forth, watching over their surroundings looking for someone to harass.

"Tell me again why we decided to come into the cursed place," Keagan whispered at me as we turned our faces away from a passing group of soldiers.

"Because in the wilds they just kill you without question. At least here we have a better chance at keeping our heads on our shoulders." I grabbed his arm and pulled him with me into an alley that gave us a reprieve from the consistent appearance of soldiers.

"We could have just killed them before they killed us. This city means death for our kind. There's no way we can fight our way out of here if they try to jail us for shit charges they love makin' up."

"Aw, is the little wolf scared?"

"Scared? You want me to howl and call them all? I'll last longer than you will you little —"

Before he could finish, I spun into him and had him up against the brick wall. My knife was at his throat and his golden eyes were wide open. I brought my finger to my lips to tell him to be silent as a large group of about a dozen soldiers marched past the exit of our alleyway. Once they were gone, Keagan went to move away but I kept my knife where it was. Keagan snarled and I grinned. "You really are on edge, eh? Even you know how to take a joke."

Keagan swatted my arm away. "This place is dangerous, O'. I'll be much more up for jokes when we're well clear of this damn city."

"So you are scared then." I gave him a cheeky smile and while the lycan had a scowl on his face at first, it eventually turned into a smirk.

"Just shut up and lead us out of here already," Keagan grumbled.

I swiftly brought my knife back into my belt and nodded before re-entering the crowded streets. Slowly but surely, the two of us reached the border. It was just on the outskirts of the city, a small garrison watching the road. It was a mix of soldiers from Fleuris and Tulp, their uniforms differentiating them from each other. I counted twelve from each country, and they were inspecting everyone that was travelling down the road. As we approached, a soldier appeared to have an argument with a civilian before that same civilian ran past the group of soldiers. The man he had been arguing with readied his rifle quickly and killed the forest sprite before the poor Tórán could get even a dozen feet away. Soon enough it was our turn, and I couldn't help but get anxious. Some people were just walking by the soldiers without a word sent their way, so we both tried to just walk on through. Keagan and I kept our heads down as we maneuvered down the road, until two soldiers in Tulp's orange and blue uniforms stepped in our way.

"Hold on you two. What business do you have in Tulp?"

"Just seeing an old army friend. Haven't seen the fool in a few years, figured I'd make the trip and say hello." I hoped that mentioning I was in the army would ease their suspicions.

"Army friend, eh? What division?"

I didn't know what to say. If I lied and got caught, we'd be in trouble. If I told the truth, we could be in even more trouble. Either way, it didn't matter. Before I could decide on what to say, the soldier questioning me removed my hood and recoiled as if I had the plague.

"*Duivel*! We don't need any more of you *vuiligheid* in Tulp. There's more than enough of you. Turn around *stuk stront*."

"Sir, please. My friend is sick, I don't know how much time he has left. I would like to see him before he passes." My calm tone and simple request did nothing for us.

"Now your friend is suddenly sick? I don't care if your friend dies tomorrow. He can rot in Hell. Anyone who is friends with *Duivels* is either a *Duivel* themselves, or a *verrader* of Deus the Creator."

"Oh, fuck Deus. The bastard didn't create anythin'. Now stop givin' us a hard time and let us pass you prick."

I knew the longer this went on the less patient Keagan would get, but I had hoped he would keep quiet. Sadly, he hadn't, and now he had given these soldiers reason to jail us or kill us. There was a good chance we would have to fight our way out of this.

"*Duivels* have no authority here! If we say you don't get to pass on through, you don't. Take your blasphemy elsewhere before we remove your tongue and feed it to your little green friend!"

Keagan pushed past me. "Tell you what. Go about one hundred paces out and train your rifle on me. If I reach you, we get to go through."

The soldier laughed, his friend joining in. "Sounds like someone wants to die. Very well, *idioot*."

The man began walking to the agreed upon distance. I wanted to say something, but I had to admit that my way wasn't really working so far. If this got us through without having to take on two dozen soldiers, then I'd be incredibly thankful. For his size, Keagan was incredibly quick and agile, so I knew there was a good chance he would be okay. Still, it was risky; yet if he was successful, we could possibly get to Tulp without much violence. The soldier reached his spot on the road and turned around. Keagan removed his cloak and his shirt before shifting into his feral form. He snarled as he waited for the test to begin. Another soldier raised his pistol into the air and fired, signaling the beginning of the challenge. Keagan's enemy fired right after the signal, trying to catch the big lycan off guard. Keagan just rolled quickly to the right before charging on all fours at the soldier. He fired another shot, this time sending Keagan to his left. The soldier would have one more chance to stop Keagan before he reached him. With Keagan roughly a quarter of the starting distance away, the soldier connected with his shot. Much to my surprise, the stubborn brute didn't even flinch. The soldier threw his gun to the ground and began to run away from Keagan. Within a couple seconds the soldier had the lycan leaping onto his back, dragging him to the stone road.

Before I knew it, nearly two dozen rifles were pointed at my companion. So much for not having to fight our way out of this. I drew my knives and quickly dispatched the closest guard. The yelp he let out, along with the blood that spewed from his neck, drew the soldiers' attention off Keagan enough for the lycan to close the distance and attack. They were caught off guard, and despite us being heavily out-numbered, Keagan and I made quick work of them. When I finished off the last one, I turned to find Keagan in his tame form, blood covering his hands and mouth. He ripped off the coat from one of the soldiers he had killed and wiped his hands and mouth clean, the stain of blood still coloring him in a shade of red. His somber look reminded me of something that was easy to forget about Keagan. The lycan was confrontational as can be, a brute in his own right. He loved boxing and fighting, almost leaving for Korblum one year to join the fights there. However, Keagan never enjoyed killing. The lycan had nightmares from his time in the army, and he kept count of every person he's ever had to kill. Our current situation made me realize that I hadn't really talked to him about the accident that caused his torture back in Cloque.

"Keagan? Are you alright?"

He tossed his shirt over his head and wrapped his cloak back over his shoulders. He walked towards me, then past me. "Let's get goin'. Other soldiers must have heard that."

Blood was already seeping through his shirt where he had been shot, the wound on his shoulder a ghastly one. He needed tending to, but he was right. More soldiers would be coming to check out what had happened here. We needed to get a move on now, before they arrived. Keagan and I pushed ourselves into a brisk jog, leaving the bloody scene we had created behind. It was a difficult path to have taken, but we had made it to Tulp.

# Chapter Eight

## Olwen

Leuw, Tulp | December 13, 1798

Leuw wasn't perfect, but it was safer than Etoile. It was prettier than Etoile too. The city was made up of small, narrow houses that found homes on patches of land left alone by calm canals. Some have called it a lesser version of Leonessa, but I had only ever been to Leuw so I couldn't compare them myself. I had stayed in Leuw roughly three years ago during one of Fleuris' first campaigns during the war. We didn't find too much resistance, the country being known more for its merchants and artists than its army. We had finished a battle in a large field just outside the city, and a few others and I were sent to formally accept King William's surrender. They wouldn't risk any human soldiers to a possible ambush in the city, so they sent me and others like me instead. We were led by a higher-ranking human officer of course, but Tóráin made up the majority of the force at the officer's back.

King William was actually not too bad. What I mean by that is that he wasn't an abhorrent ass like his son, who he had also named William. It was tradition in their line for the first-born male to be named William, and the son was the fifth of his name. He was rude and crass and was now the new King of Tulp after his father died roughly a year after his surrender. Believe it or not, my short time in Leuw was actually a nice reprieve from the constant fighting that followed us as we moved into Korblum. It hadn't changed much, but it did seem to be doing much better than when I was last here. Well, the rich were doing better at least. There were still plenty of poor folk begging in the streets and doing all the hard labor; many of them being people who called themselves Tóráin. It was faster to get around the city by boat, but I refused to force another Tórán to row us around. Keagan was of the same mind as me, so we walked instead. I struggled to keep myself from helping those I could as we made our way through the unique pathways, crossing many short bridges that connected one piece of land to the other. Seeing so many in such poor situations made me concerned for the friend that we had come looking for.

The last I had heard from sweet old Roo, he was working as a cobbler in a small shop near the more eastern edge of town. I was hoping I had remembered correctly since I really didn't want to have to ask anyone — human or not — for directions. We had been scouring the east end for about an hour or so until finally I spotted a hanging sign with 'Noach's Shoe Repair' on it. I waved at Keagan, indicating I had found our destination. I walked up to the door, opened it, and stepped in as a small bell above me rang to announce my arrival.

"Just a moment! I'll be right with ya." The voice came from a satyr that quickly went from one room in the hall at the back of the shop to another.

"Not to worry, Roo, I'm in no hurry," I shouted back.

I heard something fall in the back of the room as Keagan entered the small building, the bell sounding off again. Rooney came stumbling out, adjusting his glasses as he looked me over. I took my hood off to help him.

"Wenny?" he asked.

I nodded, a big smile on my face as I was happy to see my old friend.

"Wenny!" The satyr's arms opened wide before he wrapped them around me tightly.

"Hello, Roo." I laughed as I patted his back, hoping he would let me go some time soon. Thankfully, he eventually did let me go. It was lovely to see him but I really wasn't the best with physical affection. At least not with the majority of people.

Roo took a couple steps back as he looked me over with his hands on his hips. "My word ya look great! To what do I owe the pleasure of such fine company?"

"Is it just you here, or is the owner in one of those rooms back there?" I asked as I looked around the small place myself.

"Oh Noach? Nah the old grump went home early today. Just me here."

I trusted Roo, but I sent Keagan to check the back just in case. Who knows if anyone had gotten their claws into the sweet satyr since I last saw him. When

Keagan came out of the last room in the hall and nodded, I grabbed Roo's hands so as to better get a hold of his attention.

"You remember how I'm part of a rebel group back in Fleuris, yes?"

Roo nodded. "Of course. Great thing that is. Wish we had one here. Noach treats me well, but there are many of our kind that are not so lucky. Even a good number of humans struggle to have good lives here. They say we are in a golden age here in Leuw, but the truth is — as it is with most of Tulp — the richest humans are the only ones living well."

I smiled, knowing now that Roo was the right person to come to. "Well funny you would wish that because my friend and I have come to start a Resistance chapter here in Tulp. I was hoping you would know how I could go about doing that."

Roo adjusted his glasses and wiped the sweat from his brow with a small towel he kept draped over his shoulder. He seemed anxious at first, but he appeared to calm himself before waving at us to follow him to the back of the shop. Roo led us into a tiny room full of shoes and tools, adjusting his vest and fixing his glasses once more as Keagan and I filed in after him.

"You had to pick the smallest room?" Keagan grumbled.

I gave the lycan a swift punch to the arm. "Shut up."

Roo forced a smile as he brought his hands together over his stomach. "Sorry, friend. I'd take us elsewhere, but I think every room in this place would be small to a lycan of your stature."

"It's okay," I said. "Ignore him, Roo. What can you tell us about setting up a Resistance chapter in Tulp?"

The satyr's bushy eyebrows raised high on his forehead, and he cleared his throat before speaking. "Right. Yes. Well, I'm not the best person for something like that. I'd help where I could, but ya need a true leader in the community to get any real traction. There's this water sprite that works at the docks on the north-western end of Leuw. Her name is Cordelia. She's the person ya want to chat with."

"How do we find her?" Keagan asked.

Roo quickly reached into his pocket and pulled out a watch. "Ah yes, four o'clock. Cordelia can be easily found at the docks until five, sometimes six. After that you'll either find her at a bar or at one of the three orphanages in the city. You'll have a much simpler time if ya catch her at the docks though, so ya best get a move on if ya want to ensure catching her."

I sent the satyr a big smile before grabbing a hold of his hands. "Thank you, Roo. That is plenty helpful."

I waved at Keagan, and we made our way back to the front of the shop, Roo shuffling after us, his hooves clicking on the hardwood floor like a horse.

"One thing before ya go. If you miss her at the docks, I'd try The Lucky Whale Inn first before going anywhere else. She really likes singing at that one."

I thanked Roo once again, this time coming forward and giving him a quick, one-armed hug. Keagan then opened the door and held it open, waiting for me to go through.

"Be safe! Both of ya! Good luck!" Roo whispered loudly as I made my way out of the shop.

The door closed and Keagan groaned. "I had hoped we would find a place to get some drink and some meat."

I rolled my eyes. "Yeah, well this is more important. Come on, we'll get there in time if we run."

Keagan leaned to one side, then the other, stretching out in preparation for our sprint. "Isn't this goin' to draw attention, two Tóráin racin' through the streets of Leuw?"

"Do you have to question every damn thing I say?" I asked as I jogged into the open street.

"Hey, you're the lady wantin' to be so damn secretive."

Our pace was quick, but not too swift to draw attention. It took us more time than I had hoped, but we arrived at the docks just as the sun was nearly done setting. I was hoping that we would catch Cordelia here instead of having to search for her all night. Sure, we could just wait until tomorrow, but I didn't want to waste a day if I didn't have to. Keagan and I made our way onto the docks as fellow Tóráin unloaded and reloaded the ships anchored in the port. It was a different kind of port than one would be used to, seeing as it wasn't on a sea's shore. Running through Leuw was a large canal; large enough, and deep enough, for four galleys to sail side by side comfortably. Breaking off from The Nord Canal were smaller canals that led to docks. There were eight branches that broke off from The Nord Canal, each of them varying in size. After mistaking another water sprite for Cordelia, we were directed to the smaller canals at the east end of the port.

We dodged workers as they carried crates to new homes, gathered fish, and other things that one would expect to find people doing at one of the busiest ports in the world. Westen Port, it was called, and if you weren't careful, you'd get shoved into the water while trying to navigate the docks. Luckily, the two of us escaped getting wet long enough to spot a water sprite shouting orders at two lycans.

"Oi! Watch how you handle that! King William's wine, that is. Don't go droppin' any of it, you hear me? I stuck my neck out for you two last week and I ain't 'bout to do it again!"

She had dark green hair resembling seaweed tied up into a horsetail. Her skin was a soft, pale blue and the gills on her neck fluttered when she yelled. Her grey eyes were piercing even from this distance, and she dressed herself much like I did. Most would say it was a style more akin to the attire of males — save for the leather corset — but I found it more comfortable to wear a shirt and pants instead of a flowy dress. Even skirts bothered me. I always had a cloak on me too, even in the summer months. It was nice to see that we shared the same style of attire. Her dark blue lips flapped as she continued to shout out orders to everyone around her as if she owned the place. It was odd seeing a Tórán in such a role. It instantly made me respect her, and I knew that this water sprite was the one we were looking for.

"Excuse me!" I shouted as I made my way towards her. "Are you Cordelia?"

The water sprite spun around to face me, her hands on her hips and a toothpick resting in her mouth. "Who's bloody askin'?"

"A new friend, I hope." I smiled at her, but my grin faded as the sprite twisted her face at me and removed the pick from her mouth.

"Yeah, that's cute and all but I was hopin' for a name." The sassy sprite pushed by me and came to stand in front of Keagan. She looked him up and down as she rested a hand on his chest. "Wouldn't mind gettin' more than just a name from this one though."

"Name's Keagan. The friendly one over there is Olwen. You'll get more from her than you will from me." Keagan tapped at his arm ring; a gift commonly given to male lycans by their wives.

Keagan's wife, Cliana, died of sickness only a few months after they were married roughly seven years ago. You would think he would have moved on, still being more than young enough to find a new partner, but he didn't want to. He turned down every woman who ever threw themselves at him, and he always touched his arm ring when he did.

"Well that's disappointin'." Cordelia spun around and went to untangling a large fishnet. "What do ya want?"

"Ever thought of havin' a better life? One more like those rich pricks have? Or at the very least for things to be more even around here?" I cringed when Keagan spoke, worried that we were too in the open to discuss such things. Thankfully, I wasn't alone in feeling that way.

"Oi! You tryin' to get me in shackles? Don't come stormin' my docks and shoutin' 'bout revolution type things."

"Your docks?" Keagan crossed his arms, a condescending grin on his face.

Cordelia wrapped her cloak around her before hopping up to take a seat on a closed barrel. "They might as well be. I don't formally own 'em, but I damn well should. I run this port. Make sure things happen the way they're supposed to happen. It's somethin' I take real pride in, ya know?"

"And you're treated well?" I figured it was my turn to ask a couple questions, despite her clearly liking Keagan more than me at the moment.

Cordelia's face changed and her posture slouched. In the short time of knowing her, she had held herself high with the confidence of someone who was in charge. Now, she looked like every other downtrodden Tórán we had encountered in Leuw. Something I had said had caused her to change. Cordelia let out a deep sigh and put the net she was working with on a stack of crates next to her. She tucked the small knife she was using back into its tiny sheathe and brought her hands together.

"Honest answer?" Cordelia sighed before continuing. "No. I ain't treated well at all. Nobody like us is. Those lycans I was givin' shit to over the King's wine? I only do that 'cause if they damage even one bottle, King Willy will have 'em flogged, starved, and eventually killed. The Tóráin walk on eggshells in Tulp. It all looks pretty and such, but the only people it's nice for are those rich nobles and their fat king." Cordelia looked over her shoulder at the setting sun and hopped off the barrel. "There's a better place to talk 'bout things like this. Let me take ya to Young Wolf Pub. Its owner is technically a human but good ol' Strahan runs the place. His parents died when he was a pup, and the nice fella Godewyn took him in and raised him as his own son. Strahan was only four at the time. Come on, we can talk about anythin' ya like over there. Safe place that is."

Cordelia pushed on past Keagan and me, walking at a brisk pace down the docks. I looked at Keagan and he shrugged before following her. I followed Keagan, and together we made our way to Young Wolf Pub. It wasn't too far from Westen Port, but the sun was gone by the time we got there. I gave a quick look around the outside of the place to see if anyone had followed us before going inside. The moment we walked through the doors there were people shouting Cordelia's name as they raised their mugs in the air. It wasn't just the Tóráin patrons that did this. I counted half a dozen humans all raising their mugs too. It seemed that Cordelia was well-liked by the people of Leuw. Well, at least that was the impression I was getting. She was exactly the person we needed to be talking to. I was so excited to begin that I tried to do just that the moment we sat down at a table in the far corner of the pub.

"Hey, hey, hey." Cordelia raised a hand in the air to stop me from speaking. "First we get some drink and some food. Then we talk. Strahan! The usual, love! Make it three!" Cordelia pulled out a pipe from her pocket and packed it with a paste before bringing a match to it.

"Where did someone like you get Star Leaf wax?" Keagan beat me to the question.

Cordelia took a big inhale and puffed out smoke rings into the pub's ceiling. "Friend of mine works on one of the ships that goes to the desert lands to the far south. What's the bloody place called again? Lutis! That's it! He goes to Lutis and when he comes back here and sneaks me some Star Leaf. Every couple months or so, but he usually gives me enough to last. King Willy and his nobles buy so much of the damn stuff they hardly notice some of it missin'."

"Here you go, Cor." A large lycan with flowing light brown hair and a short, thick beard took three mugs off the tray he was balancing on his hand. He also took three bowls of steaming stew off the tray and placed one in front of each of us.

"Thanks Strahan. Always a pleasure dear." Cordelia took out a small satchel and poured out a few coins onto the table.

Strahan smiled and swiped them, quickly depositing them into the pocket on the large apron he wore. "The pleasure's all mine. Enjoy."

No talking happened for a short while. The moment Strahan had said 'enjoy' Cordelia dove into her stew. In that moment my stomach grumbled, and I realized just how hungry I was too. The three of us happily ate our stew and drank our beer in silence. Eventually we were all fat and happy, sitting back in our chairs with a fresh mug of beer placed in front of us by Strahan. Cordelia was back to smoking her pipe, leaning back on her chair with her feet up on the table. She let out an exaggerated breath before spitting in her pipe, cleaning it out with her cloak, and pocketing it. She let out an exasperated sigh before taking her feet off the table.

"So!" she said as she leaned on the table, her chin cradled by her hands and her elbows firmly on the wooden surface. "Why did you come lookin' for me? No lyin'."

I looked at Keagan and he waved me on, insisting that I tell Cordelia our mission. I described to her what had transpired with Weylyn and the others in Draca and expanded on that information when I told her about the conversations

had in Cloque. She never twisted her face once — which I took as a good sign —
but when I finished, she seemed bothered.

"Right. So, you want me to start a resistance here in Leuw. Cause problems
throughout Tulp. All so that some queen can come here and shake things up?"

"Well, yes. Basically." I felt like I should have said something better than that.

"Are you up for it?" Keagan asked before taking a huge gulp of his beer.

Cordelia bit her lip and looked at Keagan and me, bouncing back and forth
between the two of us until letting loose a small smile. "I wouldn't mind things
bein' shaken up a bit."

"Really? Great!" Cordelia's smile faded just as soon as it had appeared, causing
me to feel silly for being so excited. "What's wrong?"

"Jacob De Vries. A right prick that one. His head witch, Grada, ain't so
pleasant either. De Vries is a high-rankin' officer in the king's army. Not too high,
but high enough to make any chance of a revolution a small one. Damn near non-
existent. There was a riot a year ago, and thanks to De Vries' military smarts and
Grada's magic, they snuffed out anythin' that may have spawned from it. Not to
mention they saw to all the punishment dealt out to those who participated. If you
want to weaken Tulp, you need to weaken Leuw. To weaken Leuw, you need to get
rid of De Vries and his little witch friend. They oversee the entire city, especially
the docks. If they were gone, we could steal more goods and give 'em to the poor
and hungry. We could maybe build somethin' strong enough that could aid
neighborin' towns to cause a little chaos of their own. But, it won't be easy."

I looked at Keagan and smiled before bringing my attention back to Cordelia.
"We'll figure something out. You give us all you know about Jacob De Vries and
Grada. We'll take care of the rest."

Cordelia grinned from ear to ear, and this time her smile stuck around for a
while. She raised her mug into the air. "To new friends."

Keagan crashed his mug into hers. "To new friends!"

I smiled, bringing my mug into theirs. "To new friends."

# Chapter Nine

## Weylyn

Lombardi, Malvene | December 13, 1798

I spotted the mountains to the south many miles away. I had never seen them before, and to be in the presence of the Great Western Folds was immensely humbling. My father had described the landscape to me many times, having viewed it himself back when he had been recruited for the Fleuris army. He used to tell me that we would witness the grand sight together one day. Seeing the giant mountains now was bittersweet. It had taken us over a week to reach the small town of Lombardi, but I think we made good time. Finally entering Malvene had me nervous. I was anxious to start all over again. It was easier in Fleuris. My father's defiance in front of King Louis sparked a fire in those who had laid dormant for years. Many rode that wave of passion forward, leading to The Resistance being formed shortly after. It wasn't by any means easy though, my predecessor Darby had made sure to tell me on a consistent basis all of the obstacles he had to overcome to create The Resistance.

He had fought in the army with my father, along with Ossian and Uncle Benen. He was one of the largest and strongest lycans I had ever known. Darby spent his entire time as leader grooming me to be his successor, which at the time felt silly. We all used to joke that Darby wouldn't die for another four decades, despite him nearing his fifties at the time. It was a cruel joke when he was captured after a member of The Resistance had been tortured into revealing Darby as our leader. They publicly tortured him for weeks. General Rosspier had just successfully dethroned King Louis, and he wanted to make a statement to everyone in Fleuris, human and Tórán both. They left Darby on that stage for over a week. One night, General Rosspier's second in command, Major Carierre, just walked onto the stage and shot Darby in the head. There was no crowd. No one for him to look to in his final moments. We tried to recover his body, but it remained under the watchful eye of roughly twenty guards. Many wanted to storm the stage, but my first order as leader of The Resistance was to do nothing. Only worse things could come from us showing such a public display of strength. We peacefully begged to let us bury him, but they refused. Instead, he stayed on that stage for a few more days before they tied him up similar to how they tied up Tóráin and witches over a century ago. Wood was eventually gathered a few more days after that, and then they burned him.

His death forced me into his position, taking his place at age twenty-three. For six years I've led The Resistance, and now I had the job of creating a new one, in a new country. It's been ten years since I've seen Ossian, but I do remember that he was always good to my father and me. I was really hoping that he would have some insight as to how we could get started in Malvene. I just hoped he still lived in Leonessa. It was roughly a year or so since I had heard from him via letter, and I knew that plenty could happen in such a long time. Thankfully, I had many more days to worry about all that and more, seeing as we were probably another seven or eight days away from reaching Leonessa. The place would be much different than little Lombardi, the town inhabiting one of the many valleys that led into the mountains behind them. Houses even stretched up onto the mountainsides, some so high it made me tired just thinking about making the trek up and down every day.

"Aren't that many humans here, or is it just me?" Brina looked around, trying to perhaps find more humans lurking just outside her vision.

"Lombardi used to have more humans, until the wars with Fleuris back in the year seventeen-seventy-six. Humans felt too vulnerable on the other side of the mountains, so most of them retreated south to cities like Tordoro and Azuvipa. The Tóráin saw a chance at a place of their own, and so many either stayed or made their way here. Our fathers told us about it whenever they talked about their time in the army. Don't you remember?"

"Obviously not. Do they have good tea?" Brina asked with a smile.

I laughed. "Better. The place has great wine. Supposedly all of Malvene does."

"Another bit of information you were fed while spending time with your father I assume?" Brina teased as she led the way to the only place in town we would find a room to spend the night, The Solitary Summit Inn.

"I was fed years full of stories while spending time with him. The amount of information only grew when Darby, Ossian or Benen were around. I couldn't help but learn something new. You would know just as much as I do if you weren't too busy running around the city to ever sit down and listen to them." I skipped a few paces to be next to Brina and wrapped my arm around her shoulders for a playful hug as the two of us made our way up to the front door of the inn.

It was a good-sized building, sitting atop a well-sized hill. There was no staircase leading to the door, but a path had been carved out by the frequent footsteps of the establishment's loyal patrons. I opened the door for Brina and she stepped in, with me following in behind her, both of us welcoming the warmth of the place. It was approaching winter, which meant crisper winds, but that was intensified by being so close to the Great Western Folds. We found a table in the corner and sat down, happy to finally rest and get warm. We had travelled all day and were well prepared for a hot meal. We still had some food of our own — we had stopped in Gralion a couple days ago — but we had enough coin to enjoy some good food without having to make anything ourselves.

A large crashing sound caught both of our attention. By one of the tables roughly in the center of the inn was a human on their hands and knees. A few cups were strewn out on the wooden floor, along with massive pools of beer and wine. The woman was struggling to gather the cups while the surrounding Tóráin laughed. Even the other barmaids, a lycan and a forest sprite, openly jested at the poor girl. I figured it was just a bunch of drunken fools laughing at someone's mistake, which was common in most establishments similar to this one. That was until the woman stood up with the cups on her tray and began making her way back to the bar, only to be clearly tripped by a harpy with a patch over one of his eyes. Again, everyone in the place laughed. I realized that this young woman was the only human in the inn. Once I noticed that, I knew what was truly going on here.

Brina tried to stop me, but I pushed past her arm and went over to the barmaid as she was cleaning up the cups from the floor. The room quickly became void of the common laughter, with many people mumbling to each other instead. I handed her one of the cups and smiled. The woman responded by hiding her face from me as if the sight of her would render me blind. I took the tray of cups from her and held my hand out. After a few moments of waiting, she finally took my hand and allowed me to help her to her feet. I put a comforting arm around her slender shoulders and walked with her back to the bar. She said nothing as she began re-filling the empty cups, two with beer and three with wine. As she moved from one barrel to another, her hair flew, and I caught sight of a welt on the side of her face.

"Who did that to you?"

Silence. The woman placed the newly filled cups on her tray and began walking over to the table with the harpy that had tripped her. I grabbed a hold of her arm, tightly enough to stop her but gently enough for her to know I had no intention of harming her.

"Give me the tray. I'll bring it over."

A burly satyr came out from the room behind the bar and crossed his arms, a sour look on his face. "Hey! You can do whatever you want with her after she's done serving tables. She's cheap too."

I tried to keep myself as calm as possible. Keeping a hold of the young woman, I turned to address the clear owner of the place. "How much to have her right now?"

The satyr grinned, thinking he had a horny lycan on his hands. "Four liras."

It was a steep price, equivalent to four Fleuris francs. It was absurd to ask so much. So much so that I thought about just leaving the situation alone. One quick look over to the young woman with light brown hair covering her bruised face told me I couldn't walk away. "Two francs."

The satyr twisted his face again, upset that I hadn't taken his absurdly overpriced ask. "Fleuris folk, eh? Five francs."

I took another look at the barmaid before countering. "Three francs, and I'll pay double the price for my drinks and meals."

The owner of the inn played with his thick mustache as he pondered my offer. Eventually he crossed his arms and nodded his head. "Deal."

I took out my pouch where I kept my coins and reluctantly took out the agreed upon price. I left the coins on the bar before taking the tray from the woman's hands. I then brought it over to the table it was meant for. Met by looks of judgement and spite, I set down the tray of drinks for the five Tóráin at the table. I wanted to pour each of their drinks over their heads for what they had done to the poor girl, but I restrained myself. I went back over to the bar where only the young woman stood, the owner and my coins no longer visible.

"If it's not too much to ask, I would be very thankful if my friend and I could have something warm to eat. A hot tea for her and some wine for me. Get yourself something to eat and drink too. I'll help you bring it all over to our table."

The woman remained still for a moment before nodding and getting to work. She quickly prepared two bowls of stew before I had to insist that she prepare one for herself as well. Last came the tea and the wine, the barmaid choosing a cup of beer for herself without me telling her to do so this time. Together, we brought over our meal and placed it all on the table. She remained standing, only sitting when both Brina and I had insisted for her to join us. With all of us seated, I took a big gulp from my wine before smiling in the woman's direction.

"What's your name?"

"Camilla," she said quietly.

I reached out to grab her hand in an attempt to comfort her, but she pulled away. I sighed. "Who gave you that welt on your eye, Camilla?"

She moved some of her hair away from her face before responding. "Did you really pay more than three francs to just talk to me?"

Brina sent me a shocked look when she heard what I had done, but I waved her off before she could say anything.

"Yes, I did. I promise you that I just want to talk and give you some reprieve from the harassment." I smiled in an attempt to show her I was genuine.

"I never have any reprieve from the harassment. It's just how things are in Lombardi," Camilla said.

"Why do you stay here if you're treated so poorly?" I asked. "Not that you should have to leave, but it seems like it would be in your best interest to do so."

Camilla took up the wooden spoon in her hand and brought some stew to her lips. She chewed on the chunks of vegetables and meat before washing it all down with a couple sips of her beer. "I can't leave."

"Why not?" Brina asked.

"My father died last year. He was hunting in the mountains when they found him. He must have fallen or something. Now it's just me and my younger brother, Dario. The little coin I make working here keeps us alive. Even if I did want to leave, I doubt the two of us would make the trip to Tordoro or Azuvipa on our own."

"This is no way to live. No being should be treated like this. I understand what you have lived through, we both do. Is there anything we can do for you?" I wanted nothing more than to see Camilla happy and healthy.

Camilla finally made some eye contact and allowed a small smile to show itself. "You've already done plenty, and I don't even know your name."

"Forgive me. I'm Weylyn. That's Brina."

"Well, Weylyn and Brina, know that I'm thankful for what you've done tonight. It's nice to be among kind people. I had almost forgotten what it was like."

We all began eating then, hunger taking the three of us over. Many in the inn watched with judgement in their eyes, others went back to whatever they were doing before Brina and I had arrived. It wasn't until our bowls were clean and our cups empty that I began feeling helpless again. I had paid for Camilla's freedom tonight, but tomorrow she would return to the same owner and the same patrons. There were so few humans living in the town I doubt she even had much support, and it began to make me wonder just how other humans were treated here. Some back home would love a place like this, where the Tóráin appeared to rule over humans, but it wasn't for me. Many of my kind want revenge for what's been done to us, but all I want is peace. Equal opportunity for a happy, healthy life for both Tóráin and humans alike. Before I knew it, I was pondering a crazy idea that had popped into my head. Soon after, it was coming out of my mouth. "Why don't you and your brother come with us?"

"Weylyn what are you —" Brina tried to argue with me, but I cut her off.

"We're going to Leonessa. You could come with us there, or we could part at Azuvipa. Or any other small town or village you like. I'm sure anywhere in Malvene is better for you than here."

"I couldn't even think of asking that of you." Camilla had allowed her hair to cover her face again, scooping at nothing in her bowl.

"You aren't asking. I'm offering. We'll get you and your brother a horse and you can travel with us until we reach Leonessa, or until you find a new place to call home."

I caught a small smile creeping onto her face before she responded. "Well, I think I have an aunt that lives in Azuvipa. Perhaps I could find her there."

"Yes! Azuvipa it is then! So, you'll come with us?" I was excited at the thought of removing Camilla from this horrid place.

The young woman moved her hair from her face to reveal the biggest smile she had shown us so far. "Yes. Yes, I'll join you. When do you leave?"

I sent Camilla a smile of my own. "Tomorrow morning. Is that enough time for you to gather your things?"

"Weylyn, I don't think —" Brina once more tried to interject but I waved her off again.

"Hush Brina. It'll be fine. Is that enough time, Camilla?"

The young woman nodded. "Yes. I believe so."

I grabbed a hold of her hand and squeezed it in a kind manner. "Wonderful. Go to your brother. Tell him the good news. We'll see you here in the morning."

Camilla stood up from her seat, excitement taking her over. "Okay, I will. A satyr named Dorian has a farm just on the northern outskirts of town. That's probably your best bet at finding a horse for sale here. Thank you so much, Weylyn. Truly."

"Thank you, I'll go see him early tomorrow morning. Now go and get yourself ready!" I laughed as I waved her along, a large grin on my face as she grabbed her coat from a hanger by the door and left the inn.

"This is a mistake, Weylyn." Brina had her arms crossed as she leaned back in her chair.

"How could this possibly be a mistake? This is a good thing. She needs help, and we're more than capable of providing it."

"You know I admire your kindness. Many do. But this is not part of our plan. Spending most of our coin on Camilla is reckless. Not to mention we'll have to buy more food if we're taking on another two people. We shouldn't be doing this."

I rolled my eyes. "You can't honestly believe that. You've witnessed firsthand how she's been treated here. She can't stay. If she were a Tórán you wouldn't be challenging my decision."

Brina remained silent for a while. I could tell that what I had claimed had bothered her. Eventually, she cleared her throat and responded. "Not everyone is like you, Weylyn. Many of us have an instinctual contempt of humans. Sometimes, when a human is being treated like we are, it feels like justice is being served. I'm sorry, but I just don't believe we should be going so far out of our way to help one human whose life is a bit hard."

"I understand the hatred many have for humans. I have some hatred of my own. But this world doesn't get better by replacing one tyrannical race with another. We don't have peace through revenge. Despite all of the harm us Tóráin have endured, we have to keep compassion and kindness in our hearts. Human or not, we all deserve a certain level of respect. We all deserve a proper level of health and freedom. That is what I believe The Resistance to be about. That is why we're doing what we're doing. We're fighting for equality, not a change in power. We're helping Camilla and Dario reach Azuvipa, and then we're continuing on our way to Leonessa. It's the right thing to do, so we're going to do it."

Brina nodded after a large sigh. "Alright."

"Good. I'm going to go grab us a couple rooms." I stood up from my seat and when I did, the harpy with one eye stood from his chair too.

I began my walk over to the bar to deal with the prick who ran The Solitary Summit Inn, but my path was blocked by the harpy and his friends. Two lycans stood a bit taller than him, a forest sprite was to his left, and another harpy stood at his right.

"Where are you going? Looking for more humans to save, traitor?" The harpy with one eye played with a small knife in his right hand.

"Just grabbing rooms. Long day for me and my friend. I'd appreciate it if you let me pass." I smiled at him, hoping that they would all just leave me be.

"Human lovers ain't welcome here," The red-haired lycan said, spitting on the floor afterwards.

"I just want to sleep tonight. I'll be gone from this entire town tomorrow morning." My smile was gone now thanks to how annoyed I was getting.

The harpy with one eye took a step forward and pointed his knife at me. "Sleep somewhere else. Maybe that whore Camilla will let you spend the night for free."

I was just about to punch him before I felt a firm hand on my shoulder. Brina had joined me, her other hand firmly on the hilt of her own knife. "It's alright, Weylyn. We'll find somewhere else to sleep."

"Best listen to your friend. Want directions to Camilla's place?"

The harpy's words had me wishing to see everyone in this place punished in some capacity for what they had done to Camilla. Brina and I could have done some punishing of our own, but no good would come of it. I slowly backed away, keeping my eyes on the one with the knife to make sure he didn't come at me when my back was turned. Once there was enough distance between us, the harpy and his friends laughed and sat back down, calling for another barmaid to bring them more drinks. Brina and I gathered our things and left The Solitary Summit Inn. It was colder than most nights had been, the wind coming off the mountains shocking me after being in the warm inn. I decided that we would just head over to Dorian's farm now, hoping to convince him to allow us to purchase a horse and maybe stay in his barn for the night too.

Brina and I made our way to the northern outskirts of town. The closed off fields were empty, save for the thin layer of frost that covered the ground. Between them was a small house, with a large barn not too far from it. We approached the house, and made our way to the door. I knocked on it a couple times and waited. It took him a few minutes, but Dorian answered the door with a rifle in his hand.

"Who the Hell are you?" He was in his night clothes, showing that he had already gone to sleep or he was just about to.

"Travelers. We need a reliable horse, and a place to stay for the night if possible. Your barn would be fine. We can pay." I took out my satchel and shook it so he could hear the coins inside it.

"Horse is four liras. As for a place to stay, there's The Solitary Summit Inn in town."

The idea of spending another four francs was debilitating, but Camilla and Dario needed that horse. "We were turned away from the inn. They...had no rooms available. Come on. Four francs for a horse and a night in your barn."

"Francs? I'd make a stink about dealing with Fleuris folk, but it's late and I'm bloody tired. I don't have the energy to haggle. Four francs for a horse and a night in the barn it is. See you in the morning." The satyr grumbled something under his breath as he closed the door.

"Well that turned out well." I smiled at Brina, but she didn't smile back.

"We went from sleeping in a warm bed with more than enough coins in our pockets, to sleeping in a cold barn with more than eight francs less than what we had this afternoon." Brina had her arms crossed over her chest, a clear indicator she was upset.

"Oh, stop being so sour. Come on." I led the way to what would be our home for the night, with Brina close behind.

We entered the large barn, thankful for the reprieve from the brisk winter-like winds and looked for a couple piles of hay to lay on. The moment I laid down I realized just how tired I was. It was a lot to take on Camilla and Dario, but I still felt really good that we had. They deserved a better life than the one they were living, and I was glad that I could help them find it. I closed my eyes and thought of Rosalie, just like I did every night. Her image brought me enough peace to relax and let sleep take me.

# Chapter Ten

## Rosalie

Cloque, Fleuris | December 14, 1798

Dealing with the aftermath of Keagan's rescue without Weylyn or the others to help me was hard. We ended up losing a few members of The Resistance to imprisonment and death, so there was a lot to take care of. Assan, Baithan, Dempsey, Glenna, Nola, and Tully had all been taken prisoner during the chaos we had caused for Keagan's rescue. Teague and Lynn had been killed. Those who had been captured might need to be freed if they weren't released within the usual three week period, and those who had died needed funerals. As always, The Resistance paid for the funerals of those who died for the cause — a tradition that was started after The Great Riot ten years ago. Once Teague and Lynn's funerals were planned and carried out, I did my best to make sure everyone was informed of The Resistance's new instructions. All plans were to be cancelled, and every member was to lay low while we waited for the increase in soldier activity to die down a bit. The presence of Fleuris militia was stronger in every major city in Fleuris, but the number of soldiers patrolling the streets in Cloque was too much for us to handle. They even came by the funerals we had for Teague and Lynn, no doubt hoping to catch us plotting something. Mind you, that wasn't really new for them. Anytime a member of The Resistance was killed, soldiers would casually patrol nearby in the hopes of capturing someone like Weylyn or Olwen.

General Rosspier and his army had no idea who Weylyn and Olwen were exactly, seeing as nobody has ever identified them as even allies to The Resistance let alone first and second command. I'm sure they had their suspicions, seeing as Weylyn and Olwen — along with Keagan, Brina, and Dwyer — were fairly well-known members of the Tóráin community in Cloque. Every time someone was captured, I worried that they would tell a soldier or even General Rosspier himself what Weylyn or the others were to The Resistance. After what was done to Darby, it made us all even more tight-lipped; nobody wanted to see that happen again. We all believed heavily in The Resistance and what the group meant for so many people. None of us had it in us to say anything that would lead to its downfall, no matter how much they tortured us.

I admired every tortured Tórán's willpower and loyalty, and Keagan was no different. The lycan had only been in Bastion for a short time, but he was one of the worst looking prisoners we had ever freed. Still, he assured us that he didn't say a word while he was imprisoned. Seeing the poor shape he was in made me sick, and it made me horrified to know that they had only had a few days with him. I could only imagine what those vile people could do in three weeks. I had never witnessed the torture that wasn't publicized, but I was always aware of the aftermath. Most prisoners they released couldn't walk on their own, either because of how badly they had been beaten, or because they were starved of food and water for so long. I was usually one of the people who tended to them, so I knew just how much damage was done when spending time in prison.

Reading was something I liked to do to distract myself from all the horrible things happening in the world, and I found myself craving the pages of a book lately. It calmed me, and it removed images in my head that were formed from either bad memories or worried assumptions. Thankfully, I was recently gifted one of the books belonging to 'L'Art poétique' by Boileau, a rare poetry series which praised reason, logic, and moral correctness. It was rare, because King Louis had gone through the libraries of Cloque and burned many books he felt would inspire the revolution to continue. These books were on his list, but thankfully my good friend Hubert had saved a copy from the flames. Hubert ran the largest public library in all of Cloque, and he had saved many books from King Louis' fiery wrath. I was truly enjoying this particular book and its thought provoking verses. It challenged the usual way of poetry and literature and strived for something greater. I could see why King Louis had dubbed it a book that could entice people to revolt. I was just reading a verse about rhyme, Boileau describing how reason can enhance your poetry, when I heard a knock on my door.

"Come in!" I was at The Flying Pig, taking some time away from caring for my parents. I had spent most of the day at the hospital and being with my parents just drained me even further. They had both gone to sleep after an early supper, so I had grabbed a lantern and made my way to the pub for a drink and some reading.

"Sorry to bother you, Rosalie, but we've got a problem that requires your attention." It was Dwyer, the older, black-haired lycan standing in the door with a piece of rolled up parchment in his hand.

"No need to apologize, Dwyer. What's wrong?" I got up from my seat by the lantern I had brought with me and carried the light over to the table in the room.

"Looks like Ross is gonna start some trouble." He slammed the paper onto the table and began rubbing his gray-speckled beard.

I opened the note, reading what it said out loud. "I, your leader and provider, General Rosspier, will be speaking to the masses of Cloque on the twenty-eighth of the month of December. The speech will be made at the ruins of Geôlier Castle . All citizens are invited to gather and witness the wise words of their leader. May Deus love and protect you."

"Did you show it to her?" Moya entered the room looking like she had just run across the city. She didn't need Dwyer to answer once she noticed I was holding the paper. "You know what this means right?"

"All we know is that he's going to talk to the city about something. We don't know what he will say, and we don't know what this means. Not yet anyway." I rolled the paper back up and left it in the middle of the table.

Moya put her hands on her hips. "'Lee, they posted those all over the city. Every corner of every street has one plastered on it. They want everyone to see this."

I sighed. "Of course, they want everyone to see it. They don't want nobody to show up. They just want a crowd so General Rosspier can feel good. Don't worry so much, Moya."

It was Dwyer's turn to try to convince me something was truly wrong. "You don't understand. No one has done anything in front of that damn building since King Louis had Conri tortured there. We burned the bloody thing to the ground, and it's been left that way for a decade. Even King Louis knew how doing anything in regard to that building would cause problems for himself. He avoided it until he was killed. Ross has avoided it until now. What changed?"

I rubbed my eyes with my thumb and pointer finger. "I admit the location is unexpected, but we can't assume anything until we gather more information."

Moya threw her arms in the air. "What more information do you need? Any intelligent Tórán knows exactly what that bastard is planning on doing. He's going to use that cursed building behind him as a backdrop while he spews lies about us to the humans of Cloque. No good will come from this. Surely you know that, Lee."

I put my hands on my hips. "We have ears inside Joieternelle Palace. We've figured out General Rosspier's plans through this avenue before, we can do so again. For all we know he's grown bored inside that palace of his and just wants a crowd to cheer his name again. I'll send out our spies to find us more information, until then keep an eye out for posters and take them down when you aren't being watched. The less people that go, the better."

I could see that both Dwyer and Moya weren't completely content with my decision, but they eventually nodded in agreement. Dwyer took the paper off the table and stuffed it into his pocket.

"Whatever we manage to take off the street we'll burn," the older lycan said. "I'll make sure nobody gets caught doing so."

"I'll inform our spies that we need information on this specifically. I'll let you know if they discover anything." Moya came over and gave me a hug before leaving the room.

Dwyer gave me a short bow, something that could have been done out of respect or mockery, and he too left the room. I was just about to sit back down with my book when someone else knocked on the door, coming in before I could give them permission to do so.

"There you are!" It was Claire, my friend from the hospital. "I came here as soon as I found that you weren't home. I stopped by to drop off your parents' medicine and when I checked in on them your mother had a horrible fever. She's at the hospital now, Doctor Bernard is tending to her."

I quickly shoved my book into my handbag and grabbed the lantern off the table. "How long ago did you bring her to the hospital? Is Doctor Bernard hopeful?"

"I don't know, Rosalie. I came looking for you the moment I knew she was in good hands. However, I feel as though it would be in your best interest to make your way there quickly. I hadn't felt a fever that hot in some time."

I pushed past Claire and urged her to hurry. My parents had both been sick for some time, but this was still a shock. My mother had been relatively well when I left her only a couple hours ago. To be honest, I was more worried about my father when I had left than my mother. They both weren't doing so well, but for my mother to suddenly take a turn for the worst was causing me to become emotional. Tears began to fill my eyes as I pushed through the front door of The Flying Pig and began my journey to Landry de Cloque Hospital. I silently berated myself for leaving my parents alone, which only made me feel worse. I should have stayed with them. I was angry with myself the entire trek to the hospital, Claire sending kind and hopeful words my way in an attempt to ease the blame she knew I was putting on myself. It was sweet of her to do so, but nothing would shake the guilt from me. I needed to get to her. I needed to make sure my mother was okay.

# Chapter Eleven

# Olwen



Our plan to get rid of De Vries and Grada was an ambitious one that not everyone was on board with from the start. Naturally, I figured we would just kill De Vries and Grada, however Keagan wanted to see if we could remove them without killing them. 'My nightmares are full of enough people screamin' at me,' he had said. Respecting Keagan's request, Cordelia and I entertained this idea, and we ended up sitting on something for a good while. The idea was to kill just one of them and hope the act scared off or weakened the other enough that they wouldn't be a problem anymore. With that plan in mind, we discussed who was more likely to be scared off, who was easier to kill, who would be weakened more by the other's death, and so on. Cordelia stressed who these people were throughout that conversation, and it became clear to us that our plan wouldn't work. We concluded that even with one of them dead, the other being alive would be too much of a risk. Cordelia even had a thought that things could actually end up worse.

With us unable to grant Keagan's wish, we fell back to the original plan: Jacob De Vries and his witch Grada were to be killed. Our only problem was that neither of them were ever really alone long enough for an assassination to be successful. They were together often, a fact that could actually be helpful; however, they were heavily guarded around the clock. We needed to gather as much information on them as possible to try to find a way to get to them. Thankfully, some questions being asked turned in rumors which stated that the Tultch noble and his witch were a couple despite De Vries being married. He and his wife had no children, so I wouldn't feel bad for taking their father from them. We didn't get much of anything on Grada aside from the possible affair she was having, but we discovered that De Vries had an eye for shiny things. The person we spoke to called him a collector, but to me he was just a greedy bastard who wanted to flaunt his wealth. We took all of this information into account as we devised our new plan to eliminate the duo.

We had agreed on this new plan a few days ago, inspired by something that Cordelia had brought to my attention. She said that De Vries and Grada had both come to the docks that day to inspect one of the cargo ships that had arrived at Westen Port. After being asked if this was something that occurred often, Cordelia had informed me that it was rare. My thought was to attack them at the docks during one of these rare occasions, but they were still joined by at least fifteen soldiers according to Cordelia, which made it difficult to guarantee the deaths of our targets. That was the difficult thing about all of this; we needed to be sure that by the end of our attack, De Vries and Grada were dead. If we failed to kill either one of them, we ran the risk of creating an even greater villain. The docks were our best option though, so I took my time to think on how we could maybe make it work.

During a late-night meal at The Lucky Whale Inn, I asked Cordelia if we could get De Vries and Grada inside a ship — just the two of them. According to the sprite, the next ship that was due to arrive was captained by a dear friend of hers who she called Big Casper. From the story she told, it seemed as though the two were more than just good friends; especially when she got to telling us why he was called 'Big' Casper. Cordelia suggested him not only because she knew he would likely let us use his ship, but his cargo would probably be good bait for De Vries. Cordelia explained that Casper was one of the few captains that travelled to the far, far south. Further than Lutis even. His destination was a strong, united group of tribes at the end of the world known as Motea. Word was that they looked different than the humans up here, a darker shade even than the tawny brown skin common in Lutis. They were supposedly very kind, but also very firm, staving off early attacks from Tudrose and Fleuris back when Motea was discovered around thirty years ago.

Motea was well known for its diamonds, something the nation had plenty of. The rich absolutely adored shiny things, but we knew that De Vries would love to get his hands on some. Only very high-ranking nobles and royalty could afford mass amounts of the shiny rocks, and after a quick discussion with one of the maids in his home we discovered that De Vries didn't have any. And so, we began to carry out a plan. We gave a note to a sprite serving as a maid to Jacob De Vries citing that we wanted to give De Vries some of the king's diamonds at half price. Supposedly, Mr. De Vries wasn't a big supporter of King William. Those who worked for the noble spread the rumors of him often fantasizing about taking the crown from King William. We figured that if he had the chance to steal from the man, he would. No doubt he would bring Grada with him, both for security and because the two went everywhere together. Cordelia was convinced that they would take the bait, and the confident sprite was soon proven right. Not long after sending the note, she was approached by a human holding a letter for her from De Vries and Grada. The note we had sent had told them to give 'the loud water sprite at the docks' their answer. They agreed to come alone, into the lower decks of Casper's ship, all so they could get their grubby hands on some diamonds. Would there be any diamonds for them? No. Casper was way too smart to risk losing any of King William's purchase. It didn't matter though, because they wouldn't leave the ship. Cordelia would bring the two targets below deck, her human friend Eva would be the mysterious seller, and Keagan and I would wait in the shadows until the right time to strike.

As good a plan as it was, De Vries and Grada were late. Really late. Late enough for me to begin to worry if they had changed their minds or worse, decided to send soldiers to jail us for selling King William's diamonds. I was just about to say something to Eva when I could hear Cordelia's voice. It sounded like Cordelia was talking to someone, and she didn't seem under duress. They had finally come. This was it. I nudged Keagan and grinned. He nodded in return, but he didn't smile back. He just returned his attention to the gap in the crates that allowed him to see the steps that led down from the second deck to the third. I watched the stairs through my own opening, happy to see three pairs of boots make their way down. A voice that wasn't Cordelia's filled the room.

"Ah, this must be the seller! *Prachtig*! Let's make this quick, shall we? This ship smells like salt and sweat." His voice was of a higher pitch than most men, but I figured that it must have been De Vries.

"Hold on there. This is quite the sale here. How do we know the second we show you the goods that you won't call in an army?" I could only see her midsection, but I managed to spot Cordelia putting her hands on her hips after she had said what I had told her to say.

"Ugh. You're kind is so paranoid. You're lucky to even be in De Vries' presence, and you accuse him of trickery? I knew *bedelaars* weren't bright, but you do seem quite dim." I noted what must have been the voice of Grada, and I realized I didn't like her very much.

"Before insults start flying, it would also make me feel better to know that no soldiers will be rushing in during our sale. If it isn't too much of an inconvenience for the Lord and Lady." Eva spoke calmly, more like an educated merchant than a dock worker.

"Fine, fine. You see this bracelet?" I couldn't but I imagine that the others could. "See how it softly glows green? It means there's soldiers nearby. Grada."

I saw Grada take something out of a small bag she had with her. She was quick with it, but it looked like one of those fancy little mirrors rich folk kept so they could look at themselves whenever they wanted to. "Captain Visser, remove all soldiers from the docks."

A voice too quiet to tell what it said was heard before the loud clap of the small mirror being closed. Silence took over the room for a short moment until De Vries spoke.

"See? No more glow. Now can we get on with it?"

"Alright, here's the diamonds." I saw Eva's middle move a bit to her right before slowly spinning forward.

"Odd looking diamonds. Aren't they supposed to be clear? Are these special?" De Vries bent over to look at his diamonds, giving me a good look at his clean-shaven face and blonde curls.

"Those aren't diamonds you fool! It's sugar!" Grada shouted. "You pesky things. I knew this was all part of a scheme. I'll have you tortured for months for this."

That was as good a cue as we were going to get. Keagan and I stormed out from behind the crates, Keagan in his feral form and me with my saber drawn. Our attack had Grada shifting her attention to us, just barely holding Keagan and I still before we could reach her. She laughed as De Vries drew his saber from his hip and took a step towards Cordelia. Grada began stretching and twisting the two of us, causing Keagan to growl in pain and me to lose my grip on my sword. Thankfully, our secret weapon did her job. In all the chaos, Eva had been left alone long enough to jump behind a stack of goods and pick up the pistol I had left there for her. She was a bad shot and only caught Grada in the shoulder, but it was enough for us to break free of her spells. I quickly picked up my weapon and charged De Vries, who had been startled by the gunshot. We dueled, he and I, both of us using swift and calculated attacks in an attempt to kill the other. De Vries caught me with a punch that sent me reeling a bit, giving me just enough time to watch Keagan swipe at Grada with his claws.

The witch was blocking his blows with magic, much too weak from her wound to fully control him now. To be honest, I was surprised she had lasted this long. I didn't have much time to think about them though, seeing as De Vries made a quick follow up stab as he tried to end our scuffle. It took me a few more tries, but eventually I disarmed him. He had caught my arm just barely with a good slash beforehand, but it was nothing I couldn't handle. In the end I still had all my limbs, and my enemy had no weapon. He put his arms up to beg, and I hesitated for a brief moment. Keagan's words roared in my head and for a second I thought that maybe we could just tie the two up and have Casper dump them in Motea somewhere. My reluctance to finish the duel had De Vries pull out a knife and lunge at me. Before he got anywhere close to me, a knife lodged itself into his head. I looked in the direction it had come from and saw Cordelia standing next to a pile of crates. I turned my attention to Keagan and Grada now, the witch strewn out on the floor with gashes on her arm and her chest.

Keagan loomed over the witch and snarled. "Surrender. Leave this country and never return, and we'll let you live."

"That's not what we agreed on!" Cordelia stepped forward to end it herself, but Keagan turned around quickly and growled at the sprite.

Cordelia backed off and Keagan returned his attention to Grada. "At least let her answer."

I put my hand on my hip. "Well? You want to live or die, Grada?"

The witch spat on the floor. "You think because witches were hunted just like you that we have pity for you, but we don't. Many of us now see the mistake we made bringing you here. We were nearly worshipped before you came along. Everyone now knows what horrible little *beesten* you all are. Even if I did leave this country, I would never stop making your insignificant lives miserable ones. Wherever I go, humans will thank me, and your kind will fear me. Me, Grada the —"

I stabbed her in the neck. I could have stabbed her in the heart, but that meant there was a chance the bitch would keep talking. I hated people like her. Her words had me feeling like an idiot for letting Keagan's talk of mercy nearly get me killed moments ago.  As much as it would bother the lycan, I knew he would eventually agree that the world was better off with these two people dead. I pulled my saber out of Grada's neck, causing the witch to gurgle. She held her neck, trying to stop the bleeding, but it wasn't long before her dead eyes stared me down and her choking stopped. Keagan knelt by her as he shifted into his tame form, and closed her eyes with his fingers.

Cordelia cleared her throat as she stepped forward with her arm around Eva's shoulders. "Right well, those soldiers are goin' to be wonderin' what happened to their precious cargo. Best toss 'em overboard with cannonballs chained to their feet and send Big Casper on his merry way."

"We should get you out of here too. They'll think you had something to do with this won't they?" Eva asked.

Cordelia kissed the woman's forehead and gave her a one-armed hug. "Ah, they don't suspect anythin'. I wore a hood and a scarf and talked all fancy when the soldiers were around. They'll have no idea it was me."

"You know, maybe we don't dump the bodies. At least not here. You said there were rumors Grada and De Vries were lovers right? Just send Casper on his way and he can dump them far from here. People will think they just ran away together. What do you think, Keagan?" I put a hand on his burly shoulder hoping to give him some support amidst the clear discomfort he was in.

"We could have just captured them and done the same thing." The lycan stood up and waved his hands in the air to dismiss the subject. "I don't care what we do. They're dead. Just make a decision quick. I'm goin' to make sure we're clear to get the Hell out of here." He made his way to the stairs, mumbling something under his breath the entire way up to the second deck.

Cordelia took her free arm and wrapped it around my shoulders. "I like your idea, Olwen. A romantic getaway for the dead lovebirds, it is! Come on, I'll tell Big Casper and then we'll make for The Lucky Whale. I feel like singin' tonight."

I forced a smile and shrugged her arm off me before stepping over the bodies and trying to catch up with Keagan. Cordelia and Eva were close behind and I could have sworn I heard the two kiss. I don't know how someone could find death and blood romantic, but to each their own I guess. When we got to the top deck, Casper was waiting there for us. Cordelia then told him how everything had gone and our planned next steps.

"Well, who am I to say no to my treasure of the sea, eh? I'll dump 'em up the coast near Fjorhest. No one will be the wiser." He winked at us before shouting for his crew to get ready for open waters.

The four of us exited the ship via the plank the crew had set up and the moment we touched down on the dock a blonde lycan with long hair, and a beard in a short braid, tossed the ropes off the dock and ran up the plank. A whistle sounded and two strong human men removed the plank from the ship Casper called The Blue Mistress. Cordelia had provided us with a short story on how that name came to be, and I wasn't surprised that it involved her being naked. Keagan was moping but I knew he would be alright once he had a drink or two in him. Eva seemed energized by the whole encounter while Cordelia acted as though our reward for today was a bucket full of diamonds. My hair had come loose from the horsetail I had it in, so I tied it back again and tucked the loose strands of my hair behind my ear. My hood was brought over my head next and I looked around at the busy docks before lowering my head and following Cordelia down the docks. What we had done was dirty work, but necessary. Now I had the task of turning Cordelia into a resistance leader, a task that may be more difficult than this one had been.

# Chapter Twelve

# Olwen

Leuw, Tulp | December 17, 1798

"Another! Another!"

The crowd was enjoying Cordelia's singing and, if I was completely honest, so was I. It was a pleasant counter to the gritty work that we had done only a few hours ago. Keagan was actually smiling now thanks to the three beers he had swimming in his belly. During every song Cordelia had come over and kissed Eva, the meeting of their lips taking advantage of the brief pauses between verse and chorus. She wasn't the only one though. Cordelia kissed the head and cheek of many as she performed; whether they were human or not, male or female, it didn't matter. Of course, there were some who were either not interested or just plain shy, and Cordelia kindly respected their wishes, putting an arm around them and belting out more verses instead. Cordelia was indeed well-liked, but I wondered if she could truly lead.

Silently in my head, I debated whether Cordelia was leader material as she sang and danced around the place. She was singing an old song in our native Séúbua. The song was called '*Buachaill Óg Amháin*' which meant 'One Young Boy' in the common tongue. It was rare to hear someone sing a song in our language. One, because most soldiers liked to arrest you for doing so, and two, because not many even knew our old ways of speaking anymore. Once the hunting of the Tóráin was

74

over, humans made sure to strip away whatever connection we had to our homeland. They tossed everyone under the age of twenty into schools to be taught the common language. Some were even forced to learn their country's native tongue as well. If you spoke our language in public, you were beaten or imprisoned, or both. Some families resisted this aggressive conformity and taught their children Séúbua as well as many other things.

My mother was a stubborn sprite, and her mother was an even greater pain in the ass. They were both smart enough to keep such things secretive, but they taught my siblings and me as much as they could about our old home. Songs, recipes, stories; everything was taught in our language. I used to quietly sing for my parents when I was young, and when I got older, I became brazen and sang at bars and inns that called themselves safe havens for the Tóráin. It was risky to sing these songs in public, even in a place that claimed to be safe, but I still did it. I felt proud to do it. I stopped a long time ago though, and my reason for doing so was clawing to the forefront of my mind. I thought I was doing a good job at hiding it, but when Cordelia and I locked eyes across the room, the sight of me had her drifting off. She snapped back to attention quickly and finished her song before calling for everyone to have a drink in her name. The slim water sprite made her way over to the table Keagan and I had claimed and sat down.

"Don't like my singin'?"

Keagan scoffed. "O' doesn't like anyone's singin'. Don't take it personally."

He was technically wrong, but it saved me from explaining the real reason why I had been bothered, so I went along with it. "Yes, please. Don't take it personally. Just not my thing."

Cordelia looked me over with her silver eyes. I thought for a moment she might push for a different answer from me, but she eventually shrugged and took a sip from her mug. "No offense taken, love. Everyone's got their dos and don'ts."

Keagan took a big gulp from his mug before setting it down on the table. "You have a beautiful voice. It's a shame I didn't understand what you were sayin' though."

"Didn't peg ya as one of those kind of Tóráin. The real shame is how many are just like ya. My entire life I've been surrounded by our language. Sometimes ya forget that others weren't as lucky." She turned around and waved at the bartender before putting up three fingers.

"Cliana's father used to mutter to himself in Séúbua. I think I heard someone sing in a bar once when I was younger too. Singer was a forest sprite like you, O'. Fancy that, eh?" Keagan had a smile on his face, but I must have done a horrid job at concealing my emotions again because his smile went away, and his hand came to rest on my shoulder. "You alright?"

"Ya drink too much already?" Cordelia asked just as a barmaid reached our table with the three new drinks the sprite had ordered.

"No, no. It'll take more than what I've had for it to be too much drinking for me. I once beat Keagan here in a drinking contest a couple years ago." I was hoping that the statement would take the attention off me, and I was happy when Cordelia's eyes lit up and a fit of laughter came out of her.

"A sprite beat a lycan in a drinkin' contest? Oh, how do you even show your face in bars anymore? I mean don't get me wrong, I'm glad ya do, but man that's embarrassin', ain't it?"

Keagan grumbled and removed his hand from my shoulder. "She cheated. Plus, I had been drinkin' prior to our challenge. I'd beat her any night of any month if we were to go again."

"Oh? Why not have the rematch now? Celebrate our victory, yeah?" Cordelia had a massive grin on her face, but I had to douse her excitement.

"What victory? Sure, we eliminated De Vries and Grada, but there's still plenty of work to do. To be honest I'm wondering if you'd rather sing and drink your nights away instead of leading this new resistance we've fought to create." I had my arms crossed now, showing everyone at the table the time for fun was over.

Cordelia raised an eyebrow. "Is that right? Ain't nobody better for this position than me, love. I can promise you that. There's no harm in havin' a bit of fun. But, if it's business ya want to be talkin' 'bout, then business it is. What do we do now that our troublesome twosome is off on a romantic getaway to the depths of the sea?"

I had expected more pushback from her. Honestly, I had even expected some arguing on Keagan's front as well, but both seemed attentive and ready to work this all out. The surprise of it had me reeling a bit before I could gather myself and figure out what to say next. What do we do now? It was different in Fleuris. Everyone just kind of came together after Conri's execution. Getting the people of Leuw to join something without a spark like that could be a problem. Although, if anyone knew the lower class of Leuw, it was probably our dear friend Cordelia. Accepting that, I found where I wanted to start.

"We need people who want things to change to join us. Specifically, people you trust." I finished off what was left of my drink and shoved the empty mug into the middle of the table before grabbing the new one Cordelia had ordered me. "Got any ideas?"

Cordelia leaned back in her chair and ran both hands through her long, green hair. She took a deep breath and sighed, shaking her head as if she was trying to psych herself up for something. She leaned forward again and rested her elbows on the table. "Ya know, ya have some fans here in Leuw. Plenty of folk here wishin' for a resistance of our own. Tóráin mostly, but some humans aren't too happy with how things are either. Findin' people to join won't be a problem. What I want to know is what we do with all of 'em."

"The quick answer is make life difficult for the upper class for a change," Keagan said after downing more of his beer. "The long answer involves your knowledge of the city."

"Keagan's right. You know what spots being hit would do the most damage. The key is to hit spots that hurt the enemy hard enough to weaken them, but not so hard that it has them sending the entire army into the streets looking for you." I caught Keagan smile at my first statement, the grin on his face remaining there while he spoke again.

"Although sometimes that happens even without you meanin' for it to, so you'll need a safe place to lay low just in case."

Cordelia shook her head. "No hidin' for me. I'm at the docks every day from sunrise to sunset, sometimes earlier, sometimes later. If I'm ever not there, people start askin' questions. If things get crazy, my safest place to be is at the docks. Now for other people, I'd say Young Wolf Pub would be a good hideaway. Trust Strahan with my life."

"Fair enough. Since you know them so well, the docks may be a good place to start. Redirect some goods, spoil others, keep some for bribes when needed. Maybe even get some sea captains on your side too." I grabbed my mug of beer and took another sip before continuing. "Whatever you can do to weaken Leuw will spread to other towns and cities in Tulp."

"When Tudrose comes, it would help to have a friendly force inside the country already causin' trouble. You could be called on to cause riots or unrest in the city durin' the attacks. Maybe even join Tudrose's army. Think people will be up for that?" Keagan had shifted just his hand and was picking at his teeth with one of his claws.

"I told ya. Ya have fans here in Tulp. What happened ten years ago inspired a lot of people, probably in other countries too. We just haven't had the courage to do anythin'. But once word spreads that De Vries and Grada are gone, people will join this little rebellion of ours. I promise ya that when Tudrose comes to rid us of the bastards who run this place, we'll be ready to help in whatever way we can. I'll make sure of it." Cordelia raised her mug in the air. "To The Resistance."

Keagan and I raised our mugs together and we both echoed Cordelia's toast. The three of us all downed our drinks, turning the mugs over to prove we had finished.

"So what's next for you two? Keepin' me company still, or back home to good ol' Fleuris?" Cordelia took out her pipe and began preparing it as Eva came over and sat in her lap.

"Neither. We're headin' south to Korblum in the hopes of replicatin' what we've done here." Keagan grabbed a piece of bread from the center of the table and took a bite.

"You'd be headin' for Adler then, I imagine. I think I might know where ya could start, if ya don't have any plans already."

I had allowed myself to slouch in my chair a bit, but what Cordelia said had me sitting upright again. "No, please. We didn't really have much of a plan at all. What's your suggestion?"

Cordelia smiled as she squeezed her arm around Eva's waist. The young woman rested her head on Cordelia's shoulder and the sprite inhaled from her pipe before she blew out a plume of smoke into the air. "Harpy I used to know called Seig. She lived here for a couple years, but she moved to Adler to join the fights there. Hell of a fighter that one, but she's more than just a brute. Talked about goin' to Fleuris to help your little rebellion before she ultimately decided on goin' to Korblum instead. It's been about five or six years since she left, so who knows what's become of her, but if you're lookin' for a leader of a resistance in Korblum, that's your lady."

"Seig. I'll be sure to remember that name. Thank you for all your help, Cordelia." I stood and extended my hand in thanks.

Cordelia's eyebrow raised at the gesture, but she handed Eva her pipe so she could reach over and grab my hand in a firm grip. "My pleasure."

"When are you planning on leaving?" Eva asked.

I looked over at Keagan but he shrugged his shoulders. "Up to you, O'. You're the boss."

I couldn't help but smirk at that statement before turning my attention to Cordelia and Eva. "I'd imagine tomorrow morning. The sooner we get all these chapters of The Resistance set up, the faster they'll spread. The faster they spread, the sooner Tudrose attacks. I'd say for us to stay, but I think it's best for the two of you — as people who know the country much better than us — to set up the foundations for it all. We've done our part by giving you the space and time you need to get things going."

"So soon?" Cordelia pouted before grinning from ear to ear. "Well, that just means we need more drinks before ya go! Del'! Another round for me and my friends here!"

I was tired and wanted to rest, but I figured I could have one more drink. A drunk Keagan needed to be watched too, so it was best I stuck around. Last time I left him in a bar on his own he nearly died. I doubted any issues would arise at this place, but I was known to be quite paranoid. A short, burly man who must have been Del' brought us our drinks himself. He got a quick kiss on the cheek from Cordelia before waddling back to the bar. I grabbed my mug in my hand and took a deep breath, trying to allow myself to relax. We had done a good thing, and it hadn't taken us a year to do it. This was worth celebrating.

# Chapter Thirteen

# Weylyn

Leonessa, Malvene | December 21, 1798

We said goodbye to Camilla and Dario near Azuvipa. It was nice travelling with them, even though Brina was still sour about how much money we spent. She did little to hide her frustration our entire journey east. Her mood changed when little Dario insisted on giving her a hug before they left. Brina had been short and cold with Camilla most of the time, but she lent her ear to Dario's babbling. She led the horse with the young boy in the saddle and listened to everything he said. He would often tell her to lean in closer because Brina was the only person he wanted to hear what he was saying, and she would happily oblige. Dario was only six years old, but he still turned out to be quite the conversationalist. Sure, he spoke about things aimlessly and told stories that weren't all that interesting, but he rarely flubbed a word. He had a good grasp of the common language and I made sure to compliment him on it. Camilla worried how either of them would do in Azuvipa though, seeing as they weren't very fluent in Malvenian. Her father taught her basics, but they never had much of a need for the language living in a town highly populated by the Tóráin. I did my best to encourage Camilla though, telling her that I was certain she and Dario would be alright.

I wanted to accompany Camilla and Dario into the city to be sure they found their relative, but Brina wouldn't let me. She pointed out who led Azuvipa, a man known by Tóráin in nearly every country. Francesco Ventossa was Duke of Azuvipa, and he had a mind very similar to another bastard back in Fleuris named Tristan Frollo. The two both enjoyed harming and imprisoning our kind, both of them known to cling to the very old way of thinking when it came to my kind. They believed we needed to be removed, or at the very least controlled, and they went about doing so in their own ways. Magistrate Frollo used the law to murder and torture any Tórán he could get his hands on, while the Duke of Azuvipa used the hospitals to find his victims. Francesco Ventossa would take injured or sick Tóráin and experiment on them, often resulting in the death of his patients. He even lured vulnerable and desperate Tóráin with promises of coin or food in return for testing his new medicines. His potions were known to either kill you or drive you mad. Going into a city run by such a vile, powerful man was a risk we couldn't take, and so I had to watch the two of them leave for the city on their own.

It only took us a couple more days to reach Leonessa, a city that wasn't necessarily safe for people like Brina and me, but it was much less risky of a place than Azuvipa. The majority of Malvene's cities and towns functioned the same way as those in Fleuris did. Soldiers were always suspicious of our kind and paid little attention to the atrocities humans committed. Lycans, sprites, satyrs, harpies, and goblins were all among the poorest citizens. There were some that were lucky to have a human or two care for them enough to give them a good wage, but the majority of our kind barely scraped by. Leonessa turned out to be a beautiful city, full of canals both wide and narrow. However, I knew that — just like every other city — there would be a section of the place that appeared more run down than others. That was where I would find the majority of the Tóráin population. Brina and I had to roam around the city for most of the afternoon and quietly ask a few questions along the way, but we eventually found the part of Leonessa we were looking for.

Ossian never gave me his address for some reason, always telling me to send my letters to a place called The Gondola's Dock. Evening fell on us, the sun swiftly vanishing under the western horizon, but we couldn't find the place. I was forced to wonder if the establishment had perhaps changed its name in the last couple years. Of course, there was also a chance it had been burned down, or something of the like. My thoughts worried me, and I started to doubt we would find Ossian. After deciding to risk asking about his whereabouts and receiving no answers even from our own kind, most of my hope vanished altogether. Brina eventually suggested we just start going into every pub or inn we could find in the area, all with the hope that we would find him. We investigated four such places before coming to our fifth one. It was late now, probably nearing midnight soon, but Brina urged me to not give up.

"We have more than just tonight to look for him," she had said. She wasn't wrong in saying so, but I couldn't fend off the worries that flooded my mind.

I had thought that we would have found Ossian by now, or at least met someone who knew him. Sure, the city was big, and even the poor area of the place inhabited a large area, but I still felt the way I felt. You see, Ossian — if he was anything like I remembered — would stick out like a sore thumb anywhere that had a group of people gathered around and drinking. He was scholarly, or at least as scholarly a Tórán could become. Ossian was the only creature, human or not, that I had ever seen bring books to a bar. Not just one. Multiple. He used to say how he enjoyed reading at bars because it was more difficult to focus. I thought that would be a reason to not enjoy reading at bars, but Ossian loved challenges. He and my father would challenge each other often, usually with trivia questions or chess. The two of them had carved their own pieces out of wood, neither of them able to afford the fancy ones humans played with. There was an old rumor that King Louis had human-sized pieces on a large board in one of his villas. It was said that he had all the pieces made save for pawns; he used imprisoned Tóráin instead. When they were taken by their opponent, they were beaten, or killed in some cases. The pieces moved on their own too, thanks to a spell his witches had used on them. It was never proven to be true, but it had never been proven to be untrue either.

I shook my head a little and blinked a few times to wash the thought out of my head, forcing myself to focus on my immediate surroundings. Brina and I had entered a bar called The Boatman's Reprieve a short time ago and we had decided on staying there for the night. Brina took that as a sign we could stop searching for Ossian, at least for tonight, but I couldn't relax like she had. I had drifted off into my mind a few times, but it was never any fun anyway. When my thoughts weren't dragging me away into make belief scenarios fueled by fear and despair, my eyes were scanning every spot of The Boatman's Reprieve. I just caught sight of a satyr's legs when commotion that had started off to my left snatched my attention. Brina had gone off to one of the tables and was now protecting a goblin from three other Tóráin.

"Stay out of this she-wolf," said a male lycan with short black hair and a thick mustache.

"Yeah, mind your own business!" A male forest sprite waved at Brina with a look of disgust on his face.

"No. Not until you tell me why you're attacking him." Brina had an arm extended behind her, making sure her ward stayed out of harm's way.

"We don't have to tell you anythin'. Move aside before we make you." The person who spoke was a tall, muscular satyr with large horns and shoulder length brown hair. I had spotted him first when we entered seeing as he was pretty hard to miss.

I made my way over, my hands in the air to try to bring some calm to the situation. "Friends, please. We don't want any trouble. My name is Weylyn, and that's Brina. You are?"

The large satyr rolled his eyes. "Listen close, Weylyn. That goblin owes me coin and I mean to either collect or make an example out of him. If you and your friend here want to get in the way of that, then we'll make an example out of you too."

Nobody said anything for a bit, the three of them and the two of us standing across from each other, waiting for someone to make the first move. The lycan mumbled something under his breath before turning into his feral form, which prompted Brina to do so as well. The sprite drew a long knife, and the satyr cracked his knuckles while stretching out his neck. I was the last one to ready myself, shrugging off my coat and allowing my body to morph into the feral shape of a wolf. Before anyone could do anything more, a voice rang out through the crowd. Everyone had gotten quite excited to see a tussle, but whoever this voice belonged to was calling for it to end.

"Alright, alright. Enough posturing. We all know how tough you are Larkin, no need for any examples." The short, slender satyr had a messy mop of brown hair surrounding the curved horns on his head, save for the grays by his ears. His face was covered by a thick beard the same mix of brown and gray too. He extended a hand outward to the goblin Brina was protecting and helped him to his feet. "Gair, how much do you owe him?"

"Ten lira. I told him I had the money, but I was robbed by these two humans last week and —" The older satyr waved at Gair until the goblin stopped talking.

He pushed past Brina, took out a pouch from his coat, and poured some coins into his open hand. I could hear him muttering to himself as he shifted the coins around before putting a few back into his pouch and extending his fist. "Here's twelve lira. Take the extra two and go cause trouble in another establishment."

Larkin put out an open hand and accepted the coins from his fellow satyr and grinned. "Come on boys. We'll head over to The Muttering Goat. Good ol' Loller makes better food than this place anyways."

The lycan in the group shifted back to his tame form and picked up his coat from the floor, his shirt stretched out. The sprite pocketed his knife and chuckled with a smug look on his face. Larkin led the trio out of the bar as Gair shook his savior's hand and thanked him vigorously. The kind satyr just nodded continuously until he managed to finally send the goblin on his way. The situation now solved, our peace maker approached Brina and I as we both shifted and picked up our coats.

"You said your name was Weylyn, right? You wouldn't happen to be the son of Conri, would you? Or are my eyes tricking me?"

Mention of my father's name had me lock eyes with the satyr and realize who he was. "Ossian! Ah I thought it was you. Hard to tell with that thing on your face. We've been looking all over for you!"

"I'm not a very easy satyr to find. That's by design, you know. Sorry. Please forgive me for being so hidden these last couple years. Damn me for doing so." Ossian adjusted his glasses as a smile crept onto his bearded face. Quickly he was laughing and taking steps forward with his arms open wide. I met him halfway, the two of us engaging in a long overdue embrace. Lycans matured in their mid-twenties, so Ossian had missed my growth spurt and my body filling out. He'd also never seen me shift, so I could see why he was uncertain at first if it was really me. Ossian looked a bit different too. The bit of gray in his hair was new, as well as the wrinkles on his forehead and the edges of his eyes. His glasses and thick facial hair were certainly different too, Glasses were one of the few good things to have come from our kind coming to this dimension. Back home, if you had poor sight, you just had poor sight. It was a shame the majority of humans were so vile. They were capable of such helpful things when they chose to put their energy into something other than violence.

"That was kind of you to do that for Gair. Although, I'm not sure it's so smart for you to carry so much money around like that," Brina said as Ossian and I ended our hug.

Ossian moved his coat to the side to show off a pistol. "I'm quite capable of taking care of myself, dear Brina. It's a pleasure to see you as well. I'm not surprised you two are together. Always attached at the hip when you were young."

Brina and Ossian hugged each other then, the two of them only splitting after a couple of pats on each other's backs. Ossian silently indicated he wanted us to follow him, and so we did, all the way to a table closest to the hearth. The satyr dragged over two chairs from another table before taking a seat in one of his own. He grabbed the three books that sat on the table and stuffed them into a large satchel on the floor next to him. He made a loud whistle I remembered him doing often while looking over at the bar. Ossian held up three fingers for a short time before bringing his attention to Brina and me.

"So! To what do I owe this fine gift of much welcomed company?"

"Well, is this a safe place?" Brina asked after looking to her left and then her right.

Ossian's eyes grew wide and he made an 'o' with his lips. He leaned in closer to us both. "Resistance business?"

Brina and I both nodded. Ossian leaned back in his chair and laughed. He then showed us his hand with his first finger raised as a sign for us to wait a moment. The satyr stood up onto his chair and spread his arms wide open. "King Ludovico Almani! May his testicles fall off like sour fruit from a dying tree!"

"May he drown in his own bathwater!" Someone shouted amidst the patrons in the bar.

"May he grow a pair of tits and be forced to nurse baby goats!" A sprite shouted.

An older human actually got onto their own chair and raised their cup into the air. "May the *asino* rot in Hell."

Everyone cheered then and raised their cups and mugs into the air. Ossian chuckled as he got down from his chair and sat down. A barmaid came over to our table with three cups of wine and a platter of dried meat, fruit, and a loaf of bread. She was human, but I was glad to see that she was treated much better than Camilla had been. I had caught her raising a fist in the air when everyone raised their drinks to the hopeful misfortune of the King of Malvene. The woman had light brown hair done up into one large braid that hung down over the front of her left shoulder. She had a smile on her face as she placed our food and drinks on the table, trying to hold back a fit of laughter.

"I've heard many insults sent the King's way, but you, Ossian, always shout out my favorites. Don't worry about paying for this with lira by the way. Consider getting rid of Larkin and his *bruti* payment enough. *Goditela*!"

Ossian raised his cup at the woman before taking a sip from it, smacking his lips together afterwards. He reached over and grabbed a handful of grapes, popping one into his mouth. "That answer your question?"

"I believe so." I chuckled as I said it, still caught off guard by the open slander of Malvene's leader.

"Good. Now, what Resistance business has you travelling all the way to Leonessa?" Ossian asked as he popped a couple more grapes into his mouth.

I leaned over and grabbed a piece of dried meat, took a bite, chewed it, then swallowed it before answering his question. "We grew tired of the way things are. Not just in Fleuris, but in most countries. We want to make real change and realized that we couldn't do it on our own. So, Brina, Rosalie, and I all went to Tudrose to see Queen Sophia to ask for her help."

Ossian's eyebrows raised as he took another sip of his wine. "Quite a drastic move that is. What help could Tudrose possibly give you anyway?"

"An army. Led by a leader who believes in a world where the Tóráin and humans have an equal opportunity at a good, healthy, prosperous life." Brina had grabbed the bread and was breaking off a piece of it for herself. "Do they have tea here?"

"Not a wine drinker, yet you speak the words of a drunkard. Go over to the bar, you'll find a short and curvy woman by the name of Greta. She'll get you some tea." Once Brina left our table, Ossian turned his attention to me. "You can't be seriously planning on waging war on all of Kosavros."

"Not all of it. Just the countries that need a change. Tudrose, Linne, Fruberg, Weidel, and Czermak have all transformed into countries that allow our kind to at least remotely flourish. Sure, not every citizen is for it, but the ones that matter are. Kings and queens are giving people like us a chance to live our lives without fear. All we want is to add to their ranks, by whatever means necessary."

Ossian shook his head. "I don't know, Weylyn. You know I'm all for some pushback against the established order. You know the disdain I have for humans like the one who executed Conri. But war is a terrible thing. Nothing good ever comes from it. Surely Queen Sophia was smart enough to know that. From what I've heard, she's quite intelligent."

I shot a welcoming smile to Brina as she came back with a mug full of tea before returning my attention to Ossian. "Yes, well, that's why we're here. She knew that war would be messy, and so we came up with a plan to lessen the mess. Fleuris has many that are prepared to cause chaos throughout the country if Tudrose invades. What we hope to do is to provide gunpowder to other countries in the hopes that when Tudrose — the spark — comes along there will be a mighty explosion. Weaken the country in however many ways possible, maybe even convince enough people to rise up with the Tudrose army and fight with them when they arrive. I sent people I trust to Tulp and Korblum. Rosalie is keeping things working back in Fleuris while Brina and I take on the responsibility of Malvene and Stelpina. I was hoping you could help."

Ossian took a gulp from his cup. He reached over to the platter of food and grabbed some berries, eating them in silence. My father's old friend looked lost in thought as he stared at the gathering of food before him, blindly grabbing berries from his hand and depositing them into his mouth. Brina sipped on her tea in between chewing on her bread as she patiently waited for Ossian to respond. I, on the other hand, was tapping my fingers on the table impatiently. We had come to Ossian because I believed him to be a friend and ally. I thought he would be jumping to help us in any way possible, but his hesitancy worried me. If Ossian wouldn't, or couldn't help us, I feared we would be in Malvene for quite a while. Some time passed until he finished the rest of his wine and lunged at me, bringing his hand onto my own to stop me from rattling my fingers.

"Please stop that. I've been trying to ignore it but it's one of those things that just bothers me to oblivion." He leaned back onto his chair and put his hands on the table. "What you want to do is something I can get behind, but my fighting days are well behind me. I wouldn't be much help in your current crusade, and I would be even less useful if Tudrose reaches Malvene. With all that being said, the only assistance I can provide is in the form of information."

I was feeling sour during the first bit of his speech, but the way he ended it lifted my spirits. "That's fine! Information can be even more useful than an old satyr swinging a rusted sword around."

Ossian scowled. "I'll have you know that I was quite a terror when I was your age. Be careful what you say. You'll be as old as me one day, you know."

"I was only joking around, Ossian." I tossed a grape at him as I chuckled. "Tell us what information you have."

"Well, like I said, I won't be much use when it comes to the physical aspects of a revolution. However, I know someone who could be. He's got a fair number of followers too. He has passion, but he could benefit from some guidance. I believe a satyr named Quaid is just what you're looking for. He has the potential to cause a big enough ruckus here to entice some resistance in Tordoro, maybe even Azuvipa too. The only problem is that he was imprisoned roughly six weeks ago during a small riot. King Ludovico has him tortured publicly once a week to deter others from following in the large satyr's footsteps. You'd have to free him if you want any type of resistance to form here."

Brina chewed on a piece of dried meat. "Perfect, we'll wait until he's set to be tortured again, gather some of his followers, and steal him off the stage. Simple."

Ossian displayed the look of someone who hadn't told the entire story. He began fiddling with his fingers, but thankfully I didn't have to push for him to come out and say whatever it was I knew he hadn't said yet.

"Well...you see...that may not work. He was tortured two days ago. Now, you might be thinking 'no worries, Ossian, we'll just wait a few days', but I don't think you can. I have heard that Quaid's followers have continued to cause trouble despite the weekly torture, and so King Ludovico is debating on a more drastic display." Ossian looked only at me. "A display similar to the one King Louis made roughly ten years ago."

Brina crossed her arms and leaned back in her chair. "Well then maybe we don't save him. It's cruel, but what happened in Fleuris sparked The Resistance. Maybe, if Quaid is killed by King Ludovico, the people will rise like we did."

I was going to protest the idea, but Ossian waved at Brina to dismiss her suggestion before vocalizing his reasoning for doing so. "No way. The people of Malvene are different. We've been broken down more. Many Tóráin see Quaid as a bright light in a country full of darkness. He dies, any hope of a revolution dies with him."

"Then we free him from his prison," I said as I slammed my hand down on the table. "We've done it before in Fleuris, we can do it here in Malvene."

Brina just nodded in agreement before taking a drink of her tea. Ossian grinned and clapped his hands together. "Good! I'll introduce you to some of his friends here. Afterwards, I believe I have the drawings for the architecture of the prison somewhere. You know me, I collect everything. Don't ask how or why I have them, just be glad I do. We'll sort something out and take action tomorrow. No sense in waiting around when the good lad could be killed any day now, right?"

"Right. Tomorrow it is then." I downed the rest of my wine and smiled at Brina. She smiled back as she took another bite out of a piece of meat.

It was going to be difficult — prisons were some of the most secure buildings in any country — but Brina and I would manage. We needed to. It seemed our entire plan relied on it.

# Chapter Fourteen

## Weylyn

Leonessa, Malvene  |  December 22, 1798

It was well into the night, the sun having set long ago, and a crisp wind came through our group, as the five of us made our way down Palazzo River. We passed under a small bridge and pushed on a bit more until we were approaching the northeastern side of the palace. Our plan was as thought out as it could be within the short amount of time we had. We had gotten to work right away, going over the drawings Ossian had of the Palazzo del Re as well as a map of Leonessa. We determined an entry point, a path in and out, and an escape; hopefully every decision we had made was a good one. Our group had grown too, Ossian insisting we include a human named Ezio, who was apparently a very dear friend of Quaid's. The young man's father, Ugo, actually owned The Boatman's Reprieve, and he kindly offered up his cellar as a place to hide Quaid after we rescued him. Two more Tóráin joined us as well: lycan brothers by the names of Cathal and Lorcan. Cathal was the older of the two and had army experience, while Lorcan was still young and yet to mature. Everyone in the group had a part to play, and if we all did our jobs well enough, we could be in and out without any problems.

"Alright. Ready your hooks," I instructed.

Brina, Ezio, and Cathal all followed my order, everyone taking out their hooks from under their cloaks. There were other prisons in the city, but the perceived worst criminals were held in a small prison on the top floor of Palazzo del Re. The jail was known as Cieli de Piombo, named after the lead rooftops which made the temperature in the cells cold during the winter and hot during the summer. Ossian believed that Quaid would be held in those cells instead of Il Pozzo, the cells on the bottom floor of the palace that were damp and dark. According to the drawings Ossian had obtained, the seven cells that made up Cieli de Piombo were on the eastern side of the building. Our safest and quickest way to get there was from the roof.

"Everyone have their necklace on?" Brina and Cathal reached at their necks and showed off the charmed pieces of jewelry Ossian had gifted us. Supposedly, they would help us if we ran into a witch. Ossian refused to say how he got them, claiming that it wasn't important.

Seeing that everyone was ready, I gave the go ahead. "Alright Brina. You first."

We took turns spinning our hooks before tossing them at the roof of the white stone building. We all tugged on our respective ropes to make sure our tethers were secure enough before I gave the signal for us to start climbing. Before I made my climb, I looked over at Lorcan and saw the disappointed look on his face.

"Hey. Don't get grim. You're one of the most important people in this group. We need you to be here once we get Quaid. We shouldn't be long. If we are, or whistles sound, leave so you don't get caught. Understood?"

The teenage lycan stood straighter and nodded. "Understood. Good luck."

We didn't expect things to go wrong, but there was a chance that they could, so I welcomed the well wishes. Not only were we entering the building that housed the King of Malvene himself, but the two people who oversaw the defense of the Palazzo del Re were not to be messed with. No one knew their true names. All that was known was that they were a man and a woman, one a soldier in the army and the other a witch. They were called The Crows — a duo that both humans and Tóráin feared a great deal. The two of them also carried out the torturing of prisoners on the stage set in the largest city square named after Modello de Virtù Demarco. They would undoubtedly be somewhere in the building, but we hoped to avoid them. The cover of darkness and the late hour would be our ally, and the added protection against the witch thanks to the necklaces would definitely help.

I had to climb quickly in order to catch up to the others, but we were all on the rooftop at about the same time. I took out another hook and led our group over to the other side of the roof. Once I was sure the hook was secured, I tossed down the rope and waited. We had no idea what the patrols would be like, so our biggest risk was going into this place half blind. When nobody tugged on the rope and no voices came from below, I went to lower myself down and onto the top balcony of the courtyard, but Brina stopped me.

"Let me go first," she whispered.

I nodded and moved out of her way. Brina lowered herself off the roof and climbed down the rope, swinging slightly to get over the railing and through the opening onto the top balcony. Again, I watched and listened to see if we had been made. Instead, when I peaked over the edge, I caught sight of Brina's hand sticking out of the opening with her thumb in the air. I mimicked the signal to the other two on the roof with me and lowered myself down next. Ezio followed, and last to reach us was Cathal. I led the way down the closest hall to an iron gate that led to the seven cells. I was surprised to find nobody guarding it. Perhaps we had gotten lucky, and this was only a brief moment when the prison cells were unattended. I used that thought to urge me forward in haste, waving at Ezio to come over and pick the lock. It was nerve racking waiting for him to unlock the gate, but after looking left and right for more minutes than I would have liked, Ezio removed his tools and pushed the gate open.

"*Accesso accordato*," Ezio said as he extended his arm into the entrance to the prison.

I didn't know what he had said, but I took it as an invitation and went through. The others followed close behind and together we peered into the small, open holes in the doors. It wasn't until we got to the final one that we found our target. Brina had claimed the prisoner to be Quaid, and Ezio confirmed it after having a look himself. I quickly came over to the cell and shouted in a whisper, trying to be heard and unheard at the same time.

"Quaid? Are you alright?"

I watched the large shape adjust itself and move closer to the small bit of light a nearby hanging lantern provided. Ezio could tell just from his shadow, but I needed more than that. Thankfully, the small amount of light was just enough to brighten the large satyr's image so I could confirm it was Quaid myself. We had been briefed on his appearance, just so everyone knew who we were looking for. Quaid had thick, round horns, shoulder length reddish hair, a thick beard, and his eyes were two different colors. This satyr, albeit bloodied and bruised, had all these features. His blue and brown eyes both were wide open, no doubt surprised someone had actually come for him. He pushed his face close to the open hole in the door and looked around as best he could. He looked panicked.

"How did you make your way past Greagoir without a scratch? Did you kill him?"

We all looked at each other with confused expressions, unsure who Quaid was talking about. There had been no one watching the cells. Regardless, if Quaid was worried about this Greagoir, then he must be trouble. It appeared as though we had gotten lucky and caught a time when Greagoir was away from the prison, so it would be smart to make the best use of our time. Before I could instruct Ezio to begin opening the door, a loud, deep voice rang throughout the hallway.

"What do you think you're doing?"

I turned towards the front gate and found quite possibly the largest lycan I had ever seen in my life. He had to be nearing nine feet tall, and he was so wide I doubt he could enter the hallway without turning sideways first. The lycan was in his feral form, resembling a wolf like every other lycan would. His head was massive, surrounded by a large, black mane. He had a scar over his right eye, but it wasn't the only one. Countless scars that resembled magical runes were carved all over his skin. All he wore was a rough pair of pants that had been torn at the knees, exposing his furry legs. It was obvious now why Quaid was so surprised we had reached him without injury.

"Ezio, start opening the door. You two watch him. I'll handle this." Before anyone could argue, I tossed my cloak off my shoulders and sprinted towards Greagoir. Shifting into my feral form as I ran, I tackled the massive brute before he could call out to anyone.

I considered myself a fair-sized lycan. It wasn't common for others to be taller or stronger than me, so fighting someone who was both of those by a wide margin was a difficult task. We wrestled on the floor for only a moment before he threw me off him, sending me down the hallway we had come from earlier. Quickly recovering, I kept my eyes on Greagoir as he got to his feet and growled. Both of us charged at each other this time, the hallway wide enough for Greagoir's large frame. Right before we collided, I pounced on the wall and leapt off it, bringing my arm under Greagoir's chin and dragging him down to the ground. He roared as he fell onto his back, clearly unhappy that he was bested. Foolishly, I had admired my good work too long, and Greagoir spun around, swiping at my legs with his massive arm. I fell, landing on my ass. Now on all fours, the large lycan clawed at me. He just missed my thigh as I pushed myself back and away from the small knives he called claws. I tried to get to my feet, but before I could, Greagoir leaped from his crouched position and caught me. He pinned my arms down with his massive hands and reared his head, showing off his teeth during a thunderous growl.

"A good try, but you can't kill me. Around here, I do the killing." He came at me with his jaws wide open, going for my neck. I gave one last struggle, but I couldn't move.

The next thing I felt was not what I had been expecting to feel. My arms were free, and my neck wasn't torn to shreds. Cathal and Brina were quickly helping me to my feet as Greagoir shook his head by the wall. The white stone had some red on it, which meant the large lycan must have hit his head from the impact of Cathal and Brina coming to my rescue. His injury didn't hinder him for long though. A pale purple light shown from the scars on his skin, with every bit of the lavender radiance going to the injury on his head. The three of us had taken steps back as this happened, unaware of what was going on. It was easy to know now though. Those witch runes had just healed him, something that would make this fight even more difficult. But there were three of us and only one of him; surely, we still had the advantage. Greagoir turned to face his trio of adversaries and roared in an attempt to intimidate us. Instead of cowering in fear, the three of us all had the same idea to charge him.

The massive lycan knocked Brina to the side with a backhanded swipe and clawed at Cathal, forcing him to dodge to his right. The forced detour had Cathal lose his balance and stumble. The only one to reach Greagoir was me, and I made sure to make the most of it. I charged into him with my shoulder, trying to push the beast of a lycan into the wall again. I moved him a bit, but the real blow dealt was when I took a bite out of his side. Greagoir barely grunted before punching me in the side of the head, causing my jaws to release their hold on him. The blow dazed me, making me unaware of when or where the next attack would come. I watched Brina grab the massive lycan's arm before he could land his next strike, bringing his hand to her mouth to bite off three of his fingers. Again, barely a grunt came from Greagoir, as if he didn't feel the pain we were inflicting. A large fist met with Brina's face, sending her reeling before Greagoir pushed me onto my back after exploding forward. I watched as Cathal jumped onto our attacker's back, sinking his teeth into a meaty shoulder. Again, the lycan jailor recovered, punching Cathal with his now two fingered fist and throwing him off his back, my ally landing on top of me. Greagoir stepped back, and the soft purple glow rose from his scars once more.

"Quickly! Before he recovers!" I shouted.

Brina and Cathal both charged him with me, and together we clawed at parts of the body we knew were vulnerable. Cathal went for the same arm he had already injured, while Brina went for the large tendon in Greagoir's ankle. Both of their attacks stopped the purple light from shining and brought the giant lycan down to a knee. I took my opening with great speed, leaping up and over his head. I caught his neck like I had before, spinning around and landing on his back. I got my arms in tight and wrapped my legs around his massive middle. He struggled to fight us off; Brina and Cathal were each holding an arm to restrain him and I had a firm hold on his neck. He snapped his jaws furiously until I finally managed to out muscle him. He began to thrash less, weakened by the lack of air, which allowed me to twist his head quickly and snap his neck. Our massive foe went limp and fell to the ground, the three of us releasing our holds on him before trying to catch our breath. We checked on each other briefly, all of us thankfully escaping without any major injuries, and then made our way back to Ezio and Quaid.

"You're alive." Quaid was tall, just a bit shorter than me, but he was slouching. You could tell that he lacked much energy.

"Yes, we're alive. And you aren't in a prison cell anymore. Now that we've established the obvious, can we get a move on please?" Brina rotated her shoulder and released a low grunt as she shifted back into her usual form.

"No. We must free the others," Quaid said.

Now in my tame form as well, I brought my eyes to the satyr. I gave him an intense stare down, telling him I had no time for arguing. "We came here for you. We have you. Now let's go before anyone discovers that massive body we left in the hall."

Quaid shook his head, unphased by my display. "I'm not going anywhere without the other prisoners here. They deserve freedom just as much as I do. Greagoir should have the keys on him, so we won't have to pick every single door."

"Our escape plan doesn't involve six more people. We can't leave the way we came if we free them." I was growing impatient now, worried that we would be caught if we continued to bicker about this.

"Then we'll find another path to freedom. If you aren't going to free these people, you might as well lock me back in my cell."

I began to see the immaturity that Ossian had warned me about. It was admirable of Quaid to wish to free his fellow prisoners, but leaders had to make hard decisions. Sometimes you won't be able to save everyone. Sometimes you have to just save who you can and move on. Sadly, we didn't have time for me to educate Quaid on the ways of leading, so I sighed and made my way for Greagoir's corpse. Thankful to find the keys in a deep pocket of his tattered pants, I took them and went back to the group. I tossed the keys at Quaid.

"Free your friends. Be quick about it."

Quaid nodded before making his way to the first door. It didn't take long for our group of five to become a group of eleven. There was no way all of us would fit into one gondola. We had no other choice than to try to sneak our way out of the place another way. I hoped that having Greagoir around meant that The Crows didn't feel they needed to garrison the Palazzo del Re too heavily. It was a foolish thought, seeing as King Ludovico and his family lived here, but what was a rescue mission without a fool's hope? I looked over our group and I was happy to at least see that everyone could walk on their own. Two of the other sick prisoners were lycans, another two were forest sprites, one was a harpy, and another was a human. I wasn't overjoyed at having a strange human with us, afraid that he might alert his kind to our escape in the hopes to maybe get on their good side. Despite my noted distrust, Quaid vouched for him. The satyr claimed that the man was a priest who was preaching that King Ludovico's treatment of Tóráin was unholy. I didn't have time to ask more questions, so I just accepted it and moved on to planning our next move. Our best bet was to make for the Docks of Modello de Virtù Demarco and grab a couple of new gondolas, escaping east down the shore, towards Dafnes River. A group so large would be difficult to keep hidden, but we had no choice.

Thankfully, right below us was a small armory. I figured that if we were to have to fight our way out of here, some weapons could be of some use. It would be guarded, but eleven of us could overwhelm them quickly enough. At least that's what I was hoping to be true. I waved at everyone to follow me since I had memorized the drawings Ossian had shown us last night and again this morning. We went down another hallway until we reached a set of stairs. I told everyone to wait at the top while I descended them alone to make sure the way was clear. Much to my surprise, the place seemed almost deserted; it was so empty. I certainly wasn't complaining, seeing as things were much easier for me if we never had to encounter any soldiers. However, when we reached the armory, there were two guards standing on either side of the door. There was no way for us to sneak up on them, so we would be forced to close the gap between us quickly. They were about sixty feet away, maybe seventy, but Brina and I could do it. I silently counted to three before jumping out from the dark corner we were hiding behind and charged the one on the right. Brina's man was the one on the left, and I was happy to see him collapse with my target at roughly the same time. We remained in our tame form, using our knives instead of our claws this time. Our feral form didn't really serve stealth very well.

We made it into the armory, and everyone grabbed something, whether it be a sword, a knife, or a pistol. A few of the prisoners took one of each just to be sure. All of us armed and ready for a fight if one presented itself, we moved out of the armory after hiding the two bodies within. I led everyone slowly through the building, until a clatter of falling metal and porcelain erupted behind us. We all turned around to find a maid surrounded by broken plates and fallen utensils. All of us stood in silence, hoping that nothing would come of the situation and we would all go our separate ways. That wasn't the case. The woman screamed out for soldiers to come, sending my group and me sprinting. We came across a group of four soldiers, but instead of fighting them I just guided our group another way. We would exit into the Square of Modello de Virtù Demarco instead, but we had no other choice. That was until another five guards blocked our path. Choosing to avoid conflict yet again, I led everyone back south towards the docks, hoping that we could still escape. We were lucky, failing to encounter any more soldiers despite the constant whistles sounding off. We made it all the way outside, but our path was blocked by two figures. Before we could charge them, roughly twenty soldiers came to stand next to the duo. We were surrounded.

"And just where do you think you're going?" asked a woman in a black and violet dress, while admiring the painted nails on her right hand.

All twenty guns were fixed on us. They surrounded us in a circle, with the two people I assumed to be The Crows just outside of the ring of rifles. I had no idea how we were going to get out of this.

"I say this with the utmost amount of honesty. You did well to get to this point. No one ever has." The man wore a long black robe that stretched all the way to the ground. It was dark even with the little light we had, but I could catch the gleam from the golden stitching that lined the openings of his robe.

The woman looked away from her nails and pouted. "There was that *fastidioso* alchemist many years ago."

The man had a look of disgust wash over his face. "Ah yes, *L'alchimista*. His escape was what eventually led to us being in charge of this place." He adjusted the large furs he had on his shoulders and displayed a fiendish grin. "How rude of us to not introduce ourselves. I believe you call us *I Corvi*, no? The Crows? I don't know why, but I feel that such an occasion requires a more intimate greeting. *Mi chiamo,* Morvolio."

"And my name is Morana." The woman curtsied in a mocking fashion.

"And your names are?" When nobody said a word, Malvolio spat on the ground. "*Animali!* Such poor etiquette. Fine. Let us not make a mess of the streets, yes? Lay down your weapons, keep your fangs to yourselves, and we'll let you live. Sure, you'll be in a prison for the rest of your life, but that's better than death. Right?"

"Not when the prison is run by you two. I'd rather die than go back to that cell." Quaid spoke up from behind me, a long saber in his left hand.

"Death ruins all the fun!" Morana put her hands on her hips and frowned. She quickly changed her posture, going back to inspecting her nails. "But if you want death, then fine."

"*Soldati*!" Malvolio shouted as he raised an arm in the air.

I gave a quick look at Brina. We said a silent goodbye to one another, knowing there was no way out of this. However, we weren't going to just stand there and let ourselves get shot. We both nodded at each other and gripped our swords tightly, picking an opponent to charge at. All of us readied ourselves for the end, an end that we would make our enemies work for. A shot fired, filling the cool night air with the loud snap a gun made. Every soldier pointed their rifle in the direction of the gunshot as one of the twenty fell to the stone path, blood leaking from his head. I didn't wait to see if the others would join me. With two quick strides I was striking down one of the soldiers with my sword. I quickly shifted, swinging my hand in the direction of the next closest soldier, my claws forming just in time to catch his neck. I was happy to hear more commotion, meaning that others had taken advantage of the distraction as well. Gunshots fired off and grunts and wails from those on the bad end of them filled the pathway between the docks and Palazzo del Re. More soldiers came running into the fight from the palace, roughly another ten or so. They lined up and readied to fire into the crowd, not caring who their bullets struck. Before they could do so, one of them dropped dead thanks to a gunshot wound to the chest. They all aimed at the shooter, giving me and Quaid enough time to close the gap between us. More soldiers were running at us from the city square, but they were all brandishing swords, accepting the melee combat we had initiated.

I snapped the neck of an attacking soldier and heard a bullet whiz past my head. I spun around to find a man in uniform falling to the ground. Looking for the shooter, I turned to find Lorcan walking into the light the palace's lanterns gave off. He smiled at me, proud of the help he had delivered. Before I knew it his smile was gone, a bullet bursting through his head. A loud howl sounded out, and I watched as Cathal charged Malvolio. Morana couldn't fully stop him thanks to the necklace Ossian had given him, but she managed to slow Cathal just enough for Malvolio to spin his pistol around and shoot Cathal in the head too. I looked around quickly and noticed that not many of us had survived this fight. Brina, Quaid, the harpy, one of the sprites, me, and Ezio, were the only ones still alive. There were only about ten or so soldiers left at the moment, so I took a chance at going for The Crows. I thought to catch them off guard, coming from their far right while their attention was to their left. At the last second Morana spun around and stuck out her hand, making me feel as though I was running through waist high water. Malvolio spun around with his pistol, but before he could fire, a sword went through his chest.

No one was holding the hilt of it. I followed Morana's sightline and found Quaid, who was no longer holding his saber. Malvolio fell to his knees before falling onto his face. Morana shrieked as she spun her arms around in various patterns, purple magic swirling around her as she did so. From the lavender whisps came six daggers of purple smoke. The witch sent her arms out to her sides quickly, shooting the six daggers out in various directions. One caught the lone sprite in the neck, another caught the harpy in the wing, while a third lodged itself into Ezio's shoulder. A fourth fell into a soldier's body after Quaid moved the poor man into it; another came at me, but I moved just enough for the blade to give me nothing more than a nasty cut on my neck. The final one found its way into Brina's back, the blow stunning her. She fell to her knees, leaving an opening for the soldier she was fighting. I followed in Quaid's footsteps and quickly picked up a sword from the ground before throwing it at the man, killing him before he could run Brina through with his own saber. Quaid finished off the last two soldiers, leaving just Morana.

The large satyr had found a new sword and was now walking towards the witch. The harpy was pulling the magic blade out of his wing and Ezio was on his knees panting. I watched the human pull the knife from his shoulder just before I began making my way over to Morana as well. She tried to restrain Quaid and me, her spell only slowing Quaid while having no effect on me at all. She must have used a lot of her energy with that knife trick. I managed to reach her quite easily, with Quaid not far behind. She fell to her knees and started laughing. The cackle was unsettling. It made me hold back from killing her. The insanity in her laugh had me taking a step back as Quaid took a step forward.

"Ah the overgrown goat! I'll miss our time together the most." Morana said through her laughter.

"I won't miss it at all." He ran his saber through the witch's chest and her laugh faded. She fell to the stone path like Malvolio had, and so the last of our enemies had been killed.

"Just sit still and let me help you!"

I turned around to find Ezio trying to remove the blade from Brina's back. Brina refused to remain still, insisting that she could do it herself. She was on the ground and looked incredibly pale. The blade had done more damage than she was letting on. I quickly got to her side, pushing Ezio away.

"Brina, I'm here. Let me take the knife out, okay?" She mumbled something under her breath, but she eventually nodded.

She was laying on her left side, the knife lodged in the right side of her back. It wasn't the first time Brina had been stabbed, but this knife was made of magic. I took a quick look at Ezio and the harpy and noticed that they looked even more pale and drained than they had before. I needed to get this knife out of Brina and we needed to get out of here.

"Okay, Brina. On the count of three. Ready? One." I pulled the blade out and blood began to leak down her back.

"Ah you bastard! I knew you wouldn't count to three."

The entire knife evaporated into thin air — abandoning its solid form — as I knelt down and began to help Brina up. I put her arm over my shoulders and allowed her to use me as a crutch. She was very weak, something that truly worried me. Quaid, already quite weak from his weekly tortures, was trying to help both Ezio and the harpy on his own. Together, we slowly made our way towards the gondolas to make our escape. I wanted to bring the bodies of Lorcan and Cathal with us at least, but I began to feel drained as well. Everyone who had been injured by Morana's magical knives was losing energy quickly. We all slumped into the nearest gondola as Quaid began pushing us off into more open water.

"Go to The Boatman's Reprieve. Ugo said we can use his cellar to lay low," I told Quaid as I felt myself drifting off, noticing that the others had already passed out from whatever magic was hindering us. "Find the satyr Ossian. Tell him we need a witch. Quickly."

# Chapter Fifteen

# Weylyn

Leonessa, Malvene | December 23, 1798

I struggled to open my eyes. I saw a dark roof, and the air smelled of alcohol and rat shit. I looked around to find Ossian lounging next to me reading a book. When he noticed I was awake he quickly closed his novel and sat up.

"Easy now. Had quite the injury you and your friends did."

"What happened?" I rubbed my eyes in the hopes that they would adjust to the harsh light of the lantern sitting next to me.

"You all passed out on the gondola. I had to carry each one of you off the boat and into the cellar." Quaid's voice carried from about ten feet away, the satyr sitting up with his back against a large barrel. "After that I did as you asked and told Ugo we needed Ossian to find us a witch."

"Yes, and it took some real convincing, but I managed to get my friend to come see you all. You're all very lucky. All of you would have been dead soon if she hadn't got here when she did. That Morana cursed you with a spell of draining. According to my friend, it saps your energy until you die. To do the spell so many times takes a strong witch. She said you're all lucky to be alive." Ossian adjusted his glasses and smiled.

"Does that mean Brina's alright?" I went to bring myself upright a bit, but Ossian put a hand on my chest and urged me to lay down. "Easy, Weylyn. She hasn't woken yet, but she'll be fine. You were only nicked by a blade, the other three were stabbed by one. Give them time."

I conceded and turned my attention to Quaid. "Thank you for saving everyone. I owe you my life."

Quaid chuckled. "You saved my life just as much as I saved yours. You owe me nothing. Consider us even, lycan."

"Has Ossian told you why we freed you?" I tried again to sit up, but the room spun around when I did, so I accepted my fate and let myself back down, staring up at the ceiling of the cellar.

"I only mentioned that you needed his help. I figured you two should discuss details together," Ossian said before picking up his book again.

"Well, what help do you need?" Quaid took a sip from a cup he had sitting next to him.

I gave him the same speech I had given Ossian, informing him of Tudrose and our plan to remove all leaders who would see their countries treat the Tóráin worse than cattle. He said nothing while I spoke, never interrupting. Eventually, I reached the end of my speech. "And so, I think that with your place among the Tóráin in Leonessa, you could lead them. Cause enough trouble for when Tudrose finally arrives. What do you say? Are you with us?"

It took him some time, but Quaid finally answered me. "I've been fighting this fight for a while now, believe it or not. Nothing's changed. What would make this time any different?"

"Well, being a more organized group instead of just causing riots every week would help. You could attack food stores, free prisoners, ransack armories. There are more effective things to do than just running into the streets and screaming. Plus, when you weaken Leonessa and, hopefully, the rest of Malvene, it opens the door for Tudrose to come in and get rid of those who oppress you."

"I see," Quaid said. I turned onto my side to get a better look at the satyr. He was rubbing his beard and staring at the ground beneath him. He took his time to say more, but it was worth the wait. "Alright. You want a true resistance here in Leonessa? You got one. The death of The Crows will actually make things a bit easier. If word spreads that it was this newfound rebellion that's responsible, it could create an influx of members. We'll make life Hell here for those who deserve it. I can't make any promises about other cities in Malvene, but I can assure you Leonessa will be weak and ready for the taking when Queen Sophia comes with that army of hers."

I returned to the position where I was flat on my back and let my arms stretch outwards. I took a deep breath and let out a great sigh. Quaid had quite the job ahead of him, but he had passion. I'd also be giving him a few tips, which would help him of course. The Malvene chapter of The Resistance would be up and running quickly I imagine, with or without Brina and I sticking around. It was a dangerous and almost deadly endeavor, but we had done what we had come here to do. The longer we stayed here in Malvene, the longer our task in Stelpina would take. Quaid, Ezio, and Ossian could handle things here. Brina and I needed to be on our way to Stelpina. It had been some time since General Rosspier had said or done anything drastic to hinder the Tóráin further, but it was only a matter of time until he did. The bolder General Rosspier gets, the more undaunted other leaders become. Once the treaties were signed after the war ended roughly two years ago, the other countries watched General Rosspier like he was their parent. They mimicked what he did, adopted his policies and laws. The man had more power than he knew. This war we were about to wage wasn't just to bring an end to General Rosspier and free Fleuris, it was for everyone. The longer we took to start this war the more people would continue to suffer.

"Hello? *Cosa è successo*? Am I dead?" Ezio's voice filled the cellar as a shape in the distance began to move.

There were two lanterns down here with us, the one near me and the one at the other end of the room. Together they cast soft light and ghastly shadows. When I had leaned over to speak with Quaid, I had spotted three other shapes laid out on the cellar floor. Ezio was the second shape from where I was. From the looks of it, the one closest to me was Brina and the one furthest from me was the harpy, his wings making him a bit easier to identify. Quaid stood up from his place next to the large barrel and shuffled over to Ezio, shushing him and preventing him from sitting up. He began telling Ezio the same story I had been told when I woke up, so I tuned them out. I turned my attention back to Ossian, who was deep in his book.

"How long was I out?" I asked.

Ossian stopped reading, peering over his glasses to give me a look that told me he didn't enjoy being disrupted. Still, he sighed and closed his book once more. He reached into a bowl next to him and tossed me a peach. I managed to sit up without the room spinning, taking a bite out of the fruit when I was certain I wouldn't fall over. Ossian then reached over by the bowl again, only this time he offered me a cup. "It's December twenty-third. When I came down here the sun was already gone. So, a little under a day."

I took the cup from him and brought the liquid to my lips. The wine warmed me, the feeling causing me to have another sip before putting the clay cup on the stone floor next to me. "How long until I stop feeling like someone is smacking my head with a rock?"

Ossian laughed. "That, I do not have the answer to. It will depend on your strength as a lycan I imagine. From what I know, you should be fine soon."

"Good. So long as Brina is strong enough to do so, I think it would be good for us to try to leave before dawn." I took another bite of the peach, its juices dripping down my chin.

"Can't sit still. Your father never could either, remember? Always one thing to another. I'm surprised he ever found time to play chess with me." He leaned forward and put a hand on my thigh. "Stay. At least for another day. You're both strong, you more so than her, but you both need to rest. Eat. Drink. Read if you like. Just rest."

"Fine." I had no energy to argue with Ossian, however something he said had made me curious. "Why do you think I'm stronger than Brina?"

Ossian laughed again, stopping to take a drink from his cup before answering. "I don't think you're stronger. I know you're stronger."

"Okay, well then how do you know I'm stronger?" The argument over specifics annoyed me more than usual thanks to the throbbing behind my eyes.

"Ah, I can't say. Told Conri I wouldn't." Ossian almost seemed upset.

"Oh, just tell me, Ossian. He won't haunt you. As his son, I absolve you of your promise. We have a day to pass. How do you know I'm stronger?" Before I was just curious, but now I realized I had stumbled onto something special, and I wanted to know what it was.

Ossian played with his beard as he visibly struggled to contain this piece of information. He muttered to himself while fixing his glasses before downing what was left of his wine. My father's old friend looked over at Quaid and Ezio to make sure they were occupied before sliding closer to me. He took a deep breath in, let it all out, and rubbed his hands on the odd short pants that satyr's wore. Supposedly they never wore clothes back home, only taking to the tradition after humans had deemed their previous arrangement indecent. His legs and hooves out to his side, Ossian sat facing me.

"What has your father told you about your mother?" the satyr asked.

An odd question. I had no idea what this had to do with anything, but I answered anyway. "Only that she died when I was two years old when she tried to stop a group of humans from robbing a forest sprite. I don't remember her much if I'm honest."

"No. Your mother was executed much like your father was. She was caught speaking our language in public with another lycan and a satyr too. The three of them were tortured in the efforts of making them renounce their former language and culture. The other lycan eventually did, but the satyr and your mother refused. They ended up killing all three of them. It broke your father, but it's also what drove him to be such a pillar of the community."

I shook my head, rejecting what I was hearing. "First of all, I don't believe you, and second what does this have to do with my strength?"

"What reason would I have to lie? If you choose to not believe what I tell you, then do so. I don't need to tell you anything. Do you want me to tell you what all this has to do with your strength, or am I a liar who can return to reading his book?" Ossian had a big scowl on his face that caused the wrinkles in his forehead to be more dominant.

He was right in that he had no reason to tell my lies. I was young back then, and it would make sense that my father would tell me a different story to protect me from the truth. "I'm sorry, I don't think you're a liar. It's just a lot to take in. Please, continue."

Ossian stared at me over his glasses for a while before bringing them closer to his face. He was probably making sure that I didn't change my mind before he spoke, but I felt like a child who had interrupted his teacher. The satyr took my cup in his hand and sipped from it before putting it back on the stone floor.

"Right. Now, as you know, there are some who still practice the culture and language we practiced before we came here. Their numbers have dwindled over the years, but they can be found. Your mother and her family were one of these few. They were well known and well respected in the Tóráin community in Cloque for many reasons; however, had everyone known their true nature they probably would have been better protected. You see, in order to bring lycans and sprites and satyrs and others to this world, we needed gifted magic users. We called them *Draoithe*. In the common tongue of this world, they're known as Druids. Druids from every race participated in the spell that would open a gateway between our world, and this one. Together, those Druids — with the help from the witches of this world — created a way for our kind to escape the elves. Druids came here with members of their respective race, and the magic they had learned kept many of us safe during The Great Welcoming. It is said that there is a very small number of Druid bloodlines still alive today. However, your mother belonged to one, and so do you."

I didn't know what to say. I could tell that Ossian was waiting for a response, but I truly couldn't come up with one. What does someone say to that? If I was being completely honest, I didn't even fully understand what he was telling me. I would never admit it out loud though, fearful that Ossian would only lecture me further. I ran over all the information and only when I felt I had a good understanding of what was going on did I open my mouth to speak. "So, I'm strong because I have Druid blood? Can I wield magic like they did?"

Ossian massaged his chin for a while before responding. "In our world it was called *Fáthfhuil*. In the common tongue of this world, we call it Mystic Blood. But to answer your question, yes, the blood that runs through your veins is why you are so strong. As for wielding magic? Theoretically, you should be able to cast spells. However, you would need to be taught how to do so, and no witch is going to risk teaching a lycan how to use magic."

The whole subject had me even more curious than before. "How many other bloodlines are there? Do you know where they are?"

Ossian adjusted his glasses again. "I don't know. It's not really talked about all that much, which is both a gift and a hindrance. We stopped keeping track of the whereabouts of Mystic Bloods long ago to keep them safe, but they were very important parts of our culture. *Draoithe* were our leaders and our teachers. It would be a great boost to our morale to have them be a focal point in our community once more, but they are still hunted by the humans, so we keep these sorts of things quiet."

It made sense why we would make it hard to find someone with such a tie to our old world. Humans were vile, always killing for sport. If they ever found out someone had Mystic Blood, they'd probably hunt them and their family until the end of time. I found myself in that moment of sadness dreaming of a day where we could celebrate Druids again, but I knew it was a dream that would never be realized. The humans wouldn't allow it. To be honest I still wasn't sure there would ever be a time when the Tóráin could go about their lives without worrying about being tortured or killed. I shook my head, choosing to send away the negative thoughts that had taken me over, and made the decision to focus on my mother instead. "So, I can thank my mother for my strength then?"

Ossian chuckled. "You can thank her for much more than that."

"Thank who for what?" Brina's voice interrupted our conversation.

Her waking up had me lifting myself to sit up straighter. The room spun a little bit at first, but it eventually stopped. I caught sight of Brina rubbing at her eyes as she tried to sit up too. Ossian had shuffled over to her quicker than I thought he could move and put his hand on her shoulder as he tried to keep her on her back.

"Ossian? Where's Weylyn? Is he alright?" Brina sounded as if she was merely talking in her sleep, her questions all slurred together.

"I'm fine, Brina. We were all hit with a nasty spell. Just lie down and relax." I watched as her head snapped over to where my voice had come from.

"Are we in Ugo's cellar?" Brina asked softly.

"Yes," Ossian answered as he stood up. "Weylyn can catch you up. I'm going to go get you some tea to drink. There's a bowl of fruit to your left if you're hungry. Just take it easy until I get back."

Ossian came back over to me and shot me a quick smile as he bent over to pick up his book. He went over to the far end of the cellar where the dark covered a set of stairs. I heard him knock on the doors three times before a big rectangle of soft light shone into the black room. I watched the satyr climb out of the cellar, disappearing into the light before the door dropped back down. I could only hear Quaid and Ezio muttering to each other for some time until Brina's voice broke the relative silence. "What were you talking with Ossian about?"

I took some time to answer, wondering what I should say. Eventually, I chose the response that I thought was the safest. "Nothing."

# Chapter Sixteen

# General Rosspier

Cloque, Fleuris  |  December 24, 1798

I had been so focused on my letters that my tea had gone cold. The realization had me snapping my fingers and pointing to the teacup on my desk. The maid came and quickly grabbed the porcelain cup and scurried off. Other nobles used beasts to serve them, but I didn't trust them. They were vile things, every single one of them. Each with their own selfish motives pertaining to greedy plans. No matter how much you gave the creatures, they were always wanting more. You would think that they would be thankful to not be hunted anymore and move on with their lives. They came here expecting an oasis that they could rule the same way they had ruled their previous lands. My ancestors made sure to show them just how wrong the bastards were.

This was a world led by humans; a world made to benefit humans. Sure, there were those of our race that were lesser than others, but the world needed people to do the dirty work. Those humans, along with the *Diables*, were always complaining that they weren't getting enough money, or enough food, or enough firewood. They were never saying thank you to those who provided for them. They always want what we have, and the simple truth of the matter was that we could easily do what they did, but they could never do what we do. They lacked the education, the courage, the willpower, and the etiquette.

Those creatures and their filthy human allies believed that everyone who wasn't them just rolled around in gold coins all day. In my case, I had a country to look after. Fleuris was the largest country in Kosavros, and it required my utmost attention for it to continue to also be the best country in Kosavros. I had fought long and hard over the last forty years or so to make this country the best it can be. Ever since I joined the army at sixteen, I fought to see Fleuris prosper. I helped create laws to make my country a safer, more civilized place. I even overthrew the king when it was apparent that a monarchy was no longer beneficial to our fine nation. I made the sacrifice of becoming our new leader, devoting my life to leading these forever ungrateful citizens who lack even one patriotic bone in their body. We had to force those beasts into the army, none of them possessing the intelligence required to realize that they needed to fight for their home on occasion. I wasn't entirely surprised though, considering that they fled their previous home instead of fighting for it.

With so much weighing on my shoulders, I needed to find things to break up the constant stress. Looking over letters from kings, nobles, soldiers, and merchants made me feel good. It reminded me of my power as a leader. It also reminded me of our success during the last war. It was a pathetic showing when nations decided they would declare war on me because I dared remove the monarchy. Our superior army defeated them all quite quickly, resulting in favorable treaties being signed. We were entitled to local goods all across Kosavros. Fleuris was the center of the world, and I was her leader. As her power grew, so did mine, and that made me a happy man. It was good to have power. Anyone who doesn't want power lacks the ambition to ever become something more than a fly on a piece of dog shit. Power was everything in life, and if you had it, you would do well to hold on to it. I reached the rank of general faster than anyone ever had, and I led our army through multiple important wars. We won because of my gift for battle strategy, and my ruthlessness. There was no place for mercy when it came to war.

Despite knowing this, it took a letter from my two friends in Leonessa to remind me that I was being much too merciful as of late. They told me how they had captured a blasphemous, renegade goat who was leading riots in their canal riddled streets. It had taken them some time to finally capture him, but they claimed it would be well worth the wait. They described how they would torture him for the public to see, keeping him alive so as to do it again the following week. It was to be a sign of power, a display that said 'you will end up like him if you replicate his actions'. It was done to inspire fear and respect. The whole thing had made me realize that I was long overdue for such a display. The small riot that led to an escaped prisoner a few weeks ago told me that the respect level among the citizens of Cloque was low, and that needed to be adjusted. As I combed through more recent letters, I continued to think of what I would say during my speech, wishing for it to be perfect. I read the last letter, a notice from a merchant that he would have more of his stock than usual when he arrived next week, before removing my glasses.

"Jon!" I called out as I placed my glasses onto the large desk.

"Yes, General." I pushed out my chair and stood, turning to find Jon standing erect and saluting.

"How are the preparations for my speech?" I asked.

Jon remained still. "They are proceeding as planned, General."

I rolled my eyes and waved at him dismissively, causing him to end his salute. "There isn't anyone else around, Jon. While I do enjoy it, the formalities aren't necessary. You're free to address me casually."

Major Jon Carierre had been my closest ally since I was in my early twenties. We rose amongst the ranks together, his rise being a bit slower than mine of course. We have known each other for over thirty years, and he was the only person I truly trusted. My own wife had tried to warn King Louis of my coup, something that landed her in prison. She died there soon after — thanks to an infection of some sort. I had a daughter, Adeline, but after what I did to her mother, she left the country. I never bothered looking for her. The only one who stuck by me was Jon. I trusted him to enforce my laws and squash all resistance. He helped me keep Fleuris prosperous.

"Have the prisoners said anything yet?" I inquired.

It upset me to see Jon shake his head. "No. Two died from infection. One yesterday, the other this morning. The other four only shout in pain. No names are given, not even their own."

I poured myself a glass of champagne before offering one to Jon. He hesitated, but eventually accepted it. I took a sip from my tall glass as I thought of a solution. "See if The Dove can get anything out of them when she returns in a few days."

"I'll try tomorrow." A hooded figure walked through the open door and came to sit in one of my chairs.

"Speak of the devil and she will come." Jon took a sip of his champagne and sat down in the chair opposite of our new guest.

I came around the lounge chair positioned between Jon and our friend and sat down. "Now, now, Jon. Play nice."

"Oh, there's no trouble here. Right?" Jon crossed one leg over the other and smiled.

"I don't believe in your devil, and even if I did, I know he would not be me. The devil I believe in is made up of many, taking form in the foul things you allow to live amongst you." Her voice was somehow both warm and intimidating at the same time. Roughly eight years of knowing her and I still haven't gotten used to it.

"You're home early. Did *le joli oiseau* fail to find what she was looking for?" I swirled my champagne in my glass, allowing the sweet aroma to fill my nostrils.

The witch's lip curled in disgust as she stood up from her seat, walked over to the bottle of champagne, and picked it up. She pulled out the glass stopper and brought the bottle to her lips. She let out an exasperated vocal expression of a thirst well quenched before taking another gulp from the bottle. She brought it with her back to the seat she had claimed earlier and crossed her legs.

"This isn't my home. And no, I didn't find what I was looking for. The trip was awful. There were barely any prisoners for me to examine."

Jon coughed, apparently choking on his drink. "They let you into their prisons? *Sont-ils fous?*"

The Dove smiled. Below her nose was all that was visible thanks to a mask she wore. I had never seen her full face, and I imagined that it was because of some nasty scar or something. It was white, just like everything else she wore, but it was in the shape of a rising sun. The rays were animated slivers poking upward past her forehead and outward past her cheekbones. There was gold lining it too. It seemed expensive for a witch, but I never asked her how or where she had purchased such a thing. The Dove was her own woman, and her life was more mystery than certainty. I didn't even know the woman's name.

"You know very well that they didn't let me in, you fool. I broke in. It was all a wasted effort anyway." She took another big gulp from the bottle and wiped away some champagne that had evidently missed her mouth.

"I am sorry to hear that, *mon amie*. Will you be staying long enough to accompany me during my speech? *Le jour spécial* is only *quatre* days away. I'm expecting at least a few *Diables* to allow anger to lead them into a decision that gets them arrested or killed. You wouldn't want to miss that would you?" The delivery of my question was a bit shaky, but only because the witch had turned her head towards me like a hawk locking onto its next meal when I mentioned the *Diables*.

"Don't call them that. And stop saying so many words in that tongue. You know I hate it when you do. Calling them devils is a kindness they don't deserve.

They are much worse than that. They are an intense filth that requires holy cleansing. They are cowardly hounds and goats, conniving little faeries and blasphemous chickens. I honestly think I hate the vile imps the most. All of them are a disease born from The Dark that The Light must purify.”

The Dove’s crimson eyes stared at me. The contrast between her red eyes and her pale clothes only made the blood-colored circles stand out more. She took a deep breath before finishing off the bottle of champagne she had stolen. The Dove leaned forward and calmly placed the empty bottle on a small table that was an equal distance from all three of us. Only then did she continue speaking.

“As for accompanying you, I know as well as you do that the only reason you want me there is so that nobody tries to assassinate you. I’ve been informed of the small riot that led to a hound being freed from your most secure prison. These creatures do not fear you as much as you wish them too it seems, and so you want me there. ‘The Dove’. You hope that they fear me enough to deter any violence against you directly. This is all about your protection, with no actual benefit to me or my mission.” She leaned back and took out a knife from her belt. She balanced the point of the sharp blade on the tip of her first finger as she waited for my response.

“They wouldn’t dare try anything, with or without you there. You aren’t really needed. If you have better things to do then go do them.” Jon was agitated and letting his impatience get the better of him. He cared very little for The Dove, and sometimes he did a poor job at hiding that fact.

“While I agree that any attempt on my life would be snuffed out like a bucket of water falling over a candle, The Dove speaks the truth. I would feel safer with her by my side. Look, I have a plan and if everything goes according to that plan, we’ll have a nice show to watch in less than a week. If you aren’t busy, I would love for you to join us. I promise you’ll be entertained.” I didn’t need to tell her everything, mostly because I didn’t trust her but also because I knew she didn’t care.

The Dove pursed her thin lips and tapped on the pale leather armor she wore on her chest. The woman was just as capable as a fighter as she was a witch, something I had witnessed firsthand. Most women wore tight, linen corsets and dresses, with only a few opting for the pants or tights men wore. The Dove’s ensemble was a mix of flashy nobility and a ruffian archer from years ago. Leather armor dyed a pale white accompanied by a flowing white cloak and colorless long gloves that she wore under her bracers, which were also void of any color. The designs on her armor were foreign to me, but I just assumed they were witch symbols and nothing more. The pale palette extended down to her boots. The thick, short leather skirt she wore, along with the tall greaves that graced her lower legs, was all dyed white. The Dove continued to tap on her breastplate while making a weird clicking noise with her mouth. Eventually she stopped, standing from her seat so quickly it made Jon jump and spill some of his drink. It startled me as well, but my drink was long finished, and I held only an empty glass.

"Fine. I'll join you. I'll go visit your prisoners now instead of tomorrow. I planned on taking the train to go visit Magistrate Frollo and Ravenna in Etoile. I had a letter here waiting for me saying they have some new prisoners for me to dissect. I'll leave tomorrow and be back in time for your little speech." The witch didn't wait for any response to her leaving the city so soon, knowing full well no one was going to question her about it.

The Dove and her flowing white cloak left the room quickly, leaving just Jon and me in the room. Jon finished what was left of his champagne and huffed before getting up from his chair. He straightened out his coat and began doing up a few buttons. "I should be present for these interrogations she plans to have with my prisoners. I don't trust her to tell us if they say anything."

I remained on the lounge chair, perfectly comfortable where I was. "Please be careful what you say around her. She has no care for anyone, and I'm afraid I can't stop her from killing you if you piss her off. *Elle est sauvage et folle*, Jon. Remember that *s'il te plaît*."

Jon made his way to the open door, stopping in the entryway and turning around. "Tell me again why we put up with her?"

I smiled. "Because she's good at what she does."

Jon nodded. "Right. Good luck with your speech. I'm sure I'll hear a draft of it soon."

"Yes, yes. I think I'll work on it tomorrow. It's too late now and I'm much too tired. Do me a favor and tell someone to get my bedroom ready for me." Again, Jon nodded. He spun around and almost knocked over a maid who had returned with a hot cup of tea to replace the cold one I had sent away earlier.

She mumbled an apology and bowed out of the way, allowing Jon to leave the room. The maid waited obediently just outside, waiting for permission. I took my time granting her entry, enjoying the power I had over the woman. Eventually I waved her in, and she quickly came over and placed the teacup and saucer on the table before me. She took a couple steps back and waited to be dismissed. This time I didn't make her wait, my wish to be alone being more powerful than my need to show off the control I had over her. She left the room and closed the door at my request. I reluctantly sat up, tired from a long day, and reached for the cup of tea. Its warmth was welcome, especially in the cold month of December. The fire I had lit hours ago was barely alight now, smoldering in the hearth that sat opposite of me. I took a sip and began going over the plan I had concocted. It made me smile.

# Chapter Seventeen

# Olwen

Adler, Korblum  |  December 24, 1798

It was a relatively easy trip to Adler from Leuw, so at least we had that going for us. Keagan and I had arrived earlier in the day, which gave us time to look for this harpy friend of Cordelia's before night came. The city of Adler was known for many things, but its most popular draw were its fighting arenas. There were both formal and informal fighting pits all over the city, on both sides of the dividing river called The Hauptfluss. Whether you were north of the river or south of it, you would have no problem finding a place to watch a fight. Luckily for us we didn't have to search the entire city trying to find Seig. There were notices all over the place promoting Adler's newest bout. 'Seig the Sharp' versus 'Kyran the Black' was listed as the main event at the famous Kampfhalle. The arena was north of The Hauptfluss in the western end of the city. By the time Keagan and I reached the arena and paid for our entry, other fights had already started.

We were in the right place, but how we would get to Seig was something we needed to figure out. I led us through the building, looking to see if there was any chance for us to find Seig before her fight. She was listed as the champion, so she must be a capable fighter, but the stakes at the Kampfhalle were different from every other arena. Everywhere else, you won a fight by your opponent submitting or being knocked out. At Kampfhalle, each fight was to the death. It made me wonder if Seig was the right person for us to be looking for, seeing as she had chosen this path of unnecessary violence. Some Tóráin enjoyed the fights, but they were mostly for the entertainment of humans who just wanted to see two Tóráin beat or kill each other. I understood that most fighters did it for the money — many of them needed their pay to survive — but those who fought for the fun of it worried me.

Still, we searched for Seig. That was until soldiers caught us in an area we apparently weren't allowed in. I had thought that they would try to arrest us, forcing Keagan and I to fight our way out of another sticky situation. Instead, they informed us that the owner of the arena would decide what our punishment would be. Some would be worried, but I saw this as an opportunity. If anyone knew where Seig was, it would be the one in charge of the fights here. The four soldiers escorted us to a staircase, taking us up three flights of stairs to the top floor of the Kampfhalle. They brought us down a hall, passing entryways to fancy seating areas that only the rich could afford. Eventually they stopped in front of one of the openings, with one of the soldiers instructing us to stay where we were. He entered what must have been where the owner was taking in the fights and I quickly heard a discussion begin; however, I couldn't make out what was being said. Less than a minute passed before the same soldier came back into the hall and ordered us to follow him.

We didn't have much say in the matter, seeing as the two soldiers behind us had pistols lodged in our backs. The entryway was large enough for Keagan and me to walk in at the same time. On the other side of it was a large viewing area, but only two seats. There was a fat man with a tall glass of something in his hand in one chair, and a thin woman in a slim green dress sat next to him in the other. We were brought before them both and told to bow. I could hear Keagan growl as he followed me in leaning forward. Again, with guns to our back we really had no other choice. The round man raised his drink in the air and laughed, spilling it all over as the crowd cheered. I peeked over my shoulder to see a water sprite celebrating their latest win. A nudge from the pistol behind me had me looking straight ahead again.

"Mr. Vogel here tells me that you were lurking about my arena. Why?"

The owner's voice was of a higher pitch than I had expected for his appearance. I had almost let a smirk slip by, the irony of it all something I found quite amusing. While trying to keep myself composed, I received a jab in my back from the muzzle of a pistol. I was thankful Keagan hadn't spoken yet, knowing that he wasn't the most political speaker. A quick look in his direction had me receive a supportive nod. I cleared my throat and hoped that this whole thing didn't end with us in a prison.

"We're terribly sorry for lurking. Perhaps we can start this relationship of ours on a better foot? How about an introduction. My name is Olwen, and my friend is Keagan. You are?"

His face twisted into a sour expression, and I realized that I may have offended him somehow. His words confirmed my suspicions. "Who am I? *Ist das dein Ernst? Bist du dumm*? You come into this arena, and you don't know who I am? I am Arne Dietrich, Owner of Kampfhalle, Bringer of Blood, Giver of Spectacles! Now, Olwen, answer my damn question."

Well, we weren't in prison yet, so I'd say things were going well so far. I took a moment to smile, bowing again only this time it was voluntary. "My deepest apologies. My friend and I have travelled from outside of Korblum in the hopes to see a friend of ours. She just so happens to be your champion. Always knew she had it in her to be a champion one day. Just want to tell her how proud we are, give her a hug, maybe go out for drinks later after her win tonight. Nothing fancy. Only problem is we don't know where she is. Maybe you can help with that?"

The woman next to Arne scoffed at my request, which told me I may not like the answer I was going to get. The rotund man adjusted the very obvious wig on his head and laughed. He waved at a water sprite that was standing in the corner holding a large bottle. Arne tried to contain himself as the maid poured him more of his drink. He struggled to hold the glass still, telling me he was probably quite drunk already. I thought quickly of how we could maybe use that to our advantage somehow while Arne took big gulps from his cup. He eventually stopped, before leaning over to the woman next to him. She had a look of disgust on her face for only a moment, then it went away as she wiped away the drink that had missed Arne's mouth.

"Seig has no friends," Arne announced. "When she came here, she burned her past and gave everything to becoming the best fighter in the world. You, and your pet *Hund*, are lying. I have very little patience for *Teufel*, and none for *verlogene Teufel*. Mr. Vogel, take them anywhere but here. If they are found in my arena again, shoot them."

I was about to protest, but a goblin came running into the room. "Master Arne! Master Arne! I must speak with Master Arne!"

The overweight drunkard stopped drinking from his glass and glared at the goblin. "*Verdammt nochmal*! What's wrong now, Breasal?"

The goblin flinched at Arne's voice. He held his hands up to protect himself from an expected swing, which told me all I needed to know about their relationship. "It's The White Wolf, merciful Master Arne. He was in a brawl outside the building. The cheater took out a hammer and bashed in The White Wolf's leg. They've taken him to Bewohnerin Hospital. He's our fourth fight of the night, and our second just finished. We need a replacement, or we have to cancel the fight and return the bets."

I was surprised at how quickly Arne managed to get out of his chair. He stomped over to Breasal and cuffed him on the side of his head. "Return the bets? Did your *krankhaft* mother drop you on your head when you were a *hässlich* infant? We don't return bets. Find someone else to fight."

Breasal was shaking now, his hands up protecting himself again. "I-I've looked kind, understanding Master Arne. There's no one."

Again, Arne cuffed the poor goblin and I heard Keagan growl next to me. I reached out and grabbed my friend's hand, hoping it would calm him. Arne loomed over Breasal now, forcing the goblin to fall to his knees in fear.

"An entire city full of fucking fighters and you can't find me one? What good are you? You *Teufel* are all the same. Damn useless, the lot of you!" Arne screamed before going to hit Breasal again.

"Stop!" I shouted. Not only had I had enough of him beating Breasal, but I had also seen an opportunity. "I'll take his place. I'll fight. But if I win, you let Keagan and I see Seig before her fight."

Arne still had his hand in the air, only putting it down once he gave a short kick into Breasal's side. The fat prick stepped towards me and looked me over in a way that made me very uncomfortable, seeing as he took his time looking at my chest and below my waist. He walked around me, and I could feel his eyes almost undressing me. It made me want to spin around and punch the bastard right in the nose, but I stood still like they had trained me to do in the army. He stopped his tour in front of me, leaned in, and showed off a smile that had two gold teeth. He sniffed the air dramatically and I could have sworn I heard him moan.

"You'll do. Deal." He slowly pulled away and picked up Breasal by the collar of his shirt, throwing him towards the exit. "Tell Keera the Brutal she has a new opponent."

The soldiers started leading us away, but I resisted. "How do I know you'll honor our agreement?"

Arne raised his hand and the soldiers stopped. He waved at the woman who had said nothing the entire time. She got up from her seat and came over to me. Putting her hand on the side of my neck, she muttered something under her breath. I felt a sudden sensation that felt like someone had poked me with a hot iron. She went over to Arne and did the same, causing the man to curse and push her away. He pointed to the glowing blue mark on his neck and forced a smile.

"There," Arne said in a sour tone. "An agreement with a magical touch to it. Be the last one standing and I'll let you see Seig. Now get out of here." The soldiers started to take us away when Arne stopped them again. "Not you. You stay here with me to make sure there's no tricks."

Keagan wasn't a fan of us being separated, and neither was I, but we had no choice. He tried to close the distance between us anyway, which prompted Mr. Vogel to point his pistol right at Keagan's face. The lycan raised his hands in surrender and stepped back. I was escorted out of the room and into the hall, and Keagan was left with Arne and his witch.

"Kick her ass, O'!"

I shook my head and laughed. The lycan just couldn't keep his mouth shut, even with a pistol pointed at his head. The soldiers took me down the flight of stairs again, down a long hallway, and through a large black curtain that divided the pathway from a much larger room. The place was empty, save for two dead bodies just left there like waste. The room was soaked with blood, plenty of it staining the floors and some sections of the walls. This must be where the fighters entered and exited their fights.

"Hand over any weapons you have." One of the soldiers shoved me and held out his hand.

"My weapons? What the hell am I supposed to fight with?" Despite my disagreement with being disarmed, I obeyed the command that had been given to me.

"There's no weapons at Kampfhalle. You use what your maker gave you." He took my saber and my knives, and the soldiers left the room through the big, black curtain.

I went over to the bodies, looked around to make sure I was alone, and spoke softly so no one could hear me just in case. *"Éist liom a Dhuosnos, a Thiarna an Bháis, a Rí Dhubhaigh, a Ghlacadóir na Marbh, agus a Thabharthóir Suaimhnis. Iarraim ort teacht, súil ghéar a chaitheamh ar chlann Anu agus do bheannacht deiridh a thabhairt."*

It was a funeral prayer my grandmother had taught me when I was young and was something I had plenty of practice saying. I said it three times, as was the custom. Just as I finished, the crowd outside cheered, signaling that yet another fight had come to an end. I turned around to find a tall, copper haired lycan standing behind me. She was in her tame form, but all she wore was a rough pair of short pants and a wrap around her chest. No point in wearing a shirt if it's just going to get all torn from turning, I guess. She had an intense expression on her face and her eyes were locked onto me. I took a couple steps back and almost tripped over the dead bodies.

"You're lucky I'm not human. If they caught you speaking our language, they'd skip the fight and just shoot you." The female lycan crossed her arms over her chest, her forearms seemingly the size of my thighs.

"You know Séúbua?" I stepped away from the bodies but made sure to keep my distance from my new guest.

"*Tá a lán eolais agam faoinár gcultúr.*" She smiled, happy to show off her knowledge.

"You practice the old ways! It's rare these days to find someone else who does. I only know of a few others outside of my known family." I eased the tension in my body, curious to know more about her.

"We do seem to be a dying breed," the lycan said as she extended a hand my way. "My name is Keera. You are?"

I grasped her hand tightly and gave it a small shake. "Olwen. Keera...Keera the Brutal?"

Keera instigated the mutual release of our handshake and gave me a mock bow. "The one and only."

"Don't take this the wrong way, but I had expected someone with that name to be a little rougher."

The lycan shook her head to move some of her long, amber hair from her face. "Not every fighter is a boor looking to drink their opponent's blood. However, my dear Olwen, I can assure you that I am quite rough once that cage door is closed."

I laughed, but more so out of anxiety than happiness. It was going to take a lot of effort to beat Keera and I was having doubts on whether this was a good idea. I was confident in my abilities as a fighter, having led my own company during the last war. The doubts sprouted more from the respect I had for my opponent than the lack of belief I had in myself. I was thinking of something to say when the double doors at the end of the room burst open. Two soldiers came through, each carrying one end of a corpse. They waddled over to us and dumped the body of a strong looking satyr onto the pile of dead they had accrued during the night so far. They left through the same doors they had entered from, but another soldier in Korblum's red and white uniform held one of the two doors open.

"You, green one. Got a ring name for me to tell the announcer?"

I thought about it for a quick second before smiling. "The Banshee."

I caught Keera react to the name out of the corner of my eye, knowing that she would know the meaning behind the name. There was an old story in our culture that spoke of a female sprite that had been cursed. Anyone who saw her would experience death in some capacity the next day. Humans would have no idea what the meaning behind the name was, but the story of The Banshee was even known by those Tóráin who didn't practice the old ways. Mothers and fathers loved using the tale to scare their children, often telling them that if they didn't go to sleep The Banshee would come visit. It was a way to honor my culture without getting shot on the spot. The soldier who had asked me the question twisted his face when I answered as if he was trying to figure out whether he had misheard me. He eventually shrugged his shoulders.

"Approach the doors," the man said. "Wait behind them until you hear your name called. Make your way to the arena and wait for the bell."

The soldier slammed the door behind him and the sound of the crowd grew quieter again now the barrier between us and them was there again. I turned to face the fresh body, claw marks and a missing right arm up to his elbow telling me he had fought a lycan too. I jumped when Keera put her hand on my shoulder. She started reciting the same prayer I had said over the other two, so I joined in. Once we were done, the two of us made our way to the doors. I could hear an absurdly loud voice working the crowd up before he finally announced Keera's name.

"See you out there, Banshee." Keera the Brutal left through the doors, pushing both open at the same time.

It wasn't long until I heard my name called out. "And her opponent! A new fighter! The Banshee!"

I opened the doors and was hit with the loud booming of the crowd. There must have been thousands in the massive arena, all hungry for more violence and death. I spotted a section that appeared to be dedicated to the Tóráin, but the rest of the viewers were human. I made my way down the path lined by tall walls to a large domed cage. When I walked through the opening, two soldiers on either side of it let go of the ropes they were holding, and a sliding door fell down like the blade of a guillotine. Locked inside the ironclad structure, I started to get a grasp for what I had taken on. The screams from the crowd were so many that it all blended together in one loud wave of sound. I could feel the level of it all in my chest, and my heart started to pound.

"Ladies and gentlemen, boys and girls, beings from another world! Prepare for a furious display! Keera the Brutal, are you ready?" I looked around for the source of the booming voice and found a well-lit area not far from us with a man standing on a platform with arms open wide.

Keera shifted into her feral form, her comely facial features changing into a snarling snout covered in fur. She raised her right arm into the air and the crowd cheered.

"Banshee, are you ready?"

I looked around the arena — a difficult thing to do well thanks to the iron bars of the cage we were in — and eventually spotted the area where Arne might be. I thought I could see Keagan, but I wasn't sure. Regardless, I took a deep breath and readied myself for what would be the fight of my life. I raised my own right arm in the air and again the crowd cheered.

"The fighters are ready! Is this crowd ready?" Everyone in the audience erupted into the loudest cheer I had heard so far. "Alright then! Fighters! Go!"

Before I knew it Keera was on me, swiping a clawed hand at my head. She was clearly two feet taller than me, and she definitely outweighed me. Finding leverage in this fight would be difficult, but I knew I could do it. The one thing I had over Keera was speed. Every time Keera swiped at me, I was quick enough to duck and dodge out of the way. She chased me all over the cage, until some boos began raining down on us.

"Damn it, Banshee. You won't win running away. Fight back, or the bastards will just shoot us both and call it a draw." Keera growled and lunged at me, causing me to dive and roll out of the way once more.

It wasn't really possible to read how she felt from her face, but I could tell from her desperation and her breathing that Keera was beginning to lose her patience. That, accompanied by the knowledge we would both be killed if I didn't even try to land a blow, had me change my style. The next time Keera came at me I ducked and sidestepped to my right, punching Keera in her ribs before jumping back to avoid a backhanded strike. My own strike didn't seem to phase the lycan one bit, which told me I had a long way to go. Again, Keera swiped at me, and I continued to bob and weave until I found a good opening again to counter into a quick succession of three punches: left to the stomach, right to the stomach, left to the jaw. The attack had Keera growl and I thought she might charge me again, but she didn't. My counters had her slowing down, waiting for me to give her an opening. She was a good fighter, and I dreaded the moment she would catch me, but I felt like things were going well so far.

Keera had the reach advantage, so getting inside was difficult. Thanks to my speed, I managed to get in and land a few shin kicks and body punches before slinking back out. That was until I got overconfident. A kick I landed had caused Keera to stumble, so I went for a leaping punch to her face in the hopes of staggering her further. Her large, clawed hand met me in the air, the lycan roaring as she swatted me across the fighting grounds. My back hit the iron bars hard and all the wind in my lungs escaped at the same time. I struggled to breathe as I looked up, Keera stalking me from about a dozen feet away. She knew I was hurt and saw no point in charging forward. I had barely gathered myself before the lycan was on me. She grabbed hold of the braid I had my hair in and tugged on it hard, lifting me off my feet and swinging me into the cage again. I fell to the floor in a heap, any air I had managed to get into my lungs escaping once more.

I could hear the crowd cheering for Keera now, no doubt happy that she had finally gotten her hands on me. They wanted a show, and what I had been doing wasn't what they were looking for. The audience wanted to watch someone get torn apart piece by piece. They wanted blood. Keera took her time to get to me, once more grabbing my braid. I needed to stop her from sending me into the cage again. I kicked at the top of her knee to put her off balance enough for me to jump upward, knocking my elbow into her snout. I took the opening I had made and grabbed the arm belonging to the hand that had a hold of my hair. I dropped myself to the ground forcefully, sending Keera careening face first into the iron bars. I slithered out from under her and stumbled away, touching the back of my head. When I looked at my hand, I saw blood and realized that the cage had done some damage to me. I had bought myself some time to recover, so I did just that and waited for Keera to get back to her feet.

She roared again and charged, swiping furiously at me with her claws. Shaken up from my interactions with the iron bars of our cage, I wasn't as balanced or as quick as before and Keera caught my arm pretty good. Four deep slashes bled quickly up near my shoulder, and it hurt to keep the arm moving. Knowing I needed to push back a little, I tried to surprise my rival with another leaping punch. This time, it landed, and Keera was caught so off guard that I followed it up with a few more punches and a couple shin kicks before taking a step back. She limped on her right leg, and I took the opportunity to charge her again. This time it was Keera who dodged the incoming blow, spinning to her right and coming back at me with her claws as I sailed by, giving me fresh wounds on my back. I fell to the floor, the pain sapping my energy. I tried to get to my feet, but a swift kick came into my ribs as the crowd cheered for Keera once more. She gave me another kick for good measure, sending me spinning onto my back. She bent over and grabbed me by the throat, lifting me into the air as she strangled me. Her claws began to dig into my skin, and I couldn't help but let out what bit of a yelp I could due to the grip on my throat.

The crowd yelled Keera's name louder and louder, all while my vision began to blur. I was losing, and if I didn't do something soon, I was going to die. I struggled to look for an opening, until I remembered something Weylyn had taught me. It was a wrestling hold his father had taught him. With my last bit of strength, I wrapped my arms around the arm raising me into the air and kneed Keera in the face as hard as I could. The blow had her reeling enough to put me down on my feet, but her hand still firmly grasped my throat. I jumped off the floor and kicked at both of her knees with all I had, falling onto my back as Keera collapsed. Keeping my hold on her arm, I pulled her into me, grabbing hold of her head and forcing her into my stomach. I put my legs on either side of her, bringing my left leg in to eliminate her shoulder just like Weylyn had shown me years ago. With her shoulder out, I bent my right leg over the back of her neck and crossed my left leg over my right ankle. Knowing she was in trouble, Keera swiped at me, her claws catching the side of my head and my ear. When it didn't have me ease up my hold, she clawed again, this time jamming her claws into my side and moving them further inward as best she could. It was painful, but I kept squeezing. In seconds, Keera went limp just like I had when Weylyn showed me the move. I knew that she would only be out for a bit, so I had to hurry.

I unwrapped my legs and swung my hips to bring Keera on her back with me mounted on top of her. I took a brief moment to inspect the injury to my side, but I pushed through the pain and began punching her in the head as hard and as often as I could. With each punch my vision blurred more as tears began to fill my eyes. The crowd began to cheer for The Banshee until I finally had no more strength left in me. Keera's face was swollen, her tongue hanging loosely out of her mouth. She was unconscious, and she slowly shifted back into her tame form. I stood up from my position and took a couple steps away from Keera. The crowd began to grow quiet, after a voice called for silence. Eventually everyone was hushed, and only the voice of Arne Dietrich could be heard.

"Well done! Good show! Finish her off, and you'll get what you're owed!"

I looked back at Keera. The fights in Kampfhalle were to the death. I knew that, and yet finishing this fight felt like taking things a step too far. I stared up at where the voice had come from, exactly the location I had thought I saw Keagan earlier. I slowly — and reluctantly — made my way back to Keera. I lifted her up by her shoulders and wrapped my arms around her head and neck. The crowd started chanting the word 'death' and the image of the corpses in the room flashed before my eyes. I imagined Keera's body thrown on top of them like nothing, and my stomach lurched. These were living beings. My own people. Tóráin with lives that had the potential for things greater than killing each other for people's entertainment. We were more than this. I was more than this. I tried to push through and be done with it, but I couldn't do it. I threw Keera's body back to the ground and stood up.

"Our deal was for me to be the last one standing!" I shouted up at Arne amidst a collection of boos. "As far as I can tell, I'm the only one standing in this cage! I won!"

I couldn't see his face, but I imagined just how twisted it must have gotten. He motioned for the crowd to be silenced and once they were quiet again, he spoke. "*Du hast gewonnen*? You didn't win anything! Fights here are *zu Tode*. To the death that is. You want to win? You snap her neck!"

"No! I will not! The terms of our agreement have been met! You are bound! Now give me what I came here for!" I yelled.

"The Merciful Banshee!" someone shouted from the Tóráin section. Surprisingly, the rest of the crowd began chanting it. Eventually they just shouted the words 'mercy' and 'victory'. Again, shouts for silence could be heard, but the crowd would not stop. Everyone grew quiet once a gun fired off though.

"You *Schmutz* think you have any say in what goes on around here? I'm the King of Kampfhalle! I make the rules! You lost! *Soldaten*, get in there and —" Arne's order was cut off as he began to scream in pain.

A woman's voice broke out. "The deal was last fighter standing! Those were your words, King of Kampfhalle! The sprite is right! You are bound! You must honor your agreement!"

"You treacherous *Hure*! I'll have your damn head for this!" Again, he screamed in pain, and I remembered the burning sensation on my neck when the witch had placed the spell on us both. "Fine! Fine, damn it! You win!"

The crowd cheered again, only to be silenced by another gunshot. No longer afflicted by pain, Arne's voice rang out again. "You may have won, Banshee, but the rules are the rules. The loser dies. *Soldaten*!"

I spun around at the sound of the gate rising to find four soldiers entering the cage. Two held rifles with bayonets on each of them. The other two were empty handed, although a sword and a pistol hung from each of their belts. I took a step forward but one of the ones with a rifle trained his gun on me and ordered for me to step back. I was forced to watch as the other one ran his bayonet through Keera's chest. He stood over her for a few seconds before seeming annoyed that she hadn't stopped breathing yet. He muttered something under his breath and pointed his rifle at her, shooting her in the head. The crowd booed once the gun went off. The two soldiers whose hands were free picked up Keera the Brutal and carried her through the open gate. Much to my surprise, another gate opened on the opposite side, and the remaining soldiers ordered me to leave through that one. I kept my attention on Keera being carried away.

"*Go dtuga Tiarna an Bháis abhaile thú, mo chara.*"

"What did you just say?" The soldier raised his gun a bit, nearly aiming it right at me.

I realized I had just spoken Séúbua loud enough for a human to hear. I quickly waved at him, insinuating that there was nothing wrong. "Nothing. Just saying goodbye to a friend."

"Get moving before you get the chance to say hello again." He motioned with his rifle towards the open gate.

I slowly made my way through it, my injuries starting to hit me now as my energy began to fade. I went down a path similar to the one I had walked on to enter the cage until I reached another set of doors. I opened them and entered a room that resembled the other one, only this one was free of dead bodies. There was a table with bread and fruit, along with jugs of what smelled like beer. I graciously grabbed a piece of bread and poured myself something to drink. The pain in my side and the scratches on my back screamed and I desperately wanted something to dull the ache. I ate the bread quickly — eager to have something in my stomach despite feeling nauseous — and then I grabbed an apple afterwards. I rotated between biting into the apple and sipping from one of the jugs as I waited to be instructed on where to go next. There were a few stools by the table, so I sat down on one despite wishing to just lay on the floor. I sipped on my beer and tried to stay conscious, feeling myself sway back and forth. I was feeling everything now, and the beer was doing little to slow it down.

"O'! Are you alright?" I looked over and saw Keagan entering the room from a side door, with Arne's witch next to him.

Seeing a friendly face had me foregoing all efforts to stay strong, and I collapsed forward. Keagan managed to get over to me just in time to stop me from falling on my face. I could feel the throbbing from all the slashes Keera had given me. It all burned. I had been injured before, severe cuts and even a gunshot wound, but all of this at once was draining me faster than anything before. I was exhausted, physically and emotionally. I let Keagan cradle me in his arms, wishing to just go to sleep.

Keagan shook me. "Hey! Hey! You stay awake, now. Annika, can you help her?"

"Hold her still."

I felt a warm air wash over my face and the throbbing from where Keera had clawed me began to fade. The warm air came to my arm, then down to my side. Keagan brought me into his chest and my back ached greatly until the warm air I had grown to like washed over my injuries. Keagan loosened his hold on me a bit so I fell back into a cradled position, and I watched as Annika hovered her hands over my chest. She muttered words I didn't understand, a blue glow radiating from her hands. I began to feel less tired. She remained doing this until she wavered, catching herself before stumbling to over. Keagan reached out to her, but she waved him off.

"I'm fine." Annika put a hand on my shoulder. "How are you?"

I forced myself to sit up, surprised by what had just happened. I knew there were some witches that were strong enough to heal injuries, but they weren't exactly easy to find. Keagan kept his hands nearby to catch me if I fell over again as I thanked Anu for keeping me alive. I brought my knees to my chest and lifted myself up onto my feet. I lost my balance for a moment, but I recovered well enough. I looked over my body and found only scars instead of open wounds. I ran my fingers over the raised skin on the side of my head as I investigated what Annika had done to me. "Appears I'm alright, thanks to you. May I ask how you're here helping me and not on your way to a prison or dead? Arne seemed livid.".

"That bastard ordered his guards to take her away. I stepped between them and told him that wasn't happenin'. He changed his mind and thought it would be better to just have us both killed, but before he could officially give the order, I managed to convince him otherwise." Keagan helped Annika stay steady, her balance askew.

"Yes. Keagan said he would take me as his own prize, far away from Korblum. He added that Mr. Dietrich would never see either of us ever again. Clearly in a drunken stupor, Mr. Dietrich claimed he was tired and didn't care for talking anymore. He just wanted the situation to be over. So, he ordered me to cast a spell binding us to keep our word to never return. The fool is so dull that I convinced him nobody could break the spell. After hearing that he was more than happy to send us on our way." Annika softly pushed Keagan away to try to stand on her own, and I was glad to see she was successful.

"I see. Seems we got quite lucky that Arne's lack of patience outweighs his need for blood. Thank you, Annika. I owe you one." I smiled and extended my hand.

Annika grabbed hold of it and gave it a small shake. "You don't owe me a thing. I was happy to screw over that *fettes arschloch*. I've grown tired of this line of work. Keagan has told me why you're here, and I want to help. The world will be a better place when people like Arne Dietrich don't have the power they have now."

I was a bit bothered that Keagan had told a stranger, a witch no less, what we were up to, but I tossed it aside. I would get mad at him later if I wanted to. Now, there were more important things. "Good. Can you take us to see Seig? Or is Arne going to kick us out now that you ended the spell?"

Annika smiled. "Oh I didn't end the spell, it just stopped hurting him. If he tries to stop you from seeing Seig, the pain will come back. When I promised to never come back, I also promised to put an end to that spell after tonight. We'll be fine. Come on. Follow me."

Our new friend took us out another side door. It led to a hallway lit by torches instead of lanterns, eventually ending at the top of a staircase. Annika led us up the stone steps for a short while until we came to a door at the top. The witch knocked on the door three times, and a voice called for us to enter. Annika opened the door, and we all went in. The room was a fair size, fit with a desk, a window, and a bed. I was still tired despite Annika's helpful spell, and I wanted nothing more than to climb into that bed and sleep. However, not only was that a silly thought considering our situation, but someone was sitting on the bed already. Her large, black wings were tight to her body and her bare legs and feet hung off the tall bed just above the floor. Black feathers from her knees up the side of her thighs could be seen from a slit in the odd dress she wore. There were no sleeves nor was any fabric on her shoulders. What held the dress on her was a chain attached to the fabric which circled around her neck like a necklace. The sides had small slits that exposed her toned midriff; the long bottom of the dress split from the hip by a large slice in the black fabric. She still wore a deep red, boned corset too, which only showed off her impressive figure even more. Her hands were holding each other and resting in her lap, her nails long and sharp like the talons of a hawk. The harpy had thick, black hair that cascaded over her shoulders and her bright yellow eyes seemed surprised to see us.

"Who the Hell are these people, Annika?"

Our witch friend put a hand on Keagan and mine's shoulder. "These two have gone through a lot of trouble to speak with you. This is Keagan, and Olwen. I think you'll like what they have to say."

Seig flashed a playful grin that showed the small sharp teeth that harpies had. "Oh is that so? Well, I've got a fight to get ready for soon, so you'll have to be quick."

I didn't know when or if a soldier was going to come get Seig for her fight, so I spoke quickly. "We're from The Resistance in Fleuris. In the efforts of trying to keep a long story short, we're here for your help. Our leader went to Tudrose and struck a deal with Queen Sophia. The deal was that we would incite rebellion in Tulp, Korblum, Stelpina, and Malvene. In return, Queen Sophia would attack these countries, saving Fleuris for last. The goal here is to replace current rulers and regimes with better people to put it simply. Tudrose wouldn't claim any country for themselves, they would just see that the transition of power is made properly. The Resistance wants a world where Tóráin don't have to live in fear anymore. We want a world that gives our kind just as much an opportunity to thrive as it does humans. Some countries have already made strides to seeing this dream come true. We need you to help us take the next step."

Seig put her hands to her sides and allowed herself to lean back a bit. "So, what's the point in these rebellions if Tudrose is going to attack anyway? Why go through all that trouble?"

Keagan crossed his arms over his chest. "Because Tudrose doesn't want to risk any of their precious soldiers if they don't have to. Our rebellions would weaken the countries, while also providin' a force of fighters that can join the attack when Tudrose comes."

"I see." Seig stood up and walked over to a chest by the window. She opened it and began to slip on a pair of boots she pulled out of the old trunk. "What do you need my help for?"

"Your friend, Cordelia, pointed us in your direction. She's taken up leadership of the Resistance chapter in Tulp. She thought we could enlist you as the leader of the Korblum chapter we hope to start." I prayed that Seig would just say yes, and we could go find somewhere to rest for the night.

"Cordelia? Well as much as I can see her leading a rebellion, I'll have to inform you that I cannot." Seig removed her corset herself — a feat worth admiring in and of itself — and replaced it with a thick leather chest plate that looked to be specially made for a harpy. I guess the champion had a few perks that the other fighters didn't. "You see, as much as I would love to help you, I'm stuck here. The fighters here at Kampfhalle are all placed under a spell that links us with Arne Dietrich. When he calls, we have to come running, or his witch makes us feel a pain you never want to feel."

I was confused. "His witch? Isn't that Annika? She's no longer working for Arne. She can free you."

Seig laughed as she slid on fingerless gloves that had a thick piece of leather attached to them to protect her forearms. "Oh no, Annika here is just one of Ulla's underlings. Ulla has her students watch over the games mostly, unless there's a big event like three or more fighters in the cage at the same time. Or if there's a high-profile guest coming to Kampfhalle. She's the one who controls everything, and Arne controls her. Don't ask me how, because I don't know. But I can't do anything to help you so long as Ulla and Arne are around."

"What if we got rid of them? Would you leave the fightin' cage behind?" Keagan asked.

Seig stopped getting dressed and her eyes opened wide. "You could do that?"

I looked at Keagan and he nodded, showing his support. I stood as straight as I could and smiled at Seig. "It may take us some time, but we'll figure out a way. We always do."

A knock at the door came followed by a rough voice. "Seig, you're up. Get a move on before Arne throws another fit tonight."

Seig waved at us to all to come in tighter. "Alright. I'm in. You get rid of Ulla and Arne, and I can finally be done with this and put my energy into something I should have done years ago. You give me my freedom, and I'll give you a rebellion."

"You got it," I whispered.

"Now go out and win your fight. Be a shame if all this ended in you dyin' tonight." Keagan grinned, showing that he was trying to be funny.

Seig came up really close to Keagan and softly let her nails slide down the side of his face without leaving a scratch on him. "Oh, my poor friend, don't you know? Seig the Sharp never loses."

# Chapter Eighteen

## Rosalie



I had spent most of the night at my father's home, tending to him during his coughing fits until he finally fell asleep. I didn't manage much rest of my own before I left early in the morning. It worried me to leave my father alone, but a friend of mine had offered to watch him around noon so at least he wasn't by himself the entire day. The bouncing between my father, my mother, and The Resistance was overwhelming, but I had no other choice. I would be at the hospital until evening before making my way to The Flying Pig to be caught up on the details of the day. If I was lucky, I would find some time to sleep. Then I would go to my father's and the cycle would start all over again. The weight of it all sat heavy on my shoulders. It felt like I was physically carrying buckets of stones around, so much so that my body ached just as much as my mind did. I stretched out my neck with the hope of relieving some of the tension as I tended to my mother, her skin still awfully pale. As I looked her over intently, I found myself thinking of all the things that could happen today; none of them were positive. Recent events had caused me to become quite depressed, and my paranoia had reached new levels. On top of dealing with my parents' health, I was also forced to handle this whole mess with General Rosspier, which had caused quite a disturbance amongst the Tóráin community. Sadly, our informant had only gathered that The Dove would be present during General Rosspier's speech. There was no answer as to what his speech entailed, but many expected the worst.

The most frantic and worried was Dwyer. He believed that General Rosspier planned to lay down new laws, further restricting the lives of all Tóráin in the country. He also suggested that amongst these new laws would be punishments for humans caught aiding the Tóráin. Dwyer was known to have plenty of conspiracy theories in his head, but these expectations probably weren't as far-fetched as his other ones. We didn't know exactly what was going to be said tomorrow, but we knew that it would be nothing good for the Tóráin or their allies. The fact that The Dove would be there was even more worrisome. The Dove was rarely seen in public, and if you did get a good look at her you were probably in danger of being arrested or killed. She was General Rosspier's favorite torturer and hired killer. You wanted nothing to do with The Dove, especially if you were a Tórán. She was known to be exceptionally cruel, and the idea of mercy had never crossed her mind. Nobody had ever seen her face, and nobody knew much about her. There were a few stories placing her in different kingdoms over the last twenty years or so, but considering how secretive and sneaky the witch was, there was no telling how much of her story lay hidden in the shadows of history. She seemed to have even become a ghost for a few years, with only horror stories told of her ferocity, until she landed in Fleuris around the same time General Rosspier usurped King Louis. The Dove being present during General Rosspier's speech gave everyone a reason to worry, that I knew for sure.

I sent thoughts about the entire situation out of my head for now as I squeezed water out of a rag and into the bucket by my mother's bed. Bringing the damp, cold, cloth to her forehead, I softly pressed it onto her skin in hopes to ease her fever. The damn thing had plagued her since she arrived at the hospital, briefly breaking once a couple days ago before roaring back with a vengeance. I sat on the chair at her bedside and held her hand, watching for when she would wake up. I would have to tend to other people soon, so I tried to shut everything else out of my head and just go over pleasant memories between my mother and me. My attempted peace was cut short when I heard someone clear their throat behind me. Turning around, I found Claire standing there.

"You have visitors, Rosalie," she said. "I snuck them by Dr. Vernier, but you'll have to be quick. You know how he is about the Tóráin."

I knew all too well what Head Doctor Vernier's views were on the Tóráin. He not only charged them to be treated at this hospital, he also refused to allow visitors. When Tóráin died here, they were tossed out back with the dirty waste buckets. No one would even tell you that your loved one was there, forcing you to come check every day and night. It was cruel and unjust, but some of the nurses and a couple doctors had found ways around these rules implemented by Dr. Vernier. It was risky though. The last nurse that was discovered treating the Tóráin for free was sent to prison for thievery, Dr. Vernier claiming that the nurse was pocketing the coin for herself. Tóráin knew how dangerous it was for them too, so for someone to come visit me in this place, their reason must be important.

"Bring them in, I'll bring the curtain around." I stood up and went over to the tattered cloth that hung from iron rings looped onto a pole. The pole bent in a 'u' shape, allowing one to bring the long curtain around the bed to provide privacy. Not all areas of the hospital had them, but thankfully Dr. Bernard had pulled some strings to get my mother here.

I sat back down once the curtain surrounded my mother and me, and impatiently waited for whoever it was that came to see me to enter the enclosed space. I couldn't help but roll my eyes when Dwyer broke through the cloth, followed by Moya and another lycan by the name of Nessa. The three of them stood over my mother on the opposite side of me, with Moya speaking first.

"How's your mum?" she asked as she gently put a hand on the wet towel on my mother's forehead.

"Not any better. Not too much worse. She's fighting, and that's all that matters." I held my mother's hand again, watching her face in the hopes that my touch would wake her.

"Glad you think that way. You said you would tell us this morning what the plan for tomorrow was, but you never stopped by the bar. You do have a plan, don't you?" Dwyer had his arms crossed over his chest.

I closed my eyes and reared my head as I cursed. "I'm sorry. I forgot. But to answer your question, Dwyer, we don't need a plan because we aren't going to do anything."

"What the Hell does that mean?" Nessa grumbled.

I sighed and put my eyes on the three of them. "What that means is that we are to lay low. Lower than we have been. Whatever General Rosspier is planning on saying, it's probably best that all Tóráin are as hidden away as possible when he says it. Tell people to stay indoors if they can. Once we have more information after the speech, we'll have an idea as to what to do next."

"You can't be serious. You want us to cower in our homes? You're too busy with your human family to give a damn about us. We can't just hide. We need to show them we won't stand for any more punishment for crimes we never commit."

Dwyer received a supportive display from both Moya and Nessa, full of mumbled agreements and shoulder pats.

"I care about your kind just as much as I care about my mother. Most of my life has been dedicated to helping the Tóráin. This is the best decision for all of us. Learn to be patient, and I promise you'll be rewarded in the end." I wasn't sure about that last part, but I recognized I needed to reassure Dwyer and the others somehow.

"Patient? I was patient back when you were a child. My patience runs thin now, as does others. While Weylyn and Olwen are off seeing the world, our kind is suffering. We cannot stand for more of it. We will not." Dwyer had his hands on his hips and his voice was louder than before.

"Lower your voice!" I said softly. "Look, I am not saying to stand by and let General Rosspier do whatever he wants. I'm just saying that tomorrow is not the day to openly stand against him. Weylyn and Olwen are enacting a plan that will end the suffering for all of the Tóráin. Again, please, be patient."

Moya shook her head and Nessa mumbled something under her breath. Dwyer rubbed his bearded chin before pointing his finger at me. "You are unfit to lead The Resistance. You do not have our best intentions in mind. You're much too focused on other things. I am hereby relieving you of your position and taking command of The Resistance."

I stood from my chair. "You can't do that!"

Dwyer looked at Nessa and Moya, letting a smile creep onto his face before crossing his arms over his chest. "I just did. You stay with your humans. Us Tóráin are going to take control of our lives again and show General Rosspier we aren't cattle made for herding. Tomorrow, The Resistance will make a statement heard around the world."

The curtain opened and Claire's head popped in. "Rosalie! Dr. Vernier will be making his rounds here soon. Your friends need to go."

Before I could say anything, Dwyer and the others left through the opening in the curtain, and I was left alone. I tried to distract myself from what had just happened by grabbing the cloth off my mother's head and dunking it back into the cool water. I squeezed out the excess liquid and my hands shook as I placed it back on her warm forehead. The curtain opened again, only this time it was the friend that was supposed to be watching my father.

"Rosalie?" Her face was somber and withdrawn.

"Dorine, why are you here?" I had an idea, but my heart couldn't take it.

"Your father. I got there around noon, just like I said I would. I found him in his bed. He wasn't breathing. It looks as though he went in his sleep. I'm so sorry." She came over and wrapped her arms around me as I cried.

I had lost my father, along with the group the love of my life had entrusted me with. My mother was on the brink of death herself, and I had no idea when, or if, Weylyn would return. I allowed Dorine to hold me, leaning into her as I let all the stress and pain I was experiencing flow out of me. This was not how things were supposed to go. I came to the realization quickly that all I could do was cry now and pray that Weylyn returned home soon and my mother recovered. I was more alone now than I had been mere minutes ago, and the feeling of wanting to sleep for a week had changed to wishing to sleep for months. Any appetite I had before all this had long faded, and my heart hurt. I had lost my father, I was losing my mother, and I had failed Weylyn. Many people were going to die tomorrow because of Dwyer and the others, humans and Tóráin, and I couldn't do anything other than watch it happen.

# Chapter Nineteen

## General Rosspier

Cloque, Fleuris | December 28, 1798

We positioned the stage right before Orfèvres Bridge. The usual wooden platform stood between Geôlier Castle and Savoir Estate. This gave my crowd the ability to stretch the entire boulevard from the bridge to the front doors of the Chapel of Saint Fils. It wasn't as open as Dame Square, but my voice would carry that far and beyond; people on the steps of Sainte Mère Cathedral would hear the wonderful mixture of words I had brought together. All of *Le Coeur de la Ville* would hear their savior's voice and cheer. While in front of the stage held my audience, behind it was a bridge lined with armed soldiers, ready for whatever may happen today. It was done both as a precaution, and as a show of strength. Thousands had come, and I knew that they weren't all here to show their support. Those who came here with evil inside them needed to see what true power looked like.

Everything was ready, all the city needed now was my voice. I took a deep breath before making my way up the wooden steps at the back of the stage, cheers breaking out as my image crested over the timbered platform. The Dove and Jon were already standing on the stage silently waiting. I stopped next to Jon and saluted him. Jon saluted in return, as well as the rest of the soldiers on the bridge and the few on the stage. I made my way to the front of the platform and noticed the line of soldiers that were there to keep the crowd back, as well as the line of ten witches that stood behind them. None of them were in the front, nor could I honestly spot any of them amongst the closest members of the crowd, but the *Diables* were here. My hope was that there were plenty who had braved the brisk temperatures of the late December morning, since part of my plan involved them too.

I opened my arms, stretching them out to my sides to welcome all who had come. The crowd began to calm itself, and they became as silent as a crowd of thousands could be. They all waited for my first words, and I enjoyed the feeling I got from making them wait a little longer. It felt like I had the entire city in the palm of my hand. Eventually I decided that my plan had waited long enough to come to fruition, and I began my speech. "*Gens du Fleuris*! Citizens of Cloque! I, General Rosspier, have come to you today to speak on a matter that needs your attention! The world as we know it is changing, but the changes being made are not beneficial to humanity! These changes will only bring about war and hardship for our kind, and the *Diables* will see that a new world rises where humanity is the lower class! The *parasites* that infected and latched onto our world centuries ago have lived off humanity's hardworking, innovative, efficient, productive, ingenuous people for far too long! And now, there are some who would see their status continue to rise! Countries such as Tudrose, Linne, Fruberg, Czermak, Weidel, and those discolored barbarians who think themselves nobles down in Motea, have all allowed the *Diables* to take more of what you all deserve! I find it quite amusing that they seem to love these *cafards* so much, yet when I offer those who feast on Fleuris to these countries, they claim they have no space for them! If they are such 'splendid people' then surely, they could find room for them, no?

"The truth of the matter is that this world will not move forward until the *Diable* problem is solved! The solution will begin here, *dans le royaume merveilleux de Fleuris*, in its grandest and most beautiful city of Cloque! We must once and for all dismiss the idea that *Diables* have been anything but leeches living off the hardworking bodies of humans of every country! *Désormais*, they will be forced to model themselves after the superior people in this world, or else they will succumb to a tinderbox of unpleasantries that only they themselves will be responsible for."

I adjusted my coat and my hat, taking a dramatic pause to suck in my audience even further. They had cheered at certain moments, but they were always quick to quiet down, eager to hear what I might say next. There appeared to be movement in the crowd several hundred feet away, but I was probably just seeing things. The crowd was so large and so vast, it was easy to think you saw it move. The people were like a sea of living beings, and just as the sea was untamable so was a bustling crowd. I decided that I had allowed enough time to pass by and cleared my throat before giving them the finale of my speech.

"One last thing I would like to say on this fine December morning might be memorable to those who have heard me speak in the past. Throughout my life, I have predicted many outcomes, especially on the battlefield. *Et la vérité est*, this country has become a battlefield! Many have called me, *un prophète* but there have been just as many others who have been derisive towards me for it. During the short time it took me to rise through the ranks of *les militaires*, it was the *Diables* who responded to my predictions with jeers and mockery when I told them I would one day become general, and eventually leader of Fleuris. They laughed when I told them that I would one day, among many other things, see to it that the *Diable* problem was settled. All they saw was a young human spouting nonsense, their laughter uproarious, but, *mes magnifiques frères et soeurs*, I do believe that for some time now they have struggled to release those same laughs they had so easily bestowed upon me years ago."

I had to squint, but I was certain now that there was considerable movement in the crowd. Something was going on, but I refused to allow it to stop me from finishing my speech. I opened my arms wide, raising them high in the air like a priest would during a mass.

"*Aujourd'hui*, on the morning of *le vingt-huit Décembre*, in the year *dix-sept quatre-vingt-dix-huit*, I will show you a prophet! If the *Diables* in the north, and the south, continue to strive to plunge nations into states favorable only to their kind, then the result will not be a world led by nightmares, and thus *la victoire* of the *Diables*, but the utter destruction of their kind in all of the known world! I cannot speak for other nations, but Fleuris is no longer willing to watch humanity suffer so that this precarious *groupe d'êtres maléfiques* can profit from humanity's successes and achievements, or satisfy its predetermined need for usurpation. The *Diables'* call to support those in their community will be overcome by a much higher actuality! Humans of all walks of life and of every country, behold your incessant rival! Today, a new age begins! It begins with the new level of *justice* our country will look to bestow upon all the *Diables*!"

I waved at the back of the stage, and The Dove brought forward a trembling creature. Its skin was greenish and small horns escaped its head. The sight sickened me and had me say a quick prayer to Deus for protection from such evil.

"No! No! I'm innocent! It was The Dove! She killed him! I swear! I —" He stopped shouting once my pale bird put a knife to his neck, the beast choosing to toss his arms in the air in surrender instead.

I turned to the crowd, now getting much busier and rowdier. "This *Diable* was caught in the murder of a high ranking noble! He entered the poor man's home and murdered his entire family, all to steal some gold from the good man's coffers! No trial is needed for this vile thing, *pas d'interrogatoire*! Our recent process of punishment only gives their kind chances to rob you of justice by setting them free! No longer! As of this day, the humans of Fleuris are judge, jury, and executioner! Make the country safe from their greedy, selfish hands! *Je vais te faire avancer*! Together, we will put an end to their incursion!"

The crowd had gotten excessively busy, and I caught the glint of steel amongst my audience. The *Diables* were coming towards the stage, a large group of them in fact. My words had inspired many of the humans being shoved aside to block their way, and the evil things began to cut them down. I quickly turned away as I saw plenty of those dog people show their true forms. In one swift motion I drew my pistol and shot the prisoner The Dove was holding right between his eyes. The Dove let him drop to the wooden stage in a heap. Blood spatter covered her white hood and mask, but she hadn't even flinched when I fired. She calmly stepped forward as the crowd roared in response to recent events and moved me aside.

"Witches! Keep those hounds still! Soldiers, take out the dogs and the chickens first!" The Dove shouted from the top of the stage and those she had barked orders at readied themselves down below her.

"*Soldats*! *Avancez*! Protect your General!" Jon shouted back at the small army on the bridge.

I smiled at the idea of them ripping through the insolent bastards who had tried to ruin my speech. Indeed, they had tried, but I had finished just in time. The good humans of Cloque have heard my words, and they will spread them throughout the country. I expect my words to travel to other nations as well, and so inspire my fellow leaders to enact the proper restrictions to ensure that humanity withholds its rank in the world. I was just about to laugh, giddy at how well everything had gone so far, when a bullet whizzed past my head. It made me duck, and Jon ran over to me. "Come on, General. You should get to Joieternelle Palace at once. We'll handle this act of treachery."

I grabbed the clothing on his shoulder tightly. "No. You will come with me. Let The Dove do what she does best."

I turned around and went over to the pale witch. She looked at me as I stood by her side, her eyes wide with surprise that I was still here. I just smiled and motioned at the crowd, some of the rebels now having reached the front line of soldiers and witches. "Why don't you go have some fun?"

The woman grinned. She rarely smiled, and I found that it unsettled me when she did. "Gladly."

She jumped down from the stage with the grace of an acrobat and began dismantling the rebels that crossed her path. I felt Jon grab my arm and I reluctantly turned away. I was enjoying watching The Dove cut down those fiends. Jon and I went into the advancing army, the soldiers splitting so that we could make our way through. Jon called for the back line to follow us, roughly twenty or so soldiers. Everything had gone the way I wanted it to. My speech would go on to inspire the humans of the city to stand up for our country and livelihoods. As I had said in my speech, today was the dawn of a new age. An age where it was clear who was superior, and those below them did as they were told. An age of prosperity. An age of control. An age ushered in by the great General Max Rosspier.

# Chapter Twenty

# Olwen

Adler, Korblum  |  December 29, 1798

The next big event at Kampfhalle was tonight, and we had it on good authority from a report yesterday that Ulla would be here. It was The Duke of Adler's birthday, and so naturally he had decided to celebrate with an event at the largest fighting arena in the world. He had dubbed it a masquerade party; the like was popular in Leonessa and required guests to wear elaborate masks. They usually involved dancing, but I guess fighting was a form of dance. Ulla and Arne — our two targets — being here at the same time was great, and having a reason to hide our faces from the increased security outside the building was incredibly lucky. Keagan, Annika, and I had all entered the building without any trouble. Our plan involved the main event: Seig versus five other fighters in a free for all fight. The brawl for the chance to call yourself Kampfhalle's champion would be the final fight of the night, so we had time to prepare. It wasn't just us three working this plan of ours; Breasal was in on it too. Annika had suggested we enlist his help, seeing as he had access to all the fighters and the majority of the building. He was to inform the fighters that tonight was the night we were making our move.

In total, there were twenty-six fighters currently under Ulla's spell, including Seig. There were only sixteen gladiators scheduled to fight tonight, which meant we could insert the others in strategic points throughout the building. Six would be

in the crowd, and the other four would be with Annika. She and her four warriors
would watch an escape route the witch said Arne had just in case anything crazy
were to happen. The sad part about all of this was that since our attack was planned
for the main event, people would still die in the matches leading up to it. We had
waited for Breasal to bring us their responses earlier in the night. Surprisingly, not
one of the fighters were upset that they could possibly miss out on their freedom.
They accepted their role for the night and promised to put on a good show. They
were all taking a risk in aiding us fight for their freedom, and I knew as well as they
did that not all of us would be raising a drink in celebration if our plan worked.

There were six fights in total scheduled for tonight, and the fourth had just
begun. It was time for us to get into position. Annika had already left to meet with
her group outside the building's exit that Arne could possibly look to escape from.
Keagan and I stood in one of the hallways and waited for Breasal to join us. Not
many soldiers passed us by, but they didn't really seem worried about us anyway. It
wasn't until I spotted the last person I wanted to see that I grabbed a hold of
Keagan's shirt and pulled him in close. My back against the wall and Keagan
pressing up against me, I watched Arne walk towards us. He was accompanied by a
woman with silver hair, her piercing green eyes peering through her fancy white
mask. She wore a long, deep red dress which matched the chosen attire by Arne.
There was also another man, who looked much stronger than Arne did. He was in
clothes suited more for a ball than a fighting arena and held his nose high in the air
like all high-ranking humans did.

"I really could have just had her brought to us, Duke Lehmann." Arne looked
straight ahead as he led the trio towards us.

"*Alles ist gut*, Lord Dietrich. This way I get a small tour of the great
Kampfhalle. Seeing *das Zimmer des Champions* will be a lovely treat for a lover of
the arenas like myself." The Duke turned his head to look at me as they
approached, probably catching me staring at him and the others.

I panicked and brought Keagan in even closer, kissing him. I hoped that the
display would show us to be nothing more than some random couple trying to find
some alone time in the hallways. I kept my eyes closed for only a few seconds,
peering out past Keagan's face afterwards to see if my quick thinking had worked.

"*Pfui*! Their kind has no manners. *Ich bitte um deine Vergebung*, Duke
Lehmann. You shouldn't have to witness such depravity." Arne must have been
talking about us, seeing as nobody else was really around.

"Sadly, I have almost grown used to their disgusting ways. No need to
apologize. So, a question. I heard her wingspan is nearly *fünfzehn Fuß*! *Ist das*

*wahr?*" The Duke's voice got quieter as the trio moved past us and towards the stairs we had taken to go see Seig five days ago.

"Um...good cover." Keagan's voice brought me away from Arne and the others and back to him, realizing then that the lycan had not consented to this quick plan of mine. My face went hot.

"Sorry. I just thought that —"

"You don't need to explain it to me. At least we know that Ulla and Arne are actually here." Keagan was still fairly close to me, and my hands were still on his chest.

I took my hands away and tucked a loose tuft of hair behind my ear. "Right. Yes, that's...um...good to see."

"Not interrupting, am I?" Breasal's voice had Keagan taking a quick two steps back and me stepping away from the wall.

"No," I said. "Not at all. Are we ready to start?"

The goblin nodded, his black eyes looking up at me. "Yes, miss. Everyone knows, I just finished telling the champion. I'm quite thankful for this mask of mine. Made sneaking past Master Arne just now much easier. Everyone is ready, everything is in place. I just need to take you down to the entrance to the cage."

"How did you convince Arne to allow another fighter into the main event?" I asked.

"I just pointed out that Duke Lehmann was turning thirty-seven today, and that perhaps having seven fighters in the match would be a kind nod to that. 'The more in the cage the more death, and the more death the more cheers,' he had said. Told me to find someone. Little did he know I had already found you!"

I smiled. "Good job, Breasal. Come on, we should get a move on. Sounds like the fourth fight is over."

The cheering from the crowd was louder than the regular noise you would hear during the fight. Someone had definitely won, which meant our time to enact our plan was closing in. Breasal just nodded and motioned with his gray hand for me to follow him. Just as I took my first step forward, I felt a large hand grab my arm.

"You're sure it shouldn't be me in there?" Keagan asked.

"We've been over this. It needs to be me in there. Are you sure you're okay with your part in all this?" I put a hand on his arm and kept watch on his eyes.

"All I'm sayin' is that you nearly died last time." The lycan forced his frown to turn into a smile. "Plus, we both know I'm a better showman than you."

"Keagan." I knew why he was hesitant about this plan. "They need to die. And you're the only one strong enough to push through and see this through. The bracelets Annika made for all of us will allow us to resist Ulla and her students enough to give you time to reach her and Arne. Please tell me you can do this."

His eyes avoided mine. "That's not what's botherin' me. I know what needs to be done. I'll do it. Just...all the guns will be on you and the others. Who knows how many students Ulla brought with her? The bracelets will help, I just want to be sure that I'm not the only one to make it out of here alive."

I sighed. This was new for Keagan. He rarely allowed himself to worry about uncertainties. You could just point him in a direction and off he would go. Well, most of the time anyway. But it was more common for his stubborn ego to get in the way than worrisome thoughts. For some reason, his mind was holding him back this time and I needed him to be in a much different place than he was in now. I put a hand on the side of his face and made sure his eyes were watching mine. "I promise I will see you on the other side of this. You do your job, I do mine, and then it's back home to Cloque to see the others. You good?"

Keagan nodded. "Yeah. I'm good. Let's do this."

I patted his bearded cheek and smiled before turning around. I followed Breasal to the same place I had been before. On our way there, I made sure that I had my four Melters in my pockets. They were little packets of gunpowder and sulfur, enchanted by Annika. I had used them once before when Weylyn and I freed a prisoner from Bastion. All you had to do was cut off the piece of string that had been dunked in enchanted blue paint, wait a few seconds, then toss the rune covered satchel at any iron structure. The result would be the metal melting away like snow in the spring. It was how we were going to escape the large fighting cage and get into the audience. I didn't know if four was the right amount to make a hole big enough for all of us to get through, but I couldn't have carried more without soldiers noticing. By the time Breasal had brought me down to the same room as before, the crowd was cheering loudly again. Just as we came through the curtain, the doors on the other end opened and a satyr who had his neck bent at a horrible angle was carried into the room. He was tossed on the pile of four other bodies, and the soldiers called for us all to be ready. Seig would enter from the other side of the cage, so it was just me and the other five fighters.

Before he left, Breasal gave me a hug, a clever ruse to hide the fact that he was slipping a knife into one of my pockets. One by one we were announced to the crowd. First was a female lycan named Boudicca the Defender, then a female satyr named Enyd the Lively. After her came the male forest sprite Kenneth the Fair, followed by a male harpy named Fergus who went by the arena name The Red Talon. The usual ten seconds between entrances passed by and Moyra 'Sea Star', a female water sprite, was announced. I had decided to keep my mask for the fights, unsure if I would be recognized. Also, if I used The Banshee as my name again, Arne would be alerted much sooner than I wanted him to be. I needed a new name, so I had told Breasal to make sure I was introduced differently this time. As I had before, I spoke the prayer over the dead bodies and stood watch over them until my name was finally called.

"And now, a surprise entrant into our main event! A seventh competitor in honor of Duke Lehmann! Put your hands together for Rilea the Valiant!"

I pushed through the doors with a smile on my face. Rilea was my mother's name, and she was one of the most courageous people I had ever known. When my father was killed by drunk soldiers, my mother didn't even flinch. Her children all needed someone to rely on — we were still young sprites at the time — and my mother gave us all she had. She put on the same smile every day, never letting us see her in a weak position. My mother was my hero, even though we didn't always see eye to eye. I was proud to find a way to honor her. We weren't on the best of terms when she died, but I hoped that she had forgiven me in the afterlife and that she would protect me once more. Anu knew I needed all the help I could get to come out of this unscathed.

The crowd mostly cheered, but there were also some boos. It was common for the crowds to boo newcomers, something I had learned about from friends who had fought before, so I wasn't all that bothered by it — I wasn't here so people would cheer for me anyway. I made my way down the tall hallway and through the open gate to the cage. Memories of my fight with Keera rushed to the forefront of my mind and I found myself wishing we could have freed her before her death. All six of us stood in a circle as we waited for the final introduction to ring throughout the arena. The crowd grew silent, eagerly awaiting the final fighter.

"Ladies and gentlemen! Our final entrant, for our final fight of the night! You all know her, you all love her! Give a roaring welcome to your champion, Seig the Sharp!"

The entire crowd erupted as the gate on the opposite side of the cage opened. It only took a few seconds for Seig to make her way into the cage with the rest of us. Our audience cheered as Seig took her place in the circle we had all formed, none of them aware of how their next few moments were going to be awfully different from what they had expected. I made sure to look at everyone in the cage, waiting for them to look at me before giving a quick nod. Everyone nodded back, and I knew we were all ready for what was to come next. The bell rang and the people surrounding us broke into loud cheers once again. Kenneth and Moyra went after

Boudicca, Enyd charged Fergus, and Seig was on me faster than I could blink. It was all part of the plan, but it was still nerve racking to have a very strong — and quite capable — harpy dive onto you. I went onto my back and Seig stood over me, bringing her wings around us to give me cover. To the audience, their champion had gained the upper hand on the newcomer. In reality, the start of something special in Adler was about to begin.

I quickly pulled the four Melters out of my pockets, along with the small knife Breasal had given me. I held them all in one hand and severed the blue colored rope on the satchels with my knife. They began to sizzle and the runes on the bags began to glow the color of a cloudless afternoon sky. Seig hopped off me and I kicked up into the air to land standing on my feet. I quickly tossed the Melters at the cage and they exploded just at the right time. Each Melter was good for a blast radius of four feet. I had managed to get a good spread on my throw, and within seconds there was a gaping hole in the large cage. The crowd had already begun to panic, climbing over one another to escape. I quickly ran forward and jumped up to catch the ledge of a wall roughly eight feet high. The hole was at the top of it, leading directly into the now emptying seats. I pulled myself up and after two quick hops from row to row, I was close enough. Arne's round shape was at the edge of the balcony, shouting for his soldiers. I grabbed the tip of my small knife and chucked it up and forward. The fat man was more spry than I had thought, but he was even more cowardly than previously decided. He grabbed Duke Lehmann and pulled the man in front of him, forcing The Duke of Adler to take the knife instead.

Whistles were now blaring as soldiers entered the main area of the arena, rifles cocked and loaded. Before the others and I could go any further, we were struggling to move even with our bracelets. Ulla was standing where Arne had been, with two women on either side of her. Each one of their hands were glowing red as they held us all relatively in place. They wouldn't be able to do it forever, but if the soldiers were given the order to kill on sight instead of arresting us, we were screwed.

"*Attentäter*! All of them! They killed The Duke of Adler! *Töte jeden Einzelnen von ihnen*! I don't care who they are! Kill every damn Teufel in this arena!" Arne's shrill voice condemned many of us to our deaths.

I wasn't expecting him to order the deaths of non-fighters. I could already see certain soldiers taking aim and firing at the section where Tóráin were. This man needed to be stopped, but at the moment there wasn't much we could do. Roughly fifteen or so soldiers had their guns trained on me, Seig, and our fellow fighters. I continued to struggle to move in any direction, but the witches' hold on us was too strong. That was until the witch on Ulla's left fell back after being hit by something. I moved my eyes to look to my right and found a few Tóráin had joined the fighters from the section in the crowd. The order to kill all Tóráin in the arena probably inspired them to join the fight, which was a pleasant turn of events. The injury to one of the witches weakened their hold enough for me to fall to my right, dodging the bullets sent my way. I gave a quick look behind me to see if any others had been so lucky and was sad to find that Kenneth, Enyd, and Moyra were strewn out on the seats and not moving. The rest of us continued to charge the balcony, which sent Arne running.

I pushed myself harder to get there faster, but again I was unable to move. The injured witch had returned to her position next to her teacher and the trio was holding every Tórán back. Those of us with bracelets were still moving, but slow enough that the soldiers who had missed us last time would have a very good second chance at hitting their mark this time around. Again, the soldiers aimed for us, but a blood curdling scream had them flinch and look to the balcony. Keagan had Ulla's neck in his jaws for only a second before he tore his head away, ripping out a massive chunk of the witch's flesh. Blood erupted onto the witch to her left, causing her to scream as well. The witch to Ulla's right began moving her arms in a certain pattern, but Keagan's claws were swift, catching the woman before she could cast her spell. The remaining student of Ulla's ran away, covered in her teacher's blood. Seig, Fergus, Boudicca, and I reached the balcony as the others spread out amongst the arena to chase down the retreating soldiers. Keagan was covered in blood, the red liquid making his copper fur a dark crimson.

"You alright?" Keagan asked.

"Thanks to you." I bent over and pulled the knife out of Duke Lehmann's chest. He wasn't meant to die tonight, but he wasn't what I would call an innocent man. Plus, his absence would help in the rebellion efforts going forward. "We should hurry after Arne just in case Annika and the others have trouble."

I made my way to the exit of the balcony, expecting the others to follow me. I traversed the hallway until I reached a set of stairs. I went down multiple flights of stairs, turned right, sprinted down that hall and took another right. Our group finally went down the short hallway that led to a set of double doors. I burst through them to find six dead soldiers on the ground, along with a lycan fighter. Arne was being held off the ground by Annika, her hands emanating a soft blue glow. When she noticed us, she made a quick movement with her hands and Arne fell to the ground, collapsing to his knees. I had thought he would be furious, cursing every one of us for what we had done, but what we witnessed was quite the opposite.

"Please! Please, let me go! I'll pay you whatever you want! I'll leave Adler and never come back! Whatever it is, just tell me and I'll do it. Just don't kill me!" The pompous ruler of Kampfhalle had turned into what most people like him were. At their core, they were all cowards.

I walked around the defeated noble and stood in front of him. "I'm afraid that none of that is what we are after, Arne. You have committed many crimes against the Tóráin, and now you must pay for them."

"Crimes? What crimes? Fighters came to me looking for glory! You all did! I gave you what you wanted. You should be thanking me for all I've done for you!"

Seig scoffed. "You believe enslaving Tóráin and forcing them to fight to the death was helpful to us? You must be joking."

Arne had gained a bit of his previous charm, his disdain for us all pushing through his cowardice. "Don't you act like you didn't know what you were signing up for. You all knew the rules of Kampfhalle. So what if Ulla bound you to me. You are my fighters, fighting in my arena! I own you!"

"Not anymore. We're done killing each other for your entertainment. Humans can fight for scraps from the rich's table. We will no longer be doing so." Seig spread her wings and approached Arne.

I stepped aside, letting Kampfhalle's champion stand before her former owner. She flapped her wings and rose roughly four feet off the ground. The harpy raised a taloned hand in the air, ready to come down and tear Arne apart, but she stopped. She smiled as Arne whimpered and went back to begging for his life. Seig lowered herself back down to solid ground, then bent down and grabbed Arne by the chin.

"You have wronged many of us, so much so that each fighter here would have the utmost right to kill you. However, there is one most deserving to be the one to take your life and end your tyranny." She pushed his face away from her before taking a couple steps back. Following Seig's eyes had me looking at a certain someone, and the sight brought a smile to face.

I was more than happy to see who was stepping forward holding a long dagger in their right hand. His tattered clothes barely stayed on his starved body and tears came from his dark eyes. Breasal shuffled forward until he was right in front of his abuser.

"You?" Arne let out a mocking laugh. "Do you even know how to use that? You're not worthy enough to end me. You're not worthy enough for anything! You're just a stupid, ugly, evil, little —"

Arne's insults stopped when Breasal stabbed him in the throat. Breasal pulled the blade out and blood oozed out of the arena master's neck. He clutched at his injury, desperately trying to stop the bleeding with his hands. He fell to his side, gurgling and choking, until he finally stopped. His eyes were wide with fear, staring at the one responsible for his death. The goblin cleaned his dagger on Arne's pants before tucking it into his belt. More whistles and shouting could be heard as reinforcements were arriving to the arena. We all needed to be far away from here; there would be no rebellion if we were arrested or killed.

"We need to get out of here before soldiers find us," I announced to everyone standing around Arne's corpse.

"The sewers! We'll make for Bloody Knuckles Inn through them. Good old Klaus will keep us hidden there. He gives me food even when I can't afford it!" Breasal was already at a nearby sewer grate that he struggled to lift.

"Better than avoiding soldiers in the streets." Having now shifted back into his usual form, Keagan went over and lifted the metal cover with ease, tossing it off to the side.

We all hopped in after Breasal, the goblin insisting he knew where he was going. Our previous plan was to just find our way to Bloody Knuckles in via the streets, but if Breasal could guide us through the sewers we were better off taking that route. We had no light though, so we had to keep one hand on the wall and one hand on the person in front of us while Breasal guided the group onward using the excellent vision goblins had in the dark. It took some time, but eventually Breasal called for us to emerge from a nearby sewer grate. I chose to go first to make sure it was safe, and I was thankful to see nobody within eyesight. We all piled out of the sewer and followed Breasal to a good-sized building with a hanging sign out front with 'Bloody Knuckles Inn' painted on it. The man named Klaus who we had met only yesterday was behind the bar when we entered, and when he noticed the blood on our clothes, he quickly directed us to the back room. He gave us a lantern and two jugs of beer before closing the door behind him. There were only three other people in the bar area: a lycan, a harpy, and a satyr. They all had stood up from their seats and hurried us into the back room, so I highly doubted they would say anything if soldiers came looking for us. We drank the beer quickly, and soon some of us were laying on the floor sleeping. Eventually, it was only Seig and I awake, with Keagan being the last one to try to sleep.

"You must see me as a monster for killing so many of our kind." Seig was staring into the lantern while playing with a feather that had fallen off her wings in her hand.

"I don't see you as a monster. Once Ulla had you under her spell you had no choice. The person I question is before the spell was cast. Cordelia said you had thoughts of coming to Cloque to help with the rebellion there. Why did you choose this life over that one?"

"Believe it or not, I was afraid. I wanted to help, but the fear of getting caught and tortured was unbearable. Tóráin in Tulp all know very well the things that go on in Etoile. If that cursed city is any indication of the horrors that await in Fleuris prisons, I wouldn't blame anyone for wanting to avoid that place. Oddly enough, fighting never scared me. I was good at it, and that made me feel invincible. I figured maybe, if I went to Korblum, I could get into Kampfhalle and use my winnings to help those in Fleuris that way. Of course, I was quickly reminded of the cruelty and mischievous nature of humanity once I was given barely more coin than other fighters and bound to that bastard by Ulla." She turned her attention to me with a stern look on her face. "I want to make things right."

I took a deep breath, looking Seig's face over as I remembered how scared I was when I was forced into the army at eighteen. I was more scared about what Fleuris' soldiers would do to me than Korblum's or Czermak's. The Tóráin were mistreated everywhere for a long time, until things eventually got slightly more optimistic for us in certain countries. Still, even after many years passed by and other countries evolved, Fleuris remained one of the worst places for non-humans. The people there genuinely hated us, and many maintained the belief that we should be hunted like we had been before. It was a ruthless place, and I didn't blame anyone for wanting to avoid it. To fear Fleuris was a smart thing to do; it wasn't something to be ashamed of. I decided to take Seig's hand in mine, caress the small feathers on the back of it with my thumb, and look her in the eyes.

"You don't need to make anything right. You were right to fear Fleuris. If I were to think only with my head, I would never go back. However, I have friends there that need my help. My heart lives there. I have a responsibility there. Now, you have a responsibility here. You have friends who need your love and your leadership. Leading this rebellion will ask a lot of you, but I believe you are more than capable." I thought to add a smile at the end, hoping to convince her that I was being sincere.

Her yellow eyes moved so that they looked at the flame in the lantern and not me. "But...I've killed so many of us. How could they ever trust me?"

"I was in the army for the majority of my years from eighteen to twenty-four." I looked over at Keagan, watching him sleep for a moment before continuing. "Keagan was in the army just as long as I was. The two of us have killed many

Tóráin in our lives, and yet we are high-ranking members of The Resistance. You know why? Because the Tóráin see that we spend every day trying to bring about a world where no one else will ever have to do what we were forced to do. You can be that person for the Tóráin here in Korblum. Show them that you want a world where Tóráin don't have to fight in arenas in the hopes to have enough coin to eat the next day. Fight for a world that's better than this one. Fight for them, and I promise that they'll fight for you."

Seig took a moment, but she eventually smiled. She gripped my hand tightly before patting it with her other one. The harpy took a deep breath in before letting the air out of her lungs slowly. She looked at Keagan, then back to me, the smile still on her face. "You two must feel lucky to have each other. You know, to have someone who understands what you've been through."

I watched Keagan's arm twitch a couple times before he settled again. "My closest friends either never fought or didn't fight as much as I did. One, oddly enough, is a human named Rosalie. The second is a lycan by the name of Brina, who served in seventeen-ninety, but she managed to avoid the last war in a similar way my other friend did. He's a lycan named Weylyn. He was...important to say the least, so he faked an injury and claimed to have a limp leg so he wouldn't have to go fight. I met Keagan close to the end of the last war, and when I tell you I hated him, well I mean it."

Seig's face adopted a confused look. "I don't understand. Are you and Keagan not friends?"

I watched as Keagan twitched, grumbling and growling in his sleep before going still and silent once more. "When I met him, he was ignorant, rude, crass and reeked of beer. He had been fighting with another unit during our time in Malvene, and they were ambushed. Only he and another three Tóráin survived. They were all thrown into my unit, which I led. Well, technically Captain Monet led our unit, but I was the one who led us into battle. I didn't like Keagan much, until one night when he partially shifted into his feral form during his sleep and nearly killed the sprite sleeping next to him. I woke him up, and once he was calm and back into his tame form, he apologized. He looked shaken and disoriented, and for some reason in that very moment I took pity on him. We got to talking, and he admitted that he had nightmares every night of the people he's killed, both human and non-human. He and I talked throughout the night and come morning I had a new respect for the lycan. Keagan still acted like an asshole the next day and those afterwards, but I knew it was all to hide the pain that he had inside. When the war ended, I convinced him to come join The Resistance. For the last two years he's continued to be rough and foul, but he's also given his blood for a better world. I admire him for that. To answer your question, yes, Keagan is indeed my friend. He drives me crazy sometimes, but I do feel a bond between us. I'd give my life for him, and I know he would do the same for me."

Seig nodded her head for a bit before staring into the lantern's light once more. "I hope I can build friendships like that here. I'll need allies like that if this whole rebellion thing is going to work."

"If I can have the friends I have after all I've done, I know that you'll find allies just as loyal and brave as mine. You're strong and you have a heart that yearns for a better life for all Tóráin. I think you'll do great things here, all while forming bonds you'll hold dear for the rest of your life." I had been watching the light with Seig, but I moved my eyes onto her once I finished speaking.

Seig caught the movement, and when our eyes locked, she smiled. "Thank you, Olwen. It's a shame you won't stay here longer. Do you still plan to leave tomorrow, even with soldiers probably crowding the streets after what we did at Kampfhalle?"

I smiled back before looking at the light in the lantern. We could stay here longer and help, or even go back to Tulp and help there, but Rosalie would no doubt be needing us back home. It was best for us to return to Cloque and allow the seeds of rebellion we had planted to grow on their own. I took a deep sigh, causing the small flame in the open lantern to waver slightly.

"Yes, I think it's best we make our way home. I'm sure you'll do just fine without us. Each rebellion is its own, and I believe you and the others will do a wonderful job discovering what needs to be done here. Although if you're looking for suggestions, personally, I'd start with ending the other arenas in the country."

Seig laughed. "I was thinking the same thing. Maybe I am going to be good at this." She reached over and put a hand on my shoulder. "Thank you for what you've done here, Olwen. I promise you that when Tudrose arrives, whenever that may be, there will be a force here in Korblum ready to fight with them."

I extended my wide-open hand. "May your victory be glorious and swift."

Seig smiled before she grasped my forearm in a warrior's embrace . "Glorious and swift indeed."

# Chapter Twenty-One

## Weylyn

Balowe, Stelpina  |  December 30, 1798

Travelling through the Great Eastern Folds had us see more snow than when we had made our way through the Great Western Folds a little over two weeks ago. Brina and I had arrived at Balowe around noon today, beginning our search for Sullivan the moment we stepped foot in the city. Ossian hadn't given us much to find his goblin friend, aside from telling us he lived west of Lake Balowe. We did our best to remain discreet as we questioned fellow Tóráin on his whereabouts, keeping our hoods over our heads and only approaching those who weren't within earshot of a soldier. We didn't know if asking for Sullivan would alert a guard in any way, but we figured it was best to be cautious. It wasn't until sunset that we finally got a lead to follow. A lycan told us that a goblin named Sullivan lived in the most western district, close to a pub called The Rusty Pickaxe. We made our way there, and quickly realized a change in our surroundings.

This district was very much on the outskirts of the city and was in even worse shape than the area we had come from. It appeared that the majority of the north-western districts of the city were heavily populated by Tóráin, however I hadn't seen even one human since we arrived in this one. The houses and streets became smaller and more run down the further west you went. After a while of searching for The Rusty Pickaxe, I had come to the realization that this segregation was done on purpose. The Tóráin were forced westward, into poorly built homes that lined a dirt road, far from the center of the city. I had thought back to when we arrived at the south-eastern area of Balowe, trying to remember if we had passed by any Tóráin on our journey to the opposite end of the city. Sadly, I could not remember seeing any lycans, harpies, sprites or any other non-human races of people. I didn't have much knowledge of Balowe since it wasn't the country's capital, but I was starting to learn that this place was just as bad as every other city we had encountered on our trip. If Tóráin were being forced into the outskirts of the city, away from humans, I could only imagine what else was going on here.

I tried to focus on finding Sullivan, despite wanting to stop for every person I thought looked like they needed my help. It was hard to be in a place like this and do nothing for those suffering. Many we saw were poorly dressed for the winter months and appeared to be starving. Brina and I were far from nobility, but in this place, people must have thought we had somehow climbed the ranks among the humans just because of our clothes. I was proven right in thinking such things when those we approached to ask about Sullivan's whereabouts cowered and scurried away. Thankfully, we eventually found the pub we had been directed to. Sitting on the cold, frosted ground outside the place was a goblin wrapped in a thin blanket. He was smoking a pipe that gave off the vibrant smell of a cheap weed poor folk smoked called Scutella Leaf. It was common everywhere, with both Tóráin and humans using it to forget about the world. Those who smoked it usually ended up passing out, although I think that's the goal for most of them. I knelt down in front of the goblin, and he blew the smoke from his pipe into the sky before shooting me a large grin.

"Hello traveler. You lost? Folk dressed like you don't really venture this way. You must be heading east, right? It's getting late, you might as well just spend the night at Ol' Rusty's here and continue on your way in the morning. You probably won't like the food. If Sean even has any left."

"Actually, we're looking for a friend of ours. A goblin named Sullivan. Someone told us he lived near here." I held a smile to convince him I was friendly, despite him blowing a fresh plume of smoke directly into my face.

The goblin took a few puffs of his pipe before releasing smoke circles into the air above him. He then scratched his bushy left eyebrow with the mouthpiece of his pipe while scrunching up his face to show he was thinking hard. It didn't take long for his eyes to open wide and a fresh smile to present itself. "The grumpy one who gives me half his meals during our afternoon break at the mines! I knew I knew that name! Now that I've remembered, I kind of feel ashamed I ever forgot. Rough goblin that one, but he ain't heartless."

"Yes, yes. Do you know where we can find him?" Brina asked from her looming position above me and our new friend.

He looked up at Brina, looked her over, and took another puff from his pipe. "Nope."

I couldn't help but roll my eyes. This was the closest it seemed we had come to finding Sullivan and I really didn't want to have to continue asking people about his whereabouts. "My name is Weylyn. What's yours?"

The goblin seemed hesitant at first, but he eventually answered. "Niall. There's another goblin in town with the same name, but all you have to remember is that I'm the better looking one."

"Well, Niall. It is very important that I find Sullivan. Can you do me a favor and think hard on where I can find him?" I reached in my pocket and pulled out an apple I had been saving.

Niall snatched it out of my hand without hesitation and took a large bite out of it, having dropped his pipe in his lap in the process. He quickly picked it up to take another puff before taking another large bite from the apple. The goblin tapped the fruit against his thin lips a few times before his eyes lit up again. "Ah yes! Turns out I do know! I was there this morning actually. How could I forget that? Ah well. Sullivan lives in the house on the corner of the street. Right over there." He pointed to his left, having me look in the same direction and spotting the house the goblin had just described.

"Thank you, Niall. You have a good night now." I stood up as Niall gave me a mocking bow from his seated position.

Brina and I left the front of The Rusty Pickaxe and made our way a short distance down the street to the corner house.

"People smoke too much of that damn plant. It really ruins your mind after a while. I never understood the allure," Brina said as we approached our destination.

"It brings a sense of calm to people who crave not having to think. We all have our vices, Brina." I walked up to the front door of the corner house and knocked on it three times.

It took some time, but a goblin with thick, dark grey hair opened the door. He wore a poorly crafted robe over a worn shirt and ripped pants. His eyes squinted as he looked over Brina and I with the lantern he had in his right hand. "What the Hell do you want?"

"Are you Sullivan?" Brina asked.

"Depends on who's asking." He continued to look us over; his face scrunching up told me he wasn't very pleased with what he saw.

"A friend of mine in Malvene told me that you might be able to help us with some business we have here in Stelpina. He's a satyr named Ossian. Sound familiar?" I really hoped we had found the right person. Ever since Niall mentioned there was another goblin with the same name as him, I had begun to worry that there were multiple Sullivans in town too.

"Ossian? The one with his head so deep in a book he'd forget he needs to eat?"

I smiled. "Yes! That Ossian. So you know him then?"

"Of course, I know him. Satyr saved my life. Any friend of his is a friend of mine. Come on in, the fire won't last the night but there might be some beer somewhere." Sullivan beckoned us to enter his small home and we gladly obliged; even if it was still cold inside, at least the wind wouldn't catch us.

Sullivan's home wasn't very big. It was only one room, with a small cot in the back corner and two chairs next to the nearby hearth. The goblin went over to his bed and picked up bottles, vocalizing his joy in finding one with something still in it with a high-pitched hum. He came over to me and held out the bottle he had chosen.

"Hope you don't mind drinking from the bottle. There isn't much left but it's yours, nonetheless. I'd offer you a seat, but I only have one chair that wouldn't collapse under you." Sullivan took a seat in the smaller of the two chairs, placing the lantern on a small table in between them.

"I'm fine to stand." I motioned to the empty chair. "The seat is yours, Brina."

She didn't argue with me, swiftly taking her place in the larger of the two chairs by the fire. I took a sip from the bottle Sullivan had given me before lowering myself to the floor. With my back up against the wall, I sat next to the fire and took another sip from the bottle before breaking the silence that had taken over. "So, you said Ossian saved your life?"

Sullivan snapped to attention, having been staring into the remaining flames of the fire. "Yes. Back when the army of Fleuris was making their way through Stelpina many, many years ago. They wanted to attack Leonessa without going through Azuvipa, so they struck a deal with King Niklaus' father, King Armand, that granted their army safe passage through our land. They stopped in Balowe on their way further east before they made their way through the mountains to end up on Leonessa's doorstep. Long story short, I had gotten into some trouble with a few Stelpina soldiers. They were ready to shoot me in an alley for what I had done, but Ossian called out to me as if I were his aid. He took full responsibility for what I had done. Unable to kill a soldier of Fleuris, even if it was a Tórán, the soldiers simply reported the incident to Ossian's commanding officer. Ossian was whipped three dozen times as punishment. He's lucky he wasn't killed. I went to thank him before they left, but he insisted that there was no need. We kept in touch through letters over the years, but I haven't heard from him in some time. Honestly I was beginning to wonder if he had died."

"Oh no. He's very much alive. Head in a book as usual." My announcement caused Sullivan to chuckle a bit before his face took on a more serious look.

"Dangerous place this world is. Especially for Tóráin. You never know when a human might decide that your life should end. I'm glad he's well." Sullivan shifted in his chair before crossing his arms over his chest. "Now, what's this about him sending you to me for help?"

"Have you heard of The Resistance in Fleuris?" Brina asked after taking a drink of water from her flask. "Weylyn and I are —'

Sullivan put his hands out in front of him as if he were trying to slow a charging horse. "Woah there. I don't know what Ossian told you, but those days are long behind me. I'm too weak to be getting involved in that nonsense nowadays. Sure, I was spry and strong before, but life takes its toll on you. Even more so when you live a life like many here in Balowe have lived. Best to just follow the laws as well as you can and try to live as good a life as possible."

"We aren't here to ask you to fight or anything like that. We have a deal with Queen Sophia of Tudrose. If we can start up chapters of The Resistance in Tulp, Korblum, Stelpina, and Malvene, then Queen Sophia has agreed to wage war on these countries. She would insert people into positions of power that consider the Tóráin more like people than animals, all in the hopes to have a world where people like us don't have to be afraid. I have friends dealing with Tulp and Korblum, and we have already started something in Malvene. Ossian seemed to think you would know how we could do the same thing here in Stelpina."

My words had Sullivan's face twisting and his head shaking. "While that all sounds lovely, you're a fool to believe your little dream can ever become reality. We'll always be Tóráin, my friend. No matter who leads the country, no matter what laws are passed, our kind will always be looked down upon. No amount of rebellion will change that. Take it from someone who fought for years against tyranny, only to end up a widow, a slave, and a father who outlived his children. Nothing good comes from rebellion, Weylyn. Nothing at all."

This was far from what I had expected. When Ossian directed me to Sullivan, I thought he would be just as ready to help as Ossian had been. Mind you, the satyr was still a little hesitant at first, but Sullivan was completely and utterly against the idea of being involved in this. It was disappointing, and I could feel my entire body begin to slouch in defeat. This lead was supposed to work out and help us do here what we had done in Malvene and Fleuris. Despite the fire, I was cold and there was next to nothing left in the bottle the damn goblin had given me. If I was to be completely honest, I was ready to just walk out of here. The pub nearby would, hopefully, at least have something to drink and maybe even something to eat. Annoyed that we had searched all day for someone who was not willing to help us, I shifted myself to get ready to stand. Before I could, Brina spoke, and I found myself staying where I was.

"Ossian described someone who would be excited to hear what we had to say. What happened? I know you mentioned loss in your life, but Weylyn and I have both lost as well and yet we fight even harder than before. Is it the slavery? I thought slavery was banned in Stelpina years ago." She had asked much of the goblin, and for a second, I thought he was ready to shout at us to leave.

Instead, his face softened, and I saw a tear fall down his face. He fell deeper into his chair and let out a deep sigh. "Three years ago, I might have been happy to hear from you. Ten years ago, I would have been even happier. Fifteen and twenty years ago there's a chance I would have kissed you. A good part of my life was spent fighting for a better life for my fellow Tóráin. I started in Nours, having been born there. Eventually, my parents saw my actions as too risky to support, and they forced me to leave the city else they would report me to the military. I bounced from village to village for some time, even debating on leaving the country, but I eventually landed in Balowe. It was here that I found my wife, as well as where my two children were born. I knew that Tóráin, especially goblins, were forced to work the mines here, but I thought that I could help those who were suffering. My wife, Sheela, admired and supported my dream to one day free those enslaved here.

"Eventually, we had Imogen, and then after her came her brother, Craig. When Ossian saved my life, Sheela and I had already lost our sweet Imogen to Strawberry Fever. Craig had managed to avoid it, but it was only two years later that he was murdered by human children. They say he fell and drowned in Balowe Lake, but other Tóráin claim to have seen the children throw him in and keep his head under the surface. Even with that loss in my life, I still pushed through. The speeches I gave in pubs throughout town inspired our people to call for an end to slaving at the mines. Our cry for justice eventually reached Baron Frederick Frei, a noble who had a soft spot for the Tóráin. He had already managed to convince a few other nobles to join him before finally convincing the leader of Balowe, Count Eric

Fankhauser, to end slavery in this city. We thought it was a big win, and so my dear Sheela and I went out to a local pub not far from here. Tóráin of all kinds came to celebrate our freedom, but we were joined by angry humans who thought it was a bad thing that we were free. They slaughtered everyone who was there and burned the place down. Sheela was shot in the head, and I got hit in my stomach. I managed to escape thanks to a lycan named Sean. We were the only two that survived.

"One of the worst parts of it all was that nothing really changed. The Tóráin as a whole were still forced to work the mines and serve humans. They pay us now, but barely. We work Monday to Saturday, with only Sunday to rest. We're still getting sick. We're still starving and we're still getting attacked by groups of humans that are being encouraged by Count Fankhauser. That man is responsible for every bad thing that's happened to me, and every other Tórán in this damn city. He may not have infected my daughter, or drowned my son, or murdered my wife, but his propaganda and need for control over the Tóráin has infected this place with a cursed sickness that destroys everything good. And it all happened even with me fighting for years. So, when I tell you that nothing good can come from fighting back, you now know my reasons for believing that."

I didn't know what to say, so I stayed silent for some time. Sullivan's tale had silenced Brina as well, both of us saying nothing in response to what the goblin had shared with us. It was a sick joke among our kind that every Tórán had a sad story to tell, but Sullivan's was truly depressing. He had fought and lost, a fate I have feared for some time now would be my own. I couldn't ever bring myself to be mad at him for not helping us. A part of me believed that if my fight had taken my parents, Rosalie, and those closest to me, I would lose my will to fight too. I understood how his mind could only see darkness. I had the same feeling he had now back when my father was killed. It was Rosalie, Brina, and Darby who had pulled me out of it and showed me there was still light; that there was still hope. Olwen came into my life soon after and she only pushed me to fight for that light even harder. I realized then that everyone who would have helped Sullivan see the light had been taken from him. There was still a fighter in there, I knew there was, we just needed to help him. I got up just enough to take one big step over to Sullivan before bringing myself back down on one knee.

"I'm sorry that you have had to endure all of that, Sullivan. Forgive me, but what has ever stopped you from avenging your family? You say this Count Fankhauser is the reason all of this happened to you, so why not make him pay for it?"

Sullivan grumbled something under his breath before answering. "You don't think I want the bastard to pay for what he's done to Tóráin living in this city? There are even humans that he's abandoned to sickness and hunger. The moment my wife was killed I wanted to slit his throat, but it just isn't possible. Nobody has even bothered to try because we all know it would result in our deaths. He's constantly surrounded by witches and soldiers."

I took a moment to nod a few times, showing Sullivan I had listened and received what he had told me before responding. "Say someone managed to get rid of him. Would that solve the problem here in Balowe?"

The goblin didn't move for some time, his eyes bouncing back and forth between me and the fire behind me. Eventually he straightened himself in his chair a bit and decided to answer my question. "If the Count were to meet his end, a new Count would be elected by the barons. They don't all agree with his beliefs, but I believe Baron Frederick Frei would be elected. Some things could change for the better if he were in charge. But it's foolish to think such things."

"Why?" Brina had decided to make her voice heard in the matter now. "If Baron Frei getting elected Count would aid Tóráin in the city, we should get rid of Count Funkhauser."

Sullivan turned to her impatiently. "Oh yes. Let us just snap our fingers and be rid of the tyrant. If it was that easy, it would have been done by now."

My interest was piqued by that last statement. "So, there are those who want the Count gone?"

The goblin scoffed. "Of course, there are! Even humans hate the man. If anyone ever manages to poison his water or somehow knife him while he sleeps, the world will be better for it. But, as I've been saying, to think his death is something attainable is a borderline suicidal thought. No one can reach him."

I looked at Brina, both of us smiling at each other, before bringing my attention back to Sullivan. "We could reach him."

Sullivan laughed. "Oh, is that right? And who are you, students of Dhuosnos? Perhaps you're both descendants of the goddess of battle, Morrig? No. You're just two lycans with big dreams. You won't get him."

I thought of how to convince him, eventually landing on something that I hoped would work. "Have you ever heard of The Crows of Leonessa?"

Sullivan's eyes opened wide. "I'd be a fool to not know of those nightmares."

Brina cleared her throat to grab the goblin's attention. "We killed them. Set their prisoners free."

Sullivan's eyes squinted as he inspected us both, looking for a sign that we were lying. He ended his leering before labelling us liars, forcing Brina and I to insist that we were telling the truth. Sullivan demanded we tell him how, and so we told him the story of how we had connected with Ossian. That of course led us to finding out Quaid was a prime candidate for leading a rebellion, which then brought us to the prison escape. The goblin's eyes opened wide when I described Quaid's jailor, and the disbelief in his face only continued as the story went on from there. When our tale ended with us leaving Quaid and Ossian to continue what we had started, Sullivan had his mouth agape and was shaking his head. He tried multiple times to begin saying something, but each time he stopped himself from speaking. He struggled to find the right words it seemed, until he allowed himself to fall back into his chair and let out a long, deep sigh.

"Well, that is quite the tale." Sullivan began tapping his chin, mouthing words to himself before shaking his head to dismiss them. Finally, he said something out loud. "Let's say that you have the skills required to remove Count Funkhauser. You won't be able to do this on your own. And you'll have to pick the right moment to strike."

I grinned, knowing that we had succeeded in dragging Sullivan out of his pit of despair. "Of course. I'm sure you can point us in the direction of people willing to help. I also believe that you have a moment in mind already."

Sullivan grinned now too, leaning forward so that our faces were closer. "I have a few ideas. We don't have much time to prepare though, seeing that tomorrow we'll all be off to the mines. Luckily for us, there's a bar full of friends nearby that can help spread the word. We'll need everyone on board for this to work."

"Wonderful. Tell us what to do, and we'll follow your lead." I stood up and extended my hand out to him.

Sullivan looked it over almost suspiciously before quickly grabbing my hand and shaking it. He hopped off his seat and made for the door. "Come on now. Much to do in so little time. We'll need to get the lycans on our side, as well as the goblins. They make up the majority of the mining workforce. It may take some time to convince them, but if you can convince me I'm sure you'll have no trouble reeling them in too. We'll start at The Rusty Pickaxe and go from there. Hurry now!"

I looked at Brina as she stood from her seat. We were both smiling, happy to have turned this visit around. It had started out rough and reached a point where I think all of us were feeling depressed. Now, we had a plan of action and a target. Sullivan began briefing us on his plan even before we could leave his house. The more he told us, the more I realized that despite Sullivan's talk of defeat, the goblin had thought of this plan long ago. Supposedly Count Funkhauser enjoyed visiting the mines on every Wednesday of the week. We would strike then and rid the city of him. Sullivan went over the details until we got to the entrance of The Rusty Pickaxe. Niall was no longer seated outside but there was the noise of a good-sized crowd coming from inside the pub. We had convinced Sullivan to rebel, now it was time to convince everyone else. It was time to awaken the Tóráin of Balowe so that they might awaken all of Stelpina. It was time to start a proper rebellion.

# Chapter Twenty-Two

## Weylyn

Balowe, Stelpina  |  January 2, 1799

It had been a difficult, exhausting two and a half days. Brina and I had decided to join the others in their trip to the mines Monday morning, figuring that it would be less suspicious this way. We had debated on joining everyone on Wednesday instead, but there were too many variables that risked us raising any type of alarm. Having two new lycans from day one was less conspicuous than having two new lycans on day three. We had been wailing on rocks — and then carrying them away — for two days now. It had taken us a little more than half a day to reach the mines, and the witches and soldiers here had gotten us started right away.

We slept in cramped buildings that prevented us from stretching out, causing our muscles to be stiff the following day. I had already started to feel for those who were forced to do this six days a week. I fancied myself as quite strong and fit, but nothing had tested my body like the last couple days had. Not only was it physically draining, but it was also mentally exhausting. Witches and soldiers continuously shouted at you, while some used whips to grab your attention or make you move faster. It was very difficult for Brina and me to not intervene when floggings or punishments were being carried out. Miners either felt the whip or were tortured by magical spells the witches cast on them. It didn't at all look like the Tóráin here were free.

Before the sun began to rise in the east, we were woken up by whistles and shouts. We were in the caves before the sun ever showed itself, and we wouldn't see it until midafternoon. Well, so long as the sky was clear. Yesterday the sky was covered in clouds that dropped about an inch or two of snow throughout the day. Who knew what this afternoon would look like? The one thing the others and I knew for sure, was that we would be carrying out our plan regardless of the weather. Sullivan had gone over it with us in detail, along with a dozen or so lycans and a similar sized group made up of a mix of other races — eight goblins, three satyrs, and two sprites to be exact.

We spent the majority of Sunday night going over the plan before sending out everyone to spread the word as best they could to avoid having to speak about it at the mines. Thankfully, it didn't take much to convince those inside The Rusty Pickaxe to help us. Many were hesitant, but Sullivan was a fairly prominent member of their community and managed to convince them with the help of Sean. It was a pleasant surprise to find out that the Sean who owned the pub turned out to be the same Sean who had saved Sullivan from the attack that resulted in the death of his wife. He was the first to speak up and throw his support behind us. With Sean and Sullivan both on board, the others came around.

Just as I managed to dislodge a good chunk of ore from the damp rock wall, whistles echoed throughout the mines. As the few soldiers that watched over our group informed us that it was time for our break, the plan we had created went through my mind once more. Our plan was dangerous but simple. Sullivan was convinced it would work, and I chose to trust him on that. Neither of us liked the idea of how much blood would cover the quarry, but we both acknowledged that this was our best idea.

"Get a move on, *Teufel*!" The soldier shoved me in the back as he and his allies hurried us out of the caves.

The sun hurt my eyes as I stepped out into open air, the smell of something cooking causing my stomach to grumble. It took more than I thought it would to avoid the line for food and make for the line for water. You rarely got both according to the other miners, another subtle attack on the Tóráin. Having to choose between eating and drinking was demoralizing, and after only three days I had learned to understand why the mood around here was so depressing. The Count, his witches, and his soldiers had worn down the Tóráin of Balowe so much that there was barely any fight in them. This plan of ours had to work, or I don't think anything else we could say or do would ever inspire them to fight back again.

Brina and I made our way through the line, keeping an eye on our target. We had assigned two lycans to each witch, with some requiring three because of the distance we needed to cover; just to be as sure as possible that we took out all the witches. There was a good amount of us here, maybe eighty or so, but a dozen witches could hold us all in place long enough for the soldiers here to pick us off before we could ever mount a proper attack. The goblins — as well as the few satyrs and fewer sprites — had no real weapons save for their chisels, and they didn't have a lycan's gift of shifting. They would need all the advantage we could give them, and eliminating the witches was a very large part of that.

"Hey! No cutting in line!" A voice I recognized as Sullivan's rang out in the open, frost-covered wasteland full of rock and ore.

"I didn't cut! You cut!" Another miner shouted.

Our plan had begun. I kept one eye on the food line and the other on my target. She was of average size, terribly slim, dressed in a dark brown dress with a pale white, leather corset. The shouting had caught her attention.

"How dare you accuse me of cutting! Don't you know who I am?" The line had begun to form into more of a gathering crowd, surrounding the two arguing Tóráin.

Kaine was the one arguing with Sullivan, and he continued to play his part well as he forced his small finger into his fellow goblin's chest. "I don't give a damn who you are. You cut. Now move!"

A satyr came to Sullivan's defense after Kaine gave the older goblin a shove. Quickly, and on cue, everyone in the food line erupted into a fictional brawl. It looked pretty real to me, and I was glad to find I wasn't alone in thinking so. Every witch focused on the ruckus around the food tent, as well as the nearby soldiers. It allowed Brina, the other lycans, and me to sneak over to the cover of large boulders and piles of ore. We waited a few moments while whistles sounded, and shouting could be heard as the soldiers tried to put an end to the fighting. The witches all had their arms out towards our little distraction, ready to restrain any Tórán that they felt was a threat. We were ready to go, but we still hadn't seen Count Funkhauser. Just as our attack window was closing, the pompous bastard made his grand entrance. Flanked by two more witches and a personal guard of six soldiers, he shouted out at the group of miners.

"If you would all rather fight amongst yourselves instead of eating, then fine! No meals today, none tomorrow! *Soldaten*, find who's responsible for this and bring them to me *auf einmal!*"

We knew there was a chance that The Count of Balowe would be accompanied by more witches and soldiers, so it wasn't too much of a surprise. It did, however, require our attacks to be perfect. Brina and I still had the necklaces we were given by Ossian's witch friend back in Leonessa, so it would be up to us to charge the extra witches. We might not reach them ourselves, but we would grab their attention long enough for the rest of our pack to kill them. At least that was the hope. We needed to move quickly now, before the soldiers and witches got control over the situation. I motioned at everyone to move out, and we all shifted into our feral forms before sprinting away from our cover. Shouts were already filling the quarry due to the skirmish by the food tent, so barely anyone noticed when the first witch was caught and torn apart by her lycan assailants. By the third and fourth screams, soldiers began aiming at us and by the eighth and ninth they were shooting at us. The tenth, eleventh, and twelfth witches all managed to turn around in time to catch their attackers, but we moved quickly and swarmed them. As the twelfth witch bled out, more shots were being fired off, but they weren't being aimed at us anymore. The remaining miners had spread out now, charging the soldiers nearby.

I looked around quickly in an attempt to find the last two witches before spotting them standing guard by a bewildered Count Funkhauser. I called for Brina and the other lycans left to join me. Five of us had been shot down in our attacks on the last three of the dozen witches, but we were still more than enough to challenge the two who guarded our main target. They were focused on the swarm spreading out and attacking soldiers, but they managed to catch us charging them with enough time to attack us first. The duo must have decided that slowing us down and relying on soldiers to kill us was the wrong way to do things. They moved their hands and arms in definitive patterns, green light shining and moving in unison with their limbs. The lycans running with me started to collapse, falling to their knees while coughing up a storm. I looked back to see vines made of green wisps emerging from a lycan's jaws before bursting from his eyes. I pushed myself to run faster than I had been, the others sensing my urgency and rushing along with me. The witches realized that we would be on them soon, and so they abandoned their attack and shifted their efforts to slowing us down. For the other lycans it was like they were running in chest high mud. Brina and I, thanks to our necklaces, were only slowed as much as a strong windstorm.

Still, the witches' efforts were enough for soldiers to pick off our friends. I heard them cry out after the guns fired, and as each one fell, the magical duo that opposed us held us back easier. Brina and I had managed to dodge the shots fired at us, but with only two lycans to deal with, the witches now slowed us much like they had slowed the others. The Count of Balowe called off the soldiers firing at us and pulled out the pistol that sat on his hip, announcing that he intended to kill us himself. I fought as hard as I could, but even with the necklaces there was no way I could protect myself or Brina from Count Funkhauser's gunfire. I continued pushing forward, but I closed my eyes when I heard him cock his pistol. The sound I had expected to hear next never came. When I quickly opened my eyes to see what had happened, I was witness to quite the sight. Count Eric Funkhauser was just now falling to his knees, with what appeared to be a chisel lodged in the side of his head. The witches had stopped their spells due to the incident, shock and fear overtaking them. They began to run, but two more chisels came flying from my right and lodged themselves in each of their backs. It brought both of them to the snow covered ground as a goblin and a forest sprite charged them. They ripped out the chisels from the witches' backs before stabbing them into the women's heads. A third goblin went over to the former Count of Balowe and pulled his chisel from the man's head. He spat on the human's corpse before looking at me and Brina.

"You aren't him, but I'm counting saving his friends as repayment for Ossian saving my life." Sullivan shook his chisel to get a thick mess off it.

I was still trying to collect myself from almost dying, but I managed to let out a brief laugh. "I'll be sure to tell him the debt is paid the next time I see him."

I looked out at the rest of the quarry and the last few soldiers left were currently being overrun by the group of vengeful Tóráin. Our plan had worked, but the more I looked around the more I realized what it had cost us. At least thirty — possibly more — Tóráin laid dead in the blood-stained battleground. I looked back at the roughly twenty lycans who had also lost their lives fighting today, and our number of dead rose. It was odd to be looking at so many of us dead while cheers began to fill my ears. I allowed myself to return to my tame form as I watched the mob of survivors raise their chisels and claws in the air. Cheers rang through the area, accompanied by a few howls from my fellow lycans who had survived. I couldn't cheer with them though. All I could think of were the next steps forward which would need to be taken in order to make sure those who died here today didn't do so in vain.

Brina approached Sullivan with an extended hand to congratulate him on a successful fight. "Seems your plan was a good one, Sullivan. What's next?"

The goblin grinned as he grabbed Brina's hand. "Hope that Baron Frederick Frei gets elected, and then spread the word to every corner of Stelpina that the Tóráin have more to live for than being a slave." The smile on his face faded as he looked out at the dead. "But before all of that, we will see to it that every Tórán who died here is given a hero's funeral."

"We'll help with the funerals," I stated as I extended my hand to congratulate Sullivan too.

He gripped my hand, but he was shaking his head. "I appreciate the offer, but I don't think that's the best use of your time. I worked with a lycan today who said his sister in Fleuris sent him a letter. Supposedly, there's some trouble stirring at home for you two."

"What do you mean trouble?" I asked.

Sullivan tossed his bloody chisel aside before putting both hands on his hips. "She didn't say what exactly. Just said that her brother probably wouldn't be hearing from her for a while because recent events had her feeling that it was unsafe to leave her house to send anymore letters."

Fleuris was a big country, and there were plenty of places that could have some occurrence that would make any Tórán feel unsafe. I needed more information. "Did he say where she lives in Fleuris?"

Sullivan shook his head. "No. Although I do vaguely remember him mentioning his sister lived in a fair-sized city during a drink at The Rusty Pickaxe, back when I first met him."

A fair-sized city narrowed it down, and none of the possible answers were good ones. If something was happening in one of the major cities, there would be a need for The Resistance. As much as I wanted to make sure those who had died had a proper send off, I agreed that it may not be the best use of our time. Wondering if the city in question was Cloque had me worrying for Rosalie, Dwyer, and the others. We needed to go home.

"Is there anything else we can do to help before we leave?" I asked.

Sullivan just shook his head. Although, before he could say anything, Brina was asking her own questions. "You're sure that this attack and the murder of the Count won't have the nobles lean to someone who would look to attack you back? I doubt they will be jumping to get a Tóráin sympathizer elected after all this. Shouldn't we stay until Baron Frei is made Count of Balowe?"

It was a fair question, one that I had admittedly wondered the answer to myself. Sullivan took a deep breath as he watched the survivors of our battle inspect those who had died. "I'll admit that there is a chance that they elect someone else, however even with this display of ours I'll be surprised if Frederick isn't named Count. He's the second richest noble in Balowe next to Funkhauser and supposedly he has a cousin that is close friends with Prince Lennel. The King of Stelpina is old and will surely die soon, so anyone who would have favor with the one who will replace him is considered quite powerful. I'm fairly certain Baron Frei will be Count Frei within the week. There may be some backlash from the other nobles about what has happened here, but they won't risk possibly not having a line to the new King's ear. You should go home and tend to things there. Let me worry about things here."

Nobles did love any type of power they could have, and a possible link to the king would definitely pique their interest. I trusted that Sullivan knew the workings of Balowe better than me, and so I conceded. Brina appeared to feel the same way, nodding her head in response to Sullivan's explanation. If the goblin believed that things would go the way we had hoped they would, then I would allow myself to believe also. I moved forward so I was standing next to Sullivan and watched my fellow Tóráin begin to separate our dead from the human dead. I put a comforting hand on Sullivan's shoulder as I tried to remind myself that freedom comes at a cost. "We lost many here today, but I know that you won't allow them to be forgotten. We'll help you bring them all back to the city and then Brina and I will begin our journey home."

Sullivan turned to me, grabbed my hand off his shoulder, and reached out to Brina. She gave him her hand and the goblin brought all of our hands together before a tear fell from his eye. "Thank you. Both of you. Not just for what you did here today, but also for instilling some hope in me again. A proper resistance group is what I had always dreamed of, and I will be forever thankful for you helping me start one. I promise you that I will use whatever life I have left to see that Queen Sophia and the Tudrose army has a proper rebellion force ready to fight with them. Together, we'll see this world become a better place for our kind."

I squeezed the old goblin's hand. "Your family would be very proud of you, Sullivan."

Brina put her free hand on Sullivan's shoulder. "I agree. Sheela is smiling at you today. I know it."

Sullivan shook our hands before setting them free. "Thank you. I think they're all just happy I found my way back to being the goblin they loved. That goblin has a lot of work ahead of him, but I think he can handle it. Come, let's help the others so you two can be on your way."

The three of us split, with Sullivan and Brina going towards everyone else while I made my way to my fellow lycans who had perished trying to reach the former Count of Balowe. It pained me to see so much death, even if it was for a good cause. I bent over and put my arms under one of the dead, lifting him into my arms. As I carried him over to one of the carts that had been brought up for the bodies, I hoped and prayed that we would have kinder sights to see when we got home.

# Chapter Twenty-Three

## Olwen

Cloque, Fleuris  |  January 11, 1799

Keagan was rotating his shoulder, testing its strength as I looked over a map of the city. Thanks to having a few days now to recover, he was healing fairly well. It had been a difficult re-entry into the country after we were surprised with the new law that no Tóráin were allowed to enter Fleuris anymore. We figured we could sneak our way in near the northern tip of the Jurigora Mountains, but soldiers had been placed there. We barely escaped them; Keagan got shot in the back of his shoulder and I broke my wrist after diving out of the way of a bullet. Things didn't get better for us as we got to Cloque. There were buildings that had been burned down, an increased military presence, and from the moment we arrived in the city to when we reached The Flying Pig, I noticed four dead Tóráin just lying in the street. Luckily for us, The Flying Pig had been relatively untouched, save for the loss of Elouan. He was the human owner of the inn, and supposedly he had confronted a group of humans who were threatening to burn the building down for serving Tóráin. They shot him before they were chased off by the patrons who had witnessed the confrontation. Ownership of the place had passed on to Elouan's son, Lucien. Thankfully, Lucien was just as much of an ally to the Tóráin and The Resistance as his father was.

We were still allowed to use the inn as a safe headquarters, but we had to be more discreet than before. The fiends who had murdered Elouan had not yet returned to make good on their threat of burning The Flying Pig to the ground, but it was best to avoid giving them a reason to. The more Tóráin seen entering the inn, the more humans would want to see the place in flames. I'm sure that there are humans out there who have always hated businesses that catered to the Tóráin, but thanks to General Rosspier's latest speech, they felt brave enough now to do something about it. Keagan and I weren't here to hear it, but the words the bastard had let loose upon the city had inspired hateful humans to show their true nature. It was upsetting to discover just how many people were unable to evolve their beliefs over the centuries. Many still saw us as evil creatures sent by Deus' demonic brother, Eous; horrid beings that crawled out of the pits of Hell to wreak havoc on this world. They sought only to see us all killed or burned — or both — and it made me wonder if what we were doing would even matter in the end.

We were starting all these rebellions, and Queen Sophia was going to come across The Great Canal and liberate these countries; will any of it make a difference? If the human citizens of these countries wanted us to go backward instead of forward, what would new leadership really be able to do? We had Tóráin gathering to create rebel armies that would assist Tudrose when the time came, but who's to say that the humans of those countries won't band together against them? What I was hearing and seeing in my short time back in Cloque was unsettling and it truly made me worry if all Keagan and I had done was a waste. Dwyer, Moya, and Odran had all died in the riot that broke out after General Rosspier's speech, along with roughly forty or so others. According to Rosalie, soldiers had taken some prisoners, but after a week of torture they were all sent to the guillotine as a crowd of humans cheered. None of them had seemingly given up any information about other members or hideouts of The Resistance, but it seems they had lost their lives for their silence.

As I looked over the map of Cloque, the few pleasant memories I would have as my eyes fell on certain places no longer came to the forefront of my mind. All I was reminded of was fire and death. We had been in the city for only a few days, but what I had witnessed would stay with me for the rest of my life. As I looked over the northern district, I swore I could smell the burnt flesh of the Tórán who had been burned there three nights ago. Word was that someone had claimed she was with The Resistance, so a mob of humans ransacked her home, shot her husband, and burned her on a pile of her belongings. Right in the middle of the street. Nobody was arrested. I don't even think the soldiers cared. Fellow Tóráin feared that if they tried to bury the poor couple that they would be murdered as well, so I had decided two nights ago to finally retrieve the bodies and bury them myself. Keagan had come to help, as well as Finn and Anya. Me and Anya placed the bodies onto a cart, and Keagan carried it. Finn had come as extra security in case we ran into trouble. Both Finn and Anya were fairly young members, but their hearts were kind, and their will was strong. I trusted them enough to have them present in some meetings between me, Keagan, and Rosalie. I still didn't tell them where Weylyn was, or where I had been, but they knew enough to be helpful.

With all the new horrors I was being forced to witness — the loss of high-ranking members doing me no good either — I was feeling much lower than I had planned to feel on my return home. I didn't expect a parade, but I had thought that I would at least have a day to just sleep and not worry about anything. I scoffed at the thought of sleep, knowing full well I hadn't been able to since I saw the burnt body of that forest sprite. The only way I knew that she was a sprite was because of her horns, everything else having melted into one charred piece of flesh. Every time I closed my eyes, I was the one burning instead. I tried to close my eyes then to see if I would see something different this time, but there I was. When I opened my eyes quickly and shook my head, I noticed out of the corner of my eye that Keagan was staring at me. He was no doubt going to tell me to get some rest. He had been badgering me about it since this morning when he found out that I had been awake all night. It was silly for him to pester me about it, since he looked like he had barely slept himself. Still, his eyes were burning a hole in me, so I figured to just get ahead of it before he gave me another lecture.

"I'm fine, Keagan," I said firmly.

He grunted as he stood up from his seat. "Yeah, and my shoulder doesn't hurt. We all need to be as well rested as we can be, especially you, O'."

I spun around to face him. "You don't think I've tried? I told you already. I can't sleep. My mind won't let me. You know what that's like more than anyone around here. Just drop it will you?"

Keagan put his hands in the air and smiled. "Consider it dropped. Just tryin' to keep a promise."

I went to say thank you, but his final statement caught my attention. "What promise?"

Keagan grabbed the bottle of wine sitting on the corner of the table and one of the cups sat next to it. He poured himself some of the red liquid, took a drink, then allowed himself to lean up against the wall. He seemed nervous to answer. No, not nervous. Embarrassed? Whatever it was, he was oddly avoiding eye contact and staring into his cup. Finally, right before I just dismissed the whole thing, he answered. "I promised myself the day we left that I would do my best to make sure you were safe durin' all of this. From the moment we left The Flyin' Pig to the moment the war was won and Fleuris was liberated."

His answer wasn't what I was expecting, and it quickly became my turn to avoid eye contact. Keagan and I had a bond due to the mutual understanding of what the horrors of the world can do to a mind, but this was oddly kind of him. Our relationship was one that usually saw us arguing with or teasing each other. I quickly peeked up from staring at the map and saw that Keagan was awkwardly waiting for a response. I grabbed the bottle of wine, clumsily poured myself a drink thanks to the splint on my wrist, and dumped the liquid down my gullet before trying to shift the seriousness of the mood in the room to a lighter one.

"Aw, the little wolf does have a heart," I teased.

Keagan scoffed. "You really think that little of me?"

Another thing said that I was not prepared for. I was tired and stressed, and this conversation that had started as a silent lecture from Keagan had developed into a serious chat that I didn't know if I was up for or not. Still, despite my wish to leave the room, I knew that I couldn't. Keagan was a rash, impulsive, reckless lycan but I didn't want him thinking that was all I thought he was.

"No. I was only teasing you." I reached out and grabbed his free hand. "Thank you for looking out for me. It's nice to know that I have someone watching my back."

Keagan nodded and I let go. Silence overtook us and it quickly became the awkward kind. I loved Weylyn, and Keagan loved Cliana, so we were both capable of emotion. However, we both found it terribly difficult to show it. That brief moment of serious companionship had us both staring into our cups, and I found that I disliked mine was empty. I filled it up again, but this time I only sipped on my drink instead of downing it in one go. I went and sat on the lone bed in the room we were in just to put some distance between Keagan and I, and suddenly I felt exhausted. The feeling had eventually just vanished after being awake for so long, but the comfort of the thin mattress and warm blankets were calling to me now. I looked longingly at the pillow, and I began to caress the sheets like you would a lover.

"Just give it a try," Keagan said from his spot against the far wall.

I sighed. "I'm just going to see things I'd rather not see."

Keagan put his cup down on the table and walked over to me. He took my cup from my hand and placed it on the table next to his. He opened the blankets and kindly pushed on my shoulder, making me lie down. Something in me allowed him to do this, and I think it was the fact that I was so incredibly tired. He knelt on the floor as I got more comfortable, better situating my head on the pillow and sliding my legs under the bottom half of the blankets. Keagan reached over me and pulled the top half of the blankets up to my chin after gently tucking my injured arm inside their warmth.

The lycan cleared his throat as he grabbed a hold of my good hand. "Death is a shit thing. Whether it's a calm passin' in the night or a head bein' taken off, it's traumatic. When I was forced into the army, I was excited. I liked fightin'. I was good at fightin'. But bein' exposed to so much death, it does somethin' to you. It's even worse when you're responsible for it. Those without much of a heart become numb to it all, but people like us feel the weight of it forever. Some more than others. My point is that we've seen things that won't leave us, and I hate that anyone — let alone someone I care about — has to be haunted like I am. I don't like seein' shit things any more than you do, O'. I get it. So, I'll just sit here with you in case you see somethin' you don't like. You feel like openin' your eyes, just squeeze my hand instead, and remember that you aren't alone."

As my eyelids grew heavy, I realized then that it wasn't because I was so tired that I had allowed Keagan to force me to try to sleep. I was laying in a warm bed, ready to brave the images I knew would greet me when I closed my eyes, because Keagan made me feel safe. I let my eyes close, and I tried to send away every memory I had of what I had seen or heard about these last few days, but it still happened. First it was the burnt corpse in the flames, screaming in pain. Then it was quickly me in her place. I squeezed Keagan's hand harder than he probably expected me to, but he didn't say anything. He just squeezed back. Eventually the image in my head began to fade and what replaced it was the time Keagan and I had our drinking contest. I slowly eased my grip on his hand, but he kept a firm hold on mine. A smile grew on my face, and I felt sleep finally take me.

# Chapter Twenty-Four

## Weylyn

Cloque, Fleuris  |  January 15, 1799

I couldn't believe just how bad things had gotten in such a short time. When we left Sullivan and Balowe behind, I had conjured an idea of what trouble was waiting for us. Never would I have ever thought things could have gotten so horrific for the Tóráin and the humans that supported them. We discovered one of the new problems when we reached Bassoir, the city that harbors the point where Fleuris, Korblum, and Stelpina borders meet. All countries had claim to some area of the city. Knowing the chaos that would come with that, Brina and I figured this would be an easy place to slip back into the country relatively unnoticed. The border walls were always busy with merchants and fellow travelers wishing to gain passage into one of the three countries, but what I had seen was truly worrisome. The trouble was mainly at the Fleuris border where we found Tóráin trying to both enter and flee the country. The Fleuris soldiers refused to allow any Tórán in, but they had no problem letting our kind leave. The problem there was that the soldiers of both Korblum at the northern border gate and Stelpina at the southern border gate were denying entry to any Tórán who approached them.

After realizing that things were much worse than we had thought, Brina and I decided that we were not getting into the country this way. In a quick change of plans, my cousin and I chose to leave and try the outskirts of the city instead. We had heard a soldier tell an angry satyr that if he was caught entering the country from the wilds, he would be shot on site — it appeared to be that our chosen route was a dangerous one. Thankfully, before we had left, a thin man with light brown eyes sunken into his face approached Brina and me. He claimed he could get us to Fleuris, informing us that he had been smuggling Tóráin to and from the countries over the last two weeks via The Flechan. I had thought we were relatively hidden, but the man claimed he had developed a talent for spotting lycans thanks to his current line of work.

The wide river the man insisted could be our salvation ran through the city of Bassoir, and the Fleuris border wall was on its shore. There was a ferry that took people across, but you couldn't get on that ferry unless the soldiers allowed you to. The mysterious man — who introduced himself as Elyas — had a boat, and he claimed that he could use it to carry Brina, me, and a few others into Fleuris. "I don't understand why your kind wants to go to that cursed country, but I'll be damned if I don't help you do so," Elyas had said. With the risk of facing the wilds our only other option, Brina and I chose to accept Elyas' offer. That night, at its darkest point, Elyas guided his boat down a small body of water not far from where he had initially approached us called Wasser River. From there, we entered The Flechan and went north. The waters were rough, and our boat small, but we made it to the small entrance to the Tarade Canal. The water broke up the wall, providing a tiny enough gap for us to row on through. We went down the canal for a while before Elyas dropped everyone off just outside the city.

We were lucky to not be caught, and I was certainly thankful for Elyas' help. He took a small family of satyrs back with him and I wondered what they were running from. As we passed through a few villages, Brina and I were exposed to the reasons why our kind were trying to flee the country. Homes were burned down, Tóráin were hung outside the entrances of villages and towns, merchants and businesses refused to serve Tóráin causing them to starve; it was horrifying. There were a few villages we passed by that hadn't succumbed to whatever poison General Rosspier had infected the country with, but the majority of the places we saw or heard of from travelers had to be avoided. Our food ran out two days early, and we didn't want to risk entering a community — no matter how big or small — in fear of what the humans who lived there might do. The scariest thing for me was that if this was what the towns and villages looked like, the cities must be far worse. I worried for Rosalie, Dwyer, Moya, Odran, and the others. I even wished that Olly and Keagan were as far away from the country as possible. It was very clear to Brina and me well before we reached Cloque that the country was far more dangerous for the Tóráin than it had been when we left.

I decided that we would enter Cloque late at night, when the number of guards would be smaller and easier to slip by or engage. We had heard from a couple of lycans that they were arresting any Tóráin trying to enter the city, so we needed to be careful. Once the moon and stars were bright and everything else was dark, Brina and I left the wilds we had been hiding in and made for the south gate of the city. We didn't go towards the guards though. Instead, we made for a nearby canal that delivered water to the southern district. I got in the water first, then Brina slipped in behind me. We slowly swam towards the tall walls until we reached a eight feet wide, four feet tall opening closed off by an iron grate. We pushed on it together, and it lifted up as we came through. The Resistance had needed ways to help prisoners escape the city, and with some hard work over a few weeks, we had found one in this grate. We filed the piece off, then attached our own. We had added the hinge, allowing for the grate to lift. It was deep in the thick walls, so no one would ever know the change unless they swam up to it.

Now inside the city, we had to be careful with where we exited the canal. We had to swim underwater for a fair distance, both of us gasping for breath as we broke the surface well away from the guards on the wall. Brina and I left the water behind us, tossed our wet hoods over our heads and prayed for a warm fire soon. The cold was harsher up here, and swimming in the near freezing water had us both shaking vigorously. I felt the hair on my head and face begin to freeze as Brina and I began our journey to our meeting point. We had determined before we left that someone would wait on Mascarons Bridge for us to return, or for a letter from us to arrive. I had no idea if anyone would be waiting there for us, but we had to make that bridge our first stop. We had no idea what was going on in the city, so we couldn't assume that The Flying Pig or any other of our safe places weren't compromised. We had to weave our way in and out of alleys to avoid soldiers still patrolling the streets, but we made it to the bridge. It was very late and from the two bodies we had come across in alleyways I figured it was much too dangerous for our people to be out at this hour. It was because of this that I wasn't surprised to not find anyone on the bridge, save for the odd drunk human or stray cat. It was risky, and we were both freezing, but I decided that we should wait here until sunrise just to be safe. Brina had challenged me on my decision, but eventually she conceded and the two of us sat down with the stone railings on our backs and we cuddled to keep warm. Sunrise wasn't far away. The early twilight of morning had already begun to creep on the eastern horizon. If nobody came, or the cold became too much, we would make our way to The Flying Pig.

"Hey! What are you two doing?"

I opened my eyes and realized that the cold had drained me so much that I had fallen asleep. Brina had passed out too, the lycan lifting her head off my shoulder and mumbling to herself. The morning sun struck my eyes hard, causing me to squint at the four soldiers standing over me.

"Hey, I asked you a question! Answer it, or I'll arrest the both of you *tout de suite!*"

My eyes finished adjusting and I got a good look at the four of them. They had their rifles armed with bayonets and at the ready. The guns weren't pointed at us just yet, but it wouldn't take much for the soldiers to do so. I obviously didn't want any trouble and quickly gave the one who was yelling at us a smile.

"Good morning, sir!" I said loudly. "Appears me and my friend here drank too much last night and thought the bridge was a good place to catch some shut eye. Terribly sorry about that. We'll head home right away." I helped Brina to her feet as she feigned the effects of a long night of drinking.

"Why are you all damp and such?" the soldier on the far right asked.

I looked at my clothes clumsily. "Well would you look at that. Must have fallen in the river at some point, eh? Such a fool I am as a drunk. Probably dragged my poor friend in with me. Best get home and get a fire going!"

I went to lead Brina through the guards but the one on the far left stood his ground and gripped his rifle. The one who had yelled at us spoke next. "Where did you get so drunk last night?"

The question was an odd one for a soldier. They usually didn't care where or how you got drunk, they just wanted you off the streets. This must have to do with the bad changes occurring in the country, so I tried to keep my eyes hidden and be careful with my answer. "A friend's house, sir. Lovely home. Nice and welcoming, you know? Probably should have just stayed there and avoided getting all wet."

"*Cet ami était-il humain?* How did they come by enough *l'alcool* to get you two so drunk that you would fall into *La Dame* in winter and not rush to the nearest fire?"

Asking a question in Fleuran meant these soldiers still believed us to be human. Rosalie had tried to teach me some of the language from time to time, but I wasn't very good at it. The words '*ami*' and '*humain*' I knew though. They were asking if my friend was a human, amongst the other odd questions they posed. I didn't know how to answer any of them in a way that ended with Brina and I being allowed to leave. If this was how they were treating humans, I could only imagine how they were treating Tóráin. While I was struggling to find something to say, Brina broke the silence. "Heavens I'm cold. I'd really like to be on my way home. I'm quite sober now and rushing to the nearest fire is literally the only thing on my mind right now."

The soldier raised his fist and all of them pointed their rifles at Brina and me, forcing the two of us back a couple steps. Our backs were up against the stone railing of Mascarons Bridge and their bayonets were much too close for us to escape without getting stabbed. One of them cocked their rifle and the others followed suit.

"Look me in the eye. Both of you," the lead soldier ordered.

When Brina and I reluctantly obeyed, the man spat on the ground. "*Diables*! I knew it!"

He kept his rifle fixed on us as he nudged the soldier next to him. The man lowered his rifle, leaning it on his shoulder as he removed a pair of restraints from his hip. Just as I was about to try to say something that would get us out of this mess, the soldier on the far right grunted and grabbed at a small knife in the side of his neck. He dropped his rifle and fell to his knees. The other three quickly turned and aimed their rifles in the suspected direction of the knife. The three of them all fired at the two cloaked figures charging at us, but Brina and I had shoved them and caused two of them to miss. Thankfully, the other one was a bad shot and his bullet whizzed by the larger cloaked figure — the soldiers never managed to get off another shot. The smaller of the duo let loose another knife, striking the one who was shouting at us in the chest. He fell to his knees as the remaining two tried to run. Brina and I gave both of them a swift punch, knocking them out. They collapsed, joining the other two soldiers on the ground. Our rescuers reached us and removed their hoods.

"Olly!" As soon as I saw it was her, I wrapped my arms around her and squeezed.

She squeezed me back, a smile on her face when I let her go. "It's so good to see you're both okay," she said.

"What are we doin' about those two?" Keagan grumbled as he pointed at the two soldiers who had only been knocked out.

Olly pulled out a knife. "They've seen Weylyn and Brina's faces and will associate them with trouble. I'll deal with it."

Keagan grunted and looked away as Olly stabbed the two men in the chest. When she was done, she began to lift one and drag him to the railing. "Well? You going to help me or just sit there and watch?"

The three of us quickly began helping her toss the four soldiers into the frigid and surprisingly deep waters of The Dame. Once they were gone, Olly gathered their rifles and tossed them into the river too. With our mess cleaned up, I was comfortable asking a question that I had been dying to ask. "Olly, what the Hell is going on?"

She sighed. "Nothing good, besides you two showing up alive and well."

Brina chimed in. "How is everyone?"

Her question had me adding one of my own to the mix before Olly or Keagan could answer. "Is Rosalie alright?"

Keagan and Olly's faces both adopted somber looks and my heart jumped into my throat.

"Dwyer, Moya, and Odran are dead," Olly said. "Elouan too, along with many others. Rosalie is fine, but both her parents succumbed to their illnesses while you were away. She'll be at The Flying Pig. Hasn't left the place in weeks."

Brina came forward and asked a question of her own. "How did Dwyer and the others die? What happened?"

Keagan put his arm around Brina's shoulders and began leading her forward. "Enough questions for now. Let's get the two of you in front of a fire before you lose your limbs to winter's bite."

Olly came next to me and put a hand on my arm. "Yes, a fire first. Then I'll answer every one of your questions. A lot has happened, Weylyn, and almost none of it is good."

I grabbed my best friend's hand and squeezed it tight. The gesture appeared to have startled her at first, but she quickly squeezed my hand back and sent a smile my way. I smiled back before looking ahead of us. "We've survived harsher times before, so it stands to reason that we'll survive whatever this is too."

# Part Two

## The Spark

# Chapter Twenty-Five

## Weylyn



Every day felt like a lashing from a whip. Each morning, afternoon, or night some news reached us that made my stomach turn and a newfound rage boil within me. There was only so much we could do, and thanks to the fear that General Rosspier had managed to spread, there weren't many of us left. Multiple members renounced their support for The Resistance in the hopes that they would be left alone by the gangs that had formed in the city. They weren't just here in Cloque, but all over Fleuris. General Rosspier had given a speech each month, ensuring to keep the hatred and brutality towards the Tóráin at a high level. Many homes and businesses had been burned down, and hundreds had been murdered in various ways. With our limited numbers and an increased requirement of keeping our heads down, many of these horrid events had been allowed to happen with little to no consequences. All of Fleuris was experiencing hardship, save for those rich enough to avoid such troubles. The Tóráin were suffering the most, but our human allies were also being attacked. Even people who didn't support us were being affected by what was happening. When I left Cloque all those months ago I thought it was the beginning of better times, but for the last few months things have appeared to only get worse.

We were all taking things personally; everyone had the idea that it was their fault that the country was in the shape it was in. From Keagan thinking his rescue caused the more extreme measures, to Rosalie believing none of this would be happening if she had stopped Dwyer and the others from rioting. It was unhealthy to beat ourselves up in such a way, but we were all stubborn and any attempt to tell us that it wasn't our fault fell on deaf ears. Thankfully, every one of us belonged to a specific group of people who were determined to undo our mistakes. We all had stepped up, no matter the level of risk involved. Each high-ranking member of The Resistance knew it was up to this group to fix what was going on. We allowed ourselves to feel a small high when we saved someone, which was good. The group needed to celebrate the victories, even if they were hard to come by and often surrounded by failures.

Just three days ago we had ambushed a caravan transferring prisoners from outside of Cloque to Bastion — for what soldiers called interrogation but we all knew was just mindless torture. We set the six prisoners free, gave them some provisions, and wished them luck. The next day we received word that members of a group of extremists called the Hunters of Deus had murdered and burned a family of four Tóráin. The youngest of them was a child of only six years old. The small high we were riding from our rescue of the prisoners quickly vanished after being brought that news. We had all taken it hard, just like any other news of similar information in the past, but Keagan was especially upset. I nearly had to fight him to keep him from going out into the city to hunt the group responsible.

While we were dealing with all the negativity in Fleuris, it was always a welcoming sight to read letters from our friends in other countries. Cordelia, Seig, Sullivan, and Quaid all sent us updates every few weeks or so regarding their progress in their respective nations. Thankfully, things were going much better for them than they were for us. They had their losses of course, but they had all managed to build a fairly solid resistance of their own. I relayed everything our allies told me to Queen Sophia in a letter of my own, each time hoping to receive a response saying that she would begin a war effort like she had promised. Instead of granting my wish, she had only stated her want for greater influence in the countries. We would be due for a letter from her in about a week, and I hoped that with winter behind us Queen Sophia would be more open to moving forward. New laws and restrictions had already been made in our allies' nations, which would only make things for them more difficult. The sooner Queen Sophia kept her promise, the better it would be for everyone. However, until her letter arrived, all I could do was be thankful my friends and allies were safe and take the days ahead one at a time.

Today was turning out to be quiet, which could be either good or bad. A quiet day could mean nothing bad was going on, but it could also mean that we just weren't aware of what was happening. An informant could have been captured, a messenger could have been killed, or the humans of Cloque could have just decided to not be monsters today. Anything and everything was possible, something I had learned quite quickly over these last few months. I could go the rest of the day without receiving word of anything, or someone could knock on my door right now with news of any nature.

"Weylyn? You in there?" I would have cursed myself for seemingly summoning company, were it not for who had arrived.

"You don't have to knock, Rosalie," I said.

She entered the room and closed the door behind her. With a basket hanging from her arm and all of her hair draped loosely over her left shoulder, she came and sat down at the table with me. The basket was placed on the table and opened up, a plate of dried meat and fruit making its way out thanks to Rosalie. She took the basket off the table before grabbing a piece of meat and offering it to me. I took it, realizing that I hadn't eaten yet today.

"What's the special occasion?" I asked in between chewing and taking another bite.

"I need a special occasion to have a meal with my handsome love?" She smiled at me before taking a bite out of an apple.

"Not at all. Just hasn't been something we've done for a while." I grabbed the bottle of wine on the table and poured it into the only cup I had.

"That's exactly why we're doing this. We need to take advantage of days that don't bring further darkness into our lives. We have to remember why we're fighting and who we're fighting for. Plus, I know you haven't eaten since yesterday." She stole the cup out of my hand, taking a sip from it before handing it back to me.

"That's true." I took a sip of wine before reaching for some grapes. "How do you know I haven't eaten?"

Rosalie gave me a look that implied I was stupid. "You know I talk to Lucien, right? He tells me when you haven't eaten, or when you've been drinking too much."

I grinned as I chewed on a couple grapes. "I didn't know Lucien was your spy."

"He's not my spy," she responded quicky. "I've just had him watch you when I can't."

I let out a small laugh. "That's what a spy does, Rosalie."

Rosalie gave me a playful punch in the arm. "Whatever. I wouldn't need him to watch over you if I knew you would take care of yourself."

"It's difficult to do so when things are the way they are," I said solemnly.

Rosalie grabbed my hand and squeezed it until I looked at her. The green irises of her eyes eased the tension I had been feeling all day, and the smile she sent my way calmed my anxious mind. I leaned over and planted a kiss on her forehead. "This was a very good idea. Thank you."

Rosalie brought my hand to her lips and kissed it. "You're welcome."

I didn't know how long this moment would last, but I was still happy to have it. With all that had been happening, Rosalie and I rarely had moments like this now. Even at night we would be so tired that we'd both choose sleep over anything else. To have some time to just enjoy some food and wine along with some conversation that didn't involve death and suffering was a welcome change. I began to enjoy this moment so much that I forgot about all the thoughts that had been preventing me from doing anything else today other than sit around and worry. It just made me appreciate Rosalie even more. The world around us was in shambles it seemed, but so long as I had her by my side, I knew that we would fix it.

# Chapter Twenty-Six

# Weylyn

Cloque, Fleuris | April 24, 1799

We had to keep hoods over our heads, but Brina and I were out with other patrons in the bar. Being cooped up in a room for so long wasn't great, so it was nice to be out and interacting with people. Patrons of The Flying Pig were allies to The Resistance, but thankfully nobody had pointed out the relation to any soldiers or groups. The Flying Pig remained one of the few places untouched by everything, but we still needed to be cautious. We stayed quiet and made sure not to draw any attention to ourselves, just in case someone in here felt like causing trouble. We were lucky that lycans looked fairly similar to humans, so it was easier for us to blend in. The other races had a more difficult time, which usually resulted in them not showing up, or spending their time in one of the rooms Lucien had available. Either way, The Flying Pig was still somewhere Tóráin could view as a safe place for them.

Rosalie had joined us not too long ago, having finished her shift at the hospital. We were all drinking our favorite drink and remembering times that weren't so dark. It was a good reprieve from the usual interactions I had become used to. An older man had just spun the tale about the shark he caught in the sea to the south when he was much younger. Before that, a middle-aged woman told our group about how her mother was once requested to sing for King Louis, but she refused because their beliefs regarding the Tóráin differed too greatly. Even Genevieve, one of the few witches that were allies to The Resistance, wove a story about when her parents had discovered she had the gift of magic. I was always fascinated by witches and how they came to be. That intrigue had only grown with my discovery that I could possibly cast spells of my own. As a witch, your magical ability wasn't hereditary, nor was it something just anyone could achieve. You had to be born a certain way, and you wouldn't know until you matured. Only female humans were granted the gift of magic, but it seemed that both sexes from my world could be born with this ability. I had wished to ask Genevieve some questions after her story, but I didn't want to raise suspicion.

A story that didn't have anything to do with magic, or hunting, or singing, came from Rosalie now. She was telling us about how she had helped deliver a baby this afternoon. She was just reiterating to everyone how sweet and strong the mother was when the main door to The Flying Pig burst open. The rain from outside had drenched the man that stood in the doorway. Everyone had initially tensed up, recognizing the uniform of a soldier. However, it didn't take long for the majority of the patrons to notice the man was an informant of The Resistance. Durant was a guard at Bastion for half of the week and a guard at the eastern gate of the city the other half. He had been valuable in the past, especially in the last few months. I was usually happy to see him, the two of us actually getting along quite well. However, we weren't supposed to meet for another three days, and it was fairly late in the night. When I got closer to him after leaving my table, I noticed his shoulder was bleeding.

"Durant what happened?" I asked as I inspected his injury. "Who shot you?"

The poor man was gasping for air, probably having run all the way here. "Other soldiers. I didn't announce to them why I was leaving my post. They ordered me to stop when I ran past them, but I couldn't. They shouted at me, yelling that I was possibly a prisoner who had stolen a soldier's uniform. They shot at me. One of them didn't miss."

"What in the world had you risking getting shot at?" Brina asked, having followed me over to see Durant.

"He can tell you in the back while I fix him up. Come on now." Rosalie pressed a rag to his shoulder and began to guide him to one of the rooms in the back of the building, but Durant pushed her off.

"No! No there's no time! Weylin, you need to get out of here. The Dove knows who you are. She knows what The Flying Pig is. A prisoner broke under her torture tonight and told her everything. She's coming!"

Before I could say anything in response to what Durant had said, the main door burst open again. Eight soldiers entered the room and quickly fanned out, training their rifles on everyone. In the middle of them came the one Durant had tried to warn us about. The Dove was in her usual all white, old leather armor. The pale mask she wore covered most of her face and her cloak flapped in the wind that came through the open door. She had her sword drawn, resting at her side. Durant got between me and our adversaries before pulling out his own sword. "Go Weylyn! We'll hold them back."

The Dove laughed. "We? You poor thing. You're alone. Nobody in here is going to help you defend that disgusting hound. Weylyn, Leader of The Resistance, you are under arrest. Come quietly, and I'll let the others here live."

I weighed my options quickly. Handing myself over would mean certain death, and The Resistance would lose any morale it had left. However, I couldn't risk anyone being killed because of me. I went to take a step forward when a loud gunshot exploded to my left. One of the soldiers collapsed, and when they all turned to fire at Lucien behind the bar, more gunshots came. Some had resulted in Lucien being killed, one of the bullets finding his head. Others had come from the pistols of our patrons, taking out three more guards. A brawl quickly broke out as patrons charged the soldiers and The Dove. I saw that we actually outnumbered them, and instead of running like Durant had suggested, I made my way straight towards The Dove. If we could eliminate her tonight, it would be an enormous win for all Tóráin. The woman had cut down three patrons before I reached her. Our blades caught each other, and I pushed her back until a strong force sent me reeling. Her free hand glowed white, and I was reminded that The Dove was also a witch. Still, Brina and I could handle her. We also had Genevieve, who I saw send a ghostly knife into one of the remaining soldiers.

Brina came to stand next to me and I watched The Dove put her sword away. She held her hands in a peculiar position as white light emanated from them. Her sword out of the way, Brina and I decided to shift into our feral forms. We were stronger in this shape, faster too. We both still had the charms we had gotten from Ossian's witch friend, so I figured we had a chance. Brina charged first, and The Dove quickly raised her right hand, sending Brina into the roof. She pushed at me with her left hand, but I withstood the attack and continued on. The witch tried the same thing again, but it only interrupted my progress for a moment. I charged from where I had managed to get to, only a dozen or so feet away from her, and when I leapt at her with my jaws ready to tear into her neck, she held me still in the air. She pulled out a dagger and smiled.

"You're a strong one," she said with a grin. "I'll have plenty of time with you soon, but who's to say I can't have a little fun right now?"

The Dove stabbed into my shoulder before pulling the dagger out aggressively. The act saw a few droplets of blood fly onto her face. She spat like an unpleasant taste had just filled her mouth and her eyes widened. She hesitated for a brief moment before she licked my blood off her weapon. The witch gagged before spitting out what she had just tasted. Her red eyes were staring holes through me. "You have —"

The Dove went flying backwards and I fell to my knees. Brina quickly picked me up, no longer in her feral form, and began ushering me behind the bar. "Come on! We have to go!"

I pushed off Brina and turned to see Genevieve with her arms stretched out in front of her. The light surrounding her hands glowed green. Her black hair was flowing in a wind that only seemed to strike her, and I could see her nose was bleeding. I was going to help her when Rosalie put both hands on my chest and pushed me back.

"No, Weylyn!" Rosalie's hand then came to find my cheek. "She's going to give us time. Hurry! We have to go!"

I looked down at Lucien's body, and then over the bar at all of the other patrons. They had all risked their lives for mine and it was my job now to make sure it wasn't for nothing. Genevieve was suddenly sent flying backwards, and I noticed that The Dove had recovered. She began to run towards us when, again, she was sent hurling towards the far wall. I looked back at Genevieve who now had a cut on the side of her head. She looked at me with extreme urgency. "Go! I can't hold her off forever! Go!"

I turned and left, silently thanking Genevieve for what she had already done, and what she was going to do. Brina, Rosalie, and I hurried through the room behind the bar and burst through the rear door of The Flying Pig. There was a lone horse tied up nearby, and so I came up with a plan quickly. "Rosalie, take the horse. You know our hidden escape, yes?"

Rosalie was resisting me as I guided her over to the horse. "The small canal and the grate. What about it? Weylyn what are you doing?"

"You'll take the horse there," I said. "Brina and I will be right behind you."

"Oh no way am I leaving you. Surely the horse can take the three of us —"

I kissed her. My lips parted from hers and I put my hands on either side of her face. "We don't have time to argue. Get on the horse and make for our exit. Don't look back. Swim out for a distance and wait for us. If we don't show up within five minutes, make your way to Tudrose."

Rosalie was reluctant and I could see in her tear-filled eyes she wanted to argue more, but she quickly got up into the horse's saddle. She gave me one last look before kicking her heels into the mare's sides. She rode fast down the street before making a right turn. Brina and I both changed into our wolf-like forms. While we usually remained on two feet, this shape allowed for us to run on all fours as well, giving us speed that we needed. We sprinted after Rosalie, and I wished that she would reach the meet up spot untouched. As Brina and I rushed through the night streets towards our escape I thought of everyone we were leaving behind. They wouldn't know what happened here tonight. They wouldn't know if we were alive or where we were. I thought of Keagan and Olly, knowing that they would return from the western town of Endeuri and not find us here. It pained me to leave them, but we had no choice. I hoped that when they returned, they would find out about The Flying Pig before going there. Hopefully, there would still be other places that were safe for them to hide. The Resistance of Fleuris was in their hands now.

# Chapter Twenty-Seven

## Olwen



The city felt different. I didn't know what it was, but I felt it the moment we passed through the grate and onto the other side of the wall. Something had happened, I knew it had, just like I had feared. Weylyn and I had argued for an entire afternoon — and almost an entire night — when he told me I was leaving. We had received news that the head of the town of Endeuri was turning Tóráin into slaves. He was forcing them to do unspeakable things and he needed to be stopped. Weylyn believed it was a good idea to send his best soldier to kill the bastard, but it was that reasoning that had me disliking his decision. I argued that his best soldier needed to be here, on the front lines of this battle. Cloque was without a doubt the heartbeat of Fleuris. The state of the city influenced every other place in the country. The worse Cloque got, the more difficult life became everywhere else.

Eventually, Weylyn won the argument — the stubborn prick — and he had even convinced me to take Keagan along too. It was weird having Keagan with me on that mission, seeing as killing isn't his favorite thing to do. He didn't play any other part in the assassination other than greeting me when the task was done. It was so damn easy, anyone else could have done it well enough. I had wanted nothing more than to get back here as quickly as possible, because I just knew that something bad would happen while I was gone. As Keagan and I were making our way through the streets, I was praying that I was wrong.

It wasn't long until I saw it. A pile of crispy rubble in the place of where The Flying Pig once stood. Someone had burned the place down, and there was a surprising number of soldiers in the area. Immediately I thought the worst. I think Keagan noticed my anxiety because he put a hand on my shoulder and gently squeezed. I grabbed his hand as I stared at the one place I thought was safe from General Rosspier's vile reach. Every possible scenario passed through my mind until I found it hard to breathe. I began shaking and a pain in my chest became sharp as if someone was stabbing me in the heart. Horrible thoughts of what could have caused quite possibly the safest place for the Tóráin to burn down had my legs weaken, and I nearly fell before Keagan caught me. He pulled me deeper into the shadows of the alley we were hiding in and rested me up against the wall. He held my arms to keep me steady and watched me closely until I nodded to let him know I was alright.

"I know this is hard, and there's nothin' I want more than to make those soldiers tell me where Weylyn and the others are, but we can't stay here."

I found myself smiling. "Since when are you the calm and collected one?"

"I've been watchin' you. Well, that and Genevieve has been givin' me this potion she says helps keep me calm. She's actually pretty nice. I usually avoided her because, well, she's a witch, but after gettin' to know her she isn't half bad."

"Watching me? I'm a mess. My recent episode here provides wonderful evidence of that." Keagan went to say something, but I put my hand up to stop him. "Let's see if we can find Genevieve and the others. Would hate for you to miss out on whatever she's giving you. I like a Keagan that doesn't rush into things headfirst like a lunatic."

"Where should we start?" Keagan asked as I began to lead us down the alley.

"We'll start at Genevieve's place then work our way north towards The Fancy Fox. Let's hope there's still a safe place somewhere in this damn city."

We lurked in the shadows of the city for hours, finding more dead bodies in the street than allies. Genevieve wasn't at home, and the few places that had previously been known to be safe havens for allies no longer were. Whether the building had been burned down sometime after Keagan and I had left, or the people who own the building were suddenly no longer supporting The Resistance, it damaged my morale heavily. Our final place to look was The Fancy Fox, a pub owned by a long-term ally of The Resistance. If anyone was going to help us, it would be Verill. By the time we reached the front door of the bar it was so late that it was undoubtedly a couple hours away from the dawn of a new day. Before I opened the door, I silently prayed for Verill to be okay. The Fancy Fox still standing was a good sign, and when we entered the pub and found Verill standing behind the bar, I felt a great sense of relief. Keagan and I still kept our heads low and our hoods up just to be safe as we made our way over to the bar.

"Can't decide whether to ask you about your night or wish you a good morning! Peculiar hour to be wandering in here, but don't you worry. We don't pry into people's business here at The Fancy Fox." Verill went from grinning ear to ear to a shocked expression when I revealed some of my face from under my hood.

"We know, Verill. That's why we're here." I gave him a small smile and he looked over at Keagan, who I imagine revealed some of his face too due to Verill's expression.

"In the back. Both of you." The old yet still well-built man ushered us to the back of the pub. "It's not safe for your kind. Hurry now before someone sees you."

There were four doors for four rooms at the back of the establishment. There were plenty more upstairs, but these were reserved for The Resistance. Verill knocked on one of the room's doors in a certain way and someone I recognized opened it.

"Finn?" I asked.

The lycan rubbed his eyes sleepily before realizing who had just spoken to him. "Olwen? Keagan! Please come in!"

He opened his door fully as Verill knocked on the large wooden barrier barring the entrance to the room next to Finn's. Keagan and I entered the small place Finn must be calling home lately and sat down at the small table. Verill poked his head in, announcing that he would bring some food and drink to us, before making way for Anya. She must have been in the other room, sleeping just like Finn, but her eyes were wide and her smile big when she came over and hugged me.

"Oh, thank all that is good in this world, you're alive," the young water sprite said as she squeezed me tighter than I wished her to.

I patted her back, the unexpected gesture making me feel uncomfortable. "Why wouldn't we be? What happened?"

Anya released me and her face was void of the smile it had just moments ago. She began to say something but stopped as she looked over at Finn. Eventually she gave up and went to sit on the bed. Someone knocked on the door in the same way Verill had earlier, causing Finn to go open it before saying anything either. Verill brought in a tray of dried meat and bread, as well as two jugs of beer with four cups. He placed it on the table and made sure to tell us to call on him if we needed anything else. The kind old man left the room and Finn began pouring everyone a drink. I was beginning to get irritated that no one was answering my question. Thankfully, Finn spoke once he had sat down on the bed next to Anya and took a drink from his cup.

"To be completely honest, we aren't entirely sure," he said.

"What the Hell does that mean?" Keagan asked before I could.

"It means that nobody knows anymore than what is apparent. Soldiers found out about The Flying Pig, and they burned it down. Lucien, Genevieve, Brina, Rosalie, and Weylyn are all missing. They were all at The Flying Pig, as usual. Many think they're all dead, their bodies being burned along with the pub. We have no way of knowing for sure, because there's so many damn soldiers guarding the place." Finn stopped talking to take another drink from his cup.

Anya took the pause as her chance to add her voice to the conversation. "It didn't take long for the news to spread across the city. Many allies refused to help us, claiming if Weylyn was dead, so was The Resistance. There are only a few places that we know who still support us. So far only Finn and I have shown up here. We don't know how much the soldiers know, but we're hoping that they only knew about The Flying Pig. I'm sorry. I know this is the last bit of news you want to hear."

The sprite looked ready to cry, causing Finn to put an arm around her. Keagan and I stood there in silence. I didn't know why he didn't say anything, but I was trying to find a way to tell myself that Weylyn wasn't dead. All the evidence pointed to him and the others no longer being among the living, but surely there was something we had missed. If we could prove at least Weylyn was alive, perhaps some of our support would return. I decided on what I needed to do, but I knew that nobody was going to like it.

"We don't know that they're dead," I said. "I'll sneak by the guards and search the rubble for them myself."

Keagan took my hand in his and shook his head. "No, O'. There's no need for that. We know what happened. No point in riskin' your life."

I pulled my hand away angrily. "You're that willing to just accept rumor as truth?"

Keagan sighed. "No, I'm not. Weylyn's alive. Probably the others too. I do think Lucien was the type to go down with the ship though, so to speak. Weylyn, Brina, Rosalie, probably Genevieve too. They all got out. At the very least, Weylyn escaped. You really think that General Rosspier wouldn't be paradin' his dead body around the city by now? They're guardin' that rubble to make sure nobody finds out the truth. Weylyn is alive, O'. We just need to figure out where he is."

Keagan did speak some truth. It wasn't like General Rosspier to miss out on a chance to show off his power. If he had indeed killed his rival, he would have shouted it to every corner of the country. The fact that Weylyn's disappearance was merely a rumor pointed to the chance that he was still alive. I shook my head, to remove any negative thoughts that challenged me as I chose to remain hopeful. I would keep hope alive and believe that Weylyn and the others escaped somehow. If they had indeed found a way to elude their deaths, Keagan was right; we needed to figure out where they would have gone. It didn't take long for me to decide on where I believed they went, seeing as it was where I would go if I were them.

"They went to Tudrose," I announced to the room. "Or at least they're going to try to go there."

"Tudrose?" Finn exclaimed. "Why would they go there?"

Keagan answered his question before I did. "Because it's the safest place for them right now. Especially if General Rosspier knows who Weylyn is."

I took a sip of beer before adding to what Keagan had said. "Exactly. As long as our alliance with Queen Sophia is still valid, Tudrose is indeed the safest place for them."

"What alliance?" Anya asked.

I was reminded that we hadn't included Anya and Finn in our small circle of people who possessed this important information. They would need to be informed now. It looked like our numbers had only gotten thinner over the last few days, and I needed people that I could trust now more than ever. Well, trust was a strong word, but I needed people I felt were loyal to The Resistance. Finn and Anya were newer members, but they were always willing to do anything asked of them. Despite their need for knowledge, it wasn't the top thing on our to do list.

I put my empty cup on the nearby table. "That can be talked about later. Right now, we need to figure out how many allies we have left in the city and where they are."

"After we all get some rest. We can start our search in the mornin'." Keagan gave me a look that told me he was specifically talking to me.

"Oh fine. Few hours of sleep and then we get to work. If Weylyn is going to Tudrose, perhaps he can convince that procrastinating queen of theirs to start the war effort she promised us. If that happens, we'll need to be ready." Finn and Anya both looked like they had more questions, but I quickly raised my hand to stop them. "In the morning. I promise we'll talk more in the morning."

Keagan and I left the room and asked Verill for one of our own. I hated to admit it, but I had trouble sleeping without someone there with me. Keagan had trouble sleeping too, so it made sense for both of us to stick together. Verill unlocked the door to an empty room and lit the lantern on the table. He bid Keagan and me a good sleep and left us. I kicked my boots off and tossed my cloak aside before quickly getting under the sheets of the bed. Keagan removed his cloak and used it as a blanket as he laid down on the floor next to the bed. He put his hand up on the mattress and I grabbed a hold of it, closing my eyes. I squeezed Keagan's hand just like I had been doing for months now as horrible scenes of violence and death filled my mind. I remained strong as I squeezed the lycan's hand tightly, until the images finally subsided and sleep took me.

# Chapter Twenty-Eight

## General Rosspier

Cloque, Fleuris | April 27, 1799

It was hard to not be annoyed by recent events. Not only had the bastard leading this silly and troublesome rebellion against me evaded capture, but The Dove had disappeared as well. The witch didn't always tell me where she was going, but vanishing during such a time was unacceptable. It was disrespectful and downright rude. I've always known that witch's struggle to be sophisticated, but never had I ever met one that was as barbaric as The Dove. She was almost as bad as those things that lessen the beauty of this great country. I only put up with her because of her battle prowess, plus it pays to have the best assassin and torturer on your side. Those Resistance bastards were always so damn silent, but she had finally cracked one of them. She should have told me when she found out about Weylyn. I would have sent a thousand soldiers to the damn place, and we would have the beast in a cage where he belongs. Instead, I was here without any new information on Weylyn's whereabouts, lacking the presence of my greatest asset.

"*En veux-tu?*" Jon asked as he poured himself some tea.

"No. Give me some of that drink from northern Tudrose. The strong one." I pointed over to the many different drinks I had available to me in my study.

Jon went over and grabbed the small, wide bottle with the amber liquid. It was harsh and tasted of oak, but it had just what I needed to ease my mind. I took out my pipe and filled it with Star Leaf wax as Jon poured some of the harsh liquid into a nearby glass for me. I took a few puffs from my pipe before taking a sip from my glass. I couldn't help but let my face twist up. The stuff was much stronger than wine and beer, and despite having had it many times before, I still was surprised by its intensity.

"Stressed out, are we?" Jon smirked as he took a sip of his tea.

"Don't mock me. You think it's easy to run a country while also keeping every other one around you in line? Tulp, Korblum, Stelpina, Malvene. Every single one of them complaining to me and claiming that my inability to remove The Resistance here in Fleuris allowed for the disease to spread to their countries. *C'est épuisant*. Always having to ease their childish minds and remind them that humans are the superior beings. One little act of defiance and they begin to crumble like dry bread. You know they're asking for me to fix it for them? *Comme des enfants qui demandent de l'aide à leur père*. They want our military sent to their countries to help get their lands under control. They ask for help, yet they do it while insulting me. Did I tell you how King Franz and King Ludovico have both accused my recent efforts to control the beastly population of those lesser beings to be the reason why their rebellions have caused so much trouble? *Bâtards ingrats*! I should have taken both of their countries and absorbed them into an empire of Fleuris."

Jon chuckled. "You would have, had you not realized how much trouble it would be for you to manage three countries worth of people. Remember what you said during the signing of the treaties?"

"I'd rather have friends who owe me a favor than subjects who owe me their loyalty." I laughed a bit too, recognizing the hypocrisy in that last statement of mine. "I could still just break the treaty, invade, and name a new king of my own liking."

Jon shook his head. "No war. We can't. At least not yet anyway."

I was surprised by this response. Major Jon Carierre never shied away from war. I had come to believe he even enjoyed it. "What do you mean we can't?"

"The people you imprison and chase out of our country make up a large amount of our labor force. They work the lumber mills, the fisheries, most of the farms, the mines, and the factories. With their choices to rather hide and run than work, our economy has slowed. Humans are having to pick up the slack and —"

"And they'll do a better job than those *Diables* ever did. Let them hide. Let them run. It took me a few years, but I finally realized what this country needed to reach its full potential. You know what that thing is, Jon?" I took a moment to take a puff from my pipe and a drink from my glass, the liquid causing my face to twist once again.

Jon thought of an answer for a while as he sipped on his tea. After a length of time that I felt was much longer than he should have needed, he responded. "I don't know, Max. What is this *magique* answer to all our problems?"

"Purity. A country full of humans and void of *ces Diables*. A country full of followers of Deus without any possible trace of heathens believing in false gods. Fleuris is on its way to being even better than it was before, and it's because the *vils demons* that came and tainted this land are on their way out."

Jon put his cup down on the table in front of him and sighed. "There's only so many times you can poke a sleeping bear with a stick until it wakes up."

My face twisted again, only this time it wasn't because of what I was drinking. "What the Hell is that supposed to mean?"

Jon looked at me with a serious expression on his face. "Be careful how much you push them. Any group of people can only take so much until they strike back. We've seen this throughout history. I can't see why they would be any different."

I downed the rest of the amber liquid in my glass in two gulps and stood up from my seat. "But they are different, Jon. The groups you talk about were humans. They had a strength in them that these things do not. They are weak, simple-minded, disposable, evil creatures brought here by *ces stupides sorcières* to ruin our world. The Grand Coven thought they could seize everything for their own with their army of beasts, but even they discovered just how useless they all are. I will push them as much as I wish, because there is nothing they can do to stop me from doing so."

Jon bowed his head, conceding to my will. I don't know where that nonsense had come from, but I was glad I had sent it away. Jon was my dearest ally, but even friends needed to be put in their place every now and then. This country was mine. This world would be mine if I chose to claim it. In the end, I decide who lives and who dies; a power the mighty Deus has gifted me. Together, we will cure this disease, with or without Jon. So long as Deus was by my side, I could do anything I wanted. No one could stop me.

# Chapter Twenty-Nine

# Weylyn

The Great Canal | April 28, 1799

We would be in Tudrose soon. Captain Kenley had informed us that we would reach the shore city of Conquest by noon, which would allow us to continue to put some distance between us and Cloque. We were probably safer in Tudrose than we would be anywhere else, but I was still worried. The Dove was dangerous, and I seemed to have piqued her interest during our fight. The fact that The Dove was most likely tracking us made me want to get to Draca as soon as possible. What brought me some peace was knowing that the only people that could currently harm us were on this ship, and everyone was kind as could be. They were all hardened sailors, with many of them having ancestors who fought during the naval battles roughly one hundred years ago. Despite their rough exteriors, many of them were compassionate people. There were only four other Tóráin on the ship besides Brina and me, and as far as I could tell they were treated wonderfully. They weren't favored in any way, but there were no signs of them being beaten or underfed. Captain Kenley had told us that his crew has been together for nearly seven years now, and they were quite the tight knit group.

It had been a pleasure sailing with them, despite the swaying of the ship as it battled the waves of The Great Canal. Oftentimes during conversations with some of them, I had forgotten why I was on this ship in the first place. They were excellent sailors, according to Captain Kinley, and they also turned out to be wonderful storytellers. They told us tales of how they came to be a member of The Crimson Wind's crew, battle stories from decades ago, and an interesting mention of a shark they once saw that was apparently the size of a whale. Many other interesting bits of history and knowledge that they had gathered throughout their lives filled our voyage with pleasant, peaceful moments. I almost had a thought to throw everything away and just become a crew member myself, but the sea didn't agree with me. As enjoyable as the company was, my stomach still rejected the constant rocking the waters caused. Unable to live a life full of carefree sailing, I chose to just admire the time I had available to me. Many stressful, risky, and dangerous moments awaited me in my future, so it was best to appreciate the peace I had now.

We would be due for a meal soon, Seger no doubt cooking up yet another delicious breakfast for us. I had woken up early and made my way above deck to watch the sunrise. It made me sick, but I was starting to wish I could travel by sea more often just for the view. I watched the sun peak out over the wet horizon and color the clouds pink and orange in silent solace. I was so lost in thought that when someone cleared their throat behind me, I jumped.

"Woah, sorry there mate. Lost gazing at the pretty lady waking up, were we?" Captain Kenley came and leaned forward on the railing that separated us from the water below. He wasn't wearing his black hat or his deep red coat. In fact, he wasn't wearing anything above his waist. All he had on was his pants and his boots, and he held a pipe in his hand that he enjoyed smoking quite often.

I leaned on the railing next to him. "It's quite a captivating scene. Can you blame me?"

Captain Kenley took in the smoke from the earthy Angel Root he loved so much and blew it out into the sea air. The half-naked sailor stroked his thick beard for a short time before letting out a deep sigh. "If my life was full of horrid images and fear, I would allow myself to be lost in a rare peaceful moment too. No, Weylyn. I don't blame you one bit."

When Brina, Rosalie, and I were in the Fleuris port town of Comaine looking for someone to take us to Tudrose, we didn't have much luck. Thankfully, we had run into a crew member of The Crimson Wind in a pub. Lynwood had overheard us trying to convince another captain to take us over and said his captain would be happy to have us aboard his ship. Of course, I didn't trust him at all, but we needed to get to Tudrose so we followed him back to The Crimson Wind to meet Captain Kenley. Much to my surprise, he was a Tudrose citizen who had been an ally of

The Resistance since our group formed. He hadn't worked with us directly, but he claimed to have supported our fight for many years, even before The Resistance. Lynwood had been honest back at the bar; Captain Kenley had accepted us aboard without even hearing why we were attempting to flee the country. After some discussions during our trip, I had come to realize the captain of The Crimson Wind exuded compassion and wanted a world of equality almost as much as I did. His care was genuine, and it had led me to respect him greatly.

"Thank you for taking my friends and I to Tudrose," I said. "You have no idea how much we appreciate it."

Captain Kenley nudged me with his left elbow. "Ah, Weylyn, how many times do I have to tell you that there's no need to thank me? You folks needed help, so I helped."

I turned around, resting my back on the railing instead of my chest. "Sorry. It's just we don't really get much help. Especially as of late. I'm just not used to it."

The captain of The Crimson Wind spat over the edge of the ship and shook his head. "Absolute shame that is. Anyone who is more used to harm than help has lived a hard life. I wouldn't wish it on anyone."

"Yeah, well, that's the life of a Tórán. Shame or not, it seems as though we're destined to be hunted until the end of time. It's hard not to only see a world where nothing will ever change, even if The Resistance is somehow successful. It could be hundreds of years in the future, say the year two thousand for the sake of my point, and still my kind will not fully be accepted. There will always be those who have hate in their heart, who have been taught by their parents and their parents before them that Tóráin are evil. That we're lesser because of how we look or where we came from. In times like this, it's hard to believe that we can change things." Unexpected tears welled up in my eyes and I blinked them away as quickly as I could. "Some days I wake up and wonder why I'm fighting so damn hard."

Captain Kenley cleared his throat before taking a puff of his pipe and turning around, resting his back on the railing like I was. "When you wake up and you ask yourself that question, I'm curious what your answer is."

I had to think about it. I had been doing it for so many years that it had become a subconscious response to just get ready and take on the day. After a short while, I eventually gave up. "I don't think I really say anything. I just ask the question, and then next thing I know I'm getting dressed and going about leading The Resistance."

Captain Kenley coughed out a plume of smoke and I realized that I had only told him that I was a member of The Resistance, not its leader. I had a pit in my stomach form as I became worried that he would change his mind and bring me back to Fleuris. There was no evidence to support my anxiety, but it was there, nonetheless. Once Captain Kenley gathered himself, he scratched his hairy chest and smirked at me.

"I knew you were special," he said. "From the moment I saw you in my cabin that day in Comaine. Leader of the fucking Resistance. To be honest, your outlook on life is a tad gloomy. Expected you to be radiating hope like the sun gives off light."

I scoffed. "I haven't felt real hope in years. I fight for the Tóráin because my father did. Every day I'm just trying to make him proud by giving my life to this cause. My dream is for the world to be a certain way, but my mind is more dominant than my heart. It tells me a truth that's hard to find any falsehood in. My most common belief is that things will never be the way I dream them to be. It's hard to combat the feeling that no matter how hard I fight, we'll fall short. I'll fall short."

Captain Kenley let out a long and exasperated breath before stepping away from the railing. He came to stand in front of me, before putting his free hand on my shoulder. "Let me tell you something my father used to tell me. There will be times in your life when you can't sail. When that happens, remember you can row. There will be times when you won't be able to row, so remember you can swim. There will be times when this world makes it so that you can't even do that. In those moments remember that any movement forward, no matter how you do it, can sway the fight in your favor. Every step forward you take, can bring you one step closer to your goal. Nobody knows when or how you'll reach it, but so long as you keep moving forward, you'll eventually get there. So it takes hundreds of years, it doesn't matter. What you are doing today is inspiring hundreds of thousands, now and in the future, to fight for the same ideals."

"That's incredibly kind and I'm thankful for your words." I avoided his intense eyes, looking down at the deck beneath our feet. "You just don't know what it's like —"

Captain Kenley took his hand off my shoulder, giving me a slight shove as he did. "To lead? I'm the captain of a ship, Weylyn. I used to command a naval squadron for Queen Sophia's father. I'm a leader too. Have been for a while. I know the pressure it brings. I also know that people look to us for inspiration, for strength, and for guidance. Give those you lead these things, and they will make this dream of yours come true. Trust me. What you're doing matters."

It was hard to believe just how old Captain Kenley was. To have served Queen Sophia's father King Henry, he must be at least fifty, maybe even sixty. His shoulder length hair was a dark gray and his body was still built like a young man in his twenties. His eyes had the shimmer of a child, and he had the heart of someone who had yet to experience loss or pain. His words had been wise ones, and they sounded like something my father would have said. I still had my doubts, but what Captain Kenley had said gave me some much-needed strength. I think he even gave me a bit of hope. Maybe he was right. Maybe what we were doing did matter. We didn't know, and we wouldn't know until we had completed our goal. Until then, I decided that I wouldn't allow myself to get caught up in the depressive, anxious episodes I had willingly accepted into my life. I would sail, row, swim, or Hell even slowly float my way forward. I felt the fire in me that had been lit the day my father was executed, and I was thankful for Captain Kenley showing me what it felt like again. I think with all that had happened over the last few months, that fire had been dampened by rains and harsh winds full of despair and fear.

I found myself lunging forward and embracing the old sailor. "Thank you, Captain Kenley. Truly. This lycan was in dire need of your words. You, and your father, are wise men."

Captain Kenley laughed and patted my back. "Oh, you're quite welcome, lad. I like to use the word experienced, by the way. Wise makes me sound old."

I chuckled as I freed him and took a step back. "And experienced doesn't?"

The captain of The Crimson Wind wagged a thick finger at me. "Don't get all smart with me. I may be grey, but I'll give you a proper beating if I need to."

I put my arms up in surrender as I caught Brina pop out from the hatch that led below deck. She waved a hand at us as she called out to us. "Breakfast is ready, you two. Better come get some before Flint and Callum eat it all."

"Come on." Captain Kenley motioned towards where Brina had shown herself with his pipe. "You can tell me why the Leader of The Resistance of Fleuris is on my ship sailing for Tudrose over some hot stew. And don't tell me you're evading capture. You can do that well and easy in your own country. Leaving means you've got a reason to, and this experienced sea captain is curious. I lifted your spirits, now you owe me."

I was going to say something smart, but I figured it was best to just comply with his wishes. He was an ally and I had grown to trust him. I knew he wouldn't tell anyone why we had chosen to flee to Tudrose. If anything, I think he would be quite happy to know. Instead of arguing, I chose to ask a question that I had been itching to ask since he mentioned it.

"Only if you tell me how a leader of a naval squadron ends up ferrying goods and runaway Tóráin across The Great Canal."

Captain Kenley laughed. "You drive a hard bargain, but I'll comply. Quite the story that is actually."

We made our way towards the hatch and descended into the depths of The Crimson Wind in search of food. I had awoken today to a great bout of anxiety that required the sight of a rising sun to give me any sense of relief, but after my conversation with Captain Kenley I felt lighter. Admitting what I had felt to someone was a massive weight lifted off my shoulders. I felt rejuvenated. I felt ready for whatever came next.

# Chapter Thirty

# Weylyn

Draca, Tudrose | April 29, 1799

I was nervous. I would be forever thankful to those who had aided The Resistance throughout our existence, but an alliance with Queen Sophia and Tudrose was monumental. Their army was considered one of — if not the — strongest in the known world. Many believed that it was only because of their rulers' compassion that they hadn't taken every country for themselves. They probably could have taken the far south nation of Motea, but they abandoned that war effort because Queen Sophia's grandfather King Thane didn't feel the blood being spilled on either side was worth it anymore. He looked to peace instead, even aiding the darker-skinned citizens of the southern country when Fleuris decided that they didn't care about how much blood was being spilled. King Thane, his children, and their children after have valued peace over war for a long time, but they always kept their army ready. Fleuris and Tulp formed an alliance against Tudrose years ago, but they were promptly defeated. Tudrose's strength was well-known and well-respected. Having them on our side was vital.

This meeting with Queen Sophia was one of the most important moments in Tóráin history. I truly believed that we needed to make our move as soon as possible before things got worse. We couldn't wait another month to see how things were. I needed to convince a peace seeking queen to wage war on over a third of Kosavros. Tens of thousands, possibly more, depended on me succeeding today and the stress of it all had me feeling like I was carrying a massive boulder on my shoulders. We had arrived in Draca last evening, and immediately made our way to The Palace of Paragons. After some trouble convincing the guards to let us in, we were finally met by one of Queen Sophia's advisors. Edith had met us last time we were here and thankfully remembered who we were. She regretfully informed us that we would have to wait until the morning to see Queen Sophia, so we were forced into two rooms for the night. The beds were just as comfortable as the last time, but I couldn't bring myself to sleep. The pressure I had placed on myself had caused me to twitch and fidget all night. My breath was quick and hard to come by; my chest and head still ached.

We had been woken up in the morning with a fresh plate of fruit, which Rosalie had happily dived into. My stomach was in a twist, but I convinced myself to have a pear and a few grapes. Brina joined us in our room and the three of us followed Edith to the throne room. I continuously went over ways I could try to convince Queen Sophia to finally take the plunge and send out her army, but everything that I thought of failed in my mind. Rosalie must have noticed my struggling, because she laced her fingers through mine and squeezed my hand until I looked at her. She mouthed the words 'it's okay' to me and I allowed myself to ease up a bit. I managed to successfully calm myself down instead of making myself worse the rest of the way, until we reached the doors to the throne room. Right away panic set in again and it felt like my stomach was in my chest. I tried to take some deep breaths as Edith snuck inside the doors, leaving the three of us in the large hallway. Brina put a hand on my shoulder and Rosalie hugged my arm before getting up on the tips of her toes and planting a kiss on my cheek.

"We already know she's on our side, Weylyn," Rosalie said as she squeezed my arm tightly.

"All we can do is tell her our situation and make the best pitch possible. We'll deal with what she says after she says it." Brina patted my shoulder before putting both hands on her hips.

I managed again to release some of the tension that had built up inside me just in time for the doors to open. A guard on either side pulled the large slabs of wood outward, giving our trio a clear path to Queen Sophia. She sat on her throne, wearing yet another red dress, and two people stood to her left. Guards in metal armor stood along the carpet that led to the throne like statues, none of them moving a single muscle as we passed by them. When we got close enough, I looked to Edith and she smiled, which for some reason encouraged me to feel a small sense of calm. The human next to her was a sour looking man with a thick mustache and short, grey hair which only graced the sides of his balding head. He stared us down and I began to feel anxious again. Thankfully, the torturing silence ended when Queen Sophia smiled and raised her hand, wiggling her fingers as she did.

"Hello my unexpected guests," she said. "It's a pleasant surprise to see you here again."

"What do you want?" The old man grumbled through his facial hair.

"General Wyman, I told you that you could be a part of this meeting so long as you were polite. You are not off to a good start." Queen Sophia took her attention off the grumpy soldier and directed a smile at us. "My dear friends, what brings you here on such short notice?"

I didn't know how to begin. I started to feel lightheaded, but two things centered me. Brina put her hand on my shoulder again, and Rosalie gripped my hand. I felt their support, and with that, the support of every Tórán out there who needed our help. I cleared my throat and took a breath before answering Queen Sophia's question.

"The Fleuris leadership has discovered me as The Resistance's leader," I announced. "We were attacked by The Dove and forced to flee Cloque. We were hoping to find a safe place here in Tudrose, and to perhaps discuss the progress on our eventual war effort."

"Our?" General Wyman scoffed. "What contributions do you think you've made to be able to call a possible war effort on Tudrose's behalf yours as well?"

Queen Sophia sighed. "Despite General Wyman's complete lack of manners, he touches on a subject which I am forced to bring up. I do not yet believe that these rebellions you have started are strong enough to really help Tudrose avoid casualties. When it comes to your safety, I am more than happy to set up more permanent accommodations for you and your friends."

I heard Brina mumble something under her breath, but I couldn't make out what she said. No doubt she was upset at what Queen Sophia had just expressed, and she wasn't alone.

I squeezed Rosalie's hand to gain some courage before responding. "With all due respect, we didn't intend to stay in Tudrose for too long. Our hope was to be moving south with you and your army to begin fighting a battle that is long overdue. Before —"

General Wyman groaned. "Do wolves have bad hearing? The Queen already told you —"

"General Wyman!" Queen Sophia's raised voice had everyone in the room slightly cower. "I believe you have said quite enough. Leave us!"

The man looked prepared to say something, but he stopped himself. He turned to face Queen Sophia, bowed, and left through the big doors we had entered from. Queen Sophia stood up out of her throne and Edith took a step back before bowing slightly. The Queen of Tudrose walked over to me, stopping about five feet away. She sighed deeply before smiling at us. "I am terribly sorry. General Wyman is not as well-mannered as I would like him to be. You were telling me about your hope to be moving south?"

There was something about her being so close that made me begin to sweat. I told myself that I was being given a chance here to convince her to change her mind, and I couldn't blow it. "Before we were attacked and forced to flee, we had received news from the other rebellions. All of them have continued to grow their numbers. They're efforts continue to weaken their respective nations, stealing guns, ammunition, and food among other things. This is all good news, as I'm sure you'll agree, but it isn't the main reason why we feel the time to attack is now. Fleuris continues to murder and torture Tóráin, and I fear things will only get worse. Because of what Fleuris is doing, other countries are getting bolder. The rebellions are finding it more difficult to maintain a foothold in their respective nations, and I fear that if we wait, our best time to attack will have passed us by. If Tulp, Malvene, Korblum, and Stelpina all decide to adopt General Rosspier's ways of treating our kind, The Resistance's influence will lessen. If it lessens, you won't help. If you won't help, I firmly believe that the Tóráin will cease to exist in these countries. Please, don't let these tyrants win. Don't let my kind suffer even more than we have for centuries now. We deserve a better life than we've been given, I know you believe that too. I beg you, as one leader to another, help me save my people."

Queen Sophia put her hands on her hips and bit her lip. She turned around and went over to Edith. The two began whispering to each other, no doubt discussing what I had just asked of them. After some time, Queen Sophia came back over to Brina, Rosalie, and me. She smiled, which I didn't know was a good sign or not. My stomach was in my chest once more and I could feel the air leaving my body. After what felt like an eternity, Queen Sophia gave her answer.

"Your plight is a good one, Weylyn," the Queen of Tudrose exclaimed. "I can feel the passion in your words. You deeply care about the people you are responsible for, and I respect that a great deal. I too care very much for my people, and that is why I am so hesitant to lead them into war. Some might call it selfish, to value your country's people over others, but I see it as loyalty. They look to me for protection, and as their leader it is my job to give it to them. In saying that, I am reminded of the protection you are required to give your people as well. Seeing as you cannot keep them safe alone, I have decided to help you. The Tóráin of Tudrose would never forgive me if I stood by and watched their kind suffer. I'll have that ill-mannered grouch General Wyman ready the army. In a few days or so, we'll begin our mission to save your kind from those who would seek to harm them."

I couldn't believe what I had just heard. It stunned me, leaving me frozen in place. I tried to form a response, but words had become foreign to me. Queen Sophia adopted a look that told me she had expected a response much sooner than I was giving one and I panicked, worried that she might rescind her offer.

"Thank you!" I almost shouted. "Your kindness will not be forgotten."

Suddenly, a woman in a blue cloak burst into the room through the small door to the right of the throne. She wore a boneless, black leather corset over a white shirt along with a deep blue skirt. She stormed in, making her way towards everyone. "Sorry I'm late! Slept in. Won't happen again, my Queen. What have I missed? Anything —"

The woman stopped abruptly. She clutched at her many necklaces with a hand covered in rings as she slowly stepped towards us. Queen Sophia moved aside, and the new woman stood directly in front of me. Her pale face had small wrinkles near her eyes, but besides that she looked like she was in her mid twenties. A small strand of her dark brown hair had escaped the bun she had it in and was invading the left side of her face. The woman's eyes were as blue as the sea, staring at me for quite some time until she finally spoke.

"You have Mystic Blood," she said.

That was the last thing I had expected. Brina and Rosalie vocalized their confusion next to me as I tried to find the right words to respond with. As everyone tried to grasp what the woman had just said, Queen Sophia stepped forward and put a hand on the woman's shoulder. "My friends, this is Lady Mirlena. Apparently, she is just as good at introducing herself as she is arriving to a meeting on time."

Lady Mirlena took a step back, but she kept her eyes fixed on me. She extended her hand in my direction after blinking rapidly and shaking her head. "Sorry. As my lovely, forgiving Queen has just stated, I am Lady Mirlena. I serve as Queen Sophia's advisor from time to time. You must be Weylyn. We didn't get to meet last time you were here."

I cautiously grabbed her hand and was surprised to discover the woman had a very firm grip. "Pleasure to meet you. Now, about what you said just now —"

"You didn't know?" she shouted in surprise.

I had wished for this knowledge to remain secret, but it was apparent that Rosalie and Brina knowing was unavoidable now. "I knew. Only for a few months now, but I knew. How do you know?"

"I'm a witch. I know things." She smiled, turning around and making her way over to Edith. She wrapped an arm around the woman, who seemed uncomfortable in the witch's embrace. "Why don't we have something to eat while we chat? I'm starving."

I caught Queen Sophia roll her eyes before shooting us a smile of her own. "Yes, well it does seem we have something to celebrate. We can eat and drink with the hopes that the coming days are full of victory and void of loss."

"Great! So you finally agreed to fight then! I'll have a drink or two to that!" Lady Mirlena kept her arm around Edith as she guided the woman towards the small door she had entered from.

Queen Sophia insisted we join her, and the four of us followed the other two. I could feel Brina and Rosalie itching to ask me about what had been revealed. Worry filled me that they might be angry with me for not telling them, but then I realized that they may not even know what Mystic Blood is. I focused on the fact that we had been successful in convincing Queen Sophia to march south. The news helped me relax, and a bit of hope seeped into my heart. We were moving forward, and I was happy to do so.

# Chapter Thirty-One

# The Dove



The whimpering was pathetic. I rarely interrogated humans, but the two I had taken on in the last week or so were changing my view on things. For years I had been told how much stronger humans are than those hounds and faeries and other useless things. So far, from what I had seen, humans were weaker. Always begging for their lives and promising to say nothing if I let them go. It was sickening. Not to mention annoying. I had gagged this one and he still made more squeals than a pig being flayed alive. I guess I did have to admit that they could take a fair bit of punishment, despite their desperate cries for me to stop. I had asked people in a more civil manner if they had come across a group of two lycans and a human woman; I had been sent here. Claims were made that this man had come into contact with Weylyn and his friends. He would tell me what he knew before the end. He would break eventually, and then I would have what I needed.

It was still a surreal feeling to have finally found another creature with Mystic Blood. They were so hard to find, and I was beginning to wonder if there weren't any more left. Discovering that Weylyn had Mystic Blood had given me new life, and I needed to find him as soon as possible. I would have been on him sooner if that bitch back at the pub hadn't gotten in my way. Almost every single witch out there was just as problematic as the creatures they brought here all those years ago.

Despite that woman's interference, I still managed to pick up their trail the following afternoon. I hated having to wait, but I needed to recover the strength I had lost from my engagement with that foul witch friend of theirs. Mystic Bloods were strong. I didn't need to take any risks, and I knew that I could eventually catch up to them thanks to some tracking spells I placed on his blood.

Those spells had led me north to the city of Comaine where I discovered a group resembling the one I was tracking had left for Tudrose. I hadn't been in this country in months, and before that it had been many years. Being back here was unnerving. I wanted to be out of this country as quickly as possible, and this man was holding me up. I had him blindfolded so he didn't know where he was, and a piece of cloth was jammed into his mouth. He was stripped of his clothes, and he had small cuts all over his body thanks to my knife. His wrists were tied together, the rope that bound them hanging on a hook that hung from the ceiling of the barn. From what I could guess, he had sold Weylyn and his friends some horses. The man was a farmer just on the outskirts of town, and for some reason he had been incredibly reluctant to tell me where Weylyn and the others had gone. I brought my knife to his fingers, planning to begin removing his nails next, when a voice filled the smelly animal home.

"Uncle Milton, what's going on?" A little beast with green skin and tiny horns on her head stood in the entryway to the barn with a shocked look on her dirty face.

The man struggled at the sound of her voice and screamed into the cloth gag. The young thing tried to run, but I quickly stretched out my hand and made the door close. I held it shut as I walked over to her, the silly thing continuing to push on the exit until she resorted to calling for help. I was quick, placing my hand over her mouth and setting the tip of my knife to her throat.

"You scream one more time and he dies. Then, I'll kill you just for the fun of it. Understand?" The girl let out a muffled declaration of agreement and I took my hand away before using it to guide her back to where her uncle was tied up.

How he was her uncle, I didn't know, seeing that she was clearly a faerie and he was a human. Had something changed? Could humans and that filth actually create offspring now? It didn't matter. The important thing was that I had just got my hands on what would give me the information I needed. Maybe he didn't care what I did to him, but I imagine he cared what I did to her. I took his blindfold off to let him see the knife I had at her throat and removed his gag.

"Oh, Fia," the man said through a sigh. "Stay calm, okay? Everything is going to be alright."

I moved my blade so it pressed up against her skin, and by his reaction I must have drawn some blood. "Answer my questions and I'll let her live."

"Alright! Alright, I'll tell you. I gave two horses to the group you described, but I don't know where they were headed. I promise, that's all I know!"

I groaned, realizing that I had to show him I was serious about my threat to end the faerie's life. I went to put my knife to her eye when the girl's voice stopped me.

"North! They're headed north! I heard them talking while Uncle prepared their horses. They make for Draca, the capital. Please, that's all we know, just let us —" I cut her throat, not wishing to hear her speak any longer.

The human struggled to get to me as his pet bled out before his eyes. I couldn't help but smile, his adoration for the evil little thing was something I found amusing. He quickly gave up, resorting to weeping like a child instead. I had debated on leaving him like that, forced to watch the faerie's dead body for who knows how long. It would serve him right for delaying me so much. However, I didn't want him telling anyone about our little chat, so my knife found his neck too. I cleaned my blade on the dead child's dress and sheathed it on my belt. I went over to one of the stalls and grabbed the reins of one of the horses. Jumping onto it's back without attaching a saddle, I kicked into its sides and made my way for the road leading north. I was perhaps a day behind, maybe less, but I still had them. That Mystic Blood would be mine, no matter who — or what — got in my way.

# Chapter Thirty-Two

## Olwen

Cloque, Fleuris | April 30, 1799

We were waiting for a few hours now, which had me worried. The information we had received was from a credible source, but the group of soldiers and prisoners we were waiting for were late. Keagan had wanted to just abandon the mission not too long ago, but I wanted to wait just a bit longer. I would hate to have left and missed an opportunity to save lives. Losing Weylyn hit The Resistance hard, but there was still a fair amount of us left still willing to fight our oppressors. We wouldn't know for some time if he and the others really went to Tudrose, but it was what we were sticking with. While he was away, the burden of leadership fell to me, and I decided that we wouldn't cower in small rooms the rest of our lives. Tóráin were being brought to Cloque as prisoners for months now, but it had reportedly picked up as of late. There were more of our kind being sent to Bastion every day, crowding cells and giving General Rosspier's torturers more than enough subjects to work on. They claimed that we and our allies were being tortured to gain information on The Resistance, but we knew that the majority of the time it was done simply because they found it enjoyable.

After re-establishing contact with fellow members throughout Cloque, more knowledge of the happenings of the city became known to us. One of those things came from a soldier at Bastion who claimed that they were expecting a good number of prisoners coming from the south today. It was risky to show ourselves so soon after the attack on Weylyn at The Flying Pig, but I couldn't allow roughly three dozen Tóráin to be taken to Bastion. We were capable of stopping them from reaching the city, so I quickly hatched a plan to ambush the soldiers who guarded them. Keagan, Finn, and ten others had joined me on this rescue mission, and I was hoping that would be enough. According to our informant, there were roughly fifteen or so soldiers guarding the prisoner. A witch also travelled with them, which made things a little more difficult, but not impossible. The Tóráin would be chained, so they wouldn't be much help to us. It was our eleven against their probable sixteen. A risky endeavor, but I had won battles with worse odds before. I was just thankful Keagan had decided to come.

This time last year, I would have wanted Keagan as far away from this mission as possible. However, in the last few months I had seen him change. He controlled his anger better, he thought more clearly, and he was having better sleep than I was. I don't know what happened, but I was thankful for whatever it was. Keagan had always possessed skills that were useful for missions like this, but his impulsivity and aggression would get the best of him. Not to mention it was rare for you to find him sober. I had asked him what caused the change, but he just said how he 'wanted to be better'. I didn't push him on the subject, knowing much better than to press my luck with his newfound peace. He still got angry and impatient, but his emotions didn't rule him anymore. It was odd to see this side of him, but I had to admit I enjoyed it much more than the side he had shown everyone for years now. The truth of the matter was that I felt safer with Keagan around. I trusted him to not just watch my back, but to also watch over everyone else. His fighting skills in both his forms were strong, and with a mind void of beer fog, he was quite formidable.

Still, his dislike for killing had inched its way into his mind before this mission. He had suggested we jump the guards and knock them out. In his opinion, the soldiers and the witch guarding the prisoners didn't need to die. For the prisoners to escape, their guards just needed to be asleep long enough. We had argued over what quantified as a necessary kill, to the point where Keagan had decided he wasn't going to come. He had felt this way before, even when he was drunk as can be he avoided significantly harming anyone. He got into his fistfights here and there, but he never took it too far. His accidental kill had haunted his dreams for days. Now, with less beer in his belly and a mind that takes more time to think, his mind for avoiding killing was even stronger. However, despite all of this, when I got ready for today Keagan was right there with me.

"What changed your mind?" I had asked.

The lycan grumbled in response, saying nothing before leading us out the back door of The Fancy Fox. He still hadn't answered me hours later and, with all the time on our hands, I had been wondering about what it was.

"So, you going to tell me why you came here today, or are you taking that to your grave?" I gave a quick look over at Keagan to see his reaction to my question and I caught him rolling his eyes.

"Why does it matter?" he asked. "I'm here, aren't I?"

"Oh, come on. We could die today, and I'd never know what changed Keagan The Gentle's mind." He gave me a look that told me he was annoyed, but I nudged him with my elbow to let him know I was only joking around.

Keagan looked away towards the road we were watching before groaning loudly. "Fine. All night I had nightmares of you and the others dyin'. I had to carry each of your bodies back to the city and bury you all by myself. I decided when I woke up that I was tired of losin' people. I came here to make sure as many of us make it out of this alive as possible. There. Happy?"

I couldn't tell if he was annoyed by my pestering or because of how long we had been waiting for this group to come down the road. Regardless, I needed to reassure him that it was safe for him to admit things like that. "Yes, I am quite happy. You know you can tell me stuff like that right? There was no need to hide this from me, Keagan The Protector."

I nudged him again and I caught a smirk sneak onto his face. "Yeah, yeah, Olwen The Annoyin'. How much longer are we goin' to wait here? Doesn't look like they're comin' this way, O'."

It was possible that they had taken a different road, but it wouldn't have made sense for them to. This road was the most direct way to Cloque's southern gate. They were coming this way; I knew they were. "Just give it time, before you know it, we'll be back at The Fancy Fox having a drink to celebrate our —"

A bird call made me silent. Someone was coming. All five of my companions looked at me once the sound reached us, looking for directions. I'm sure the others were doing the same to Finn on the other side of the road. Sure enough, a procession of soldiers and prisoners came over the hill and began walking between us. They were all on foot, save for a soldier at the front and the witch in the back. They were mounted on horses, the witch watching over the prisoners to make sure they all stayed under control. Keagan and I were responsible for the witch, with everyone else set to take on the soldiers. I let out a similar bird call, and the five of us fired our stolen rifles at the soldiers guarding the prisoners. One of the shots took down the mounted soldier, preventing him from riding to get help. The others met their marks too, bringing their total from what appeared to be eighteen to thirteen. With the odds evened a little bit, all eleven of us charged out with swords, knives, or claws.

The witch was caught by surprise at first, but she gathered herself quickly. She held out her hands, the purple glowing magic from them slowing our attackers. The soldiers managed to ready their rifles to shoot, and I was already seeing graves I would have to dig because Keagan and I hadn't gotten to her fast enough. I had to focus on the witch, despite my wish to help our friends. The guns fired, and I winced as I continued on my path to the witch. I spotted a strained look on her face as she struggled to make sure the prisoners were incapacitated. On top of slowing her attackers, the witch was strong enough to slow all the prisoners as well. The only thing we had going for us was that the witch couldn't hold everyone for long. I went to throw a knife at her, but she raised her left hand, and my knife went flying past her. Recognizing her own life was in danger, she abandoned her efforts with the others. The prisoners began to cheer as our friends took on the soldiers. Keagan leapt at the witch, his jaws wide open and his claws outstretched, but she swatted him away before he reached her. Still, Keagan crashed into her horse, knocking the animal and its rider over.

I charged forward to catch her while she was down, jumping over Keagan and the horse to reach her. Before I could land on my target with a new knife, she sent me over her head, forcing me to roll on the hard road. I gathered myself quickly and charged at her again. This time she held out both hands and, even with my charm, the witch held me in place. She stretched my arms and legs out to the side and pain filled my joints.

"You filthy rabble! You'll pay for interfering in our —" She immediately screamed as Keagan sank his teeth into her neck.

The red-haired lycan held her with his massive hands and pulled, tearing out half of her neck with his jaws. Blood erupted from the witch's neck, and she fell to the ground in a heap. More cheers came from the prisoners as I realized that we had been successful. From what I could see, five of us had died; two sprites, two lycans, and a satyr lay dead. It was upsetting that we couldn't all be victorious together, but they knew what they were getting themselves into. They'd be glad to have given their lives so that others would be set free. Keagan came over to me to make sure I was alright, and he assisted me in putting both my shoulders back in place. It was painful, but I kept quiet. I didn't need Keagan hovering over me all day checking to see if I was alright. We made our way over to the prisoners who were being released by a key Finn must have taken off one of the guards.

"Who leads you? I must speak with whoever leads you!" A female harpy shouted into the crowd.

"You can speak to me, friend. What's wrong?" I put a hand on her arm as Finn removed her shackles in an attempt to calm her.

"It's Valarc. The town south of here? Something's happening in that place. Something dark. Baron Laurent mysteriously died a week or so ago, and his son Jean took his place. Ever since, he's increased the military presence in the town and searched harder for Tóráin. Before, we were relatively fine — given the times — but Jean is not like his father. It seems he wants every Tórán taken away. But they aren't just arresting everyone. They're taking their blood too, before sending them all to Cloque. Anyone who tries to escape the town is either captured or killed. You need to put an end to it. Please!"

We had heard of blood being collected by soldiers here and there, but never had it encompassed an entire town. Something was indeed going on there, and I believed it started and ended with Jean. If I could get rid of him, I imagine this craziness would end, or at the very least stop long enough for people to flee. It was a quick decision to make, but those people needed help.

"I'll go there myself and stop whatever is going on. I promise you. Now go, all of you. Head to the borders and try your best to leave the country. There are smugglers in the cities and towns, you just need to find them. Hurry now!"

The harpy grabbed my hand and kissed it before making her way into the trees with the others. They would have a hard time trying to escape Fleuris, but there were avenues to take that could lead you away from what was happening here. As the prisoners ran away, we began hiding the soldier's bodies in the forest that bordered the road. Keagan watched the others carry the corpses away before he put a hand on my shoulder.

"So, when are we leavin'?" he asked.

I shook my head, gently taking his hand off me. "No we. I'm going alone. It'll be faster that way. Besides I need someone I can trust in Cloque to watch over things while I'm gone. I'll be back before you even realize I'm not around."

It was Keagan's turn to shake his head, his beard and neck covered in the witch's blood. "No way, O'. I don't like that plan one bit. You need someone to watch your back."

"What I need is for you to say, 'okay Olwen, whatever you say' and let me do what I need to do." I took one of his big hands and wrapped both of mine around them. "I promise you I'll be careful. If at any moment I think what's going on in

Valarc is too dangerous for me to handle alone, I'll leave and get help. Just don't let the city burn down while I'm away, you hear?"

Keagan twisted his face in disagreement and growled under his breath, but he eventually nodded. "Fine. You keep your word damn it. If it's too much you come back here, and we'll deal with it together."

"Deal." I squeezed the hand I held tightly and smiled at Keagan, hoping that my grin would ease his worrying.

I didn't know what awaited me in the small town of Valarc, but I knew I could handle it alone. I'd be back in a couple days, and everything would be fine.

# Chapter Thirty-Three

# The Dove

Draca, Tudrose | May 1, 1799

I did my best to blend in, knowing full well if I was noticed things would become very troublesome for me. I was a known member of the Fleuris Regime, plus I had killed a few people here over the years. I had to abandon my mask, something I hated to do, and I exchanged my white cloak for a black one that I had stolen from a guard I took out when entering the city. I could have just worn some different clothes, perhaps hid my armor in a room at an inn, but I refused to part with it. My mother had given it to me before I left home, and I would not risk losing it. I used the dark cloak to keep my attire hidden as I began asking around the southern end of Draca for those who I hunted. I learned to hate my luck when a soldier said he had ordered a group similar to the description I had given to not race about the city on their horses.

"I asked them where they were off to in such a rush, but they refused to tell me at first," the soldier had said. "When I threatened to make an arrest, they admitted they had business with the Queen. Don't believe that for a second, but if by chance they were telling the truth and I had delayed them, I would have gotten an earful from Queen Sophia."

"How long ago?" I had asked.

"Not too long," the man said. "Maybe a day? No more than two."

If they were off to see the Queen of Tudrose, they had no doubt made for The Palace of Paragons. The place was where Queen Sophia called home and was probably the most secure place in the entire country. I expected a large military presence when I went to scope out the place, but it was even busier than I had predicted. Something was going on, and I just knew it had to do with Weylyn being here. He and his friends must have come here looking for protection, hence the increased number of soldiers on the grounds. Possibilities of what had gone on since Weylyn had arrived here flooded my mind as I stepped aside for a group of four soldiers to go by.

I hid behind a tree, one of the many that inhabited the royal grounds. It wasn't the dead of night — the sun was still setting — so I had to be careful how I found my way through the guards. Of course, it would have been easier to wait until darkness could keep me hidden, but I still didn't know where Weylyn was or if he was even still here. I needed to survey the place when people were still awake and hope to discover my target's whereabouts. I waited for the soldiers I had avoided to leave before peeking my head out. The way was clear for me to move closer to the building, so I took my opening and sprinted over to some bushes. I was the closest I had ever been to the royal building, but I was still too far to know anything of value. I stayed in the thick brush for a short while to make sure nobody had seen me run over before peering through the nearest bush. A group of six guards were marching my way, so I had to retreat fully into my hiding spot.

"I still can't believe we're actually doing this. You know she has every meal with him? His manners are probably horrible."

"Maybe she just tosses his food on the floor and he licks it up like a stray dog."

The soldiers all laughed as they passed by me. They must have been talking about Weylyn. It was good to know that he was indeed still here. The only thing left to discover is where I could find him. I broke out from the bushes and made for a tree closer to the building. I quickly climbed up into the thicket of the branches and leaves to ensure I was hidden well. Watching the guards patrol the entrance had me thinking of how I was going to get inside. After some time spent amongst the branches and leaves, I decided on a plan. It would be risky, but I figured it was my best bet; plus, I didn't want to stay in a tree all evening. I dropped out of my hiding place and quickly made my way over to the two guards watching the entrance to the palace.

"Hey! What are you doing out here?" One of the soldiers shouted at me as I approached.

"I've been searching everywhere for a man named Weylyn. I was ordered to give him a letter. A soldier told me he was in these fields, but I couldn't find him. Do you know where he is?" I kept my cloak tight and prayed that they wouldn't ask to see the letter.

"Hand us the letter and we'll see that the man gets it. Weylyn, was it?"

Before I could respond the other soldier inserted himself into the conversation. "Hold up. Ain't Weylyn that dog that came here a couple days ago?"

The soldier who had shouted at me before had his eyes light up as he realized his friend was right. "That he is! What business do you have with a hound from Fleuris? You a spy or something? Is he a spy?"

I shook my head. "No, no, no! Neither of us are spies. My friends, I have come a long way to deliver this letter, and I was told to make sure I only give it to Weylyn. Please, I am tired and aching for a beer. Do you know where I can find him or not?"

The two guards looked at each other until the one on the right shrugged his shoulders. The one on the left of the entrance pointed to his right. "Saw a tall, wild looking fellow walking with Lady Mirlena not too long ago. They were making their way towards the courtyard. Might find them there."

I smiled before bowing my head multiple times. "Oh, thank you kind sirs! Thank you! Have a pleasant evening!"

I quickly turned away and made my way to the courtyard. I wanted to sneak past the oncoming group of guards ahead of me, but I was worried that the ones I had spoken to were watching me. I just put my head down and kept at a reasonable pace until I passed them by. Nobody said a word to me. I guess they assumed that someone this close to the royal home of their Queen must belong here. Fools. I didn't care though, seeing as it benefited me; I approached what looked to be the courtyard unchallenged. The sun was nearly gone now, and some soldiers were beginning to light lanterns and torches. If it was just Weylyn and a weak noble woman, I could possibly take what I needed right now. I had the element of surprise and I could easily get the jump on the mutt before he even knew what was happening. I grinned as I thought of finally getting my hands on what I had been searching so long for. After passing another group of unsuspecting soldiers, I found myself in the courtyard. I could hear people talking, and slowly made my way towards the voices. I couldn't help but curse when I found who they belonged to.

There was just enough light given off by the lantern they had with them for me to see that one of them was indeed Weylyn. I would have been ecstatic if it weren't for the woman he was with. I didn't know her by name, but I knew her face. I had encountered this person before, many years ago. She had stopped me from getting what was mine back then, and now she was standing in the way again. This Lady Mirlena was a witch, and an incredibly powerful one at that. Our battle had occurred over a decade ago, so I could only imagine what new things she had learned. The bitch had nearly killed me when we fought, and I remember wishing that I never had to face her again. Some would go after her, wishing to get revenge or something like that. Not me. I was smart. I was taught that there was always someone out there stronger than you, and that you needed to respect that. Trying to attack Weylyn now would be incredibly dangerous, and with all the soldiers around too, it was best I stayed away. So instead of attacking, I listened. Most of it was just trivial things, but eventually something was said that caught my attention.

"Are you nervous about our trip to Tulp?" Lady Mirlena asked.

"A little bit," Weylyn said. "I don't have much experience in war, but I am capable. I've had enough fights in my life to know what to do in one. The size of it all is what I think worries me the most. So much can happen, you know? Will you be coming with us?"

It was interesting to find out that Weylyn had apparently avoided the conscriptions over the years. It was possibly something I could take advantage of. The talk of war and Tulp now made the increase in military presence around here make sense.

"Yes!" Lady Mirlena's strong voice carried well. "I'll be with the Queen during the battles to keep her safe. I've had my fair share of violent encounters too, believe it or not, but I have yet to experience a true battlefield as well. It will be a new experience for the both of us."

"Well," Weylyn started, "if all goes according to plan, it stands to say that we'll be gathering quite the amount of experience over this campaign. I hope we have enough energy to take on everyone."

Very interesting. Both of them were inexperienced in the large battles that make war what it is, and they would possibly be separated during fights. It appeared as though Tulp wasn't the only country on Tudrose's list, and I wondered then if the rebellions in Fleuris' neighboring countries had opened the door to a war campaign by Tudrose. It took a lot to get Tudrose to fight, at least that's what history says. For them to wage a campaign as ambitious as this one, there must be something big at play. Tudrose was friendly with the evil creatures that had come to this world, so it was possible they were doing this to help them, but it had to be more than that. Queen Sophia's motives would be something I thought of later. For now, I knew that Weylyn would be coming right back to Fleuris. I could just go and wait for him to arrive, then take him for my own during a battle when he was vulnerable and alone. Lady Mirlena would be distracted protecting the Queen, so no risk there. Even if the woman did manage to stay by Weylyn, I would probably have Ravenna with me. With that witch's strength on my side, I would defeat her. It was risky to let Weylyn fight all these other battles before reaching Fleuris, but my alliance with General Rosspier had burned any bridges I might have held with the other countries' leaders. I wouldn't be able to join the fight without having both sides after me. In Fleuris, I had my best chance at getting what I needed from Weylyn.

I waited for the two of them to abandon their seats and leave for the palace. The sun was completely gone now, so I had the cover of darkness to help me escape the royal grounds without ducking into bushes and climbing trees. It felt horrible leaving something I had worked so long and hard for behind, but I convinced myself that this plan of mine was the best course of action. It was too risky to go after Weylyn while he was under Lady Mirlena's protection, and I needed to wait until I could take as many advantages as possible. Besides, with all the death that inevitably comes with war, I'll be able to cast the spell right after I take what I need from that disgusting hound. His Mystic Blood would be mine soon enough. I'm sure of it.

# Chapter Thirty-Four

## Rosalie

Draca, Tudrose | May 3, 1799

Weylyn was off meeting with Queen Sophia and General Wyman to discuss army stuff, so I had decided to spend some time in the courtyard. Edith had been kind enough to show me to the library within the building, allowing me to choose a book or two to read. I was reading one of the novels I had chosen now, enjoying the warm spring air. It was quite an intriguing read. From what I had read so far, the story focused on an orphan girl named Emily, who is separated from the man she loves. She's then confined within an old castle belonging to her aunt's husband. It was a good, romantic thrill; just the type of book I enjoyed. Mind you, I tended to enjoy most books, but the fact that this one was written by a woman just made me like it even more. Men tended to dominate everything, so it was always a pleasure to appreciate and support a woman's hard work.

I was just getting to an intense part when I heard someone clear their throat behind me. That person turned out to be Brina. The lycan came and laid down next to me on the warm grass, shooting me a smile as she got comfortable. She didn't say anything. She just looked up at the sky and watched the few clouds fly by in silence. I gave her a couple minutes to say something, but when she remained silent, I went back to my book. Right as I began to read the next line, Brina decided to speak.

"Nice day, isn't it?" she asked.

I sighed and put my book in my lap. "You're bored, aren't you?"

Brina used her elbows to lift herself up a bit. "What? No! Why would you say that? I'm just coming over to spend some quality time with my friend."

I couldn't help but roll my eyes. "Why didn't you go with Weylyn? You're always stuck to him like burrs on cotton anyways."

"He insisted I find some time to unwind and relax today, pointing out that we should take advantage of our time in Draca before moving out with the army." Brina picked at blades of grass and flicked them away into the soft breeze.

"And have you found some time to unwind and relax?" I asked.

Brina sat up now, playing with a blade of grass between her fingers. "Of course I haven't. How can I? All I can think about is the coming war, not to mention what could be going on back home. I'm not like you. I can't just pick up a book and forget about everything."

I realized the conversation was going to be longer than I had hoped, so I placed a ribbon on the page I was on and closed the book. After placing it next to me, I shifted so that I was facing Brina more head on. "I don't forget everything. I just push it back and let something else take over for a while. It doesn't always work either. I understand your stress. I worry about the war and our home too. However, Weylyn is right. We need to rest our bodies and our minds while we can. The road ahead will be hard, Brina. Weylyn and I, along with everyone back home, are going to need you at your best."

Brina was silent for a bit until finding her voice again. "We have no idea what's going on back home. I know we had to leave, but it feels wrong. We might not be back in Fleuris for months. Who knows how much worse it'll get without us there? We don't even know if Olwen, Keagan, and other members of The Resistance are okay. Plus, Weylyn is refusing to send a letter telling them we're safe in the fear it could be intercepted and result in another person's torture or death. We're disconnected, during a time when we shouldn't be."

I shuffled over to get close enough so I could put a hand on Brina's shoulder. "I don't like that we're apart either, but we've been apart before, haven't we? We survived and so did The Resistance. We'll survive this too. I'm sure Olwen has everyone safe while she continues our fight in Fleuris. Our job now is to make sure we help Tudrose win this campaign. Try to focus on right now. Let the past be the past and allow the future to reveal itself when it chooses to. What can you do right now?"

Brina stared at the grass in her hands as she thought about my question. "I don't know. What I do know is that I'm certainly not going to read a book with you."

I had been meaning to ask Brina something since we left Cloque. It never seemed like the right moment, but I figured now was possibly the best considering she was bored and looking for something to do. I changed my position so that I was on my knees and put my hands on my thighs. I adjusted my skirt a bit and made sure my back was straight to show Brina I was serious. "You could teach me how to fight."

Brina's left eyebrow rose as she turned to look at me. "Teach you how to fight? You already know how to defend yourself. Weylyn made sure of it."

I rolled my eyes. "No, not that fighting. I mean war fighting."

Brina shook her head and began the process of getting to her feet. "Oh no, no, no. No way. No way Weylyn ever lets you fight in an actual battle."

I got up with her, adjusting the leather corset I had on before crossing my arms over my chest. "Excuse me? No way Weylyn ever lets me? Since when has Weylyn ever had control over what I can and cannot do?"

Brina pointed at me. "Since you wore dresses and read books on a nice spring afternoon. You aren't made for war, Rosalie. It's best you just stay back and let us handle it."

I was starting to get upset. "The last time I stayed back and let you handle it, people died."

Brina blinked in confusion. "What in the world are you talking about?"

"Last year, when you and the others left to start the rebellions. I was left behind and look what happened. If I could fight like you, I could have gone instead. One of you would have been in Cloque. Hell, Keagan would have done a better job at stopping that riot from happening than I did."

Brina grabbed a hold of my hand. "First of all, what happened was not your fault. Dwyer and the others were going to start that riot no matter who was in Cloque watching over things. Second, not knowing how to fight in a war doesn't make you useless. We all have our strengths and our weaknesses. What your saying is silly, Rosalie."

I pushed her hand away from me. "Silly? You know what it was like having to watch people I care about leave on a dangerous mission? I was left behind because I was useless. I don't want to be useless anymore, Brina. I want to help fight for the Tóráin just like you and Weylyn do."

Brina took a deep sigh as she put her hands on her hips. "You aren't going to let this go, are you?"

I put my hands on my hips and stuck my nose in the air at her. "If you don't teach me, I'll still end up on that battlefield." When Brina groaned and looked away, I grabbed her hand so she would look at me again. "I want to fight for those I love. I want to fight for a group of people that I have cared about my entire life. A group that my parents cared about too. Please, Brina."

Brina mumbled something that I didn't quite make out before taking her hand back and crossing her arms over her chest. "I have one condition."

"Anything!" I was so happy I didn't care what it was.

"You don't fight until we reach Fleuris. I need time to make sure you're ready for the horrors and dangers that war brings."

I wasn't so happy anymore, but as long as I was eventually fighting for my home, and those I love, I was content. It wasn't exactly what I wanted, but it was better than a no. "Fine. When do we start?"

Brina grabbed my arm and kicked my legs out from under me, sending me careening onto my back. "The moment you get off your ass."

# Chapter Thirty-Five

## Olwen



I arrived at Valarc in a reasonable timeframe, but everything seemed to go downhill from there. I was caught trying to enter the town at first, which resulted in me being shot at and chased into the woods. I was in a tree for the majority of the night, waiting until the rising sun was nipping at the horizon's heels before I tried again. I managed to slip by the guards that time around and went directly for Joan's Courage. It was one of only two inns the town had. I had been told by that harpy, Nora, that I could find an ally in the owner of Joan's Courage, Jacques. My luck continued to fail me however, seeing as Jacques had been killed after being accused of helping the Tóráin. With Jacques gone I had to deal with his grieving wife who spent more time crying than giving me any useful information. It wasn't until the barkeep, Gerard, overheard us that I gained some news. Although, of course, it wasn't news I wanted to hear.

"Baron's left town I'm afraid," the stout man had said. "*Mon frère* is a guard at *la maison du bâtard*, and he was complaining that he had been left behind."

"How many days until he's back?" I had asked him.

"*Cinq, je crois*," Gerard responded.

"That's five, yes?" I was forced to ask.

*"Oui!"* Gerard exclaimed, before he scrunched up his face and shook his head. "I mean, yes. Sorry. Five days is the time you'll have to wait. You're more than welcome to hide away here."

The safest place for me — as well as any Tórán in the town — was somewhere hidden away. I accepted Gerard's offer and chose the cellar of Joan's Courage as my new temporary home. I waited in that cramped space for what felt like weeks; it wasn't until this afternoon that I was told the Baron of Valarc had returned. After being given some vague layout of Laurent's villa by Gerard, I left the cellar when the sun went to sleep. I skulked in the shadows of the town for a decent distance until I reached the building that housed my target. It was extremely hard not to just run in, but I managed to contain myself long enough to pick up on a route the soldiers outside were taking. It didn't take too much longer until I snuck past them. I tossed a rock away from me, which caught the attention of the soldier watching the door I intended to use to get inside. It was the server's door, used by maids and kitchen workers. For some reason, it was the least heavily guarded and the soldier they had left to stand watch was easily tricked. He went out looking into the bushes of the small garden nearby and I snuck over to the door. Thankfully, it wasn't locked, and I slipped inside.

I entered what appeared to be a kitchen, with only two lanterns giving the room any light. One was on a small table near me, and the other was with a cook chopping up vegetables for tomorrow's morning stew. He had heard the door open and close, so his eyes were on me. My hood was still up, and I imagine that the lantern cast a shadow over my face because he asked who I was. It was clear that I wasn't a soldier, and I assumed that no one else was expected at this hour. I didn't say anything, pretending I hadn't heard his question as I began walking to the door which exited the room. The cook shakily lifted his knife, and I stopped my advance, raising my hands in the air.

*"Dis-moi qui tu es ou j'appelle un garde."*

I didn't understand what he said save for one word. He had said something about a guard, so I quickly sprung into action. I swiftly got over to him, grabbed his wrist with my right hand and whacked him in the mouth with my left one. I managed to remove the knife from his hand and put it against his throat.

"Listen close. I don't want to hurt you. I'm here for the Baron. You're going to tell me where he is. Do that, and I'll let you live. Call out for a guard, and I'll kill you. Understood?" The man looked at me with wide eyes and nodded as much as he could.

When the cook remained silent I cleared my throat and he immediately began speaking. "Top floor, fourth r-room from the...stairs, on your left side. That's his st-study. If he isn't in there, he'll be in the...room across the hall."

I moved the knife away from his throat and the man let out a great big sigh. His relief was short lived though. I brought the hilt of his knife to the side of his head and knocked out the poor cook. I struggled to drag him into a darker corner of the room before blowing out the lantern he had been using. I went out the door and was happy to find a set of stairs not too far down the hallway. I slowly made my way up the staircase; I was ready to run into any soldiers but, luckily, I went unnoticed. Walking as silently as I could, I passed by three rooms until I reached a fourth one. My sword now in hand, I burst through the door ready for a fight. My entrance was met with a surprised look by a man who could only be Jean Laurent. It may not make much sense, but he looked like someone who would kill their father to gain power. Something about his ill-kept beard and the blank stare he gave told me he just wasn't right. Only people with serious issues killed family members. It wasn't something common amongst our kind, but humans apparently did that sort of thing more often than you'd think. He spotted my sword and went to call for help, but I quickly threw the blade forward, piercing his shoulder and the tall-backed chair he sat in. The blow pinned him to his seat, while also sending him into enough shock that he gave up on calling for his guards and chose to gasp for air instead.

I made it quickly over to him, jumping over the table he sat at and landing in his lap with my knife at his neck. "Hello, Jean."

"Please don't kill me!! I'll give you whatever you want! *Tu veux de l'argent? De la nourriture? D'être libre? Tout ce que tu veux est à toi*!" Jean tried shifting his position but the knife at his throat and sword in his shoulder only made him wince and groan.

"I want to know why you killed your father. It must have something to do with how you're treating the Tóráin. Tell me or I swear I'll —"

He lifted the one arm he could as he continued to beg. "No! No! You don't want me! I'm just a pawn. I'm doing this for The Dove. She wants resilient *Diables* to test on. Something about a spell she's working on? *Je ne sais pas*, I'm not a high enough ranking member. I was hoping that taking over from *mon père* and sending her more prisoners would change that. Please, I'll stop. *J'emmerde la sorcière*! Let me live and I'll tell you where to find her."

I pushed my knife closer to his neck, drawing a small bit of blood. "How about you tell me where to find her first, and then we can discuss letting you go."

Jean seemed reluctant, but I knew what to do. After a quick elbow to the sword lodged in his shoulder sent him into a painful fit full of groans and cursing, he gave in. "Etoile. I was supposed to meet her, along with other members, in Etoile, *le quinze de ce mois*." I nudged the blade jammed in his shoulder again and he groaned angrily. "The fifteenth of this month. The meeting is at ten o'clock at night, on the highest balcony of the building next to the courthouse, overlooking the courtyard. That's the Magistrate's villa you know! He's probably part of it all too! I bet he's very important actually, and I just gave him and The Dove to you. So, surely you'll —"

I quickly swiped my knife across his throat, sending his words into unintelligible gurgles. I slid backwards off him as blood spilled from his neck before pulling my sword free. Jean slumped into his chair as he gripped at the wound I had opened up, blood flowing through his fingers. Eventually, he slid down so far that he slipped out of his chair and ended up on the floor. It had taken longer than I wanted it to, but the Baron of Valarc was no more. Hopefully, now that he was gone, the town would become safer for my kind. It was hard to ever know where The Dove was, so this knowledge being dropped in my lap was a rare gift. If I could rid us of The Dove, General Rosspier would be weakened. It also seemed that I could put an end to whatever horrors the witch was up to. I couldn't let this opportunity pass me by. As I slowly shut the door to the former Baron's study, thoughts of what The Dove could be up to filled my head. By the time I opened the door to leave the building — and surprised the soldier now standing guard with a swift punch — I was leaning towards a plan of action. Once I slipped by the patrolling soldiers guarding the grounds, I was convinced. I had to go to Etoile.

# Chapter Thirty-Six

# Weylyn

The Frigid Sea  |  May 8, 1799

The Frigid Sea was earning its name. Summer was approaching, and yet the breeze that rushed over and through the ship had it feeling like fall. Luckily, we had made the turn towards Tulp and would be out of the winds by tomorrow afternoon. I didn't know which I wanted to face first: another day at sea or my first real battle. Brina, Olly, and Keagan had told me many stories, so I had some idea of what to expect. Little good that did me though, seeing as all of their stories were horrific. I had killed before today, and I would kill tomorrow, but something about all out war was different. It sounded more chaotic and less forgiving. Blood and death surrounds you, and if you survive long enough, your body begins to just act on instinct. The prospect of experiencing that made my stomach lurch even more than the rocking waves. It was why I was awake and not sleeping like the others. I just couldn't get my mind to rest long enough for sleep to take me, so I abandoned the idea and came up for some salty sea air. The skies were mostly clear, and the moon was full, the stars shining in all their lovely constellations.

It had taken some time to finally get here, to this moment, and I tried my best to appreciate that. The years I had spent fighting for a better world for the Tóráin were culminating into a war campaign to finally make some real change. I had hated finding ways to avoid conscriptions over the years, watching as my kind was dragged off to fight in a war they didn't believe in. I had begged Darby to let me fight with Brina in the war that eventually led to General Rosspier taking over, but he refused. I debated for a while on just going anyway, however Rosalie had convinced me that it was more important for me to be next to Darby in Cloque than next to Brina on a battlefield. Of course, Darby died and then I had to take over leadership of The Resistance. That role forced me to elude war once more, and I still held some regret for doing so. Being able to finally join Brina and other Tóráin in fighting for a cause we all believe in was very special to me. Despite being nervous, I was still very proud to stand next to them tomorrow.

"The full moon is special to your kind, right?" Lady Mirlena had somehow snuck up on me, causing me to jump at the sound of her voice.

I gathered myself, clearing my throat before answering. "My father made sure we watched every single one we could. He never said why, but I didn't really care. I just enjoyed spending time with him."

"It is said that the goddess Odarian uses the moon as her home, where she prepares select dead to be reincarnated. Strong warriors, great leaders, passionate lovers, people like that. Lycans, satyrs, harpies, all of the races that came here had a chance to be given a new life in Odarian's revolving castle on the moon." Lady Mirlena smiled when I sent her a look of confusion.

I couldn't help but smile back. "How do you know all that? I'd never heard of Tóráin believing in reincarnation before."

The witch let out a deep sigh before responding. "My parents died when I was five years old. I was forced to live with my widowed aunt in northern Tudrose. When I took my next step in my journey to adulthood at age twelve and it was revealed that I was a witch, she kicked me out. I had no home, no family. After making my way south and stealing some coins from an unsuspecting merchant, I bought a room in an inn in a town called Salwic. Some men were acting all creepy around me, but they were chased away by a friendly, yet also quite intimidating, lycan. She turned out to be fairly old, although she didn't look it. Her hair was still long and red, wrinkles barely managing to take over her face. She had convinced me to tell her my story, and after hearing it she offered to take me into her home and raise me. She taught me everything she knew, and she knew quite a bit."

"That must have been weird," I said. "A human being raised by a Tórán I mean."

Lady Mirlena tapped the side of her head with her finger. "A witch being raised by a Tórán. It wasn't as weird as you would think. I owe that old lycan so much. If it wasn't for her, I wouldn't be where I am today."

I could see on her face that she was saddened by our conversation, and I felt compelled to ask a question I believed I already knew the answer to. "Where is she now?"

Lady Mirlena sniffed, wiped away tears from her cheek, and looked up at the sky again. "If I had to bet my life on my answer, I'd say she's on the moon with Odarian waiting to be reincarnated."

"I'd like to think my dad is there too. He deserved a better life than the one he had. Maybe his next one will be better." I watched the moon and recalled all the times I spent watching it with my father.

"If we succeed, every Tórán, reincarnated or not, will have a better life than before." She put a hand on my forearm and looked at me. "Are you nervous? For tomorrow I mean."

I scoffed. "By both of us being here instead of sleeping, I assume you're just as nervous as I am."

Lady Mirlena chuckled. "Excellent observation. Maybe we should both try to fix that. Won't do us any good to be exhausted for our first battle now will it?"

I took a deep breath and looked up at the moon again. "You go on ahead. I think I'll spend just a few more moments remembering pleasant memories."

I heard Lady Mirlena's feet take her away from me, but something had crossed my mind earlier and I had finally mustered up the courage to inquire about it. I spun around and was happy to see the witch was still above deck.

"Lady Mirlena!" She turned back around and smiled at me. "How did you learn to control your magic living with a Tórán? Did she know a witch that trained you?"

The kind woman grinned from ear to ear. "Another story for another time, Weylyn. I have a final question of my own actually. Your father. What was his name?"

"Conri," I answered.

"As in Conri the Defiant?" she asked.

The name made me feel proud. "Yes."

"Quite a strong name. He's proud of you, Weylyn. I'm sure of it." Lady Mirlena opened the hatch that led to the lower decks of the ship, but another question came to my mind.

"Wait! What was her name? The lycan who raised you?"

Lady Mirlena froze, holding the door open. She stayed like a statue for a few moments until looking at me with fresh tears in her eyes. "Brigantia. Named after the goddess of poetry."

I smiled. "Beautiful name. I'm sure she's proud of you too."

"Goodnight, Weylyn," Lady Mirlena said. "Should I not get the chance, good luck tomorrow. May the gods watch over you."

I lowered my head in thanks. "And may they watch over you as well. Goodnight, Lady Mirlena."

She finally began her descent to the lower decks where dozens upon dozens of hammocks and bed rolls were laid out for everyone on board. The idea of sleep was enticing, but I wanted just a bit more time with my father. I raised my head and stared at the soft glow that emanated from the big, silver circle in the sky. I let the memory of my father's voice soothe me and allowed his image to give me strength.

# Chapter Thirty-Seven

# Weylyn



"Are you sure I should be here?"

I couldn't help but ask the question. We were making our way into Royal Daum, the palace that housed the monarchs of Tulp. Our battle had taken place a less than ten miles from the western beach. Tudrose's army pushed Leuw's soldiers east across hilly tundra until we finally found victory just inside a vast forest. While we had been fighting there, a group of rebels led by Cordelia had attacked a caravan that was trying to sneak King William and his wife out of the city. They had brought them both back to Royal Daum and held them there until our arrival. Queen Sophia had decided to give King William a chance to keep his throne and would discuss the terms of him remaining the leader of Tulp today. When she had requested that I join her, I was hesitant. I obviously agreed to accompany her, but it felt odd to stand next to a human queen as an apparent equal.

Queen Sophia sighed before sending me a reassuring smile. "I told you already, Weylyn. This war effort is inspired by what The Resistance has done for your kind. Our terms are your terms. You represent all Tóráin and their interests. Not only do I believe you should be here, but I also believe your presence is more important than my own."

It was my second time being told by her about my place in this whole campaign, and yet it was still hard to believe. I had dealt with the pressure of being the leader of The Resistance all these years well enough, however representing every Tórán in these countries was a newfound weight that I wasn't sure I could bear. Still, I was determined to do the best I could. I wasn't sure that me being here today was more important than the leader of the winning army, but I accepted that my presence was necessary. This was mainly about making life better for the Tóráin, and the only way for their voices to be heard today was through me. The first, gruesome part of this was over. The next step — quite possibly the most important one — was next. It was easy to win a war. It was extremely difficult to change the outlook of an entire country afterwards.

"I just hope things go smoothly," I responded. "From what Cordelia has told us in letters, it doesn't seem that King William is the most reasonable man."

Queen Sophia let out a small laugh. "I have heard the same. He will agree to our terms or be removed. Either way, things in this country will change. We'll make sure of it."

I didn't know exactly what she meant by 'removed' but hearing her say 'we' was something that made me smile. It told me that she, a human leader, and I, a lycan, were working towards the same goal. It wasn't new for Queen Sophia to speak like this, but it was a surreal feeling every time she did.

"Oi! The conquerin' heroes have arrived!" A female water sprite dressed in commoner's clothes shouted just as we began climbing the stairs.

As we got closer, I realized she had a pearl necklace around her neck and a ring on her right hand. Both of which were much too rich for someone dressed like her to own. Queen Sophia must have been eyeing the contrast in her appearance like I had, because the sprite ended up commenting on it.

"Oh, like my new gifts, eh?" she said as she flaunted her jewelry. "King Willy and his wife gave 'em to me in exchange for me to let 'em go."

"You let them go?" I shouted.

The sprite laughed. "Gods no! I agreed to their terms, but I lied of course. It's made 'em both quite sour to be honest. Oh! Forgive me! I ain't even introduced myself! My name's Cordelia, but my friends call me wonderful. You must be Queen Sophia of Tudrose and the famed Weylyn of The Resistance!"

Keagan and Olwen had told me about Cordelia. I had thought this unreserved water sprite had been her, but I didn't expect her to be so...brazen. To be honest, having the first thing she told Queen Sophia be that she lied to and stole from King William probably wasn't the best first impression.

Queen Sophia surprised me by chuckling and holding out her hand. "A pleasure to meet you, Wonderful."

Cordelia grinned from ear to ear. "Oh, I like this one!" She grabbed Queen Sophia's hand and shook it before sticking out the same hand to me.

I grabbed it and gave it a shake. "Thank you for preventing King William from escaping. It really saves us all a bunch of trouble."

Cordelia waved her hand at me. "Ah don't mention it. Trust me, it was my utmost pleasure to see that justice is served. Speakin' of which, shall we go inside? Ol' Willy and his lady are waitin' for us."

Queen Sophia looked at me and I nodded. She brought her eyes back to Cordelia and smiled. "Lead the way."

Cordelia opened both doors at the same time. Queen Sophia, me, and the dozen soldiers that had accompanied us entered the room. The curved ceiling was tall and had squares of paintings strewn about it. Large, burgundy curtains were pulled back to let in the sunlight from tall windows. To our left sat the throne of Tulp, with who I assumed to be King William seated on it. His wife, Queen Hemina, stood next to him. They were defeated and embarrassed, yet they still held their noses to the sky. The two Tóráin who had been guarding the entrance from inside the room closed the doors behind us and we made the short journey over to the leaders of Tulp.

Queen Sophia inclined her head. "King William. Queen Hemina. Lovely to see you both."

King William spat in response to Queen Sophia's greeting. "Keep your sarcasm to yourself. You know very well that this meeting is in no way lovely. Now explain to me why the Hell Tudrose has stooped so low as to join forces with these *kwaadaardige wezens*."

"Evil creatures?" King William appeared shocked to discover Cordelia understood Tulp's native tongue. "Aw, Willy. Has anyone told ya how much of a sweetheart ya are? Oh? What's that? People only call ya a fat coward?"

King William erupted from his throne and pointed at Cordelia. "*Jullie zijn allemaal onbeleefde, ondankbare afval*! It's as if you forget what your lives were like before humans foolishly chose to be merciful to your kind. No etiquette. No respect. You're no better than wild animals! No wonder you were hunted for so long!"

Cordelia's smile vanished and she went for the knife at her waist. I quickly put a hand on her wrist to stop her and chose to add a calmer voice to the conversation. "I think that's quite enough of that. We didn't come here today to throw insults at each other."

King William turned his attention to me. "Oh no. You came here to take over the country instead. What will it be, Sophia? Is this *hond* meant to replace me? Your love for mercy has driven you mad."

"He is a lycan, not a dog. His name is Weylyn. He leads The Resistance in Fleuris and is here to speak on behalf of all the people which you feel justified in mistreating. He is not here to replace you, nor is that my intention either. We came here to talk." Queen Sophia's tone was strong and commanding, her face having adopted a firm expression of judgement.

"When people wish to talk, they don't bring an army with them," Queen Hemina chimed in.

King William seemed exhausted from his outburst and retreated back to sit on his chair. "My wife speaks the truth. I will only ask you one more time, Sophia. Why did you attack Tulp? Why align yourself with such beings?"

Queen Sophia cleared her throat and took a step toward King William. "As you may already know, Tudrose has led the countries of Kosavros in recognizing people like Weylyn and Cordelia as equals. I have made it a goal of mine to do my best to see that all of their kind is treated well. Weylyn came to me late last year and proposed an idea to quicken the pace at which the Tóráin were becoming more respected members of our communities. For some time, although I agreed to help him and his kind, I did my best to avoid violence. However, it has come to my attention that things have progressively gotten worse for the Tóráin in most countries, and I refuse to go backwards. I don't wish to take up too much of your time, but if you're interested in the answer as to why Tulp was targeted as part of this campaign, I'm sure Cordelia could enlighten you. Why align myself with Weylyn and the others? Because I believe that every person in this world deserves specific rights. No matter how they look or where they're from. Whether they can cast spells or not. Everyone deserves to be treated with a certain level of respect and understanding."

I took a step forward and continued Queen Sophia's speech when it seemed as though she was finished. "We are here to see if you're willing to take the step forward this world needs to take, in order to become stronger and more united than ever. Queen Sophia and I would like to see if you're willing to move away from the past, and work towards a brighter future for everyone."

Queen Sophia looked over at me and smiled, apparently pleased I had chosen to speak up. Someone who wasn't pleased at all was King William. "A brighter future for everyone? Queen Sophia. At first, I thought you mad but now I see you are just gullible. This *zwerfhond* has tricked you into making the strongest countries of

Kosavros weak, so that he and the other *Duivels* can take over. By the end of this campaign of yours, you will see. They will take revenge on us for what we did hundreds of years ago. They'll enslave humanity. They'll murder us for no reason other than to see us bleed. They are *Duivels*! Eous has sent them to rid the world of Deus' greatest creation. Humanity."

Cordelia snorted. "I'd pick a fuckin' worm as Deus' greatest creation before a human ya stuck up windbag."

King William swiftly pointed at Cordelia. "*Zie je*? You see the venom that this snake spews? They will spread their vile ways across Kosavros and beyond. Save us all now and kill these two, and those who follow them!"

Queen Sophia ignored King William's disrespectful tirade. "Is it safe to say that you, as well as Queen Hemina, refuse to take the necessary steps forward?"

King William spat at Queen Sophia, his saliva catching the Queen of Tudrose in the face. "I will never encourage the uprising of Eous' *Duivels*. I will now, and forever, fight for humanity and their Deus given right to rule this world as we see fit. We have allowed the *Duivels* to live among us and we have received nothing but insolence and complaining. Perhaps what General Rosspier is doing in Fleuris is the right way to do things."

I took a step forward, but Queen Sophia turned quickly and held out a hand to stop me from advancing. She looked over to one of her guards. "Arrest King William and Queen Hemina please."

I watched the soldiers in their red and white uniforms march forward and seize the rulers of Tulp. They both resisted at first, but they quickly succumbed to their fate. King William was being taken away by the soldiers, but he wasn't going quietly. "You'll regret this, Sophia! *Let op mijn woorden*! Humanity will look back on this day as the beginning of the eventual Hell you will allow to run amok in our world! May Deus forever deny you entry into his hallowed hall and may the *beesten* you favor stab you in the back in thanks for all that you will give them!"

Once King William and Queen Hemina were removed from the room, Cordelia laughed quietly to herself as she sauntered up to the throne and sat down in it. She extended her arms and grinned. "Well, what do ya think? Looks good, no?"

"I don't think the best way to go about things is to make William look correct in any way. No doubt he isn't the only one in this country that believes what he does. Naming a Tórán as head of Tulp would only feed their outlandish theories." I hated saying such things, but they were true.

"Weylyn is right." Queen Sophia announced in agreement. "While Queen Wonderful does have a lovely ring to it, I must say that we have to find another avenue forward."

Cordelia crossed her arms and pouted. "You're all no fun, ya know that? If I don't get to be queen, then what are we doin'?

Queen Sophia and I looked at each other, both of us about to speak but neither of us able to find words to say. We had both been hopeful that the leaders of these countries would value their power so much that they would comply with our demands. It turned out that our expectations of how much in love King William was with ruling were ill-informed. The country couldn't go leaderless, and Queen Sophia had been adamant that she and Tudrose would not be colonizing any nations. We set out to free those who felt shackled — physically and spiritually — all while making the upper levels of society more diverse and accepting. Remembering why we had come here gave me an idea for what to do, but I was nervous to suggest it. I didn't want it to look like I was taking over in any way. What King William had said made me anxious to say anything now, fearing that his words had possibly stirred up doubt in Queen Sophia's mind. My internal struggle must have showed itself to the other people in the room because they both gave me inquisitive looks.

"What is it, Weylyn?" Queen Sophia asked.

"Yeah, what's goin' on in that beautiful head of yours?" Cordelia added.

I took a deep breath and tried to reassure myself that Queen Sophia was on my side before speaking. "We're striving for equality, right? That's our main goal. We don't want the Tóráin to take over, we just want to be viewed as equals. And the people of Tulp are known to value their independence more than any other country. According to history books I was forced to read when I was younger, the people of Tulp have long disliked the idea of a monarchy since before the Tóráin arrived. So how about we show the world that we truly are about equality and compromise. Abandon the monarchy and replace it with a council of people. Twelve let's say. Six Tóráin, six humans. Poor and rich, male and female. What do you think?"

The confidently casual water sprite tapped her chin with her finger. "Well...I guess that could work. I mean Queen Cordelia sounded much more lovely, but I could settle for Council Lady Cordelia."

Queen Sophia smiled. "I think that is a wonderful idea, Weylyn. How will we choose the remaining members?"

I shrugged. "Why not let the people have a say? Allow them to nominate people from their community, and we'll meet with them to determine who would best suit the roles we are looking to fill."

"Ya can't stay here too long, Weylyn. The longer ya stay, the more time ya give other countries to prepare for your attacks. Even if they ain't got contacts in Leuw, word will spread faster than the juiciest piece of gossip." Cordelia broke out a pipe and stuffed it with a paste she procured from a small jar.

"Cordelia is right. We can't stay to oversee the forming of this council ourselves. However, I could leave Edith here to do it for us. I'll leave a battalion or two of soldiers behind to help keep the transition peaceful, but I believe there won't be too much push back on this. We might have the odd angry mob here and there, but we can sort that out well enough. We'll have to send out letters to other cities and towns of Tulp to ensure everyone has their chance to be represented. I'll get Edith started on things right away."

Cordelia had laid herself out horizontally across the throne, her legs hanging off one armrest while her back leaned against the other. She blew a plume of smoke into the air and sighed. "Well, I'm glad that's all sorted out. Shame I won't be here to see it all happen though."

Queen Sophia and I looked at each other in confusion. I put my hands on my hips and sent my baffled expression Cordelia's way. "What do you mean you won't be here? You agreed to be a member, didn't you?"

"That I did," Cordelia admitted as she lifted herself up and swung her legs around so she was sitting on the throne properly again. "However, I don't intend to stay here while you're out there playin' hero. This special sprite ain't one to quit while she's ahead. So long as there's more to do, I'm doin' it. Tóráin here in Tulp may have been helped, but those in other countries are still in trouble. I didn't do all I did these past few months just for the Tóráin in Tulp to be treated better. I did it for every livin' Tórán across Kosavros. I'm comin' with ya. A few of my friends are comin' too. We want to help give other members of our kind what we brought about here in Tulp."

Queen Sophia sighed. "That is very admirable of you, but I think you are most useful staying here. Tulp isn't suddenly a better place just because William and Hemina are gone. This transition will take time, and it will need people like you to help see that it is as smooth as possible."

Cordelia waved her hand at Queen Sophia. "Oh fish shit. Eva and the others that are stayin' behind are more than capable of handlin' things here. Plus, this friend of yours, Edith was it? She and your soldiers will make sure nothin' crazy happens. The only people that are goin' to hate this new change are snobby nobles and crazy extremists. Thankfully, the human poor and my fellow Tóráin outnumber 'em heavily. Tell people who have been unheard most of their lives that they now have a voice, and they'll do anythin' to hold on to the ability to scream. My place on this new council will be waitin' for me when I get back. I'm comin' with ya. My mind is already made up."

I looked at Queen Sophia again and she shrugged her shoulders, seemingly at a loss for words. Sticking my hand out towards Cordelia, I smiled. "It will be our pleasure to have you along with us."

The water sprite took a puff from her pipe and blew out the smoke she didn't inhale. She looked at me for a moment before smiling and walking over so she could grab a firm hold of my hand. "The amazin', exquisite services of the beautiful and witty Cordelia are yours, good sir. You're welcome in advance."

# Chapter Thirty-Eight

## Weylyn

The Graafschap, Tulp  |  May 12, 1799

The sun was still rising from its slumber, barely peeking over the many hills of a land the people from Tulp called The Graafschap. Despite the early hour, I was already out and about. We probably wouldn't begin packing up and moving out for another hour or two, and the majority of our army was still sleeping. I had been awoken by a soldier who claimed Lady Mirlena was asking for me. To be completely honest, I was surprised; I wasn't sure that the woman could wake up this early. I desperately wished to remain asleep, cuddled next to Rosalie, until we continued our march south. However, I didn't want to be rude and ignore Lady Mirlena's request. She had been quite kind to me, and those I care for, so I wanted to keep the friendship we had and not upset her. Soldiers, both human and Tórán alike, spoke highly of Lady Mirlena's skills and I found that having her as an ally was in the best interest of everyone. People almost seemed to fear her, which was odd because she was incredibly friendly.

I followed the soldier who had called on me to Lady Mirlena's temporary home. We swiftly walked past a multitude of tents and dead campfires. We even walked by Queen Sophia's massive tent, which was guarded by roughly a dozen or so soldiers surrounding the entire thing. We made it to the base of a good-sized hill and began the trek up towards the tent that rested at the top of it. The witch had positioned her residence away from the immense group of tents. It wasn't so far as to be considered on its own, but it was distant enough to notice the clear intention to be separated. I didn't know why she had chosen to do this, and I guess it really didn't matter. Witches were strange, especially this one. Not many knew why they did what they did, but we always assumed it had a magical reason behind it. Knowing Lady Mirlena the little that I did, it would be safe to guess that she wanted to be away from noises that might wake her. The woman enjoyed her sleep and everyone around her was happy when she had gotten lots of it; the witch was quite grumpy when she was tired.

"Lady Mirlena? Weylyn is here, as requested." The soldier shouted at the closed flaps that kept what was inside the tent a secret.

"Thank you! Come on in, Weylyn!"

The soldier left back down the hill and I took a deep breath before making my way towards the entrance. Any conversation I had with Lady Mirlena seemed to leave me exhausted afterwards, and I was already tired as it was. I opened the flap and stepped inside and was hit with the scent of a bitter orange. A kettle was floating next to Lady Mirlena, a small fire licking only the iron base. The witch was wearing a blue dress void of a corset or frills, and her hair was messily draped over her shoulders. When she saw me enter, she smiled, before turning her attention to the kettle. She waved her hand and the flame disappeared. A protective mitten on her other hand allowed her to grab the handle of the hot iron and pour the liquid into two cups she had resting on the small table before her.

"Doing magic so early in the morning is exhausting, but I didn't feel like going out to the fire outside. Sometimes you just want to stay away from the chill, early morning winds, you know?" When I didn't say anything, the witch waved her hand at me before picking up the two cups of tea. "Never mind. You don't need to hear the complaints of a middle-aged woman. Let's talk about something else, yes? Did you know that there's old folktales of this land being inhabited by beings smaller than goblins? They say that people can hear them laughing and singing at night. Did you happen to hear anything?"

I accepted the cup of tea Lady Mirlena offered me. "No, I don't think I did."

The witch pouted as she moved some hair out of her face. "That's a shame. Neither did I."

Lady Mirlena beckoned for me to sit with her on a mass of blankets laid out on the grass. Welcoming the idea of not having to stand, I eased myself down, making sure not to spill my tea. Once seated, I took a sip from my cup before breathing in the warm steam emanating from it. I realized then that the scent of bitter oranges I had smelled upon entering the tent came from the tea.

Lady Mirlena took a sip from her cup before smiling at me. "Well, still, it's fun to imagine the little ones dancing among the hills. Wouldn't you agree?"

I allowed myself to imagine tiny people prancing about the hills with mugs of beer in their hands, all while singing song after song. I looked away from my tea and smiled at Lady Mirlena. "It's nice to imagine a race of people who aren't weighed down by humans."

The witch sipped from her cup before putting it down next to her. "Had I known you were so grim in the morning I would have prepared us some wine instead of tea."

I averted my eyes as Lady Mirlena began braiding her hair. "Sorry. It's a habit I'm trying to break."

The woman laughed. "Oh no need to apologize. Grim times make grim people. Hopefully, my news will lift you up a bit."

I perked up. "What news?"

Lady Mirlena grinned. "I am going to teach you how to use magic."

I nearly spat out the tea I was drinking. "You're going to do what now?"

The witch rolled her eyes as she completed the simple braid she had been working on. "Oh come on. You don't know? Mystic Bloods are descendants of Druids. You all have the gift of magic wielding. I figured it might be beneficial for you to learn some."

I rubbed my eyes with my right hand. "I know that. Well, sort of. I heard it put as more of a suspicion than a fact though. Wouldn't learning magic only put a larger target on my back?"

"Perhaps." Lady Mirlena stroked the braid of hair hanging over her shoulder. "We can keep it secret if you'd like. You told me about your run in with The Dove and I realized that if you could wield a bit of magic of your own, it might help you out should you encounter her again."

The idea of possibly having a better chance at defeating The Dove was appealing. She was General Rosspier's deadliest weapon. Knowing some magic could maybe help me with ordinary witches too. "Alright. But we'll keep it as secret as we can. I don't know what sort of trouble could be caused by soldiers discovering a Tórán was casting spells, and I don't want to find out."

Lady Mirlena clapped her hands together. "Very well! Secret magic lessons it is then. Care to get started before we have to move out?"

I choked on the last bit of tea I was drinking. "What, now?"

The witch brought her legs forward and crossed them before fixing the wrinkles in her dress. "Why not? No better time than the present I say. Come on! I'll give you an introduction, then get you to try something small. Nothing crazy, I promise."

"Alright." I sighed as I straightened my back. "What do I do first?"

"First, you listen." Her hand glowed blue as the kettle floated over to each of our cups and poured the two of us more tea. "Magic is something that exists in both worlds, and it appears to be similar in certain ways. The main similarity, is that only certain people can wield magic. Believe whatever you wish when it comes to how those people are chosen, the fact of the matter is that not any old twit can do what we can. Many witches have theorized what makes us different over the centuries, but the general consensus is that it has something to do with our blood. It appears as though it is the same way with the Tóráin. However, your magic wielders are bloodlines, while the lineage is much more random for humans. Just because your mother was a witch, doesn't mean you'll become one too. Oh, and only female humans are born with the gift of magic, something that apparently doesn't apply to Mystic Bloods.

"Magic is more chaotic in humans than it is the Tóráin, showing itself when a girl reaches the moment of her first bleeding. Without proper teaching, the girl can cast magic unknowingly. An untrained witch is dangerous and is a large reason why we are feared almost as much as your kind are. In contrast — from what I was told — Mystic Bloods could go their entire lives without ever knowing they could wield magic. There was no age when their abilities would show, with some Mystic Bloods having begun magic training as young as three years old. It is because of this that Mystic Bloods have hidden themselves so well amongst ordinary members of their kind."

I blinked repeatedly, trying to make sure I took in everything she was telling me. A question came to mind. "Do we learn magic differently?"

Lady Mirlena's eyes lit up. "Wonderful question! The best way to answer that is to explain magic itself, at least our current understanding of it. Think of magic as an element, much like fire, water, air, and earth. Ancient witches believe that some women are born with this fifth element in their blood. This gift develops over time, until finally revealing itself once the girl matures. It happens this way all over the known world, and probably even in places we haven't discovered yet. There is one difference between magic and the other elements though. Magic is its own element, yet it also encompasses the other four. Hopefully that makes sense with time. Took me a while to understand that bit."

That was confusing, but there was something else she had told me that I chose to question. "All over the known world? But my kind didn't appear in the desert land to the south when the witches brought us to your world. Other places to the far east too. There must not be any witches there, right?"

"A very common misconception." Lady Mirlena paused to take a sip of her tea. "Lutis, as well as the eastern nations you bring up, have always had witches, they just never dabbled in the type of magic other nations did. I know that the witches in Lutis saw your world as a cursed place, one that their gods would punish them for engaging with. I'm not certain why eastern nations refused your world, but I wouldn't mind betting that it was for the same reasons as Lutis. There are indeed witches all across the world, all able to cast spells of their own."

Before Lady Mirlena had begun speaking, I was expecting to be bored. I had never been one for learning or reading, something Rosalie was constantly trying to change. However, the more the witch told me the more interested I became. The more interested I became, the more questions I seemed to come up with. "How do you cast spells? Is there a special language you use?"

Lady Mirlena downed the rest of her tea and groaned as she adjusted her position on the floor, reaching over for a pillow to place under her. Once she was comfortable again, she smiled. "Sorry. I much prefer my bed back home. I fear I've gotten used to luxury. Anyway! To answer your wonderful, intelligent question, yes and no."

"Yes and no?" I asked.

Lady Mirlena rolled her eyes. "Let me finish. So, technically, you can cast spells in any language you wish, modern or ancient, it all works. However, a witch's full power is realized when she uses one of the ancient languages to cast her spells. Nobody really knows why; some have their theories. But the fact of the matter is that ancient languages appear to give you more control and more strength when casting spells."

"What language do you use?" I asked.

Lady Mirlena clapped her hands together. "Yet another lovely question. Good to know you're paying attention! Well, for me it was difficult. Usually, a witch is trained by another witch, and so she would use the ancient language of her teacher. Depending on where that experienced witch is from, that language could be Dafnek, Planin, or Old Lutisan. There are others but I don't need to list them. Since I was taught by someone who wasn't a witch, I had to learn in regular old Tudish. It wasn't until my teacher passed on from this life that I found a new one who taught me the old language of Tudrose called Septennic. That's what I use now."

I took a moment to ponder some of the things she had said, some of them conjuring questions that would take us away from our current subject. I chose to remain on task with a question I hoped would show the strength of my wit. "So, Mystic Bloods would use Séúbua to cast spells then? Or is it different with my kind?"

Lady Mirlena pointed at me and winked. "You catch on pretty quick! Surprisingly, it isn't different with your kind. Well, not entirely. Mystic Bloods do indeed use their native language when casting spells, but that is all they can use. Any other language won't work. However, not every magic user needs to recite incantations to cast spells. Some are powerful and skilled enough to simply will them into being. But that is usually for the case of exceptionally experienced witches."

I thought about what Lady Mirlena told me for some time, making sure to commit this all to memory so I wasn't looking like a fool later on. Lady Mirlena seemed content to let me absorb everything, and so we sat in silence for a short while. Eventually, I decided to ask another one of my questions. "So, I could just say some words and my hands would glow too?"

The witch laughed. "Sadly, no. It isn't that simple. You have to connect with the magic in your blood in order to use it. Actually, I think that's enough history on the matter. Care to give something a try?"

I was suddenly extremely nervous. I couldn't help but imagine myself causing the entire tent to erupt into flames or something of the like. Ossian had said Mystic Bloods were stronger than normal Tóráin. Were we stronger than your average witch too? What if I said the words wrong? What if I hurt Lady Mirlena? What if I hurt myself? I was beginning to wonder if I was ready for all of this when Lady Mirlena reached over and grabbed my hand. She smiled softly and her eyes gleamed in a way that assured me everything was alright.

"It's something small. Not dangerous at all. It's how my teacher taught me." She plucked a blade of grass from the ground and placed it into the palm of my hand. "All you have to do is make that float."

That seemed easy enough. A blade of grass couldn't kill anyone; at least I didn't think it could. I pushed my anxiety to the back of my mind and readied myself to try magic for the very first time. "What do I have to do?"

"Well, the process is a little different for your kind than mine. Our magic is always just sitting there ready to be used, much like a lake full of water. For Mystic Bloods, your magic is at the bottom of a well. You need to reach for it before you can use it."

A new question came to the forefront of my mind. "How do you know so much about Mystic Bloods learning magic?"

She waved her hand at me, dismissing my question. "That's a story for another time. Now, I need you to do your best to focus. In fact, why don't we use that well metaphor. Imagine your magic is at the bottom of a deep well. Picture yourself lowering down into it. Once you reach the water at the base, see it absorb into your body like a sponge. When you feel ready, focus on the blade of grass and say '*Eitil*'."

I nodded, trying to void my mind of everything else but this imaginary well of magic water. It took some time, but finally the clutter was gone and only the well remained. I climbed into an abnormally large bucket and began to slowly lower myself down. My surroundings became incredibly dark, but I continued to go deeper into the well. Eventually, my feet felt the cold water at the bottom, and I hopped out of the bucket. Now, with everything but my neck and head submerged in the water, I focused on absorbing the liquid like Lady Mirlena had suggested. This took some time, and I was beginning to get frustrated. No matter how much I tried to imagine it, the water remained where it was. Eventually I abandoned it all, opening my eyes and turning my hand over to let the blade of grass fall to the ground.

"I can't do it," I announced.

Lady Mirlena plucked a new blade of grass, took my hand, and placed it on my palm. "Magic is believed to be fueled by our emotions. In my early stages, my anger or sadness would cause things to float or burst into flame. After some time, I learned to control those emotions and channel them when I needed to. When I use my magic, I choose to focus on a memory that makes me feel an emotion very strongly. It's best for that emotion to be happy, but it can also be anger, or sadness, or fear. Whatever makes you feel the most. Think of something when you're down in that well amongst the water. Try again."

I took a deep breath and closed my eyes. I was still frustrated, but I took the time to calm myself before trying again. I followed the same path just as easily as I had the last time, ending up back in the cold water. Wet and cold, I went through my memories to find one that could work. The memory of my father's death showed itself, and I could feel the water entering my skin, but I shook the image away. The water that had entered my body left, and I was right back to where I started. I didn't want to be fueled by anger and pain. I had seen the path that took people on, and it led to a place I didn't want to go to. I continued to go through my memories until I landed on one I didn't even know I had. It was my mother, with me in her lap. She was in a rocking chair and had me wrapped in a blanket. I was young, maybe two? I remembered being scared; maybe I had a nightmare? That fear began to fade quickly as my mother sang to me in what sounded like our native language. I could feel her chest rise and fall with each breath she took. The warmth of her body and her voice soothed me, until I felt an immense sense of peace. I felt safe, along with an overwhelming amount of happiness. As I snuggled into my mother, the cold water seeped into my skin. Eventually I stood on the bottom of the well, now completely dry. I opened my eyes and found the hand that was holding the blade of grass was glowing a deep amber.

I made sure I was confident in remembering the word Lady Mirlena had told me before finally whispering it. "*Eitil.*"

The blade of grass began to rise from my hand, but it wasn't the only thing. The pillows on the ground and our two cups began to rise as well. I panicked and the image of me and my mother vanished. Everything fell to the ground and Lady Mirlena looked at me with wide eyes. "Well then. It looks like you found your memory."

"I'm so sorry. I should have focused on the grass better." I picked up a new blade by my foot and held it up in the palm of my hand. "Can I try again?"

Lady Mirlena laughed, but I think it was more out of nervousness than joy. She stroked the braid that rested on her shoulder and bit her lip. After letting out a deep sigh, she nodded. "Alright. Just go slower, yeah? Really give yourself enough time to focus on the grass before saying the word."

I did it ten more times. It took me four tries to finally get only the grass to levitate. After that achievement, Lady Mirlena tasked me with trying to do it with a small stone. It took me until my last try to lift it, and only it, off the ground. I found myself immensely exhausted, as if I had marched all day already. I was even panting, gasping for air like I had just ran a great distance. I was sweating and I felt slightly dizzy. Lady Mirlena must have noticed me wavering, because she aimed her hand at a good-sized bag next to her bed roll. The bag floated over to her, and she reached inside, muttering to herself as she looked for whatever she was after. She pulled out an herb, along with a wooden mortar and pestle. She ground the herb up and the smell of sage filled the area around us. She put the remains into her cup before pouring some tea into it and handing the drink over to me.

"Drink this. It'll help." I took the cup and she smiled. "Using magic uses up our energy. Certain spells require different amounts of it. It takes time, but eventually we learn just how much energy is needed for each spell, so we don't overdo it.

Plus, you build up endurance the more you practice. You've done enough for today. We can try more tomorrow morning."

Before I could say anything the sound of the tent's flap opening had me turning around to find a young boy entering. "I gathered as much purple heather as I could mother. Oh, I'm sorry. Should I wait outside?"

Lady Mirlena grinned at him and stretched out a hand. "No, no. That's wonderful news about the heather. Come here. Meet a friend of mine."

The boy came and sat in her lap. He had hazel eyes and brown, curly hair. He couldn't be older than eight, but I could be persuaded to believe he was ten. His body was indeed the size of a boy around ten, but his face still bore the innocence of a young child. He smiled as Lady Mirlena squeezed him tightly.

"This is Weylyn," Lady Mirlena said. "He's the leader of The Resistance in Fleuris."

The boy's eyes opened wide, and a smile washed over his face. "You're the reason we're out here! I've always wanted to travel, but mother says I'm too young. But, since she had to go, I got to come too!"

His joy made me chuckle. "Well, I'm glad I could help you achieve your dreams. Although, I'm sure your mother would prefer your trip was taken under better circumstances."

"Oh no. Mother has always talked about making other countries treat your kind better. Always complaining that Queen Sophia is too much of a —"

Lady Mirlena put a hand over the boy's mouth. "This little gossip is my adopted son, Arthur."

He pushed the hand away from his mouth and looked up at the woman it belonged to. "You don't have to always introduce me as your adopted son. You may as well be my birth mother."

I was surprised by the fact that I was only learning now that Lady Mirlena had a child, but my lack of energy prevented me from pursuing the story behind it. "Well, Arthur, it has been my pleasure meeting you, but I must be going. Perhaps I can still catch a quick nap before we start heading out today." I stood up, prompting Lady Mirlena to remove Arthur from her lap.


Both of them got up and on their feet. Lady Mirlena put her hands on her son's shoulders and smiled. "Yes, get some rest if you can. I look forward to seeing you tomorrow morning."

"Can't wait." I waved goodbye at the two of them and exited the tent.

Luckily, the camp was still relatively quiet. A few soldiers here and there had woken up already and were taking in the morning air. I wouldn't have much time to rest, but if I hurried back, I should have a few minutes to lay down. However, I wondered if my mind would let me sleep. It had been given so much to think about thanks to my meeting with Lady Mirlena. I was learning magic. The idea still seemed outlandish to me even though I had clearly been casting spells for what must have been only a little less than an hour. She had been in awe at how quickly I had picked up on it all, claiming it took some magic users weeks — or in some cases months — before they could properly control their power. It was extremely rare for someone to get a good handle on it within less than an hour. We both wondered if it was just easier for Mystic Bloods, and the thought was one of the many that inhabited my head. I came to grips with the fact that I probably wouldn't be able to sleep, but I did enjoy the idea of at least laying down with Rosalie for a short while more.

# Chapter Thirty-Nine

## Olwen

Etoile, Fleuris | May 15, 1799

I had enough time to stop by Cloque on my way to Etoile to inform Keagan of my plan. He was happy to see I was alive, having been worried I was gone for so long. Of course, that happiness evaporated when I told him I wasn't staying. Just like with my previous plan of going alone to Valarc, Keagan vehemently opposed me going to Etoile alone. We had quite possibly our biggest argument ever over whether or not I was even going, let alone by myself. Eventually, wishing for us to not end up breaking the bond we had, Keagan submitted. Our agreement was a compromise of sorts. I would enter Etoile and enact my plan on my own, but Anya would travel there with me and wait at a rendezvous point outside the city. If I didn't show up at our selected time, Anya was to find out why and then report back to Keagan. Anya, Keagan, and Finn all informed me that whether I was captured or killed on this mission, the remaining members of The Resistance would attack Etoile to either rescue me or avenge me. It was admirable of them to say such things, but I asked for them to focus on more lives than just my own. I knew they wouldn't listen to me though. I wished for them to remain safe, so the idea of them all risking their lives for mine had me mounting even more pressure on myself to get in and out without a scratch.

It had actually been quite nice travelling with Anya. I wasn't overly social, so I had thought that being stuck with a person that I still wasn't fully used to would be upsetting. It was a pleasant surprise for things to turn out much differently. Anya was ten years younger than me, but she had fought in the most recent war, so she wasn't naive. The girl still had some joy in her, despite being dragged into the military when she was only fourteen. This was all thanks to Fleuris being in need of fodder in its campaign against half of Kosavros four years ago. When they ran out of Tóráin aged eighteen to forty to throw at the enemy, they forced our younger people into the army. They took some as young as thirteen, and in some cases twelve. It caused what is known as the Riot for Dead Youths. Anya's mother and father, having escaped the military due to both of them being in their fifties, died during the riot.

Many other Tóráin who had decided to fight against the conscription of their children also perished that day. Somehow, Anya had survived. A battlefield was no easy thing to come out of alive, and it didn't get easier when she returned home. She came back to a dead family and a new law that spawned a six-month period known to the Tóráin as The Great Dread, which only ended because nobles were beginning to lose money; Tóráin make up a massive percentage of Fleuris' labor force. The only thing humans — especially rich ones — cared about was their money. Luckily for Anya, and every other Tórán in Fleuris, the nobles convinced General Rosspier to remove the Diables Loyalty Act and end The Great Dread.

It was an extremely debilitating and horrific set of events for anyone to endure, but to do so at such a young age while still having a spark of hope in your heart was admirable. Thanks to it being just the two of us for the longest stretch of time in the months we've known each other, Anya and I actually bonded quite quickly. We connected over our experiences with war, and we talked about what we did to stay alive and help others during The Great Dread. She told me what she remembered of her parents, and I said what I felt comfortable saying about my own. Our conversations made the journey a pleasant one, and before long we came to the outskirts of Etoile. I left Anya on a small hill just outside of a decent-sized, wooded area. She had given me a hug before I left, something that I was very surprised by. Just as I wasn't a voluntarily social character, I wasn't really a hugger that much either. That type of communication and displays of affection were saved for a select few in my life, but I had happily embraced Anya back. She was perhaps not on the level of friends like Weylyn and Keagan in terms of trust, but we had grown fairly close over our few days of travelling.

"Please be careful," Anya requested.

"I'll be back so soon you won't even have time to miss me." I broke our hug and shot Anya a quick smile before running off towards Etoile.

I managed to sneak inside the infamous city by climbing into a trader's cart and hiding under the blanket that covered his goods. With how the Tóráin were being treated across the country I didn't want to try to enter Etoile out in the open. I hopped out of the cart once I felt it was safe to and hid in one of the many alleys of the city until nightfall. I managed to elude the few soldiers standing guard at the Magistrate's villa by climbing the walls of the courthouse and jumping over into the garden of the fancy home. It was a rough landing, but I was lucky enough not to injure myself. I had such a miserable time with that broken wrist I had back in January that I really wanted to stay healthy for at least a couple more months. Plus, not getting badly injured before trying to kill one of the most dangerous people in our known world was an important goal of mine.

I took the small watch I had out of my pocket and checked the time. The meeting would be starting soon, so I had to get into position. It took me some time, but I managed to climb the stone walls all the way up to the third floor. As my eyes peeked over the stone floor of the fairly large balcony — which would be better described as a terrace — I noticed nearly a dozen people all dressed in white. They were all seated facing a tall, extravagant mirror. I quickly ducked when I saw who was next to the mirror, causing me to nearly lose my grip. I waited there, frozen, listening for any sign that someone was maybe coming to investigate. Eventually, I peeked through the stone railings again at the woman standing before the gathered crowd. It wasn't The Dove, but it was someone who was possibly just as dangerous.

"Quiet down everyone! The meeting is about to begin!" Ravenna, the witch Magistrate Frollo raised to despise my kind just as much as he did, shouted at the crowd.

She wore a deep purple dress with a black, boned corset accentuating her figure. Scars covered her exposed arms, and she adorned her neck and fingers with many pieces of jewelry that were either black or violet. Her hair was as dark as a jackdaw's feathers, tied up in a braid that extended from her head all the way down to her lower back. The witch's lips were colored black, and her eyes were a bright blue. She was just as intimidating as you would expect one of the most dangerous witches alive to be. She would definitely make my task more difficult if I couldn't get at The Dove without fighting her too. I would still wait though, not yet willing to concede this wasn't doable. The small gathering of people clad in white had become silent, and Ravenna was now casting a spell on the mirror.

Arriving late, it seemed, was Magistrate Frollo himself. He was covered in a white cloak as well, the cloth billowing in the wind he left behind him as he briskly made his way to the mirror. *"Veuillez m'excuser, les amis.* Something came up. Is everyone here?"

"Whoever was loyal enough to come, has come." Ravenna said, with what sounded like a touch of displeasure.

Magistrate Frollo hadn't seemed to pick up on his daughters tone. "Good! *Merveilleux.* Where is The Dove?"

Ravenna's glowing hands continued to make patterns around the mirror. "She'll be here soon."

"How is she not here yet? Why would she tell us all a specific time only for her to be late?" Right after he had asked his question, Magistrate Frollo jumped back a step from the mirror. Everyone there bowed their heads, Magistrate Frollo included. "My Lady."

"Tristan. Always a pleasure. Is everyone here, Ravenna?" A voice that sounded distant, yet close at the same time asked the witch.

"Baron Jean Laurent, Baron Renard Lavigne, Lady Celine Garnier, and Baron Hubert Monet are the only ones who haven't come, Bright One. Everyone else is accounted for."

Bright One? Who were they talking to? And where was The Dove?

"Excellent. Those who have decided not to come will be dealt with at a later time. Now, I am here to speak to those loyal to our cause." Lavender light began to emanate from the mirror until it formed the shape of a woman my kind knew all too well. "Those who have come will be happy to know that I have had a breakthrough in my research. Something has led me to discovering the location of someone with the blood I have long been searching for. While it is all but certain I will have it, I do believe it is best to continue what you have been doing. This person I have found may not be the only one that possesses Mystic Blood. The more I have of it the stronger chance of the spell working. I'd like to know how everyone's operations are going. Lady Blanchet, would you care to start?"

My own thoughts drowned out the woman now speaking to the glowing purple image of The Dove. Everything about what I had just heard sounded bad for the Tóráin, not to mention my target wasn't even really here. I had discovered what was being done to the prisoners who were sent to Bastion though. Whatever kind of spell that required Mystic Blood was something big, and I had a feeling that it wasn't going to be good for Tóráin or humans. I had been told about Mystic Blood by my grandmother when I was little, so I didn't remember too much of what she said. All that was coming to me was that Mystic Blood was rare among the Tóráin and that those who had it were stronger than regular members of their race. I think my grandmother had even mentioned something about them being able to wield magic, but it was said that only the Druids could do that, and their family lines were long dead. Wait. Maybe those with Mystic Blood had Druids as their ancestors! That would explain why it was so rare. But it didn't make any sense, my grandmother had told me all the Druids who brought us here were killed during The Great Welcoming. Too many thoughts were running through my head, and I was beginning to get lost in them. I realized that if I wanted answers to my questions, I needed to get my hands on someone.

Ravenna was my first choice, but a fight with her was incredibly risky. I could follow any of the people here and question them, however I doubted they would know much more than I did. If I really wanted answers, I needed to go after someone higher up; someone like Magistrate Frollo. I wasn't sure if I could get to him tonight, but I was certainly going to try. I watched and listened to two more nobles tell The Dove of their progress until it seemed that everyone had spoken. I was hopeful that the meeting would end now, my body beginning to ache from holding myself in this position for so long.

"That's everyone, yes? Good. That concludes the meeting." The Dove opened her arms to the small gathering before her. "Go in peace and may we all find Heaven soon."

Heaven? What did Heaven have to do with all this? I hadn't pegged The Dove as a zealot, but it was looking like she and this group of hers could belong to the group known as Deus' Chosen. They believed that if a portal to my ancestral world could be opened, then a portal to Deus' home in Heaven could be opened as well. Was that the spell The Dove spoke of? It would explain the need for something as strong as Mystic Blood. I had nearly a dozen questions lined up and ready to ask as I waited for an opportunity to get my hands on the Magistrate.

The nobles all rose to their feet and began leaving the room that was attached to the terrace. The Dove's violet image watched them leave before turning to Magistrate Frollo. "I trust that everything is going well in Etoile?"

He nodded quickly. "Yes, Bright One. Those demons try to flee Fleuris nearby every day. I'll send you a new group to deal with in the next few days."

"Don't bother. I'll come there. I find that if I stay in the capital too long, I get an overwhelming itch to kill everyone here." The Dove turned her attention to Ravenna now. "You can show me if you've made any progress on what we've been working on. I'll be in Etoile in a few days. Make sure you have that wine I like, Tristan. I'll need it."

"Of course! I cannot wait to host you again. Safe travels." Magistrate Frollo bowed dramatically.

The image of The Dove was sucked back into the mirror, leaving just Ravenna and Magistrate Frollo.

"Well, it's late. I'm going to sleep, father." Ravenna went over and kissed the older man on the cheek.

He returned the gesture before letting out a sigh. "I think I might have a drink before turning in. These meetings always make my nerves run wild. *La Colombe* wasn't even truly here, and I was still worried about upsetting her."

Ravenna began walking away from her surrogate father, taking steps backwards so as to still face him. "You worry too much. Get some sleep." The witch turned around and made her way to the exit with her back to Frollo. "*Bonne nuit!*"

This was my chance, but I had to be cautious. Magistrate Frollo had a pistol on him, and if he managed to fire that off the entire estate's garrison would be on me in seconds. Not to mention Ravenna was still close by and could possibly hear a struggle. I needed to be quick and efficient. I watched my target turn to face the open air and take in a few deep breaths. He stood there for some time, admiring the clear night sky and all the stars that littered the black veil, until finally returning to the room. I kept my eyes on him as he went over to a small table that appeared to have multiple bottles of alcohol ready to be poured. The time was now. I quickly pulled myself up and over the railing, doing my best to move swiftly while also remaining as quiet as possible. Just as he went to take a drink of what smelled like whiskey, I kicked at the back of his leg to bring him down to his knees and put my knife to his throat.

"You made me spill my drink. Do you have any idea how expensive that is?"

Not what I had expected to hear him say, but I didn't let his apparent disinterest in my knife deter me. "I have questions, and you're going to answer them. Shout, and I kill you. Go for a weapon, and I kill you. Understood?"

Magistrate Frollo put his glass down on the floor and slowly put his hands up, both actions causing me to nearly cut his throat. Any movement could mean the beginning of a struggle, and I couldn't risk that. I knew better than to underestimate my opponent. He was well past his prime, but the man was a feared commander in Fleuris' army before he became the Magistrate of Etoile. I wanted answers, but I wanted to get out of here alive more. If I had to kill him without gaining any knowledge, I would. At least the world would be rid of one more monster.

"So, what are you? *Un chien ou une chèvre*? We're up fairly high, perhaps you flew in here like a *pigeon*? *Non*? Oh, you must be one of the colored *Diables*! Can't be one of those *petits monstres*, you're too tall."

Every word he said made me angry. Not only was he ignoring me, but he was also taunting me. There were rumors that the man was insane, and he was starting to prove those rumors true. Who antagonizes the person holding a knife to their throat? Colored demon, eh? Fine. I slowly moved around him, keeping my blade pressed to his neck, until I was facing him. I pulled out a throwing knife with my free hand and stabbed him in his thigh. He bit his lip, refusing to make any sound in response.

"Feel like answering my questions now?" I twisted the blade, managing to get a small groan out of him, but he soon started to chuckle to himself.

I ripped the knife out and jammed it into the side of his knee. The blow got a considerable groan out of him this time, but before I could ask him anything he spat in my face. Blinding me for that brief second gave him enough time to grab my hand and push the knife away from his neck. Having quickly regained my eyesight, I watched as Magistrate Frollo pulled the smaller knife out of his knee and went to stab me in the stomach. I dove away, just barely avoiding the strike. I tried a strike of my own, but he caught and twisted my hand until my wrist gave out, causing me to drop my knife. He quickly pounced on me and tried to stab me in the face. I brought up my hand, the blade sliding through until the hilt brought it to a stop. The point of the knife was terribly close to my eye, but a swift punch to my attacker's injured leg gave me enough leverage to push him off me. He scrambled for the knife lying on the floor, but I quickly pulled the blade out of my hand and leaped onto him before he could reach it. I put my knife to his neck once more.

"What is The Dove planning?" I asked.

Magistrate Frollo scrunched up his face in disgust and pushed at my hand, causing the knife to catch the side of his neck and give him a nasty cut. He reached over for the blade still free on the floor, and I reluctantly stabbed into his neck. The shock of the blow didn't deter him, as he still struggled for the knife. I quickly stabbed him in the neck again, but he continued to reach for it. Blood spilled from his injuries, and I cursed as I stabbed my small knife into his eye. His struggling stopped, and I was left with no more answers than I had before this encounter. I should have known that he wouldn't tell me anything. I ripped my knife out of his head and rolled off him to lay on my back. I was breathing heavily from our fight, so I gave myself a brief moment to recover before grabbing the blade off the floor and putting it back in my belt. I leaned over and began searching Magistrate

Frollo's body for anything that could lead me to my next mission, and I eventually found something in his coat pocket.

It was an envelope, and inside it was a letter with plans for a structure of some kind. I quickly read what was written and horror struck me. It was a letter from General Rosspier, instructing recipients of the letter to begin making temporary camps to house imprisoned Tóráin. It spoke about his plan for initiating a new law called the Diables Labor Act. It gave soldiers and nobles free reign to force the Tóráin into these new camps, making them do work that was being left undone because of everyone either being killed or trying to flee. Nothing about this seemed good, and as much as I wished to learn more about what was going on with The Dove and her followers, I needed to return home. I shoved the letter in my leather corset and took the white cloak that the Magistrate had taken off before our fight. Free of blood, the cloak would hopefully allow me to vacate the villa without much trouble. I went back out onto the terrace and began my descent, hoping that I got back to Cloque before anything bad happened.

# Chapter Forty

## Olwen

Cloque, Fleuris  |  May 20, 1799

Anya and I had caught sight of Cloque when the sun was directly above us. We debated over whether we should wait until the cover of night to enter the city, or just risk it and go in during the day. The argument was brief and the young sprite eventually conceded. I didn't want to wait any longer. The more time I spent out of the city, the more anxiety I felt. You would think a Tórán would want nothing to do with the place and stay away at all costs, yet I couldn't wait to enter. My friends were in there, and after what I had discovered in Etoile, I needed to make sure they were alright. It was very risky to try to sneak into Cloque in broad daylight, so we had to be careful. The two of us entered the canal further away from the wall than usual. The long swim had me wishing I was a water sprite like Anya.

When we got close to the outer walls of the city, we silently went under the surface. When my need for air caused my lungs to nearly burst, I slowly allowed my horns, eyes, and nose to be free of the cool water. I had managed to get just a meter away from the tunnel that would provide us cover from the guards. I saw Anya safely inside it, waving at me to hurry over. I doubted the soldiers on the walls were going to look directly down at the canal, but I played it safe and went back under the surface for a few more seconds. I came up for air right next to Anya, and the two of us pushed the grate open before swimming to the other side.

We needed to endure another long stretch underwater in order to avoid the guards. Thankfully, nobody noticed two blue and green females poking the tops of their heads out of the canal. To be honest, the streets where we popped up seemed more dead than usual. I looked back and even noticed that there weren't as many guards on the city's side of the south gate. Something was different from when Anya and I had left Cloque. The two of us slowly climbed out of the canal and cautiously made our way north towards The Fancy Fox. As we maneuvered our way through alleys and side streets, the lack of people continued to be noticeable. It wasn't until we ran into a harpy, who cut into the alley we were navigating, that we found out what was going on.

"What are you two doing?" he had asked. "Trouble is coming. General Rosspier is encouraging his minions again in front of Sainte Mère Cathedral. You'd do best to hide for a couple days or so. Do you not have somewhere to go?

"We're fine," I responded. "Has General Rosspier spoken already?"

The harpy was thrown off by my question, but he answered it all the same. "No. Soon though. Now if you aren't coming with me, get out of my way."

He pushed through Anya and I, grumbling to himself as he tried to hide his wings with an oversized cloak most harpies tended to wear. After he had passed us by, I gave a look to Anya and she swiftly shook her head. I didn't stay to argue. I was curious if General Rosspier would be announcing his new plan to the public or not. Of course, he didn't have to. He could just start it and let people find out as time passed them by. It was how all laws had come to be. They were created away from the public eye and then suddenly dropped on the masses. However, I could see the advantage of announcing this to his followers. Not to mention the man was so vain that he probably wanted to hear the applause he would get for his announcement. In my honest opinion, it was very likely that he would say something, and I wanted to hear it. I wanted to get a grasp on how the crowd reacted. There were some humans who had slowed their support for General Rosspier's encouraged civilian justice, and I wondered what his words about these camps would do.

I was almost certain that Keagan had someone there already to listen to what General Rosspier was saying, but they could miss something important. These speeches were hateful and divisive, but sometimes they gave us an insight into the General's mind. Plus, he was so pompous and proud that he had given us information on the apprehension of a small group of Resistance members to the south last time he spoke. We managed to save a few of them thanks to him. The biggest thing that I got from these speeches was motivation. Every vile word that left General Rosspier's mouth gave me another reason to fight back. It was hard to keep going, especially with the way things were. Having something that pushed me forward every month was good. As Anya and I made our way towards The City's Heart, I couldn't help but smile at the thought that General Rosspier would hate knowing that his speeches were actually encouraging Tóráin to stand against him. He wanted to spread fear to my kind. He had been mostly successful, but there were still some of us who stood bravely in defiance.

"Are you sure about this?" Anya asked as she pulled me back into the shadows of the alley.

We were finally at Court Bridge, and I could both hear and see the crowd that had gathered to hear General Rosspier speak. "Oh we'll be fine! Come on, I don't think he's started yet."

I grabbed a hold of Anya's hand and dragged her out of the alley and onto the bridge. From there we could see the stage that the General had made for his speech, as well as the large assortment of soldiers guarding it. There were at least twenty or so on the stage with him, and probably four times that amount surrounding the raised platform. I spotted who I assumed to be Major Carierre standing next to General Rosspier. The stage was void of the usual image of The Dove, who was no doubt already in Etoile trying to deal with the fact that Magistrate Frollo was dead. I wondered if she even cared. The woman was as cold as ice according to our spies in Joieternelle Palace. My thoughts about The Dove vanished the moment I heard General Rosspier's sickening tone stretch across the crowd.

"*Les bons humains de Fleuris*! I come to you today with good news! I have taken into consideration your feelings on something you all have been quite vocal about! Last time I was on this stage, I spoke about ridding the *Diables* from our country! As much as you all enjoyed the idea, many others pointed out that we humans shouldn't be forced to do the grueling work made for *ces Diables*! You didn't see why us superior beings should be lowering ourselves to such a level! *N'aie pas peur*, for I have thought of a solution! *Ce matin*, I initiated a new law in Fleuris! The Diables Labor Act will give my soldiers the right to remove *ces horribles bêtes* from their homes and toss them into select locations! These camps will ensure that those inside them will do the hard labor necessary for the day, freeing humans to live their lives the way we were made to live them!

"*Vous êtes tous des enfants exceptionnels de Deus*! You have led me to a path of enlightenment! I realize now that the *Diables* were made to be slaves, not hunted! They were brought here to ease the pressure of our lives, and allow us all to ascend to a higher level of existence, both socially and spiritually! Deus has tricked his brother Eous into delivering a workforce for The High One's greatest creation!"

Anya nudged me. "Okay, I think we've heard enough. Now let's get out of here."

I shrugged her off. "We're fine. I want to see if he says anything about what The Dove is doing. We still don't know if General Rosspier has any connection to it."

"Fine. You stay and risk your life. I'm leaving for The Fancy Fox." Anya pushed by me, quickly walking back over the bridge we had partially crossed.

I was trying to push Anya's words out of my head when I heard a girl shout. The noise had me spinning around to find six soldiers surrounding Anya.

"Get your hands off me!" Anya shouted as I swiftly got closer.

"You deaf, *Diable*? General Rosspier said we can do whatever we want. Now, before we take you to one of these new camps, play nice." Two soldiers grabbed Anya by her arms and put the poor girl in a vulnerable position.

"Hey! Leave her alone!" I shouted at the soldiers as I drew my sword.

The soldier fixing his pants and tightening his belt grinned. "Oh look what we have here! Another one! *Attention les gars*, she might stick you before you stick her!"

There was only six of them, so I felt fairly confident, but I didn't want them to hurt or possibly even kill Anya. I gripped my sword tightly, deciding there was no way I was leaving my friend to these beasts so long as I still lived. "Final warning. You let her go and none of you die."

The soldier that had addressed me nodded at the other guards and one of them gave Anya a swift punch to the side of her head. The girl instantly went limp, and I was charging forward as the large man put Anya over his shoulder. The remaining soldiers all drew pistols and fired at me. I dove to my right, but one of the bullets hit just enough of my left arm to go in one side and out the other. I quickly pounced at the closest soldier, and we engaged in a brief battle as the others readied their pistols for another shot. I saw the large soldier who had Anya toss her up onto a horse before getting into the saddle himself.

"Take *la pute* to Camp Liodorleu! We'll deal with this one." One of the soldiers yelled at the man up on the horse.

Seeing him race off with Anya set fire to a rage inside me that had me cutting down my dueling partner. I used his body as a shield to close the distance between me and the others when I heard one of their panicked voices.

"Help! Over here!" they shouted.

One of them sounded a whistle, causing me to peek out from my fleshy cover to see the soldiers I was charging had retreated, the distance between me and them still too far to risk revealing myself. I looked behind me, and I could see the crowd parting. More soldiers would be on the way. My eyes went to the direction the horse had ridden off to, and I silently apologized to Anya for putting her in danger the way I did. I also made sure to promise her that I would see her rescued, before pushing the limp body at the soldiers in front of me and sprinting for the stone railing of the bridge. I leapt over as gunshots whizzed by, luckily none of them catching me before I dove into the cold waters of The Dame. Bullets followed me in, the afternoon sun giving enough light near the surface for me to see them swim past me. I allowed the calm current to guide me forward as I swam underwater and out of the sight. Eventually, I had to come up for air and as I peeked out at my surroundings, I realized that I was under the Bridge of Michele L'Archange. I could see Sainte Mère Cathedral in the distance, along with a large group of soldiers spreading out to find me. I continued to let the current guide me west, slipping out onto the stone shores just before the river dipped south.

After climbing up the stone steps to reach the streets of Cloque, I quickly ducked into an alley to gather myself. Right away I began berating myself for being so reckless. We should have gone straight for Keagan and the others. That had been what I wanted to do so badly before we heard about General Rosspier's damn speech. Why the Hell was hearing that bastard speak so damn important to me? I rubbed my eyes before forcing myself to move, the question never leaving my head. As I weaved my way through alleys to get to The Fancy Fox, I continued to search for an answer. Was there something wrong with me? I had found every way possible to validate making that speech a priority. For what? To hear him call my kind devils? To hear him say things I already knew? I finally came to the conclusion that it was what happened in Etoile that had caused my lapse in judgement. The truth of it all, was that General Rosspier wasn't my greatest enemy anymore. The Dove had taken his place thanks to her mysterious plan involving my kind and some special spell. I wanted to see if she was here, even though I knew she wasn't. I wanted to hear General Rosspier speak about it, even though I was almost certain he had no part in what The Dove was doing.

I had allowed my need to take down The Dove drive me to a path that I usually would not have taken. What's worse is I put Anya in danger. Now she was being taken to a place called Camp Liodorleu. I intended to rescue her, as well as any others that I could. I didn't know how or when, but I was hoping that Keagan, Finn, and the others possibly had some information that would help. I reached The Fancy Fox with the sun still beaming in a partially cloudy afternoon sky. The second I burst through the door, I made my way to the bar.

"Ah, Olwen! Good to see you back in one piece. Where's Anya?" Verill's face got grim when I ignored his question in favor of asking one of my own.

"Where's Keagan?" The panic in my voice had Verill quickly leaving the bar and making his way to one of the few rooms he had available.

Verill knocked on the door in a special pattern, and Keagan answered it. He had a big grin on his face as he came forward and hugged me. "O'! Glad you're back!" I could hear him sniff the air before gently pushing us apart. "Where's Anya?"

I pushed by the lycan and entered his room. I heard Keagan knock on Finn's door and when I turned around, I saw Keagan nod in my direction. Finn came into view, and he entered the room quickly, stopping when he realized I was alone. I could see he was struggling to ask the question he probably didn't want the answer to. Anya and Finn were very close, much in a way that Keagan and I were.

"Where's Anya?" Keagan asked Finn's question for him as he closed the door.

I felt ashamed saying it, knowing that it was mostly my fault. "She was taken by soldiers when we entered the city. I couldn't stop them, Finn. I'm so sorry."

"How could you not stop them? You and Anya are both capable fighters. You alone are more capable than nearly any remaining member of The Resistance. Were there dozens of them? How was she caught? Do you know where they're taking her?" After Finn had so much trouble blurting out his first question, his new one's just fell out of him like water out of a tipped over bucket.

I raised my hand to tell him to calm down. "Easy, Finn. General Rosspier was giving a speech at Sainte Mère Cathedral. I thought it might be a good idea to find out what he was going to say. We got close enough to hear a good bit before some soldiers surprised us. They got a hold of Anya and knocked her out. Before I could get to her, her kidnapper rode away. I heard one of them shout for him to take Anya to a place called Camp Liodorleu. I jumped into the river to avoid getting captured myself and I immediately came here."

"You should have immediately come here the second you entered the city," Keagan grumbled.

I threw my hands up in the air. "Yeah well, we didn't, Keagan. I can't go back in time and change that. What we can do is try to figure out how we're going to save Anya and any others taken to this place."

"Camp Liodorleu must be that new place they were building north of the city. Why would they take people there though? Is Bastion full or something?" The worry in Finn's voice had vanished, giving way to a more focused tone.

"I found this on Magistrate Frollo's body after I killed him." I pulled out the letter and the plans from a pouch hanging off my belt. Keagan and Finn both gave me a look full of shock from my statement. I waved them off. "Long story. Just look at the letter will you."

Keagan unfolded the letter and the plans for the camp set to be built near Etoile. I watched him and Finn read it together, fidgeting impatiently as I silently begged for them to read faster. I felt like every second we wasted here made our chances of saving Anya less and less.

Keagan looked away from the letter and nodded. "Yeah, that's definitely what that buildin' to the north is. They started workin' on it the day after you left for Valarc. We had no clue what it was for. This is a problem."

I pulled my hair away from my face and let out a deep sigh. "It's all part of this new Diables Labor Act General Rosspier has introduced. They're turning us into slaves, Keagan. Every Tórán is being brought to these camps and forced to work."

Finn had a shocked look on his face. "What are we going to do?"

Keagan folded the letter back up and put it on the nearby table. "We'll scout Camp Liodorleu ourselves tonight and see if we can come up with a plan to free Anya and as many others as we can. Camp Liodorleu is outside the city walls, so it will be easier to free people from there instead of going door to door throughout the city now."

"Shouldn't we at least try to save some people now?" The worry had returned to Finn's voice. "What if Tóráin die in that camp before we free them?"

I put a hand on the young lycan's arm. "We can't think like that. Keagan is right. Our best bet at getting people away from Cloque is freeing them from the camp instead of trying to wrangle everyone in the city. We'll go check things out tonight."

A knock on our door had Keagan opening it a crack, which let in Verill's nervous voice. "Soldiers are going door to door. They'll check these rooms. Best get you three in the cellar."

I grabbed the letter off the table and followed the two lycans out of the room. Verill led us to the cellar door and held it open while we descended the steps. The darkness and smell of alcohol reminded me of the days I spent in the cellar of Joan's Courage back in Valarc. I hated that it had come to this. As the three of us tried to get comfortable, I thought of Anya. I remembered the promise I had made her before I jumped into the river. I told myself then that I would do anything to see that she was safe. I would make things right. I would save her and as many others as we could before bringing this damn country to its knees for what it has done to us.

# Chapter Forty-One

## Weylyn

Höllentore, Korblum | May 23, 1799

The battle had begun, but we remained where we were. It was hard to watch others fight, however Queen Sophia had created a plan and we had to stick to it. A scout had returned to us before we entered the valley informing us that Korblum's army would no doubt meet us in the morning. With that knowledge, Queen Sophia and her war council decided to send two brigades ahead to hide in the forests which bordered the great valley: one brigade on each side of the open field. These brigades were named Unity and Peace. Both were heavily populated by the Tóráin but, according to Brina, they weren't in any way like the Diables Division of the Fleuris army. These groups of about fifteen hundred or so soldiers had formed themselves, choosing to train and fight together. They were made up of Tóráin and humans who highly respected each other. The leader of Peace was a human by the name of Colonel Albert Smith and the leader of Unity was a forest sprite named Colonel Seamus. The fact that a Tórán had reached such a rank in the army had surprised me — as well as Cordelia and Brina — and his position led us to deciding to fight with Unity. I felt a sense of pride standing next to Colonel Seamus. Especially when he and Colonel Smith had offered up Peace and Unity to undertake this mission before anyone could be chosen.

Höllentore, the name of the valley that had become our battlefield, split the Quellen Mountains in half, and is bordered by the Neidern Forest to the south-west and the Vocken Forest to the north-east. According to Lady Mirlena — who was well-versed in the histories of every nation — Höllentore had been a battlefield many times throughout Korblum's history, dating all the way back to the great Luilan Empire over a thousand years ago. The Luilans had called the place '*Portae Inferi*', which is the Planin phrase for 'The Gates of Hell'. They had called it that because of how vicious the warriors from old Korblum were during their wars. The Quellen Mountains had served as a natural border between the old kingdom of Walula and the Luilan Empire, with the valley being the only clear way to enter without travelling around the mountain range. After hundreds of years, well after the Fall of the Luilan Empire, the newly formed Kingdom of Korblum gave the place the same name but in their native language of Korblan. Höllentore continued to live up to its name throughout the years, being a frequent Hell-inspired battleground during, and after, the time of the Kingdom of Korblum. It only made sense that we would now add our blood to the land as well.

We were to remain hidden in the trees and wait until the trumpets sounded. The goal was to ambush Korblum's army, attacking their left and right flanks. Their cannons were our target as well. They had already taken out a few of our own artillery, and stopping them would be vital to our victory. To give us the opening we required, the main army would initiate a false retreat. At the sound of those trumpets we would charge. I could smell the scent of gunpowder and blood, as I'm sure every other lycan here could. We would be called upon soon. A few minutes passed us by, and it started to look as if Korblum was winning. Sure enough, the trumpets to retreat sounded and the mass of red uniforms all began moving away from their enemy. I looked at Colonel Seamus seated on his horse, the sprite holding his arm high in the air. We had arrived at our spot on time thanks to horses, but not everyone had decided to ride theirs into battle. Lycans could run close to the speed of a horse in our feral form, harpies could fly, and satyrs were more comfortable on their hooves than the horse's; humans, sprites, and goblins were the only ones that were riding into battle. Cordelia had taken up her position on horseback with the rest of the cavalry to the left of Colonel Seamus while Brina and I, along with the rest of the brigade, were prepared to charge on his right.

Colonel Seamus dropped his arm quickly as he broke out of the trees that had been providing us cover. The cavalry raced off after him, with the rest of Unity not far behind. I sprinted on all fours towards Korblum's unexpecting army with over a battalion of Tóráin next to me. Whistles began firing off as Korblum realized they were being flanked on both sides, and gunshots followed soon after. The main army had abandoned their fake retreat and attacked the front of Korblum's forces. The cavalry that Colonel Seamus led aimed for the rear of the army, while the rest of us charged directly into its side. I could hear screams coming after the sounds of guns firing, telling me that not all of us would reach our enemy, but it only made me run faster. The sooner we reached them the quicker we would force them into melee combat. Soldiers quickly held out their rifles with bayonets on the ends of them like spears in the hopes to halt our advance. The satyrs crashed into the soldiers holding the pointy rifles as they all foolishly raised them to try and spear the lycans who had leaped over the front line's attempted barricade. Harpies flew over top and dove into the mass of black uniforms as lycans clawed and chewed apart those nearest to them. In such close quarters, it was difficult for the soldiers to pull out their sabers and use them well enough. The few that did would feel less dangerous thanks to us lycans having some protection. Tudrose's army had thick leather armor they provided for their lycans, as well as any other close combat Tórán. They were the only ones who did this, according to Brina, and I was quickly thankful for it when a soldier slashed at my stomach and left only a scratch on the armor.

It was hard to tell how long we fought for. Tracking time was a skill that was easily lost during battle. It was one of the many things I had learned back in Leuw. I was able to put everything to use when we were attacked just inside the northern border of Korblum, although the force we faced was much smaller than the one here in Höllentore. I kept my head moving and my eyes open, trying to keep up with the mayhem that took over every battlefield. After grabbing a man's sword arm, spinning him around and making him cut his own throat with his sword, I turned around just in time to block a stabbing bayonet with my arm. The soldiers deeper in the ranks of Korblum's army had kept their rifles at hand instead of drawing their swords, using them like spears in between trying to shoot you. The tip of the bayonet stuck out one side of my thick forearm for a moment before the soldier pulled it out aggressively. Blood spilled from my arm, which had me quickly putting my left hand over the wound. I took a breath and said the words Lady Mirlena had taught me to say.

*"Leigheas mé."* I felt the tendons and muscle repairing as I moved slightly to the left and caught the follow up stab from the Korblum soldier.

With my arm now healed and my hand firmly holding the man's gun, I pulled him towards me. He stumbled headfirst into my chest before letting go of the gun and backing up. He didn't have any fear in his eyes despite knowing he was about to die. Instead, there was anger — more like hatred actually. He spat in my face as he stood defiantly before me. My intention was to kill him, but one of his allies swung at me with a sword. I turned my attention to my assailant, blocking his blow with the rifle I had stolen. With a quick spin of the rifle, I disarmed the soldier before running the entire bayonet through his chest. A sharp pain erupted from my left side as I turned around to see the man who had spat at me with a sword in his hand. Half of the blade was inside me. He pulled it out and went for another stab, but I found the strength to move out of the way. I grabbed his extended arm and twisted quickly, the bones snapping. The man yelped and fell to his knees. I lifted him up to his feet by his broken arm and snarled in his face. The defiance he had in his eyes was still there. Again, he spat in my face. Some would call him brave in the face of death, but I knew that bravery had nothing to do with it. This was pure hatred. Hatred for me and those like me. I wanted to return the hatred he had for me in the form of more pain, but my energy was fading from the blow he had injured me with earlier. I brought my free hand to his throat and swiped my claws across it before letting go of his arm. He collapsed to the ground, desperately trying to hold in the blood leaking from his neck.

"Weylyn!" I recognized the voice.

"Colonel Seamus?" I asked as I looked around with blurring eyes.

I held my side and noticed that I had bled quite a bit, and my energy was slowly leaving me. I didn't have much time, so I had to act quickly. Focusing as hard as I could, the pain from the wound and the fear of death trying their best to distract me, I held my hand firmly on my injured side. I allowed myself to fall to a knee, before both of them rested on the bloodstained grass.

"Weylyn!" I heard what sounded like swords clashing before a grunt was released by whoever lost. Next thing I knew someone had their hand on the side of my neck. "Weylyn! Hey! You alright?"

I didn't answer. I kept my eyes closed and did my best to focus. The more time that went by, the less energy I had to use. More sounds of swords clashing and guns firing filled my ears until I blocked them out too. What I was doing was dangerous, but it was necessary. Whether I didn't heal myself and bled out, or was cut down with my eyes closed, I was dead. I had to try. It was harder to do because of the severity of the injury, but I finally felt confident enough to tap into whatever energy I had left and hope that it was enough.

"*Leigheas mé*." The little energy I had left all went to my wound to repair it. The next thing I knew I was falling over, and my mind went to sleep.

I woke up to someone slapping me in the face multiple times. I opened my eyes slowly as I moved my head away from the person's hand. "I'm alright! Stop it will you."

I noticed that I had returned to my tame form and that the only people around me were allies. They were moving forward, continuing the assault on Korblum's forces. My vision was blurry at first, but I soon recognized Brina. Looming over me in her tame form, she brandished a good cut on her left arm.

"Oh thank the gods you aren't dead!" She exclaimed before embracing me roughly.

"Since when could Tóráin heal themselves?" Colonel Seamus asked as I noticed him standing over me.

I struggled to find the words to explain, but the sounds of triumphant trumpets filled the air instead. They blared the tune of victory, and many of those around me stopped what they were doing to raise their arms in the air and cheer. Knowing we had won allowed me to feel a sense of relief. I had no energy left in me to continue fighting. I was surprised that I had even opened my eyes. I felt at my injured side and shook my head in disbelief when there was no wound to be found. I would have died if Lady Mirlena hadn't taught me the spell to heal injuries. Brina tried to lift me to my feet, but I remained mostly limp, completely and utterly spent.

"Set him down, Brina. Let him rest. We won." Colonel Seamus put a hand on Brina's shoulder and she lowered me back to the ground.

My cousin held my head in her lap. "You're sure you're alright?"

I laughed. "I'm fine. Just tired."

Brina moved stray strands of hair from my face. "Sleep if you need to. If you can. I'll make sure you're looked after."

I closed my eyes. "I know you will."

# Chapter Forty-Two

## Weylyn

Adler, Korblum  |  May 25, 1799

I had slept until last evening, waking up briefly to be greeted by a distraught Rosalie and a worried Brina. Cordelia was there too, alive and well, as well as Queen Sophia, Lady Mirlena, and Arthur. They had all been waiting for me to wake up. Mostly because they wished to be sure that I was alright, but also because Queen Sophia had refused to meet with King Franz until I was ready to go with her. I told her she didn't have to do that, but she insisted that I was just as important as she was. I admired her immense respect for me. Very few humans would admit that a lycan, or any Tórán for that matter, was just as important as they were; especially when that human was the leader of an entire country. Regardless of why everyone was there, it warmed my heart to see all of them safe. Knowing how close I had come to death made me recognize how easily someone else could have died, and so I thanked whatever gods would listen for keeping my friends safe. After a bit of chatting, along with some food and drink, I informed Queen Sophia I would be ready to go with her in the morning. I slept well that night, holding Rosalie close and admiring the little things in life more than usual. When I awoke this morning, I still felt a little tired, but I was more up for travelling than I had been the day before.

While I was resting, the army had dealt with the dead from the battle and moved forward to Adler. During our fight, Seig and the rebel forces had initiated a battle of their own, fighting the city's garrison amongst the streets. Just like us, they were victorious, taking control of Palamfluss, the castle where King Franz ruled from. The bulk of our army camped outside of the city, but a good number of soldiers — I'd guess maybe five thousand or so — entered Adler with Queen Sophia and me. The soldiers helped Seig's rebels keep control of the city while the Queen of Tudrose and myself went to the eastern end of Adler, where Palamfluss rested on the shores of Haupt River. Seig met us at the gate, the harpy woman looking much more powerful than I had imagined her. She still held a feminine beauty, but her physique openly displayed her strength. Seig welcomed us warmly and was now leading us to where we would meet King Franz and his young son, Prince Wilhelm. King Franz had divorced his first wife after she could not give him children, and he had Wilhelm's mother executed when it was suspected that she had been hiding the fact that she was a witch. According to Queen Sophia, no real proof had ever come forward, but King Franz was rash and quick to make decisions. He also always believed he was right.

We arrived at an intricately carved set of doors made of a wood that was a darker brown than the usual oak. They were different from all the other doors we had passed by, and their deep color provided a strong contrast to the bone white walls and ceilings. Two intimidating lycans stood guard, both in their feral forms. One had a dark amber color to them while the other was as black as the night sky. Their golden eyes were fixed on us since we turned the corner and began walking down the hall. It made sense as to why they were ready for a fight, knowing what was waiting behind the door they guarded. King Franz had demanded to speak with Queen Sophia once his home was taken by Seig and the others. The man and his son weren't fully detained yet, hiding in the throne room with roughly twenty or so soldiers guarding them. They all had rifles aimed at the door, and after a few Tóráin died trying to storm the room, nobody wanted to go in. Seig had told us that she would rather let them rot in there than send Queen Sophia and I inside. However, despite her worries, she had conceded to Queen Sophia's determination to speak with King Franz.

Seig banged on the door with her fist. "Queen Sophia is here, Franz. You got what you wanted now tell your soldiers to stand down!"

"No one commands me but Deus himself! Send *die Königin* in, and only her. I will stand down when I wish!" King Franz's voice was strong, reaching through the walls well enough that it was incredibly easy to hear what he said.

Queen Sophia stepped towards the doors and put a hand on its carved surface. "King Franz, enough of this foolishness! The fight is over! Have your soldiers stand down and we can discuss terms!"

King Franz didn't respond right away this time. Silence enveloped everyone as we waited to hear from the deranged King of Korblum. After a couple minutes, his rough tone shouted from the throne room again. "You've won one battle, Königin Sophia! My soldiers from every corner of the country are on their way to free their *König*, that I know! If you want to prevent any more of your people from dying, you'll follow my instructions and come in here alone while my *Soldaten* stand ready!"

Queen Sophia stepped away from the door and waved for Seig and I to come close so she could whisper her question. "Do we know if more soldiers are coming? Would they really try to free him even though we've taken the capital?"

Seig's face squirmed as she thought before answering. "Our informant did say that soldiers had been called upon from other cities and towns in the country. They don't know they've lost yet, but I can't imagine they would fight to free him. Most humans are blunt blades, but surely they would see they've lost. Oh...sorry. Obviously, you aren't one of those humans, Queen Sophia."

"It's alright, Seig," Queen Sophia responded. "I know many blunt blades myself. What do you think we should do, Weylyn?"

I was caught off guard by her request for my opinion. It was her life she would be risking, surely my stance on the matter didn't mean much here. Nonetheless, I crossed my arms and thought about what had been said before providing an answer. "Even if there is a force coming our way, they wouldn't stand a chance against us. You said it yourself that we would be facing the bulk of Korblum's army, and we beat them. We have the city under our control. I don't see the leverage King Franz seems to believe he has. I wouldn't succumb to his demands. There's no need to."

Queen Sophia nodded. "I agree that his threat of another force is lackluster. However, I would like to avoid losses to our numbers if I can. I need to deal with King Franz before his reinforcements arrive. I will not go in there alone to do so though."

"So lie." Queen Sophia and I both gave Seig a quizzical look. She rolled her eyes, apparently annoyed that she had to explain herself. "Tell him his army isn't coming. Say you've sent riders in the direction of every main city with the message that King Franz has surrendered and is negotiating terms with you already."

"Why would his reinforcements believe a Tudrose soldier?" Queen Sophia asked.

"Tell him we sent one of his own that we captured during the fight," I suggested.

"Yes! We can say that you promised the messengers riches and land in return for them convincing the reinforcements to return home!" Seig said excitedly.

Queen Sophia said nothing, only nodding before turning around and knocking on the doors again. "King Franz! This army that you believe is coming? Well, you are wrong to think so! We sent your own soldiers to inform them that you surrendered already and that terms are being discussed! I have offered them quite a handsome payment for doing as I ask, so I am sure my messengers will convince your remaining forces to return home! It is over, King Franz. If you want your soldiers to remain there, then fine! But at least allow me the comfort of having a few of my own in there as well! Let us end this and move on!"

Again, there was silence for a couple minutes until King Franz finally responded. "*Meine Leute* would never believe I would surrender! They are coming, I know they are! However, I will entertain your suggestion! You can do your best to sway me, but I will not concede this country to you or any of *der Müll* you fight with!"

Queen Sophia stepped away from the door and waved at the soldiers that had accompanied us inside. The twelve of them moved to stand at the doors in a column of three by four. Queen Sophia stood behind them, with me and Seig on either side of her. The four Tóráin who had accompanied Seig filed in behind us followed by the two large lycans at the back. The soldiers at the front of the column we had formed eased the doors open and a single gunshot sounded off, causing the men to quickly retreat.

King Franz's voice echoed from the large room on the other side. "Consider that your only warning, *Königin von Tudrose*! You try anything and you'll be as dead as crops in a drought!"

"Warning received, King Franz!" Queen Sophia shouted back before insisting the soldiers open the doors again.

No gunshots were heard this time around. The soldiers entered with their rifles angled in such a way that would not provoke an attack, but also at the ready enough should an attack occur. When I entered the large room, I noticed that King Franz's soldiers had their rifles at the same angle. The estimated number of twenty soldiers had been a tad under as I counted two dozen soldiers: a dozen men on each side of King Franz and his son Prince Wilhelm. I could tell from the grimace on his face that King Franz wasn't happy about how many of us had entered, but it was too late to force us back out. He still held a numbers advantage over us, but it would be incredibly reckless to instigate a fight when you were practically in the middle of it. King Franz held up his hand to halt our advance before standing from his seat and walking towards us, his son and another man in fancy robes flanking him. Without saying a word, Queen Sophia grabbed my hand and forced me to follow her forward as well; I noticed quickly that she had done the same to Seig. King Franz's face, along with the faces of his cohorts, twisted in disgust as they watched Queen Sophia have two Tóráin accompany her. Eventually their trio stopped, which had our trio halting roughly fifteen feet away from them.

King Franz shook his head in disbelief. "What madness has Eous infected your mind with Königin Sophia? I thought our friendship would prevent this from ever happening. You're telling me you threw that relationship away for these...these...*Biester*?"

"I have only ever tolerated you, King Franz. I would not call that a friendship. And no madness has entered my mind. Quite the opposite, I think. I could tell you why I have done what I have done, but I think it is best you heard from someone else. Weylyn?" Queen Sophia looked at me, which had me casting a quick glance at King Franz.

A trio of angry, spiteful faces looked back at me as I gathered myself before speaking. "My fight began with King Louis of Fleuris. It has continued with General Rosspier. Through that fight for equality, my eyes were opened to the hardships of my kind all over Kosavros. Korblum presents a path for the Tóráin to obtain riches and respect through the arenas. This is false. All the arena brings is pain. Fighting is the only way to barely make a living in Korblum for my kind. The treatment of the Tóráin in this country is akin to rabid dogs. We are more than that. Queen Sophia has lent us her help to teach that fact to this country and others. My kind is just as entitled to a healthy, safe, prosperous life than your kind is."

The man to King Franz's left spat at my feet. "*Blasphemie*! The creatures of Eous deserve nothing! It is only through the teachings of mercy by Deus do we gift them what they already have!"

"Archbishop Hann is right." King Franz turned his attention from me to Queen Sophia. "The fights are my gift to these people. It gives them purpose. It gives them a dream, something to aspire to. It makes them hard and strong. *Über alles*, it provides them an avenue for penance for what they are. Korblum is not like other countries, Königin Sophia. You know this. We do not imprison and torture them. We don't kill them on a whim. Many of those who achieve high status as *Kämpfer* are even loved by their fans. Korblum is, and has been for a long time, a good place for *die Teufel* to live."

"A good place to live?" Seig said, her wings flaring out a bit in anger. "Your words are no better than poison! Your words and the words of your people infected me and many others all across Kosavros. We came here hoping for money to help sick loved ones and to perhaps gain even a small amount of respect. Instead, we were forced to injure, maim, and eventually kill our own kind for humanity's enjoyment. And I'm sure you'll say that if we didn't like it, we could have just stopped, but that isn't true, is it? We were either bound by magic or poverty and hunger to enter those arenas. My kind has more to aspire to than entertainment for rich humans who view us as expendable beings. The ones who should be looking for ways to repent are those who trick my kind into a life of violence. And love? Humans like you don't love us. You never will. You love the blood spilled and the heads rolling. You love the ending of our lives and the beatings we take before. The arenas are closed. We won't fight each other only to be just as mistreated and hungry as those who don't. You speak of blasphemy? I speak of hypocrisy. Don't claim you offer a good life while you do nothing to prevent a bad one."

King Franz was visibly upset, as well as his son and the archbishop. Seig's words had riled them up and I could tell things were getting tense now. I watched the soldiers behind the King of Korblum and noticed them all slightly lower their rifles as their leader became angry. They knew him well enough to know that if his temper flared, an order to fire on us would be given. I tried to think of something to say to ease the tension in the room, but I realized that nothing I said would make things better; Tóráin speaking had been what escalated the situation. Thankfully, Queen Sophia took a small step forward and held a hand up in an attempt to calm the three men before her.

"Alright, clearly there is a difference of opinion here. However, the battle has already been decided. Tudrose, along with The Resistance, has taken your capital King Franz. Your reinforcements will not come. We are here to discuss terms. Ours are as follows. The arenas, every single one, no matter how big or small, will no longer be used. Tóráin in Korblum will have other ways of making a living and will be treated as equals. The rich will help the poor, both Tórán and human alike, to create a more balanced country. Do you accept these terms?"

King Franz spat at Queen Sophia's feet. "That's what I think of your terms. My reinforcements will arrive, and you will be forced out of my country. *Die Teufel* are below us. They always will be. They're *Biester* bred for the sole purpose of violence. Take away an outlet for them to release their nature and they will run rampant, killing everywhere they go. Help me rebuild the arenas *dieser Aufstand* has burned down. Lend me witches to keep them in line. These things need to be controlled, Königin Sophia, not let loose."

Queen Sophia sighed. "So, to be clear, you refuse to accept these terms and remain King of Korblum?"

King Franz grinned as I noticed the soldiers behind him grow tense. "You want a straight answer then? Fine. Here's my answer."

The series of gunshots that followed his statement flooded my ears. The King of Korblum had quickly pulled his pistol from his hip and fired it at Queen Sophia. The action had caused every soldier in the room to fire as well. I had not been hit by any of the bullets that whizzed by, but many others were not so lucky. The soldiers had taken most of each other out, but this confrontation wasn't over. I instinctively moved toward King Franz to stop him from firing again, while two lycans leapt by me as they raced for the remaining soldiers. I heard screams ring out as my feral form ripped my shirt and coat, right before my fangs dug into the King's neck. I got up quickly to see Prince Wilhelm and Archbishop Hann on their knees, begging to be spared. The two lycans had made quick work of the few soldiers that hadn't been killed by the initial gunfire, and almost all of the soldiers on our side were dead or dying. My fellow lycans, covered in blood, came to stand over the two cowering humans which allowed me to address something that needed my attention. King Franz had fired at Queen Sophia, but his bullet never found its target. Seig, no doubt noticing the growing chance of a fight like I did, had moved in front of the Queen of Tudrose.

I shifted as I swiftly moved towards the two of them. Queen Sophia was on her knees, firmly pressing her hands on Seig's chest in an effort to stop the bleeding. The wound was above her heart, but she would still die soon if nothing was done. I quickly pushed everything out of my mind as I moved Queen Sophia's hands away from the wound. Placing my own hands on the bleeding hole left by the bullet, I spoke the word I had been taught and felt the energy in me move into Seig. Having kept my eyes closed to remain focused, I opened them when I felt a small object press against my palm. I took the bullet in my fingers and tossed it away as Seig opened her eyes. She moved to get up but Queen Sophia and I both eased her back down.

"Am I dead?" The harpy asked.

"No. And neither am I, thanks to you." Queen Sophia leaned forward and planted a kiss on Seig's forehead.

The harpy blushed as she cleared her throat. "Yeah well, without you this whole thing crumbles so I figured it was best to keep you alive."

Queen Sophia smiled. "Whatever your reason was, I'm still incredibly thankful."

Seig looked down at her healed wound and back at me. "How did you do that?"

I shook my head and smiled. "A discussion for another time. What matters is that you're okay. Do you want to try to stand again?"

Seig nodded and moved to get up with some help from Queen Sophia and myself. The color in the harpy's face had returned well enough, as well as her strength. She was still wobbly once she reached her feet, but with our help she managed to steady herself. A group of Tóráin burst through the doors behind us with rifles and swords at the ready. They were allowed to be shocked and stunned for only a few moments before Seig was shouting orders at them.

"Take these two away and lock them in a room somewhere," she said pointing at the archbishop and the prince. "We'll deal with them later. Tend to the dead as well."

I took a deep sigh as I watched the Tóráin follow Seig's orders. "Well, it seems like yet another country needs new leadership. Do you think we can convince Prince Wilhelm to abide by our terms?"

"No," Seig said as she knelt down next to a slain water sprite and closed it's eyes. "The man is more of a boy, and he idolizes his father. He's also known to be a devout follower of Deus much like the rulers of Korblum usually are. It's possible you could manipulate his feeble mind into doing what you want, but I have a feeling that type of thing isn't what you're after."

Queen Sophia knelt down to check on a soldier before moving her hand over him, making the holy symbol of a blessing which resembled the number eight. "Your feeling is a good one. So long as this current family remains in power, their intense feelings towards your kind will remain thanks to their dedication to Deus. Manipulated or not, the hate for the Tóráin will continue. I don't think Korblum would accept a leadership group akin to what we established in Tulp though. They'd want a king."

Seig put her hands on her hips. "Tell me again. Why aren't you just conquering these countries and ruling over them yourself? It would make things much easier."

"Because that isn't why we're doing this," I answered out loud. It had been something I meant to say silently in my head, and I was nervous now about possibly offending or upsetting Queen Sophia.

She smiled at me, putting me at ease, before addressing Seig. "Weylyn is right. We're looking at building a better world, not an empire. Were I to conquer these countries and take them as my own, it would only take my death to have someone lesser than me have control over most of Kosavros. It is much better for this campaign to institute rulers native to the country who can better guide the people of their nation towards a peaceful, balanced, caring world. Motea, the exotic land far south of here, has lived in peace with your kind ever since you arrived. They are proof that this peace we are fighting for is possible. This plan needs multiple people from different countries working together to create a world that both humans and Tóráin enjoy living in. It will not work any other way."

Seig nodded as she walked over to King Franz's bloody corpse. She stood over him for some time as Queen Sophia and I watched a great pain take over her face. For a moment I thought the harpy might kick him or spit on him, but she did something else that was unexpected. Seig squatted down low and stared at the former king with her elbows resting on her knees. Letting out a deep sigh, she reached over and closed his eyes. After slowly rising up from her low position she walked back over to Queen Sophia and me.

"This country needs more than just someone willing to abide by our terms. They need to want to change things. I can't think of anyone better than a noble from the eastern part of the country. His name is Baron Ehren Fuchs of Ruteimwass. He has long been against the arenas and has often provided help to fighters who no longer fight, whether because they didn't want to anymore or they couldn't. He gives them honest work or even land of their own in rare cases. Someone I grew very close to while working my way up through the ranks had a wound in his arm fester, resulting in amputation. He couldn't fight with only one arm, so he made the decision to leave for Ruteimwass, and Baron Ehren gave him a job as a stableman in his personal stables. He sends me letters every month telling me how kind the Baron is and how I should, if I could ever escape it, leave fighting behind and come live with him." Seig seemed to drift off in thought before smiling, her eyes shimmering with unshed tears. "In my opinion, if it means anything to you, if you want someone who will bring true change to this country, make Baron Ehren the new King of Korblum."

Seig sniffed away her rising emotions and cleared her throat as she moved by us to grab the feet of a dead forest sprite before helping a satyr carry the poor soul out of the room. It was just me and Queen Sophia now, save for the dead bodies in the room.

The Queen of Tudrose put her hands on her hips. "Well, I think this Baron Ehren sounds just like the man we're looking for. What do you think?"

I was staring at the doors Seig had left through, the look on her face when she had suggested Baron Ehren still present in my mind. I opened my eyes wide and took a deep breath before letting it out in an exaggerated release of air. Turning my attention to Queen Sophia, I smiled and nodded. "It takes a lot for my kind to believe a human has our best interests in mind. If Baron Ehren is as good of a man as Seig and her friend believe him to be, then I think we should trust their judgement. Plus, King Ehren sounds like a strong name. I think it'll work."

Queen Sophia's right eyebrow rose up. "Do I have a strong name?"

For some reason I didn't say yes right away and my failure to respond quickly had frozen me in a state of silence. As I fumbled to find words again, Queen Sophia laughed and reached out, squeezing my wrist with her small hand.

"Oh relax, Weylyn! I was only teasing you. Come, let us get back to the others so I can send a messenger to Baron Ehren to inform him of his new position. We will stay in Adler until he is crowned King of Korblum and then make our way south to Stelpina's capital, Nours."

I followed Queen Sophia out of the room with all of the dead bodies still laying inside it, wishing to find some water to clean myself off and rinse my mouth out as soon as I could. You needed to be willing to accept a certain level of violence in order to be effective in battle as a lycan but, no matter how horrible the person was that it belonged to, I still hated the feeling and taste of blood.

# Chapter Forty-Three

## General Rosspier

Cloque, Fleuris  |  May 30, 1799

"Can you believe it? They really thought that I would help them! Why would I? What need of a military alliance do I have with a country that can't even stop *une bande de voyous* from burning down their precious fighting arenas?"

Jon put down his cup of tea after taking a small sip. "What about Stelpina and Malvene? Have they asked for our help too?"

I rolled my eyes. "Of course, they did. They're all so weak still from what we did to them a few years ago. Their *Diables* cause so much trouble that they can't help each other without risking losing control of their own nation, so they ask *leur père* for help like helpless children."

"We could send them a few Demi-brigades from the south army in Gralion." Jon leaned back and crossed his right leg over his left.

I scoffed at the suggestion. "And waste our soldiers? No, The Bitch of Tudrose and her *animaux sauvages* will eventually extend too far when they try to take my country from me. I will put an end to them then. For now, let the other countries fall. Let their soldiers die and people suffer. *Je m'en fiche.* All that will ever matter is the prosperity of Fleuris."

Jon uncrossed his legs and leaned forward so that his elbows were on his knees. "But what if us aiding those countries now prevents that army from ever reaching

Fleuris soil? *Nous avons les chiffres.* Together with Stelpina and Malvene you would stand a very good chance at winning."

I spun away from one of the tall windows in the room so that Jon could see in my eyes that I meant what I was about to say. "You do not think I know that? I'm one of the best military minds ever to be a part of this country! Of this world! I know exactly what I can do to see this *petite campagne* of theirs brought to an end! Leaving our country void of our army would only give the *Diables* a chance to fight back. We have them under control thanks to the camps. The only reason any of *ces monstre*s even exist still is because the remaining humans in the workforce decided they deserve to be rich without all the work necessary to obtain wealth. Because of them, I have to keep *ces maudites bêtes* in this country, and I have to hand out money to those who don't deserve it."

"They only think that way because you told them that humans are so far above the hounds, and goats, and all the other servants of The Dark." The Dove stood in the entryway, leaning up against the frame of the door.

I was going to respond, but I had no patience to deal with her today. Not everything I had said during my speeches had resulted in perfection, but it was rude to point that out. I was doing a better job than any other leader in Kosavros when it came to dealing with the *Diable* problem, and that's all that really mattered. Eventually, I would convince the poor to return to work and then this beautiful country could finally remove the blemish caused by those monsters. I took a deep breath to compose myself before straightening out my shirt and continuing my conversation with Jon. "Fleuris comes first. We need to be as strong as we can be, and we are strongest with *les Diables* under our boot. We are staying within our own borders."

The Dove stepped away from the entrance to my study and sauntered over to the table that had a teapot and two more cups available. After she poured herself a drink, she took four heaping spoonfuls of honey and deposited them into her cup. The witch had a sweet tooth, taking in more sweets than one would expect to be normal. She still held an exceptional figure despite her eating habits though, no doubt by the ways of some blessing by Eous. Witches were useful, but they were all cursed. Once the *Diable* problem was removed from Fleuris, witches would be next. Of course, I kept this to myself. I didn't even tell Jon about it yet. Witches were not only powerful, but I found most of them to be quite rash and moody; probably because they were all women. I didn't need a rumor leading to a horde of witches on my doorstep. Fleuris would be free of Eous' dark influence in due time, all thanks to my wisdom and determination. In that moment I would ascend to the position of Deus' General, taking the place of the archangel Michele. I would show Deus that I was more effective than his idolized daughter, and he would lend me gifts to aid me in my campaign of ridding all of Kosavros of his brother's evil touch.

"Max? *Tu vas bien?*"

Jon's voice had me blinking vigorously before shaking my head to remove myself from my foreseen future. "*Oui, je vais bien.* Just thinking of how wonderful things will be once all of this is over."

"Jon's right." The Dove said in between chewing on a small cake she had plucked from a plate. "You could end all of this sooner if you just marched east and formed an alliance with Malvene and Stelpina."

Jon's face soured. "You don't get to call me that. I'm Major Carierre to you."

The Dove rolled her eyes. "Oh get off it. It's just a name."

I ignored the small spat between the two of them and focused on what The Dove had said prior to their bickering. "Since when do you care about military strategy? Even when you fought for me years ago you barely entered half of the battles waged."

The Dove sucked on her fingers, removing whatever was left of the sweetness from the cake she had eaten, before leaning back in her chair and crossing one leg over the other. "First of all, I didn't, nor will I ever, fight *for* you. We are tentative allies. Our goals somewhat align and so I tolerate you and you tolerate me. Second, I don't care about military strategy. I care about obtaining something of mine that could be much easier to get my hands on if we joined the war."

Jon rolled his eyes before crossing his own arms across his chest. "And just what nonsense are you after now? Something to fix the face behind that mask you wear? What do you need? A Queen's toenail?"

I had fully expected the witch to draw a blade on Jon, but instead she downed the remainder of her tea and stood from her seat. "What I'm after is my business. Whether we wait for them to come here, or we go after them there, it doesn't matter. I'll have what I need eventually. I can feel it in my bones."

I grumbled as I poured myself something a bit stronger than tea from another table. Some would say it was perhaps too early for wine, but they didn't endure the stresses I did. "For the last time we are staying here. Let the bastards deal with their own countries and I'll deal with mine. Whether they come for us next or last, it won't matter. We will win and they will lose."

The Dove smiled. "And I'll get what I want."

Jon let out a deep sigh and raised his cup of tea in the air. "To an impending victory then."

I raised my glass of wine as well before taking a hefty drink.

# Chapter Forty-Four

## Olwen

Camp Liodorleu, Fleuris  |  June 4, 1799

It was an incredibly risky plan on my part. Keagan wasn't on board with it, but I had gotten myself arrested and forced his hand. After surveying Camp Liodorleu for days, I concluded that our best bet for saving people would be to have someone who knows about the escape plan on the inside. There was no way for us to ever get a message to someone, and even if we could, we would never know if they were up for trying to breaking out. We had witnessed a few attempted escapes, and they resulted not only in the death of the intended escapees, but also a random member of the large group that had not tried to flee. It was a brutal tactic to deter people from trying to run, and it had seemingly worked.

In the last five days, not one person had attempted to escape. However, even without much reason to randomly kill those within the camp, the fires could still be seen every other night or so. Dozens of people had been killed at Camp Liodorleu alone since we had been watching. Worst of all was that age didn't matter to the soldiers doing the killing. What looked like a family of satyrs tried to escape about a week ago. They shot the mother and father, as well as a child that looked barely old enough to be a young teenager. The mother was carrying a young one who couldn't have been more than two years old. The child cried loudly, and it only stopped when the soldier pulled the trigger on his pistol and all you could hear was the echo of a gunshot.

It was easy to get myself caught. The law was that all Tóráin were to be sent to the camps that Fleuris had built across the country. The difficult part was to ensure that I was taken to Camp Liodorleu. There were two camps for the citizens of Cloque: Camp Liodorleu to the north and Camp Pétarouges to the south. The risky part was trying to not get killed on the spot, something the soldiers had been known for doing on occasion. I couldn't appear to be escaping from somewhere or causing trouble, but even just being spotted in an alley could result in your death. You never knew how the soldiers were going to respond to you. This was a major reason why Keagan was so against all of this, claiming that it was just as likely for me to be killed right away than it was for me to be brought to Camp Liodorleu. It feels silly to say, but I was thankfully brought to Camp Liodorleu after I allowed myself to bump into a soldier during his group's patrol in the northern area of the city. I could have just approached him with my hood off and my green skin out in the open, but he could have seen that as a threat. Soldiers had nervous trigger fingers, the fear that General Rosspier had instilled in them mostly responsible. We were wild animals to them now, and we were being treated as such.

They had all trained their rifles on me as soon as my hood fell off my head. I had faked a fall, putting myself on the ground in the hopes to appear as vulnerable as possible. A soldier came forward and clapped my wrists in iron before taking my cloak off and wrapping it around my head. I thought they meant to strangle or suffocate me, but instead they guided me on foot to a new destination. I had no idea where they were taking me, and it wasn't until a long while after that I heard soldiers talking.

"Found this one trying to sneak by us on patrol. Another green one." Someone pushed me forward and I stumbled, landing hard on my face.

"We'll put her with the others. *Bon travail, soldat.*"

I felt two people lift me to my feet by each of them grabbing one of my arms. Another push in my back came shortly after, but this time I managed to keep my balance. It was haunting how quiet the place was. I had gotten myself caught in the evening, just as the sun was setting, after informing Finn that I was leaving. I told him to wait to tell Keagan for a short while, giving me enough time to get caught and hopefully brought to the correct camp. The second my head was released from the wrapping of my cloak, I looked around and was relieved to find myself in Camp Liodorleu. The iron shackles around my wrists were removed before another shove came into my back. I allowed myself to fall into the mud the afternoon rain had created, giving myself some space between me and the soldier who had shoved me. The place would be quiet enough for Keagan and Finn to hear my signal even though they were hiding in our lookout spot in the surrounding forest. It was a risk for me to do this, but Keagan and Finn needed to know that I was successful in getting inside. They needed to hear it, or no help would be coming. I quickly brought my hands to my face and let out the bird call we had decided on.

"You little bitch!" A sharp pain sprouted from my side from the kick I received. The soldier crouched down and grabbed my face with his hand. "Why did you do that? Who are you calling? Answer me!"

I smiled at him. "Just letting the world know I'm still alive."

The soldier stood up quickly and took a step back before aiming the point of his rifle at my face. "You won't be alive for much longer."

I heard the click of the cocking of his gun so quickly that I didn't even have time to prepare myself for my death.

"Hold! I know that voice. Olwen?" I didn't recognize the man's voice, but it had caused the soldier in front of me to lift his rifle away.

A hand grabbed my left arm at the elbow and helped me to my feet. The man I saw in the glow of the lantern he had with him had a face I didn't recognize either. This human somehow knew me from my voice, so I must know him, but I couldn't for the life of me match his clean-shaven face to a memory. His eyes glowed the brown color of tea and he wasn't wearing a hat like the other soldiers. As my eyes inspected him further, I noticed that he wasn't wearing a regular Fleuris uniform. He wore the clothes of a unit of the Fleuris army that I knew very well, having served most of my time in it. The Specters wore loose clothing, usually of green or brown shades. We would look like hunters, but we were much more than that. The Specters were the only part of the army that used guerilla tactics, something Fleuris had learned the Tóráin were quite good at. Forest sprites were especially good at this form of warfare thanks to how we embraced the feel of the woods and hills. We were extremely effective, so much so that the majority of the unit is made up of sprites like me. There are humans too of course, but sprites and lycans filled out a good chunk of the soldiers. I remembered many from my time in the army, however the majority of those I knew were dead.

"You don't remember me?" the man asked. "We fought together as Specters. The name Wyatt doesn't ring any bells for you?"

I struggled to find some memories of this man. So many people with so many names flooded you during war, and you rarely bothered to remember them since there was usually a good chance one of you would be dead the next day. The name

Wyatt did seem familiar, but the feeling was so faint I wondered if I was forcing myself to remember him. I worried that if I didn't recall who he was soon, he would let the soldier kill me. Before I could make a fake expression of recollection, the man spoke again.

"Ah well I'm not surprised." The man chuckled as he moved some hair from his face. "How could the famed Demon of the Wilds ever remember such a forgettable man like me? Even if she did save my life."

I hated that name. The human soldiers had given it to me because of my effectiveness. I was so angry from the use of it now that I almost missed the last thing Wyatt had said. Thankful to have heard it, I finally remembered who the man was.

"Oh! Yes, now I remember! Dunkel Forest in Korblum! You got bit by that viper and I sucked the venom out of your leg before it spread to your heart. You still barely made it. Made every soldier watch their step a whole lot more after that scare." I tried to force a bit of a laugh to ease some of the tension I felt.

Wyatt didn't laugh with me. In fact, he didn't even smile. "Yes. The event that earned me my new name amongst The Specters. Do you remember it?"

I did, but I didn't want to say it. I knew he didn't like it, and I had even insisted that they retire the silly name. Wyatt squeezed my elbow tightly now and gave me a rough shake before repeating his question. I was confused by his aggression.

"Wee Wyatt!" I shouted. "There, I said it Why would you make me say that? You hate that name."

"Yes, Wee Wyatt. A name that has followed me for years. They claimed I cried like a child, begging for someone to save my life. 'Saved by your mother,' they said. I was left to be the joke of the group while you went on to essentially lead it." A quick punch to my gut caught me off guard, taking my breath away. "I've always hated you for that."

I gasped for air before responding. "I saved your life you idiot! Most people would be thankful!"

The back of his hand struck the side of my head, causing me to wobble a bit. "You ruined my reputation!" Another strike came, this one making me stumble to my left. "You ruined any chance of me moving up the ranks!" A third strike knocked me to my hands and knees.

"I tried to get them to stop! I never wanted you to be ridiculed like that. Would you rather I had never helped you? You'd be dead if it wasn't for what I did." A pain in my ribs told me he didn't care for what I had said.

I didn't have time to gather myself before another kick to my side sent me sprawling onto my back. I could have fought him. Every one of his strikes would have been relatively easy to counter, but I couldn't do anything. Fighting back would almost guarantee my death, and there were people that needed me alive. All I could do was take the beating and hope Wyatt would be done with his revenge soon. More kicks followed the previous ones. My legs, my sides, my arms, and even my head found the harsh touch of Wyatt's boot.

Eventually, Wyatt came to sit on my chest. "Having your life saved by *Diable* is worse than death." His right hand came down, striking my left cheek. "I would have rather died than lived this life of ridicule." His left hand struck my right cheek. "I can't make you feel the pain I've felt over the years, but I can try." A firm jab struck and broke my nose, the crunch allowing a stream of blood to pool out of my nostrils.

"I'm sorry, Wyatt," I said as tears filled my eyes from my injured face. "I was just trying to help you."

My sight was obscured by the water in my eyes, but I caught the sound of a knife unsheathing before noticing the glint of steel in the lantern light. Wyatt's hand held my face down as he carved what felt like the letter 'w' into my right cheek. "A little reminder for what you did. But don't think that's the last bit of reminding you'll get from me. You see, I run this place. You and I have all the time in the world to make amends."

Wyatt got off me before lifting me to my feet. Drained from the beating I had endured, I struggled to keep up with his swift pace which ended up in him essentially dragging me towards one of the longhouses. He opened the door and shoved me in. "See you in the morning, Demon of the Wilds."

The door shut and the darkness of the place enveloped me. Not one lantern was left for us, and I felt as if I was laying on five or six people. I apologized as I tried to get off them, but kind hands stopped me. The soft whispers of people waking up to the late arrival of another prisoner filled the large room. Fingers traced my face and eventually reached the horns on my head. I never flinched away, knowing that the people in here were allies.

"What's your name sprite?" A soft, female voice asked me.

"Olwen." I looked around even though I couldn't see well. "I'm looking for someone. A water sprite named Anya. Is she here?"

Whispers broke out as my question was carried across the multitude of people crammed into the place. My heart raced as I waited, hoping that I hadn't been too late.

"Olwen?" The voice was louder than a whisper and full of joy.

I could hear the grunts from people as someone from the other side of the longhouse made their way through everyone to get to me. She said my name a few more times, my responses guiding her towards me. I knew that it was Anya, but I still held the worry that it was just someone who knew Anya and me. It wasn't until I felt her hand touch my arm that I knew for sure it was her. She wrapped both arms around my neck and I welcomed the act happily.

"Olwen! How in the world did they ever catch you? What —" Anya had broken from our hug to put her hands on each side of my face, causing her to feel the wound on my cheek. "Who did this to you?"

I smiled, even though I knew she couldn't see it, and gently took her hands away from my face. "An old friend wasn't too happy to see me again." I held her hands in mine, wishing then for my eyes to let me see my friend's face again. "Are you alright?"

She squeezed my hands tightly. "It's hard, Olwen. How they run this place? It's wrong. I'm lucky to be alive to be honest with you."

"Well, I'm here to tell you that we all won't have to endure this place for much longer. Keagan and I have a plan. Finn too. We're going to get all of you out of here. It'll take some time, but if we stick together, we'll survive. I promise."

# Chapter Forty-Five

## The Dove

Cloque, Fleuris  |  June 6, 1799

There was nothing more I wished to do than to go after Weylyn, but the level of risk on my part was high. Tudrose was strong, and the countries they planned to engage were no pushovers despite their weakened states. There were just too many factors that weren't in my favor. The dog would come to me soon enough and — with Max's army on my side — I would get what I needed from Weylyn. However, I refused to solely rely on leaving this all up to chance. His arrival was uncertain, so I needed to continue looking for someone who might replace him. Countless vials of blood littered my room, each one to be tested by a certain assortment of spells taught to me by my mother. It wasn't the easiest or quickest way to check them, but the alternative made my stomach turn upside down. The blood I needed had a special taste to it, bitter like the ruby berries from my home, but also acidic. It made your tongue tingle and your throat burn. My mother had a vial of the rancid stuff, and seeing as it wasn't enough for our mission, she used it as part of her lessons. She made me taste a drop of it once a week for five years until she was certain I knew the taste well.

Mystic Blood was one of the most powerful ingredients, probably because of the evil that was called upon to make it. The Dark is powerful; very dangerous when left unchecked. My mother was Champion of The Light, and that title had been passed on to me. It was my responsibility now to find those with Mystic Blood, but I wasn't going to subject myself to that horrid taste if I didn't have to. Plus, the taste of regular blood was no appetizing flavor either. Ingesting blood was for creatures of The Dark, and I would not lower myself to their level. I had promised my mother I wouldn't at the ripe age of six. It was incredibly rare for someone in my family to ever be seduced by The Dark, but it had happened. People I looked up to had chosen to mingle with creatures of The Dark and practice their culture. They were shunned, as they should be. I would not develop any practices that would relate me to those beasts and traitors, so I was left with the long and advanced spells my mother taught me.

They involved many steps, but I had them remembered so well that I sometimes dreamed about them. I spoke the words and mixed in the right ingredients. Thankfully, it didn't take much of what I had stored to test the vials. The ingredients these spells required came from another world. Witches had saved them and kept them secret for decades, and I had stolen a great deal of their collections. My mother had given me a good amount of what I would need before I left, but I figured it was good to grab whatever I could whenever possible. I was desperately hoping to find someone other than Weylyn; someone more vulnerable. Relying on Weylyn's arrival only made me anxious, mostly because I didn't have any more ingredients for a very special spell. That spell had guided me across this world towards those with Mystic Blood, and my last stop was Fleuris. The only reason I continued to search was because the spell had told me there were three creatures of The Dark possessing Mystic Blood to the lands in the west.

It had taken me to Tudrose, Fruberg, Korblum, Malvene, and even far south to Motea. Each time I failed to find what I was looking for. Well, save for Tudrose. I had found what I was looking, but I failed to procure what I needed. And so, my last chance was here in Fleuris. So long as those who the spell had locked onto remained in Fleuris. Weylyn could be the only one still alive. There was no way to know now. The only way to find someone else was to continue my work, something that had gone much easier now that I had Ravenna testing blood as well. She was loyal, and she knew me on a level no one else in this world did. She was the only one I trusted, and the only company I enjoyed having. My mother would no doubt disapprove, seeing the relationship between Ravenna and I as a distraction. My mother forced me to form relationships most of my life, but she had changed her tune when the time came for me to begin my training to be the Champion of The Light. She claimed that only the mission mattered, and that everything else meant nothing.

She was a devout follower of The Light, my entire family had been for centuries. Despite that being the case, I wasn't as strong of a believer as her. I still served my family well and I followed the belief that The Dark needed to be removed from existence, but I did believe there was more to life than what I was sent out for. My mother expected me to only ever think about the mission, and to hate everything about this world that didn't have to do with The Light. Even though her teachings were forever being spoken in my mind, I still found myself enjoying things that I shouldn't. Ravenna was one of the more promiscuous joys, but I had solemn ones too. I enjoyed the night sky more than the afternoon sky. I enjoyed sneaking in the shadows more than engaging in all-out war. The one that my mother would no doubt be most ashamed to find out was that I enjoyed killing. Even though my family was responsible for the deaths of many creatures of The Dark, we were taught to never enjoy the act. It simply needed to be done in order to preserve The Light. Those of us who enjoyed taking a life, even if it was one poisoned by The Dark, became known as Reapers. A group that operated for The Light but would never be a part of it when they died.

Still, even with all my transgressions, I know my mother loves me. She used all her strength and knowledge to teach me and prepare me. It would be pleasant to feel her embrace again. It had been so many years since I felt her lips on my forehead. She had planted a kiss on my forehead every morning since the day I was born. My memory was so strong that I could have sworn I felt her kiss me, and my fingers went to touch the spot. I felt foolish for doing so, knowing full well that nothing had happened. And yet, there wasn't one part of me that didn't wish that something had. This road was a long one, but there was hope now that it would be finished soon. Even if I couldn't find the other two Mystic Bloods, I believed that Weylyn would indeed reach Fleuris. I would find him on the battlefield and take his blood for my own, using it to finally achieve my goal: bring forth The Light.

# Chapter Forty-Six

## Rosalie

Offnetore, Korblum | June 8, 1799

It was a pleasant change to have the sun out in the sky, untouched by dark clouds. It had rained for the last two days. Add that to the attack a few days ago and our trip from Adler to Nours was a miserable one. King Ehren's coronation had been such a pleasant event, and yet every day after it was miserable. Everything was difficult since we had left Adler, but sleep was something that had become quite evasive. My exhaustion was all thanks to the ambush near Braben Forest; I had been woken up to the sounds of gunfire and screaming. A force from the southern Korblum city of Monschwarz had hidden themselves in the Braben Forest, waiting to ambush us in the night. Reports said that they poured out of the trees like ghosts, killing people in their sleep. They had gotten caught at some point, and gunfire woke everyone up. The battle was well on its way when I woke up to Weylyn standing over me in the shape that gave him wolf-like features. He had woken up mere moments before I had and was calling for me to come out of my sleep-filled sate. When he looked back to see me getting to my feet, he quickly ordered me to grab the knife under the pillows. Once I had it ready, Weylyn's large hand gripped my free one and pulled me out of the tent.

Weylyn intended to take me to Queen Sophia's tent, believing I would be safest there. The fight had not yet reached our tent, but the shouting and gunfire was coming from the direction of our destination. I was terrified, clutching the knife in my hand so tightly I thought I would break the handle. All of it was so fresh in my mind still that I found myself experiencing each moment over and over again. Passing by the tents this morning reminded me of passing by them that night, and the emotions I had felt at the time began rushing back. Before I knew it, my mind reached a certain point that haunted me so much that my breath quickened. I suddenly felt light-headed, causing me to grab hold of Weylyn's arm as I stumbled. Weylyn was quick to catch me, preventing a fall, and brought one of his gentle hands to my chin. He lifted my face so he could inspect it, searching for an answer to his question before he even asked it. The palm of his hand slid up to cover my cheek as his fingers tickled the edge of my ear, the golden hue of his eyes grounding me to the present.

"Are you okay?" he asked. "There's a couple hours left before we move out. Maybe you should head back to the tent and grab some rest if you can."

I shook my head. "No way am I going back to that tent alone. I'm fine."

Brina had her arms crossed as she looked at me from behind Weylyn. "I can go back with you if you want."

I gently broke free of Weylyn and straightened myself out before taking in a deep breath of summer air. "That's kind of you, Brina, but it isn't necessary. I'm fine. Truly. Come on."

I began leading the way towards Lady Mirlena's tent, which was still outside of the general mass of the army despite what had happened. Luckily, she had decided to set up camp west of the main group of tents instead of in the forest to the east. She would have surely died, being all alone against the sneak attack from the Korblum soldiers. This hadn't persuaded her to change her habits though. The witch liked her privacy and general quiet. She was an odd person, but she had a wonderful heart. She had given me something to help me sleep last night, which was sweet of her, however I had decided not to take it. The worry of another attack and the possibility of dying in my sleep prevented me from even thinking about taking a sip from the tiny flask. After a short while more of walking, the three of us arrived at Lady Mirlena's tent. There was a smoldering campfire outside of the temporary home and the smell of a variety of herbs surrounded the entire place.

Weylyn stepped forward. "Lady Mirlena? It's Weylyn. Rosalie and Brina are with me too."

"Come on in!" Lady Mirlena shouted from behind the cloth of the tent.

Weylyn went in first, Brina next, and then I followed in behind them. Lady Mirlena was on her knees, patting Arthur's flush faced with a wet rag.

"How's he doing?" I asked.

"He'll be alright. It isn't anything serious. Every now and then the little one has the same sickness wash over him. It usually passes within a couple days. He just needs rest." Lady Mirlena left the cloth folded on Arthur's forehead before getting to her feet and walking over to a teapot. "Anyone want some tea?"

Weylyn and Brina both refused, but the thought of some warm tea was comforting, even with the higher temperatures of summer. "I'll have some, please."

Lady Mirlena poured a cup for herself and then one for me. She held out the small teacup and I graciously reached out and held it in both my hands. The warmth soothed me as I raised the cup to my lips and sipped on the tea. The taste and smell of jasmine filled my senses, and I felt the tension in my body ease slightly.

"So, would we be able to train today?" Weylyn asked with a tentative yet hopeful tone in his voice.

Lady Mirlena's face twisted as she considered his question. "Oh, I don't know, Weylyn. I think Arthur needs my full attention."

"I don't mind watching over him." Everyone looked at me with expressions of curiosity on their faces. "What? I'm a nurse. I can tend to him while you two do what you need to do."

Brina crossed her arms and smirked. "You're just trying to get out of your training."

I put my free hand on my hip in defiance. "I am not! I'm trying to be helpful."

Weylyn smiled before turning his attention to Lady Mirlena. "Well?"

She took some time to think, but eventually the witch's shoulders dropped in defeat. "Fine. But we won't be long. Just a short lesson. Come on. The sooner we begin the sooner we can finish."

Lady Mirlena went over to Arthur and bent down to plant a kiss on his cheek before coming over and giving me a hug. "His favorite book is under the pillows. I usually read it to him when he wakes up."

I nodded and Lady Mirlena smiled at me before waving at Weylyn to follow her out of the tent. I took another sip of my tea before making my way over to the makeshift bed Arthur was laying on. I lowered myself down to sit next to him, putting the back of my free hand on his cheek to feel his temperature. He still had a fever, but he did appear to be sweating which was a good sign that the fever was breaking.

Brina sighed. "Well, if you're going to play doctor then I'm going to go find something else to do. Unless you want me to stay with you, of course."

For a moment I wanted to ask her to stay, but for a reason I didn't know, I found myself craving some time alone. I enjoyed having someone with me, especially after what had happened, although I felt like I needed to not rely on Brina and Weylyn so much. I wanted to go to battle with them. How could I possibly do that if I constantly needed someone to watch over me? "No, no. It's alright. Taking care of someone is when I'm most comfortable. What will you do?"

Brina ran her fingers through her hair. "Not sure. Maybe I'll go see if Colonel Seamus is awake and willing to chat. You're sure you'll be okay?"

I waved Brina away. "Of course, I'll be okay. I'm stronger than you think. Tell Colonel Seamus I say hello."

Brina nodded before turning towards the flap of the tent and exiting through it. The gentle morning breeze flowed through the tent, filling the silence that had taken over with the soft sounds of cloth rustling in the wind. I set my cup down next to me and pulled out the book Lady Mirlena had mentioned. The cover was a colorful depiction of an old warrior fighting a giant of some sort. 'The Tale of Bodulfr' was written in fancy letters under the image, and I felt compelled to read it myself. It was obviously fiction, and I did enjoy a good fantastical tale. I set the book down for a moment to tend to Arthur. I removed the wet cloth from his forehead, submerged it into the pale of water nearby, rang it out, and put it back where Lady Mirlena had left it. I brought the blanket draped over him up to his chin and put my ear to his chest. It sounded well enough, much like someone on their way to recovery, so I felt comfortable laying down next to Arthur with his book in hand. I had finished the first dozen or so pages before a voice grabbed my attention.

"Be careful." The boy's voice was soft and weak. "If you read it now, you'll want to read it forever."

I put the book aside and sat up, turning my attention to Arthur. His eyes were open, although they did look irritated by the heat of his body. He had removed his arms from the embrace of the blanket, having folded his fingers together over his chest. The boy had a smile on his face, something I found not many sick people could manage. I didn't know the extent of his sickness, so I was unaware of how much Arthur suffered, but Lady Mirlena had been very concerned since he fell ill the morning after the attack near Braben Forest. Leaving him with me told me she believed him to be in less danger, but the smile was still unexpected. If I were sick, woke up, and found my mother wasn't at my bedside I would be upset. Arthur seemed unbothered by Lady Mirlena's absence, starting to let loose a small chuckle.

"Why are you looking at me like I've risen from the dead?" Arthur asked with a cheeky smirk on his face.

I blinked repeatedly, realizing that I had been so lost in my mind that I had forgotten to do so. "Sorry, I just...I didn't expect you to wake while your mother was away. How do you feel?"

The boy coughed. "I'll live. Thankfully, mother gives me stuff to drink that has me sleep most of the time I'm sick."

I took the cloth from his forehead and began gently patting the sides of his face and neck with it to provide him some relief. "Are you in any pain?"

Arthur let out an exasperated sigh. "Only when it's at its worst. I promise you I'm okay. Where's mum?"

I put the cloth back above his brow and stopped looming over him. "She went to give Weylyn another lesson after I offered to watch over you." The information appeared to upset him. "What's wrong?"

He remained silent for a while, his eyes avoiding mine, until he finally answered me. "I just wish I could do magic like them."

I felt this conversation may last a while, so I laid back down next to Arthur. Laying on my side with my head resting on my hand, I sighed. "And why would you want that? Not everyone likes witches."

Arthur turned onto his side to face me, cuddling into his pillow instead of resting his head on his hand like me. The cloth on his head fell, and he tossed it aside with an annoyed look on his flush face. "Travel far enough and you'll find someone who doesn't like you. It doesn't matter if you're a witch or not."

His answer caught me off guard. Arthur very much had the image of a boy his age, but it often tricked you into thinking his mind was immature. The boy was wiser than most people three times his age.

"I suppose you're right. However, you never answered my question. Why do you wish you could wield magic?" I watched as Arthur's eyes averted mine again, and a look of what appeared to be shame took over his face.

Arthur let out a small cough before clearing his throat. "It's the only way I can help people. I'm not a noble so I'll never be able to change laws. Plus, not knowing when my sickness comes would make being a soldier hard. If I had magic, I could do things. Save people. Humans and Tóráin."

His purity made a big grin stretch across my face. "Oh, Arthur. You don't need magic to help people. You don't need to be a soldier either. Take me for example! I don't have any magical capabilities, and I'm not wonderful with a gun, but I help people as a nurse. And when I'm not taking care of people's bodies, I'm doing my best to take care of their minds. I'm sure you give your mother strength by just being you, and that strength allows her to do what she does."

Arthur sighed as he rolled onto his back. "But I want to be a hero. Like Bodulfr! I want to save a kingdom from an ogre and slay a dragon."

I laughed. "Is that why you like this book so much? The ogres and the dragons?"

Arthur seemed offended. "No! The poem is much more than that. It teaches the reader a lot about how to live."

Having not read the book, I was intrigued to hear what Arthur had discovered. "Tell me then. What has The Tale of Bodulfr taught you?"

Arthur came back onto his side, his eyes shining with new life from his excitement. "It's a story about the cycle of time. How even great kings and heroes grow old. It's about respect, loyalty, and honor. It's about being the best person you can be by protecting people from dangers."

Something I had read in the first bit of the book felt contradictory to what Arthur had just said. "But doesn't Bodulfr go looking for fame? He wants to be remembered. Maybe he only does all those heroic deeds for himself."

The boy shook his head. "No, no. I thought the same thing, but my mother corrected me. She tells me that Bodulfr isn't doing things for himself, he's doing things because he wants respect. Respect is a good thing to have, and it's always better than fear. Bodulfr uses his strength and skill to save people and keep them safe, so that they'll respect and honor him. They'll be loyal to him, and then they can all protect the world together."

I didn't feel opposed to what he was saying, but I did want to see what more wisdom waited behind those eyes of his. I chose to challenge him again, testing his wit. "I don't know, Arthur. That sounds like someone who just wants power so people will follow him and do what he tells them to do."

The boy rolled his eyes, and I couldn't help but smile at his passion on the subject. "No, Bodulfr never wants to be king. He just lived a life of honor and respect, which made people want to follow him. I don't want to spoil the story for you, but he only becomes king because the one before him and the prince die. The people choose him as their king. And then, before he dies after killing the dragon, he makes the only warrior who stayed with him the new king. Power isn't the story, Lady Rosalie, it's respect and loyalty. That's why I like it. That's why I want to be like Bodulfr. If I can be a great enough hero, then people will follow me, and I can teach them how to respect everyone. They may not like everyone they meet, it would be silly to expect that, but at least there will be peace."

I sighed, almost in awe of the maturity of the young man. I reached out to grab a hold of his hand with a smile. "Your wish to help people is admirable. Your dream to have people respect each other is inspiring. I don't know which path you'll take to get there, but I think the world would be incredibly lucky to have a hero like you. You're wiser and kinder than the majority of people I know of already, and I really do believe you will only get better with age. Can you do me a favor, Arthur?"

The boy smiled, appearing to look better than when our conversation had started. "Of course, Lady Rosalie."

It was sweet of him to call me that. The title was above me, but he had insisted on giving Weylyn, Brina, and I the titles of lord and lady anyways. I took a deep breath and let out a long sigh as I released his hand and put my own on his warm cheek. "Promise me that you'll never give up on that dream, and that you'll never abandon making that wish come true. So long as you believe in a world better than this one, never stop fighting for it. Whether you have magic or not, you do that for me okay?"

Arthur nodded. "I promise."

"Good!" I rolled over to grab the book that held the story we had been talking about so much. "Why don't I just continue on reading then? Or should I start from the beginning?"

"I know the story," Arthur announced as he shifted his position. "Just continue from where you were."

I rested the book in my lap after sitting up. I flipped through the pages to find my place and cleared my throat. "Alright, let's do this."

# Chapter Forty-Seven

# Weylyn

Granfelden Valley, Stelpina | June 13, 1799

It was a hard-fought battle. News had spread and our element of surprise was long gone. Stelpina had managed to properly gather a formidable army to challenge us. They met us in one of the valleys amongst the forested Soljuren Hills. Queen Sophia and her war council were surprised to hear that news, having expected the enemy to wait until we exited the hilly region to attack. However, a few members did concede that the valley could be advantageous to them. Those suspicions rang true. While our army marched south across Granfelden Valley, Stelpina's army sat waiting for us with the hills to their backs.

They placed cannons on those hills, giving them an advantage over ours, as well as soldiers to fire upon us from afar. Korblum was known to have a better army than Stelpina — being the larger and more advanced country of the two — but Stelpina had more time to prepare. They had planned for us to come this way, no doubt knowing we would avoid the larger cities. Their army was roughly the same size as the one we had faced back in Korblum at Höllentore, and the placement of their cannons were cause for worry. We had lost all but two of our cannons in the fight against Korblum, and even with the few King Ehren had provided us we were still severely outmatched when it came to artillery.

Tudrose was known for its discipline and skill, but the enemy's cannon fire proved to be better early on. Our infantry charged theirs to start, Stelpina's army waiting for us to reach them while cannonballs rained down on us. Our cannons were out of range of theirs, something that proved to be a massive hindrance. It broke the strength of our advance, and we had lost more than we would have liked by the time we reached the dark blue mass of our enemy. Peace and Unity were amongst those brigades that had been sent in. I watched as soldiers to my right and left were gunned down during our advance, and I couldn't help but let a touch of doubt enter my mind. Tudrose hadn't lost too much so far on this campaign, and our army had received reinforcements from both native soldiers of our previous enemies and rebels willing to join our fight. However, between deaths and soldiers left behind to ensure our sacrifices weren't for nothing, our army had dwindled. We were still the clear favorite by numbers, but the Stelpina army outnumbered our artillery four to one. We also had a clear disadvantage in battlefield position. I knew from the moment the whistles and trumpets sounded that this would be, both figuratively and literally, an uphill battle.

As I walked through the blood-soaked field, the battle played over and over again in my head. The sight of a dead horse reminded me when Stelpina's cavalry hit us. They must have split into three, because it had sounded like we were getting charged at from both sides as well as from the front. Images of their soldiers rushing through the mess of battle wielding their sabers was still fresh in my mind. My hand moved to my shoulder, looking for a wound that was no longer there. I had been caught by one of the many blades swung in my direction, and barely had time to heal it. I credited that moment to my training with Lady Mirlena. It was easier for me to access my magic now, which was useful during battle. You rarely had any time to think, let alone concentrate on trying to heal a wound. I had been lucky to find the time. The would was deep, and had I not been wearing the leather armor given to me, there was a good chance I would have lost my arm completely. Despite being able to heal my arm, it had drained me more than I expected. The thought brought me to the event that happened after, and I felt myself fall into a state of sadness.

Our cavalry had joined the fray shortly after the enemy had, the trumpets sounding their charge being followed by cannon fire. Enough of them reached the battleground to even out the fight a bit, at least that's how it felt. There were more soldiers in red and white around me than those in royal blue, which told me we must be doing well. It only lasted for a short while though. Soon the colors around me began to even out, bringing our battle to a feverish level of chaos. Everyone was involved now, and the cannons continued to fire on our back line. I fought with everything I had, but I was slowly becoming surrounded. I had charged into battle with Brina on my left and Seig on my right, the harpy having joined us along with many of her followers, but the mayhem had separated us. My energy was waning, and a stab to my thigh had brought me down to a knee. That's when a roar rang through the noise of battle, preceding one of the soldiers around me getting tackled to the ground. A lycan I did not recognize joined the attacker, as well as a water sprite. I took the small window of opportunity provided by the distraction to heal my leg, the act leading to the world before me spinning for a moment.

The brief spell of dizziness faded just in time for me to swat away the swing of an enemy's saber. After slashing at the man's face with my claws, I noticed who had come to my rescue. It was Colonel Seamus who had tackled that soldier. The lycan and sprite that had joined him were both dead, and he was fighting off three soldiers by himself. I took a step forward but again the world spun in on itself. I stumbled and fell to my hands and knees. I looked up with blurry vision and saw Colonel Seamus get stabbed in his side. I quickly tried to get up, but I fell again. Too weak to help, I watched one of the soldiers dressed in blue swing their saber and behead the brave Colonel. Tears welled up in my eyes as I remembered his headless body slumping to the corpse covered ground. I blinked them away, but more followed. I resorted to wiping my eyes with my bloody fingers. The red substance only irritated my eyes, which caused me to curse out loud. After blinking furiously, the irritation subsided, and my vision returned to normal. I needed my vision to be its best right now. I wasn't just aimlessly wandering the battlefield. I was looking for someone. We had been separated, and the reason why filled my mind as I continued my search.

After the Stelpina soldiers killed Colonel Seamus, they turned their attention to me. I called upon what energy I had left and managed to stand. My legs were shaking, and I felt that if I tried to move, no matter how slightly, I would find myself on the ground again. Still, I tried to stand as erect as possible. I was head and shoulders above my enemies, and I hoped that my size might intimidate them. Two Tudrose soldiers attacked before my assailants could, distracting a couple of them. Still, there were two more with their eyes fixed on me. Despite my best efforts to look imposing, I knew they sensed my weakness. One of the two Stelpina soldiers survived the attack from the duo of soldiers dressed in red and white, joining his allies as the three of them took a step forward. A gale of wind blew by me then, and a force pushed back one of the soldiers. A small ball of flame crashed into another, sending the man screaming and clutching his seared face. The remaining attacker turned around and retreated, not wishing to suffer the fate of his friends. The one who had been knocked over by the forceful wind went to get up, but he was stopped by a quick stab into his chest. Cordelia turned around to give me a quick smile before she returned her attention to the Stelpina forces before us. She stood guard as someone put their hand on my shoulder. Lady Mirlena's eyes were quickly inspecting me, looking for injuries.

"Are you hurt?" The witch had asked.

"No. Just weak," I had answered.

Cordelia fought off an attacking soldier as Lady Mirlena lowered her head and closed her eyes. I felt a warm sensation on my shoulder, the feeling spreading throughout my entire body. My weariness wasn't completely gone, but I had at least felt capable of walking without falling over. As the energy Lady Mirlena gifted me rejuvenated my strength, I caught sight of Colonel Seamus' head. His eyes were still open, staring at me.

"Come on, let's get you off the front line for a bit," Lady Mirlena had suggested.

I didn't want to abandon the sprite that had saved me, but I doubted I would survive. I was strong enough now to at least defend myself, but Lady Mirlena, Cordelia, and I were somewhat separated from the majority of our army. We needed to retreat. I just nodded, too upset to speak. Lady Mirlena called after Cordelia and the three of us made for a more favorable position. Eventually, our army had gained the advantage and pushed through. Stelpina's army began to retreat, and we followed after them until we reached their cannons. Cheers broke out as the only remaining soldiers in blue uniforms were either on their knees in surrender or fleeing south across the hills. We had won, but I did not join everyone in the celebrations. I had experienced something new, and it was something I had dreaded ever since this war began. Olwen and Keagan had talked about it, as well as Brina: the hardest part about war was having to watch your friends die. I hadn't known Colonel Seamus for long, but I admired him greatly. He inspired me, and I found myself wishing to impress him every time we met. I would have been upset at his death if he had simply passed on in his sleep, but he had died in a more horrific manner. The added guilt of not being able to save him after he had saved me only added to the sorrow I felt.

The moment we had won, I began my search for his body. The confusion that war caused had me disoriented. I couldn't tell where I had been when the brave forest sprite gave his life to save my own. The battlefield was large, and the bodies appeared to number in the thousands. I had searched for well over an hour, at least that's what I assumed. It could have been longer, or shorter; time had escaped me. During my search, only the battle occupied my mind. It wasn't until the sun was beginning to set that I finally found his body, his severed head nearby. After taking a deep breath, I stepped over to the Colonel's head and picked it up. I brought it over to his body and placed it nearby. If someone would have asked me why I did that, I wouldn't have much of an answer. I just felt that he needed to be whole when the others found him. He needed to be whole when he was buried during a proper funeral. I would insist he got one, despite them being a luxury during war. Bodies were buried in a mass shallow grave, with a few words said over them by the few priests that accompanied the army. As I knelt by Colonel Seamus' body, I promised myself that the sprite would receive a funeral worthy of a hero.

"Weylyn? Are you alright? I'm so sorry, I should never have allowed us to get separated. Next time I'm never leaving your —" Brina stopped talking abruptly, no doubt recognizing who I was mourning.

It was good to know Brina was alive. I realized that in my mission to find Colonel Seamus' body, I had completely forgot to look for Brina. I grew angry with myself then, the feeling eventually turning into shame. I didn't even look at my cousin, too guilt-ridden to face her. She admired Colonel Seamus as much as I did, possibly more. I had failed her too. Brina knelt down next to me before placing her hand on mine.

"I know what you're thinking," she said. "It isn't your fault, Weylyn."

I shook my head. "No, it is. I could have saved him, but I was too busy saving myself. I was too weak. He should have just let them kill me. He'd probably still be alive."

Brina squeezed my hand. "None of that. There's no telling what will happen during a battle. Death is a lead actor in the play called 'War', and there's nothing we can do about it. We will mourn him, but we will not belittle his sacrifice. He made his choice. You have to honor that, as well as his legacy. We'll make sure his name isn't forgotten."

I looked up from Colonel Seamus' body and absorbed the sight before me. Thousands of bodies, bloodied and mutilated. Humans and Tóráin alike, all dead because of a dream. I started to wonder if I had made the right choice coming to Queen Sophia. I wondered if war had been the best path. The struggle in my mind spilled out, and I found myself asking Brina a question I desperately needed an answer for. "So much death. So much pain. Is it worth it? In the end, I mean. Say we win and the world changes for the better. Will all this death be worth it?"

Brina sighed as she patted my hand, squeezing it tightly before answering. "No war will ever be worth the amount of death it causes. No matter how righteous the cause, the loss of life that litters the path of war will always be painful. But this is the way of the world. It's the only language understood by tyrants. It was this way back home, and it's this way here. War, and the death it causes, is inevitable. All we can do is honor those who die so that a better world can come forward. Respect them forever and keep their memory alive."

# Chapter Forty-Eight

## Weylyn

Nours, Stelpina | June 14, 1799

We had carried out every funeral custom known to the Tóráin. It was as nice of a ceremony as we could manage. When the last bit of dirt covered Colonel Seamus' body, I was happy to feel that we had honored him as best we could. The sprite was a special figure in Tóráin history, and the ceremony was reflective of that. Directly after Colonel Seamus' funeral was concluded, Queen Sophia and I rode for Nours. The two of us were accompanied by Brina, Lady Mirlena, General Wyman, and roughly three brigades of cavalry. We had planned for the possibility of some resistance when we reached the city, and it was good that we had. A fair-sized garrison met us in the outskirts of the city, hoping to fight us off. The attack was futile, especially once rebel forces attacked the small army from behind. We were victorious twice in as many days, this time losing relatively less soldiers than we had the day before. The garrison surrendered not long after the battle had started, and we entered the city. We were making our way to a place called Kleinerturm, a small castle on the other side of Turkis River which the monarchs of Stelpina called home. However, we were intercepted by Sullivan and a lycan I remembered being called Kiara.

"Lovely to see you again, Weylyn," Sullivan said with a smile. "And even more lovely to meet you, Queen Sophia. I am happy to inform you both that King

Niklaus has formally surrendered. However, you're going the wrong way to meet him."

"What do you mean? Has he run off?" Queen Sophia asked before I could.

Sullivan shook his head. "No, Queen Sophia. He has merely changed the venue of your gathering. He was escorted by a group of Stelpina soldiers to the Cathedral of Nours."

"A soldier informed us that the King of Stelpina will be waiting for you to meet him there to discuss terms," Kiara added.

"Leaving the security of a castle in favor of a church is odd, is it not?" Queen Sophia asked as she looked to General Wyman.

The General of Tudrose had a sour look on his face. "It could be some sort of trap, My Queen."

"Oh, it's almost certainly a trap," Sullivan grumbled.

Queen Sophia sighed. "Well, trap or no trap, we need to speak with him. I'm sure we can do something to make this a safer discussion than previous ones."

Despite our collective distrust in the situation, Queen Sophia ordered our large group to make for the Cathedral of Nours. The incident in Adler had not hindered her bravery at all, and her confidence almost seemed to have grown. General Wyman suggested that she just arrest the King of Stelpina and be done with it, but Queen Sophia refused to not give King Niklaus a chance to keep his crown. She still believed that one of these leaders would agree to our terms and make our jobs much easier. Queen Sophia chose to believe that moving to a church meant that King Niklaus planned for a peaceful meet, but everyone else couldn't shake the feeling that negotiations would somehow end up in violence. I feared for all our safety, but it was Queen Sophia's that mattered the most to our cause. Without her, we probably didn't have an army. Tudrose would be weakened without their queen, which could cause all our work to eventually be undone. However, despite being aware of how reckless it was to put herself in such dangerous situations, Queen Sophia refused to stay away. She remained adamant that she and I be the ones to discuss terms with the current leaders of each country we entered.

We arrived around mid afternoon, the sun trying to peak through dark clouds that threatened us with rain. The temperature in the air was surprisingly cool for this time of year, and the weather cast a shadow on the church which made it appear incredibly unwelcoming. The high spire that reached for the sky towered over us as we approached the two large doors. A retinue of six soldiers, Queen Sophia, Lady Mirlena, Sullivan, Brina, and I entered the suspicious building just as the first few drops of rain began. Queen Sophia had ordered General Wyman to remain outside and ensure nobody entered or exited the church until they were done. He wasn't happy, something that was easy to determine since the man was incredibly opinionated and found it difficult to keep those opinions to himself. His temper wouldn't serve us well in negotiations, and so he remained outside with the rest of the small army we had brought with us.

Before we had entered the building, an order was called out from the man General Wyman had chosen to lead the guard. From the front of our group, he called for more soldiers to join us. The moment I entered the church I looked around for a reason why he would give out such an order, discovering twenty or so Stelpina soldiers standing in the shadows on either side of us. They lined the walls under arched pathways, the intricate statues carved in the columns watching us as intently as the soldiers were. Their numbers were still greater than ours, but Queen Sophia had refused to have too many Tudrose soldiers enter the church with us; she claimed it would be received poorly and negatively impact negotiations. It was hard, but I pulled my attention away from the opposing guards to take in the rest of my surroundings. The roof was tall, at least fifty feet high, with curved arches littering the ceiling. Pews were lined up on either side of a red carpet that ran from the front doors, all the way to the other side of the cathedral. At the end of the carpet was a raised, stone platform with three stained glass windows towering above an altar. Three figures stood in front of that altar, all three of them men. One was clearly a priest, while the other two were definitely royalty.

"Come! Come! Welcome, Queen Sophia! I am honored to treat with you in such a holy place. It's beautiful, isn't it?" King Niklaus had his arms out in greeting, but I doubted anyone here would even think of embracing the man.

"Quite a lot of soldiers to have in a church do you not think so?" Queen Sophia shouted from behind the soldiers that guarded her.

As we made our way closer to the King of Stelpina and his counsel, the Tudrose soldiers that had joined us spread out amongst the pews and fixed their eyes on the guards that flanked us. When we reached the second to last row of the long wooden benches, Queen Sophia stopped her advance. The soldiers in front of her moved to either side of their Queen and kept their eyes on the three men before them. The aisle we had traversed was wide enough for three people to walk side by side. Lady Mirlena and I flanked Queen Sophia, while Brina and Sullivan filed in behind us. I could see the disgust on the face of our three hosts when they noticed me, Brina, and Sullivan. The priest was especially perturbed, making a holy sign with his hand to keep him safe from the evil he believed was before him. King Niklaus lowered his arms, bringing them over his plump belly and lacing his fat fingers together. He looked around at the force we had brought with us, appearing displeased at our numbers.

"We all want to be kept safe, do we not?" King Niklaus asked with a smile on his face that you knew was fake. "You have been on quite the war path, and I heard what you did to King Franz. Can you truly blame me for having guards?"

Queen Sophia spoke calmly and directly. "King Franz tried to kill me. He failed. So long as you don't plan on such an action yourself, I can guarantee that you will be safe."

"Why do you have *Moindres* with you? I had heard rumors that you fight this war for them. I laughed when I heard it. Surely, they aren't true, or was I wrong to think of you as a sane, servant of Deus?" The priest asked his questions with a tinge of disgust and disbelief.

"Ah, Archbishop Pierre Abadie. I have heard of your teachings. I must say that I do not agree with them." Queen Sophia gave the older man a quick smile that I knew was meant to make him feel more uncomfortable than at ease. She turned her attention back to King Niklaus as she proceeded to answer the archbishop's questions. "These Tóráin are my friends and allies. Your rumors were slightly true. I am not fighting this war for them, but with them. Together, we are using a firm hand to guide Kosavros into the future. A place in time where Tóráin and humans live lives that are relatively, if not exactly, equal. There are many things wrong with how the poor are treated in this world, and every Tórán is a member of the poor. I am here to see if you would like to be a part of this new world being ushered in, or not."

The only man yet to speak let out a small fit of laughter. "So, you want to make the *Moindres* rich? That's why you're attacking countries that you are at peace with? They don't deserve the niceties that we already bestow upon them. What could possibly make you think they deserve more?"

"Her mind has been poisoned by these creatures, *Seigneur Roi*. That one there is *une sorcière*. She must have cast a spell on the Queen of Tudrose. It is the only answer to such blasphemy." The priest made his protective signs again as he stepped closer to his ruler.

"Or maybe she isn't blinded by a religion that preaches the extinction of people simply because they're different from you!" Sullivan shouted from behind Lady Mirlena.

"Keep your *animaux* quiet, Queen Sophia. They have no place to speak here. In fact, I request that you remove them from *ce lieu saint*. Their presence darkens a light that should never be infringed upon." The man who had laughed was now pointing to the doors we had entered from.

When nobody moved, he nodded to the soldier closest to his right and every guard dressed in blue aimed their rifles at someone in red. The soldiers loyal to Tudrose aimed their rifles at those loyal to Stelpina and a standoff began.

King Niklaus raised his hands in the air. "*Tenir*! I gave no order! Stand down! *Tout le monde*!" The soldiers cautiously raised their rifles and pointed their bayonets to the short ceiling above their heads. King Niklaus shot the other man an angry glare before letting out a deep sigh and turning his attention to Queen Sophia. "I am sorry for my son's lack of etiquette. This is a surrender. There will be no more fighting. What are your terms?"

"Not to worry. Weylyn, Leader of The Resistance, will formally submit our terms." Queen Sophia looked at me and I nodded in response. We had discussed shortly after our meeting with King Franz that I should submit our terms going forward. I wasn't ecstatic about the decision, but I understood the reasoning behind it. The terms meant more coming from a member of the people they looked to help.

I cleared my throat and began the speech I had prepared earlier. "King Niklaus of Stelpina. Today, we meet to discuss the terms of your surrender. We, Tudrose and The Resistance, will accept your surrender under the following terms. All slavery must end. You might try to pass off the poorly paid labor given to the Tóráin as jobs, but we both know what it truly is. The Tóráin, as well as other members of the poor, are to be properly compensated for whatever work they do. They are to be cared for in a more similar manner to how nobles are cared for. We understand that rank cannot be completely abolished, but the gap between beggar and noble must be lessened. The livelihoods of those you have willingly squished beneath your boot must become better. These are our terms. Do you accept them?"

Archbishop Abadie spat on the ground while Prince Lennel twisted his face in hatred. No matter what I had said, they would be offended and displeased. King Niklaus seemed the more reasonable of the three, even though he clearly wasn't without fault. He had allowed for these atrocities to run rampant in his country, doing nothing to combat these old, horrid tactics to belittle and demean those which nobles and zealots believed below them. King Niklaus had much to atone for, but the expression on his face was different than the men flanking him. He appeared to actually be considering the terms, which was new for our campaign.

King Niklaus eventually took a deep breath and let it out in a loud, exasperated sigh. "*J'ai décidé*. While I do not view your kind as humanity's equal, I cannot deny that our intention was to essentially enslave you. This will change. However, I

cannot promise that I will be able to lessen the gap between beggar and noble. That
is a tall task for anyone in our position. Perhaps we can find a place in the middle
somewhere. Why don't we return to Kleinerturm and feast together? We can talk
more about —"

"No!" Prince Lennel came behind his father and raised a knife to his throat. "I
will not stand by while my country falls into the evil hands of *Moindres*!"

The Stelpina guards once again lowered their rifles, and another standoff
ensued. Queen Sophia raised her hands in the air as a sign of no ill intent. "Prince
Lennel, please, find some reason. You hold your father at knifepoint. Calm yourself
before this becomes a situation you regret."

The archbishop stepped in front of Prince Lennel and King Niklaus, disrupting
the Tudrose soldiers' sight on their target. "You will not fire upon us holy patrons
in *cette maison de Deus*! Lower your rifles!"

"You lower yours first!" Sullivan shouted.

"Silence, demon! My prince, keep your resolve, do not submit! Deus is with
us!" Archbishop Abadie raised his hands up and outward, closing his eyes before
beginning to mutter what I assumed to be prayers.

"Lennel what the Hell are you doing! Release me!" King Niklaus struggled
behind the archbishop, but Prince Lennel only tightened his grip.

It looked as though he spoke some words into his father's ear before he glared
down at us from the raised platform he stood upon. He looked quickly to his left
and his right multiple times before displaying such a grin that I felt would haunt me
for a few days at least; it was full of hatred and malcontent. In one swift motion he
slid the knife across his father's throat and the Tudrose soldiers trained on him
fired. All but one ended up shooting the archbishop instead, Prince Lennel getting
grazed by a bullet that appeared to catch the side of his head. The injury did not
seem to deter him though, for amidst the chaos of more gunshots the Prince of
Stelpina drew his arm back and threw his knife at me. I was pushed aside just as
quickly as the knife travelled, collapsing against the pew to my right. More
gunshots were heard as the soldiers fired at Prince Lennel, killing him. I caught
sight of him falling to the stone floor in front of the altar before realizing what had
just happened. Queen Sophia was leaning heavily on me, the hilt of Prince Lennel's
knife in her shoulder. Brina, Sullivan, and I all helped the Queen of Tudrose down
to the floor as Lady Mirlena inspected her injury. Her face twisted in a way that
someone's face would twist when they caught the scent of a stables. I quickly
became exposed to what Lady Mirlena was reacting to, as a strong scent of
something I had wished never to smell ever again filled my nostrils: diseased flesh.

"Queen Sophia, we need to get you out of here. This wound is magical in nature," Lady Mirlena said as she continued to inspect the blade in her queen's arm.

"No. I'm fine. With those two gone, we need to figure out who will look after Stelpina." Queen Sophia's voice was soft and haggard.

Despite her apparently weakened state, Queen Sophia reached over and tried to remove the blade from her arm.

"No! Hold still. I'll remove it." Lady Mirlena coughed as the stench became stronger.

"Well hurry up. We don't...have...all...day…" Queen Sophia's eyes rolled into the back of her head as she went limp in my arms.

Lady Mirlena quickly removed the blade from the Queen's arm and swore the moment the blade vanished into green dust, leaving only the black handle behind. "Decay magic! I need my herbs! You two! Pick up your Queen and follow me! Now!"

"Wait! Weylyn." Queen Sophia had come back to us, but her eyes remained closed, and her breath was rank like the smell that surrounded her wound.

"I'm here." I held her head gently as two soldiers positioned themselves at her head and her feet. Lady Mirlena had her hands firmly on the wound and was muttering a language I recognized as the one she used for spells.

"Decide who leads Stelpina. I trust you." Before I could say anything, Queen Sophia fell limp again.

"Come on! Keep her steady and stay with me." Lady Mirlena began leaving down the aisle with the two soldiers carrying Queen Sophia.

"She's going to be okay, right? Lady Mirlena? Surely we can wait for her to decide!" I called after them.

"Figure it out, Weylyn! I don't have time to feed your confidence! She told you to sort it out, so sort it out! Come on you bastards, quickly! We have a long way to go! Move!" Her orders were followed quickly by the two soldiers who quickened their pace to match Lady Mirlena's.

General Wyman had charged through the doors mere moments ago and had made his way halfway down the aisle before going the opposite way with his Queen. I could hear him shouting orders as the doors to the cathedral opened and closed. The remaining soldiers in the building looked to me, having heard that I had been left in charge of the situation. I didn't know what to do or what to say. Thankfully, Brina spoke up.

"Start clearing out the church. Find out if these soldiers had family and inform them of their deaths. Bring the King and Prince back to their home and let their bodies be prepared for their funerals. Carry our dead out and bring them back to the camp." Brina had given the orders, but the soldiers didn't move. They stared at me, waiting.

"What she said. Get to it." It felt odd being looked at the way the human soldiers had stared at me. I was used to giving orders to fellow Tóráin but giving orders to human soldiers was new territory that I never thought I would ever journey into.

"So, what are we going to do about leadership?" Sullivan asked.

I took a deep sigh as I ran my fingers through my hair, trying to think of something. "I don't know. Do you have any ideas?"

Sullivan appeared taken aback by my question. "You want little old Sully to make someone a king? That's too much responsibility. Knowing the way my decisions in life have gone, I'd probably pick another tyrant in disguise."

"Don't say that, Sullivan," I said. "You've led previous rebellions before. You've led this one here in Stelpina. You have a good mind and an even greater heart. Surely you must have someone in mind, no? I don't know Stelpina as well as you do."

Sullivan rubbed the small beard on his chin as he looked at me with thoughtful eyes. "Your words are very kind, my friend. If you're forcing me to give a name, I would provide you with one you've already heard of. Count Frei has done well to end atrocities committed against our kind after being promoted from Baron. Why not promote him again to King?"

I would be lying if the idea hadn't crossed my mind already. However, I thought that it could be bad to give someone so much power in such little time, so I didn't say anything. Now that Sullivan had suggested Count Frei, I voiced the worries that had kept me from suggesting his name myself. "Would his rise to such power be too quick though? Would people even follow him?"

Brina put a supportive hand on the old goblin's shoulder. "If Sullivan believes the man is worthy of such a position, I trust his judgement."

Sullivan cleared his throat. "Well, I agree that usually such a hurried rise to power can sometimes corrupt the individual in question. In fact, I have learned that throughout human history, those who rose to such strength often ended up having ill intentions to some degree. However, I just don't get the sense that Count Frei would allow himself to be corrupted. He has a genuine heart and has only used his newfound influence to make the world a more inclusive place for every race and every walk of life. He would do wonders for Stelpina. Having been part of a noble family for years will no doubt help him be respected by his peers too."

I took only a few moments to think on what Sullivan had said before making my decision. "Right. It's decided then. Send word to Count Frei that he is to come to Nours to be crowned the new King of Stelpina. He must, however, accept the terms we gave King Niklaus, as well as one other term I've decided on."

Brina and Sullivan both looked confused. It was Sullivan who spoke up though. "What term would that be?"

"I want him to name you the new Count of Balowe," I said as I placed a rewarding hand on Sullivan's shoulder.

"You're insane. Even a man as forward-thinking as Count Frei wouldn't accept those terms. Leave me out of it." Sullivan shrugged my hand off and crossed his arms.

"No. You deserve a reward for all you've sacrificed for the Tóráin. It's about time that one of us was recognized as a noble. I can't think of anyone else more deserving of nobility than you, Sullivan. Those are the terms to him accepting the crown. I have a feeling he might surprise you. Just send a rider with that offer and we'll see what he says." I turned around and began walking towards the exit.

"Where are you going?" Brina shouted after me.

"I have to see if Queen Sophia is alright! Send the letter! I'll see you both back at the camp later!" I opened the doors to the rest of the city and was struck by a torrent of rain.

Soldiers were still standing guard outside despite the weather, and I rushed over to them calling for a horse. I could have just run there in my other form, but a horse would be quicker. I stayed in my tame form and jumped into the saddle of a horse a soldier brought over to me. I kicked my heels into the mare's sides and raced off for the camp, praying to whichever gods were listening to have Queen Sophia be alive when I got there.

# Chapter Forty-Nine

## Olwen



Loud booms filled the camp as a summer thunderstorm raged outside. Despite the constant rain all day, Wyatt still insisted on us working at the lumber mill and nearby farmlands. The storm brought a cooler than usual wind that, when combined with the downpour of rain, made many of us extremely cold. They didn't allow us to warm ourselves by a fire or give us dry clothes. Anyone who complained was beaten by the soldiers, and when one sprite refused to stay down, he was shot. Any sign of defiance was met with the swift pull of a trigger. It had been this way for some for days, weeks for others. Those who had it the worst were what the soldiers called 'Wyatt's Favorites'.

The bastard had singled out a chosen few that he would abuse for sport. I was one of these people, probably the most 'favorite' of all. The abuse given out by Wyatt harmed your body and your mind. It was much crueler than a mere punch to the face or kick to the ribs. I knew these punishments well. Each morning I would be dragged out of the longhouse by my ankles before being deposited at the area we were allowed to relieve ourselves. Wyatt would instruct me to go about my business while he fired shots in my direction. There was little for me to send out of my body, since we were barely given any food or water. Still, I would be shot at until I relieved myself.

Being forced to dance while being hit in the stomach with whatever blunt weapon he could find, cleaning the soldier's latrines while being peed on, and being hung upside down by my ankles while soldiers chucked mud — and other things — at me were just a few acts that Wyatt had enjoyed subjecting me to. It was all horrible, but I would much rather endure those things than be killed or forced into different situations that other Tóráin had experienced. The worst among them was when Wyatt instructed a lycan to have sex with a pig on one of the farms. The poor lycan was to follow that order or be shot. Wyatt had managed to get him to remove his clothes and get close to the pig before killing him anyway. He had made everyone there that day watch, so that we knew what would happen if we got on his bad side. Almost every time he abused or embarrassed someone, he would make sure to use it as a threat to everyone else. Wyatt had always been a bit of an asshole, but he had evolved into someone with a mind full of evil intentions. He enjoyed what he was doing to people. He enjoyed it even more when it was me that he was torturing. I would actually rather him focus more on me than the others. I shuddered thinking of what he had done to the younger ones.

The sickening thought filled my head and I had to quickly push it out. I had nearly set out to kill Wyatt the moment I had heard, but Anya reminded me of why I was here. Staying alive was the main goal in this place. We needed to stay alive until Keagan came so we could all be free. Perhaps I could kill Wyatt, but the remaining soldiers would butcher me for all to see. They'd probably kill more of us as further punishment for my actions. No, I had to stand aside. For now, anyway. I pushed as best I could, trying to replace the horrifying images in my head with something pleasant. I had found that thinking of times where Weylyn and I had spent time together were most helpful. I missed him greatly, but at least I knew he was alive. Well, I suspected he was. I had overheard soldiers talking about Tudrose's advance through Kosavros. They spoke with disgusted tones about a dog that Queen Sophia was fighting the war for. It didn't mean that Weylyn was alive, but I had chosen to take it that way. In my mind, Weylyn — at the very least — escaped that day and went to Tudrose for help. Now he was cutting through countries with Queen Sophia, leaving behind a better world in his wake. He would reach Fleuris at some point, we would see each other again, and I would tell him how I feel. It was something I had decided on a couple days ago. I knew nothing would come of it, and I suspected he may already know, but life was too short to keep secrets from loved ones.

I thought of our anticipated reunion as I coddled a young lycan named Duna. I had grown close to her, especially after her father was killed a day after I arrived.

She was sixteen years old, by no means a child, but she required a certain level of positive attention to combat the negative experiences she was having. She was one of Wyatt's Favorites too, and as I thought of what he had done to her my teeth began to grind. Again, I had to push the thoughts aside. There wasn't a moment that passed by that I didn't want to rush out of this longhouse, kill the guards outside, make for Wyatt's quarters, and slit the bastard's throat. Not being able to was the greatest torture I had been forced to endure in this place so far. Duna began coughing, and she woke from the fit.

"If we don't die from a bullet, we'll certainly die from sickness," Kayne grumbled. The satyr was older than me, but not too old to be ineffective. He was still strong and nimble, even in his deprived state. He was one of the first people to say they would attempt to escape with Anya and I, even doing his best to convince others to join us.

"She isn't going to die, Kayne. Stop scaring the poor girl." I moved Duna's dark hair from her face and held her closer to me in the hopes of keeping her warm.

"She's not a damn child. I was in the army at her age. She knows just as well as you and I do that the longer we stay here the more likely we'll never leave." Kayne let out a loud sneeze, sniffling afterwards as he recovered from it.

"We'll escape. Have a little more faith, you old grouch." Anya's voice was only a whisper, but it carried well enough. I could tell she wasn't as close as Kayne was, but she was obviously close enough to join our conversation.

Duna had fallen asleep for only a moment before her nightmares took over. They jolted her awake, the poor thing breathing heavily and quickly. I shushed her in an attempt to calm her, but when that didn't work, I chose to do something I hadn't done in a long time. I began to rock her in my arms and softly sing. The song was one my mother had taught me. I could feel Kayne glaring at me as the words of our old language came out of my mouth and into the longhouse. He no doubt saw it as another excuse for the soldiers to beat or kill us, and he wasn't necessarily wrong. Had they heard me, I wouldn't be surprised if they walked in and shot me right away. I knew that, and yet I didn't stop. My singing was calming Duna, and eventually she fell back to sleep.

"That was beautiful, Olwen." Anya didn't sound as far away as before; the sprite had probably moved closer.

I scoffed. "It's probably the last time you'll ever hear me do that."

"Good," Kayne grumbled. "I don't need to get shot because of a fool's singing."

Anya ignored him. "Why? You sounded wonderful. I'd sleep much easier hearing that at night instead of taunts from the soldiers."

I sighed. "You'll just have to remember it, Anya. To be honest I'm surprised I broke my promise. I never thought I would. But it won't happen again."

"What promise?" Anya asked.

I would rather Kayne not hear, but I didn't mind telling Anya. Keagan and Weylyn knew why I didn't sing, and I found Anya was a closer friend of mine than I had anticipated. We had leaned on each other a fair bit during our time in Camp Liodorleu. To be honest I don't know if I would be able to endure everything without her here. I closed my eyes as I prepared myself to tell a story I had rarely told. I took one last deep breath before starting.

"When I was younger, maybe a year less than Duna, I was incredibly reckless. My father had died a couple years before, and I had taken up being a thief to help my family eat. On top of that, I was singing at bars to earn some money. I sang songs in the common tongue mostly, but when it was just Tóráin I would sing in Séúbua. It was incredibly risky, and when my mother found out I was doing it after my twin brother Devlin told her, she stuck Devlin to my side to keep me from doing it. However, my brother's consistent lack of support only pushed me to sing in Séúbua more. I even started singing when humans were around. Majority of them were allies to the Tóráin and rather enjoyed the songs I was singing anyway, so I saw no harm in it. That was until one night in April when I was getting ready to sing at a tavern called The Broken Glass.

"Before I began, the doors burst open and six Fleuris soldiers marched in. They informed everyone that they had been told someone was singing songs in a language they shouldn't be, and how that person should come forward. A kind lycan by the name of Kennon quickly tried to take the fall for me, but the soldiers pushed him away. 'We're looking for a green one,' they had said. Before I could say anything, my brother was stepping forward admitting that he was the one singing. Despite my continued confessions, the soldiers refused to believe me. They took my brother away to Bastion and held him there for weeks. It wasn't until June that I caught word of the execution of a forest sprite happening in front of Bastion. I made my way there, having discovered the news only an hour before his scheduled death, and got there just in time to see a battered, swollen face of a male sprite being secured into a guillotine.

"The blade fell, the crowd of mostly humans cheered, and I fell to my knees. I stayed there until soldiers came to shoo me away. I wanted his body, but they wouldn't give it to me. They claimed he was property of Fleuris and would be dealt with 'in a manner that fits his station'. That manner they spoke of was being tossed into a shallow grave and burned, along with the other prisoners they had executed that day. I returned home and informed my mother of the news. She rightfully blamed me for Devlin's death, something my younger sister Tawnia also chose to do. She was only six at the time, but the hatred in her eyes still hurts me more than most things. They both wanted nothing to do with me anymore, and I was kicked out onto the streets of Cloque. I found out through some friends a couple weeks later that my mother had been overcome with grief and hung herself. I returned home to take care of Tawnia, but she was nowhere to be found. I later discovered that she had contracted the disease Strawberry Fever and was in the nearby hospital. I went to see her, which resulted in her throwing a violent fit as she blamed me for our mother's death as well as our brother's. About three weeks later I was notified by a nurse friend of mine that Tawnia had died."

"Oh, Olwen. That's...I don't know what to say. You don't blame all of that on your singing, do you?" Anya had managed to find me in the dark, grabbing my arm in an attempt to comfort me.

"Of course, I do. I promised myself that day to never sing again. If I wasn't singing, my brother wouldn't have been in prison. If he wasn't in prison, he wouldn't have been killed. If he was still alive, my mother wouldn't have taken her own life. If my mother was around maybe my sister would have had more to fight for. They're all dead because of me, and that's just something I'm going to have to live with." I wiped away a tear that had fallen down my cheek, hoping that the darkness surrounding us kept the action hidden.

"You shouldn't think that way. Two family members made decisions of their own, and one succumbed to a deadly disease. I don't blame you for any of their deaths." Anya squeezed my arm a bit tighter, showing her support.

I patted Anya's hand gently. "That's kind of you, but I do. My actions led to their actions. It's my fault they're dead."

Anya resorted to rubbing my arm now in an attempt to soothe me. "Olwen, don't —"

The door to the longhouse burst open and soldier's stormed in. They tossed someone inside and fanned out, holding their lanterns high to get a good look at everyone. Eventually one of them reached me, and the soldier pointed in my direction. "There! Found one! Oh, they're all here I think!"

A man not dressed in the regular uniform of a Fleuris soldier stepped through the people laying on the floor and came into the light of the lantern; it was Wyatt.

He smiled. "Ah, there she is. The Demon of the Wilds herself. You three wouldn't happen to be Kayne, Anya, and Duna, would you?"

I went to spring up to my feet, but Wyatt quickly pulled his pistol out and aimed it at me. I stared him down with a look I was praying would strike him dead. "Do whatever you want with me. Just leave them out of this."

"I'll take that as a yes. *Emmenez-les dehors*!" Wyatt turned around as soldiers came to grab the four of us.

Duna, half asleep and confused, was already crying. Anya was struggling as much as she could without provoking the soldiers to shoot her. Kayne was arguing that he wasn't in fact Kayne, and that there was a misunderstanding. Having been dragged out of this longhouse so many times now — day and night — I had grown numb to it. I let them take me wherever they planned to take me as I prepared my mind for what was to come. The rain was coming down so hard it was difficult to hear the soldiers instructing us to move faster. We all stumbled through the mud towards The Trees, a set of wooden poles sticking up out of the ground where prisoners were tortured or killed. It wasn't a good sign for us to be brought to this place. The soldiers stood each of us in front of a pole of our own before stepping back a few paces, their rifles ready to aim and fire at Wyatt's command.

"Strip." One word that instantly made you feel less than an animal. It wasn't the first time I had heard the order during my time in Camp Liodorleu; it was one of Wyatt's favorite forms of embarrassment.

"Is this really —" Kayne stopped arguing the moment Wyatt raised his hand in the air and the soldiers aimed their rifles at each of us.

Reluctantly, all of us removed what little clothing we had. Everyone was given a dress of some sort, one piece of cloth to cover ourselves. The layer of clothing slipped off my shoulders and fell down to the mud-covered ground squishing between my toes. The cold rain hitting my naked body was unsettling, the feeling of discomfort only increasing as I spotted the soldiers' grins in the lantern light. Even with it being summer, the storm had caused conditions that had me beginning to shiver. My hair was soaked, gripping to my scalp, neck, shoulders, and face.

"It has been brought to my attention that a group of *imbéciles bestiaux* are planning an escape of some sort. Don't try to argue. I won't believe you. You're out here because I want to know whose brilliant idea it was to escape. Who is stupid enough to actually think I would let any *Diables* escape my camp?" Wyatt looked at each of us, but nobody said a word. His shoulders slumped before he lazily took out his pistol. He waved it in the air as he spoke. "Come on now, we haven't got all night. You tell me whose idea it was, and I let you live. How's that for a deal?"

Nothing but the rain and thunder could be heard for a few moments until a voice broke through. "Okay, okay! It was all Olwen's idea! She bewitched me somehow! I would never think to —"

The shot from Wyatt's pistol went through Kayne's face and out the back of his head, causing the satyr to slump down to the soaked ground. The act caused Duna to scream and her crying intensified. Wyatt looked up to the sky in annoyance before marching over to Duna and putting his pistol to her forehead.

"*Silencieux*!" he shouted. "The only thing worse than a snitch is a whining *chienne*!"

Duna continued to sob. "Please, sir. Please. Just let me go back —"

Another gunshot filled the camp, followed by a bright flash of lightning in the distance.

"You bastard! She was a harmless child! How could anyone have such disregard for a life to do something so —"

Another gunshot rang through the air, and I felt my legs fall out from under me. I fell to my knees at the same time Anya's body collapsed. Tears mixed with raindrops as an overwhelming amount of grief took over my body. Someone was yelling at me, but I couldn't fully hear them. The image of Kayne, Duna, and then Anya being killed before my eyes was burning itself into my mind. Suddenly, my grief turned to unbridled rage and I burst to my feet with newfound energy I hadn't had in days. I moved right for Wyatt, but I quickly stopped my advance. Wyatt had drawn his sword, and the tip of it was pushing up against my throat. The blade had nicked me before I could stop, and I felt the warm blood trickle down my neck along with the cold water falling from the sky.

"There she is! The Demon of the Wilds reborn! Don't be angry with me. You did this. You're responsible for this. Their blood is on your hands, Olwen, not mine." He stepped forward, pushing the blade into my neck, causing me to step backwards until my back was pressed up against the pole. "I could kill you too, but what fun would that be? Consider this your punishment. Live with the guilt of getting these three killed."

I was shaking, not from the weather, but aggression. "I'm going to kill you. Maybe not today. Maybe not tomorrow. But one day, I'll watch the life leave your eyes."

Wyatt pretended to be scared with a silly facial expression. *"Si sinistre*! If you're done making what we both know is just an idle threat, you can get to work on cleaning this mess up. Bring the bodies to the pit."

He took his blade away from my throat and turned his back. I would have struck then, but the soldiers had their rifles trained on me. I took my eyes off of Wyatt only to locate my clothes amongst the mud. I was about to toss the clothing over my head when a shout stopped me.

"No! After you're done, Demon of the Wilds. Let the rain wash away your sins!" He let out a bellow of laughter after that last remark as he made his way back to his quarters.

The soldiers remained where they were, watching me as I made my way over to Anya. I knelt down next to her limp corpse and brushed my fingers over her face to close her eyes. I moved her hair away and wiped the blood covered mud off her face. Sitting there next to my fallen friend, I looked up and over at Duna's body lying about ten feet to my right, then turned to glance at Kayne who lay dead double that distance to my left . I returned my attention to Anya and leaned over to plant a kiss on her forehead.

I rested my head on hers and closed my eyes, trying to feel a soul that I knew had already passed on. "I'm so sorry, Anya. I'll make sure he pays for this. I promise. *Codladh go sámh, mo chara.*"

"Get a move on, *Diable*!" a soldier shouted at me.

I took a deep breath and leaned back. After moving the wet strands of hair out of my face, I put an arm under Anya's back and another under her knees. I lifted her as I extended my legs, nearly slipping because of the mud under my naked feet. The soldiers urged me to move faster by waving their rifles in the direction of the pit where dead prisoners were burned. I blinked away tears and held my head high as I passed by them, cradling my friend in my arms.

# Chapter Fifty

# Weylyn

Nours, Stelpina  |  June 16, 1799

"I'm going to find something to eat. Care to join me?" Rosalie sent one of her precious smiles my way.

"You know I can't," I said as I smiled back. "Despite how much I would love to."

Rosalie's shoulders slumped and she lifted her chin like a child who had just been told they couldn't have sweets for dinner. "Oh, come on. She's going to be fine, Weylyn. Lady Mirlena said so herself. We'll be quick, I promise. You need to eat."

I looked away from Rosalie to look over Queen Sophia. "She's like this because of me. I have to be here when she wakes up."

Rosalie sighed and put a hand behind my head before taking a seat in my lap. "How many times do I have to tell you that every bad thing that happens isn't your fault? You put so much responsibility on yourself that you take on things that you don't need to." She brought her left hand to rest on my cheek before making my eyes meet hers. "That foul Prince Lennel did this to her. Only he is responsible."

Rosalie leaned in and gave me a kiss that warmed a soul that was feeling awfully cold lately. When our lips parted and she leaned back a bit, the beautiful woman looked over my face for a couple moments before planting a comforting kiss on my forehead. Rosalie then proceeded to get off my lap, fixing the simple dress she wore. "I'll go get us some food. If you need to stay here, then I won't make you leave. Just don't beat yourself up the entire time I'm gone, okay?"

I sent her as kind a smile as I could muster. "I promise I'll do my best not to. Thank you for understanding."

Rosalie returned my smile before spinning around and making her way to the door. She left the room, leaving me alone with Queen Sophia. We had moved her to Kleinerturm, the weather proving too troublesome to treat her at the camp. It had been alternating between heavy rain and brisk winds for a couple days now. She was put in the guest room of the small castle, a decent sized room with a hearth and a bed big enough for two people. I watched Queen Sophia lay in the middle of that bed, blankets up to her shoulders. Her right forearm laid across her stomach, softly rising and falling with each shallow breath. Her left arm was no longer there. A bandage wrapped around the stump left behind was all that remained. I remembered General Wyman's reservations when Lady Mirlena had declared they needed to remove the Queen's arm to prevent the curse from spreading. He insisted that Lady Mirlena wasn't doing enough to save her, and that she was acting out of desperation rather than reason. Eventually, Lady Mirlena ignored him and ordered the nurses she had gathered to prepare Queen Sophia for amputation.

The smell and look of her arm at the time was revolting. Her skin had turned a deep, dark green with boils and puss covering from her shoulder to her elbow. Lady Mirlena had spent roughly an hour speaking spells and rubbing ointments made from her herbs into the wound, but it had only slowed the spread. I was there when the witch removed Queen Sophia's arm with an axe. I had expected the Queen to wake up, screaming in pain, but she laid quiet on the table beneath her. She had been asleep ever since her last words in the cathedral, and many of us worried if she would ever wake again. Lady Mirlena said that the amputation should stop the spread, and that Queen Sophia would eventually wake. Even with that news, I was still finding it hard to be hopeful. For a couple days now, the Queen of Tudrose was as pale as death itself; her lips were a soft blue and her body still wasn't as warm as it should be. Were it not for the rise and fall of her stomach, you would think she was already dead.

The only bit of relief any of us had was when Lady Mirlena had come by to check on Queen Sophia and I asked if a small amount of color had returned to her skin. I had been hesitant to say anything, thinking that it was maybe just the way the lantern and fire from the hearth cast a certain glow on her, but after a short inspection of her own, Lady Mirlena admitted that I was correct. The witch had said it was a good sign that Queen Sophia was recovering. I agreed with her at the time, trying to be positive about the situation, but I couldn't get over the fact that Queen Sophia wouldn't fully recover. She could regain the color in her skin, warmth could return to her body, and her eyes could open, but she wouldn't be whole. She had lost her entire left arm. General Wyman feared that it would make her appear weak, inspiring her enemies to become bolder than before. Lady Mirlena had insisted that it would make her look stronger. That the world would see a woman who faced death and won. My heart sided with Lady Mirlena, but my mind caused anxieties that led me to worry about General Wyman possibly being right. Regardless, all we could do right now was wait for Queen Sophia to wake up.

A knock on the door broke me away from my thoughts. "Who is it?"

"It's Sullivan. I've brought someone who wishes to meet you."

I didn't feel like meeting people, but at least it would distract me from my thoughts for a while. "Come in."

The door opened and the goblin I had come to admire walked in, followed by a man of average height. Sullivan wore richer clothes than I was used to him wearing, and the man with him was dressed even more fancy than he was. I realized who the mystery man was from the crown on his head.

"Lord Weylyn! A pleasure to meet you. Sullivan has done nothing but speak highly of you. I am —"

"King Frederick Frei of Stelpina. The crown gives you away." I forced a smile as I grabbed his offered hand.

King Frederick shook it kindly as he laughed. "Yes, I imagine it does. Still doesn't feel real. Sullivan told me that it was you that decided I was to be given this incredible honor. I want you to know that I am both immensely humbled and incredibly gracious. I'll do whatever I can to see that Stelpina evolves into something better than it has been in the past. I promise."

The man had kind, brown eyes and his hair was a fair, light brown. His face was void of hair save for his bushy eyebrows and the thin mustache resting on his upper lip. The make of a person had more to do with how they looked, but King Frederick appeared to be a welcoming, kind person. There was no feeling of judgement or disgust when he looked at you, and his eyes gleamed with excitement and intrigue. I nodded in thanks at first, but when I saw that King Frederick appeared uncomfortable that I hadn't said anything, I added a vocal response to his statements.

"Sullivan suggested you for Count of Balowe and King of Stelpina," I said. "You should be thanking him more than me. I am thankful that you would promise such a thing though. I can't even imagine many people in your position saying those words without trying to withhold the need to vomit."

"Did he?" King Frederick turned and grabbed Sullivan's hand in both of his and shook it. "Thank you, Lord Sullivan! I have strived to be as much of a friend to your kind as I can be. To be thought of in such a light by you is immensely appreciated."

Sullivan gave the new King an uneasy smile as he respectfully retrieved his hand from the man's grasp. "That's wonderful. Just keep on doing what you're doing and I'm sure more Tóráin will think of you the same as we do. Now, not to be rude, but we don't have a lot of time. Can't be away from your crowning party too long without people asking questions."

"*Ja, du hast recht.*" King Frederick's eyes fell on Queen Sophia after the grand smile on his face faded away. He adopted a somber expression before speaking. "I did come to meet you, Lord Weylyn, but I am also keen to know how Queen Sophia is doing."

I had stood up from my chair to greet the new King of Stelpina. From my higher vantage point, the Queen of Tudrose appeared incredibly frail. Even though the curse had not spread throughout her body, it had caused her to lose some of her weight, making her slightly thinner than before. She was only a couple inches taller than five feet, and the loss of weight, as well as her entire left arm, made her look incredibly small in the good-sized bed. From what I saw, I would say that Queen Sophia wasn't doing very well at all. However, those who knew more than me about health and magic had insisted that she was slightly improving. I chose to say the more positive opinion of the two in my head.

"She's strong," I announced. "We're confident that she'll recover."

King Frederick nodded. "Yes. Yes, that's wonderful news. I look forward to speaking with her. I would love to stay and chat with you some more, but I fear Lord Sullivan is right. There are those who wish to kiss the new King's ass in hopes of receiving greater favor than they had before. I must go, but I would like to leave you with some information, if I may."

I nodded, and King Frederick nodded in return before standing a little bit straighter and smiling. "As *König* of Stelpina, I, *König* Frederick Frei, grant The Resistance access to my resources. I will need troops to keep my country safe but should any wish to join you in your fight, they may. Food, other supplies. All will be made available to you and your supporters. Now, while this could be enough for some people, I felt the need to take one step further with a few specific things that may anger some people, but they will accept them regardless. I have begun work on a reparations act that will see the poor of Stelpina — mostly the Tóráin who were barely paid at all — given funds to revitalize their livelihoods. Craftsmen will begin making the slums of cities better, so that they resemble the homes of richer folk more closely. Also, I will be passing a new law that will punish people for using hateful slang to address your kind. Words such as *Geringere* and *Moindres* will be outlawed in Stelpina, as well as any other harmful terms people bring from other countries. Finally — as requested by you — Lord Sullivan here will be named Count of Balowe. With me in Nours and Lord Sullivan in Balowe, we will make this country one that both humans and Tóráin will be happy to be a part of. As for you specifically, you and your friends will always have a place here in Kleinerturm as honored guests. I hope all of this is to your liking." King Frederick put a hand over his heart and bowed slightly.

I struggled to find words. Sullivan had talked to me through spoken and written word about the character of Frederick Frei, but experiencing it now had me shaken. I had no idea how he would get any other noble to agree with all of that, or how he would prevent a negative reaction from the human citizens of the country. However, the more I thought about it the more I chose to dismiss the questions I had. This wasn't something to analyze and strike down with negativity. King Frederick's announcements were things to be celebrated, and so I chose to do just that. I allowed myself to smile and feel proud for, apparently, making the best choice I could have made in making Frederick Frei King of Stelpina.

"That is quite a bit of information, King Frederick," I said with a smile. "Please know that all of it is greatly appreciated by me, The Resistance, and all the Tóráin that we fight for. When I joined The Resistance, I dreamt of moments like this. Your words have made one of my dreams come true, my friend. This is all wonderful news."

"What's wonderful news?" The weak voice of Queen Sophia pulled my attention away from King Frederick, bringing me to quickly sit on the edge of the bed.

"Queen Sophia? It's wonderful to hear your voice." I put a hand on hers and watched as the Queen of Tudrose's eyes fluttered open.

Her eyes were bloodshot and tired, but it did look as though more color had returned to her skin. Her lips weren't as blue, and her breaths appeared to be stronger. She began to cough, and I quickly poured a cup of water and brought it to her lips. Queen Sophia allowed me to lift the drink into her dry mouth before giving me a small smile as thanks.

"Where am I? Is everything —" Queen Sophia noticed that her left arm wasn't there, and I saw the panic rise in her eyes.

"Sullivan, go find Lady Mirlena." I didn't wait to see if he left, but I did hear the door open and close. "Easy now, Queen Sophia. You've been through quite the experience."

Tears began to fill her eyes and her body shook as her hand touched the empty space where her arm should be. Her fingers ran along the bandage covering her shoulder as she sniffled and whimpered. "How? What?"

I cleared my throat, the woman's emotion causing some to stir in me as well. "The knife that Prince Lennel threw at me, the one that you saved me from, was cursed with a decay spell. Lady Mirlena did her best, but the curse threatened to spread throughout your body, which would have killed you. The decision was made to remove your arm to prevent the spread. Thankfully, it worked. I'm so sorry. You should have just let the knife hit me. You don't deserve this."

Queen Sophia's shimmering eyes looked at me quizzically. "And you think you do?"

I didn't answer. Instead, I lowered my head and avoided her gaze. She reached out and grabbed my arm tighter than I thought she could. "Nobody deserves this, Weylyn. However, it sounds like this curse was a deadly one. I'm glad I got in the way of it. This campaign needs you more than it needs me."

I couldn't believe what she had just said. She must still be delirious from being sick. She didn't seriously believe that did she? The woman was the queen of the strongest country in Kosavros. It was her army winning these battles for us. "I'm sorry if you see this as me being rude, but you're terribly wrong. You lead this campaign, Queen Sophia. Without you, it never starts. Without you, it ends."

Queen Sophia was staring at her injury when she began to respond. "You still don't see how important you are in all of this, do you? Weylyn, without you, The Resistance fails. As much as you would like to see it as you were joining my army, it has always been my army joining The Resistance. I may command the army, but you are the spearhead leading the charge. From setting terms to fighting in the battles, you are leading these people forward. I did not choose to fight a war for you. I chose to fight it with you. I may be more advanced than other leaders in policy pertaining to treating the Tóráin better, but I am not one of you. The Tóráin see you, and they see hope. They see a reason to fight. You mean everything to this campaign. It is why I moved between you and that blade. Now stop making my sacrifice seem foolish instead of heroic. I should be paraded down the streets instead of being lectured like a child."

She smiled at that last bit, knowing that she was being cheeky. I couldn't help but smile too. All she had said was incredibly kind, and I did have to admit that it had some truth to it. I bowed my head in surrender. "Thank you, Queen Sophia. Your words humble me."

"Just Sophia is fine from now on," she said before a small coughing fit took hold of her again. When it stopped, she forced a smile and continued. "I don't want you thinking you're any less than I am anymore. We're equals as far as I see it. We'll just agree that we're on the same level and move forward with that premise."

I nodded. "Just Sophia it is. Thank you. Truly. You're waking up after nearly dying, discovering you lost an arm, and you've spent all your time making me feel better. I feel like a bad caretaker."

Sophia laughed. "Well, if you want to be a good one, get me something stronger than water."

Just as I was pouring her a cup of wine that Cordelia had brought Rosalie and I earlier, the door to the room opened. Lady Mirlena entered, with Rosalie close behind. Lady Mirlena came to the other side of the bed and sat down.

"How are you feeling?" The witch asked as she put a hand on Sophia's forehead.

"We've been worried about you." Rosalie came to stand next to me, draping an arm around my shoulder.

Sophia looked at the bandage on her shoulder before sending a warm smile at everyone in the room. "I think I'll live."

# Chapter Fifty-One

## Olwen



It was difficult to keep track of how many days had passed by, but I knew that Keagan would arrive any day now. I hoped I was right. There was no telling how much longer Wyatt would be entertained by my suffering. He had begun discussing my death with me, and I was sure it was only a matter of time until he acted on his threats. The worst part was that I sometimes wished he would just do it already. The days were hard before Anya's death, but they became increasingly more difficult afterwards. Even if I could fight through my nightmares enough to find some sleep, it would be disturbed by Wyatt having me woken up in the middle of the night. Every night since he took Anya, Duna, and Kayne from me, he had me relive the moment. Some nights Wyatt would come to watch me strip down again before soldiers aimed their rifles at me. Every now and then they would shoot, laughing each time I flinched. Gunfire used to be on the same level as birds singing in the trees for me, but now the sound shook my bones. It caused moments of that night to flash before my eyes. Every time. Just when I thought it couldn't get any worse, Wyatt had decided to start bringing out randomly selected Tóráin with me for the last six nights. It was always me and one other, with the unlucky person being killed in the same manner Anya and the others had been.

My days weren't much better. The abuse continued on, and the work we were subject to felt more strenuous each day that passed by. Wyatt had lowered everyone's rations by half after he had discovered people were thinking of escaping. He publicly blamed the decrease in food and water on the Demon of the Wilds, which had members of my own kind treating me like an enemy. Very few helped me during work, and even less spoke to me. Nobody wanted to be seen with me in fear of gaining Wyatt's eye. The number of people still willing to try to escape was very few, and it saddened me deeply. The others either didn't trust me, or they were too afraid of Wyatt to even think they could be free of this place. People were dying of exhaustion, starvation, and dehydration. Not to mention Wyatt's pistol was responsible for quite a few deaths as well. There were many who had reached the point where they hoped their death came from a bullet to the head instead of suffering like the others. When I had arrived, there was still a fair amount of hope amongst the people here. Wyatt had managed to break almost all of them down in a bit more than two weeks. Their hope had vanished.

I listened to people whispering nearby as I waited to be taken out to The Trees again. They spoke of a young boy that had collapsed and died earlier today. He was a satyr, probably around the age of eight. His name was Brady. The soldiers poked at his body with their bayonets to see if he was still alive, at least that's what I was telling myself. One of the people whispering appeared to be the lycan who had been instructed to carry the body back to Camp Liodorleu to be burned like so many others. It sounded like he was quite emotional as he spoke about the experience, a pain I knew all too well. Not only had I been forced to carry Anya, Kayne, and Duna to their grave, but I also had to do the same for the poor people Wyatt was killing to make my nightly torture more like that horrid night. I had been around death before, especially during my time in the army, but this was different. The bodies I had carried ranged in age from under twelve to over fifty. Wyatt didn't care how old you were, nor did he care whether you had followed orders or not. He chose his killings on a whim, which kept everyone in the longhouses in a constant state of fear. I stopped listening to the whispers and went inward, trying to bring Brady's face to the forefront of my mind. When I was happy with what I had, I whispered a small prayer for him. It pained me that it was all I could do.

"Olwen?"

The soft voice had me open my eyes quickly, even though I could barely see anything. "Tal?"

I felt someone grab my arm. "Is this you, Olwen?"

I put my hand on hers. "Yes, Tal. What is it?"

Tallulah was a water sprite that was part of the small group that still wished to be free. She was probably the only person I had left that I could genuinely call a friend in this place. It made me wary about speaking with her during the day. I didn't want Wyatt to notice our friendship and use it against me. Too many people had died because of me already.

"Is it tonight?" Tallulah asked.

I squeezed her hand. "I don't know, Tal. Maybe. It doesn't look like it though. Try to get some rest. The soldiers will be coming for me soon and I don't want them to take you too."

"Stay strong, Olwen. Our freedom will come soon. I know it." The water sprite's hand let go of me and I heard some shuffling to my left as she made herself as comfortable as she could.

I sat there in the dark for some time, but I began to wonder if Wyatt had forgotten to have me tortured tonight. Maybe he was purposely waiting longer than usual? It had been at least an hour — maybe two — and still neither Wyatt nor his soldiers had come for me. I was exhausted, so I abandoned my seated position in favor of one that had me laying on my back. My head was on someone's leg, but that was just how things were. Even with all the death that had run through this camp, there were still too many of us to sleep comfortably in the longhouses. I felt the person shift their leg under me before they swept it away quickly, causing my head to fall to the wooden floor. The jolt snapped me out of the sleepy state I was in and had me mumbling curses to myself. I remained where I was for what felt like another hour until I started to feel sleep take me. I tried to keep my eyes open, expecting Wyatt and his goons to come in at any moment, but eventually my exhaustion won the battle and my eyes closed.

I woke up to gunfire and yelling. Whistles and trumpets blared as I sat up quickly, looking around the dark longhouse. The tiredness that clouded my mind vanished swiftly and I recognized what was happening. Keagan had finally arrived, and it was time for us to go. I immediately addressed everyone in the longhouse. "Anyone who wants to be free of this place, come with me. I promise you that you'll be safe. Hurry!"

I didn't wait to see how many were following me. I knew that we had a limited amount of time. The forces that Keagan would have gathered from the villages that surrounded Cloque wouldn't have been enough to fully defeat the garrison at Camp Liodorleu. However, they would give us enough of a distraction to sneak away. The thought of being free from this place had given me a boost of adrenaline that I had not felt in weeks. I was alert and ready as I quickly opened the only door in the longhouse. Knowing where they were thanks to my many nights of torture, I leapt onto the soldier to my left after striking the soldier to my right with a swift right hook. I wrapped my arms around the neck of the soldier I had tackled and gave it a quick twist. The snap I heard told me I could let go of him and make for the next guard. I was happy to see that I didn't have to. Tallulah and a few others had subdued the soldier themselves. I returned my attention to the man whose neck I had snapped, taking his sword and pistol. I removed the bayonet from his rifle and handed it to the person nearest to me. The pistol was in case of emergency, but the rifle wasn't necessary. Gunfire would only alert the soldiers to our escape. After a couple other Tóráin took the sword, pistol, and bayonet from the other guard, I motioned for them all to be quiet by putting my finger to my lips. I then waved for them to follow me before making my way to the other longhouse.

I told everyone to remain in the shadows as I made my own way to the guards. By the time they saw me, my sword had torn through them. A swift slice to the neck to one followed by a sharp stab to the other's chest and they both fell without firing off their rifles. I opened the door and called to the large open area. "If you want to be free of this place, come with me. Hurry, we don't have much time!"

I left the guards to be robbed by someone else once I heard the rustling of people getting up. A goblin, two sprites and a harpy split the weapons amongst themselves. The sight of the wingless harpy still triggered me into a feeling of sickness. Wyatt had kept all the harpies' wings tied up at first, but about ten days ago he had decided to cut their wings off completely to make sure none of them would escape. Many harpies had died from the mutilation until Wyatt started cauterizing the wounds so that a few would live on to be tortured and killed another day. I waved at everyone to follow me, and we swiftly met up with the rest of our group of hopeful escapees. I led a group of roughly one hundred people towards the back of the camp. The razor wire that encased the place blocked our exit, not to mention the spells that had been placed on it. I rubbed the tip of my pointer finger as I remembered how Keagan and I had discovered such enchantments during our scouting. If you touched the wires, your skin would burn like it was covered in acid. It was all too thick to weave through without getting cut and burned. There were three layers of it too, about half a dozen feet thick. Knives couldn't cut the wires either. Thankfully, Finn was right where we had planned for him to be.

He was accompanied by a woman I did not recognize. She had her hands outward, glowing a soft blue. They must have found the witch during their journey, which would really help make Finn's job safer. I heard someone shout in pain about a dozen feet away from me before someone wondered out loud how we were going to get through the enchanted barrier. The witch must only be strong enough to weaken the spell where Finn was working, which told me the spells placed on the borders of the camp were incredibly strong and probably performed by multiple witches.

"Guess you're happy to have found a witch!" I shouted to Finn.

"Olwen, this is Marie. Marie, Olwen!" Finn cursed as he struggled to get one of the wires to cut. "I thought we'd be saving more people, where is everyone?"

A feeling of guilt washed over me. "The rest are too afraid to get caught. I can't force them to come."

"Where's Anya?" The question made my stomach turn and my heart race even more than it was already.

After my lack of an answer made the lycan stop what he was doing to ask me for a second time, I forced the only response I felt was appropriate. "I'm sorry, Finn."

The lantern he had brought was dim, but I could see how dejected the response made him. He and Anya were close. Very close actually. I had dreaded the moment I had to tell him I failed. He shook his head quickly and returned to cutting the wires. He didn't say anything, but I could hear him stifling back his sadness with sniffs and coughs. Finn was cutting through the wires with a special pair of scissors we had ordered from a blacksmith that was an ally to The Resistance. They were massive, roughly fifteen times the size of regular scissors. The blades were thick, and the handles were long. Finn held each handle at the end, snapping through the wires as quickly as he could. When we arrived, he was already through the first layer of razor wire. It took him a bit longer to get through the second layer, until he finally cut through the third layer that barred our path. He carefully moved the wires out of the way, something he was able to do thanks to the witch, until there was a big enough hole for everyone to get through. I ushered people into the gap as gunshots and other sounds of battle continued to fill the camp. When the last person made their way through, the only one left was myself. I hesitated, looking back to the front of the camp where the battle raged on.

"Olwen, let's go!" Finn yelled at me.

I looked over at The Trees and the night Anya was killed acted itself out in my mind. Turning my attention back on Finn and the others, I saw the lycan shake his head in disagreement. "No Olwen! Keagan and the others are doing their part. Do yours and help me get these people out of here."

I sighed. "Get them to the rally point, Finn."

I began sprinting towards the fight as Finn called after me. Eventually I heard him curse before shouting for everyone to follow him. I did want to see that everyone was safe, but I trusted that Finn would make sure that they were. My place was elsewhere. I had made a promise that night, and I decided tonight was when I would make good on it. As I got closer, I could see two forces locked in battle. Soldiers in towers fired upon their enemy down below as the rest of the garrison fought in front of the entrance to Camp Liodorleu. The force Keagan had managed to gather was a formidable one, a size that I had not expected. The battle appeared to be even so far, and that in itself was a victory. Thankfully, there was only one witch that lived here at Camp Liodorleu. Esme was up in one of the towers doing what she could to slow the Tóráin attacking the Fleuris soldiers. I quickly climbed the ladder that led up to her and about six guards. I stabbed Esme first, the green glow emanating from her hands fizzling out as I removed my blade from her back. The attack caused the soldiers to panic, some trying to bring their rifles into the enclosed space of the tower while others drew their swords. I fought all of them, the rush of energy I felt surprising me more than anything. I had a burst lip and a cut on my thigh, but the tower was mine. I quickly made my way back down the ladder and snuck over to the other tower that flanked the entrance to the camp. I dealt with that group more easily, contracting no other injuries during the fight.

With the towers dealt with, I could see that our force was making some ground. The lack of bullets and magic raining down on them allowed the Tóráin force to push through and gain a slight advantage. It was reckless of me, but I attacked the back of the Fleuris garrison myself. It caused confusion amongst their ranks, so much so that the Tóráin Keagan led in front of them pushed further in. Eventually, much to my surprise, shouts of surrender began to erupt from the Fleuris force. The initial plan was to cause enough chaos for a while until retreating into the woods. Instead, we had beaten the garrison into submission. It was a pleasant victory, but that wasn't what I had come here for. As the Tóráin around me cheered and howled, I began searching through the ranks of soldiers now on their knees. There were some dressed differently than the regular soldiers — causing me to get excited for nothing — but eventually I found him. Wyatt was on his knees with a sour look on his face. He was shouting slurs at everyone around him, despite having apparently surrendered. The verbal attacks eventually upset a nearby lycan enough where he raised his clawed hand in the air in preparation of a killing blow.

"Stop!" I shouted. The lycan looked at me and snarled, but I stared him down until he submitted.

"O'?" Keagan's voice rang out in the night, and I felt a moment of happiness. The red-haired lycan burst through the crowd, his jaws and hands covered in blood. He had cuts all over him; a pretty nasty one on his left side. "You're okay!"

He shifted into his tame form as he made his way over to me. He hugged me tightly, but I didn't embrace him back. I was incredibly happy to see Keagan, and we had so much to discuss, yet my mind was elsewhere. Keagan set me free and stood back, a quizzical look in his eye. "What is it? What's wrong? Are you hurt?"

I put a gentle hand on Keagan's left arm and moved him to the side so I could set my eyes on Wyatt again. He had a small cut on his forehead and his mouth was twisted in disgust. He hawked up a big wad of spit and sent it my way, the liquid hitting me in the face.

"Demon of the Wilds," he said as he clapped his hands together in a mocking applause. "Responsible for the death of many. Both human and *Diable* alike. May Deus curse you for the rest of your miserable life."

Keagan looked at the man angrily, knowing full well that I hated that name. His eyes opened wider ever so slightly, and I knew he recognized who the man before him was. He hawked up a wad of spit of his own, sending it into Wyatt's face. "Wee Wyatt. Cried over a snake bite. Saved by his brave mother. Whined about the whole thing like a little bitch for months."

Wyatt wiped the bloody spittle from his face and grinned. "Keagan the Bloodthirsty. The Red Wolf. The Butcher."

Keagan snarled and returned to his feral form. His lip curled, baring his blood-stained teeth as his golden eyes glowed in the light from all the lanterns nearby. He took a step forward with a rage I had not seen in years. He hated those names more than I hated mine, and his temper was less manageable than my own. He would have killed Wyatt had I not stood between them, my hands placed firmly on Keagan's hair-covered chest.

"No, Keagan! You don't want to do this. He doesn't deserve it." I turned around once Keagan reluctantly shifted back into his tame form. I grabbed Wyatt by his wavy locks and pulled him towards the camp. "He deserves something much worse."

Wyatt had managed to struggle enough to free himself from my grasp, but when he tried to run Keagan and a group of lycans stood in his way. With one on each side of him, they grabbed his arms tightly and dragged him after me. I came to a place I didn't want to be, but I knew it was necessary. The Trees were a place I had come to fear, a place that haunted my mind while both awake and asleep. I wanted to be far from this place, but I had a promise to keep. I motioned for the lycans to put Wyatt up against one of the wooden posts before crossing my arms and smirking. "Strip."

"You think you're better than me, but you have more darkness in you than I do. Deus tells us that your kind are demons made by Eous. *Vas-y*! Prove everyone right. Show them what the Demon of the Wilds does to a surrendered soldier."

His words upset me, and I wondered for a moment if I was going too far. I questioned if revenge was the answer. And then, I saw Duna. Then Kayne. Then Anya. And after them I saw Dowe, Cattlin, Lollar, Taney, Ethna, and Hagen, the six who had perished the last few nights in this very place. Wyatt had made sure I knew their names before they were killed so that I would only feel more guilt from their deaths. I pulled out the pistol I had on me and cocked it; the barrel aimed right between Wyatt's soulless eyes. "Strip."

Wyatt growled, his grin vanishing. When he didn't move, I fired off a shot that whizzed by his ear before shouting my order again. "Strip!"

"O' what are you —"

"Keagan!" I felt tears welling up in my eyes as I stared at him, the pistol in my hand shaking slightly.

I didn't need to say anything else. Keagan could see that I needed this. He inclined his head and took a step back, watching as I shot another bullet by Wyatt to tell him to hurry with removing his clothes. The cloudy sky opened up for the first time in a couple days and rain fell down on us. It wasn't as harsh as the rain that night, but I felt like the gods were making the moment poetic. I watched as the vile man who had caused me so much trauma and pain over the weeks began to shiver from the cool breeze that rushed through all of us. His hair, along with the rest of him, was soaked just like we were that night. I kept the pistol trained on him and waited, letting the rain and wind cause him as much discomfort as possible. Wyatt egged me on, calling for me to show everyone who I really was. I thought of the little time I had spent with Anya and how close we had become. She meant a great deal to me. Duna had felt like having a little sister again. Kayne, oddly enough, reminded me of a friend I had lost during the war. We hadn't spent a great amount of time together, but we might have if it weren't for Wyatt. He had robbed me. He had hurt me. He had humiliated and tortured me. Not just me, but many others as well. I allowed everything he had done to me and everyone else in this place to run through my mind, reminding me why I was doing this. Despite all of that motivation, I still struggled to pull the trigger. His words were holding me back. I didn't want to be like him. I didn't want to be known as the Demon of the

Wilds anymore. I was better than that. More than that. I was just about to give up the idea of his execution when Wyatt started laughing.

"I knew it." The grin on Wyatt's face stretched from ear to ear and it made me sick. "You don't have it. You never did. Everyone always thought you were the greatest, but I saw through you. You aren't strong. You never were. You're just a useless, horned, *monstre* that pretends to be heroic. You're a fraud. You aren't a hero, or a leader. You're just some *bête vaine* that thinks it's better than us. Others may not see it, but I do. You're weak, *Diable*, just like that whiny *chienne* and that blue *pute* you let me —"

The gunfire interrupted him, and the bullet wound between his eyes made sure he wouldn't ever speak again. Wyatt slumped to the ground like the others had, and I allowed my pistol to follow him. Suddenly, all of the energy I had felt disappeared, and I nearly fell over. Keagan caught me, but I pushed him away as I forced myself to stand.

"Go get everyone else from the longhouses," I instructed. "Bring them to the woods with the others."

Keagan's face was one of concern. "O', are you —"

"Just do it, Keagan," I said.

The lycan nodded and shouted orders to those around him to do what I had asked while I stood there and stared at Wyatt's dead body. The pain I had was still there. The trauma I had didn't feel any lighter. Nothing had changed for me. It didn't make anything better, but I had kept my promise. Those he had killed were avenged, and now everyone else would be free of him. That's all that mattered.

# Chapter Fifty-Two

## General Rosspier

Cloque, Fleuris | June 24, 1799

Lady Adelyn Amboise had supposedly requested I wear something especially fancy for tonight's dinner, but my military uniform was good enough for me. Count Bellamy Amboise, the Lady's father, had insisted the woman be my date for this evening. I knew he was just trying to gain some power, no doubt wishing that I would develop a liking for his daughter and make her my bride. If I was honest, I had little intention of marrying again. However, Lady Adelyn was a young beauty and her hips looked strong enough for children should I wish to have some again. I hadn't tossed the idea completely away just yet, despite her need to be heard all the time. The woman loved talking and felt her opinions were wanted by everyone she met. Her personality irritated her father, but in his letter, he had described his hope that it would please me. I did like a challenge, and instilling discipline was one of the things I enjoyed most in this world. As I adjusted the medals on the left side of my chest, I found myself smiling at the idea of bending someone to my will. Perhaps tonight would be quite exciting.

"Max? Everyone is here. Lady Adelyn is waiting for you at the bottom of the main staircase. Probably best to not have her standing alone much longer." Jon didn't wait for me to respond, retreating through the door he had entered while leaving it open so I would follow.

I looked over myself in the tall mirror in front of me and made some last second adjustments to my hair before testing my smile. Supposedly it was overly proud to give yourself compliments, but I thought it just displayed your confidence. I gave myself a few encouraging comments on how I looked before turning around and making my way out the door that Jon had left ajar. I swiftly made my way down the hallways that led me to the main staircase, slowing my pace so that I could appear more regal than hurried. As Jon had said, Lady Adelyn was standing at the bottom of the steps. I cleared my throat to gain her attention, and the young woman quickly spun around to watch my descent. Her bright red hair was done up in a fancy braid, decorated with yellow ribbon and gold berets. The dress she wore was a slightly darker shade of yellow, with a pale corset to accentuate her comely shape. Her chest was large and her hips wide, a body type that seemed common amongst the people from Amnites. She looked up at me with bright blue eyes and her thin lips stretched into a smile as I reached the final steps that separated us.

"My Lord Rosspier." She curtsied, but quickly stood back up. "Or is it General Rosspier? Oh, I've made a mistake already, haven't I?"

Her wish to address me in a manner I enjoyed pleased me. I forced a welcoming smile and held my hand out for her to take. "I prefer General, but Lord has a lovely ring to it too. Shall we?"

A redness in her cheeks that had surfaced began to subside as she smiled cautiously. The young woman took my hand and held her head high like all nobles loved to do. "Lead the way, General."

I led us to the dining hall doors, where Jon was waiting for us. He entered the room himself while we waited outside, and I could hear him introduce us to my guests. Two soldiers opened the tall double doors, showing me the long table that had roughly two dozen people seated at it. Plenty of the necessary silverware was laid out before everyone, as well as the plates and bowls that anxiously awaited the food my chef had prepared. I believe his name was Mallon. I didn't allow my mind to wonder about it any longer than a couple seconds, knowing his name didn't matter to me. Whatever it was, the man had cooked us all a great banquet. I counted six whole chickens presented on the table, as well as plates of steamed vegetables, freshly baked loaves of bread, and an abundance of fruits. Oysters, salmon, and sardines were also visible, as well as pies full of duck and boar meat. The entire room smelled wonderful, and I could tell from the heat emanating off the majority of the food that it had just been brought in. The sight of everyone seated at the table rising to their feet joined the lovely sound of adoration people made by clapping their hands together in applause. I could have told them to stop, but I waited to see how long they would go on. I was happy to discover that they continued for nearly a minute until I finally raised a hand in the air to instruct them all to stop.

"*Seigneurs et Dames, amis et alliés, jeunes et moins jeunes*, I welcome you to my home. It is so wonderful to have you all here. Please, take your seats." I went to help Lady Adelyn with her chair as I called out to the servers nearby. "All of you standing on the walls better make sure nobody's glass is empty at any point tonight. I want everyone here to go to sleep drunk and happy!"

Some more applause came from a good amount of the guests, no doubt happy to consume food and drink they didn't have to pay for. They were all the richest families of Fleuris and — surprising no one — they were also the most greedy. They valued their riches more than the members of their own family. I'm sure that the majority of their reasons for coming here this evening was either to suck up to me like a dog or suck on me like a leech. I wasn't fooled in the slightest. I knew nobles well. They were always out for their own personal gain. Still, whether it was faked or not, they were all here to remind me how wonderful of a leader I was. I would accept all the flattery and absorb every bit of praise sent my way tonight because I deserved every syllable of it. In fact, I felt as though I should remind everyone here why their lives were so wonderful.

Once I had Lady Adelyn seated, I remained standing in front of my own chair at the head of the table. Some people had begun to reach for the food, but they were quickly stopped by others. Eventually all their eyes were on me, waiting for me to speak. I gave them all the smile I had practiced in the mirror before extending my arms out to my sides like a priest would during mass. "I know the food is enticing, and I am quite hungry myself, but if you would humor me for *juste un moment*. I would like to point out the luxury we all are about to experience *ce soir*. I would also like to point out the reason for said luxury. Fleuris has always been strong, and I believe we have earned a great deal of respect from other nations for possessing that strength. When I took over from King Louis, I did so to make Fleuris even better than it was. *Il a fallu du temps*, but I have finally fixed our *Diable* problem, with a more permanent solution waiting to be brought forward. Our country is free of those *parasites maléfiques*, locked away in cages like the animals they are. Once the humans return to their jobs, which I am certain they will do soon, we will have no more need for *ces Diables*. We will eradicate them, like we should have done centuries ago. The purity of our country is returning, and once it is fully realized, we can focus on spreading our bright light to the rest of the world. *Pour le moment*, I ask that you thank Deus, *et moi*, for gifting you a country so holy and bountiful."

A man wearing a gold chain with a large pendant of Deus' seal known as The Trinity raised his glass of wine high in the air. *"Gloire à Deus!"*

Count Amboise quickly stood from his seat and raised his glass of wine as well. *"Gloire au général Rosspier!"*

Everyone cheered and raised their glasses to toast our god and I in the same light. The action brought a genuine smile to face, and I finally felt appreciated for all I had done so far. The nobles had done nothing but complain at the beginning of all this, whining that they had to part with a bit of their wealth in order to keep the striking labor force happy. They were quick to bring those complaints to an end when I offered them compensation from the royal treasury. Jon had thought that foolish, but if I wanted the mob to love me and the *Diables* to be gone, it was necessary. So long as the lesser humans adored me, the army respected me, and the nobles were loyal to me, nothing would get in my way. I raised my glass to all of them, pandering to the crowd as a host had to do no matter how far above them he was. After finally taking my seat, everyone went after the food in front of them. It was like watching pigs who had learned a certain level of etiquette. Jon was seated to my right, as always, and Lady Adelyn was to my left. Her father was next to her, and her mother next to him. Seated to Jon's left was his wife, Coraline, and next to her was the holy man who had spoken already. Sat next to the zealot was a woman that was either his daughter or his new wife; she was young enough to be either.

The banquet began and the two violin players I had ordered for the night began to play. Everyone focused on their meals for the first hour, especially once the sweets were brought out. Once the food was all gone and their bellies were full, conversation truly began, and their voices challenged the violins for supremacy. A few nobles had risen from their seats and come to speak with me, while others simply shouted down the table. Lady Adelyn lived up to her father's description, continuously inserting herself into conversations that did not concern her. I had planned to lecture her after the first interruption, but the redness of her lips and her pale chest gave me a grander idea. I chose to leave every unnecessary insertion of opinionated speech alone until later tonight. I figured I would lecture her then on all her transgressions, and then, if I felt up to it, bed her. It was uncommon to bed a woman you weren't married to, especially as a noble, but I didn't care. What was Count Amboise going to do about it? He wanted me to fancy her. Bedding her was probably the greatest bit of flattery I could offer. If anything, he would probably be happy.

As the night went on, families kindly excused themselves before making their way to their designated rooms. Joieternelle Palace had plenty of guest rooms to accommodate such a party, which only encouraged people to drink more knowing they had a bed not too far. Eventually, the majority of guests had departed. Even Jon and Coraline had excused themselves by now, as well as Lady Adelyn's parents. The young woman stayed with me, even though I could tell she was tired. The procession out of the dining hall continued until there were only five of us left in the room. Lady Adelyn remained to my left, with Baron Brice Varon of Roudor to her left. To my right sat Lady Serena Blanchet of Cidesnutes, and to her right Count Hamelin Fortier of Unprodoit. We were discussing current events, which had led us from the current war Tudrose was waging to how things in Fleuris were being conducted. Brice, Serena, and Hamelin all had differing opinions, but they were smart enough to express themselves politely.

"Deus teaches us to serve one another and care for them as he cares for us. I can't help but wonder if some sort of divine punishment is waiting for those who have harmed *ces créatures*," Baron Varon exclaimed.

Lady Blanchet took another drink from her glass before setting it down on the table. "Those teachings are for humans. In case you have forgotten, those *bêtes sauvages* out there are not human. They are nothing but a means to an end. One where humans ascend to Heaven with Deus."

Count Fortier of Unprodoit rolled his eyes. "Oh, who cares what's done with the *Diables*? So long as I still have my riches and a belly full of boar and wine every night, *je suis content*. Those things have never affected me or my life before all of this started, and it won't affect me once it comes to an end. You all think too much. The real problem is Tudrose. Worry about them."

"I think a case can be made for all of you. Perhaps the answer is somewhere in the middle? *Un compromis* between everyone that sees us all pleased." Lady Adelyn smiled as she spoke, apparently still lively enough to keep up appearances despite the late hour.

I patted her hand as I ignored her comment, much like I had done throughout the night, and addressed the three nobles before me. "I'm sure that everyone has their own opinions on things, and that's quite alright. *Cependant*, the only opinion that truly matters here is mine. I'm sure you can all agree that I am the most qualified to lead this country forward into a state of even more grandeur and splendor. The filth of this country will be washed away with purifying waters of divine justice. Deus *et moi* stand together against this threat upon our country, and I will continue to fight alongside him until the problem is solved. As for Tudrose, they march through Kosavros with evil intensions, guided by Deus' vile brother. They stand with the *Diables* as if they were equal to us. Their blindness to the truth and their betrayal of Deus will lead to their downfall. There is nothing to worry about. When they come, they will lose, and we will spread our influence to every corner of the world. Now, *veuillez m'excuser*, as I think it's time for your host to head off to bed. Lady Adelyn will be joining me."

I held my hand out as I stood from my chair, annoyed that I had to suffer through conversation with so many people tonight. The young woman looked at me with confusion on her face before looking at the other three people in the room. I watched as they all just stared back, no doubt also shocked that I planned for her to join me. Lady Adelyn began to speak but stopped. She did this a couple times before taking a deep breath and taking my hand. I bid the remaining guests goodnight and led Lady Adelyn to my bedroom. I silently prayed for the woman to keep her opinions to herself for the rest of the night and follow my instructions. Maybe if she did well, I would consider what Count Amboise was hoping for. An obedient woman at my side wouldn't be all that bad. Besides, I believe I deserve a reward for all I've done.

# Chapter Fifty-Three

## Rosalie

Arlenburg Pass, Stelpina | June 27, 1799

The last couple days had been a welcome change, with clear skies and a warm sun taking over from the rain. The tall mountains that surrounded Arlenburg Pass were supposedly mere hills compared to some of the mounds of rock we would see the further we ventured into the Great Eastern Folds. We would have been deeper into the mountain range by now, but our march for Leonessa had been slowed. Queen Sophia had required roughly two more days of rest after King Frederick's coronation before she was able to travel. On top of that, we had stopped in Balowe for a day to get Sullivan situated in his new position, only for him to insist on coming with us instead.

"Sean can keep the seat warm for me. My place is with all of you until this is over," the old goblin had said.

"What happened to being too old for war?" Brina had commented quickly.

"Turns out a good meal everyday and a warm bed does wonders for the body," Sullivan had said with a big grin on his face. "I feel like I'm twenty years younger! I used to be quite strong back in my day you know. I'm coming with you, and I won't hear anything else but thanks for my decision."

On the morning of the twenty-second day of June, we left Balowe behind and began our long trek to Leonessa. Weylin had told me that the path we were taking was one the Fleuris army had used years ago in an old war with Malvene. It made our journey to the capital a bit more strenuous and long, but it took us past Azuvipa. In avoiding the city, we would also avoid the garrisons and forts that littered the surrounding land. Not having all those possible skirmishes kept our army fresh and ready to take Leonessa. It was common knowledge that Azuvipa's forces may have already moved to Leonessa, since Malvene had a copious amount of time to prepare for us, but nobody was certain. It had also been wondered if King Ludovico had abandoned his throne and fled Leonessa in favor of Azuvipa. General Wyman spoke up during that particular war council meeting — one that I had graciously been allowed to join — and claimed that King Ludovico was known as a proud ruler. According to the old general, leaving his throne behind was not something King Ludovico would do. All of that and more was discussed, but Queen Sophia was not present for any of it.

Despite being able to travel, Queen Sophia still spent a fair amount of her time sleeping. Even with Lady Mirlena's help, the curse had left her very weak. Queen Sophia had entrusted Weylyn to speak for her during the war council meetings, something General Wyman was not overtly happy about. Weylyn and the Tudrose general argued a fair bit over what Queen Sophia's opinion on certain matters would be, but cooler heads always seemed to prevail and nothing ever came of it. I had taken it upon myself to take care of Tudrose's Queen, tending to her every hour of the day. She had healers that could do it instead, and Lady Mirlena visited her often, but I found that I needed to look after her. I still felt guilty for not being able to nurse my parents back to health and being away from my hospital for so long had me itching to take care of someone. I had assisted the healers after battles, but this sort of healing was much less traumatic. Back home, I barely dealt with the injuries that you would discover on people during war. My expertise was illness. Coughs and fevers, things of that nature. Queen Sophia had indeed lost her arm, but what ailed her now was a lack of strength. She needed help getting out of her bed to relieve herself, along with the simple tasks of drinking and eating. I had to move her arm and legs for her to try to build back the muscle she had lost from the curse, and every now and then she would have horrible coughing fits that scared everyone who witnessed them.

Lady Mirlena insisted that Queen Sophia was indeed getting better, but I wondered just how long it was going to take until she would return to her former self. She had managed to sit up on her own last night — which was incredible to see — but she had passed out shortly after having a small drink and a couple bites of bread. Weylyn worried about her all the time, and I was sure that he wasn't alone in doing that. It had been my job to reassure him, as well as the others, and keep everyone's spirits as high as I could. As for who was keeping my spirits up, Weylyn was an obvious supporter. Surprisingly enough, the other person bringing a smile to my face the most as of late stormed through the flaps of Queen Sophia's tent, followed by his mother.

"Lady Rosalie! How's the Queen?" Arthur shouted as he ran in and gave me a warm hug.

"Hush, Arthur! The Queen needs her rest." Abandoning the look she had adopted to scold her son, Lady Mirlena gave me an exasperated smile. "You're sure that you're okay to watch him?"

"I don't need to be watched. I'm not a child," Arthur argued as he sat on the bed Queen Sophia was laying in.

I couldn't help but chuckle at the boy's defiance, playfully shaking his hair about with my hand. "Oh, the little bugger doesn't bother me. I'll be fine."

Lady Mirlena nodded. "Alright. I won't be too long. When Weylyn and I are done, we'll both come by, and I'll tend to Queen Sophia for a bit before we begin packing up to move out."

"Wonderful. We'll see you when you get back then." I sent a smile Lady Mirlena's way to assure her everything was alright.

"Teach Lord Weylyn something fun today!" Arthur shouted.

Lady Mirlena quickly brought her finger to her lips, adopting yet another stern look. The boy put his hand over his mouth after mouthing the word 'sorry'. His mother shook her head in disbelief of her son before waving goodbye and leaving through the flaps of the tent. Some of the sun shone through the fabric of the temporary home, but when the flaps opened sunlight lit up the place as if there was nothing around us at all. Since yesterday evening, I had only left the enclosed space for a few minutes earlier in the morning to warm up some water over one of the fires outside. Our surroundings were fantastical, and I dreamed of a world where I could visit such landscapes for reasons more positive than being on a warpath. I craved to go out and feel the sun's warmth on my face, but it was an experience I would have to wait a couple more hours to have. For now, my place was watching over the Queen of Tudrose and the wise little boy named Arthur. Well, he wasn't so little. He had gone through a small growth spurt since we had met, and I could swear his voice was slightly deeper than usual. He was perhaps a little young for such things to happen, but it made sense that his body would try to appear as old as his mind. I stood up from my chair and went over to where the teapot was.

"Would you like some tea?" I asked as I poured myself a cup.

"No thank you. I had some with my mother already." He turned around to face me, a large grin on his face. "Some wine would be nice, though."

I rolled my eyes as I chuckled. "Nice try. You know your mother doesn't want you drinking that stuff yet."

It was Arthur's turn to roll his eyes. "Oh yes. I'd have one sip of the stuff and be so in love that I'd have a bottle of wine in my hand every moment of every day."

The more time we spent together the more comfortable the boy had become around me. Some of the things he said were surprisingly crass, and I had discovered that sarcasm was his favorite thing. Mind you, when you got to know the woman raising him, Arthur's sarcastic personality didn't really surprise you all that much. They were both strong-willed, headstrong, opinionated people who spoke openly and confidently. They held very little back, and they have a certain type of humor that some would consider rude. I found them both enjoyable to be around, but especially so with Arthur. Every conversation I had with him, he seemed to surprise me. Whether it was his knowledge of the human body and alchemy, or some wise words on a subject you'd expect from a person in their sixties. The boy was a joy to be around, and I had grown quite fond of him. Weylyn had also come to like Arthur, the two often spending time together during our marches. It was perhaps silly, judging that I was slightly old enough to be the boy's mother myself, but I saw him as one of my closest friends. We had bonded heavily during his sickness, and that bond had continued to strengthen after he became healthy again. I liked to think that he enjoyed my company as much as I enjoyed his.

"Your mother knows what's best for you, Arthur. You'll have plenty of time to drink all the wine you want once you're a few years older." I took a sip from my tea before returning to my chair by Queen Sophia's bedside.

Arthur looked at Queen Sophia's bandaged shoulder before turning his eyes on me. "Will we still be fighting this war in a few years?"

I was taken aback by the question, but I gathered myself quickly enough to answer. "It's gone by fairly quick so far. We should approach Leonessa in a few days time, maybe a week? After that, who knows."

Arthur shook his head. "No. Even I can tell that this war could be over before winter. What I meant was the fight for people like Lord Weylyn to not have cursed blades thrown at them."

The boy thought of things that someone his age usually didn't think of. Most would just see this war as any other war; one group wanting to defeat another group in battle. However, Arthur was aware of the reason for this struggle, and he knew that it spanned a field that withheld more than just a war of swords and guns. Before I could say anything, Queen Sophia began coughing. She woke up, her right hand shaking as it came to rest on her chest. Much to my surprise, the woman managed to sit herself up quickly. Her coughing fit began to subside, and once I knew she was alright I got up to grab her a full cup of tea. I filled the cup I was using, figuring I could pour myself a new one later, and brought it over to Queen Sophia. I brought the warm cup to her lips and titled it, pouring some of the hot liquid into her open mouth. She surprised me again when she began to hold the cup herself. I hesitantly let go of it, keeping my hand close so I could help her if she needed me to, and watched as her shaky hand lifted more of the tea between her lips.

"How are you feeling?" Arthur asked.

Queen Sophia smiled. "Better. I think your mother's spells are finally doing something for me."

"My mother's spells aren't the only thing helping you get better." Arthur looked at me and smiled.

Queen Sophia tried to laugh but ended up having another short coughing fit. After I got her some more tea to drink, the fit passed and the Queen of Tudrose addressed the young man's statement. "You're quite right, Arthur. I'm positive that Rosalie's care has restored my strength just as much as those spells, if not more."

I bowed my head. "Thank you, Queen Sophia. That's very kind of you to say."

Queen Sophia managed to stretch a smile across her face. "Kind, and necessary. I truly am thankful for you. Now, before sleep inevitably takes me again, tell me about your morning. What were you doing before I so rudely interrupted you?"

I was about to tell her that she hadn't been rude at all, but Arthur spoke before I could. "We were talking about the war."

Queen Sophia's eyebrows raised. "Were you now? What about it?"

Arthur briefly glanced at me, appearing to ask permission to say what he wanted to say. I just nodded, encouraging him to speak freely. Arthur grinned and returned his attention to Queen Sophia. "I had just asked Lady Rosalie when people will stop throwing cursed blades at people like Lord Weylyn."

Queen Sophia took a sip of her tea before answering. "My hope is that the answer is 'not for much longer', but it is hard to know for sure. I know some think that things will never change, but I have more faith in people than they do."

"So even after this war is over, you'll still have to fight. Would there be another war? Would I have to fight?"

The Queen of Tudrose glanced at me, silently communicating our shared admiration for the curiosity Arthur possessed, before bringing her cup to rest in her lap. "Yes, we'll still have to fight. If it were up to me, war would never have been needed, but sometimes there's no avoiding it. War has happened abundantly in the past, and it will no doubt find a way to break into this world again in the future. As for whether you'll fight in said wars, that's up to you."

Arthur looked visibly encumbered. The answer Queen Sophia had given him had truly perplexed the boy, and he was trying to make sense of it. Why people would choose war over anything else was difficult even for some my age to comprehend, so I could only imagine the trouble someone Arthur's age would have. Still, his face eventually untwisted, and he straightened his back before speaking again.

"I'd fight for a world where cursed blades aren't thrown at anyone," he said. "But, I would rather find another way to stop those people. War doesn't have to always be the answer, does it?"

Queen Sophia's shoulders slouched, and I could see she was growing tired again. "I would love to tell you no. I would love to be able to say that war isn't necessary in the world. However, no matter how hard you try to avoid it, it seems as though it's inevitable at times."

Queen Sophia began to slide down, her strength leaving her. I grabbed the cup from her hand and set it on the floor before leaning over and easing her onto her back again. I cleared her hair from her face, her skin no longer as pale as it was a few days ago. Arthur shifted a bit forward so he could grab Queen Sophia's hand.

"I hope that one day that isn't true," Arthur said.

Queen Sophia closed her eyes with a smile on her face, her expression returning to a neutral look as sleep took her again. I put my hand on Arthur's shoulder and he let go of the Queen's hand.

"She's going to get better, right?" the boy asked.

I brought him in for a small hug, my left arm wrapped around his shoulders. "With you helping me look after her? She'll be better before you know it."

# Chapter Fifty-Four

## Olwen



A gentle shake woke me up. I slowly began to rise from the makeshift bed I was laying on, but I snapped to attention once I noticed the commotion engulfing our group. There was somewhere between two to three thousand of us, and almost everyone was on edge. Keagan was standing next to me, watching over everyone from the small hill we had deemed our spot to rest. Something was happening. Everyone was looking to the south, which wasn't a good sign. Those who had guns had them pointed into the thick woods, while the others brandished swords or bows that we had made since deciding on making this area our camp. I noticed that some lycans had shifted into their feral forms, their hulking shoulders and large heads looming over everyone else. Keagan remained in his tame form, but he had a rifle ready in case he needed it.

We had stationed scouts roughly half a mile out, all of them equipped with enchanted whistles thanks to Marie. The whistles were made to be louder, but only the Tóráin could hear them. Our scouts would hide high in the trees and watch for anyone coming our way before sounding their whistle, alerting the main camp of a possible attack. We had been lucky so far that no one had found us, mostly because of the rain that had covered our tracks, but it seemed as though our luck had run out.

I stood next to Keagan with a saber in my hand and waited for our uninvited guests. We watched for some time until those furthest south began waving their arms at Keagan and me. The crowd began to part, making way for a human of average height dressed like a hunter. He made his way to us quickly, stopping a few feet away to salute. Keagan and I both waved him off and he let his shoulders slouch. The man pulled out a container and took a few hefty gulps of whatever was inside. He gasped for air after his drink and forced out a smile.

"It's good to see you standing on your own, Olwen," he said. "You had many of us quite worried."

I could have forced a smile, but I found it required too much energy to do so. I was still incredibly drained, even though it had been roughly a week since we escaped Camp Liodorleu. Keagan had been pressuring me to allow Marie to aid me in some way, but I refused to accept any help until the others were healthy. There were people that needed the witch's assistance more than I did, so I sent her their way whenever she came by to check on me. I didn't blame Keagan for wanting me to get a boost of some sort though; I wouldn't want to watch someone I cared about be a shell of themselves either. Being free of the camp and Wyatt's torture, I didn't feel as obliged to hide how weak I truly was anymore, so it was apparent to everyone how much I struggled. I had finally allowed my body to succumb to the torment it had endured during my time in that wretched place, beginning the process of healing the best I could from such an experience. I spent the first few days sleeping, as much as I could thanks to my nightmares. It wasn't until a couple days ago where I could comfortably and confidently stand on my own without leaning on Keagan for support.

"What do you have for us, Soan?" Keagan asked.

The man nodded multiple times. "Yes, yes. Well, sadly, there isn't much good to say save for one thing."

"What's that one thing then?" I asked.

Soan forced another smile. "Well, I haven't heard of anything regarding a search happening. Soldiers did come by that cursed camp to find it empty save for all the bodies. However, it doesn't seem as though the Fleuris army is doing anything about it. Well, not directly anyway."

I suddenly felt lightheaded. Angry with myself for not recovering faster, I grabbed Keagan's arm to keep me from falling. I ignored the look he gave me and kept my attention on Soan. "What's that supposed to mean?"

The man waited, watching to make sure I was alright before he answered. "The other camps, at least those around Cloque, have increased the number of soldiers there. On top of that, my allies say that there seem to be more fires raging that usual in the camps. I fear that instead of chasing your group down to punish you, they're simply taking it out on everyone else."

There was a thought for us to attack the other camps once we were strong enough, but the increase in military presence would seem to put an end to that idea. Even if we did free another camp, it appeared as though we would only be killing more of our own people. The news bothered me, and I grew angry with myself for not being strong enough to do something. Keagan growled as he turned and kicked at the ground angrily.

"Keagan!" The lycan's change in position caused me to fall over since I had slowly been relying on him more and more to stand.

Keagan turned around quickly and came over to help me get back on my feet. "Sorry, O'. You sure you don't need to lay down maybe?"

I shook my head. "No. I'm fine. I don't need to do anything but listen to Soan's report."

Keagan's face was sour, but he put his arm around my waist and allowed me to wrap my arm around his middle so that I could remain standing. Soan was looking at me with pity in his eyes and I hated it.

"Is there anything else?" I asked sharply.

Soan blinked furiously before shaking his head. He went to turn away but stopped, spinning back around with his finger pointed in the air. "*Attendez*! There was something else. I don't know what it means in the slightest, but I did find it odd."

Keagan and I both insisted the informant get on with it, and Soan's face twisted with confusion as he told us what he knew. "There are reports of people in white robes going to the camps to obtain Tóráin blood. Did...did this ever happen to you while you were...you know...imprisoned?"

I hadn't talked about my experience in Camp Liodorleu with anyone. Not even Keagan. I meant to, but I couldn't bring myself to say anything just yet. Talking about it would only make me relive everything and they weren't experiences I wished to have again. For now, the most anyone knew was that my time in Camp Liodorleu was a bad one and that Anya had died, along with many others. The news Soan had delivered did intrigue me though. It piqued my interest so much to the point where I risked thinking back on my imprisonment. I never remembered seeing anyone in white cloaks, but people did go missing from our group for a short while before returning. I didn't remember anyone talking about people dressed in pale clothing taking their blood though. Maybe they were knocked out beforehand?

I wasn't sure. Regardless of whether it was happening at Camp Liodorleu or not, I had a suspicion over who was behind it all.

"As far as I know, my blood wasn't taken," I said. "There is a chance it was and I just don't remember, seeing as me and many others were often beaten so much that we were knocked unconscious. The same goes for people in white cloaks. I don't remember seeing any, but only the gods know what happened to us when we were knocked out."

Soan had a somber expression on his face. "That sounds quite unpleasant, not knowing if things have happened to you or not I mean. I'm sorry."

"It's fine. Was there anything else?" I asked.

"No," Soan answered. "I'll leave you to rest now, but before I do, do I have any new orders, or should I just keep my eyes open for everything?"

"Just absorb all that you can and report back in a few days, Soan. Make sure nobody follows you." Keagan extended his free arm to shake Soan's hand.

Soan reached out and grabbed it. "As you wish. Just so you know, nobody notices me, Keagan. I'm just a lonely hunter out looking for some food. But, to ease your mind, yes. I will make sure nobody follows me."

Their hands separated and Soan was about to leave when I called out after him. "Wait! Find out if The Dove is in Cloque. Check with our informants at Joieternelle Palace and Bastion."

Soan looked confused. "Um...okay? Can I ask why?"

I rolled my eyes. "Just do it for me. You can do that for me, right?"

Soan abandoned his baffled look and nodded. "*Oui*, I can. I'll look into The Dove's whereabouts and keep an eye on everything going on in and around Cloque. I'll report back in a few days. Stay safe and stay strong, *mes amies*."

"You too, Soan." Keagan watched the human walk down the small incline before turning his attention towards me. "Why the Hell are you keepin' tabs on The Dove still? We have bigger things to worry about right now."

I wanted to storm away from him, but I hated to admit that he was probably the only reason I was even still standing at this point. For some ridiculous reason, the progress I had made had abandoned me and I was struggling to not fall over. My legs were slowly giving out and it felt like my head was floating amongst the clouds. So, instead of running from Keagan in defiance, I stuck my tongue out at him like a four year old. Keagan's face hardened but he didn't say anything. He just guided me back to the pile of leaves and branches we had used to make beds for us and helped me down. I rested my back up against the tree my bed of leaves brushed up against and brought my knees up to my chest. I sat there and looked out and around at our group and sighed. Keagan slumped down the tree and sat next to me. He looked at me, but I looked away, knowing that another lecture was coming from a lycan who believed he had suddenly become wise or something. Every lecture coming from Keagan was rich, since it was usually me lecturing him.

Eventually his voice broke our silence. "Even if you were strong enough to go after her, your place is here with these people. They need you, O'."

I continued to keep my eyes away from Keagan's. "She's behind all of this, Keagan. I know she is."

"This is all General Rosspier's doin'," Keagan replied. "You heard his speeches. You even saw his letters to the nobles. The Dove is just an assassin who hates our kind and enjoys torturin' us. I doubt she's got any say in what General Rosspier does."

I turned my head around quickly to glare at him. "She's more dangerous than you think. Did you forget what I told you about that meeting? This grand spell she's planning? Those people in white cloaks are her followers, Keagan. The bitch is probably behind the camps. If I can put an end to her, maybe the camps will be closed, and everyone will be let go."

Keagan sighed. "Look, O'. There isn't much in this world that I wouldn't do to get my hands on The Dove. Killin' isn't what I love doin', but I do have a list of people that I know need to exit the land of the livin'. The Dove is probably right up there with General Rosspier. The problem is that she's probably ten times more dangerous than General Rosspier. The Tudrose army will eventually come to Fleuris, and when they do, they'll beat that pompous general into submission and everythin' will get better. The Dove will either die or run away. Our job right now is to keep as many people as safe as we can."

I was frustrated and tired, but I chose to use what little energy I had left to try to convince Keagan I was right. "Going after her does exactly that! Removing The Dove and whatever sick, twisted plan she's trying to act out protects our kind from death and torture. She managed to hide from me back in Etoile. She isn't going to escape me again. If she's in Cloque, I'm going after her and ending this."

Keagan threw his head back in frustration. "Oh come on! You can't truly believe that killin' The Dove will make General Rosspier just go, 'alright every Tórán goes free, so sorry'. Riskin' your life to maybe do somethin' that won't fix the real problem in the end is reckless and I won't let you. I let you go to Camp Liodorleu and look what happened. You won't even tell me what went on in there. You're just gettin' more and more careless, and it isn't like you to be that way. I'm supposed to be the reckless, emotional one. Since when did our roles switch?"

There was a lot to address there. I didn't have the energy to argue, but I had to comment on some of the things Keagan had said. As much as I wanted to just grumble to myself and go back to sleep, I took a deep breath and responded. "You didn't let me go. You don't have any more control over me than I have over you. That's how we've always been. We're stubborn. I know that very little of what I say won't change your mind, but what happened to me was because I decided to go in there. It was my decision, which means what happened is on me. Now, I know that General Rosspier is an evil bastard who won't stop doing what he's doing just because The Dove is dead but losing her weakens him. It probably scares him too. Maybe it makes him make a mistake. I don't know. What I do know is that The Dove is doing something that may be even worse than what General Rosspier is doing, and I need to stop her. Maybe our roles have changed. Maybe I got tired of losing people because I was too hesitant or too passive. Maybe you realized how being reckless and emotional puts not only you, but others at risk too. Maybe we're just going through some shit. I don't know, Keagan. What I need from you isn't a lecture. What I need is the support of possibly the only person left in this world who I can trust. I need to do this. I need to kill her. I feel it in my bones, Keagan. She's dangerous, and she needs to be stopped as soon as possible."

Keagan looked like he was going to argue with me some more until he sighed and put his arm around my shoulders. He pulled me in, and I reluctantly let him hug me. I was mad at him for challenging me so damn much but feeling the warmth of a friendly body was a comfort I had not had in a long, long time. I had felt strong with Keagan nearby, knowing the power he possessed. Now, I felt safe. I didn't think he was going to say or do something stupid that would force me to save his ass for the hundredth time. I trusted him to protect others; to protect me. Feeling that sense of security had my eyes struggling to stay open. Keagan cleared his throat, the noise holding my sleep at bay for a moment more.

"If you're goin' to do this, you'll need your strength," he said softly. "Try to get some rest, and tomorrow you're goin' to let Marie help you recover. Those are my conditions. You don't go until you're strong again."

I wasn't happy with his terms, but I just wanted to sleep so I submitted. "Fine. Thank you, Keagan."

"Yeah, yeah. You're goin' to do whatever you want anyway. Might as well just save us all the headache and support you."

I laughed. "Glad you finally understand."

Keagan squeezed me tightly and I closed my eyes. Images of moments from my past began showing themselves in my mind. Horrors from Camp Liodorleu came next. First my experiences with Wyatt, then the deaths at The Trees, and finally, the worst one. I reached over and grabbed the hand holding my shoulder. Keagan wrapped his hand around mine and let me squeeze it. This moment played the most, and it scared me the most. It haunted me the most. You'd think killing Wyatt would be a happy memory, but for me it was one of my worst. In that moment I had treated him with the same malice and disrespect he had treated me and the others with. Some would say it was poetic how I killed him, but that's not how I felt. In that moment of vengeance and anger and pain, I drifted into a place that I didn't want to be. Wyatt had achieved one last victory, one that would torture me the longest. He had made me into the Demon of the Wilds. He had made me act just as evil as so many humans believed my kind to be. I had avenged those Wyatt had harmed, but it would haunt my mind for years. As I squeezed Keagan's hand, I reminded myself of something I had begun to say to help me sleep: 'every victory, no matter how big or small, requires sacrifice'. I was glad to give up a part of my soul so that those who perished because of that vile, spiteful man were avenged. As I began to drift off, I told myself that I could deal with the pain, that I would endure. Just like I always have.

# Chapter Fifty-Five

## Weylyn



Lady Mirlena and I had left before the sun began to show itself, the bright yellow ball only beginning to light our way until we were already a good distance up the mountain. The witch didn't tell me where we were going, only that I was to follow, and that today's lesson would be an important one. I didn't understand why our lesson couldn't have just happened somewhere near our camp. It was one of the more pleasant places we had rested during our campaign. An old ruin Lady Mirlena called Senzuvole Castle was welcomed by the vast waters of Sorgente Lake and the surrounding mountains of Valdestelloro. It was calm and peaceful, even though we were in enemy territory.

"Come on, Weylyn! We're almost there!" Lady Mirlena shouted from about ten feet ahead of me.

The witch was quite spry for her suspected age, and the climb so far had barely challenged her. I wasn't struggling, but I wasn't necessarily navigating the rocks with the skill of a mountain goat either. The trees were thick and there wasn't much space for a lycan my size to weave through as simply as Lady Mirlena could. The news that we would reach our destination soon was a welcome bit of knowledge. After a few more minutes of travelling, the incline that seemed never ending evened off considerably. It was that way until we were going slightly down hill, before the trees began to thin. The woods gave way to open air and a good-sized body of water. The wind was harsher so high up, especially when the trees didn't disrupt the gales that flew through you. Despite the cool wind, I was sweating considerably from our climb and the thought of taking a swim in the lake was enticing. Lady Mirlena bent over nearby and began gathering sticks, tossing them into a pile. With a wave of her hand, the sticks erupted into a fire.

"Welcome to The Great Lake of Leondoro." The witch smiled as she warmed her hands near the campfire she had made.

"It's beautiful," I said. "The fire necessary? The wind might be brisk but it's still a July morning in Malvene."

Lady Mirlena crossed her arms over her chest. "The fire has nothing to do with the cold and yes, it is necessary. It plays a part in your lesson today."

I looked around at my surroundings while trying to think of what lesson would require us to be at this specific place. Did she expect me to light the forest on fire and put it out with the water from the lake? It didn't make any sense. Lady Mirlena must have noticed the confusion on my face because she let out a bit of a laugh as she tugged on my sleeve.

"Sit down before you hurt yourself," she said. "I'll tell you why we're here."

I sat down on the right side of the fire. "How do you even know about this place?"

Lady Mirlena lowered herself down on the left side of the fire. "I study geography and history often. I like knowing things that other people probably don't. Funny, that actually ties into your lesson."

I picked up a stick laying on the dirt nearby and twiddled it between my fingers before tossing it into the fire. "When is that starting? Or are we just here for the view?"

Lady Mirlena laughed. "No, the view is just a bonus. This place seemed perfect for a lesson I think will help you as much as it has helped me in the past. It's an old magic, foreign too. Not many know it and even if they did, I doubt they would try it."

The description of this magic was intriguing. Majority of what I had been learning were overly simple spells. There wasn't anything too crazy or immensely difficult about my previous lessons. Some of our time spent together was just Lady Mirlena lecturing me on the pronunciation and history of certain spells. Today seemed like she had something special planned. I was excited at first, but I quickly grew nervous. Everything Lady Mirlena had been teaching me, I had picked up pretty fast. I was worried this would finally stump me. My excitement outweighed my anxiety, and I pressed Lady Mirlena on the subject, focusing on what had intrigued me the most. "Foreign magic? You don't mean my foreign magic, do you? Like Druid magic?"

Lady Mirlena shifted herself closer to the water's edge and removed her shoes before letting her feet break the surface of the lake. "You caught that, did you? Good. Means you were listening. Yes, this magic was introduced to witches by Druids of your world. Back when our relationship with your kind was at its strongest."

"What is it? Why doesn't anyone know about it? Why wouldn't they use it? How do you know about it?" Lady Mirlena shot me a look that told me I had clearly asked too many questions at once.

"Few know about it because it stopped being taught, they don't use it because they consider it a dark and evil practice now, and I know about it because I was lucky enough for someone to have taught it to me." I went to ask another question, but Lady Mirlena held her hand up to stop me. "What is it? Well, how best to describe it? Okay. You know how we need food and water to give us energy?"

When Lady Mirlena didn't continue, I realized she was actually expecting an answer and the question wasn't rhetorical. "Yes, I know that."

"Good!" she shouted as she moved her feet in the shallow water. "Well, everything in this world, and yours mind you, has something that gives it energy. And that energy can be called upon when you need it."

"Like the lesson with the flower?" I asked.

Lady Mirlena snapped her fingers and pointed at me. "Exactly! There's energy all around us, and we can give or take that energy as we please. Those spells were born from an old skill introduced to us by Druids of your world. Nobody really knows that, so they don't mind using those spells. They probably wouldn't use them if they knew where they came from though. Anyway, that's beside the point." My teacher turned to face me, removing her feet from the lake. She picked up a handful of dirt from the ground and left her hand open. "This magic is more raw and more dangerous, but can be very rewarding and useful. This skill allows you to draw on elemental energy."

She waved her free hand at the dirt resting in her palm. A lick of flame from the fire jumped over and floated above her open hand, right before a droplet of water plopped out of the lake and came to float next to it. A gust of wind rushed over us and lifted the dirt off her hand and into the air with the fire and water. The wind stopped flowing through our little campsite, save for Lady Mirlena's palm. The edge of her sleeve continued to flap in the breeze as the dirt, flame, and droplet slowly spun in a circle above the witch's hand.

"Fire, water, earth, and air. The four main elements. The strongest elements. The purist elements. The skill I plan to teach you allows the user to absorb energy from them." Lady Mirlena quickly closed her hand, and everything save for the dirt disappeared. She then leaned over and dipped her hand in the nearby lake. "It's dangerous, as I've already said, but I think you can manage it."

The anxiety that I had earlier was overtaking my excitement. "Can I ask why it's so dangerous before we start?"

Lady Mirlena smiled. "Of course, you can. Drawing on, say, a flower is less risky because it only has so much energy in it before it dies. The elements are limitless in energy, although they aren't all equal. Fire is the easiest, or least dangerous, to draw from, although some would say earth is — to be honest they're relatively the same depending on the situation. Next would be water, with air being the most dangerous of the four. Before you ask me why, this scale is derived from how easily you can sever the connection between you and the element. For example, fire is easy and less dangerous to draw from because I can easily snuff out this small campfire. Air is the most dangerous, because the only way to escape it is to submerge yourself in water. They range in power too, the scale subject to change depending on the state they are in. Also, the more power the more intense the connection may be."

"I understand the first part, but the bits about their power being different depending on their state I don't get," I admitted.

"Oh? That's fine. Examples then." Lady Mirlena waved her hand around us. "The elements as you see them now, would probably have earth being the weakest, and perhaps air being the strongest. Why? Well the ground on this mountain is loose, and the wind is a bit stronger than a breeze. Now, say this fire of ours had engulfed half of the forest around us, it might take down air as the strongest. Does that make sense?"

I thought on it for a moment before speaking. "So if this lake was a waterfall or rapids, they'd be stronger than a calm wind?"

Lady Mirlena had a big smile on her face. "Yes! Being in certain states of motion and or size influences the amount of power flowing through the elements at the time you're drawing from them. It's much easier and safer to draw from something small, tame, and simple to distance yourself from. Today, we're going to start with this small campfire and see how it goes."

I was hesitant to accept this task. "Wouldn't earth be a better place to start?"

Lady Mirlena shook her head. "No. Fire is the only element that magic users can conjure and dismiss through spells."

I was confused. "But I have seen you send gales of wind at people during battle."

Lady Mirlena smiled. "You're so attentive. That is me manipulating the air around me, not conjuring it. It's different. Would you rather a lecture on this, or should we try what we came here to try?"

I smiled back and shook my head. "No lecture needed. I trust you. Fire it is. What do I do first?"

"Well, for starters, you need to be tired. The climb up here was probably helpful with that, but it'll be better if you're more exhausted than you are now. Just to be safe. Here." Lady Mirlena tossed a rock at me. "Skip it across the lake. Without using your hands."

I held the rock in my hand and reached down inside for where my magic was. I didn't need as much time to do this anymore, and I could even keep my eyes open now. I imagined what I wanted the rock to do as I focused my eyes on the small object. "*Caith.*" I said out loud. The small stone rushed out of my palm and skipped across the lake roughly a dozen times. Lady Mirlena replaced the rock quickly, and I continued to skip small stones across the lake another twenty times until my teacher was pleased.

"You're probably at a good spot now. I don't want you utterly spent. I assume you could use a little lift?" She smiled at me, and I forced a smile back. I wasn't utterly spent, but she had me throwing the rock further each time, and the rocks had increased in size as well.

"That sounds wonderful," I said, feeling ready for what was to come. "What do I do now?"

Lady Mirlena shifted her body over so that she was closer to me before grabbing my wrist. She guided my hand closer to the fire. "First, you need to feel the element you're tapping into."

I pulled away as the heat began to burn my hand. "Hey! Feel the fire? You want me to burn myself?"

Lady Mirlena rolled her eyes. "I don't want you to burn yourself. Just stay there and feel the heat. However close or far is necessary to feel it without burning yourself. Just feel it. Really feel it."

I let out a long exhale before extending my hand towards the fire. It took a second or two, but I found the sweet spot. "Alright I feel it. Now what?"

"No, no, no. Weylyn, you have to feel the fire. Its rage, its power, its fragility. Not just the heat it gives off. Feel its capability of destruction and its ability to keep you alive in the winter. Close your eyes if you have to. I'd suggest staring into it though." When I kept looking at her, Lady Mirlena ushered me to heed her instruction with an impatient wave of her hands.

Keeping my hand where it was, I stared into the flames. I chose to surrender to it in the same way I surrendered to myself when casting a spell. The act of just letting everything else go, save for the flames, had me feeling unbelievably warm. It felt like I was only a couple feet away from the sun. I could feel the skin on my body bubbling and blistering from the heat, and I began to scream from the pain before it all suddenly vanished. Lady Mirlena had killed the fire, the pain from the flames dying with it. I checked my skin for burns as Lady Mirlena shook her head.

"You just felt the danger of tapping into the elements," she announced. "You can't go too far, or they'll consume you. Try again."

She waved her hand, and the flames came back. Making sure one more time that the skin on my arms and face weren't melting, I took a deep breath and stuck my hand out again. Instead of fully letting myself go, I kept a part of me in my mind. I imagined just me and the fire, only this time I wasn't fully engulfed by it. We were separated, save for my hand which was — in my mind — in the middle of the flames. I was surprised when I didn't feel the skin melting off my bones. My hand had grown warmer than before, but it wasn't painful. Lady Mirlena's voice almost broke my concentration. "Good. Now, slowly, welcome the energy into you like we did with the flower. I emphasize slowly. It's easy to get overwhelmed."

I did as I was told. I felt the energy inside the flames and opened a door for it. It rushed in like a stampede of burning horses. I felt myself recover so quickly that my body felt like it was a part of the flames itself. I wasn't burning like last time, I just felt unstoppable. Soon after I felt jumpy and out of control. Scared, I severed the connection between me and the fire. Gasping for a breath I realized I had not taken yet, I pulled myself back and away from the campfire. Lady Mirlena began clapping her hands together with a large grin on her face.

"Good! Good! Almost got into trouble it seems, but you got yourself out well enough. You probably feel like you could run up and down this mountain five times over before the afternoon, but you did well, Weylyn. You are okay, right?" Her smile faded a bit as a look of slight concern took over.

She was right. I did feel an immense amount of energy. So much so that I desperately wanted to be rid of some of it. I spotted a stone about the size of my head nearby and said the words necessary in my mind. It was the first time I had cast a spell without saying the words out loud. The large rock flew across the body of water, skipping multiple times before crashing into the middle of the lake. Lady Mirlena looked at me with wide eyes. For a second, I thought I had done something wrong, but the woman's eyes shimmered and a massive grin swept across her face. She shook her head slowly as she laughed.

"By the gods!" she exclaimed. "I would say you're much better than okay!"

The amount of energy I felt had lessened after my display, leaving me feeling comfortably strong. "What happened to me? How did I do that?"

Lady Mirlena waved at the flames, and they vanished. She put a hand on my shoulder and adopted a more serious expression. "You experienced the dangers of this magic. Like I said before, the energy these elements possess is limitless. So long as they exist, you can keep sapping energy from them. Take on too much, and you'll die. That's why fire is the lowest of the four. It's easy to just snuff it out and cut the connection to it. You severed the bond without me doing it for you, but you still took on more energy than you could comfortably hold. Your display was a release of that energy. It can be useful to give yourself such a boost, but it's also very reckless. I would advise you to stop before you reach the level you reached today. Especially with the other elements."

"Can we try with the other elements?" I asked.

Lady Mirlena looked at the sky before twisting her face in thought. Eventually, she sighed. "We can try using earth. But you have to use up your energy again. Perhaps we can practice *Brúigh*? That one seems to wear you down well enough."

I did as she suggested, casting the spell that sent a force outward from my hand. I cast the spell over the water, sending waves and ripples into the calm lake. Eventually, I was tired enough to give using earth a try. We went through the same steps as we did with fire, and once again the damn spell nearly killed me because I went too far. Reining myself in a bit, I tried again, only to feel the same sensation of being buried alive once more. It took me four more tries until I finally created a safe bond between the earth beneath me and myself. However, it quickly became dangerous as opening up had me feeling like a mountain was falling on top of me. I felt overwhelmed, and my heart began thumping so fast that I felt it hard to breathe. Just before I nearly passed out, I felt nothing beneath me. Looking down, I noticed I was floating in the air. Lady Mirlena had her hand out towards me, keeping me afloat until she felt it was okay to lower me back down. The amount of energy within me was too much and I couldn't stop shaking. Lady Mirlena quickly put a hand on my arm, and I felt the energy inside me begin to subside. My teacher's free hand pointed towards the lake and the water erupted high into the air as if a boulder the size of twenty people had fallen into it. I still felt anxious and jumpy, but at least I could breathe more comfortably.

"I think that's enough for today," Lady Mirlena said. "We have to get back to camp before they leave anyway. You okay to head back, or do you need a minute?"

I shook my head. "No. I'm fine. I thought fire and earth would be similar, but it seems like I was wrong to think so. How does anyone even survive using water or air?"

Lady Mirlena patted my arm before getting to her feet. "It takes a great amount of control to do it, but you'll be happy to know that even experienced Druids avoided using wind — especially during storms. Only the strongest used water. Earth and fire were much more common, especially amongst witches. You did surprisingly well for your first time though. You should be proud, Weylyn. Your progress in magic is years ahead of most witches. With some more practice, I think you'll be much better at this. Just keep in mind that you should only do this in an emergency. I know I've already said it multiple times, but this magic is dangerous."

I nodded as I stood up. "Only in an emergency. Got it."

Lady Mirlena smiled as she sighed and clapped her hands together. "Good! Now, let's head back to camp, shall we? Don't want to keep everyone waiting."

# Chapter Fifty-Six

## The Dove



As I tended to do quite often now, I thought about my current situation regarding my need for Mystic Blood. A follower of mine had sent me some wonderful news regarding Weylyn's whereabouts not too long ago. Lady Eleanor was a high-ranking noble in Stelpina and she had been loyal to me for many years. Her report only confirmed the stories being spread throughout Kosavros. Followers were continuously sending me letters about a dog some were calling The Wolf of Eous and how he was murdering all these monarchs. I had suspected this was Weylyn, but I didn't know for sure until Lady Eleanor told me his name was being uttered by many people during the coronation of the new King of Stelpina. Weylyn was still alive, which meant my opportunity to take his blood was still there. However easy I had deemed that task to be, I had to admit it would be even easier to find someone in one of these camps. They were all just huddled together like herded cattle, waiting to be tested. There was one vial that had passed three of the five tests, giving me hope. I immediately set the fourth test in motion before leaving to retrieve the faerie myself. You could imagine how furious I was to find that they had killed and burned the thing roughly two days prior.

Some would say it was rash of me to do so, but I killed the soldiers responsible. Along with the two soldiers who happened to witness the murder. And there was that one hound that had seen what I had done as well. I tossed them all into the pit and burned them along with every other waste they were setting ablaze in that disgusting place. And yet, my rage ended up being for nothing. When I got back, I discovered that the blood had failed the fourth test. The soldiers had killed just an ordinary beast, which meant I had no business killing them. So long as I didn't get caught, I didn't care. In fact, I don't think I would care even if I did get caught. All I would have to do is make up some wild story and the good little general would accept it as truth. He had little choice to do anything else. What was he compared to me?

"Dove? It's Major Carierre."

I was so lost in thought amidst my tests that the knock on the door that had preceded the announcement startled me. "Go away!"

More knocking came during more talking. "Open up, Dove! We need to talk!"

Perhaps this was about those soldiers. The proud commander of Max's army would never let this go until I addressed it. I rolled my eyes and sighed as I reluctantly waved my hand at the door behind me. The latch on it opened and I heard Jon walk in before closing the door behind him.

"What is it?" I asked. "I'm busy."

"The garrison at Camp Valldeosse reported Colonel Rousseau and some of his soldiers were killed. Well, they assume as much. There was no sign of Colonel Rousseau or his guard when soldiers investigated the unexpected fire in the pit. It took me a few days, but I finally got some information worth something. A soldier told me that people in white cloaks had come by about a week beforehand."

I swirled around a vial of blood, watching it turn yellow as it failed the first test of spells. "Lovely. Care to tell me why you're here bothering me and not out looking for these pale cloak wearing individuals?"

Jon came to stand at my side, arms crossed. "I'm here because I've seen you interact with people in white cloaks before."

I tossed the failed vial in a bucket next to me and turned in my chair, mocking the Major's discovery. "Wow! Wonderful eyes you have! It still doesn't tell me why you're here."

Jon's face was stern and serious. "You killed Colonel Rousseau and those soldiers."

I put a hand to my mouth and gave Jon an exaggerated look of surprise. "What? Me? I wouldn't dare kill a soldier of Fleuris. Let alone Colonel Rousseau. I'll have you know that I quite liked the man."

Jon's face showed he was not a fan of my acting. "You probably didn't even know his name until just now. And you would kill a soldier of Fleuris. Or do I need to remind you of two years ago?"

I pretended to struggle to remember, but my memory was involuntarily excellent. I remembered the experience like it was yesterday. The foolish — or brave, depending on how you looked at it — soldier was drunk and believed he was charming enough to lure me to his bed. Sadly, his description of charming was forceful, unwanted physical affection. I don't know why Jon would be so mad about it. I had clearly warned the man that I would kill him if he did not leave me alone. He made a choice, and I killed him. His drunk allies sought to avenge the brute and it cost them their lives as well. Jon and Max were furious, mostly because many people had seen it all happen. They burned with offense for no reason, since after a couple months passed by, people stopped talking about it. I found it silly for Jon to even bring up the subject. It only brought forth the assumed precedent that if he had done nothing about my killings then, he would do nothing about my killings now.

I forced a fake smile. "Look, I know it may not look like I'm busy to you, but I am. Let's just jump to the part where you let this crusade slip into nothing but a memory. Just like old times, yeah?"

Jon wasn't smiling back. "So you admit that it was you then?"

I threw my hands in the air and stood from my chair. "Yes, yes, yes! It was me! I did it! Who gives a damn? Just replace him with one of the other thousands of soldiers you have lying around picking their noses and shouting unwanted fancies at women in the street."

"You're going to come with me and admit what you did to the General. He'll deal with you accordingly." Jon took a step forward, his boots scuffing the stone floor.

I spun around with a newly poured cup of wine in my hand and a curious expression. He probably couldn't notice the intrigue on my face because of my mask, but I showed it, nonetheless. "You don't want that, Jon."

The Major had stopped in his tracks, even taking a step back as I stared him down. "Those men deserve justice, Dove. I intend to see that they have it."

I rolled my eyes before offering him the cup of wine in my hand. When he didn't take it, I shrugged and downed the delicious red liquid myself. I turned my back to him to pour myself some more, showing Jon just how threatened I was by him. "Oh, come on. You know full well that nothing is going to happen. Max will just wag his finger at me and tell me to be more careful. If even that. You have no leg to stand on here, Jon. Just go before you embarrass yourself any more than you already have."

"I know what you're doing with the blood," Jon said firmly.

I smiled, happy to have our conversation become interesting. Jon was known to have his little spies throughout Fleuris, so there was a chance he knew something. He had finally moved me into a state of curiosity, and I found myself wanting him to speak more instead of less. I turned around, took a sip from my glass, and motioned for him to continue.

"I know about your cult that you've created," the Major of Fleuris said. "I know which nobles are members, and I know what you're telling them you can do. *C'est de la folie*. What you're doing is blasphemous and treacherous."

Hm. I guess he knew more than I thought he did. "I don't know what you just said there but I can only imagine it was meant to be hurtful. Look, I can see an argument made for blasphemous, but treacherous? That's a stretch."

"You convinced our General to make the camps! You manipulated him so that what you're doing was made easier. You're trying to rule through him instead of serving at his side." The man's tone was one that perhaps his soldiers feared, but it didn't have any effect on me.

I rolled my eyes before taking another sip of my wine. "I do not, nor have I ever, nor will I ever serve anyone other than The Light. So what if I whispered in his ear. The man makes his own choices. Don't be jealous just because he listens to me more than he listens to you."

That last bit bothered him a bit more than I had hoped. His body tensed and I could see his teeth clench as he bit back words he knew he may regret. He allowed his body to relax again before responding. "I know where I stand with Max and I know that my place is, and always will be, at his right hand."

I grinned. "Good for you! Are we done yet?"

"I was waiting for you to mess up," he said with a cocky smile. "I knew it was only a matter of time until you'd do something stupid and give me an opening to tell Max everything I know. He may have dismissed everything before, but with you killing a high-ranking officer he's bound to listen. He'll believe every word I have to say. Telling people you can open a portal to Heaven is a level of blasphemy that deserves the most severe of punishments. The only way to meet Deus is to die."

I kept the smile on my face as I fingered the hilt of my dagger. "I can send you to Heaven right now, if you like."

Jon took a step back, resting his hand on his pistol. "You're sick, you know that? There's an evil in you. A darkness that blocks out all light."

I lunged at him then with a speed I think he didn't expect me to have. I pushed him hard, his back hitting the stone wall so harshly the grip on his pistol faltered. I quickly snagged it from the holster and tossed it away, the gun landing near the closed door. Grabbing him by his shirt, I spun him before getting my leg in his path. The action had him falling to the floor before he even realized I had taken his gun away. His back was on the floor, and I was straddling him. Before he could even try to struggle, my dagger came to his neck and his arms just froze where they were. Jon's eyes were wide with surprise and fear. Good. It meant I had his attention.

"Evil? Darkness? The Beasts of The Dark are much viler than I am. You think you know darkness, but you haven't seen what I've seen. Know what I know. Oh, and don't even begin to think that humans are any better. I've watched and listened. Humans like to think that their belief in Deus makes them all so special, but they all have a darkness in them too. A darkness only The Light can break. Humans, along with The Beasts of The Dark have all committed greater atrocities than I have. They all have more of The Dark in them than me. I am the Champion of The Light, and my mission is to purge the world of the Darkness that has swallowed it and held it hostage."

Jon let his hands drop to the floor near his head. He tried to move, but my dagger kept him where he was. "You talk about humans as if you aren't one yourself. You aren't just evil, you're insane too."

I patted his nose playfully with my first finger. "Not insane, my friend. Enlightened. Now," I leaned back, keeping my knife still close enough to kill him if he tried anything, "I believe our little chat is over, but I will end it with a warning. You will stay out of my affairs and never question me like you have tonight, or I swear I will kill you. And if you don't care about your own life, then I'll kill your wife. Understood?"

He didn't say anything or give me any indication that he had agreed to my terms, but I just assumed he had. The one thing everyone knew about me was that I always meant a threat when I issued it. Call it a warning, call it a promise, it didn't matter. If I said I was going to kill someone, then you could bet all your riches and your family's lives on the fact that I was going to kill them. Jon knew this. He may be reckless coming in here the way he did, but I wouldn't go as far as to say he was stupid. I eased back, deftly getting to my feet so that I stood over Jon as he squirmed out from under me. The man stood up and immediately went over to retrieve his pistol. I was ready to toss my blade into his chest before he could even ready his weapon, but he tucked it back into its holster.

"You know I can tell Max you threatened me, on top of everything else," he said.

I had to laugh. I couldn't believe that after all that, he was still adamant to pursue this path. Maybe he was stupid after all. "Oh, you go ahead, dear. Do whatever helps you sleep at night. I don't care. Max doesn't rule me. He knows that. He fears me. And you know what? So should you."

Jon just shook his head slowly at me for a few seconds before removing the latch on the door behind him. He kept his eyes on me as he opened the door, so I gave him a little wave as he slipped outside of my room. The door closed and I instantly waved at it to close the latch. I made my way over to the bed and sat on its edge. Opening one of the drawers in the nightstand, I pulled out the mirror my mother gave me before I left home. She said it was special, but never mentioned how. I tended to use it when I needed reminding of who I was. It didn't happen often, but every now and then I would pull out this mirror, hold it by its golden handle that branched out into a golden floral border, and stare into it. I would tell myself who I was, and what I was trained for. I would remind myself who I fought for and how important it was that I completed my task. Staring into my own eyes, I removed my mask from my face and was reminded of why I wore it. I inspected every one of my features, telling myself over and over again that I was The Champion of The Light, and that no Darkness would ever poison me. The Dark is my enemy, and those born of it would be purified.

# Chapter Fifty-Seven

## Weylyn

Grapiademento, Malvene  |  July 9, 1799

Our armies met in a place called Grapiademento, or in the common language, Plains of Great Betrayal. It was a flat land that had allowed us to spot our enemy with spy glasses from about five miles away. With the mountains far behind us, yet still slightly visible on the horizon, The Resistance clashed with Malvene. Their army was large and well prepared. They had soldiers in heavy armor, almost like knights from a time before my kind arrived. The shiny metal plating was worn by infantry and cavalry, although the majority of their forces wore dark green coats. This battle was important for many reasons, but one of them was perhaps the most meaningful to me. Sophia, with the support of the brigade, had named me the new leader of Unity. The responsibility was immense, and I feared greatly that I would somehow dishonor Colonel Seamus' memory. I nearly refused, but oddly enough it was Quaid who had persuaded me to take it on. The satyr, along with about two battalions of rebels, had met us just as we left the mountains near a small town called Giacomo. Brina and the others had tried to encourage me, but it was Quaid's words about the meaning and responsibility of a leader that had me kneeling before Sophia and being named a Colonel of the Tudrose army.

Together with the rebels from Malvene, soldiers from Tudrose and Stelpina stood with rebels from Tulp and Korblum. A force made up of Tóráin and humans charged the army of Malvene and it pained me to say that it did not start out great. Our infantry was sent in first, and Malvene had countered with its heavily armored cavalry. They were slower than regular horse riders, but they hit us harder when we came together. Their armor heavily protected them from lycans, and it made it extremely difficult to kill them. Thankfully, our infantry numbers heavily outweighed their cavalry numbers, and we began to move forward. Trumpets and whistles blared as orders were sent out — barely noticeable amongst the loud booms from the artillery of both armies — with myself and those around me having not a clue what they meant. In the heat of battle, your mind seemed to shrink until all you knew was survival. You couldn't tell the difference between the tunes of trumpets or how many blasts from the whistles were sounded. All you knew was more soldiers were coming, and the battle you were fighting was about to get bigger.

Killing was still something I wished I didn't have to do, but I had to admit that I was quite good at it. The skill surely wasn't something to ever boast about, however I noticed that I handled myself fairly well. My skills in both physical and magical warfare had improved over the weeks and months. It was hard to say that I was comfortable in a battle now, but I understood how things worked a bit more and knew more of what to expect. You were going to get injured, those around you were going to die, and the momentum of the battle could shift as quickly as you could blink. Things happened fast on the battlefield and you had no choice but to keep up, or you'd most certainly perish. Brina was by my side, fighting furiously on my left, while Quaid fought with a heightened level of ferocity on my right. Cordelia, Seig, and Sullivan had all been nearby during our charge, but I had not seen them in some time. I tossed the distraction aside, focusing in on the soldiers that were trying to kill me. Slashing away a rifle pointed at me, I ran my claws across the opposing soldier's face and looked around for my next opponent. I suddenly noticed that Brina and Quaid were no longer with me, the battle having dragged us apart.

One of the heavily armored soldiers came into sight as I looked around for my friends. He brandished a thick, weighted sword that only one of the strongest soldiers would be able to wield. He cut down a lycan that charged him, before lopping the head off of a Stelpina soldier. He turned his head, and I could tell that he had discovered me watching him. His helmet had a visor that covered every bit of his face save for a slit for his eyes. He readied his broadsword in the air near his right side and advanced. I had seen just how quickly the other lycan had fallen, so I knew brute strength wouldn't be my ally here. I needed to be smart about my next move. In fact, I needed to be smart about every move after that too. The little armor I had was light, and none of it would protect me from losing a limb or — a much worse outcome — my head. I took a step back as he closed the distance between us before I had a plan in mind, continuing to retreat until the chaos of battle was at my back. The knight realized my poor positioning and I imagined him grinning before swinging his sword at me. I dove to my right, barely avoiding the thick, sharp steel that tried to remove my head. I fell upon an abandoned rifle and decided to pick it up.

It was hard to wield a weapon in my feral form, my elongated fingers and enlarged palms making it difficult to grasp any weapon comfortably. However, I realized I needed something to deflect the knight's strikes. I couldn't just dive out of the way forever. I clumsily struggled to get a good grip on the thin rifle, gripping the gun well enough just in time to move it in the way of the heavy sword coming for my side. I breathed a sigh of relief as the rifle parried the blow, remaining intact despite the strike from the sharp blade. The knight swung his sword around quicker than I figured possible, and I barely brought the rifle above me in time to block his next strike. His broadsword came down on me so strongly that — despite parrying the attack with my rifle — I fell backwards. The knight readied for another attack as I struggled to get to my feet, making sure to keep an eye on my opponent the entire time. His sword landed in the dirt instead of my stomach as I rolled to my right. The heavy blade was stuck in the ground just enough to give me a brief opening to recover. I abandoned rest when I noticed a weak spot in his armor just under his arm, in the pit between his bicep and his ribs. I quickly stabbed with the bayonet on the end of the rifle, but I missed my target and the blade glanced off the knight's chest plate.

Despite my failure, I now had a plan. The man was heavily protected , and his weapon was probably more deadly than my own at the moment, but I was quicker. After parrying and dodging more of the knight's strikes I went to block another overhand blow. The rifle finally gave way and broke in half. His blade, redirected by the broken gun, landed sharply in my shoulder. The leather armor I had on slowed it enough so that I kept my arm, but it was deep enough to cause me problems if I didn't heal it soon. Thankfully, I had the wherewithal to notice that the opening I was looking for had presented itself. Wielding the half of the gun with the bayonet in my right hand, I shoved the sharp point up into the weak spot I had noticed earlier. The knight grunted loudly as the entirety of the bayonet entered him. He removed his blade from my shoulder and stumbled backwards, the broken half of the rifle sticking out of his armpit. He stabbed the earth with his blade before reaching over and slowly pulling out the bayonet. A small bit of fear encroached on my spirit, wondering what else I could possibly do if this didn't kill the man. He tossed the rifle away, but as his hand reached for his weapon, he fell to his knees. He stayed there, with his hand on the hilt of his sword, for only a moment before his grasp on his weapon relieved itself and he fell face first into the ground.

I looked around quickly to see how Brina and Quaid were doing, but neither of them was nearby anymore. I thought to look for one of them when shouting was heard over the raucous noise of battle. "More cavalry from the west! Reinforcements!"

I had remembered many people, especially General Wyman, being concerned at the size of the initial army that opposed us. It was too small in the General's eyes, and he worried about us being out maneuvered somehow. Everyone, even General Wyman, agreed that there was no choice for us but to fight anyway. It seemed as though our worries were had for good reason. Azuvipa was known for its deadly cavalry, mainly because of its leader. Despite King Ludovico residing in Leonessa, the general of his army remained in Azuvipa. General Ercole Aloisio was known for his ruthless training regimes and his skills as a tactician. General Wyman admitted that he had dreaded facing the man more than facing General Rosspier in Fleuris. There was a folktale about the man that he had been born of old pagan gods of this world before being blessed and welcomed by Deus. Those from Malvene believed him to be unstoppable and destined for victory every time he was in battle. His victories at dueling and jousting tournaments over the last ten years or so only gave his people proof to base their beliefs on. If he and his cavalry were indeed attacking us from the west, we were in trouble. Medoa River covered our left flank, which was good but also bad. It had protected us from being flanked; however now it was possible we would be pushed into the river.

More enemies came my way and I fought as hard as I could, my body dealing with the loss of energy from healing my shoulder much better than before. The more the battle went on, the more I could feel us being pushed more to my left. General Ercole's cavalry were pushing us to the river just as I had worried. Something had to happen to change the momentum of this fight, or we would eventually lose. From listening intently to General Wyman speak at meetings, I knew that our numbers probably equaled that of Malvene at full force. Having already been fighting before Azuvipa's cavalry came charging in, there was a very good chance we were outnumbered at the moment. The army needed a spark. Something to galvanize themselves behind. A rider came into the pocket I had made, and I quickly pushed him with a spell, knocking him off his steed. I shifted into my tame form so I could ride the horse better and looked out over the battle in the hopes of seeing something to inspire me. Out in the distance, I spotted a small group of soldiers on horseback outside of the main battle. I counted seven of them, with one in the middle pointing and looking like he was giving out orders. The entire western flank shown with the silver armor of Azuvipa's soldiers. Possibly making a horrible decision, I turned my horse north and kicked into its sides.

The only way to get to who I assumed to be General Ercole was around the cavalry he had brought with him. I determined north was the easiest route, expecting to encounter more friendly forces than hostile ones. I grabbed a rifle from an enemy soldier who was prepared to skewer someone with the blade on the tip of it and pushed my ride as best I could. Eventually, I broke out of the violent mass and rode out into the open field, racing past enemy forces. It wasn't long until the soldiers guarding their General spotted me charging towards them. My actions provoked the guards into turning their attention to me, readying their rifles and firing in my direction. One of the bullets struck my right arm, while another grazed the left side of my neck. The injuries were painful, but manageable. I aimed my rifle as well, succeeding in taking out one of the opposing soldiers. Despite that small victory, another volley of bullets was readying themselves. I quickly slid over the right side of the horse and veered it slightly to the right. I had closed a great amount of distance between us, but when my enemies fired their guns and my horse cried out in pain, I was nervous. The brave animal collapsed in a heap, yet I had managed to leap off of it in time to roll through the fall and land ready on a knee. I aimed my rifle and fired an excellent shot, killing another soldier. I charged them now, running forward as they fired at me one more time. All of their shots missed, and I could now hear General Ercole scolding them in what I assumed was Malvene's native language. My last shot missed, but I was close enough to turn my rifle into a javelin and toss it at one of the remaining soldiers. Taking what strength my horse had before leaping off it had worked out wonderfully, giving me the added strength to pull off such a feat. The three remaining guards abandoned their rifles and drew their swords, each of them charging towards me. I shifted into my feral form mid stride and met them head on.

They came at me in a staggered line, almost like a sideways triangle. They were fairly spaced out, so much so that it allowed me to take them on relatively one at a time. After I dodged to my right and avoided the first soldier's swipe, I gathered myself enough to use my push spell and knock the man's horse off stride. The attack sent the beast and its rider stumbling and crashing off to my left. Seeing how well it had worked the first time, I managed to replicate the act with the second soldier. The man and his horse stumbled forward to my right this time and I began to feel unstoppable. When the third soldier approached me, I closed the gap between us quickly and leaped at him. His blade stabbed forward and gave me a deep slice to my side. Still, I had taken the man off his horse and the force of the fall had resulted in a loud crunch. The terrified horse he left behind had stopped nearby and was rearing. Shifting back into my tame form I hopped into the saddle and directed the war horse towards the, now vulnerable, General Ercole. My successful defense had surprised him enough that he was still drawing his pistol. Despite that, he managed to fire off a shot in my direction, hitting my steed in the head and sending it careening forward. Again, I managed to avoid collapsing with the horse I was riding and tumbled in the direction of the General of Malvene. Shifting into my feral form mid roll, I broke out of the fall in a four-legged sprint. I reached the leader of the country's army and lunged at him. I heard a gunshot as I stole him from his saddle, the two of us falling to and rolling on the ground. His aim was good, a bullet wound now weeping blood from my stomach proved that. I quickly healed the wound knowing full well this fight wasn't over, tossing the bullet that fell into my hand to the short grass next to me.

I could hear the soldiers I had dodged charging towards us, and I knew I had to act quickly. General Ercole was getting to his feet slowly, and once he was steady, he drew his sword and pointed it at me. "*Bestia indegna*! You're a fool for challenging me! Come now! Meet your end, *cane*!"

The man's face changed from anger to joy, and I realized what was happening. I instinctively rolled to my left, hoping that I had made the right choice. The horse charging down at its target missed me and raced on by. I turned to face the next one and deftly moved to my right just enough to avoid his swing, catch his arm, and remove him from his saddle. I swiped my claws at the man's neck and turned my attention to the General. A sharp pain just under the left of my chest — just above my stomach — had me grabbing hold of the General's arm, stopping him from pushing his blade in any further. It wasn't much, but a good amount of his sword was inside me. I did something then on instinct, something Lady Mirlena had told me was considered a darker use of the magic she had taught me. I wasn't thinking of what others would say, all I was thinking about was survival. I overpowered my enemy and made him remove his sword, but not before I took his energy from him. His tanned skin grew pale as he stumbled backwards, terrified and surprised by what had just happened. I put a hand to my wound and used my newfound energy to heal myself once more. The power I felt standing tall while my enemy cowered in fear was intoxicating and I had to shake my head to remove myself from such thoughts. It was hard not to feel good about besting those who would see you dead. Knowing that I had the ability to heal myself while others could not had given me a confidence that bordered arrogance, and while the feeling worried me, I shrugged it off for now as adrenaline from the fight.

General Ercole struggled to get to his feet, coughing and wheezing even after he was standing. He aimed his sword at me before lunging forward, forcing me to knock his weapon aside before biting into the man's neck. My teeth tore through his clothes and muscle, blood filling my mouth as it poured from his body. I let him fall to the ground with eyes open wide and looked at the last soldier from the General's guard. The man had halted his new advance only a few feet away from me. His mouth was agape as he made holy protection symbols over his body that priests would often do when they saw my kind. The man stayed where he was for a moment before urging his horse to race toward the main battle.

"General Ercole is dead! *L'Immortale è morto*! The one blessed by gods old and new is gone! *Ritirata*! *Salvati*! The battle is lost!"

Had they continued to fight, there was a good chance it was The Resistance that would lose. However, my plan appeared to work. I figured that killing their leader would disrupt them enough to allow us to overcome the odds, but this was even better. Soldiers hearing the declaration of their famed general's death began turning their horses around and retreating altogether. I had only a few moments to silently celebrate my victory, as I realized that a good-sized group of panicked — and possibly vengeful — cavalry was now charging in my direction. I had no horse to flee on, all of them either being dead or having run off. I got ready to try to sprint away as best I could when a friendly face rode towards me.

"Weylyn! Get on!" Brina was in her tame form, riding a white horse, with her right hand extended out for me to grab.

I said nothing. I shifted into my tame form and grabbed her hand as I leapt onto the back of the horse. Brina urged the beast to race off to the north, and we managed to avoid the retreating forces of Malvene. Cheers began to break out as The Resistance forces realized what was happening. It was incredibly risky, but I had succeeded. My plan had worked. General Ercole Aloisio was dead, and the morale of Malvene's forces had died along with him. The battle was won. However, my mind returned to the moment I was fighting the General of Malvene. I thought about what I had done, and I began to wonder something. I had won the battle for us, but at what cost?

# Chapter Fifty-Eight

## Weylyn

Leonessa, Malvene | July 10, 1799

"I'm still not sure you should have come, Sophia."

The Queen of Tudrose patted my hand. "You worry too much. I'll be fine."

General Wyman cleared his throat. "As much as it displeases me to admit it, I agree with Colonel Weylyn. You still aren't at your full strength yet."

"I'm sure King Ludovico would have understood if you chose to rest instead of humor the man by having dinner with him," Lady Mirlena said.

"I assure you all that I am quite alright. Now, I beg of you, leave the subject of my health alone. There are more important things that require our attention tonight." Sophia slumped for a brief moment in her saddle, which prompted me to quickly hold my arm out. She didn't fall off this time, but I still made sure that our horses were close just in case she did in the future.

I kept the reins for both our horses in my hands, making sure to be in as much control as I could. General Wyman and Lady Mirlena were right in saying that the Queen wasn't fully recovered yet. She was strong enough now to stand on her own though. She could even walk by herself for a short while, but her energy still vanished very quickly. She wasn't resting as much as before, and it was probably better for her if she was. Despite not being in the best health, Sophia had insisted on joining us and meeting with King Ludovico in Leonessa. A messenger had arrived this morning stating that the King of Malvene wished to treat us to dinner in his home, the famed Palazzo del Re. Going back to that place stirred up sour memories of the good people who had died there roughly six months ago when Brina and I freed Quaid. The satyr wasn't all too happy to return either mind you, and I think he had more reason to dislike the place than I did. The sun was just barely reaching the end of its shift as we approached our destination. It sat low in the western sky, coloring the clouds purple and orange, when we finally arrived. Memories of our fight with The Crows entered my mind as two guards and a woman in a black corset over a dark green dress greeted us.

"*Benvenuta*! It's a pleasure to meet all of you! King Ludovico is excited to provide Queen Sophia and her allies with a wonderful meal tonight." The woman looked to our left and right with an uneasy smile on her face. "The retinue of *soldati* you've brought is quite unnecessary."

We had brought a unit of soldiers with us once we received no push back entering the city. Sophia, General Wyman, Lady Mirlena, Quaid, Brina, and I were joined by three battalions of soldiers on our journey to Malvene's capital city. Despite none of us truly trusting a surrender anymore, Sophia and I still felt it wasn't smart to bring our entire force through the rest of the city. We both agreed that it would only provoke the people of Leonessa, and possibly even the King himself. So, we ended up bringing roughly one hundred soldiers with us instead of the few thousand we had started with: a compromise between the two of us and General Wyman. Those soldiers weren't the only ones left behind mind you. Rosalie had insisted on joining us, but I convinced her it was too dangerous considering how things had gone in the past. She stayed back with Cordelia, Sullivan, Seig, and the rest of the army to look after Arthur for Lady Mirlena. Despite leaving many allies behind, I could see how a group like ours might seem a little intimidating showing up for a dinner. I didn't mind it though. It was better to have them intimidated than thinking we were vulnerable.

"Just a precaution, dear. Bad experiences with the last king who offered us a peaceful meeting." Sophia pointed at the void where her arm should be, and the woman bowed her head.

"Queen Sophia," the woman said. "My apologies. I meant no disrespect."

I had dismounted along with everyone else, save for Sophia and Quaid. The satyr, just like every other one of his kind, couldn't comfortably ride a horse so he had no need of one. Sophia, despite her strong-willed nature, knew that she needed help getting on and off her horse. As I extended my arms towards her, she put her hand on my shoulder and allowed me to lower her down.

"Do not be silly," Sophia said as her feet touched the ground. "No apology is necessary...um..."

The woman perked up, her dark brown hair flowing in a breeze that flew through us all. "Giada. Giada Bruni. I am the King's personal witch and head of the security of Palazzo del Re."

Sophia took two steps on her own before weaving her lone arm through mine. I could feel her relying on me for stability and realized that the journey had probably taken a lot out of her. General Wyman and Lady Mirlena watched her closely with looks of concern, but Sophia ignored them and continued her conversation with Giada.

Sophia tried to stand a little straighter to show her strength. "What a pretty name. I assume you are here to guide us to our meal?"

Giada smiled before looking at the soldiers behind all of us. "*Sì*. But, um, I don't think we have enough food for all of you."

General Wyman spoke up. "We are not going into that place without any soldiers you little —"

"Surely you have enough food for twelve of us?" Sophia asked, cutting General Wyman off.

Twelve of us would be our group plus six soldiers: a reasonable force for a dinner. Brina and I had freed Quaid and survived an attack with only a few people fighting by our side, so surely a group of a dozen people would keep us safe enough. Giada hesitated, but eventually she nodded and flashed a comely smile.

"*Sì, dodici* is quite alright. King Ludovico is a wonderful host and will see to it that every one of you is fed and comfortable. *Venga con me*, I'll take you to the dining hall."

The witch spun around, her free hair and flowing dress flaring out from the quick motion. General Wyman called on six soldiers and ordered the rest to set up a loose perimeter around the building. Giada led our group of twelve through the archways that led to a small courtyard before entering through two attractive double doors. She took us left, to the area that Brina and I had not ventured into. Soon after, we arrived at two dark brown doors about eight feet high and possibly the same size in width. Giada peeked in before opening the doors for us herself. A large table was set with so many pieces of silverware I thought it was a prank. Plates and bowls covered each setting as well, and three bouquets of flowers with extravagant colors and shapes lined the center of the long table. Giada insisted we take our seats before leaving through the doors we had entered from. There had been an apparent dislike for the size of our group, and yet I counted twenty-one placements on the table. Even our grand number plus the royal family would leave plenty of spots vacant. All of us stood in front of our chosen seats, nobody willing to sit down and leave themselves even slightly more vulnerable to an ambush. Eventually, the doors opened, and Giada's voice filled the room.

"*Introducendo Sua Maestà*, King Ludovico Almani, *sua moglie*, Queen Mirabella, *il loro figlio*, Prince Vincenzo, *e la loro figlia*, Princess Alessandra."

The family of four entered the room together, but only King Ludovico had a smile on his face. Queen Mirabella dawned a hefty scowl while Prince Vincenzo was much too young to even know what was going on; he was probably no older than four. Princess Alessandra was older than her brother, much older in fact. Well, at least that's how it appeared; my guess was she was older than fifteen yet younger than twenty. She held herself maturely with a poise that came with age. She had a nervous look on her face; one could argue it was just the young woman being shy though. The royal family made their way down one side of the table until they reached their seats at the head of it.

King Ludovico clapped his hands together as he stood in front of his ornate chair. "*Che bello vederti*! I'm happy you've all come. I'm sure you're eager to talk about terms and all that, but I insist we eat first. Please, sit, I beg you. *Porate il cibo!*"

I looked at Sophia, who was taking the seat to my right, and she nodded. Everyone took their seats, and what I had discovered was the order for food to be brought in was quickly followed by the lovely scent of pies, vegetables, and what turned out to be roasted boar. The room was mostly silent and void of any true conversation for a while, but eventually more words filled the dining hall. King Ludovico spoke with Sophia, General Wyman and Lady Mirlena spoke to each other, I spoke with Brina mostly, and Quaid had struck up a conversation with Princess Alessandra. The soldiers talked amongst themselves, and Queen Mirabella whispered to her young son, Prince Vincenzo. We all ate, drank, and talked for some time until the food was gone and some tea was brought out. Small cakes and fresh fruit joined the warm drinks, which became a prelude to the King of Malvene standing from his chair and raising a glass of wine.

"*Che pasto meraviglioso!*" he shouted. "I am glad to have shared this food with such wonderful people. To the loveliest of guests!"

"To the loveliest of hosts!" Sophia raised her glass in the air with King Ludovico's.

"Oh, come on." Lady Mirlena blushed when she realized she had spoken out loud, but when everyone remained with their eyes locked on her, she continued.

"Can we move past all the niceties and get to why we're here already? The lack of attention paid to it all is sickening."

"I struggle to keep my meal in my stomach as I say this, but I agree with the witch. Get on with it, *amore mio*. This has been more torture than pleasure." Queen Mirabella took a big gulp from her glass, finishing off the wine that remained inside.

"I'm actually having a wonderful time," Princess Alessandra announced as she glanced back at Quaid. Her mother's glare had the girl's entire body retreat into the chair she sat in. "*Scusa, mamma.*"

"No, no, Alessandra! Don't apologize. Your mother just doesn't know a good time when she sees it! I'm glad you've enjoyed yourself, *mio dolce fiore*." King Ludovico smiled, getting a small smirk from his daughter in return.

"Good time? Stop acting like *un pazzo*, Ludovico! *Hai perso*! You've been defeated! You're surrendering to these...these…" Queen Mirabella stopped her rant when her husband grabbed her arm.

"I'm sorry, my friends. I think my lovely wife has enjoyed the wine too much." The King of Malvene smiled, and it seemed like any hostilities that were encroaching on our event were leaving.

That was until Brina spoke up. "No, please, let her continue. These what?"

I turned to face my cousin swiftly. "Enough, Brina. Let it go."

Queen Mirabella looked like she was going to respond to Brina, but a quick jostle of her arm by King Ludovico kept her silent. That silence spread throughout the room, the tension in the dining hall having grown considerably in the last few moments. Sophia slowly began to stand up, prompting a swift ascension from my seat to assist her. She waved me off, but I stayed ready to catch her if the act was too much for her.

"King Ludovico," Sophia began, "I think that a meal together was a wonderful idea. On behalf of everyone here, I thank you for your kind gesture of peace. I would, however, like to suggest that perhaps terms should be discussed now. It is getting late, and I am quite tired."

I saw General Wyman wince at the admission of weakness. Lady Mirlena didn't look all too happy about it either. King Ludovico, however, adopted a look of compassion I had yet to see form on a leader's face during this campaign. "Of course, Queen Sophia. I apologize for not considering your health better. Perhaps a smaller group of us would be less strenuous for us both."

"Absolutely not!" General Wyman shouted.

Sophia stared the man down and he inclined his head in apology. Sophia smiled at everyone before giving her attention to our host. "I think that is a lovely idea. You all can go, save for Weylyn and Quaid."

"My Queen I highly advise against such a —"

"I said you can go, General Wyman," Sophia snapped. "Take Lady Mirlena and Lady Brina with you, as well as our soldiers. Wait in the courtyard outside until we're finished."

Everyone hesitated, until King Ludovico spoke next. "*Amore mio*, take the children to their rooms. *Soldati*, you may also leave."

The few Malvene guards in the room looked at each other as Queen Mirabella prepared to scold her husband. Despite how clearly angry she was, she stopped herself when our host gave her a stern look. The Queen of Malvene stood from her seat, took Prince Vincenzo by his hand, and went over to plant a kiss on King Ludovico's cheek. Princess Alessandra stood from her chair, which had Quaid clumsily bursting out of his seat before bowing and smiling at the young woman. Her mother called after her and she went away quickly, followed by the Malvene soldiers as well as ours. Brina grabbed my arm before leaving to follow General Wyman and Lady Mirlena out the door.

"If they hurt you, I'll burn this entire place to the ground," she said.

I laughed as I gently patted her arm. "I know. Go, I'll be fine."

Brina was the last one to leave the room, the lack of people inside now making the dining hall feel more immense than before. King Ludovico sat down in his chair, prompting the rest of us to do the same, but not in our same seats. Sophia moved up to be closer to the King at his behest, and so I followed her. Quaid, on the other side of the table, moved closer as well. King Ludovico didn't seem to mind, in fact he smiled at the choice and appeared to welcome it. He poured himself some more wine, the butlers and maids who had been doing it for him having vacated the room as well.

"Before we start, I have something to say. I will try to keep it all in the common tongue so that you will understand. Forgive me if I fail." King Ludovico cleared his throat, took a sip of his wine, and sighed. "I have heard of what challenging this force of yours does to kings. Whether it be imprisonment or death, I'd rather choose a third option that has me remain comfortably in that throne not too far from this room. Know that I am willing to abide by your terms, within reason, despite the advice from my wife and other advisors not to. I have no intention of staging some sort of ambush or anything of the sort. These discussions we are about to have will be governed with peace and advancement in mind. You have my word."

I looked over at Quaid, the satyr looking back at me with just as much surprise as I had. The King of Malvene was, so far, the most reasonable of the leaders we had encountered. I still had my doubts, but I chose to believe that he indeed meant us no harm. It allowed me to relax muscles I had kept tense since the moment we entered the city.

Sophia took a sip from the cup of tea she had taken with her to her new seat before responding to King Ludovico's opening statement. "I am happy to hear all of that. I am sure my friends are too. In what you have heard about our previous meetings with other monarchs, did you happen to discover what our terms are?"

King Ludovico's face twisted as he tried to remember. "I don't recall the details, but I know you want *Caduti*...sorry. That name has become customary for your kind here in Malvene. Allow me to use the name you use instead. I know you want the Tóráin to be treated better. I remember something about giving money to the poor too. Am I missing anything?"

"I think 'treating the Tóráin better' can be expanded on with a little more detail," Quaid suggested.

"I agree. Weylyn, would you be so kind?" Sophia sent me a weak smile and I nodded.

Looking at the King of Malvene, I submitted the terms that Sophia, Quaid, and I had agreed upon. "The Tóráin in Malvene have been treated in such a way that will no longer be acceptable as our world takes a step forward. Past beliefs and fanatical religious views cannot continue to dictate the quality of life for the Tóráin. Our terms involve the end of the subjugation, oppression, and persecution of my kind. They will be seen as equal citizens and given every opportunity to have a safe, prosperous life. In that same vein, the poor of Malvene, both human and Tórán alike, will be better looked after and provided for. Priests will focus their attention on the sick, orphaned, and homeless instead of the mistreatment of the Tóráin. Nobles will adopt better ways of treating those under them instead of acting like those people don't exist or aren't important. Most of all, you, as King of this country, will work towards closing the gap between the poor and royalty instead of killing and torturing anyone who tries to see that gap closed themselves. Malvene has the potential to be a better, more unified country, and we believe that you and your people are all important in making Kosavros a stronger, happier, and safer place for every person no matter what they look like or how much money they have. These are our terms."

King Ludovico was upset by what I had said. Well, it seemed that way to me at least. No smile was visible on his face and his eyes had squinted just enough for a scowl to form. He pursed his lips and moved his eyes to Sophia, then Quaid, then back to Sophia, and then finally back to me. His head didn't move at any point, making his eyes do all the necessary work to view the expressions on all of our faces. Quaid and Sophia had adopted serious looks that told the King of Malvene that they fully supported the terms I had given. Our host licked his lips quickly before attempting to clear his throat. The act led into a small coughing fit that ended once he downed some more of the wine that he had chosen over the tea. He finished what was in his glass and then proceeded to reach over for a glass jug with some wine still left in it. After pouring the remaining liquid in his cup, he frowned, apparently disappointed that there wasn't more for him to drink. He took a small sip from his newly filled glass and let out a deep sigh as he put the drink down on the elaborate cloth that covered the table.

"You appear to be proof that not all stories told are true," he said. "Sometimes they exaggerate and sometimes they undersell. Sometimes they stretch out truths and — fairly often — they outright lie. I was told weeks and weeks ago of *un lupo* that travelled with the Queen of Tudrose, her army at his back. I was told how his savagery and dark tendencies had poisoned the peaceful Queen Sophia and convinced her to wage war on the world. Messengers told me of how you took the King of Tulp and his family in your jaws and dragged them out of the throne room as they begged for mercy. Eventually I received word about the carnage you had left behind in Korblum. How your bloodlust could not be contained, the evil inside you lashing out, causing you to slaughter the King and those who stood by to bravely defend him. More news came of your skills in battle, and how your darkness was spreading through the Tudrose army like a plague. You called more of your kind to your vengeful cause and continued on your path south, leaving a trail of countless bodies in your wake. You were pictured as unreasonable, unruly, demonic, and soon people began calling you The Wolf of Eous. People genuinely fear you, so much so that after news of what you did at the Cathedral of Nours, my *consiglieri* wished for me to flee south and ask the Papal States of Luila to assist Malvene in battle, all while hiding safely in their capital with Pope Barnaba himself.

"I have to admit that after hearing the carnage you left behind in such a holy place, supposedly murdering the King, his son, and an archbishop as well, I almost listened to them. The rumors that you had used Queen Sophia as a human shield to protect yourself from the bullets that flew through the hallowed cathedral only further depicted you as a mad creature with no loyalties at all. I was going to flee, take *la mia famiglia* with me and run, but I had a dream the night before we were set to leave. In this dream, an angel appeared to me and spoke only one word: believe. The single word spoke to a feeling deep inside me that you couldn't be as vile and monstrous as they said. I admit that perhaps I can treat my subjects, of all kinds, better than I do. However, I never was of the mind of the church. I didn't believe your kind were born of darkness and spawned purely for evil intentions. The idea that you were all Fallen like Eous always seemed wrong to me. The hope inside me, that there was more to the story being told, was encouraged to rise up by my dreams. I chose to stay and defend my home on my own. Half because I wanted to, and half because The Papal States of Luila had refused to send us any military assistance. Supposedly they're having troubles with Pumera. Anyway, that's beside the point. I chose to believe in the strength of my army, as well as my thought that the army attacking me was not led by a demonic wolf sent by Eous to plunge this world into eternal darkness. I would fight to defend my country and my family's well-being, just like any righteous, loyal, king would do. However, my fear of you was lessened. Not in a disrespectful way, but I'd say in more of an enlightened way.

"When I got word that we had lost our battle, and *i miei soldati* began to tell stories of how the Wolf of Eous butchered my general, I admit that I was nervous. I wondered if I had made the wrong choice to stay here, and I began to fear that I had made a mistake. In that moment where fear tried to take me, I followed the order given to me by that angel. I chose to believe that there could be peace between you and me. That you had not turned Queen Sophia into a warmongering tyrant. And so, with that belief in my heart, I sent out my notice of surrender along with an invitation to dinner. I hesitantly welcomed you, Queen Sophia, and your allies, and I watched. As the night passed by, I began to form an opinion on each one of you. This was the first time I had ever hosted your kind at my table, and if it is blasphemous to say such words than I guess I'll need to beg the Pope himself for forgiveness. Maybe I'll go on a pilgrimage or something. *Non importa.* What I'm trying to say is that I began to see you and your kind as equals. How you spoke during the issuing of your terms has only opened my eyes further."

"Well isn't that wonderful," Quaid interjected. "Why couldn't you see that before? It would have saved a lot of lives."

King Ludovico's face adopted a somber expression. "I know. And while nothing I say now can relieve me of my responsibility for every life lost, I will admit with great shame that I allowed myself to be lead astray. I allowed members of *la mia famiglia*, along with the Pope, to influence me so much that I believed that the right thing to do was to keep the Tóráin below humans. There have been

times in my life when the idea of making peace with your kind was put forth —
most recently by a secret group of Dafne nobles who were begging me to save them
from the Kayghuz Empire — but every time I was coerced by members of my
council into refusing such things. My choice was to fight, and I have to live with
that decision for the rest of my life. My dear mother is no doubt ashamed of me."

"Why would your mother be ashamed of you?" Sophia asked. "You said your
family taught you to look down on the Tóráin. Or did I misunderstand?"

King Ludovico shook his head. "Not everyone taught such things. My father
and uncle thought that way, but *mia madre* liked your kind. She dreamed of a
world, or even just a town, that would treat the Tóráin better. She would be
ashamed of me now because a long time ago, I promised her just before she died
that I would use my power to help her dream be realized one day. Instead, I
allowed priests and nobles, as well as my wife, to influence me during my rule as
King. I have failed my mother, and in turn I have also failed you and your kind. I
know that I cannot change the past, nor can I openly challenge it without the
Church being angry with me, but I can make changes so that the future for your
kind is brighter. I will agree to your terms. In fact, to prove my intentions to be
good and true, I'll promise something now that could get me in some trouble.
Actually, it could end up a problem for all of us, but I think we could manage it if
we work together."

Sophia raised her hand in the air before adding a new voice to the dining hall.
"King Ludovico, please. Your acceptance of the terms is appreciated. You don't
have to rush into drastic changes to prove yourself. We do not want to aggravate
those who would not agree with our partnership."

King Ludovico took a couple gulps of his wine. "You want change, don't you?"

Sophia's cheeks became flushed, and I could tell that the combination of wine
and exhaustion was hindering her mind. "Well, yes. Of course. That is why we are
doing this. I just...I do not want it to seem like we are playing sides here. Yes, our
main focus is the treatment of the Tóráin, but our goals also include humans. We
are striving for a world where everyone feels accepted and capable of wonderful
achievements."

"Whether you want to or not, you're going to upset people. Surely you know
this by now," Quaid said.

I could tell that Sophia was getting overwhelmed and frustrated, so I put a hand
on hers. Our eyes locked from the touch, and she nodded, giving me permission to
make her point for her.

"We knew from the beginning that there were going to be a lot of people that won't be happy about the changes we planned to make. The knowledge and understanding that what we're asking of people is intense and different is the first thing we needed to have before we set out on this campaign. People are going to be angry and feel like they're being pushed aside. They'll probably feel that their lives are going to become worse while those they see as less than them will rise up to heights even they couldn't reach. Our most important goal has always been to bring about drastic change to a system that is heavily unbalanced. Our second most important goal is to make sure we communicate with people and respect their beliefs, no matter how unpleasant they are. Conquering the world is an easy way to make things the way we want, but it isn't lasting. We want to work with people and educate them by introducing new ways of thinking that focus on inclusivity, unity, and equality. What Queen Sophia is trying to say, is that the path to a sustainable change in the world we live in is slow and steady. A massive change to the way things are, right away, can backfire like a faulty rifle. We need to be careful."

King Ludovico and Quaid both nodded their heads, absorbing my words into their minds. They both took a few moments to process everything I had said, until one of them chose to respond.

"I can see why you were chosen to lead The Resistance," King Ludovico said. "I can also see how you convinced Queen Sophia, along with so many others, to join you. Your words are wise and inspiring. How you speak of this new world and how to create it reminds me of conversations I would have with my mother. I understand what you have said, and yet I still believe that this needs to happen. Not only to show my loyalty to this partnership, but also to show my people that atrocities committed against your kind will no longer be tolerated." King Ludovico turned his head to Quaid. "Months ago, you led a riot as a plea for better lives. I had you imprisoned and tortured for it. I nearly had you killed for it. This was wrong. While I can admit this and look to working towards a point in time when you can possibly forgive me, there is one man who I know will not do the same. I think you know who I speak of."

"Francesco Ventossa." The way Quaid said the name, you would think the man had been the satyr's torturer during his time in prison.
"The Duke of Azuvipa," I said with a great amount of disgust. I wasn't too fond of the bastard either, having heard of the things the noble of Malvene liked to do to our kind.

King Ludovico nodded. "*Sì*. That man has nothing but ill intentions when it comes to your kind. He's quite the zealot as well. There's been rumors in the last couple years that he is not particularly happy with me. I think it would be wise to remove him, strip him of his wealth and power. Let his influence fall away into history and bring a new voice to the forefront in his place."

Queen Sophia took a sip of her tea before leaning back in her chair. She was slouching now, struggling to keep her regal posture. "But who would you replace him with? You would have to be sure that the man or woman would not challenge your new views on how to run the country. Maybe the Duke of Tordoro? Not the kindest man I have heard of, but there is a lack of any stories about him that paint the man in the same, cruel light that Francesco Ventossa resides in."

King Ludovico smiled. "I was thinking of someone else. Someone whose views I know are more aligned with my own."

The King of Malvene looked at Quaid. The large satyr stared at him in confusion for a moment before glancing back at Sophia and me. He shook his head, his curly locks bouncing around his big, curved horns. "No way. No thank you."

"Why not?" Queen Sophia asked. "You've done a good job as the leader of The Resistance group here in Malvene. Perhaps it would be even better for you and the country if you led one of its main cities."

Quaid closed his eyes, rubbing them before massaging the horns on his head. "Forgive me if I heard wrong, Queen Sophia, but weren't you just pushing for us to not make sudden, drastic changes that would piss a lot of people off? Because making me the Duke of Azuvipa is probably the last thing you want to do if you want to avoid trouble."

Sophia grimaced as she tried to shift in her seat. She had been visibly growing more and more uncomfortable as this conversation went on. "It is a massive change, and perhaps it is coming too quickly, but King Ludovico knows his people better than we do. Every country is different. Perhaps Malvene needs a drastic change for things to move forward."

"I agree," I announced. "I will admit that it worries me what might come after such a change, but maybe once the common people experience the good that you'll end up doing for them, they'll begin to accept you. Religious extremists and stubborn nobles will always be a problem for all of us, whether we're in positions of power or not. At least as Duke, you'll be able to keep things relatively under control. Having the full support of King Ludovico would also make things easier. It's not like you're taking control of the city, it's being given to you legally."

The muscular Tórán adjusted his position in his chair as he thought about what his allies had said. He appeared to be warming up to the idea of it all, shown by his random smirks as he looked up at the ceiling. There was no doubt in my mind he was realizing all the good he could do. However, when Quaid looked like he was beginning to respond, he didn't appear to be too happy. He looked troubled, worried even. Probably nervous too. King Ludovico picked up on this as well and spoke up before Quaid could.

"Look, I know it's a lot to take on," the King of Malvene said. "I would be lying if I wasn't even a little worried myself of what the reaction to this will be. However, I promise you that I will do whatever I can to ensure your safety. Members of my own personal guard, a personal witch maybe? You could even bring people you trust into your court if you wanted to. Whatever you need, I'll do my very best to provide it. *Hai la mia parola.*"

Quaid took a couple minutes to take in what the King of Malvene had just offered him, until finally he gave us all an answer. "If you all truly think this is a good decision, and you can guarantee I'll have your support when I need it, then I will accept this new position. However!" There was a collective groan let out by the rest of the people in the room. "I won't take up my position as soon as you all may want me to."

King Ludovico rolled his eyes. "And just when do you plan on taking up this position? The longer that vile man is in power, the more damage he does to your kind. I can't get rid of him without someone to take his place, so he stays in power until you accept the position."

Quaid grinned. "Someone will take his place. Just not me. Not yet anyway. I move that my dearest and closest friend Ezio watch over Azuvipa for me while I continue on with The Resistance." The satyr locked eyes with me now. "You helped my people. I owe it to you to stand with you and assist you in helping yours."

"Are you sure? Ezio is a little young, isn't he?" I asked.

Quaid laughed. "He may not be as mature in age as you or me, but I trust the man with my life. I need to see the rest of this campaign through, so I need to have someone I trust stay back to watch over things while I'm gone. This dinner is to discuss terms, right? Well, those are mine."

King Ludovico was hesitant, but when Sophia began her coughing fit his face changed to a look of compassion. He could see that Sophia needed to rest, and that this conversation needed to come to an end soon. The King of Malvene waited until Sophia's cough passed and we were all sure she was alright before he spoke up.

"I accept your terms," he announced. "Your friend Ezio will take leadership of Azuvipa away from Francesco and retain it until your return. Should some horrible outcome occur and you fail to return, then Ezio will be named Duke in your place."

That last bit put a smile on Quaid's face, no doubt addressing a worry he probably had about all of this. King Ludovico turned his head to address Sophia and I next. "With that settling that bit of business, I have one more thing to offer you. I cannot offer much, and my general is dead, but Malvene will send as many soldiers as we can spare to join The Resistance. To be completely honest with you, I never liked General Rosspier. Mind you I didn't like the man he overthrew either. What I'm trying to say is that I think Fleuris, and the rest of the world, will be a better place when that man isn't in a position of power. However that happens, I don't care. It's late and I believe we could all use some rest. Keep soldiers here if you wish to, but please, stay here for the night. Riding back to your camp in your state is dangerous for your health."

Sophia smiled. "That is an offer I will not hesitate to accept. Thank you, Ludovico. This night has turned out to be one of the more pleasant times I think we've all had in the last few weeks. I only wish that we could have avoided the bloodshed that preceded this moment."

King Ludovico adopted a somber expression. "So do I. But our intentions were unknown before tonight. As I have said earlier, we cannot change the past, but we can make a better future. I hope that our alliance made here today continues on for generations after our deaths."

"I'll drink to that." Quaid raised his glass of wine and downed what remained.

King Ludovico called for someone to come guide us to our rooms. He instructed one of the first people who showed themselves to inform those out in the courtyard what was going on. I wasn't sure if Lady Mirlena would spend the night here without Arthur, and I wondered if I really wanted to sleep here too, so far from Rosalie. General Wyman would obviously stay with his Queen, and Brina would go wherever I went. Whoever made whatever decision, whether to stay or go, it didn't really matter. Sophia was going to stay here tonight, and I think that was the best decision to make. I don't think she could handle the ride back to camp. I had a thought that she would be safe here with General Wyman and the soldiers we had brought, but I couldn't bring myself to make the decision to leave Sophia's side. Rosalie would be upset, but my place was here tonight. Even with all the happy smiles and joyous reactions to terms being agreed upon, I still couldn't fully bring myself to trust King Ludovico just yet. The man seemed reasonable and honest, but I remembered the stories Ossian had told me the last time I was here. The man in those stories contradicted the one I had met.

As I followed the maid that was leading Sophia to a room, I reminded myself of something King Ludovico had spoken about. The stories about me were exaggerated and false, so perhaps the stories about King Ludovico were also not to be trusted. I abandoned trying to decide on whether I trusted the King of Malvene to stand by his promises in favor of a more welcoming thought. Thinking of the old satyr had me wishing to see Ossian while we were in Leonessa. As the door to a decent sized room was opened and I helped Sophia into the warm bed, I thought about my old friend and how proud he would be of us for what had transpired in the last couple days. I told myself to remember to have us stop by his home before we left Leonessa tomorrow. Bringing the sheets up to Sophia's chin as her eyes closed and she drifted off to sleep, I remembered the few letters Ossian had sent me over the months. I smiled when I thought of the idea of talking to him in person again.

"Your room is just this way, sir," The maid announced as she pointed to the door.

I grabbed a chair from the nearby desk and brought it next to the bed. "That won't be necessary. Thank you, though."

The maid bowed her head and left the room. Something Ossian had said in one of his letters came to the forefront of my mind, and I couldn't help but smile.

*"The revolution is alive and well, my dear friend! We'll see a new day rise soon and I'll be happy to say that I helped make it happen. I'm proud of you, Weylyn. I'm sure your mother and father are too. Stay strong, and long live The Resistance!"*

# Chapter Fifty-Nine

## Olwen



It had taken only a couple days or so for Soan to return and tell me where The Dove was. It took a few more days after that for me to honor my agreement with Keagan. I was still weak at the time, but after as much rest as I could stomach, I was leaving the cover of the trees and making my way to Cloque. Soan said The Dove had supposedly been in her room for weeks now. Nobody knew what she would do in there, but everyone knew it wasn't anything good. No more information was given to me, save which window led to the witch's room and when was best to sneak onto the grounds.

I kept my hood up and my head down as I slithered through the city's streets until I reached my destination, luckily avoiding the soldiers that patrolled late at night. It was very late, an hour before midnight if the watch Soan had given me was correct, when I surveyed the area. Tall, iron bars rose up about fifteen feet high, forming a tall fence all around the estate. The back of the palace, which was practically on the street, was impossible to enter from. I was to go through the Royaux Gardens, the large area of trees, flower beds, and open grass south of the palace. The trees could provide me some cover — perhaps the bushes of flowers would conceal me too — but I had to make my move at the right moment if I was to be successful. Four groups of six soldiers each patrolled the Royaux Gardens, while a fifth group of six guarded the main entrance into the palace. That was the case, until eleven o'clock.

At eleven o'clock, the groups of soldiers went from five to three. The majority of the city was asleep or so drunk they couldn't walk properly around this time, so I guess they assumed they didn't need as many guards patrolling. Whatever the reason was for the change, it only benefited me. I watched all five groups of soldiers enter the building, as only three came out to relieve their fellow guards. The fresh soldiers took up their positions amongst the fancy garden and I took my eye off the spyglass. The lowered number of soldiers were probably still more than I could handle. I wouldn't be able to take them all out before someone would sound the alarm. I had to be smart. The six guards at the entrance to the palace weren't really my concern. It was the two patrolling units that would give me trouble. They were spaced out about fifty feet apart in a straight line, stretching across the width of the Royaux Gardens. The line of soldiers themselves were apart from each other by at least forty feet. The guards marched along their imaginary lines back and forth with lanterns in hand and rifles ready to fire on anyone they spotted. I took a deep breath, convinced myself that I was ready for this, and bolted out from the cover of the alley I was in like a racehorse. I leaped onto the iron fence, slipping at first before managing to get a proper grip on the bars. I climbed over as quickly as I could and landed quite gracefully on the other side. I let a small grin wash across my face, happy to see that the rest Keagan had forced on me was well worth it. Low to the ground, I surveyed the area ahead of me. Tall trees bordered a fair-sized pond nearby. I rushed to the cover of the trees and looked out ahead at the patrols.

There was no way I would be able to take even one of them out without the others noticing soon after. I had to sneak by them; a challenge I was happy to accept. I waited until the soldiers made their way to the eastern section of the Royaux Gardens and sprinted to the western side before diving into the grass. Laying there, I watched the soldiers begin their march towards me. All I had to do was remain still and hope they didn't spot my prone body nearby. I prayed that the darkness from the night and the earthy shades of clothing I wore were enough to keep me hidden. The soldiers marched by, but the light of their lanterns didn't reach me. They turned around and began their trek back to the east and I jumped to my feet as soon as they were far enough to not hear me running. I got to the next line of defense after diving into the grass halfway there. The gardens were more open here, with bushes much too small to hide behind as the only spot of cover. Eventually, the tactic I had used for the first patrol worked on the second and I made my way to the window Soan had described to me as The Dove's. Lanterns were placed around the immediate grounds of the palace, which meant I could be spotted by even the first patrol I had evaded. I had to enact the next part of my plan perfectly.

I pulled out a small pouch and tied it around my knife. I said a silent prayer to whoever would listen that Maria wasn't a bad witch before I squeezed the pouch. The loud crunch I was told to listen for reached my ears and I smiled; so far so good. I quickly aimed my knife and threw it at the wall as hard as I could, the blade lodging itself into the wooden pole that the lantern was hanging on. The force that Maria had claimed would burst from the pouch released and snuffed out the flame in the nearby lantern. The soldiers would no doubt notice this and come over to light it again. I only had about a minute until that happened. I sprinted over and quickly unwound the rope around my waist. I spun the metal claw at the end of it next to me before throwing it at the roof, the iron grasping onto one of the ornate designs that littered the outer walls of the palace. With the end of the rope tied around my waist so that nothing would be left behind for the guards to spot, I quickly began to climb up the building. I moved past two windows before reaching a third one. I pushed it open, just like Soan said I would be able to, and crawled inside.

The room was completely dark. So many different aromas flooded my nostrils, but there was one scent I hadn't expected to smell: blood. I wondered what I had gotten myself into as I removed the rope from my waist and took out a magic torch Maria had made for me, yet another useful magical trinket that I was thankful for. I licked my finger and rubbed it against the symbol painted on the thin log. I knew the symbol was disrupted when a small burst of magical flame ignited on the end of the torch. It wasn't as bright as a usual torch, but it was enough light for me to begin looking around the place. The walls were covered in herbs I recognized — things like sage and lavender easy to spot by a trained eye — but I was surprised to find things that confused me. They appeared to be plants and weeds that my mother had told me about when I was younger. One of them was a Lunum, a pale flower with crescent petals. My mother had one of them, telling me that it had been passed down by her family for multiple generations. She kept it in a simple cloth, folded and flattened between the pages of a book her grandmother had used to write multiple folk tales in Séúbua. How The Dove had come by the flower was a mystery, and it made me upset that she would possess things that — in my eyes — belonged to my kind and my kind alone.

"What are you doing?"

The voice had me spin around with my knife in my hand. Someone had entered the room without making a sound, or someone had been in here the whole time without me knowing. Either way, I knew who it was. I stood my ground and addressed the shadows. "How do you have Lunum flowers? They aren't for you. Nothing from my world is for you."

Light suddenly filled the room as multiple lanterns lit themselves. I realized the size of the place was larger than I had thought it was, and my stomach lurched when I saw what else was in the room. A desk nearby surrounded by countless vials of red liquid that must have been responsible for the smell I had noticed when I entered through the window. A bed was on the far wall across from where I stood, and across from the vials, at the front of the room by the closed door, stood a woman in white leather armor and a large white cloak. She had a pale mask covering half of her face, and her blue eyes shown in the glow of the small flames surrounding us. The Dove smiled at me.

"You're one of them then? Come now, show me which one you are. You're much too short to be a hound and your head is too tiny to be a goat. No wings as far as I can tell. Too tall to be a gnome. You must be one of those vile faeries. Horns or gills?"

I tossed the hood off my head to reveal my features in a display of pride and defiance. "What are you doing with my people's blood?"

The Dove stood there and stared at me until the small smile on her face twisted into something unpleasant. I could see anger in her eyes and before I knew it, I was pushed back so hard I nearly fell out the window. Catching my balance before that happened proved useful as The Dove followed up her magical attack with a physical one. Keeping my balance allowed me to barely move out of the way of a knife aimed for my face. My back fell into the wall behind me hard and my eyes opened wide as the witch was pointing at me with her empty hand. I lunged to my right just as a small fireball exploded from the witch's fingers and flew into the stone wall where I had been. I drew my sword with my free hand and adopted a backhanded grip on my knife. The Dove smirked, drawing her sword and choosing a backhanded grip on her second blade as well. "Always so confident. The ego of your kind is limitless. To think you could invade my privacy and get away with it. I knew you were here the moment you entered the grounds."

"I didn't come here just to invade your privacy." I began stepping to my left, which caused The Dove to step to her right. We began circling each other when the woman laughed.

"Oh you didn't come here to kill me, did you? Just you? I knew most of you lacked a certain level of intelligence, but this is truly the plan of an idiot. The only person that's going to die here tonight is you."

The Dove closed the distance between us at a remarkable speed, telling me she must have enhanced herself with magic. Her speed was unnatural, and it took all my skill and training to muster up a feasible defense. A clumsy parry led into a pain in my arm thanks to her knife. The Dove took a couple steps back before jumping at me again. Once more I barely defended, managing to fend off two strikes this time before her knife slid across my ribs. The Dove took a couple steps back again and pointed at my face with her knife hand.

"What's that scar on your face?" she asked. "It's quite odd. Did you mark yourself up like that?"

Anger filled me as I thought of the man responsible for the reminder left on my cheek. The Dove must have noticed this because she chuckled and relaxed her stance.

"You let someone do that to you?" she said before letting out a taunting chuckle. "Oh, by The Light your kind is weak."

I let out a guttural growl as I lunged forward, stabbing with my sword before spinning and swiping with my knife. The anger and pain I had deep inside me began to boil and the rage I felt propelled me forward. The Dove had lazily dodged and parried my blows at first, but I ended up forcing her back up against the wall before grazing her stomach with a swing of my sword. I felt it cut into her leather armor, but there was no blood on my blade. Her armor had done its job, yet I could tell that the attack had changed her. The witch's cloak began to sway in a wind that I couldn't feel right before a force sent me flying backwards. My back hit the stone wall hard, knocking the air from my lungs. I knew my enemy would be on me quickly, so I struggled to my feet. I wasn't fast enough this time, and I only managed to slightly deflect her sword. The blade entered the far right of my stomach. She ripped the steel out of me, and I struggled to keep my footing. My mind flashed quickly to Weylyn, and then Keagan. The faces of Rosalie and Brina came next, followed by Anya and Finn. The others at Camp Liodorleu showed themselves and I remembered their loss all over again. I thought of how my friends would have to mourn me and inflicting that pain on them became something I could not allow. The responsibility I felt to keep them all safe, along with the love I had for all of them, gave me a surge of energy.

Feeling the newfound strength within me, I lunged at an opponent who had thought the fight was over. I hounded her with strike after strike, the two of us dancing with our blades across every bit of the room. Eventually I caught The Dove again, but this time I drew blood. A low swipe to her leg with my knife brought forth a contrasting red streak to her white clothing. The injury provoked a growl from The Dove, along with a flurry of unexpected attacks of her own. We dueled again until both of us had cuts and bruises. A brief break in the action had us staring each other down. I was exhausted, but The Dove had barely broken a sweat. She must have noticed this because she smirked as she lunged at me again. Too tired to keep pace with her strikes, I received a throbbing pain in my leg as the entirety of her knife plunged into it. She ripped it out and I tried to follow up with a stab of my own, but she swatted my knife out of my hand. Hobbling, I tried my best to defend myself until the witch promptly disarmed me. I was exposed, but not yet dead. I made one last attempt at an attack with nothing but my fists, which only led into a swift counter punch to my face. I could taste blood now as the blow knocked me to my knees. I tried to get up, but my body was being restricted.

Without my intention, my body was brought upward. The Dove was a good bit taller than I was, but she wanted our eyes to meet. My feet hovered over the floor as The Dove stretched her neck. With a loud sigh, her bright blue eyes locked onto me. "You may be stupid, but you have strength. It didn't do you much good though. Any last words?"

I spat in her face. Blood and saliva sprayed on her mask mixing red with white. Her tongue moved over some that had fallen on her lips, and she spat at the floor in dramatic fashion. When she looked up at me her eyes were wide with shock. "Mystic Blood."

With me still hovering in place, she took more of the blood I had spat at her and licked it off her finger. Again, she spat out what she had tasted emphatically.

"All that time searching, and you ended up coming to me yourself," The Dove said with a smile. "Oh, this is perfect. Now I don't have to wait for that bastard Weylyn to show up."

I perked up at his name. "Why would you be after Weylyn?"

The Dove must have spotted the concern in my voice because she grabbed my face and pouted at me. "Aw is he a friend of yours? Don't worry. Now that I have you, I won't be needing him. He'll just have to die like everyone else."

Something bubbled up inside me before bursting out. The thought of this evil woman killing Weylyn sent a rush of energy into me again and it erupted into a wave of wind that pushed The Dove back and released me from her spell. I rushed forward and grabbed at her head, hoping to strangle her. We struggled, and the hood of her cloak fell off. I recoiled as if the woman was made of fire. I couldn't believe what I was seeing. There was no way it was possible.

"You...you're an elf."

The Dove reached out at me, and I felt all control over my body vanish again. I floated back to her, and she opened her arms wide, a dramatic smile on her face. Her eyes were now a deep maroon, piercing and malicious. "That I am! And I am here to finish what my kind started."

"But...how?" I asked. "How did you get here? Why follow us? You won."

Her eyes squinted, which had me imagining a great scowl taking over her face. "You think you're the only ones that can use magic? The only ones that could create those bridges between our two worlds? It was difficult, and it took us many decades, but we finally found out how to do it ourselves. The only problem was we needed your blood to do it. A couple more decades past until we found one of you. A hound. The few of you left in our world were keeping him hidden in the mountains. We captured him and used the beast to open the bridge. You see, we only win when you're all gone."

"But we left!" I shouted.

The Dove shook my head. "You escaped! Running away from our divine cleansing. So long as you survived elsewhere, you were a threat to our beloved Solas. You had to be eliminated."

"You really think that one of you is going to kill all of us? I almost killed you myself." I forced a grin, knowing the claim would piss her off.

The elf swung the back of her hand into my face. "Arrogance! Dorcha's children reek of it! I'm not going to fight you on my own. I'm just a scout. A messenger of sorts. A champion, if you like. The filth we used was old and the magic in his blood was so weak thanks to him being near death when we found him. We could only open one portal. I was chosen to come here to find more of those with Mystic Blood so I could open more portals and bring my army here to finish what we started. Thanks to you, I have what I need. This world will burn as we purge Dorcha's beasts from it."

The detestation in her voice confused me. "Why do you hate us so much? We never did anything to you."

"Oh, but you did." The Dove slowly removed her mask, revealing scarred skin that covered a large portion of her face. "Your kind did this to me, and even worse things to many others. You are *deamhain* made by Dorcha, *Dia an Dorchadais*, to mock and destroy those made by Solas, *Bana-dia an t-Solais*. You are our enemy

— my enemy — and I would follow you all to *Anslocdubh* itself if it meant ending your existence.”

I wanted to shake my head in disbelief, but her magic kept me where I was. “I always thought The Dove was crazy. I’m not too happy to find out I was right.”

The elf smiled, the act scrunching up the scar on her face. “The Dove? That is not who I am. I am Nylathari, Member of House Solana, Daughter of Queen Alavara and Champion of Solas. Your kind feared my name long ago, and I’ll make sure everyone in this world fears it again. Your kind, humans, it doesn’t matter. The way I see it, you’re all just as evil as the other. Dorcha spawned you all, infecting my world and this one. I’ll see to it that both worlds are purified, and you’re going to help me do that.”

Nylathari went over to the desk and picked up an empty vial. She sliced my hand open with her knife and collected the blood that fell out of the wound. After cleaning her knife on my clothes, she sheathed the weapon and shoved a cork into the vial before placing it in a pocket in her cloak.

I did my best to struggle, which actually had me break enough of the spell to move a bit. Nylathari caught sight of my small victory and gave me a hard punch on the side of my head. The spell broke and I fell to my knees. I was dazed, but I refused to die quietly. “Kill me if you want. You won’t win. Even if you do bring the elves here. You can’t beat all of us.”

Nylathari came down to my level and grabbed me by my hair. She jerked my head back so I was looking at her. “So eager to die. No, I’ll keep you alive for now. I don’t know exactly how much of your blood I’ll need just yet, so best to harvest as much as I can for a while.” The elf put her mask on her face and brought the pale hood over her head. “Guards! Someone’s in my room! Guards!”

She stood up and went to turn away from me. Desperately, I grabbed at her cloak and tried to stand. Nylathari spun around and hit me hard in the side of my head again. My ears rang and the room twisted before my eyes as I fell to the ground. All the energy I had was gone. My vision was blurry. I struggled to stay conscious, but all my injuries were catching up to me. I heard the door open before Nylathari ordered for the soldiers to take me to Bastion. My last thoughts were of Weylyn before pain and injury took me, causing everything to go black.

# Chapter Sixty

## Olwen

Cloque, Fleuris  |  July 20, 1799

I woke up to the sound of horses walking on cobbled roads. My wrists felt restricted, and my head felt like someone was sitting on it. Before I even thought to open my eyes, I knew I was in a carriage. The jostling gave it away. My eyes fluttered until I saw that my hands were bound by heavy, iron shackles. They were connected to the floor by a chain that would keep me bound to the carriage until we reached our destination. I was dizzy and my vision was still a little blurry, but I remembered what was going on. I was being taken to Bastion, where Nylathari would drain me of my blood like a cow was drained of its milk. Knowing full well that the process would not be as simple as cutting my hand, I was preparing myself for more torture. Perhaps I would find an opening one day and manage to kill the elf. It was the only positive thought I managed to have as I stared down at the bottom of the carriage.

The sound of horse's hooves hitting stone began to fall away into nothing as my mind slipped into the past, and the elf's image came before my eyes. There was no mistaking what she was. Even if she hadn't admitted to it, her ears were long and pointed just like the stories said. The revelation of her dark red eyes only added to the list of evidence that marked her as not human. Mix that with her incredible speed and her skill with magic and it all came together. It was maybe a bit silly of me to do so, but I grew angry with myself for not realizing this sooner. I felt like I should have known somehow. Maybe things would have turned out differently if I had.

Our conversation acted itself out in my head over and over as I made sure to remember every single word the elf had said. I didn't want to miss anything in case I ever escaped. I doubted I would ever forget those words though. The insanity and hatred behind every syllable Nylathari spoke reminded me of the story my grandmother used to tell me. It was about the time a group of elves had kidnapped her great grandfather back in the old world. I was young, and I remember being absolutely terrified of the elves. They were vicious, spiteful extremists who didn't like multiple races back home. It wasn't just those who had escaped to this world. Many more were eradicated before the elves had convinced other races — like the dwarves — to destroy us. Most notable among the elves' enemies were the giants, who were the dominant force in our world hundreds of generations ago before the elves overthrew them. Going through my knowledge of our world's history led me to something that I hadn't really had time to process all that much.

Mystic Blood was barely talked about in my family, but my grandmother had told me about it. She mentioned it in some of her stories. Mystic Blood was something that gifted the lesser races the ability to wield magic. It was different from the magic that higher races were given, and that led to the higher races such as elves, dwarves, and centaurs waging war with us. Giants were the only ones that supposedly had the ability to be born with Mystic Blood and what the higher races called Refined Blood. It's why the giants ruled for so long. They kept the peace until the elves took over, leading to a short war with the dwarves until they became allies. It wasn't until the elves convinced the centaurs to attack us too that our lives were in true peril. The elves convinced others that Mystic Blood was evil and needed to be removed. From that moment on, war raged across every corner of our world. It wasn't until great Druids of our races came together and found us a way to escape those who hunted us.

The Druids were the ones who possessed Mystic Blood. They were responsible for watching over their tribe as well as passing on the stories of history. With my grandmother knowing so much about everything to do with our world, it would make sense that she came from a line of Druids; this meant my mother was also of the same line. I was angry at both of them for not telling me about our family history for only a moment before I wisely understood why they had kept that part of their lives a secret. Not only had humans targeted people like her during the Great Welcoming and onward, but it turns out that an elf had come looking for us too. I was even more angry with myself for disobeying my mother now than I was before. Her fears when it came to recklessness when I was young made so much more sense now. She didn't want any attention brought to our family. What a fool I was. Now, I was all that was left of my family's Mystic Blood, and I was about to give it all to Nylathari. I hated myself for not winning our fight, but I also had a small sense of relief.

Discovering Weylyn had Mystic Blood was something to digest, but I was happy that Nylathari hadn't caught him. Knowing that he wouldn't have to endure the torture that I would be subject to made me feel a little better about the situation I was in. Weylyn was strong, and those around him made the lycan even stronger. I loved him and believed in him. Perhaps I would die soon, and Nylathari would be successful in bringing the elves and their allies to this world, but I knew that Weylyn had the strength to stop them. I always knew that one day he would bring about true change to this world. If anyone could unite humans and Tóráin to face this new enemy, it was him. With Weylyn alive, we stood a chance. An image of Weylyn killing Nylathari gave me a reason to smile. I raised my head to look out the window of the carriage only to discover there weren't any. The light was coming from a lantern sitting next to a soldier on the opposite side of where I was seated. He was in the royal blue uniform of Fleuris, hat and all, with his right hand resting on his pistol. A thick mustache covered his upper lip and the soft glow from the lantern helped him show off a truly sour expression.

"Don't you even think of trying anything, *Diable*," he said. "One wrong move and I'll put a hole in you."

The warning was no doubt meant to keep me in my place, but I knew that I was of no value to Nylathari dead. After a quick inspection I had discovered that the wound to my stomach had been healed. My other injuries were left as they were, with the wound on my leg being the most painful. Still, this showed me that I was more valuable alive than dead, so I didn't pay any mind to the soldier's threat. The carriage hit a large bump in the road causing us both to bounce in the air. A jingling sound caught my attention, bringing my eyes to a set of keys on the belt of the soldier assigned to me. The despair that had overcome me began to fade, and a tinge of hope creeped into my heart. I thought up a plan to escape, feeling confident in trying it out because I believed they wouldn't kill me for doing so. Not knowing how much time I had left, I quickly began coughing. The guard didn't flinch until I started gagging and choking from the coughs I was forcing out of myself. Despite my discomfort and the lack of air I was getting into my lungs, I continued on.

"Hey!" the man shouted. "Hey now! You stop that!"

I heard him cock his pistol, so I leaned back from my hunched over position to fake a gasp for air. I was only upright for a moment to see where he was holding his gun before I began coughing again, hunching over once more until I eventually stopped my fit and went limp. I fell forward, my head hitting the man's knees quite hard, and waited.

"Hey. Hey!" The guard jostled me, cursing when I didn't respond. "Oh The Dove is going to kill me. *Espèce de Diable stupide*! Don't die on me. I'll be damned if I'm killed because of you."

The soldier turned me over and I quickly sprung into action. Opening my eyes, I spotted his pistol right away. Putting my shackled hands on either side of his wrist, I crossed them over and twisted as hard as I could. A loud snap instead of a gunshot told me I had successful snapped the man's wrist. His pistol fell to the floor of the carriage as I used my flexibility to reach my legs up above me. I wrapped them around the soldier's neck as he struggled to fend me off. It only took a few moments more until I got the positioning I needed to squeeze my legs as tight as I could. My injuries from my fight with Nylathari screamed, but I held firm. The man began scratching at my legs until he passed out, the lack of air rendering him unconscious. I released him from my grip and spun myself around so I was on my knees. Quickly, I made for the keys at his hip and put the first key in my mouth. The key didn't work for either of my wrists, so I fumbled quickly for the other one. With the irons up at my face, I used my teeth and my tongue to maneuver the key until I heard a click and the iron clasped around my left wrist fell off. I did the same for my right and then went to steal the soldier's pistol and sword. I took his coat and hat as well, hoping that it would provide me a way to disappear once I escaped the caravan taking me to Bastion. I took a deep breath and told myself that this would be my best chance to escape. Before I managed to gather the courage to open the carriage door, I heard gunshots and orders being shouted.

I waited a moment before I opened the door just as a man screamed. In front of me was a Fleuris soldier who was bleeding profusely from his neck. A large, copper colored lycan was holding him still with his large hands. Blood covered his jaws as it dripped down to the red stained cobblestones. I had a thought of who it was, but it was dark and I wasn't sure if I was hallucinating. How could he have known where I was? The lycan spotted me and tossed the corpse away before shifting into its tame form. I felt tears fill my eyes as the man rushed forward and plucked me from the carriage, squeezing me in his big arms.

"O'! Gods you're okay!" Keagan put me down and held me straight with both hands on my shoulders as he looked me over. "You are okay, right? Can you run?"

I was still trying to comprehend what was going on. "Keagan, how are you here? Who's watching everyone back at camp? How did you even know I was in there?"

Keagan smiled before giving me another rough, quick hug. "Finn is back at camp. I'm sorry O', but I couldn't let you go alone. Me and a few others followed you into Cloque in case you needed help. You could imagine how glad I was that I came when we spotted you gettin' tossed into a carriage. The Dove told the soldiers to take you to Bastion immediately. We quickly ran off to set up an ambush and here we are."

The mention of The Dove had me scrambling for words. "Keagan! The Dove! She isn't who we think she is. She's worse. She's —'

Keagan cut me off. "O'! O'! When we're safe you can talk my ears off for weeks, but right now, we don't have any time for it. We're closer to Bastion than I wanted to be. No doubt they heard the gunshots. We have to go. Now can you run or not?"

I went to continue what I was saying before he had cut me off, but I stopped myself. If we were close to Bastion, Keagan was right. We needed to leave. I went to take a step forward but the wound in my thigh from Nylathari's knife had me limping. Keagan spotted this and quickly grabbed my hand. Without saying a word, he guided me to get on his back, my arms wrapping around his neck. He shifted into his feral form and sprinted on all fours away from the remnants of the ambush. Others followed after him, about five or so I think, and off we went into the night. I thought about how mad Nylathari would be about losing me, and I smiled.

# Chapter Sixty-One

## Weylyn



I had grown accustomed to waking up this early, but the way my morning had started made it difficult to stay awake. A bad headache informed me that I had drank too much last night. Quaid and Cordelia were a bad influence in that regard. Even with the throbbing behind my eyes, I didn't regret doing it. A group of us had gathered around a fire and properly enjoyed each other's company. We felt victorious, and it wasn't too proud of us to do so. We had achieved so much already, and instead of looking at the next obstacle in our path like we had been doing for months now, we decided to enjoy what we had overcome. Of course, that enjoyment had consequences, and one of them was snoring very loudly next to me.

Rosalie was never much of a drinker, but last night she had tried to keep pace with everyone else. Brina had tried to get her to stop, being the only sober one in the group, but my favorite person in this world decided she wasn't going to listen to anyone. As expected, she eventually passed out which brought our small party to an end. I carried her back to our tent and laid her down under the blankets. She had woken up then and encouraged me to join her for some romantic fun. It was clumsy because of how drunk we both were, but I never needed much convincing to enjoy any intimate moments with Rosalie. Thanks to my headache forcing my eyes shut and Rosalie snoring with her head and hand on my chest, it appeared as though more rest was in my future.

I had almost fallen back to sleep when a tired voice broke the spell I was under. "Weylyn? Are you awake?"

I kept my eyes closed and smiled. "No."

Rosalie pulled on my chest hair causing me to twitch. "Don't be smart with me, or it'll be no more fun for you."

I opened my eyes and looked down at the woman I have loved for more than a decade. Her red hair was out of its usual braid and strewn all about her shoulders and back. The lack of light in our tent tried to dampen the sparkle in her olive eyes, but it failed miserably. She had a mischievous smirk on her face as she slowly slid her hand up and down my chest.

I smiled back. "No more fun for me means no more fun for you, and we both know you couldn't last without it."

Rosalie adopted a shocked expression before sending a playful glare my way. "Is Lord Weylyn suggesting that his Lady needs him to please herself?"

"That's not what I said," I countered through a laugh.

Rosalie brought the playful smile back as she moved her hand up beside my head. She slid her body onto mine, her legs brushing up against my own. Her chest grazed mine as she held herself above me with her hands planted firmly on either side of my head. The stunning features of her face were tantalizingly close to mine, our noses practically touching and our lips so close only a paper page from a book could possibly pass between them. Her eyes stared into mine for a moment before looking down towards the imminent kiss we both knew we would share.

"You need me more than I need you," she whispered. "Admit it, and we can move on with this morning's festivities."

I chuckled. "Are you still drunk?"

Rosalie lowered herself so that her chest firmly rested on mine, but she kept her face where it was. Her hand came up to my face, the woman's slender fingers brushing up against my bearded cheek before venturing into the thicket of my hair. "I need to be drunk to crave intimacy with someone I love? Just do as I say, damn you. Or would you rather I go back to sleep?"

I couldn't take it anymore and leaned upward so our lips met. Her hair fell onto me like a waterfall as she pushed herself up again, maneuvering her legs so that they were on either side of my hips. I broke free of our kissing for only a moment to oblige her request. "Okay. I admit it."

Rosalie continued to kiss me in between her response. "Admit what?"

She ran her fingers through my hair, and I brought my hands up onto her bare hips before answering. "I need you more than you need me."

Her hips began to move and we enjoyed each other's company in an intimate whirlwind of movement. It wasn't as clumsy this time around, and as we went on, I felt my headache begin to fade away. We went on for some time until we came to a stop with both of us on our left side. My left arm under her and my right arm over her, I held her close as she pushed her body into mine. My head rested on hers, strands of red hair tickling my nose. We were breathing heavily, happy to remain in the position we were in until we recovered. Rosalie eventually began shifting herself, turning over so she was facing me. She brought her leg over my hip and cuddled into my chest. With my hand on her thigh, I kissed her forehead. After slowly walking my hand up the curves of her body, I reached her head and began stroking her hair. We stayed like that for some time until I realized how much light was coming through our tent. It was well past sunrise, and as much as I wanted to stay where I was, I had promised Lady Mirlena that my choices last night would not stop me from meeting with her the following morning. I let out a deep sigh as I realized I had to bring this lovely moment to an end. Before I could say anything, a muffled voice from under my chin broke the silence.

"You should get going before Lady Mirlena scolds you," Rosalie said softly.

I chuckled as I put a small bit of distance between us so Rosalie could look up at me. A pleasant smile stretched across her face as I moved her hair out of the way so I could see her eyes better.

"You promised me you wouldn't be late!" I said in my best Lady Mirlena impression.

Rosalie laughed. "Don't ever let her hear that voice. It's so inaccurate she might take it as an insult."

"Well it wasn't meant to be a compliment," I said.

Rosalie playfully smacked my chest. "Don't be rude! She's done a lot for you. Go on now. Get dressed and head over there. She's probably been expecting you for some time now."

"What if I would rather stay here with you?" I went to kiss her, but the woman's hand covered my face and gently pushed me away.

"We'll have all the time in the world to have this moment when this is over," Rosalie said. "Your training with Lady Mirlena is important, especially with us getting closer to Fleuris. We'll need both of your magic in the coming days."

I sighed as I looked into her eyes. I quickly planted a kiss on her forehead before turning over and slipping out of the bed. I grabbed my pants and shoved a leg through. "Weird that we're going to be back."

Rosalie sat up, bringing the blankets up to cover herself. "I don't even know if weird is the right word."

I slipped on my boots and went over to a basin of water resting on a small table. After splashing my face a few times with the cold water, I dried myself off with my shirt before tossing it over my head and sliding my arms through. I climbed back into the makeshift bed and put my arm around Rosalie, prompting her to rest her head on my shoulder.

I squeezed Rosalie as I thought about what we were marching towards. "Maybe there isn't a right word for it. All I know is that we have incredible people fighting by our side, which gives this worried lycan a small bit of hope that we'll come out on top in the end."

"I'm glad that you still have hope," Rosalie said as she nuzzled into my neck. "Sometimes I wonder if you've lost it all. Maybe you're finally believing in yourself some more."

I gently moved her head so she was looking at me. "Maybe it's all your confidence rubbing off on me."

She smiled. "It's probably that. We both know you'd be insufferable without me showing you what a damn smile looks like. You know you don't always have to brood right?"

"I don't brood," I said.

Rosalie laughed before planting a kiss on my lips. "You brood. A lot. But I still love you."

I kissed her back. "I love you too."

We began kissing more and more until I felt the urge to lower Rosalie down onto the bed again. Before I could, she broke off the dance our lips were engaged in and kissed my forehead. "Go before you're even more late than you are."

I reluctantly left Rosalie's side and climbed back out of our makeshift bed. I wrapped my belt around my waist, the holsters for my pistol and sword vacant until I grabbed the weapons and put them in their places. I made my way for the opening of the tent and turned around before leaving. "I'll see you later. Make sure you eat something soon."

Rosalie had a sour look on her face. "I'm not a child, Weylyn."

"You sure? You drink like one." I laughed as I watched Rosalie's mouth open wide in shock.

Rosalie had a scowl on her face that made her look cuter instead of intimidating. "Weylyn, you leave before I hit you so hard you'll be asleep for a week."

"Only after you tell me you love me," I said with a cheeky smile.

Rosalie rolled her eyes, but she couldn't stop a smile from creeping onto her face. "After that comment? Fine. But only so I don't have to look at you anymore. I love you."

I put a hand on my heart and bowed my head. "And I love you."

Rosalie smirked. "Get out before I throw you out."

I didn't think it was wise to tease her anymore, so I just sent a warm smile her way before exiting the tent. The valley we were in was beautiful, and the weather so far had been clear for the last couple days. The open sky made it easy to spot the flock of birds flying in unison in the distance. They flew past the rising sun, already mostly clear of the summits of the surrounding mountains. I hurried over to Lady Mirlena's tent and hoped that she had slept in like she had a few days ago. It wasn't often, but every now and then I would bare witness the grumpy attitude of a woman who would be much happier sleeping. I wouldn't say she had necessarily slept in this morning, but when I arrived at her tent the witch was taking a kettle off the flame of a fire nearby. Making tea was the first thing she did when she woke up, so either she was making more — which was entirely possible judging how much of the stuff the woman drank — or I was lucky and she had just woken up. I chose not to ask, and just pretended like nothing was wrong.

"Good morning, Lady Mirlena," I said with a welcoming grin. "Sleep well?"

She held the kettle in both hands and looked at me with a grand scowl. "You're late."

I came forward and urged her to let me take the kettle from her. She reluctantly gave it up and I led us inside. "I'm sorry. We still have time for a lesson though, don't we?"

Lady Mirlena walked over to a small table and placed two cups in front of me, remaining silent until I poured us each some tea. "Not a magical one. Maybe a history lesson would better suit the time we have. To be completely honest, Arthur woke me up in the middle of the night due to a nightmare and it ruined my sleep. I'd much rather not have to use or deal with magic today anyway."

I took a sip of the warm tea before responding. "I didn't have much sleep either. History lesson it is then. May I ask whose history?"

Lady Mirlena waved for me to follow her, and we came to sit down on the blankets that made up her bed. We put pillows under us for comfort and the woman across from me took a deep breath before letting out an exaggerated exhale. She fixed the informal blue dress she was wearing before finally answering me. "I guess you could say our history judging it kind of involves both the Tóráin and humanity. To start, it would be good for me to know what you know about your kind. Tóráin and, more specifically, Druids."

I took a moment to think before answering. "Just the stuff that any Tórán probably knows. The elves in our world wanted us dead, so we were brought here by witches. Humans didn't like that, so the Great Welcoming happened. Then things got slightly better, and our lives have been an obstacle-filled, uphill, marathon ever since. Druids I think I heard of before, but Mystic Blood specifically was something I only recently learned about from the friend of mine you met back in Leonessa, Ossian. Mystic Blood allowed Druids to wield magic, and they were the ones responsible for opening all the portals for us to escape. Humans hate them even more than regular Tóráin so they don't really show themselves. Some don't even know that they have Mystic Blood, which was the group I fell into until a few months ago. That's all I have."

Lady Mirlena nodded her head. "Right. So, a general understanding. I'll better describe everything for you. I think it's important that you have this knowledge. I'll tell you more of what I know as the days go on, but for now a basic history lesson is good enough."

Curiosity urged me to ask my next question. "How do you know more about me and my kind than I do?"

The expression on Lady Mirlena's face became a bit grimmer before she responded. "You remember the lycan I told you about? The one who took me in when I was young?"

I took a sip of my tea and nodded. "Yes. Brigantia, right?"

"Right," Lady Mirlena said as she avoided my eyes. "You had asked me before how she taught me how to use magic. I think by now you can probably guess the answer to that question. Just in case that answer is eluding you, Brigantia had Mystic Blood. She told me only a few days into knowing her, and I kept her secret for years until Queen Sophia asked for me to tell her my story. Only you and her know this bit of information. I'd like to keep it that way."

"Of course," I said. "Was she a good teacher?"

Lady Mirlena smiled. "Yes. The most wonderful of teachers. She was an excellent role model as well. I craved her praise and did everything I could to be just like her. She was strong and brave, telling me stories about her when she was younger. She was also immensely kind and compassionate. Brigantia was like a second mother to me. I enjoyed every moment of every day with her until she left this world."

The last bit of what she said seemed to upset her. I didn't know if I should say anything, but my curiosity got the best of me, and I ended up blurting out a question anyway. "What happened? Sorry, you don't have to answer that."

The woman waved her hand at me. "No, no, it's fine. Brigantia, bless her heart, was taken from this world before her time. I had been living with her for nearly twelve years, and I was an excellent student. I had learned much and mastered a fair chunk of it. Brigantia called me the best achievement in her life. Oh, that made me so proud. Anyway, my skills in magic made me overconfident in my abilities. I liked your kind even before Brigantia took me in but living with her and hearing her stories had made me wish to help the Tóráin. One day, a goblin was being attacked in the street by a group of humans. I went to stop them, but one of them managed to shoot me in my leg. They took the opening and began kicking and beating me like they had been doing to the goblin. Suddenly, the attacks stopped. I looked up and they were all on the floor writhing in pain. Brigantia helped me to my feet, the poor goblin having succumbed to his injuries. Despite being nearly seventy, she lifted me up into her arms and carried me away. Her secret was out. She had used magic to save my life and people would be looking for us. We fled our home and went to a remote village in the far north of Tudrose. We were there for a year until we were discovered.

"It was late in the night when the person attacked us. I woke up to the sounds of fighting and rushed into Brigantia's room to find her fighting a well-built, lightly armored assailant. They were tossing spells back and forth in between taking swipes at each other with claws and steel. I joined the fight immediately, tipping the odds in our favor. With Brigantia's help, I sent the attacker fleeing into the night. However, my teacher and guardian had been badly injured. She had struck her head hard, and she remained asleep for a couple days before eventually passing away. I buried her in the frozen earth of northern Tudrose and made my way south. I had promised Brigantia when she first began teaching me that when she died, I would search for others with Mystic Blood and pass on the knowledge she had. The lycan had never had any children, not wishing to put them at risk like she had been. A week or so before the attack, she gave me this pendant to help me find people like her." Lady Mirlena handled the piece of metal that hung around her neck at all times. "It's almost like she knew what was going to happen."

I waited to see if she was going to say more, but when she didn't, I responded to her tale. "I'm sorry, Lady Mirlena. Did you ever find the person responsible?"

The woman sniffed before rubbing her nose and blinking away tears. "The person that was responsible is sitting in front of you. I was reckless and forced her to expose herself. The assassin coming after us was just the way the world responds to people like her. I've had my fill of this conversation. Shall we get to the lesson?"

I wanted to challenge her thinking but thought better of it. I just nodded instead. "Yes, of course. Where are we starting from?"

Lady Mirlena pointed at her cup, silently asking me if I wanted more tea, to which I shook my head in response. She stood up from her seated position and went over to the kettle, pouring herself another cup of tea. After taking a quick sip right after it was poured, she came back over to me and sat down.

"I guess we can start with how Tóráin and humans came to meet," she began. "Many believe that the witches were the first to open the gateway between our worlds, specifically members of the Grand Coven. What they don't know is that it was actually your kind who did it first. They eventually taught the witches they managed to connect with how to do it, providing them with the necessary ingredients. This led to some witches beginning to study the uses of human energy, a thing that had been forbidden previously. They began sacrificing people, using their energy to communicate with the people from your world."

The talk of draining people of their energy had me thinking back to what I had done to the Malvene general, and I became quite uncomfortable. Lady Mirlena seemed to notice, but before she could say anything I urged her to continue. "Didn't that upset the Grand Coven?"

Lady Mirlena gave me a look that told me she knew something was wrong, but she abandoned it and continued her lesson. "Yes, it did. Especially when they found out about the blood magic these witches were practicing. That was the main ingredient you see. Mystic Blood. Witches didn't have it in their bodies, so they had to use it in their spells to open the portals. Druids of your world gladly gave it to the witches, hoping to form an alliance with our world against those who oppressed them in theirs. It was why they were casting the magic they were casting. Your kind was looking for help. They could see the way things were going, what with the elves forming fresh alliances with dwarves, who are short, bearded people similar to goblins, and centaurs who are half horse creatures with the other half resembling elves. They are all members of what they liked to call the Higher Races. They all disliked members of the Lesser Races, but elves were beginning to radicalize everyone. Eventually, discussions began to happen between Druids and witches about some sort of alliance. It was shot down by the leaders of the Grand Coven, as well as the leaders of the human countries at the time. Things got worse where the Druids were, and a group of witches all across the known world hatched a plan to bring members of your kind here anyway.

"Druids were highly respected members of the community, functioning as the tribe's healers, generals, and monarchs. Other beings, such as minotaurs and trolls, were wiped out by the time the Druids of the races who exist in this world decided to flee. In order to do so, they needed immense amounts of energy. They gathered thousands in one place and asked for half of them to offer up their lives so that others could escape. With their enemies marching towards them, the sacrifices were made, and the Druids used their energy to open the portals across the world. You could imagine the horror that crept into their souls when they were greeted by The Great Welcoming."

I shook my head, struggling to imagine the fear the Tóráin must have had during that time. "They traded one genocide for another."

Lady Mirlena nodded. "Yes. The humans of Kosavros, as well as the lands to the east, unleashed their misguided, altruistic, spiteful wrath on everyone responsible for your arrival. Tóráin and witches alike were hunted, murdered, and burned for years. Some humans pitied us and helped those they could, but a group of people that numbered in the hundreds of thousands wilted down to tens of thousands. Still a considerable amount of people, but when you knew how many there were before, the numbers made your stomach turn. Druids remained revered beings despite what they had led their people to. Many of the races gave their lives to keep them safe. Eventually, your kind realized that it was safer for their leaders to be ignored. Soon the knowledge of Mystic Blood became a rarity, and then it eventually became a legend. Those who hunted Druids assumed they were all dead, and those who protected them began to assume the same. With the ending of The Great Welcoming came a time not many of the Tóráin rejoiced for. They stopped hunting you, but you were barely more than cattle to humans. Witches and Tóráin became slaves for decades until things got slightly better in some countries. Still, anyone who knows about someone with Mystic Blood keeps it to themself. The dangers of others knowing are great. You know this firsthand. You're lucky The Dove hasn't come for you yet."

I scoffed. "Yeah and now I'm running right into her arms."

Lady Mirlena laughed. "When you do so, please be sure to shove a knife in her back for me."

"You know her?" I asked.

Lady Mirlena waved the notion away with her hand. "Gods no. I know of her. She's the worst of the worst. The world will be a much better place when that bitch dies."

I never knew Lady Mirlena to lie, but something about the way she spoke told me the hate she had for The Dove was personal. My feeling wasn't strong enough for me to challenge her on it though, so I changed the subject as best I could. "So that's the lesson?"

The witch smacked her lips. "Yup! I think so. This was just for you to better understand what people with your blood mean to everyone. Your abilities aren't just important for war, they're important for the hopeful peace that comes after it. When we meet Fleuris' army and get them begging on their knees for mercy, we'll have done something special in Kosavros. The treaty between Tudrose, Linne, Fruberg, Weidel and Czermak will extend to those countries we have freed. A new time will come, and your kind will need someone to look to. They already look at you now, but it'll be different when they know the full extent of your capabilities. I'm sure some already do, due to your spellcasting during battle."

I was confused. "Wait, what do you mean by 'when they know'? Didn't you just tell me how important it was to keep that part of me relatively secret?"

Lady Mirlena adjusted her position so that her rear was on the pillow and her legs were stretched out before her. She reached for her toes and then reached high above her head. "Did I not mention that if we're successful, the world will be better? You, and possible others like you, won't have a reason to hide anymore. You can be honored and revered like you should be."

I started the process of getting to my feet. "What if I don't want to be revered?"

Lady Mirlena scrambled to her feet. "What are you on about? People already revere you. Respect you. Love you. Many are here to follow you."

I scoffed at the statement. "I was under the impression people wanted to change things because they genuinely believed in their own hearts that the way people, especially my kind, are treated in this world is unacceptable and wrong. I didn't think people were just blindly following the dreams of a wounded dog."

The sharp burn on my face from Lady Mirlena's hand surprised me. Her face was stern, and I could swear I spotted the beginning of tears forming in her eyes. "Don't you dare, Weylin. Don't you dare. You know full well that nearly every single person in this camp wants a world better than this one. Humans and Tóráin alike are fighting side by side to see a dream realized. You think you're the only one with that dream? People aren't blindly following you. They may not yet know what runs through your veins, but I like to think they can feel it in their bones that you're special. Humans respect you and Tóráin adore you. So many here have witnessed your leadership and it has inspired them to strive for something they never thought they could have. Equality. If you want to keep this part of who you are a secret forever, that's your choice, but don't do it because you're afraid to be given the loyalty and reverence that you have earned since you joined The Resistance. You've earned their adoration, Weylyn. Please don't think otherwise."

I didn't know what to say. I was still trying to process the smack the woman had given me. The conversation had gotten to a point where I felt uncomfortable. I never wanted to lead The Resistance. I never believed I was good enough to do it. Darby tried to convince me on many occasions, but his compliments never sunk in. I took up the role as leader to honor Darby after his death, but I struggled to be the leader he was. I struggled to be the leader my father would have wanted me to be. The two of them were fearless, wise, and honorable beyond belief. Meanwhile, I choose to hide my fear through humor and feigned optimism. I struggle to learn things it seems countless people already know. Plus, I had just killed a man in such an evil manner that I couldn't shake the feeling that I deserved to die because of what I had done. My blood is supposed to make all of that not matter? As if Lady Mirlena was in my head listening to my thoughts, she lunged forward and embraced me.

"You're a great leader, Weylyn, and an even better person. I wouldn't be training you and passing on my knowledge if I didn't know that." She put her hands on my arms and separated us, keeping a firm grasp on my elbows to keep my attention. "We don't always feel like we're good enough. There's actually nothing wrong with that. It's normal. It's how we use that feeling that defines us. Either we can use it as an excuse for hiding away and avoiding responsibility, or we can use it to push us to always strive to be better. Use it as a reminder that there's always more we can do. I'm not telling you to change how you feel or change who you are. I'm just asking for you to have more faith in yourself, along with the rest of the world. The past, as I've just told you, has been dark and hopeless. Hell, you could even say the present hasn't fully scared the shadows away just yet. But the future? I know that the future is going to be brighter for everyone, because it has people like you fighting for it."

Her words were growing on me. I could sense they came from a very personal place, and for some reason that made me believe more of what she was saying. Rosalie was always telling me to believe in myself more. Hell, even angels were telling kings to believe in me. Maybe something was there. Maybe I hadn't realized it yet. Instead of trying to prove my negative thoughts as truths, I chose to allow

Lady Mirlena's words to enter and fill my mind. Not just hers, but Darby's too. Rosalie, Brina, Olly, Ossian, even Keagan gave out the rare compliment when he wasn't telling me off. Most of all, I chose to listen to my father. Every night before I went to sleep, he would tell me that I would change the world. Maybe it was time I started believing that.

"Thank you, Lady Mirlena. I didn't want that conversation, but I think I needed it." She let go of my arms and nodded before an awkward silence engulfed us. I forced a smile and tried to lighten the tension that had built up in the room. "Who'd have thought that a history lesson would have led to you slapping me, eh?"

Lady Mirlena's face grew red as she spun around and went over to where she had left her cup. "Sorry about that." She bent down to pick up both empty cups sitting in the blankets below us and went over to the kettle. "I felt you needed it."

I laughed, dramatically rubbing my cheek. "Maybe I did, But you didn't have to hit me that hard."

The witch began to pour herself some more tea. "Oh stop. I barely touched you."

Trumpets sounded, followed by shouting. Orders must have been given to begin packing up camp. Having brought my eyes to the exit when the trumpets had blared, I looked back at Lady Mirlena for permission to leave. I didn't need it, but as her student I always felt it was polite to ask for it. She took a sip of her third cup of tea and waved me off. "Go on. I need to go save Queen Sophia from Arthur anyway."

I gave a small bow, as I had tended to do at the end of our lessons, and made for the exit. I was halfway through before I stopped and turned around. "Thank you for the lessons."

Lady Mirlena smiled. "Any time, Weylyn. Any time."

# Chapter Sixty-Two

## Weylyn



We escaped the mountains and ventured across the border into the land I called home. Our army passed through with relative ease, but as we ventured further into the country The Resistance met its first challenge in Fleuris. As we approached the large city of Gralion, a sizable army was in our way. From what we could tell, the force before us was not at full strength. Fleuris was known to split its army in northern and southern halves, but what stood against us looked considerably less than what we were expecting to face. Regardless of their size, they caused enough trouble to slow us down and cut into our numbers. We eventually won the battle by overwhelming them with our larger force. They never would have defeated us, but nobody believed that was their intention. Their purpose was to try to injure us in some manner; lessen our numbers, take out a high-ranking officer, lower our morale, those sorts of things. That Fleuris force had almost succeeded in landing us a devastating blow when General Wyman was badly injured. Thankfully, Lady Mirlena had been nearby to help him, or we would have lost the commander of our army. Our other near loss that would have dealt a blow I never would have overcome rode up next to me.

"You should be resting," I scolded.

Brina twisted her face after rolling her eyes. "I told you countless times already, Weylyn. I'm fine."

"You nearly lost your arm. You would have if they hadn't surrendered in time. It still hasn't regained its proper color. You aren't out of the woods just yet."

"It was a very bad injury, Brina," Rosalie chimed in. "Even with the help from magic the damage done could become permanent."

I watched as Brina brought a hand over to her arm. We managed to stay by each other's side this time around, and we were lucky that we had. Brina was shot in her leg during the battle, and as if that wasn't enough to worry about, she had also received a deep, horrible cut to her left arm. I defended her as best I could until the yells of surrender began to break through the sounds of battle. The blade had cut through the muscle and badly broken the bone of her forearm. She was holding the limb together as best she could until I finally managed to heal it. However, defending her on my own for that long had depleted a lot of my energy. With nothing to gain more energy from — I was still too nervous to try using the elements without Lady Mirlena nearby — I healed as much as I could without passing out again. The bullet wound was tended to first, a puncture wound from a blade that had broken through her armor covering her belly next, and then I healed the broken bone in her arm. It wasn't until we reached regular healers that she was repaired with mundane practices. Having recovered well enough, I healed the wound for her this morning, but she was still having trouble moving her hand and fingers. It would be terrible if she were to lose use of her hand, especially when our most important battle was approaching. It was all very stressful and my dear cousin's stubbornness only made things worse.

Brina stopped rubbing her arm and forced a smile in our direction. "It's fine. I feel great. Good as new. The little bit of healing Weylyn gave me this morning has done wonders. You worry too much."

"I tell my mother that all the time. She doesn't like it very much, though." Arthur had come up next to Rosalie on his own horse.

The boy had been able to ride a horse on his own before, but his recent growth spurt over the past couple months made it look like he actually belonged in the saddle now. Rosalie grinned while looking the boy over. "And just what are you doing on your own? Your mother won't be too happy you've run off again."

Arthur scowled. "I didn't run off. I went to find Lady Rosalie and Lord Weylyn."

"So, I'm not worth looking for then?" Brina teased.

Arthur became extremely flush with embarrassment as he leaned over in his saddle to get a better look at Brina. "Lady Brina! I'm so sorry! I didn't mean to be disrespectful. Of course you're worth looking for."

Brina waved him off. "Ah don't worry, young one. I was just leaving anyway. I'm going to go find Sullivan. He doesn't lecture me all the time."

Brina shot me a smile so I knew she was only joking around and not truly upset. She turned her horse around and moved further back into the parade of soldiers marching through the outskirts of Gralion. I looked to my right to address Arthur, but he was gone. Rosalie pointed at where Brina had just been, and I turned my head to find that Arthur had taken her place.

"And was there a reason for setting out on your own to look for me and Rosalie?" I asked the young man.

Arthur adopted the posture and serious facial expression he liked to use when he wanted to seem more like an adult. "Well, I know that you and Lady Rosalie are from Fleuris. Lady Brina is too, but I don't think we get along as well as the three of us do. I'm not even sure she likes me. Anyway, I wanted to know what it felt like to be home again."

Rosalie spoke up first. "Brina hasn't always done well with children, but she does like you. That I know for sure."

Arthur's response was quick. "Well then why doesn't she mix well with me? I'm not a child anymore."

I rolled my eyes. "Yes, we know. But Brina still sees a young boy untouched by the world. Don't worry about it too much. As for your question, I guess you could say I'm feeling...hopeful? At least I'm trying to."

Rosalie sighed. "Well, I don't mean to speak for Weylyn, but we're both quite nervous too, I think. Afraid might be the better word to be completely honest."

Arthur pondered our answers, looking out at the field already inhabited by the soldiers ahead of us. The noon sunlight shone on him strongly, making his brown hair seem lighter than it was. A medallion he wore around his neck glinted in the light, something I had learned Lady Mirlena had made for him in order to protect him from certain magic. He squinted as he faced the sunlight head on until turning his head towards Rosalie and me. "I understand the hopeful part. We're coming here to do what we did in the other countries, and you hope it all works out. But I don't know why someone would be afraid to come home."

I looked at Rosalie, the woman looking back at me with a hesitant expression. Neither of us really knew right away how to explain it to Arthur, but when I noticed the boy beginning to shy away, I quickly spoke up to assure him that he hadn't said anything wrong. "It's an understandable question to have. We know how bad it was here when we left and, during our escape, we had a very good idea of how much worse it was going to get. We had no choice but to abandon our friends. We're afraid because we don't know what happened to them. With news of what has been going on as of late, we have to accept that there's a very large chance that they could be dead."

"Exactly," Rosalie said. "And we're afraid of losing them because not only would the void left behind be unfillable, but it would be truly heartbreaking to bring about this new world and not be able to celebrate it with those we love. It's hard not to worry about it." Rosalie forced a smile then, probably trying to make sure our answer didn't upset Arthur.

Surprisingly enough, the boy didn't seem too bothered by it. "That makes sense. My idea of home is different from yours. I'm sorry. I can only imagine how scared you are for your friends. I don't know what I would do if my mother died. And that's just one person! You have so many you care about being the leader of The Resistance and all."

I reached over and put a hand on the boy's shoulder. "Your mother isn't going anywhere, Arthur. She's much too stubborn to die. Don't trouble your mind with thoughts like that."

Arthur nodded and I let go of him, leaning back into the comfort of my saddle. We rode in silence for a short while until the young man spoke up again.

"How did The Resistance start?" he asked.

It was a subject I didn't talk about willingly, even though that day was burned into my mind like the branding on the hide of a bull. I remembered every minute of it. I didn't want to ignore the boy, but I also didn't really feel like talking about one of the worst days of my life. I ended up reaching a compromise with myself. I would tell Arthur, but in as little words as possible while hoping he doesn't ask too many questions. Right before I started, I felt a hand grab my arm and I glanced over to Rosalie. She had a comforting smile on her face, prompting me to return the gesture as I put my hand over hers for a brief moment. I turned my attention back to Arthur and blew out the short breath I had taken in a bit of a dramatic way.

"Well, Arthur," I started, "I'm going to be honest with you. The Resistance was born on the darkest day of my life. My father, Conri, was executed by King Louis. People loved my father so much that they refused to stand by and let there be no consequences for taking him away from the Tóráin community. Led by other leaders of our community, the largest riot in Fleuris history took over Cloque. Many people died that day. A lycan named Darby, who was a good friend of my father, suggested we fight back in a less chaotic and reckless way. He started The Resistance about a week after my father's death."

Without even taking a moment to think, Arthur responded. "Oh. That's horrible. I'm glad people fought back though. He must have meant a lot to your kind. Your father, I mean."

Rosalie spoke up when I struggled to come up with something to say. "He was one of the sweetest living beings I've ever known. He'd give the skin off his own back if it meant he could put an end to someone's pain. Conri was a light in those dark times."

"I like to think about how happy he is to know that his light being snuffed out only lit up thousands more." The smile I had forced onto my face faded as new thoughts came into my head. "And I abandoned those lights to save my own life when I left Fleuris."

Silence swallowed the three of us up. I didn't want to say anything else, and I was sure Rosalie and Arthur were thinking of a way to convince me I was wrong.

"We didn't have a choice, Weylyn," Rosalie said. "If you died that day The Resistance would have fallen apart."

"Yeah," Arthur added. "If you didn't leave, we wouldn't be marching right now. We wouldn't have beat those other countries. People say you won the big battle in Malvene practically on your own! You're a great leader, Lord Weylyn. Don't beat yourself up too much. It isn't healthy to always be sad and miserable. It breeds bad habits."

I heard Rosalie chuckle next to me. "Arthur, be honest with me. Are you truly only ten years old?"

Arthur raised his nose to the air like a snobby noble. "I'll have you know I'm only two months away from my eleventh birthday."

I leaned over and rustled Arthur's hair, encouraging the boy to look at me with a big smile on his face. I shook my head, yet again in disbelief of the wise nature of the young man. "You know Arthur, you're already great at the young age of almost eleven, but I believe you're going to do great things in this world when you're older."

"Oh, I agree. I'd bet my life on that prediction coming true." Rosalie sent a smile of her own Arthur's way.

"Really? You think so? Why?" You could tell the boy was both curious for an answer, but also enjoyed being complimented.

"Because you always find the better side of things," I said. "Your cup is always half full instead of half empty. This world will always need more people like you. Never change, Arthur. Please. Keep that light alive."

Arthur put his fist over his chest with his back as straight as it could be. "I promise I will, Lord Weylyn."

"There you are! I swear to you, Arthur I will take a rope and bind you to my hip if I have to go looking for you again!" Lady Mirlena came up next to Arthur and gave him a small punch in the arm. "You worry me when you run off like that!"

Arthur rubbed his arm with one hand while pointing at Rosalie and I with the other. "I didn't run off! I just went to find Lady Rosalie and Lord Weylyn! They told me that I'm going to do great things when I'm older."

Lady Mirlena tried to keep the stern look on her face, but it gave way to the smile that crept across her lips. "Did they? Well, I'm not so sure they're right about that."

Arthur's face dropped into such a state that I thought the boy might cry. His mother leaned over, grabbed his hand, and kissed it, grinning from ear to ear. "You don't need to grow up. You already do great things."

I asked Lady Mirlena how Sophia was, and she began telling me a long story starting all the way back to last night. We continued to talk afterwards, but in my mind I thought of other things. I thought of Olly and Keagan, Finn and Anya. I wondered how they were and if they were alive. Just when despair started to fill my head, Arthur's words about breeding bad habits came forward. I chose to imagine our reunion instead of what I was thinking of before. The thought of everyone being okay and us being successful perhaps reached too far away from reality, but I didn't care. Seeing people I loved and cared for smiling and laughing again was what I wanted to experience. Until the world gave me no other choice but to do otherwise, that was where my mind would be. With my friends. Safe, happy, and victorious.

# Chapter Sixty-Three

## Nylathari

Cloque, Fleuris | August 9, 1799

I looked over the drawings on the floor for the seventh time to make sure they were accurate. I kicked one of the corpses on the floor out of my way before taking a few steps forward to inspect the design riddled with different shapes and symbols. They were a mixture of Higher and Lesser runes, which made me sick. Mixing our holy magic with that of those bound to Dorcha was unsettling and wrong, but it was necessary. We didn't know the exact spell that our enemy had used, so we had to fill in the gaps where we could. After consulting a book of mine that contained the drawing of the stave on the floor, I closed the small journal and tucked it into a pouch that hung from my waist. After taking out two vials of blood from the pouch, I took a deep breath and removed the first stopper with my teeth. The energy from those Lessers that I had killed was pulsating in a pale blue orb hovering over my right hand, so everything was ready for the final step. All I had to do was pour the blood onto the stave and cast the spell with the energy I wielded, but I was hesitating. I knew this was certainly enough blood to do this, yet I had been putting it off for a few days now.

Contacting my mother was something I had waited many years to do. I dreamed every night of being reunited with her. However, in my dreams I had been successful. I would inform my mother of my success and she would shower me with compliments. The Queen of the Elves would praise her daughter for achieving the goal she made for her, a warm embrace being one of my many rewards. In reality, our conversation would go much differently. If she was still alive that is. I had no idea what had gone on in the past few decades or so. This would be my first time contacting my home, and instead of being overjoyed I was extremely nervous. Weylyn was on his way, and I was sure that his faerie friend would join him. They would come to me, and I would use them to bring forth the legions of the Higher Race Alliance to erase everyone from this world. I just needed to convince my people of that. The plan was always to contact them so they could prepare, but the hope had been that I would already have everything I needed in order to open all the portals. With this one vial of Mystic Blood, I would only have enough to open this portal for a short time. The lack of energy available to me didn't help. The five creatures were prisoners that nobody meaningful would miss, but it was nothing compared to what I would need to bring my people here. If my mother was still alive, I would have to convince her that I would have enough energy and blood to bring them here soon. I had thought about the conversation for days, already wasting too much time. I just had to cast the spell and do my best not to disappoint.

I poured the Mystic Blood onto the stave, causing it to glow a soft green. I then uncorked and poured the second vial of blood over the multiple lines and symbols. We could have used a leaf from The Tree of Solas or something of the like, but we needed to be sure someone was there to receive me when I called. It was considered too risky to have a vial of the Queen's blood, so we settled on her main advisor. With the second dose of blood, the stave glowed a darker shade of green and began to hum. I spoke the words necessary as I threw the ball of energy into the stave. A bright, white light filled the room until it dissipated into what some would think was a tall mirror. The construct hovered above the runic symbols, holding the image of a female elf studying at a desk. I almost called out to her in this world's common language, but I caught myself in time. Clearing my throat beforehand, I spoke in my native tongue as I called out to the fellow member of my kind.

"Syndra!" I shouted. "Can you hear me?"

The elf jumped in surprise at my voice and fell out of her chair when she spotted the portal. She responded in our native Cànansorcha; a sound that made me feel warm inside. "Is this what I think it is?"

I rolled my eyes. "I don't have a lot of time, Syndra. I need to speak with the Queen immediately. Hurry!"

"Right! I can summon her here, Princess Nylathari. Just a moment." The elven woman quickly went over to a mirror in her room. She cast a spell I knew well. The mirror shimmered and rippled like a pond that had just had a rock tossed into it. She stepped into the warped glass, disappearing from my sight. It only took about ten seconds or so until she came back through with someone following behind her.

"Oh, I knew you would do it! Praise Solas! We are to prepare then. How long until you open the portals for us?" I was hoping my mother would have been more interested in my well-being, but I shook off the negative feelings her first words had created and smiled.

"A few days or so," I said. "I would advise you gather everyone you can, Queen Alavara. There is a race of creatures who inhabit this world that I believe are made by Dorcha as well. They must be dealt with."

The fair features of her face turned into a look of suspicion. I wasn't sure what I had said to garner such a look, but it stayed on my mother's face as she combed her fingers through her silver hair. It wasn't until she finally spoke that I knew what troubled her. "Why is your timeline not more secure? Why the uncertainty? Were you not successful?"

I tried to keep my discomfort concealed. In a last moment of panic, I did something that I had never done before. I lied to her. "I was successful. No need to worry. This world and its people are tricky. Things can sometimes take unexpected turns. Dorcha has his claws deep in this world's very soul. Give me four days, maybe five, and I'll have the portals open for you."

The Queen of the Elves glared at me through the small portal I had conjured. She would punish me greatly for speaking falsely to her. Her bright red eyes gripped me and held me in place as she decided on whether I was telling her the truth or not. Eventually, she smiled. "Very good. Do not worry, little one. We'll see that his darkness is removed from both worlds. No one will stop us."

I bowed very low, remaining in a submissive position until I felt a hand touch my cheek. I looked up to see my mother closer to me than she had been for what felt like centuries. The white and gold threads of her dress traced the strong shape of her body. The pieces of silver armor that covered her shoulders, chest, and stomach shone in light coming from the sun from our world. She put her hand under my chin and guided me back to an upright position. When I was standing up straight, she brought her hand and arm back into her side of the portal and smiled.

"You have done well," my mother said, causing me to feel a great sense of pride and relief. "Very well, my little star. You will be revered for generations as the greatest Champion of Solas ever. Stand proud. Stand strong. I'll see you in a few days, and together we will end this."

I returned her smile with one of my own. "Thank you, Mother. Your praises humble me. I cannot wait to be by your side again."

My mother chuckled. "If you're telling the truth, you won't have to wait much longer."

I felt my heart skip a beat. "Of course I'm telling the truth. I would never lie to my Queen. We'll stand together very soon. I promise."

The portal flickered like a candle caught by a hefty breeze, but I caught the smirk on my mother's face. "Good."

The portal's edge flashed a bright white light like when it had opened, leaving nothing in its place when the light faded away. Realizing that I had been holding my breath for a while, I let out a large exhale. My tightened muscles were given permission to relax as a shaky hand wiped the sweat off my brow. I brought my mask down to rest on my face before turning around. When I did, I saw a soldier standing in the doorway. He was frozen in place with fear in his eyes. I brought my hood back over my head to cover my ears before crossing my arms over my chest.

"What did you see?" I asked him calmly.

The man's mouth opened and closed but no sound came out. I clapped my hands together in an attempt to snap him out of whatever trance he was in, prompting the weak creature to cower and cover his face. "Nothing! I saw nothing!"

I stepped forward and grabbed him by his collar. He kept his eyes closed until I shook him. "What did you see?"

The soldier began to whimper until he formed a response. "There was a magic mirror, and you were speaking some weird language, then a big flash of light came and the mirror was gone. Not to mention the group of dead bodies surrounding you and the magic looking thing on the floor." He put his hands up in an attempted surrender. "But I won't say anything! I promise! I'm a follower! All hail Deus' Chosen, Champion of The Light!"

I shook him again. "Enough! Why did you come here? I gave orders for nobody to be on this floor of the prison."

His eyes opened up and he forced a smile. "I have news for you! Good news! We caught someone. A human. He was skulking in the shadows near Joieternelle Palace."

I rolled my eyes before pushing the soldier away from me. "What does this have to do with me?"

He stumbled but managed to keep his balance in the end. Bringing his hands together, the soldier twiddled his thumbs as he answered. "We asked him what he was doing, but he didn't tell us. When we threatened to have him tortured by The Dove, he broke. He said he would tell General Rosspier everything, but only him. My guess is it's something to do with those Resistance *salauds*, so I figured to tell you instead of General Rosspier. You are still after them, right?"

If that faerie knew Weylyn, she must be involved with his little group too. I had ordered that any news on the whereabouts of The Resistance was to be brought to me directly. I knew some would go to Jon or Max, but I was actually glad to find out someone had obeyed my orders. "Take me to him."

The soldier nodded, looking nervously at the dead bodies around us. I kicked over the bucket of water nearby to erase the markings of the stave and left the main torture room with this informant. Bastion had many levels, both above and below the ground. This level was the lowest and was reserved for myself and my interrogations. The soldier took us up a multitude of levels until we were on the second highest floor of Bastion. He brought me to a cell closer to the end of the hallway and opened it for me. I stepped inside to find a man sitting in the corner with his arms wrapped around his legs. When he saw me enter, he jumped to his feet before bowing. What a fool.

"The Dove!" he shouted. "I guess you're here to take me to General Rosspier."

I drew my sword and pointed it at him. The tip of my blade hovered in front of his throat, having the cowardly human raise his arms in the air. Humans. Always so quick to surrender. It made me sick. In all fairness, it would have been foolish for him to fight me, so I guess surrendering was his best option.

"What are you doing?" the man asked. "I said I would tell him everything! Please! Just take me to him and you'll see that I know many useful things! Please don't kill me!"

I kept my sword where it was. "What's your name?"

The man was breathing heavy and fast. "Soan, miss. Lady. Dove."

I forced a smile as I pushed the tip of my blade closer to his neck. "Soan. Listen closely. You're going to tell me everything you know. If I think it's useful, I'll pass it on to the General. If you refuse, I'll kill you."

"Okay! Okay!" Soan looked around like a cornered rat before continuing. "I work for The Resistance. I'm an informant. I keep my eyes and ears open and tell them what I see and hear."

I let out an impatient sigh, silently telling Soan that what he had said wasn't enough to stop me from cutting his throat. He swallowed and shook his hands in the air as a silent plea to not kill him before he spoke up again.

"I know where they are!" His voice was a higher pitch than before now. "A whole bunch of them! Their leaders are there too! Keagan and Olwen. A lycan and a forest sprite. Olwen was actually asking about you a lot last time I talked to her. I don't know why, it seemed really odd to me that she would ask —"

I pushed my sword into the stone wall behind him, grazing the left side of his neck. The blood dripped down to his chest as the man shook with fear and went silent. "Olwen is the green one? With lavender eyes?"

Soan blinked rapidly. "I-I'm not sure about what color her eyes are."

I drew my sword back before stabbing the other side of his neck, drawing blood again. "Think harder!"

"Yes!" the pathetic man yelled. "If I had to say so, they're lavender."

This might be the faerie that slipped through my fingers. If she was a leader, it would make sense that she was friends with Weylyn. Perhaps I didn't have to wait until the battle to get the blood I needed. "Where are they?"

"Southern area of Ellova Forest." Soan swallowed before taking a hurried breath. "I can take you there myself if —"

One quick movement had his head slipping off his shoulders. I turned around just in time to see the soldier who had brought me here vomit on the stone floor. How could a soldier have such a weak stomach? I exited the cell, stepping over the vomit covering the entrance, and addressed a soldier standing guard about six feet away. "Get a unit of soldiers ready to ride out immediately. Keep as quiet about it as you can. General Rosspier and Major Carierre don't need to know. Go!"

The soldier saluted before running down the hallway. The man behind me was breathing heavily as he recovered from his sickness. "See! I told you I had good news! Should I come with you?"

I spun around and ran my sword through the man's chest. His eyes stared back at me in horror, asking a silent question that I was more than willing to answer. "You saw too much."

Ripping my sword out of his chest caused his tall, thin body to fall forward. I stepped out of the way and let him collapse to the floor. After cleaning my sword on his coat, I grabbed his leg and dragged him into the cell with the beheaded corpse of Soan. I closed the cell door and locked it with the key the soldier had used to open it. The prisoner in the cell next to Soan's was cowering in the far corner of his cell. He had probably seen what happened, but it didn't matter.

Nobody would believe a filthy goat when he said The Dove killed another Fleuris soldier. Well, maybe Jon would. Either way, it didn't really matter. If Soan was telling the truth, I would have this Olwen in my custody by the end of tomorrow. I would have all the blood I needed for the spell, and Weylyn's army would bring me all the energy necessary to cast it. I may have lied to my mother at the time, but I would make my claims be ones rooted in truth. I would have the Mystic Blood. I would have the energy. I would bring my mother and her army here, and together, we would conquer the creatures of Dorcha.

# Chapter Sixty-Four

## Olwen

Ellova Forest, Fleuris  |  August 11, 1799

"If we go through with that plan there's a less likely chance of a lot of us dying," Finn announced.

"Takin' the bastard's home won't mean a damn thing if we don't win the battle. We should leave tonight and try to get everyone to Tudrose's army," Keagan said before tearing into a piece of cooked meat with his teeth.

"Our first and most important duty is to keep these people safe," I said. "Many of them aren't soldiers, Keagan. You and I both know that war is far worse than what most of these people have experienced. There are more like them out there. We could take advantage of the battle and move further north to Camp Menteuroche and free them. A couple months ago we knew that Tudrose ships were ferrying Fleuris refugees across The Great Canal. If Tudrose wins the coming battle, we move south after freeing Camp Menteuroche. If Tudrose loses, we get as many people on as many ships as possible and flee across the northern waters."

Keagan was clearly disgruntled by my opinion, but Finn seemed less disagreeable. The young lycan took a drink from his waterskin before adding his voice to the conversation once more. "That is probably the better plan, but how will we know that Fleuris will be distracted by Tudrose? We can't venture into open areas with this many people without drawing attention."

"Soan will be here in the next couple of days," I answered. "I'm sure he'll know what's going on out there. Once we know when Fleuris' eyes will be looking south of Cloque, we'll move north towards Camp Menteuroche. Keagan? That good with you?"

Before the lycan could respond, a great commotion was heard amongst the people. The three of us looked up from the map Soan had brought us and tried to spot what was causing everyone to appear unsettled. I noticed people were looking up to the sky and pointing at something above the trees. Just as I discovered what they were looking at, a harpy fell out of the sky and collapsed onto the ground close by. I rushed towards them as they struggled to their feet. I recognized the harpy as Aiden, one of the Tóráin that Keagan had recruited. He was holding his stomach with a blood-stained hand and his face was pale. I guided him over to my makeshift bed of leaves and branches that rested against the base of a thick tree. After helping him lower himself, I moved his hand away from his stomach to investigate his injury.

"What happened?" Keagan asked from over my shoulder.

"An army. Probably two units strong by the looks of it." Aiden went into a coughing fit then, prompting Finn to offer the injured harpy his waterskin. Aiden held the container with a shaky hand and poured some water into his mouth before continuing his report. "I was going to just signal you, but then I noticed that The Dove was with them. I feared she would somehow hear our signal, so I waited to see how many of them there were before finally mustering up the courage to take flight and come warn everyone. A soldier spotted me though, giving me the bullet in my stomach. They'll be here soon."

"What do we do?" Finn asked.

"What we prepared to do. Tell everyone what's happening. Get them ready." Finn nodded and ran off, shouting at the massive group of people waiting for instructions. I looked at Keagan next to give him his orders. "Bring Aiden to Marie, then come find me. Hurry! We don't have much time."

Keagan responded by coming over to Aiden and helping him to his feet. The two made their way to wherever Marie was, and I surveyed the clearing. It used to be littered with trees, but we had cut most of them down. We knew that there was always a chance someone would come looking for us, so Keagan and I had done our best to prepare. Making the calculated assumption that any force coming after us would be coming from the south, wooden barricades had been placed throughout our camp facing our eventual attackers. Finn's orders were echoed by others, leading to more and more people rushing to complete their tasks. Soon everyone was forming up behind the barricades with weapons in hand. There weren't enough rifles or pistols for everyone to have their own, but I'd wager roughly one in three of us were ready to fire off some shots at the Fleuris soldiers coming our way. To be honest, I wasn't as worried about how many soldiers were coming — or how many guns we had — as I was about The Dove being on her way. The majority of those here were ordinary people, not fighters. The Dove would kill many of us on her own, and the only person who could stop her was me.

I went over to the nearby stump where we had been talking about our next move and picked up the two rifles resting on it. Keagan was so focused on getting Aiden to Marie that he had forgotten his. I looped the straps on both of them over my left shoulder and began jogging over to the position Keagan, Finn, and I would be taking up. Keagan had argued with me about where we would be should an attack ever come, with his opinion eventually winning out. I wanted to be on the front line, or at least the second, but Keagan stressed that it was too reckless. Everything was too reckless to him nowadays. Don't get me wrong, a big part of me enjoyed the new and improved Keagan, but it seemed like he lacked emotion at times. It was almost like he had suppressed his feelings instead of having them under control, and it worried me. One of the things that had drawn me to Keagan was his immense passion. Sure, it often led to him making stupid choices, but at least you knew the lycan cared. Lately, everything was so logical with him, and I was forced to be the emotional one, a role I wasn't entirely comfortable playing.

I was our general, and I needed to think and act a certain way; something that I was struggling with lately. To be completely honest, I didn't like being in the army. I didn't like killing people. I didn't like the smell of dead bodies and I hated the constant bullying I was forced to endure during my service in the army. However, I had an immense amount of pride for the skills I had developed during that time of my life. It had made me who I was today, and I knew how important that person was. This knowledge didn't come out of ego or anything like that; I just knew my value. Whether it was a physical battle or a mental one, I always had a level of confidence in myself that had me believing I would come out on top. I became one of the youngest, most efficient soldiers in Fleuris' army to the point that I had actually earned the respect of many high-ranking officers. My calm, collected, analytical mind helped me pick apart opponents before a battle even started. And when it did start? That same level-headed composition gave me an edge over everyone who dared come at me. And yet, despite knowing this, I've been allowing my emotions to take more control over me and my decisions. I just wasn't used to this at all. It was always me telling someone to calm down and think with their head instead of their heart. Being on the other side of it was foreign and it made me feel childish. I used to be so disconnected that people often thought I had no heart at all. That is of course very untrue, but I don't blame them for thinking such things. Only two people ever knew how much I truly cared. Weylyn, who was somewhere out there marching towards Cloque, and Keagan, who came to stand next to me with a smile on his face.

"I'm surprised you didn't just go on the front line anyway." He extended his hand out, silently asking for the extra rifle I had.

Handing the gun over to him, I sighed. "I figured I had better stay nearby to make sure you don't die."

We were at the very back of the lines of barricades we had set up. We had made ten lines of ten barricades, enough for everyone to hide behind. The more experienced fighters were placed at the front, with the weakest members of our group far behind where Keagan and I stood. Those too young or old to fight were making their way further north. They would travel to the shores of The Great Canal and try to find refuge in Tudrose, just like we had planned. Those able to stand against our enemies stood in groups behind the barricades, ready for the incoming assault on our camp. The small hill that the tenth and final line rested on allowed me to view the entire area. There were no more people running to their designated positions anymore. Whoever was staying behind to fight was ready, and those who were fleeing were disappearing into the thicket of the woods. All there was left to do was wait for our enemy to arrive. It was probably about ten minutes or so until we could hear the small army coming towards us. Not long after that, my keen eye caught movement in the trees which eventually stopped a few feet before the tree line we had crafted. The first row of barricades were about fifty feet away from the trees, all of them staggered so we could get as many guns firing at our assailants as we could.

I watched as the people closest to the barricades aimed their rifles down the holes we had carved out so our people could fire behind the safety of the wooden barriers. The Fleuris army was spread out in formation; Aiden had done a good estimate on their numbers. Two units, probably four thousand soldiers if their group went as far back as I assumed it did. This battle would be hard to win, but we had no other choice. I was perfectly fine waiting for the enemy to make the first move, until a voice filled the calm air of the afternoon.

"I came here for someone!" Nylathari stepped into view, her pale clothes breaking through the trees. "If she comes forward and submits to me, I will let the rest of you live!"

Before I could even think of saying anything in response, Keagan roared an answer of his own. "She isn't goin' anywhere, elf! Send your army at us! See how many of you are left alive when we're done with you!"

Nylathari didn't say anything, and silence took over the clearing and surrounding trees. Keagan and I had actually agreed that everyone should know who The Dove really was. They deserved to know what hunted them. Keagan calling her an elf got no reaction out of our side, and it surprisingly got no reaction out of her side either. Perhaps we just couldn't hear them — or they were too afraid of Nylathari to ever say anything — but I was sure that the knowledge must have caused at least a bit of a stir amongst their ranks. The elf covered in white turned around and faded into the sea of white and blue. We waited for a few moments until the elf's voice called for a charge. I was saddened to see that her army was still willing to fight for her. As was customary, Fleuris' front two lines fired off two rounds of gunshots before racing forward.

"Fire!" I called out. The sound of rifles firing off more shots filled the area as Fleuris soldiers fell to the ground. "Fire!" I ordered for the second time.

The second round of gunfire was just as effective as the first one, sending many opposing soldiers to the ground in a heap. There was no time to get off a third volley before Fleuris' force reached ours. Scattered gunfire continued as the sounds of steel clashing with steel joined the fray.

"Archers!" I shouted. "Loose!"

We hadn't made more than maybe a couple hundred bows, and each archer maybe had ten arrows each, but it was better than nothing. The archers in the fifth row of barricades raised their bows and fired at the mass of Fleuris soldiers. Screams filled the air as men were struck by the miniature spears just as the archers prepared for another volley. They continued to fire on the advancing army, which was pushing its way into the second row already. I could see so many Tóráin being cut down and the idea of staying out of the battle for any longer upset me.

"We need to help them," I said.

"No, O'. We stick to the plan. The arrows will cut into their numbers enough for us to push back." Keagan kept his eyes forward, watching the battle play out just like I was.

The arrows rained down just as Keagan said they would, but the army continued to advance, reaching the fourth row now. "Keagan this isn't working."

"We knew this wasn't goin' to be easy," the lycan growled.

"That doesn't mean we should stand by and watch our people die," I said angrily. "We need to get in there."

I took a step away from the barricade I was peeking around, and Keagan grabbed my arm. "Don't. Not yet."

I reluctantly stayed where I was and watched as our people continued to fall. The battle carried onward until the Fleuris force reached the eighth row of barricades. Before I could even begin to convince Keagan we should join in, Finn spoke up.

"You should go, Olwen," the young lycan said. "We can't let her catch you."

Keagan punched Finn in the shoulder. "This battle isn't over yet."

I ignored them both as I caught sight of Nylathari amidst the chaos before us. She was moving with a dangerous grace, cutting through our forces with ease. The enemy was advancing onto the ninth row now, and I prepared myself to finally enter the fray. I would make my way directly to Nylathari. If I could take her out, perhaps the army would retreat. Before I could advance, a firm hand came onto my shoulder. I turned around to see Keagan looking down on me with an expression I didn't like. I suspected what he was about to say, and I was furious about it. "Don't you dare. You said it yourself. This battle isn't over yet. If I can kill her, we can win this."

Keagan looked out at the battle before us and then back to me. "Go. Get out of here. Make for the Tudrose army and tell them what you told me. Finn and I will keep the bitch busy."

Finn took a step forward. "She can't get her hands on you, Olwen. You have to run."

I made a quick, aggressive advance on Finn that was only stopped by Keagan's strong arm. "I have to kill her!" I shouted. "That's it! I'm not leaving you here to do it for me! I'm not running."

Keagan put his hands on my shoulders and made me look at him. "Think, O'! If she gets her hands on you, things are goin' to get worse than they ever were. Be smart. You have to go."

My eyes began to blur from the tears forming up in them. The calculated brain I had valued over recent years convinced me that Keagan and Finn were right. Maybe I could kill Nylathari, but if I didn't, I will have handed myself over to her all over again. I reluctantly accepted that I had to go, but I had one condition. "I'm not leaving without you."

Finn began taking out his rifle and firing at the advancing forces. Keagan shook his head at me after glancing towards the sounds of battle.

"There's no time, O'," he said. "Get —"

"No!" I shouted quickly. "I need you, Keagan! I can't lose anyone else!"

Keagan looked back at Finn and the others firing at the enemy. Some had already abandoned the cover and charged in. Finn gave us both a quick look and smiled. "I've got this. Get out of here. Go!"

We didn't wait for any more encouragement. Keagan and I sprinted north towards where we had tied up the few horses we had. There were only three left; those who had already fled had taken the rest. Seeing the three horses made me feel guilty for not insisting Finn came with us. I wanted to look back, but I knew I couldn't. Keagan tossed me the reins of the brown mare before jumping into the saddle of a black and white stallion. I jumped into the saddle, feeling embarrassed about what I had said to Keagan earlier. I had never told anyone that I needed them before. Not even Weylyn. It made me keep my eyes away from the red-haired lycan as he waited for me to get settled in the saddle. Once we were both aimed away from the ensuing massacre, we urged our horses onward. We would have to flee north until eventually making our way around Cloque to get to Weylyn and the others. I couldn't help but feel guilty that I was going to be reunited with someone so close to me, all while so many would never get that chance ever again. Just like I had promised Anya that I would avenge her death, I promised Finn and everyone else who gave their lives for mine today that I would make sure their sacrifice wasn't in vain. I'd see to it that Nylathari was defeated, even if it required a sacrifice of my own.

# Chapter Sixty-Five

## Weylyn



Our march ended shortly after we entered the Fields of Biette. The famous
Montassinel Castle up on the hill overlooking the fields was in the distance, with a
very clear camp made not too far north of it. General Rosspier had sent a
messenger forward a couple days ago to inform us that he would be waiting for us
here, scheduling our battle for the thirteenth of August, when the sun was highest in
the sky. It was odd to me that the man believed he could dictate when and where
our battle took place, but Sophia didn't seem to mind it. In her eyes, we were
destined to fight in the coming days, so it didn't matter where or when. General
Wyman was of a different mind, believing that we should attack now while the
enemy was unprepared. Fleuris was a powerful country when it came to military
might, and even with the additions to our army throughout our campaign, it
wouldn't be the worst idea to try to gain any advantage we possibly could. General
Wyman and I nearly convinced Sophia to attack right away but — in a surprise
switch around — she ended up convincing us that rest was a greater ally than
getting the jump on our enemy. The majority of our army had been travelling for
months now, and it was no secret that everyone was tired.

Every other person at the meeting this morning was happy to accept an extra
night to rest before what many hoped to be the final battle of this venture. The

moment we caught sight of the castle and the bustling crowd in and around it, Sophia had called for us to stop and make camp. Sleep would no doubt be a difficult thing to achieve thanks to previous events on our journey. With such a large army less than a mile away, you couldn't help but worry they would attack during the night. As I began to set up camp, my mind filled itself with all the possible outcomes for tomorrow and I wasn't liking any of them. It bothered me that my instinct was still to think negatively of situations like this, despite all of the proof from previous situations that things could go well. We hadn't gotten here without some losses, but we had managed to achieve everything we set out to accomplish all those months ago.

Chapters of The Resistance were formed in neighboring countries and Sophia had kept her promise to offer her assistance when we needed it. Those rebel groups combined with Tudrose's army had led us to — for lack of a better word — liberating four countries. The world was shaping itself into a place I recognized from my dreams; the ideas and hopes that I adopted from my father. I found myself wishing that he could see all we had accomplished when I heard my name being shouted from afar. The call had stolen my attention away from helping Brina set up her tent. I focused in on where I heard the shouts coming from, ignoring everything else. Someone grabbed my arm and I looked down to see Rosalie looking up at me.

"Weylyn?" she asked. "You alright?"

"Someone's calling my name," I said.

Brina perked up from hammering a large nail into the ground to keep the tent from flying away. "I hear it too."

Rosalie rolled her eyes. "Damn you two and your good hearing." She peered behind me, getting up on the tips of her toes in the hopes to look over the tents and people that blocked her view. "Where's it coming from? I don't see anyone."

The sound of my name grew louder until I spotted a soldier dressed in the red and white colors of Tudrose riding towards us. "Here! I'm here!" I called out to him.

The soldier slowed his horse and had it trot over to us. Brina came to stand next to me and Rosalie weaved her arm through mine.

"Colonel Weylyn! Leader of the Unity brigade?" The man had a grizzled appearance, with muscles that appeared ready to burst out of his uniform.

"Yes," I answered. "What's the matter? Is something wrong?"

"There are two creatures at the eastern border of our camp. A green one, and someone who looks like you and your friend there. They claim to be friends of yours."

The descriptions gave me a rush of hope. "What are their names?"

The soldier appeared to be annoyed now. "I didn't bother to ask. For all we know they're spies, or assassins sent by Fleuris. We need you to come confirm they aren't a threat, or we'll just shoot them and be done with it."

I quickly went over to the horse I kept with me throughout our travels and hopped into the saddle. Brina did the same with her horse, and Rosalie reached her hand up at me. I grabbed her arm and lifted her up with ease to sit behind me. "Lead the way."

The man rode slower than I would have liked him to. He didn't seem to care that two innocent Tóráin could be shot if I didn't get there soon enough. I desperately wanted to urge the man in front of me to hurry, but I didn't want to upset him either. And so, our pace remained the same, more of a canter than a sprint. Eventually we got close enough to the border of the camp where I could see a group of four soldiers with their rifles aimed at two cloaked figures. I couldn't see their faces from the distance we were at, but I still shouted at the soldiers to stand down. Either they didn't hear me, or they refused to listen. Whichever it was, they kept their rifles trained on the two people with their arms raised in the air.

"I said stand down!" I shouted as we grew closer. I dismounted my horse mid stride and was prepared to yell at the soldiers again.

"Do as he says!" I stopped my hurried advance and spun around to find Sophia on her own horse riding towards us. Lady Mirlena was next to her as well, Arthur seated in the saddle in front of her.

The four soldiers raised their rifles and backed away. I got closer to the two individuals and asked a question that was eating away at me. "What are your names?"

The two of them, no longer being threatened with death if they moved, removed their hoods and I caught a better look at their faces. The moment I saw them I sprinted forward and hugged both of them at the same time. I eventually freed them from my embrace and stepped back with a large smile on my face. I began to look them over and I noticed that Olly had tears in her eyes.

Before I could say anything, she lunged forward and wrapped her arms around me. "Thank the gods you're alive."

Keagan smirked and put a hand on my shoulder. "I knew you weren't dead."

I rubbed Olly's back and grasped Keagan's wrist tightly. "Where's everyone else?"

Olly let go of me and took a step back. I felt Rosalie's fingers lace through mine and I spotted Brina come up to stand on my right side. Keagan and Olly both avoided my eyes and I knew that what they were about to say would hurt.

Olly sighed, blinking away tears. "It's just us, Weylyn."

"What do you mean?" I asked.

Keagan put a hand on Olly's shoulder before responding. "Nylathari came with soldiers and attacked us in Ellova Forest. We escaped to prevent her from getting her hands on O'."

"Who's Nylathari?" Rosalie asked.

"And why would she want Olwen?" Brina added.

Keagan took a step forward before answering our questions. "That's The Dove's real name. She's after O' because —"

"Because she's like Weylyn." We all looked over to watch Lady Mirlena walking forward, holding a pendant in her hand tightly. She got closer to Olly before expanding on what she had just said. "Your friend here has Mystic Blood."

Olly took a step back and I could tell she was uncomfortable. "Who are you and how do you know that?"

I put my hands up to try to calm my friend down. "This is Lady Mirlena. She's a powerful witch and an advisor to Queen Sophia. She's a friend."

Lady Mirlena smiled and held out her necklace. "This pendant was a gift from someone very dear to me. It tells me if someone of your kind with Mystic Blood is nearby. I thought it was just responding to Weylyn, but if The Dove is after you too, I assume it's for the same reasons she's after Weylyn."

"Do you have any idea, other than just wanting Mystic Blood, as to why she's after you?" Rosalie asked. "We have some ideas ourselves, but I wonder if it's just us being immensely negative and paranoid."

"I think that is a wonderful question, one I would love the answer to." Sophia walked up to the group while holding the reins of the horses she and Lady Mirlena had ridden here.

Arthur, from his seat up on one of the horses, added his voice to the meeting. "I want to know why too!"

Lady Mirlena spun around and glared at her son. "Hush, Arthur!"

"Nylathari is an elf," Keagan growled.

"I know that sounds crazy," Olly started, "but I saw it with my own eyes. Not to mention she admitted it to me before knocking me out. Nylathari wants our blood for a spell she plans on casting. If she gets what she wants, our lives will be in much greater danger than they've ever been."

"What do you mean she told you?" Brina asked.

"She went after The Dove after escapin' one of the labor camps. She figured if she put an end to her, the use of the camps would come to an end," Keagan responded.

"You were in one of those labor camps?" Rosalie shouted.

I glared at Keagan. "Why would you let her go on her own?"

Olly took a step forward. "He didn't let me do anything. I chose to go on my own. Still, despite me telling him not to, Keagan followed me into Cloque. It turned out to be a good choice since he ended up saving me from being bled to death in Bastion."

"How did you escape from Bastion?" I asked.

"Okay!" Sophia stepped forward, her hand up in the air before it came down to rest on her hip. "It seems you both have plenty to tell us. I'm sure you are hungry and tired. Come into the camp and we will talk about everything amongst better conditions."

Olly and Keagan both looked at me for guidance, and I just nodded before waving them closer. "Sophia's right. Come on, let's get some food in you before tomorrow comes."

We all began walking back to the center of the camp where Sophia's tent would be. I asked for one of the nearby soldiers to go find Cordelia and Seig, knowing that they would both be glad to know Olly and Keagan were alive. Perhaps I should have asked for Sullivan and Quaid to come too. If what Olly and Keagan were saying was true — and I firmly believed that they had no reason to lie — then it was probably good that everyone knew. Rosalie had gone ahead to speak with Arthur, while Brina and Keagan opened up a conversation of their own. I knew that both Brina and Rosalie had purposely done this so that Olly and I could talk alone. They knew the bond we had was strong, and respected that there were probably things we wanted to talk about just the two of us. There wasn't anything deceptive or treacherous about Olly and mine's relationship, we were just the type of people who appreciated knowing we had someone who we could say anything to. Olly and I understood each other on a level that was unmatched, and I had truly missed having her around to rely on.

The two of us were the last ones in our small procession to Sophia's tent. Olly had been rather quiet so far, which concerned me, so I decided to break the silence between us. "Well, it sounds like a lot has happened since we last saw each other."

Olly scoffed. "Yeah, you could say that."

"Anything you want to talk about just you and me?" I asked.

Olly chuckled. "I wouldn't even know where to start, Weylyn. For now, let's just say that life was hard and mean when you left."

I grabbed her hand. "I'm sorry. I shouldn't have left you and the others."

"I'm not saying that what happened was your fault," Olwen said as she squeezed my hand. "What happened to me has nothing to do with you. Don't try to blame yourself for this. The blame is mine and mine alone. Look, when I first found out you were missing, and then when I thought you were dead, everything seemed like it was coming to a horrible end. It was hard to see any light left in the dark that had swallowed us. I missed you. A lot. But then, when I was in the labor camp, I heard about a lycan leading an army across Kosavros and liberating Tóráin. I knew then that you leaving was the best thing that could have happened for our kind. You should be proud for what you've done, Weylyn."

I let go of the sprite's hand and put my arm around her shoulders. She leaned into me as I squeezed her to make sure she was close. "I doubt everything bad that happened was your fault, Olly."

"You shouldn't," she said quickly. "Pretty much everything was my fault. I don't feel like I even deserve to be here right now."

I stopped walking and came to put my hands on Olly's shoulders. When she averted her eyes, I gently grabbed a hold of her chin and moved her face so that she would look at me. "You deserve to be here. Okay? Don't you dare think otherwise."

I brought her in for a hug and squeezed her tightly. Her muffled voice came out from my chest. "I'd argue but I think I'd rather our first conversation after all that's happened be a more pleasant one."

"You sure you don't want to talk about any of it? All that's happened I mean," I asked as we separated from each other.

Olly just sighed and began walking again. I followed her in the silence that had taken our conversation over until she finally answered me. "No. Not now. There's…something else that I want to say actually."

I smiled at her as we kept on walking, catching sight of Sophia's tent out of the corner of my eye. "And what's that?"

Olly stopped walking. She turned to face me, but her head was lowered, and she was staring at her feet. She mingled her fingers together in an anxious manner and I started to become worried about what she was about to say. I didn't try to guess though. Patiently, I waited for her to speak.

"Well," Olly started. "Okay look. Over the last couple months or so I've come to discover that life is shorter than we realize. That things can happen at any moment, both good and bad, and that those we care about can vanish from our lives faster than we can blink. I knew all of this before thanks to my time in the army, but the idea has really been driven home by some…" Olly's voice trailed off for a moment before I heard her sniffle and sigh. "Some immensely unfortunate, and unpleasant, events. With this battle coming tomorrow, I just felt like I should tell you that I —"

"Hey! Are you two comin'?" Keagan was standing at the entrance of the tent, a piece of bread already in his hand.

"Go on! We'll be there in a minute!" I shouted back before giving my attention to Olly. "Look, whatever it is you want to tell me, tell me after we win tomorrow. I understand more than anyone that everything you just said is true, but we can't allow ourselves to think in such a negative way. It's something that I've had to learn during this campaign. When this is over, you and I are going to have as much beer and wine as we can stomach while we tell each other every bit of every day that we spent away from each other. Don't worry about tomorrow. Come the end of the day, we'll be celebrating a victory over General Rosspier and Nylathari. Whatever they throw at us, we can handle it, Olly. Together."

Olwen opened her mouth a couple times to respond, but eventually she shook her head and smiled. "Together."

# Chapter Sixty-Six

# General Rosspier



"And the cannons are placed along the walls?" I asked.

"*Oui, Général,*" Colonel Deschamps answered.

Lieutenant Joubert leaned over and pointed at the southern wall of Montassinel Castle, his long, blonde hair hanging low around his face. "We placed extra cannons here and here as well once we realized we had the room to do so."

Jon pointed to certain sections of the map next, indicating areas on either side of the castle. "Our heavy cavalry has gathered here, along with the heavy infantry. The light infantry and light cavalry, as well as *Les Spectres* have gathered here."

"*Très bien.* Are we waiting on anymore?" I asked Jon directly.

"*Non, Général.* Everyone is accounted for. The only members of the army not yet there are us and the two units of *Garde Du Roi* that will escort you to the battlefield tomorrow morning."

"Excellent. I believe everything is ready." I raised my glass of champagne, holding it in the air until the other three men raised there's. "To one of the grandest victories in history. Songs will be sung about tomorrow for centuries, depicting how Deus and I came together to lead our army to victory. We will make an example out of them before spreading our influence to every corner of Kosavros, teaching them all how to properly run a country. May this impending triumph be known as the beginning of a new empire, one full of prosperity and holy order! *A la victoire!*"

The three of them cheered my announcement loudly. Our glasses came together for an eloquent clink before the four of us downed what was left of our drinks. I turned away from the table and snapped my fingers at a butler waiting nearby. The man came over and filled my glass. Turning back around, I noticed everyone was still standing there. "*Va-t'en!*"

Colonel Deschamps and Lieutenant Joubert left the room promptly after sending me a quick salute. Jon stayed where he was, and I could tell something was bothering him. I could have asked what it was, but to be completely honest I didn't care to hear it. Today and tomorrow were going to be some of the best days of my life. After our victory, I would marry that pretty daughter of Count Amboise. She would provide me with many sons, and I would conquer the world, bending everyone to my will. The will of Deus himself. I had shied away from an empire before, but now I saw what Deus had planned for me. I now knew what I was made for, and nothing was going to ruin me taking the first step towards building an empire worthy of Heaven itself. Whatever Jon was thinking of saying, I prayed that he kept it to himself. It didn't look like it was going to be a pleasant thought and I didn't want anything negatively impacting my good mood. I silently told Deus to keep the man's mouth shut as I went to go sit down in one of my comfortable chairs, but my order was ignored.

"Are you sure we're going about all of this the right way?" Jon asked.

I rolled my eyes. "What the Hell do you even mean by that, Jon? Of course we're going about it the right way. That *groupe de païens* out there deserve every bit of what's coming to them."

Jon came over and sat in the chair opposite of me. "And what about our group? Our soldiers? Do they deserve what's coming?"

I couldn't understand what in the world was going on and it was upsetting me. "Do they deserve victory and prosperity? You're really asking that?"

Jon growled as he shifted in his chair. "No, Max. I'm asking if they deserve to die for all of this. Look at what this army has done. They tore through everyone they've gone up against, and now they're numbers have been replenished by Malvene. They aren't trying to conquer us. They just want better lives. Is denying them that worth sending so many of our own to die?"

Before, I didn't understand what he was saying. Now that I did, I couldn't believe what I was hearing. I erupted from my seat to loom over the man and make him feel small. "*Ce sont mes soldats! Le mien!* They do what I tell them to do! If I tell them to march, they march. If I tell them to fight, they fight. If I tell them to die, they die."

"Max, I didn't mean it like that I just —"

I raised my hand to silence him. "As for that *déchets* that you seem to think has any right asking for a better life, I will remind you of what they are. They are evil incarnate. Creatures born of the bile that festers in the maw of Eous. They have no right to this country. They have no right to this world. Humans, those who honor Deus and are loyal to him, deserve the better lives. *Ces Diables* are lesser than even wild animals. They don't even deserve the cages I provide to hold them in. The only right they have is to be eradicated from our world so that it may be cleansed of the vile shadow that their kind casts upon our bright light. They deserve to die. *C'est ça.*"

"I'd wager that they would say the same about humans." The Dove sauntered into the room as if it was her own.

With Jon's recent remarks, I had little patience for hers. "Is that an idea you share with them?"

Her eyes locked on to me quickly. "I share nothing with their kind."

I began swirling the champagne in my glass just under my nose, wafting the aroma into my nostrils before taking a sip. "Oh, I think you do. You pretend like you're so calm and controlled, but I know just how wild you are. How malicious you can be. I hate *Diables* just as much as any holy man would, but even my stomach turns at the sight of what you have done to some of them in Bastion. You're barbaric in every way. You keep your face hidden behind that mask and you skulk in the shadows like a fiend. You hate their kind so very much, but you seem to have no love for your own."

The Dove slammed the glass she was pouring wine into onto the floor. The tall, slender shape of the glass shattered, spilling the red liquid all over one of the carpets. "You insolent swine! You have no right to say any of that!"

"I have every right!" I shouted. "For years I have closed my eyes to your schemes! I've allowed you to do as you please, come and go as you wish. I've opened up my resources to you. I have even allowed you to have a voice in matters that no other woman would even be considered to be allowed to speak on. You may have made a name for yourself before we met, but I made The Dove a feared name in every home. Without me you'd still be scrounging about in Czermak like *une petite souris!*"

The witch took a step towards me, prompting Jon to stand up from his seat and put a hand on the hilt of his sword. The Dove's eyes were wide with rage. "You wouldn't have command of this country if it wasn't for me! Or have you forgotten what I did for you?"

I raised my chin and straightened my back in defiance. "You did what you did because I ordered you to do it!"

The Dove's jaw clenched as her blue eyes stared into my very soul, and I could have sworn they became as red as blood for a moment. She took another step closer, and I thought she might be attacking me. When it was clear that she wasn't, I held out a hand to stop Jon from advancing. He had his sword partially drawn and he was glaring at The Dove with a ferocious intensity. The witch's thin lips stretched into a smile as she stood only a foot away from me.

"I do what I do because it helps me get closer to my goal," she said. "I don't serve you. I serve The Light. Tomorrow, I will fight to see my mission completed. That's it. You can all die for all I care."

Jon took the statement as a threat and drew his sword from its place at his hip. He held the tip of it a short distance from The Dove's face. I saw her begin to reach for her own blade and I quickly grabbed a hold of Jon's wrist to move his sword away. I held out a hand at The Dove and tried to de-escalate a situation that I was guilty of creating. As much as I had come to loathe the witch, I knew how dangerous she was. I recognized that it was against my best interest to have my greatest weapon and my second in command trying to kill each other a day before our battle, so I cast a smile on my face as I addressed The Dove. "As long as you're killing my enemies, I don't care what your mission is, or if you succeed. Just be ready for noon tomorrow."

The Dove sheathed the bit of her sword that she had drawn and smiled back, making sure to give a look to Jon before turning and leaving the room. Jon put his sword away after going to the door and closing it. I finished off my drink and snapped at the butler to come pour me some more. As the man was pouring the light-yellow liquid into my glass, Jon came back to stand near me with his arms crossed over his chest.

"That woman is trouble, Max," he said with a look of concern. "I've told you what she's doing. She needs to be stopped."

I waved at my friend, completely over his negativity. "One thing at a time, Jon. I know she has to be dealt with, and she will be. Right now, I have a problem that she can be very helpful in solving. To put your mind at ease, I'll promise you this. After we win tomorrow, if *la pute* is still alive, I'll put out an order for her arrest. She'll be charged with treason and executed. However, until then, I'm more than happy to let her play around tomorrow while taking out a hefty number of my enemies. *Assez parlé pour l'instant.* Go get some rest. I'll see you in the morning."

Jon looked like he wanted to say something again, but he just bowed his head. He turned around and made for the door before opening it and leaving me in the room with the butler. I sent the man away as well, telling him to leave the bottle behind. I thought of what Jon had said about our soldiers and I grew angry again. What would the man have me do? Agree to the terms Queen Sophia and her dog have forced upon the other countries? Let that scum run rampant across this country once more? No. There was no other path for us to take. If they wished to take my country from me, they would have to pry it from my cold dead hands.

# Chapter Sixty-Seven

## Weylyn



The messenger had come by a couple minutes ago. We were going over plans one last time before joining the army just north of the camp. General Rosspier wished to speak with Sophia before the battle. General Wyman believed it was a trap of some sort, and while we all appeared to agree on that idea likely being true, Sophia still agreed to meet with him. She believed this was our one last chance to avoid the great numbers of dead that would litter the beautiful Fields of Biette. The messenger was told that we would meet General Rosspier between our two armies, and we all gathered ourselves before heading out of Sophia's tent. Olly, Lady Mirlena, General Wyman, Sophia, and I all made our way to the front of the army on horseback, passing by the front line and venturing out into the open space that would soon be covered in a chaotic mess of blood and violence.

I looked up at the sun, high above our heads. It shone brightly, despite the clouds that were threatening to cover it. A large mass of dark clouds to the east loomed ominously nearby. Ahead of us were three horses riding in our direction. As they drew closer, I began to assume who was riding them. General Rosspier was in the middle, his military dress the grandest of any Fleuris soldier. To his right was another soldier that I assumed was his second in command, Major Carierre. Riding on General Rosspier's left was a soldier clad in all white, a hood over her head and a mask covering her face. As the three of them came closer to us, Sophia called for our group to stop. General Rosspier instructed Major Carierre and Nylathari to stop as well, his hand raised proudly in the air.

"General Rosspier," Sophia said.

"Queen Sophia. The foolish woman who allowed herself to be tricked by *un chien*," General Rosspier countered.

"If you've called this meeting only to cast insults, I assure you that —" General Wyman stopped when Sophia raised a hand in the air and glared at him.

Sophia lowered her hand and turned her attention to General Rosspier. "Why did you call this meeting? Do you wish to discuss terms?"

General Rosspier grinned as he had his horse move a few steps closer. "Yes. My terms are these. Leave now and you will be spared. I have no quarrel with Tudrose. Take your army and leave Fleuris. Should you stay, I promise you that there will be no mercy given out today or any day in the future. You will all die here."

"You'll die too if that bitch has her way!" Olly shouted. "Mark my words I'll put an end to you Nylathari! You and your plan!"

General Rosspier and Major Carierre looked confused, confirming that they indeed weren't aware of Nylathari's plan, or her true name. Before they could say anything, the elf spoke up.

"Just another crazy faerie spitting out nonsense. This world will be better once you're all dead. I'll make sure that happens." Nylathari smirked at all of us, adding a quick wink to the end of her statement.

Olly leaned forward in her saddle. "The world will be better when you're dead you —"

"Enough!" General Rosspier shouted. "What is your decision, Queen Sophia?"

The Queen of Tudrose looked over at Olly and I before addressing General Rosspier with a defiant, strong look on her face. "Tudrose will continue to stand with The Resistance. Your tyranny comes to an end today, General. You and your allies will pay for what you have done."

General Rosspier had a grin come across his face that made my stomach twist. "Let history remember that I gave you a choice between life and death, and you chose death."

General Rosspier turned his horse around and raced back to his army. Major Carierre followed him, but Nylathari remained behind. She came closer and all of us went to our weapons. The reaction had the elf smiling from ear to ear. Her dark red eyes glared at the five of us one at a time in silence until she finally spoke, staring at Olly and me. "If you have even one brave bone in your body, you'll make your way to the castle. I'll be waiting for you there. Come alone. Come with an army. It won't matter. I'll win. You'll lose. I promise you that."

Nylathari jerked the reins in her hand to the right and spun her horse around, riding north to follow the two men she had come with. With the discussion concluded, the five of us all turned our horses around and made our way back to the army. Once we arrived at the front line, Sophia brought her steed to a halt before addressing all of us.

"Whatever happens today," she began, "I want you to know that I regret nothing. I know this is where I was meant to be, and I am honored to have you all fighting beside me. Good luck and may whatever gods you're loyal to keep you safe." Sophia gave me a quick smile before entering the army with General Wyman.

The two of them would lead the army from the rear as was the custom in war. My place, as well as Olly's and Lady Mirlena's, was elsewhere. Together we rode east along the front line until we reached Unity. I tugged on the reins of my horse to bring her to a stop before dismounting. Olly did the same, but Lady Mirlena remained in her saddle. Standing on the front line was a group of people that included friends both old and new. Brina stood a step ahead of them, taking up the leadership role I had thrusted upon her. She wasn't happy that she hadn't been made a part of our group, but she knew the importance of her gifted position as the leader of Unity. Next to her was Keagan, standing tall and proud. I was surprised by how much he had changed over the last few months, possessing an air of wisdom and maturity that I had always wished he would achieve one day. To his right stood the leaders of the groups that Olly and I had helped start last year. Cordelia, Quaid, Seig, and Sullivan all stood ready to wage war on Fleuris. We all exchanged quick nods before I turned my attention to the person I was most worried about.

"You're sure I can't convince you to stay behind?" I asked Rosalie as I brushed some loose hair from her face.

"This is my home just as much as it's yours. These are my friends too. I'm not standing by while you risk your lives. I'm fighting with you." Her eyes were fierce, showing the strength and determination inside her that I knew all too well.

I brought her in closer and kissed her, savoring the moment for as long as I could before breaking away to stare into her eyes. "Stay next to Brina no matter what. Do as she says. Be safe."

"You too." Rosalie glanced over at Olly. "Both of you."

"We'll be fine," Olly said.

"Those bastards won't know what hit them." Keagan grinned as he extended an arm toward Olly.

She brushed past it and gave the lycan a big hug instead. "Stay alive."

"Ah don't worry. I'll keep the handsome prick kickin'." Cordelia grinned as she punched Keagan in the shoulder.

"We'll keep each other safe," Seig said.

"We'll all get drunk together after today," Quaid added.

"Come nightfall we'll be celebrating the biggest victory in Tóráin history. Then I can finally lay in bed and rest these old bones," said Sullivan.

I smiled. "I hope you're all right." Whistles blared and trumpets sounded, signaling for the army to prepare for battle. "I'll see all of you later."

Olly and I both got back into our saddles, but before we could leave, Brina grabbed my arm. "You should say something to the rest of them."

I looked down at Brina before looking out at the mass of people before me. "Why?"

"Because you mean more to them than you think. Many of them are here for you. Humans and Tóráin alike have joined Unity to fight for you. Acknowledge them. Even a few words will go a long way." Brina let go of my arm and took a couple steps back.

I looked out at the mixture of people and realized many of them were looking back. As I sat there on my horse, I noticed more and more soldiers turning their attention towards me. I tried to think of what to say, eventually coming up with something I felt would be good enough. "Unity! Together, with our brother brigade Peace, we have proved that the Tóráin and humanity can co-exist. We have proven that together, we can accomplish great things! Today is our greatest obstacle, but I know that we'll overcome it. Victory today means a new world tomorrow! Fight for the soldier next to you! Fight for that new world we all crave! Stay brave! Stay strong! Stay together!"

The group in front of me cheered, which encouraged cheers from surrounding sections of the army. I gave one last look at Rosalie before riding further east with Olly and Lady Mirlena. We passed the right flank of the army and continued onward until we met up with a good-sized cavalry group made up of both Tóráin and humans. There were about forty of them I think, maybe fifty. Our task was a difficult one — and was made even more difficult knowing now that Nylathari would be there — but it was also very important to our success. The Fleuris army had chosen this place because of the advantage of having the castle. From the castle walls, they would rain cannon fire down on our army. Not only did we not have nearly enough cannons to challenge theirs, but the cannons of Fleuris would be protected by the ramparts. If we were to have any chance, they needed to be taken out.

The plan was for our force to sneak in behind the enemy once they had advanced and charge the small stronghold. Montassinel Castle was old, and its gates were nothing more than open entryways. It had long been turned into a homestead instead of a true military position, which made it much easier for us to get inside and get rid of those cannons. Still, the mission would be a difficult one and there was a good chance that not many of us would survive. Not to mention we had to sit back and watch our friends fight while we waited for our opening. It was a plan that I wasn't overly excited about, but one that I knew was necessary. Olly had wanted to hunt for Nylathari instead, but I guess the gods granted her a gift by placing the elf in our path. I would look at it as more of a curse though. From what Olly had told us, Nylathari was incredibly dangerous, and I would rather avoid her if I could. Despite my wish to stay away, it seemed that we had no choice but to cross paths with the famed assassin. I told myself that so long as we stayed together, we could beat her. We had to.

We all sat in our saddles and watched as trumpets and whistles blared, sending the soldiers from both armies forward. The battle was far from where we were, and the relatively flat land made it hard to really see the scale of everything. What I could see told me that things didn't start out well for our side. Fleuris had sent forth their light infantry, marching forward first. We had countered with what appeared to be our light cavalry. As soon as our forces began charging outward, Fleuris' heavy cavalry raced towards their enemy. We had inherited some of Malvene's famed cavalry, but our numbers were still less than Fleuris' in that regard. Add that their soldiers were more heavily armored than the ones we had sent forward, and you could imagine just how bad it was. Not to mention the cannons that fired on our advancing horse riders. The two forces met in a heavy clash and the battle began. We had countered with our heavy infantry, which was making its way across the battlefield at a slower pace than Fleuris' light infantry. Fleuris stopped advancing and waited for our forces to get closer before sending a volley of bullets their way. They shot into the mass of cavalry still engaging with one another, no doubt hitting their own soldiers. It only showed the heartless nature of their leader and how little he cared about his own people.

The two forces waged war with each other as the sounds of steel meeting steel and gunshots whizzing through the air filled our ears. The crisp scent of a coming storm wafted through my nostrils as the cannons on the walls continued to shoot a steady rate of fire down on our army. The rest of our soldiers were sent in to join the fray, but it wasn't until it looked like we might be gaining the upper hand that I saw the rest of Fleuris' army begin to advance. We waited for a short while until Olly gave us the signal to begin our charge. I had been handed a military leadership role by Sophia, but I chose to defer to Olly. She was more experienced in war than probably any member of our group and I trusted she would lead us well. We followed her as she raced towards the castle, all of our horses braying and snorting as we pushed them to gallop as fast as they could. We needed to stop those cannons before they did any more damage to our army. The fate of our new world was in jeopardy if we didn't.

# Chapter Sixty-Eight

# Olwen



Despite our best attempts to avoid the army, a group of soldiers noticed us and looked to block our path to the castle. They outnumbered us three to one, but they didn't have the heart we had. Humans constantly underestimated the Tóráin, and it made me glad to see them falling to us one by one. Still, even with all the hatred I had for them, a part of me wanted to save them. Maybe not the one's trying to stab or shoot me, but humanity as a whole. Nylathari and the elves posed just as much of a threat to humans now as they did to the Tóráin. Ending her was the most important task, and I was glad that I would get a chance to complete it very soon. Perhaps I would have had a hard time doing it on my own, but I wouldn't be alone this time around. This time, not only did I have fifty or so Tóráin with me, but I also had the person I trusted the most in my life at my side. Fighting side by side with Weylyn always made me feel unstoppable. Sure we hadn't fought in a war before, but I was happy to see that the circumstances of our fight didn't change how I felt.

Together, Weylyn and I were extremely effective. We just knew how to move together. It was incredibly easy to lose each other in the thick of battle and it was rare that people who planned to stick together ever did. And yet, there we were. Weylyn in his feral form and me with my sword, cutting through our enemies like we had done this a million times before. His witch friend was also always nearby, coming in and out of view as she cast spells, while wielding a long dagger in her right hand. The rest of our force proved to be quite efficient as well, which allowed us to eventually overcome the group that had tried to stop us from reaching our destination.

"Make for the castle!" I shouted.

A few people stayed back to finish off what was left of the Fleuris soldiers while the rest of us charged down the pathway that led up to the main entrance. Just as we approached the large archway void of any gate or door, someone came hurtling down off the wall from above. The person was surrounded by dark purple fog, but they appeared to land on their feet. A couple of our fighters charged the woman — who was clearly a witch — but they were killed with ease by tendrils that stabbed out from the violet fog. The smoke began to clear a bit and I noticed who the witch was. It was Ravenna, probably one of the most dangerous witches in the known world. I thought of all the horrible things she must have done to my kind over the years in Etoile and I charged towards her. She looked at me and I went flying back, a fellow sprite catching me so I didn't hit the ground. Ravenna raised her hand as she twisted her face in disgust, a violet glow radiating from her palm. Before anything could happen further, a rush of wind collided with Ravenna, sending her tumbling into the bushes that lined the pathway. Lady Mirlena came forward, her hands glowing a soft blue.

"I'll deal with her," she announced. "Go get rid of those cannons."

I nodded and called for everyone to follow me. Weylyn arrived at my side just as we crossed the threshold of the entrance. We stormed into the main courtyard and as I looked around for a way up onto the walls, anger filled me. I stopped my search because I had found what I was truly looking for. Nylathari was standing a little less than a hundred feet away, facing a large stave that she had drawn onto the ground. A ball of pale blue light hovered next to it. She didn't appear to know we were here yet. I grabbed the closest soldier by his shirt and brought him close. "Go find the cannons."

I pushed him away and started walking over to the elf that had nearly killed me only a few days ago. Any element of surprise I had was gone when Weylyn called after me. Nylathari spun around and smiled. Her hood was down, exposing her long, pointed ears. She took a few steps forward and removed her cloak entirely. Her body was just as fierce as I remembered. Some would say she was thin, but I knew just how strong she was. I began to think of our previous battle and I could have sworn that I felt her knife jam into my thigh again. The pain she had inflicted on me came rushing back, and I began to wonder if we should run away instead of facing her. Just when I began to allow my recent hopeless negativity to seep into my head, I saw Weylyn come to stand next to me out of the corner of my eye. He was in his tame form for some reason, sword in hand.

"What are you doing?" I asked.

"Being in my other form uses more energy when I cast spells," he said. "It's something I figured out while training with Lady Mirlena. I'm more useful this way. Trust me."

"No," I said. "I meant why are you here and not taking out the cannons?"

Weylyn looked at me and smiled. "I'm not leaving you again."

"Aw, how sweet. Such a lovely moment that I think I might vomit! Leave. Stay. It doesn't matter. Either way I'll have what I need from you in the end." Nylathari drew her sword from her hip and pointed it at us. "Come on then. Let's see if two of you pose any more of a challenge than just one."

I took out my knife with my free hand and twirled my sword before sprinting at Nylathari. Weylyn was right there with me, ready to fight the elf who hunted us. Nylathari moved with incredible speed, parrying and dodging each of our strikes with a grace that made me angry. It was painful to acknowledge how skilled she was. She fended Weylyn and I off well enough until I heard Weylyn mumble a word in our language. I caught sight of his hand glowing a shade of amber as a burst of air pushed into Nylathari and caused her to stumble. The attack gave me just enough of an opening to catch the outside of her arm with my knife. Nylathari didn't even flinch from the wound. She smiled instead, right before a burst of air blew into Weylyn and I, knocking us both backward. Nylathari then swung her right arm in the air as we gathered ourselves. Blades of white light were created around her, hovering there until she jutted her hand outward at us. The magical knives flew forward, forcing Weylyn and I to be more defensive. I caught him ducking and diving out of the corner of my eye as I knocked away a blade with my sword and rolled out of the way of another. I heard a groan and chanced a look over at Weylyn to find one of the blades sticking out of his arm. It vanished into nothing soon after, but it had hindered Weylyn enough to give Nylathari an opening.

Flames erupted from her hand and flew towards Weylyn, engulfing him in a ball of fire. I was stunned, unable to move. Before I could grieve, my best friend burst through the fire with a shimmer about him and swung his sword at Nylathari. I quickly shook off the despair that had filled me and joined in the fight once more. Weylyn had briefly told me about his — well, our — magical capabilities last night, but it was surprising to see it happen. I wished that I had experienced some sort of training so I could help in that regard, but I conceded that Weylyn was handling it fairly well on his own. In between our thrusts and slashes, the lycan was tossing in small spells with the intention of injuring or knocking Nylathari off balance enough to give us an opening. Each time Weylyn tried, the elf countered with spells of her own. Eventually, Weylyn muttered the word '*oighear*' and his spell worked after the fifth try. Ice ruptured out of nowhere and encased Nylathari's right foot, rooting her in place. I attacked, but the elf was still very capable and managed to give me a cut on my hand. The wound caused me to drop my knife, but the attacks from us didn't stop. Weylyn stabbed at her next, and she parried the blow before backhanding him in the face and sending him stumbling to his left.

I quickly recovered and leaped at my adversary, hoping to bring my sword down on her head. Before I could, the ice exploded off her leg and she stepped forward with her free hand reaching out at me. Nylathari caught me by my throat and held me in the air. I struggled as she began to choke me, eventually taking a swing with my sword. She knocked my weapon out of my hand and I resorted to clawing at her face. I ended up removing her mask to reveal severely scarred skin underneath. That seemed to anger the elf and she lunged her head forward, smacking it into mine. My vision blurred and I felt myself get tossed across the courtyard. It wasn't until I tried to get up that I realized just how far she had thrown me. I struggled to my feet, but my world spun before my eyes and I fell. I watched as Weylyn — now in his feral form — attacked Nylathari with a fury of swipes. It looked like he may have caught her with his claws, but the small victory was short lived. I was forced to watch as she dodged his next swipe and stabbed into his side, causing my friend to fall to his knees. He surprised me by lunging forward, but Nylathari stopped him by striking him in the side of the head with the hilt of her sword.

I noticed the need for me to get back into the fray as I begged myself to recover faster. I managed to get back onto my feet before sprinting towards my sword. When I spun around my heart sank. Nylathari had Weylyn leaning over the stave on the floor with her blade at his throat. Before I could take another step forward, she quickly slid the sharpened steel across his neck and his blood spilled out onto the magical drawing. She held him there until the stave glowed a pale green before tossing him nearly ten feet away like he weighed no more than a sack of bread. I caught Nylathari going over to the glowing ball of light that had grown larger as our fight had gone on, but I didn't pay any mind to it. My focus was on Weylyn. I could feel tears filling my eyes before I even reached him, dropping my sword and adding my hands to his to try and stop the blood spilling from his neck.

"With his blood and the energy from all those pathetic souls out there, my mission is complete! Don't worry, faerie. Your end is coming soon. All of your ends are coming." Nylathari laughed behind me as I tried to keep Weylyn alive.

"Weylyn! Weylyn! Come on, don't die on me. Please don't die. I can't lose you. I need you. Damn it, do something! Don't quit on me, Weylyn. Please! I love you! Come on!"

Thunder broke through the darkening sky as the storm we had expected began to roll in. A burst of blinding white light filled the courtyard and I quickly looked back once it disappeared. Hovering over the stave that was now covered in Weylyn's blood was a large opening displaying a massive group of armored soldiers. A group of them turned to face the portal before they broke apart, making way for a tall woman to step forward. They were elves, clad in golden armor and ready for war. Nylathari had succeeded. I had failed. I had failed everyone.

# Chapter Sixty-Nine

## General Rosspier

The Fields of Biette, Fleuris  |  August 13, 1799

Fools. Every single one of them. Our army cut them down like inept children trying to play war with grown men. Fighting against them was exhilarating though. I had not engaged in most battles in the last war, but I wanted to fight in this one. I wanted to watch them come forward and die at my hand. I wanted to see the field covered in their corpses and hear their cries as they were killed. With my personal guard nearby, I didn't get into the thick of it as much as I would have liked, but my pistol was empty and *Diable* blood covered my sword well enough. I could taste victory in the air until our advance slowed. The fighting became tighter and more packed together. There was suddenly less space to move, and I could tell that the control we had over the field was lessening.

It wasn't long until one of the men fighting by my side was killed. We continued to fight as hard as we could, but it began to feel as though we weren't making up much ground. I felt as though the battle was fairly even at the moment, and that just couldn't stand. We should be destroying them. They're nothing. They follow false gods and are born of the great evil in this world. It is by our righteous hand that they should be removed from this place with the lead of bullets and steel of swords. Another one of my guards fell and I grew angry with my army. They needed to fight harder. Didn't they know who their general was? Max Rosspier doesn't lose. I cut down a dog nearby before removing the horned head of one of the goats. Then, with my sword in the air, I chose to remind Fleuris who led them.

"Fleuris!" I shouted amidst the chaos. "Fleuris! Soldiers of Fleuris! *Bats-toi plus fort*! We have them! Fight for Deus! Fight for his champion, your General! Make them regret ever challenging us! *Ne lâche pas la bataille! Rallies-toi à moi! A la victoire!*"

The soldiers around me cheered and roared, inspiring those further away to do the same. They did as they were told, my words boosting their adrenaline and my holy influence guiding their hands. I felt the area around us begin to shift in our favor, and from my seat up on my stallion I could see that to my far right and far left it was the same. The morale had begun to falter, but I had brought them back. They were falling into a pit of despair and my voice rallied them to their holy cause. It continued to show that we were gaining the advantage as I led the charge ahead, casting away whatever demons dared come before me. The members of my personal guard that were left fought valiantly, and together we were the spear head that drove through the enemy's ranks. Victory was caressing my lips and teasing my tongue once more. It was close. I could feel it. I almost began to laugh at how unhindered our advance was. Just when I thought nothing could stop us, a grand number of howls and cheers broke out from the mass ahead. Soon after, our advance came to a sudden stop. Mere moments passed before five members of the famed King's Guard of Fleuris were either killed in their saddles or removed from them violently. Our army began falling back, and more members of my guard were dying.

"Fall back, General! We've pushed too far!" Jon shouted at me.

The idea of giving any more ground to these beasts and heretics made me sick. I felt nothing now but hatred and defiance. "Nonsense! They will not conquer us! They will not conquer me! Fight on Fleuris! *Avance!*"

My words provided a small boost in our aggressiveness, bringing a short halt to the enemy's advance. Perhaps others would turn around and flee, but I refused. All my life I had stared death in the face and laughed. Today would not be the day I died. Today was meant for victory. I felt it in my very soul. Deus himself told me that we would be victorious. This would not be my end, nor would it be the end of Fleuris. More soldiers and beasts rushed into us, taking out more of my guard until one of the hounds slashed at my leg. I groaned from the pain but quickly managed to cut the creature down. Before I had any time to recover, something knocked me out of my saddle, and I went tumbling onto the blood-soaked grass. I gathered myself quickly, a tad hindered by the gash on my right leg and stood ready against any who would dare try their hand at killing me. A soldier wearing Tudrose's red and white charged forward, and I deftly parried his strike away before slashing across his back as she stumbled past me. A demon with blue skin came after me next, with the result being the same. I dodged the creature's strike and chopped its arm off at the elbow before running my blade through its chest.

"Rosspier!" A loud voice growled.

I looked in the direction of the shout to find a tall creature in the shape of a wolf. It had blonde fur covering it, and it looked at me menacingly. The dainty thing next to the beast was a human woman, and she looked like she was lost. How the girl had stayed alive all this time, I wasn't sure, but her luck was about to end. The two of them charged forward, causing me to call on all my energy and skill. Some would consider me an older man, but I had made sure to keep myself battle ready. Deus had gifted me a body that refused to reflect my age and it allowed me to dodge and parry the blows sent my way by the duo. The dog caught my arm with its claws but the anger and adrenaline that had filled my body failed to acknowledge it. I went on the offensive, Deus' holy essence giving me new life. He wanted me to win. He wanted me to succeed and bring about a new world where those who opposed him were eliminated for good. His hand guided mine, and after much effort I finally landed a proper strike.

I thrusted my blade at the beast across from me before taking a quick step forward and making a deft yet powerful stroke upwards. The sharpened steel caught the creature in the face, giving me the opening I needed. Basking in my victory over the demon dog, I stabbed it in the stomach. The beast had tried to move out of the way, but I still caught it well enough. The wolf-like fiend grabbed my arm, preventing me from sliding my blade in any further. I pulled the blade out harshly, knowing that I had caused enough damage. My enemy fell to their knees as a shrill voice shouted out.

"Brina!"

I turned my attention now to the foolish woman who was clearly not a soldier. Even with dirt and blood on her, she was a comely thing, but I knew the deception of Eous when I saw it. Deus had gifted me the ability to spot evil when it tried to hide behind pretty faces and sad eyes. The woman had betrayed her own kind and the one true god of this world. She would pay for it just like all the others. As I approached her, she readied herself for my attack. I couldn't help but let out a small chuckle as I began to toy with her. A lackluster slash here, a feigned attempt at a stab there, the girl holding her own well enough. I grew bored and began to fight harder. The dirty little thing stood her ground, but after a quick stab to her shoulder and a swift slice to her leg, the woman fell to the ground. As she sat there holding the wound on her leg, she began to weep, and I was shown once more why the majority of women didn't make good soldiers.

"What a weak and foolish thing you are!" I shouted at the woman. "You threw away your life! *Fille idiote. Les Diables* don't care about you. *Aucun d'eux ne le fait*! And yet, now you will die for them. Pity, you would have been lovely to watch as you served me tea every morning." The girl looked up and spat at me. The holy rage that flowed through me for such demonic disrespect had me squatting down to grab a hold of the wounded woman's face.

"Insolent, unholy, fiend! *Traître et vil*! I'm always told how intelligent women are, and yet here I find one so dull and easily manipulated. They convinced you to join them and you tossed the health of your body and your soul away just like that! Weak! *Vous tous*! Women aren't made for war, just like those *Diables* you love so much aren't made for this holy creation Deus gifted us! You will die here, *fille naïve*. Banished and alone. There will be no salvation for you or those you fight for. You'll all die here on this field, and I promise you that I won't stop until every last one of them, and those who were seduced by them, are nothing but ashes!"

A pain emanated from my left side. I knew the feeling. It wasn't the first time I had been stabbed. I let go of the girl's face and looked down at the hilt of her knife sticking out just under my ribcage. Angrily, I let loose a swift and powerful punch, sending the bitch fully onto the grass beneath us. I got to my feet and looked around, trying to find a horse or — better yet — Jon. Before I could even cast my eyes on my surroundings for more than a couple seconds the large shape of that wolf I thought I had killed came leaping at me. The force of the tackle knocked me on my back and put me in a daze. I was given no time to fight back before I felt long, sharp teeth dig into the meat of my neck. The beast got to its feet and stood over me as I quickly tried to stop the blood spilling from the side of my neck.

"No!"

A Fleuris soldier ran into view. He wore the military dress of a major, and I realized that the man must be Jon. My dearest friend sent a furious assortment of slashes and stabs the blonde beast's way, but they were attacks full of emotion. He swung wildly and clumsily, allowing the one responsible for the blood covering my hands to easily move out of the way of his strikes. A bright, white light burst into the darkened, cloud-filled sky from the castle, before another similar light shone a small distance away shortly after. I couldn't see what was going on, my vision beginning to blur, but I could still hear fairly well.

"It's the elves! We don't stand a chance unless we fight them together!" A low, yet female voice shouted.

"Elves? You think I'm a fool? Why would I ever fight with you?" Jon's voice carried well.

"Because they want to kill you too! The female voice came through again. "The Dove! She's one of them! She brought them here! They'll kill us all if we continue to fight each other!"

I began choking more, and the little bit of air I felt I was getting was vanishing. The first droplets of rain began to fall on me as my vision became a complete blurry mess, unable to even see shapes properly anymore. I could feel the life in me fading and I began to panic, but then I remembered who I was. I was General Max Rosspier, Leader of Fleuris, Chosen Son of Deus, Heaven's General. I had died a martyr. I was going to Deus to be cheered and praised in the same light his holy image gives the world. Jon would continue my work. This world would be made free of evil even with me not there to do it myself. My teachings would influence others. I would look down from Heaven and smile on all the good work being done in my name.

"Dammit! Fleuris! Attack those from the portal! They're the new enemy! Attack with The Resistance!"

I thought hearing Jon's voice before I died would soothe me, but his last words only upset me. Hate invaded my heart and I damned them all to the cold emptiness of Hell. I choked and gurgled my last breath before a grand darkness covered my eyes.

# Chapter Seventy

# Weylyn

Montassinel Castle, Fleuris  |  August 13, 1799

Tears filled my eyes. I knew what was coming. I knew why it was happening. I had failed, and Nylathari had gotten what she wanted. The life I had lived up until this very moment began to roll through my mind like scenes from a play. Shaky memories of my father crying at night after my mother died. Spending nights looking at the moon with him as I grew older. The day I realized I loved Rosalie. The first time I kissed her. The happy thought led into what was my darkest one as I saw King Louis kill my father. The chaos of the riot that followed. Darby teaching me the patrols within the city and sparring with Brina came next. Darby's death, followed by the first time I met Olly came after that. Then Olly and Brina went off to war again and I was left to run things on my own. My first time meeting Keagan and how much I disliked him followed that. Moments from years ago continued to progressively flash across my eyes until I got to the present moment, going past my death. Rosalie. Brina. Keagan. Olly. I'd leave them. I'd leave them behind to fight a battle I had started. That was if any of them would survive today. The future was dark now, for both me and those I loved. Maybe this was just how things were meant to be. Maybe we were cursed.

"Weylyn! Weylyn, teach me how to use magic! I can heal you! Come on dammit! Weylyn!"

Poor, sweet Olly. She would blame herself for this. She always blamed herself when things went wrong. The sprite held so much responsibility on her shoulders and would never allow anyone to take some of it. There was nothing I could do to ease the pain she would no doubt feel when I died. I felt the tears falling down my cheeks mix with the rain hitting my face. I had reverted to my tame form, just like every lycan who was near death. We needed a certain amount of energy to change, and no such energy was ever available on your deathbed. I removed my hands from my neck and used one to grab Olly's arm, letting the other rest at my side. She desperately held her hands on my wound as the rain coming down on us fell harder.

"Please let me help you," she begged.

There was nothing she could do. There was nothing I could do either. I had no energy left. I couldn't heal myself. I forced a smile, trying to ease Olly's pain as best I could, just as a large gust of wind rolled through the courtyard.

"Don't you dare leave me!" Olly screamed.

Her words mixed with the rain and the wind, and it prompted me to think of something truly desperate and reckless. I was dying anyway. I could try. The storm would make it even more dangerous, but what did I have to lose? I closed my eyes, prompting Olly to scream at me some more, but I ignored her. I could feel the life in me fading as I desperately tried now to hold on long enough. Deep inside me, I called upon the magic within. I reached out to the elements around me, and I began to feel malleable, then a certain feeling of weightlessness filled me. I felt uncontrollable. I felt wild and untamable. Unstoppable. Strong. Too strong. The energy inside my body had me feeling as though I would burst and I quickly tried to sever my connection to it. The constant droplets hitting me and the gusts of wind that followed the storm above us made it hard, and I feared I wouldn't be able to stop. It was too much. Lady Mirlena had warned me. I felt my heart racing in my chest. I needed to break the connection, and in a desperate act I cast what could maybe be my last spell. In my mind I said a word that I had said to protect me from the flames Nylathari had sent my way; *bacainn*. Suddenly, I felt more like myself, embracing the weight of my body along with the tough tissue that made me what I was. I cut the connection and opened my eyes, so full of energy I was shaking. Olly was looking at me with wonder as the rain failed to reach us, the wind whistling around us.

I thought of my wounds and spoke in my head the necessary word to heal them. I felt the energy I was holding release as all my injuries began to repair themselves; my fingertips touched my neck just as the slit closed together. Any energy I had lost had returned, and I felt as strong and healthy as I had this morning before the battle. The barrier between us and the elements that had saved my life dissipated and the rain poured down on us. I tried to get to my feet, an act that had Olly doing the same. Her eyes stayed on me though, a mixture of surprise and fear. The look on her face shifted into a smile as she leaped forward and wrapped her arms around me. There was probably no person happier than me that I was alive, but I knew there was no time to celebrate. About twenty to thirty armored figures stood in front of the open portal. They obediently stood by as a tall woman had her hands on Nylathari's shoulders. The two of them were speaking in a language I didn't recognize.

"*Mo rionnag bheag. Tha mi cho moiteil asad,*" The tall elf said.

"*Tapadh leat, a Mhàthair,*" Nylathari responded.

Olly broke away and turned to face the small force I was focused on, bending down to pick up the sword near her feet. Nylathari and the elf she was speaking to noticed us, and the two smiled the same smile. From what Olly had told us last night, I knew now that this tall, regal elf was probably Nylathari's mother; Alavara, the Queen of the Elves.

"Demons of Dorcha are tricky creatures! A knife to the throat and you're still alive?" Nylathari looked at her mother, as well as the small force that followed her before looking back at Olly and me. "We'll make sure to take your heads then. Beheading your kind was a fun game I used to play with your ancestors back in my world. I'll enjoy it even more in this one."

I put a hand on Olly's shoulder as I turned into my feral form. Alavara raised her hand in the air and the elves near her formed a wall ten or so wide and three deep. Tall shields that they carried came in front of them and short spears jutted outward. We had struggled to kill even one elf, we stood little chance against more than twenty of them. Still, I looked down at Olly and she looked back at me. We nodded to each other, knowing that it was unlikely that we would survive this fight. Before we charged forward, I heard a commotion behind us. It was a bit far, but it was getting closer. I saw the faces of the elven soldiers in front of us twist in disgust. The noise behind us and the reaction from the elves had me turning around. A large group of maybe fifty Tóráin and humans came rushing through the entrance of the castle, led by Keagan. Lady Mirlena, Quaid, and Seig were also with them. They came to stand with Olly and I, Keagan putting a hand on Olly's other shoulder.

"We saw the light and came runnin' over as fast as we could. Another one broke in the western flank of the battlefield too," Keagan said.

"They're everywhere!" Nylathari came out in front of the force of elves, a large grin on her scarred face. "Just like when you ran here all those years ago. It took me some time, but I plucked what I needed from hundreds of places throughout your known world and used them for this spell. Our forces are cleansing every corner of Kosavros! Something that's even easier to do thanks to your little campaign, Weylyn. Much obliged!"

"Can you close the portals?" Seig asked Lady Mirlena.

"Yes," she said. "With Weylyn's help I think I can."

"What about all the elves that made it through already?" Keagan asked.

"I think I can add to the spell that opened the portals and have the elves and their allies sucked back into their world," Lady Mirlena said. "I'd need Higher Blood to do it though."

"Good. We'll take care of the elves while you close the portals and send the bastards back where they came from," Quaid added.

As we readied to enact our plan, a loud shot from nearby artillery invaded the courtyard and five elves received the kiss of cannon fire. I looked over from where the shot had come from, and I was proud to see two Tóráin standing near a Fleuris cannon which was aimed down at our enemy. They then ran from the cannon and began making their way towards our group from the castle walls. With them was about a dozen or so of our remaining allies from our initial assault on the castle. As I turned back around to face our enemy, Keagan howled, and our force charged forward at our opponent. I made straight for Nylathari, Olly on my right side and Lady Mirlena not far behind on my left. I caught sight of my target, pushing past another elf fighting a large, black lycan to get to her. Just as I was getting close, a force sent me tumbling into Olly. Someone growled in annoyance, and I looked up to see Alavara next to Nylathari. Olly and I quickly got back to our feet and stood ready to face the mother daughter duo with Lady Mirlena. Before we could engage, Keagan charged at Alavara from the side and his claws barely missed her face as she dodged away.

"I'll help Keagan," Lady Mirlena said as she sent her arm forward, casting a barrier on Keagan to protect him from a thrust by Alavara.

With the two of them taking on the Queen, it was again up to Olly and me to take on Nylathari. We attacked with as much force as we could, trying our hardest to do what we couldn't do before. I was now casting spells from my feral form, the energy I had gained from the elements giving me so much power I barely knew what to do with it. I mixed in a few strikes with my claws here and there, hoping the mixture of my attacks would catch the elf unawares. Still, Nylathari was evading a killing blow by either of us. The elf quickly ran her hand near her sword, and it glowed white, casting out lines of light where it slashed. Dodging and avoiding her next few strikes were hard, and eventually one of the lines caught my side. The injury burned continuously, almost as if someone was holding a torch to my ribs. Olly, after a flurry of attacks, caught Nylathari on her cheek with her blade. The elf recoiled and her sword lost the pale light that was emanating from it. We were about to re-engage when a shout caught Nylathari's attention. I looked over and saw Alavara holding her face. Elves engaged Lady Mirlena and Keagan as another one guided Alavara back through the portal she had entered from.

The injury to Nylathari's mother had distracted her, something I thought we could use. I chose to attack, and when I did, Nylathari snapped her attention back to me. Rage filled her deep red eyes as she pretended to crush something in her hand. I felt my right leg snap below the knee, then a hard backhanded swipe from Nylathari sent me sliding across the stone floor. The elf's attention was all on me as she took a step forward, but a shout pulled her eyes away. The elf quickly took two steps to her right before grabbing Olly by the throat yet again. The courageous sprite had leaped off a fallen elven soldier's back and into the air in a desperate attempt to kill Nylathari and save my life. I struggled to stand as Olly defiantly tried to stab the elf that had her feet dangling in the air. She got Nylathari in the shoulder as I collapsed again. I watched as Nylathari yelled at her attacker before shoving her sword through Olly's stomach. The elf withdrew her blade and let her opponent fall to the stone ground of the courtyard.

"No!" The roar caught both of our attention, and I looked over just in time to see a red-haired lycan leap onto Nylathari. The elf screamed as the two of them fell to the ground, and a new pain hit me as I saw the elf's steel blade sticking out of Keagan's back.

I began crawling over to where Olly was, catching sight of Lady Mirlena approaching the heap of flesh that was Keagan and Nylathari out of the corner of my eye. I put a hand under Olly's head and held her close. Her eyes were still open, her hands shaking as they held the wound on her stomach. I looked over at where Lady Mirlena was and saw her push Keagan off to reveal Nylathari staring up with blank eyes. The entirety of her neck was torn out; Keagan practically beheading the elf. I could hear Keagan groan before he waved Lady Mirlena away and started crawling over to us.

"O'! O' hold on!"

He came over and grabbed Olly's hand. I quickly went to put my hand over the sprite's wound to heal her, but someone pulled my hand away.

"No Weylyn. I need all the energy you have to close the portals. It may not even be enough as it is," Lady Mirlena said.

I shook her off. "I'll be fine. Just let me —"

She pulled my hand away again and Keagan growled at her, having shifted into his tame form already. I needed to heal them both soon before it was too late.

"You can't! I have Higher Blood thanks to Nylathari's corpse. But I need Mystic Blood too. As much as she used to open the portals." Lady Mirlena's statement angered me. I knew what she was saying, and I wouldn't let it happen.

"Take my blood then! I'll just call on the rain and the wind like I did last time, and we can close the portals."

The witch seemed a bit shocked by that bit of information, but she put a gentle hand on my arm and squeezed so I would look at her. "The fact that you survived that is next to a miracle Weylyn. I can't have you risking your life like that again. I need you to close the portals. It —"

"It has to be me," Olly said before struggling to take in a breath.

"No way. Not happenin'. Take my blood." Keagan's feral eyes were staring down Lady Mirlena, but they became calm the moment Olly's bloody hand touched his face.

"They need my blood, Keagan. It's okay. I can live with dying to save everyone." The sprite began to cough as she smiled and tried to laugh. "That's a funny way of saying that."

"No, O'," Keagan said. "I won't let you."

Olly groaned. "How many times do I have to tell you? Nobody 'lets' me do anything. This is my choice. Let me make it."

I struggled to form words. "Olly…you don't have to do this."

She looked at me, pulling out a small knife from her belt. She took my hand and forced the fingers to grip the handle. "About what I said earlier. When you were dying. I —"

I put a hand over the hand she used to make me hold the knife and smiled. "I know, Olly. I've known for a while. I-I'm sorry I couldn't give you what you wanted. I wish I could."

Olly smiled. "Then do this for me."

I realized why she had handed me the knife and I shook my head, struggling to find words. I caught Lady Mirlena bending over Nylathari's body amidst the battle still going on just as a firm hand grabbed at the knife. Olly let go, and then so did I. Keagan held it in his hand, tears in his eyes.

"I'll do it," Keagan said before sniffing and clearing his throat.

"Lady Mirlena!" I called out for her with hopes for instruction.

"Just do it there. Then come here. Quickly now!" She yelled back at me, waving her arms around as a stream of blood flowed from Nylathari's corpse to the runes on the floor.

Olly put her right hand on Keagan's chest and used her left hand to grip mine tightly. She smiled at us both before closing her eyes. Keagan swiped the knife across her neck. Blood spilled out just like it had done when my neck was cut, and I managed to call out to Lady Mirlena to tell her our task was completed. The witch looked back and reached out with her right hand. The blood coming from Olly wound up in a tendril and swam its way through the air, falling down into the symbols on the courtyard's stone floor.

"Come on Weylyn!" Lady Mirlena beckoned as the stave on the floor glowed a soft blue color.

I looked over at Keagan and the lycan nodded and smiled. He was very pale, and I knew he wouldn't survive his injury. "It's been an honor, Weylyn. I hope that world you've always dreamed of comes true."

I smiled, putting a hand on his shoulder. "I'll see you again soon, brother."

Keagan coughed, groaning as he tried to adjust himself. "Hopefully not too soon."

I nodded, taking one more look at Olly before pushing myself to stand. My leg was still broken, but my determination to make sure that Olly and Keagan didn't die for nothing allowed me to hop on my good leg. I got to Lady Mirlena and put my arm around her shoulders for support. "Now what?"

"Go to the well," she said. "Tap into yourself. We're giving our energy to the spell. It shouldn't take as much energy to close them as it did to open them. I hope. Just don't give me everything or you'll die."

"What if you need everything?" I asked.

She shook her head in frustration. "We'll know if the damn portal doesn't close! I don't want either of us dying if we don't have to. Enough death has happened today. Now focus, Weylyn. As much as you can without killing yourself. Be careful."

I closed my eyes and focused. Tapping into myself sounded odd and unsettling, but I had to do it. The more I did, the more I noticed my body. It was painful. It felt like every injury I ever had was being felt again. However, the pain was soon accompanied by a sense of joy. Every comforting hug, warm kiss, and friendly pat on the back came through at once. I was aware of every drop of blood and every teeny bit of skin and muscle and bone. As the drumbeat of my heart filled my ears, joined by the sound of air flowing in and out of my lungs, I gave as much as I could to Lady Mirlena. I became more and more limp until the witch couldn't hold me up anymore. I fell to my knees and slumped up against her leg. I watched as a ball of pale blue light just like the one Nylathari had made was hovering in front of the witch. She pushed it forward as she collapsed to her knees as well. The ball lowered itself onto the stave and a massive flash of white light burst into the sky again. When the light faded, the portal was gone, and so were the elves who were still fighting Quaid and the others.

I struggled to stay conscious, but I needed to see them again. I feared that I had maybe given Lady Mirlena too much of my energy and that I was dying. What an end that would be. I used everything I had to crawl back to where Olly and Keagan were. I faintly heard voices shouting my name as I came across the sight of Keagan and Olly laying on the stone floor of the castle courtyard. Keagan had her in his arms, both of their eyes closed as if the two were sleeping. My vision blurred even more as tears filled my eyes, recognizing again just how much we had to give up. The thought of if Brina and Rosalie had survived or not — along with the outcome of the battle being unknown — caused more emotions to flood my weakened mind. It all became too much. My eyes closed as I felt a hand on my shoulder and the image of Rosalie's face entered my mind. She was smiling, sitting next to Olly, Keagan, and Brina. My father was there too, along with my mother. I smiled as what bit of energy I had left faded away.

# Chapter Seventy-One

## Weylyn

The Field of The Brave, Fleuris  |  August 16, 1799

Everything that had happened in that courtyard was such a blur, and it angered me. The only thing that I remembered as clearly as ever was the image of Keagan and Olly laying on the wet stone floor. Other moments were mere flashes in time, brief feelings from different senses. The taste of blood, the sound of steel hitting steel, the smell of rain, the feeling of a sword tearing my skin, and the glance of Nylathari's grin. Pieces of a puzzle that refused to come together, forcing me to go over it all again and again as I painstakingly criticized myself for the decisions that were made. The entire thing was so traumatic that when I woke up for the first time, I nearly injured those looking after me. I had shifted into my feral form and thrashed about in a fervor. It was Rosalie's voice that calmed me. It was a sound I had feared I would never hear again. Her encouraging words preaching peace and control soothed me, and I reverted to my tame form.

A soldier who had been standing by the opening of the tent ran off and I looked around to try to ground myself. Brina was also by my bedside, brandishing a large bandage on the left side of her face. Her injury and the crutch sitting next to Rosalie reminded me that a battle had gone on outside of the fight I had endured. I asked immediately about Quaid and Sullivan, as well as the other rebel leaders. I asked about Lady Mirlena and Sophia too. Hell, I even asked about that grumpy bastard General Wyman.

"Not now, Weylyn," Rosalie had said to me.

"We're happy you're finally awake, but you really should rest more. You look like death," Brina had added.

I asked then how long I had been asleep, and I was surprised to hear the answer. Nearly three days now I had been out. I remembered then what Lady Mirlena and I had done, and I worried about the witch's health. I moved to get up, planning on going to find her if Rosalie and Brina wouldn't tell me how she was, but when I went to move my leg throbbed. I realized how tired and injured I still was, and so I abandoned the attempted escape. Not wishing for me to try again, Brina and Rosalie chose to tell me how the battle had gone. This story included how they received their injuries. It gave me a sense of joy to learn that General Rosspier had died. Brina told me of how she convinced Major Carierre and — through him — the Fleuris army to join with us to fight against the elves. Dwarves and centaurs had travelled through the portal as well, but they all disappeared when we closed the gateways they had arrived from. Brina and Rosalie knew that Olly and Keagan had died, but I was tasked with telling them the traumatic tale of how they had fallen. The three of us mourned our friends together until Sophia entered the tent. More things were discussed, and through the next day or so we looked to recover from what had happened.

We had the corpses of elves, dwarves, and centaurs burned. Humans and Tóráin were gathered by both Fleuris and The Resistance. Major Carierre had his soldiers brought back to Cloque to be buried where their families wished. In light of the events that took place during the battle, Major Carriere had agreed to allow us to do something special for the Tóráin who had died. There was a group of humans who would also be honored, those close to them in our army claiming they would wish to be buried here beside their friends. Everyone saw it as a grand tribute and display of respect, a sign of unity and sacrifice. On the northern side of Montassinel Castle, in the Fields of Biette, we buried our friends and allies. The burial ground would be renamed as The Field of The Brave, a decision that Major Carriere was happily in agreement with. The man had been known as a devout follower of Deus and many believed him to possess the same beliefs as his General, but Major Carierre had proven to be quite different. Perhaps it was the fact that Brina had saved his life, or maybe seeing what humans and Tóráin could accomplish when they worked together had moved him in some way. Whatever it was, I was happy that someone who appeared to not hate my kind would be in charge of Fleuris.

Bodies were gathered, graves were dug, and swords were stabbed in the earth as markers. Our fallen brothers and sisters were lowered into their final resting places, and then everyone who had gathered to pay their respects waited. They waited for someone to say something. Rosalie had insisted that I should be the one to speak, an idea that many others ended up sharing. I had thought about what to say all night, and now that I stood before everyone in the morning sun I was at a loss for words. My eyes fell to Olly's grave, then over to Keagan's which was next to hers. Moving my gaze to the right, I looked over the resting place of Seig, and then Sullivan's after hers. General Wyman's grave was next to Sullivan's, something that had surprised me. Sending his body back to Draca made the most sense in my opinion. I respected the man well enough and, before the battle had begun, he admitted that he respected me as well. I had no ill will towards the old general, it just seemed odd to bury him here. Whichever way I thought of it didn't really matter though because Sophia had insisted that General Wyman be buried here instead of in Draca.

"This is a place for heroes," she had said. "He saved my life more than once during this battle. He deserves to be here."

Next to General Wyman was a human that made much more sense to be buried in this place: Colonel Smith, leader of the Peace brigade. He fought side by side with the Tóráin and it was right for him to be laid to rest with them. We had lost so many good people in order to achieve this dream of ours, and I couldn't imagine anything I could say that would ease the pain people felt. Rosalie squeezed my hand, bringing my eyes onto her. She had tears on her face, the rising sun causing the streams to shimmer. Her green eyes looked up at me with sympathy as her lips stretched into a comforting smile. A hand on my shoulder had me turning to look at Brina, the one eye she had left wet and red from crying. I had always admired my cousin for her strength and constant support. Looking at her had me catch sight of Quaid and Cordelia a few feet away, both choosing to send a smile my way despite the dower circumstances of our gathering. The interaction had me think of the other friends who had survived, causing me to look to my left. I hoped to receive some reassurance from them, needing all the encouragement I could get at the moment.

I was greeted by encouraging looks from Sophia and Lady Mirlena. The witch had been just as weak as I was the last few days, and yet she still lent me some of her strength so I could fix injuries that had been treated mundanely. There were so many people to heal, and not enough witches capable of the spells necessary to go around. With Lady Mirlena's gifted strength, I healed my leg, Rosalie's leg, and Brina's eye. After all she had done, I was surprised to see the witch standing here under her own power. She had her hand on Arthur's shoulder, the young man staring at the graves in front of him. Sophia nodded at me, telling me it was as good a time as any to say something. I gave one more look at Rosalie before returning to my brothers and sisters who had given their lives not only for the dream of an equal world, but also to protect that world from those who would seek to destroy it. I thought of what I had planned to say, and realized it was just best if I spoke from the heart. It was scary, but it was necessary. I took a deep breath as I let go of Rosalie's hand and put my arm around her shoulders so I could hug her tightly.

"For many of you here, this place might become somewhere that grants you nightmares. It might show you flashes of memories you may rather forget. The horrors of war are many, and the fear we all had during that battle may go unmatched for the rest of our lives. Instead of looking back on this day as one full of sorrow and darkness, I beg that you view it as I believe it should be remembered. People from multiple nations, both humans and Tóráin alike, stood together against a common enemy and won. The people in these graves gave their lives to prove that a peace between our two people can unite us and bring forth a better world. Their sacrifice helped prove that we can defend that better world. That no matter what you look like or where you come from, we can all make the idea of an honorable, respected, healthy, happy life a reality.

"This place was named after a woman who a man loved very deeply. She was taken from him before her time, and so he named the area around her home after her. In honor of that act, as you all may by now know, we are naming the area north of Montassinel Castle The Field of The Brave. Many people who we loved deeply died before their time during this battle, and so this place will keep their memory alive. Let it be a sign that humans and Tóráin can share this land, this country, this world, and live in it in peace and prosperity. I bid you all raise your cups high and toast to the brave people who gave their lives so that we can experience this new world. May we live on for them, remember them, and continue to fight for the dream that they all shared with us. Hail the heroes of the new world. May their lives after death be ones full of peace and joy, and may they guide us to better times."

I kept the cup of beer I had in my hand high in the air, seeing everyone to my right and left doing the same. I said a silent thank you to the friends I had lost, and a special thank you to Keagan and Olly. They gave their lives to put an end to Nylathari and close the portals. Many have already been thanking me for doing both those things, but I continued to tell people who the true heroes of this tale were. I promised myself to make sure that they were forever remembered before bringing the cup to my lips and drinking the beer inside it. Everyone followed my lead, drinking from their cups full of beer, wine, or water. I let the cup fall from my hand when I was done, dreading the next part of the funeral. I took the first step forward, prompting thousands of others to do the same. We would all bury our friends and allies together.

A tall satyr by the name of Teag went over to Colonel Smith as Rosalie made her way to Keagan's grave. Brina went to Sullivan, Quaid went to Seig, Lady Mirlena and Sophia went to General Wyman, and I went to Olly. I took the shovel sticking out of the mound of loose dirt next to her grave and got ready before looking down at my best friend. I thought about all we had been through, and then a pain hit my heart when I thought of all that she had been forced to endure on her own. I didn't even know what she had been through since I left, Olly not even telling me how she got that scar on her cheek, but I knew that whatever it was had changed her. More tears came down my face as I told myself that she didn't have to carry that weight around with her anymore. She was at peace now, happily reunited with those she had lost throughout her life. I took a deep breath and let out a shaky exhale as I poured the dirt onto Olly's calm body, her arms crossed over her chest as was our custom.

Cordelia began to sing a song in Séúbua. I stopped in the middle of my third pouring when I realized that I recognized the tune. It only took me a moment before I remembered where I had heard it before. My father had sung the same song every night on the day of my mother's death. He didn't know I was awake, but I heard him every time. The connection made me even more emotional than I was before. Allowing myself to feel every emotion that showed itself, I continued to move the pile of dirt next to Olly's grave until it completely covered her. I dropped the shovel and lowered myself to my knees. Staring at the sword that marked her grave, I followed it down to the earth where my dear friend now rested.

"Goodbye, Olly. I hope you sing again. I hope you laugh so hard you snort like that time a couple years ago when I was drunk and tossed a dart into Keagan's ass. I hope your family forgives you and embraces you. I hope your new life treats you better than this one did. You earned this peace, Olly. Enjoy it."

Rosalie eventually came over and lowered herself to her knees too. She paid her respects to Olly, and then we stood up together to do the same with Keagan and the others. Different people went to different graves, and much of the morning was spent reminiscing about happier times. Multiple people came up to me, both Tórán and human, to thank me for what I said earlier. Some offered their condolences, and a few shook my hand and thanked me for all I had done. As much as I knew how incredible what we had accomplished was, I couldn't bring myself to enjoy it all. Not yet anyway. Soon the crowd began to shrink as people left for the camp, and Sophia approached me.

"I know I've said it many times already, but I am sorry for your losses, Weylyn," she said.

"We all are," Lady Mirlena added.

"If you need anythin', don't hesitate to ask," Cordelia said as she put a hand on my shoulder.

Rosalie had my arm draped around her shoulders, her hair in two braids that fell over her chest. "You aren't alone. None of us are. We all have each other. Together, we'll make sure nobody falls to their grief."

"Isn't today supposed to be about being happy? That's what Lord Weylyn said right?" Arthur said before his mother leaned down and kissed the top of his head.

Quaid had managed a big smile on his face. "You're quite right, Arthur. I know it's difficult for all of us, since we all lost someone dear to us today, but we should be proud of what we accomplished."

"Yeah!" said Cordelia with a smile of her own. "We should be singin' and dancin', You know, celebratin' the lives of those who made this all possible."

"Celebrating will have to wait, Cordelia." Everyone who had a smile on their face adopted a confused expression in response to my statement. "I know that many people now believe that our fight is over, but I know that isn't the case. We only liberated a few labor camps on our way to Cloque, and word tells us that there are many still running. Who knows what the leaders of those places will do once they learn that General Rosspier has lost. Not to mention that once we liberate these camps, we have to reintroduce the Tóráin back into a society that has willingly murdered them in their homes."

Sophia sighed. "Major Carriere has said that word will be spread about how the Tóráin and humanity fought together against the elves and their allies. I am sure that such news will start the warming of cold hearts."

I appreciated the positivity, but this country was unlike the others. Hate had been cultivated and nourished here long before this year, and the recent months of General Rosspier's madness had only made things worse.

My silent response to Sophia's comments were confronted by Lady Mirlena, who appeared to have been reading my mind. "It might take longer than everywhere else, but things will get better here, Weylyn."

"I know," I said. "But we still have to work for it. Things need to happen still before Fleuris is the place we want it to be. Not to mention there are other places in the world that may need our guidance. I find it hard to think of anything other than what needs to be done next."

Rosalie squeezed me tightly before going up on the tips of her toes to plant a kiss on my cheek. "What needs to be done next doesn't have to stop you from mourning your friends. Both things deserve your attention, and you don't have to choose between them. It's good that you're aware of our next steps, and I want everyone to be safe just as much as you do, but take the time to deal with this moment."

Brina wrapped her arm around my shoulders. "Olwen, Keagan, and everyone else here deserves to be celebrated properly. Come have some drinks. Sing, even though you have a terrible voice. Honor the dead today, and deal with what comes next tomorrow."

Arthur came forward and grabbed my left hand. He smiled at me, and I managed to smile back. I looked around at those who had survived our campaign and felt blessed that so many were still here. We had lost many on the way, but to still have people alive to support you was a miracle that you had to acknowledge just as much as the sacrifice given by those who were dead. I gave in then, nodding to the small gathering of friendly faces that surrounded me. There was still much to do, and despite my wish to address it all immediately, my friends were right. It was our responsibility to honor and celebrate those who gave their lives for us to live the dream we all had when we first joined The Resistance. Everyone began making their way back to camp, but I lingered just a moment longer to look at the graves. I thanked those I knew of, and those I didn't, before promising them all that I would see them honored for centuries after today. Those who lay in The Field of The Brave will forever be remembered for what they did. I would never forget them, and forever admire them.

# Chapter Seventy-Two

## Weylyn

Cloque, Fleuris | September 6,, 1799

It had been a very stressful three weeks. There was so much to be done across the country and not everyone was necessarily on board with what we were doing here. As expected, there were many in Fleuris who were against the changes being made. Humans believed that they were being robbed somehow, with the idea of Tóráin becoming their equal being so outlandish and evil that many had risen up. Pockets of resistances led by nobles who saw a chance to possibly seize the country for themselves sprouted throughout Fleuris. The only reason we had dealt with the majority of them so swiftly was because Jon was on our side. The Major of Fleuris had become the interim leader of the nation and was surprisingly quick to aid us however he could. We had spoken a lot lately, and I had been made aware of why Jon was so eager to help us.

The man lived for Fleuris. His loyalty to his country was unmatched, and all he has ever wanted is for the country to be prosperous and safe. It had taken us some time — with a few heated arguments — but eventually he and I landed on a compromise that would eventually lead to a hesitant friendship; he would try to better accept the Tóráin, and I would try to trust him more. Each of our tasks were difficult in their own ways, but I felt like progress was being made. At the very least, Jon was calling us Tóráin instead of other things, and I had accepted that he wasn't plotting against us.

We had built a good foundation for our new relationship from how the removal of the labor camps was handled. Jon had expressed right away that he had never been on board with such tactics. "Knowing that The Dove was the one who gave Max the idea only makes me want to burn them down even more," he had said. Riders had been sent out the morning after the ceremony at The Field of The Brave informing the leaders of the camps that they were to release all Tóráin. Jon had appeared to be just as furious as Sophia and I when we received word that some of the camp leaders had decided to kill their Tóráin instead of free them. Out of the twenty-one camps in the country, sixteen remained in use after our victory on The Fields of Biette, thanks to Olly and Keagan taking down one and our army liberating four on our way to Cloque. Nine of those camps freed their prisoners. Seven chose to turn their rifles on them instead. One camp in the southwest actually managed to fight back and save some of their own, but in the end we had lost roughly another ten thousand Tóráin to the hatred that lived in humanity.

Dealing with the pain of that news had affected many in their own way, but for me, horrible thoughts entered my mind. Anger had clouded my judgement and I had called for the soldiers responsible for the massacres to be publicly executed. For the first time since my father was killed, I wanted to revenge on humanity. Even now, as I looked over letters from all across the country and beyond, a great rage bubbled to the surface when thinking about what had happened. Thankfully, Rosalie and Sophia had recognized that my anger came from a place of pain, not malice, and they urged me down another path. Brina and Lady Mirlena also had a part in guiding me away from my vengeful thoughts, and Jon had promised he would make sure that those responsible would be punished. The leaders had been executed behind closed doors, and their followers were arrested. Some of them had attempted to run away or fight off the soldiers trying to arrest them, so some were lost or killed, but I eventually agreed that this was the better plan of action for us to take. As much as I believed it would be justice for them all to die, we couldn't be seen as tyrants. It was never in our plan to rule these countries with an iron fist, using fear and violence as a tool to get what we wanted. That was the old way.

We needed to reintroduce the Tóráin to the community peacefully, not as conquerors but as allies. A letter from Etoile reminded me just how difficult that was in some places, with those pockets of resistance causing problems that often led to senseless murder. It had taken time to achieve peace in the villages and towns, and it would take even more time to find a sense of peace in the cities. They had been the worst when it came to how the Tórain had been treated for the last few months, and the humans there still held a great contempt for my kind in their hearts. New programs and laws were being put into place in some areas to help in that regard, but magistrates in certain places were reluctant to follow orders. "Until there is a true ruler of Fleuris, we will refuse to put laws in place created by a foreign leader," had been the consensus of their letters. It was a problem we were running into as of late: the people of Fleuris wanted a new leader. Surprisingly enough, majority of the country was actually glad General Rosspier had died. From poor to rich, there were many humans who were unhappy with some of his decisions. Mind you, Tórain being enslaved and killed wasn't on many of their lists of transgressions, but it was an opening for us to possibly guide them our way.

Many saw Jon as a middleman though. Some even refused to refer to him as Major Carriere despite him being the highest-ranking officer in Fleuris' army at the moment. Nobles especially wanted the monarchy to be restored, but they would all vote for themselves, and no choice would ever be made. The lack of solid leadership was an issue, but until we could make a proper decision on that, we were forced to do our best. Tiny bits of progress had been made, with the rebuilding of destroyed homes and establishments being a relatively well accepted decision. Whether the humans of Fleuris wanted the Tórain living or working in these newly built places was still a problem, but as Lady Mirlena loved telling me, we'll cross that bridge when we get there. I had taken it upon myself to handle a lot of things pertaining to the running of the country, so I heard that phrase leave her lips often. Rosalie and Brina echoed her, as well as Sophia. I'm sure Cordelia and Quaid would be telling me to slow down too, had they not left for their homes and new responsibilities about two weeks ago. The only person who wasn't constantly telling me to ease up and rest was Jon. He knew just as well as I did how much work was needed to get this country to the place The Resistance wanted it to be. We had both been under a great amount of stress, me with the social and legal reforms and he with the security of the nation.

I went over a letter requesting extra soldiers to quell an attempted takeover of a smaller town west of Cloque by a group of unhappy humans. This was actually not uncommon. It was foolish for anyone to think they could just take over a town without consequences, but many of these people were desperate. They wanted to hold on to their undeserving power over my kind so badly that they were doing extreme things. I made a note of it so I could pass the information on to Jon before leaning back in my chair and stretching my arms. I looked out the window nearby to see the beginning of a night sky. I had been here for hours, toiling through countless pages of requests, threats, struggles, and acceptances. The glass on the table was empty, and I groaned at the thought of getting up. If I left this desk, there was a chance I wouldn't come back until tomorrow and there were still many letters to get through. Not just ones that needed reading, but ones that required writing too.

"I knew I would find you here." Rosalie came into view on my left side as she planted a kiss on my cheek.

"Don't go patting yourself on the back for that," I said. "I'm practically chained to this table lately."

"That's why I'm here actually." Rosalie grabbed my hand and began pulling me out of my chair. "I have a surprise for you."

I was so tired all I wanted to do was crawl into bed and sleep for three days straight. The idea of a surprise should have been exciting, but I just saw it as another possible task, and I resisted my love's pulling. "I don't know if I'm up for any more surprises, Rosalie."

She stopped pulling on me to put her hands on her hips. "This isn't a bad one. It's pleasant, I promise. Come on now, it's rude to make people wait."

I reluctantly stood up from my seat and stretched out my back. "People? Rosalie what's going on?"

She shook her head while smiling a sneaky little grin that had me smirking. "Nope. Not telling you. You'll just have to find out for yourself."

Rosalie took my hand and began guiding me out the room. We were in Joieternelle Palace, Jon insisting that Sophia, Lady Mirlena, Arthur, Brina, Rosalie, and me all stay here for the time being while we get things in order. Rosalie guided me quickly down hallways and staircases until we reached the main floor. We came over to the dining hall, the doors closed. Rosalie stood in front of them while facing me, the grin on her face having grown since our conversation in my room.

"Are you ready?" she asked.

I sighed. "Go on then."

Rosalie opened the doors to the room and a large table was laid out in the middle of it. I had eaten here only twice so far, but it had just been a small group of Sophia, Jon, his wife Coraline, Rosalie, and me. Sitting at the table was a larger group than I was used to. Lady Mirlena and Arthur sat next to Sophia, while Brina sat opposite of them. Jon and Coraline sat next to her, and then there were four people I did not expect to see. Next to Arthur sat Cordelia, with her partner Eva next to her. Across from them sat Quaid, and next to him — probably the most surprising of all — was Princess Alessandra of Malvene. There were too vacant seats with elaborate plating in front of them: the one at the head of the table, and the one on its right-hand side. Rosalie took my hand in hers and guiding me towards them as I tried to process what was going on. Eventually, as we reached the empty seats, I found the words to ask my internal question out loud.

"What's going on?" I asked.

"Today is a special occasion! Well, we're hopin' it will be," Cordelia said before sending me a wink as she raised her glass in the air.

"We can talk about that later," Sophia said. "Right now, you can just sit down and enjoy a well-earned meal with your friends."

I looked around at everyone and received only smiles. I pulled the head chair back and inspected it, wondering if this was some sort of prank.

"Oh just sit down already!" Lady Mirlena shouted. "I'm quite hungry, as I'm sure everyone else is."

Rosalie seated herself in the open chair next to me before I finally took my own seat. I inched my way closer to the table, and once we were both seated comfortably, Jon shouted something in Fleuran towards the open doors. Within thirty seconds or so, a flurry of butlers and maids entered the room, bringing in a grand number of meats, breads, fruits, and cakes. A woman came and filled up everyone's glasses with an aromatic white wine while everything was being placed before us. Once all of the dishes were placed on the table and the workers — save for three of them — had all left, Jon raised his glass in the air.

"To Weylyn, Leader of The Resistance. This is a meal honorably earned. I know just how much work there is still left to do, but I think we can all take the time to enjoy tonight. Especially you. *Bon appétit*!"

Everyone raised their own glasses, the mixing of their voices agreeing with Jon sounding like nothing but loud mumbling. Still, I was thankful for what they had done for me. I had not expected to see Cordelia or Quaid for months, possibly even years. I was eager to speak with both of them; I was especially curious about Quaid's date to this dinner. As much as certain conversations appeared to be wished for, the beginning of our meal was relatively quiet. There was some general chatter, but everyone was mostly focused on filling their bellies. I couldn't blame them. The food was incredible, and I made sure to tell the butler nearby to bring in the chef so I could thank him personally. Everyone had given the humble Marlon praises for his meal, and the man was flush from the compliments. Cordelia insisted he have a drink with us, and while he was clearly hesitant to mingle with non-humans, he accepted the offer. That was when the conversations became louder and more frequent. After some pleasant time spent with Marlon, he excused himself, citing he needed to prepare some things for tomorrow morning before he went to sleep. That was when I finally asked one of my burning questions.

"Princess Alessandra, I am curious about something," I said with a smile. "Surely Queen Mirabella didn't want you coming here. How did you come to accompany Quaid?"

The young woman became flush as she looked at Quaid before answering. "She does not know where I am."

As happy as I was for Quaid, I grew nervous. I didn't need the Queen of Malvene thinking her daughter was kidnapped or something of the sort. "No one knows you're here? How did you manage that?"

Princess Alessandra shook her head. "No, *mio padre* knows that I am here. Quaid asked him if I could join him on his trip to Cloque. He approves of us. *Mia madre* does not. She thinks I'm on a holy trip to Luila to pray."

"Ah forbidden love," Cordelia chimed in. "How beautiful. Good on ya for fightin' for what ya want."

Rosalie finished chewing on a cake before raising her glass at Quaid and Princess Alessandra. "I agree. I'm happy for you two."

I raised my glass as well, which prompted everyone else to do the same. "I pray that your mother comes around, Princess Alessandra. Still, should she not, I wish you and Quaid nothing but happiness."

"*Au bonheur!*" Coraline shouted.

"To happiness!" Jon translated.

We all echoed the cheer and everyone applauded when Princess Alessandra gave Quaid a quick kiss. Everyone took a hefty drink from their glasses with smiles on their faces. Tonight was going wonderfully, and I finally felt some of the pressure I had been under slip away in favor of unhindered joy.

"I think it is time for us to talk about you, Weylyn," Sophia announced.

"Yeah! Get to the good bits," Eva said as she leaned in closer, wrapping her arm around Cordelia's.

"What is it?" I asked.

Sophia took a breath before looking at everyone else. When her eyes fell on me, she had a big smile on her face. "I think it is in everyone's best interest that you are made King of Fleuris."

"What?" I shouted. I began shaking my head. "No. Jon is a good enough leader. He's willing to work with us and he's agreed to our terms. We need to focus on making him leader of Fleuris."

"I'm the one who proposed this," Jon said.

I struggled to find the right words. "I…don't understand. Why give up your rule to a Tórán? You were just fighting to kill all of us a few weeks ago."

"Weylyn that isn't fair," Rosalie said quickly.

"No, Rosalie, it's alright. You are correct. For most of my life, I have judged you and people like you. I was raised to believe that you are beneath me, and so my beliefs reflected those before me. However, I never shared the belief that you deserved to be enslaved or murdered. I treated you the same way I treated the poor. Leaders before him were unkind to the Tóráin, but Max was disgusted by you. His hate festered for years, eventually reaching an extreme that I could not agree with. He was my longest friend and leader of the country I am loyal to, so I didn't push as hard as I should have for him to change his ways. This was wrong of me. I knew in my heart that what he was doing was wrong, and that the hate within me for your kind was misled. Free of him, and after replacing his teachings with the memory of a Tórán saving my life, I can now look forward.

"I know the world is changing. I recognize that my views, while not as extreme as others, are still the kind that need to be adjusted. I welcome the challenge of encouraging people to accept this new world and move away from old beliefs. As I am sure many others have, I gained a lot of respect for the Tórán known as Weylyn, Leader of The Resistance, after speaking with you for some time. I see now what you stand for and I respect it. The world you want, the world we all want, is not something I can provide. Not in the necessary time, anyway. I believe Fleuris needs a king again, and I believe that you should be that king. If you choose to take the crown, you will have not only the support of my wife and I, but also the entire Fleuris military."

I knew that I should be feeling immensely honored for a man like Jon to put his support behind me in such a way, but every bit of my being refused the idea of it all. "I don't want a crown. Find someone else."

Lady Mirlena crossed her arms over her chest. "I told you he wouldn't want it."

I turned my attention to the witch. "You knew about this?"

"We all did, Weylyn," Rosalie said. "It's why we're all here."

Sophia shifted in her chair so that she was facing me head on. "It is quite funny actually. You are reacting exactly how most of us expected you would."

"You've earned this, Weylyn." Quaid said. "More than anyone. It should be you."

I shook my head. "I don't think so. I'm sure we'll find someone else better suited for the job than me. I can't be the leader of Fleuris."

"Why the Hell not?" Cordelia shouted. "Who are ya kiddin'? You'd be an excellent leader."

"He already is an excellent leader." Rosalie had left her seat and come to stand next to me. She leaned in and planted a kiss on my cheek. "You should accept, Weylyn. I promise you that you're the best person to lead this country."

I looked around at everyone, pondering what they had said. I noticed that Brina had been silent. "Brina? What do you think?"

The lycan ran her fingers through her short hair before rubbing the injured eye that had rendered her half-blind. "I don't see how a nation that was more than happy to lock Tóráin away in cages so that they can be treated worse than cattle would possibly welcome an Tóráin ruler. Even before the camps, they were content with us being killed for little more than looking at a soldier funny. It may work in other countries, but Fleuris is different. There's still a great level of hate for our kind and it has only been encouraged during our lifetime. I can see why Weylyn would be hesitant to accept the position."

Brina's words were allowed to marinate amongst the group until an unlikely voice entered the conversation. "But people can change. Can't they? Shouldn't we have faith that people will hear about what happened across Fleuris, with the elves and what not, and realize that we're better together? We've had hope for so long. Why would we stop having it now?"

Lady Mirlena leaned over and wrapped her arm around her son, squeezing him tightly before kissing him on his cheek. "We didn't lose hope, Arthur. These things are just more difficult than you think."

"They don't have to be though," Cordelia said. "We'll have Tóráin on a council in Tulp, the fights in Korblum are no more, and there are Tóráin nobles in Stelpina and Malvene. Tudrose's most trusted advisor is a witch, and the northern nations already have treaties in place with Tudrose to make life for the Tóráin better in their countries. The world is changin', Weylyn. Who better to lead us all into a new age than the lycan who has been fightin' for this for more than a decade?"

I sighed. "But Brina's right. Humans —"

"Humans will learn to love you," Quaid interrupted.

"Many of them already do," said Princess Alessandra.

"Give it time and they'll all come to see how your dream benefits everyone," Jon added.

I felt Rosalie wrap her arm around my shoulders. "They're right, Weylyn. Deep down, you must know that."

"Lead Fleuris into the age of peace you have always dreamt of," Sophia said.

Lady Mirlena cleared her throat and I looked at over at her. She had a very serious look on her face as she spoke. "It's time for you to believe in yourself the same way we believe in you. It's time for you to do what you were clearly born to do. Lead. Show people the way and I know they'll follow you."

I was still struggling with my decision, everyone's comments now leaning me perhaps a different way than before. I looked at Brina again. I needed her support if I was going to do this.

Brina's shoulders fell before she looked around at everyone, eventually letting out a reluctant sigh. "There's no doubt in my mind that you would be an incredible king. I believe in your capabilities, and in your heart. It's going to be probably one of the hardest things you will ever do in your life, but if you choose to take this challenge on, I'll stand with you. I'll always stand with you."

Now everyone looked at me, waiting for a response. I took in everything everyone had said and finally made a decision. "Alright."

Rosalie kissed me and everyone had smiles on their faces. It felt odd judging that the times we were in were still what many would consider dark. We were celebrating something that many wouldn't be able to experience, and it pained me greatly. I found I just wanted to sleep now, wanting to relieve myself from having to think about anything, let alone becoming King of Fleuris. Unfortunately, the conversation wasn't done just yet.

"I'll send out riders tomorrow morning with invitations," Sophia proclaimed.

"Invitations?" I asked. "Why? Can't we just do it quietly?"

Everyone looked at me like I was a young child who had just done something incredibly adorable. Sophia chuckled a bit before answering me. "Weylyn, we cannot do it quietly. You know that. And with such a monumental moment in this world's history, I think the rulers of Kosavros should be there to witness it. Do not worry. I will take care of it. Everyone will be pleased to come meet King Weylyn of Fleuris."

I took Rosalie's hand in mine and kissed it. "Don't forget Queen Rosalie."

Everyone looked more shocked than I thought they would.

"Formal unions between Tóráin and humans are illegal everywhere save for Tudrose, and even there they aren't the most pleasant occasions," Brina said.

"I'll be King of Fleuris, right? It's legal if I say it is. I'm not doing this without Rosalie by my side." I gave the love of my life a quick kiss, reinforcing my statement.

"Then it seems as though we'll be having a wedding as well as a coronation. If Rosalie wants us to, of course." Lady Mirlena looked at Rosalie with a look of expectation.

"Of course I want that!" Rosalie said. "Yes!"

Again, the cheer that surrounded me felt misplaced. With so much death and sadness in the last three weeks, it was hard to find a reason to feel any sense of joy. My mind fell to how much I wished Olly and Keagan could be here. Sullivan and Seig came to mind next. Then everyone that has died in the last few months appeared in my thoughts before the oddest thing happened. Something inside me told me to be happy. I couldn't explain it if I tried. As faces of those I had lost came before my mind's eye, I just felt an overwhelming feeling that it was okay for me to be happy. I chose to take it as Keagan and Olly — and everyone else — letting me know they were still with me. Allowing myself to smile, I stood up from my seat and hugged Rosalie tightly. Sophia started talking about all the preparations that needed to be made as everyone stood from their seats. Brina came over and put a hand on my shoulder and Cordelia started to sing.

# Chapter Seventy-Three

## Weylyn

Cloque, Fleuris  |  September 22, 1799

A knock on my door snapped me out of the whirlwind of thoughts spinning around in my head. "Come in!"

I looked away from the mirror I was staring into to find someone I didn't really expect to see. "Quite the get up you got there, Weylyn. You sure look like a king."

I stopped adjusting my clothes and went over to give the old satyr a hug. "Ossian! I didn't expect to see you before the ceremonies."

We broke apart and I motioned for him to come sit on the bed with me. He moved slowly before plopping down on the thick blankets. "Yes, well I wanted to talk to you before you became too important to give me the time of day."

I put my arm around him. "I'll always have time for you, Ossian."

The satyr fixed his vest. "Sure, sure. I have no idea what it's been like leading The Resistance, but I imagine leading Fleuris will be more demanding. Just let me have my moment to speak. I have something to say before you go out there."

I shifted myself so that I was facing Ossian, one leg bent and on the bed with the other dangling off the side. "What is it? Is something wrong?"

"No, No." Ossian patted my hand. "Nothing's wrong. After your father killed those soldiers to protect you, I assume you remember him taking you to his brother, Benen, yes?"

Talk of my father was uncomfortable for me, but the fact that it was with Ossian made it a bit more manageable. "Yes, I remember. He left me with Brina and Uncle Benen and told me to stay inside."

Ossian nodded. "Yes, well, you see, after making sure you were safe, he came to my home to speak with me. We knew what would happen if Conri stayed in the city. I tried to convince him to leave, but he refused. Not wishing for you to be possibly arrested as well, he chose to turn himself in. I didn't like it, but there was no convincing Conri to not do something once he put his mind to it. He told me to look after you before giving me this."

Ossian reached into a pocket and pulled out a thick, silver ring. The top of it had the image of a wolf's head in the center of a circle. The wolf's eyes were black gemstones and ornate designs decorated the sides. I recognized the ring immediately. It was the ring my mother had given my father on their wedding day. It was a customary part of the ceremony for lycans to give gifts to each other. The ring belonged to her father, my grandfather. I had long thought that the soldiers who took my father had stolen it off him. I never thought I would see it again. My hand reached out almost instinctively, and I plucked it from Ossian's fingers.

"He wanted me to keep it safe for him," Ossian said. "Why he didn't just give it to you or his brother, I don't know. He never told me why. He left before I could ask. Anyway, shortly after Conri left some soldiers came to my home looking for him. It made me worried that they were maybe watching me, so even with Conri turning himself in, I still didn't want to maybe endanger you. I stayed away. Then the riots happened, and I am ashamed to say that I got scared. I had seen so much death in my life, Weylyn. Seeing so many of our kind murdered in the streets had me fleeing the country the next day. I had a thought to mail the ring to you, but I was afraid it would be lost or stolen. And so, I kept it."

I played with the ring in my fingers as I looked it over. "Why didn't you tell me? Why didn't you give it to me when I was in Leonessa?"

"You were doing good things in Fleuris with Darby. I felt that if I told you about the ring you would want to come get it, and I feared you wouldn't want to go back. Fleuris needed you. As for why I didn't give it to you earlier, I forgot." Ossian chuckled. "My mind is old, and I grow forgetful when I'm plotting prison escapes, nursing people back to health, and meeting queens. Luckily, I remembered to bring it with me on this trip. I'm glad that I did. It belongs with you."

"Thank you, Ossian." I tried the ring on and was happy to find it fit my finger perfectly.

"I've said it before, but I'm going to say it again. Your parents are proud of you, Weylyn. Not many could have ever thought that you would be where you are today, but I know your parents did. They saw greatness in you since you were a baby. I'm sad that they aren't here to see that they were right, but I know that, somehow, they know." Ossian patted me on the back.

"Yeah," I said. "There's a few people I wish were here."

A loud knock on the door interrupted our conversation. I called for the person to enter, and Lady Mirlena opened the door. She had a fancy, dark blue dress on with a lighter blue corset accentuating her features. Her hair was done up into an elegant braid and a large smile enveloped her face. "Come on you! Everyone's waiting!"

Ossian stood up and fixed his vest again. "I apologize, the delay is my fault."

I stood up and put a hand on the satyr's shoulder. "No need to apologize, Ossian. I'm glad we talked."

"You're sure about what we talked about earlier? There's no changing your mind after without causing a giant mess," Lady Mirlena said.

I smiled. "Of course, I'm sure. Wouldn't have it any other way."

"Alright. Come on then!" Lady Mirlena waved us on before leaving the room.

I made my way down the hallway and continued to chat with Ossian. Being inside Joieternelle Palace was still weird to me but knowing that it would become my permanent home was even more odd. The wedding and coronation would be done in the throne room, witnessed by the leaders of Kosavros and a handful of Fleuris nobles who had accepted the invitation. Many had not, which was to be expected, but more had come than I thought. The two soldiers standing guard opened the doors for Ossian as he went ahead of me to join the others. I stood there anxiously until I finally found a sense of calm. With my newfound confidence, I pushed through the doors myself, everyone turning around to look at me the moment I entered.

There were people in the room who I recognized, and others who I didn't, but I had good guesses. I noticed King Ludovico and his family first, before spotting King Frederick and his wife Queen Petra. Next, was the impossible to miss King Ehren of Korblum, his long blonde hair tied back and his soft brown eyes watching closely. Others wore crowns on their heads, but I didn't know exactly who they were. I couldn't match names to faces yet, but I was sure the two tallest monarchs were King Harald of Fruberg and King Bjorn of Linne. The women with them must have been King Harald's wife, Queen Freja, and King Bjorn's wife, Queen Alsa. There was a man that looked relatively young, perhaps in his early twenties, so I assumed he and the woman with him were King Andreas and Queen Nadine of Weidel. The final ruler left was a woman, who I assumed was the oldest person in the room: Queen Zofia of Czermak. A middle-aged man stood next to her, and a younger boy perhaps around the age of Arthur was in front of him. The two were Queen Zofia's son and grandson, Prince Jakub and Lord Mikolaj respectfully. Everyone else that was there were nobles I hadn't bothered to meet yet, save for a few important people at the front.

Cordelia and Sophia stood before two chairs with tall backings. In the first row to the right stood Eva, Quaid, Jon, and Coraline. In the first row to the left stood Lady Mirlena, Arthur, and Ossian. I came to stand in front of Sophia and Cordelia and we exchanged smiles. We all then began the painstakingly long wait for Rosalie. It was only a minute or so, but it felt much longer. I was excited to marry her more than I was to be named king. We had both wanted to do this for years, and for it to finally be happening was incredible. Eventually, the doors opened again and there she was, the love of my life, being escorted by Brina down the aisle the two groups of people had created. My cousin wore something more akin to what a male would wear, but Brina had never been one for dresses anyway. Rosalie on the other hand, had always dreamed of wearing a fancy dress for our wedding and I was glad that her dream had come true. A seamstress in the city had offered to make Rosalie's wedding dress, and the woman had done an incredible job. The dress left the top of her shoulders bare, flowing all the way down to the floor. It was a light green shade — Rosalie's favorite color — and was accentuated by a dark green corset that wonderfully displayed the curves in her body that I adored. There had been some talk about how wedding dresses needed to be white, but Rosalie wanted what she wanted. It didn't bother me at all. She was more beautiful than ever before. Brina and Rosalie made their way down the aisle until I was finally able to take Rosalie's hand and bring her over to stand on my right side.

Cordelia stepped forward and addressed the room. "Today we celebrate the union of two lovebirds who are just made for each other. Together, they show us that love doesn't care what you look like, where you come from, who you worship, or where your allegiances lie. I'm honored to marry the two of 'em and honestly can't wait to see those crowns go on their heads, so let's get started shall we."

Mumbles could be heard behind us, and I couldn't help but smirk. I had learned that Cordelia will always speak honestly, even when it wasn't maybe proper for her to do so. The water sprite took my right hand and Rosalie's left hand and brought them together. She wrapped a cloth around our hands before smiling at us both. "In the name of whichever gods you pray to, I am blessin' the union of one Weylyn, Son of Conri, and one Rosalie Thomas. Do you have your gifts?"

I took my free hand and shoved it into my pocket, removing a pendant in the shape of a rose. Rosalie looked over to Eva and she handed her a small box. Rosalie opened it to show a pin representing a crescent moon. We exchanged our gifts by passing them to Brina and Eva, and then Cordelia spoke again.

"The gifts have been exchanged, the hands have been bound, and the blessin' has been made. In the eyes of your friends and those you worship, you're one. Now seal it with a kiss, will ya."

I kissed Rosalie without hesitation, bringing my free hand to the side of her face to keep her close. There were more cheers than I thought there would be, which made me hopeful for when we would meet with the crowd outside. Before we could do that, there was another order of business. Cordelia stepped aside and Sophia took her place. The Queen of Tudrose motioned for us to both kneel and we obeyed the order. Lady Mirlena brought forth a simple golden ring on a cushion, with a smaller one sitting inside it.

Sophia took the larger one in her hands and held it high above my head. "In the name of the Goddess Anu and Our Lord Deus, I name you King Weylyn of Fleuris." She brought the crown down and rested it on my head.

Sophia then took the smaller crown and raised it over Rosalie's head. "In the name of the Goddess Anu and Our Lord Deus, I name you Queen Rosalie of Fleuris." I watched as she lowered the crown down onto the immaculate braid that encircled Rosalie's head.

I could hear people whispering behind us as Sophia signaled for us to stand. The mention of our gods was probably something many here wouldn't be too happy about, but Sophia had insisted on honoring my heritage and culture in the ceremony. Rosalie and I got to our feet and turned to face everyone. The nobles in the small crowd kneeled while the other kings and queens bowed.

"Long live Weylyn and Rosalie, King and Queen of Fleuris!" Sophia proclaimed.

Everyone echoed the cheer, and it began to sink in what had just happened. I didn't have much time to enjoy it though, because Sophia was already ushering everyone out of the room so that Rosalie and I could be introduced to the public. A large crowd had been allowed to gather in the large park south of the building, but many others had supposedly spilled into the streets. We were worried about how this would all go, but there was some encouraging news that had come a few days ago involving what had happened during the battle at The Fields of Biette. Portals had opened all across Kosavros that day, and those circumstances had encouraged humans to join with the Tóráin and fight them off. Many died, much like they had at The Fields of Biette. However, the comradery shown had planted a seed that had since had time to grow. Word reached us of a growing sense of peace amongst the countries of Kosavros as of late, which was lovely to hear. There were still many problems in Fleuris, but I believed that we would eventually join the other nations in recognizing that we can put aside our differences and come together. Many out there who weren't happy with me being named King of Fleuris could possibly be a problem, but we couldn't dwell on it too much. We knew what doing this would bring, and we were prepared to prove to those who were against us how wrong they were.

We all made our way to the courtyard where a stage had been crafted. You could hear the crowd from anywhere in the building, but the sound grew louder as we got closer to the southern exit of the palace. Rosalie and I eventually stepped out into the afternoon sun and were greeted by a mixture of boos and cheers. Soldiers escorted us to the stage and, together, Rosalie and I stood before the masses. Guards formed a barrier four lines thick to keep the crowd at bay, while a line of soldiers stood behind us. After a short time of feeling like a piece of jewelry or a prized piece of meat being stared at in a market, the men behind us fired one shot into the air, silencing the crowd. I held Rosalie's hand in mine before stepping forward to address everyone. Before I could, someone shouted from the group of people.

"You aren't my king! I'll never be loyal to a *Diable*!" The claim stirred up a great number of people who began yelling similar statements.

Another set of gunfire filled the air and the crowd eased enough for Jon to step forward and speak. "Weylyn is your king, and I promise you he will be a great one! His people have been horribly mistreated by humans and yet they stood by us and fought against the invaders from another world." He held up his arm, showing everyone the stump that remained. "The same invaders who did this to me! If it weren't for a Tórán I would be dead. There are many people all across Kosavros who can say the same. King Weylyn and Queen Rosalie have my support, and they should have yours as well."

The crowd bustled a bit but there was no more shouting. I took the chance to speak to them like I had intended. "People of Fleuris! The relationship between the Tóráin and humanity has been a trying one. We have endured a great amount of abuse since arriving here, a truth that sparked a grand rebellion which led to this new regime. I know many of you may hate me, whether it be due to religion or something else, and I am sorry that you have been taught this way. I promise you that my kind has always been a warm, compassionate, hardworking, spiritual people. We hold no ill will against humans. We don't seek revenge for past transgressions. All we want is to move forward, together. We see the potential in a better relationship between my kind and yours, and we know where that potential can take us. This world can be so much better for so many people, and we want to make the necessary changes so that everyone's life can be the best it can possibly be. Tórán or human, it doesn't matter to me. We're all citizens of Fleuris in my eyes. We're all in this together. I assure you that we are not the monsters you have been told we are. All I am asking from you is to give us a chance to prove it. With some patience and hard work, I know that this new era of peace will bring prosperity and joy to everyone. As your king, with my queen at my side, I will do everything in my power to see that the poor are lifted from the depths of poverty, and that everyone is given an equal opportunity to have a healthy, happy, and safe life. All I need from you all is a little bit of faith."

I couldn't make out what people were saying, but nobody was shouting obscenities my way, so I felt like my speech had gone well. That was until a man dressed like a noble shouted from the front of the crowd. "Your kind can't make children with humans! This is well known! How are we to support your reign when it is weakened by a lack of succession?"

I turned to my right and waved at the two people standing off to the side of the stage. I had planned to do this differently, but it appeared the best time was now. Lady Mirlena came up the steps with Arthur before stopping about ten feet away and urging her son to go to Rosalie and me. The young man came to stand between the two of us and we each put a hand on his shoulder before I addressed the crowd.

"There is no lack of succession. Queen Rosalie and I have chosen an heir to Fleuris' throne. This is Arthur. He is human, like many of you here today. He is wise beyond his years, more intelligent than many, and, most importantly, he is immensely compassionate. He possesses all of the qualities we hope to encourage during our reign, and we believe he will lead this country well one day."

The large group was relatively quiet until a surprising shout came from far away. "*Gloire au Prince Arthur!*"

More people echoed the cheer before another was added to the mix. "*Gloire au Roi Weylyn! Gloire à la Reine Rosalie!*"

Not everyone was joining in, but I would say at least half of the crowd was applauding and cheering us within a few seconds of the shouts hailing Arthur, Rosalie, and I. Smiling at Rosalie and Arthur before doing so, I raised my hands in the air and prayed that I said it correctly. *"Gloire aux citoyens de Fleuris!"* The rest of the crowd cheered and I breathed a breath of relief. Rosalie had thought it smart to teach me a few phrases in Fleuran that might help endear me to the human population, and I was glad that she had. Fleuris was an incredibly proud nation, and any sign of recognition or celebration of their culture was greatly appreciated and admired. Sensing a good enough amount of joy in the crowd urged the next shout from me to come forward. "Begin the celebrations!"

Musicians spread throughout the park began playing shortly after my announcement as maids and butlers began passing out cups of beer to the crowd. I wasn't sure if we had enough for everyone, but I knew that the pubs and taverns would gladly fill up those who went dry today. Our friends all joined the three of us at the center of the stage and greeted us with hugs and handshakes. Brina stood next to Ossian with a small smile on her face, an arm draped around the satyr's shoulders. Jon had his wife Coraline beside him, her arm wrapped around his uninjured one. Lady Mirlena stood with Sophia before lunging forward and hugging Arthur tightly. Cordelia had her arm around Eva's waist, and Quaid was standing quite proudly with King Ludovico's daughter, Princess Alessandra, holding his arm. I smiled, happy to have everyone around.

"It's horrible that some people had to miss this," I said.

"They're seein' it, Weylyn. Don't you worry 'bout that," said Cordelia.

Eva smiled. "They're cheering so loud they'll lose their voices by the end of the night."

"Yeah. I bet they're having their own massive party to celebrate," Quaid added.

"With lots of wine and those little cakes everyone loves so much but are always told they can't have too many or they'll get fat." Everyone was a bit caught off guard by the detailed story Princess Alessandra had just given, but we were all quickly laughing at her comment.

Coraline pouted. "Oh now I want one of those myself."

"You already had two this morning," said Jon, prompting us all to laugh a little more.

Brina stepped forward and looked out at the crowd. The sudden movement had me turning my attention towards my cousin. Everyone slowly saw I was distracted, and soon we were all looking out at the crowd, watching a group consisting of different races of people celebrate a monumental day in history. Brina put her hands on her hips and sighed. "I really hope this is a new dawn for the Tóráin."

"Shouldn't you call yourselves something else now?" Arthur questioned.

I put a hand on his shoulder. "What do you mean?"

"Well, Tóráin means Hunted Ones in your language, right? You aren't being hunted anymore. You should be something different now."

"I suppose you're right. Any suggestions?" I asked.

"How about the Láidre?" Lady Mirlena, Cordelia, and Ossian all reacted happily to the suggested new name.

"How do you know Séúbua?" I asked.

"Mother's been teaching it to me. She helped me pick the name actually." Arthur smiled at Lady Mirlena.

"What does it mean?" Quaid asked.

"The Strong Ones," Ossian answered before Arthur could.

I pulled Arthur in for a quick hug with one arm while bringing in Rosalie for one as well with my other. "The Láidre it is then."

Brina continued to look out at the crowd. "Láidre and humans, side by side. Will it last, I wonder?"

"I think it will," Arthur said.

"We'll make sure of it," Lady Mirlena stated.

"Together." Sophia's response was echoed by the others there. The camaraderie shown by us all had me thinking of Keagan and Olly.

I kept them in my mind as I smiled. "Together

# Language
## Key

# Fleuran

| | | |
|---|---|---|
| Diable(s) | — | Devil(s) |
| chien | — | Dog |
| salauds | — | bastard |
| petite merde | — | little shit |
| Gens de Cloque! | — | People of Cloque! |
| déchets | — | trash |
| monstre | — | monster |
| dix protecteurs | — | ten protectors |
| lâche | — | coward |
| le joli oiseau | — | the pretty bird |
| Sont-ils fous? | — | Are they crazy? |
| mon amie | — | my friend |
| Le jour spécial | — | The special day |
| quatre | — | four |
| Elle est sauvage et folle | — | She's wild and crazy |
| s'il te plaît | — | please |
| Gens de Fleuris! | — | People of Fleuris! |
| parasites | — | parasites |
| cafards | — | cockroaches |
| dans le royaume merveilleux de Fleuris | — | in the marvelous kingdom of Fleuris |
| Désormais | — | Henceforward |
| Et la vérité est | — | And the truth is |
| un prophète | — | a prophet |
| les militaires | — | the military |
| mes magnifiques frères et soeurs | — | my beautiful brothers and sisters |
| Aujourd'hui | — | Today |
| le vingt-huit Décembre | — | the twenty-eighth of December |

| dix-sept quatre-vingt-dix- huit | — | Seventeen ninety-eight |
| la victoire | — | the victory |
| groupe d'êtres maléfiques | — | group of evil beings |
| justice | — | justice |
| pas d'interrogatoire! | — | no interrogation! |
| Je vais te faire avancer! | — | I will take you forward |
| Soldats! Avancez! | — | Soldiers! Advance! |
| tout de suite | — | right now |
| Cet ami était-il humain? | — | Was this friend human? |
| l'alcool | — | alcohol |
| La Dame | — | The Lady |
| En veux-tu? | — | Do you want some? |
| C'est épuisant. | — | It's exhausting. |
| Comme des enfants qui demandent de l'aide à leur père. | — | Like children asking their father for help |
| Bâtards ingrats! | — | Ungrateful bastards! |
| magique | — | magic |
| ces Diables | — | those Devils |
| vils démons | — | vile demons |
| ces stupides sorcières | — | those stupid witches |
| Mon frère | — | My brother |
| la maison du bâtard | — | the bastard's house |
| je crois | — | I believe |
| Oui! | — | Yes! |
| Dis-moi qui tu es ou j'appelle un garde. | — | Tell me who you are or I'll call a guard. |
| Tu veux de l'argent? De la nourriture? D'être libre? Tout ce que tu veux est à toi! | — | You want money? Food? To be free? Everything you want is yours! |
| Je ne sais pas | — | I don't know |

| mon père | — | my father |
| J'emmerde la sorcière! | — | Fuck the witch! |
| le quinze de ce mois | — | the fifteenth of this month |
| Veuillez m'excuser les amis. | — | Please excuse me my friends. |
| Merveilleux | — | Wonderful. |
| La Colombe | — | The Dove |
| Bonne nuit! | — | Goodnight! |
| Un chien ou une chèvre? | — | A dog or a goat? |
| pidgeon | — | pigeon |
| Non? | — | No? |
| petits monstres | — | little monsters |
| Les bons humains de Fleuris! | — | The good humans of Fleuris! |
| N'aie pas peur | — | Do not be afraid |
| Ce matin | — | This morning |
| ces horribles bêtes | — | these horrible beasts |
| Vous êtes tous des enfants exceptionnels de Deus! | — | You are all brilliant children of Deus! |
| Attention les gars | — | Watch out boys |
| la pute | — | the whore |
| une band de voyous | — | a gang of thugs |
| rébellions | — | rebellions |
| leur père | — | their father |
| animaux sauvages | — | wild animals |
| Je m'en fiche. | — | I do not care. |
| Nous avons les chiffres. | — | We have the numbers. |
| ces monstres | — | those monsters |
| ces maudites bêtes | — | those damn beasts |
| les Diables | — | the Devils |

| | | |
|---|---|---|
| Tu vas bien? | — | Are you okay? |
| Oui, je vais bien. | — | Yes, I'm okay. |
| Bon travail, soldat. | — | Good job, soldier. |
| Moindres | — | Lessers |
| Seigneur Roi | — | Lord King |
| une sorcière | — | a witch |
| animaux | — | animals |
| ce lieu saint | — | this holy place |
| Tenir! | — | Hold! |
| Tout le monde! | — | Everybody! |
| J'ai décidé. | — | I've decided. |
| cette maison de Deus | — | this house of Deus |
| Emmenez-les dehors! | — | Take them outside! |
| imbéciles bestiaux | — | beastly fools |
| Silencieux! | — | Quiet! |
| chienne | — | female dog |
| Si sinistre! | — | So sinister! |
| Vas-y! | — | Go ahead! |
| bête vaine | — | vain beast |
| Seigneurs et Dames, amis et alliés, jeunes et moins jeunes | — | Lords and Ladies, friends and allies, old and young |
| juste un moment | — | just a moment |
| ce soir | — | this evening |
| Il a fallu du temps | — | It took time |
| parasites maléfiques | — | evil parasites |
| Pour le moment | — | For now |
| et moi | — | and me |
| Gloire à Deus! | — | Glory to Deus! |
| Gloire au général Rosspier! | — | Glory to General Rosspier! |

| ces créatures | — | these creatures |
| bêtes sauvages | — | wild beasts |
| je suis content | — | I'm happy |
| Un compromis | — | A compromise |
| Cependant | — | However |
| si vous voulez bien m'excuser | — | If you will excuse me |
| Attendez! | — | Wait! |
| mes amies | — | my friends |
| C'est de la folie. | — | This is madness. |
| Espèce de Diable stupide! | — | You stupid Devil! |
| Oui, Général. | — | Yes, General. |
| Les Spectres | — | The Specters |
| Très bien. | — | Very good. |
| Non, Général. | — | No, General. |
| Garde Du Roi | — | King's Guard |
| A la victoire! | — | To victory! |
| Va-t'en! | — | Go away! |
| groupe de païens | — | group of pagans |
| Ce sont mes soldats! | — | They are my soldiers! |
| Le mien! | — | Mine! |
| C'est ça. | — | That's it. |
| une petite souris | — | a small mouse |
| Assez parlé pour l'instant. | — | Enough talk for now. |
| un chien | — | a dog |
| Bats-toi plus fort! | — | Fight harder! |
| Ne lâche pas la bataille! Rallies-toi à moi! | — | Don't give up the fight! Rally to me! |
| Avance! | — | Advance! |

| Fille idiote. | — | Stupid girl. |
| Aucun d'eux ne le fait! | — | None of them do! |
| Traître et vil! | — | Treacherous and vile! |
| Vous tous! | — | All of you! |
| fille naïve | — | naive girl |
| Bon appétit! | — | Enjoy your meal! |
| Au bonheur! | — | To happiness! |
| Gloire au Prince Arthur! | — | Glory to Prince Arthur! |
| Gloire au Roi Weylyn! | — | Glory to King Weylyn! |
| Gloire à la Reine Rosalie! | — | Glory to Queen Rosalie! |
| Gloire aux citoyens de Fleuris! | — | Glory to the citizens of Fleuris! |

# Tultch

| | | |
|---|---|---|
| Duivel(s) | — | Demon(s) |
| vuiligheid | — | filth |
| stuk stront | — | piece of shit |
| verrader | — | betrayer |
| idioot | — | idiot |
| prachtig | — | wonderful |
| bedelaars | — | beggars |
| beesten | — | beasts |
| kwaadaardige wezens | — | evil creatures |
| Jullie zijn allemaal onbeleefde, ondankbare afval! | — | You are all rude, ungrateful garbage! |
| hond | — | dog |
| zwerfhond | — | stray dog |
| Zie je? | — | You see? |
| Let op mijn woorden! | — | Mark my words! |

# Malvenian

|  | |  |
|---|---|---|
| asino | — | jackass |
| bruti | — | brutes |
| Goditela! | — | Enjoy! |
| Accesso accordato. | — | Access granted. |
| fastidioso | — | annoying |
| L'alchimista | — | The Alchemist |
| Mia chiamo | — | My name is |
| Animali! | — | Animals! |
| Soldati! | — | Soldiers! |
| Cosa è successo? | — | What happened? |
| Bestia indegna! | — | Unworthy beast |
| cane | — | dog |
| L'Immortale è morto! | — | The Immortal is dead! |
| Ritirata! | — | Retreat! |
| Salvati! | — | Save yourself! |
| Benvenuta! | — | Welcome! |
| Sì. | — | Yes. |
| dodici | — | twelve |
| Venga con me | — | Come with me |
| Introducendo Sua Maestà | — | Introducing His Majesty |
| sua moglie | — | his wife |

| l loro figlio | — | their son |
| e la loro figlia | — | and their daughter |
| Che bello vederti! | — | Good to see you! |
| Porate il cibo! | — | Bring the food! |
| Che pasto meraviglioso! | — | What a wonderful meal! |
| amore mio | — | my love |
| Scusa, mamma | — | Sorry, Mother. |
| mio dolce fiore | — | my sweet flower |
| un pazzo | — | a fool |
| Hai perso! | — | You lost! |
| Caduti | — | Fallen |
| un lupo | — | a wolf |
| consiglieri | — | advisors |
| la mia famiglia | — | my family |
| I miei soldati | — | my soldiers |
| Non importa. | — | It does not matter. |
| Mia madre | — | My mother |
| Hai la mia parola. | — | You have my word. |
| mio padre | — | my father |

# Korblan

| | | |
|---|---|---|
| Ist das dein Ernst? | — | Are you serious? |
| Bist du dumm? | — | Are you stupid? |
| Hund | — | dog |
| Teufel | — | Devil(s) |
| verlogene Teufel | — | lying devils |
| Verdammt nochmal! | — | Fuck me! |
| krankhaft | — | diseased |
| hässlich | — | ugly |
| Du hast gewonnen? | — | You won? |
| zu Tode | — | to death |
| Schmutz | — | filth |
| Soldaten | — | soldiers |
| Hure | — | whore |
| fettes arschloch | — | fat asshole |
| Alles ist gut | — | All is well |
| das Zimmer des Champions | — | the champion's room |
| Pfui! | — | Yuck! |
| Ich bitte um deine Vergebung | — | I ask for your forgiveness |
| fünfzehn Fuß | — | fifteen feet |
| Ist das wahr? | — | Is that true? |
| Attentäter! | — | Assassins! |
| Töte jeden Einzelnen von ihnen! | — | Kill every single one of them! |

| auf einmal | — | at once |
| die Königin | — | the Queen |
| König | — | King |
| Meine Leute | — | My people |
| der Müll | — | the garbage |
| Königin von Tudrose | — | Queen of Tudrose |
| Biester | — | beasts |
| Blasphemie! | — | Blasphemy! |
| Über alles | — | Above all |
| Kämpfer | — | fighters |
| die Teufel | — | the devils |
| ieser Aufstand | — | this uprising |
| Ja, du hast recht. | — | Yes, you are right. |
| Geringere | — | Lessers |

# Séúbua

| | | |
|---|---|---|
| Tóráin | — | Hunted Ones |
| Tórán | — | Hunted One |
| Buachaill Óg Amháin | — | One Young Boy |
| Draoithe | — | Druids |
| Fáthfhuil | — | Mystic Blood |
| Éist liom a Dhuosnos, a Thiama an Bháis, a Rí Dhubhaigh, a Ghlacadóir na Marbh, agus a Thabharthóir Suaimhnis. Iarraim ort teacht, súil ghéar a chaitheamh ar chlann Anu agus do bheannacht deiridh a thabhairt. | — | Hear me Dhuosnos, Lord of Death, Black King, Receiver of the Dead, and Rest Giver. I encourage you to come, take a close look at Anu's child and give your final blessing. |
| Tá a lán eolais agam faoinár gcultúr. | — | I know a lot about our culture. |
| Go dtuga Tiama an Bháis abhaile thú, mo chara. | — | May the Lord of Death bring you home, my friend. |
| Codladh go sámh, mo chara | — | Sleep peacefully, my friend. |
| Eitil. | — | Fly. |
| Leigheas mé. | — | Heal me. |
| Caith. | — | Throw. |
| Brúigh. | — | Push. |
| oighear | — | ice |
| bacainn | — | barrier |
| Láidre | — | Strong Ones |

# Cànansorcha

| | | |
|---|---|---|
| deamhain | — | demons |
| Dia an Dorchadais | — | God of Darkness |
| Ban-dia an t-Solais | — | Goddess of Light |
| Anslocdubh | — | The Black Pit |
| Mo rionnag bheag. Tha mi cho moiteil asad. | — | My little star. I am so proud of you. |
| Tapadh leibh, a Mhàthair. | — | Thank you, Mother. |

—

# About
the Author

Marc R. Micciola lives in Ontario, Canada with his two dogs Rielly and Ace. He has a great passion for hockey, movies, and books. He possesses a book collection consisting of a multitude of fantasy stories. Many of these novels are from his favorite authors: Mark Lawrence, George R. R. Martin, Tom Lloyd, and J. R. R. Tolkien. His prize possessions are his two replica swords from the Lord of the Rings films and his growing number of fountain pens. When Marc isn't writing, he's spending time with his dogs, his family, and his friends. Photography and wood art are other things that Marc enjoys doing. Marc's goal when writing any book is to put together a story that is enjoyable, emotional, and intriguing. If the words on the page make you feel something, then this author feels he's done his job.